Di Morrissey is one of the most successful bestselling writers Australia has produced. She began writing as a young woman, training and working as a journalist for Australian Consolidated Press in Sydney and Northcliffe Newspapers in London. She worked in television in Australia and Hawaii and in the USA as a presenter, reporter, producer and actress. After her marriage to a US diplomat, Peter Morrissey, they were posted to Singapore, Thailand, South America and Washington, DC. During this time she worked as a freelance journalist, TV and film scriptwriter and radio broadcaster, appeared in theatre productions and had several short stories published. Returning to Australia, Di continued to work in television before publishing her first novel in 1991.

Di has a daughter, Dr Gabrielle Hansen and her daughter, Sonoma, is Di's first grandchild. Di's son, Nick Morrissey, is a Buddhist scholar and lecturer.

Di and her partner, Boris Janjic, divide their time between Byron Bay and the Manning Valley in New South Wales when not travelling to research her novels, which are all inspired by a particular landscape.

www.dimorrissey.com

Also by Di Morrissey

Di Morrissey

The Valley

PAN
Pan Macmillan Australia

Author's Note

This is a work of fiction. All characters are creations of my imagination – with one exception. Isabella Mary Kelly lived in the Manning Valley of NSW in the mid nineteenth century and I like to think she would be pleased with my telling of her story, the salvaging of her reputation, and remembering her for the feisty and formidable woman she was.

I have also drawn inspiration from the letters and memories of my grand-parents, Jack and Louisa Revitt of Wingham, NSW, where I was born.

I hope you enjoy my valley.

DM
Byron Bay, 2006

First published 2006 in Macmillan by Pan Macmillan Australia Pty Limited
First published 2007 in Pan by Pan Macmillan Australia Pty Ltd
This Pan edition published 2008 by Pan Macmillan Australia Pty Limited
1 Market Street, Sydney

Reprinted 2009

National Library of Australia
cataloguing-in-publication data:

Morrissey, Di.
The valley/Di Morrissey.

9780330424585 (pbk.)

A823.3

Typeset in 11.25/13.5pt Sabon by Post Pre-press Group
Printed in Australia by McPherson's Printing Group

Papers used by Pan Macmillan Australia Pty Ltd are natural, recyclable products made from wood grown in sustainable forests. The manufacturing processes conform to the environmental regulations of the country of origin.

For all my family, everywhere.
Special hugs to my mother, Kay,
daughter Gabrielle and son Nick;
and to Barrie, welcome to the family.

Acknowledgments

For Uncle Jim Revitt, who shares my memories of growing up in a special little town. Thank you for your constructive and wise input (as always). And also Rosemary Revitt for your balance and warmth. Thanks to Uncle Ron Revitt-Jonach for your help in understanding artists and their work. And for darling Boris who is always there for me and now too loves the valley.

Thank you to everyone at Pan Macmillan – you're family too!: James Fraser, who's had such faith in me from book one; the lovely Nikki Christer (good pal, great editor); Jane Novak (clever, funny and the best road buddy). And always there with advice and friendship; Ross Gibb, Jeannine Fowler, Roxarne Burns. And thanks also to all the hardworking, enthusiastic Pan Mac reps.

Special thanks to Ian Robertson, who pretends to be my lawyer but is really a great raconteur, lunch companion and all-round inspiration.

Thanks to artist Katie Clemson, and to Liz Adams for her enthusiastic support and for being a great sounding board.

Thanks also go to many people in the Manning Valley who helped me in so many ways. Also: Mave and Eric Richardson, Graham and Chris Gibbons, Noel, Rachel, Jack and Madi Piercy, the Wingham Historical Society, Tom Wollard, Russell Saunders, Sue Mitchell (Manning Regional Art Gallery).

Special thanks to Maurie Garland for permission to use details of Isabella Kelly's life from his book *The Trials of Isabella Mary Kelly* (Brolga Books).

DM

The Valley

The valley was a little-known gem. Its undulating green landscape slashed by the magnificent river seeking the sea.

Those who knew this place, knew its magic.

From its first inhabitants who roamed the hills, river and valley, it was a country of ceremony, corroboree and creation. Then came white settlers with horses and cattle. They carved the first bush homes and found and felled the ancient trees. There were murders and births. Many died before their time.

As two centuries passed, the valley remained little known. Those who came, and stayed, were drawn into its embrace as to a mother's breast, were comforted and made welcome, finding peace in which to live out their lives.

The valley was special to all who knew it.

Prologue
Kelly's Crossing, 1840

THE CLOUDS PARTED LIKE a plush grey curtain leaving a backdrop of streaky winter sky behind heavily timbered peaks. Centre-stage, three figures, dwarfed by the landscape, made their way along the narrow cutting through ancient trees in a dense rainforest. The track was rough, rutted from bullock hooves, timber drays and an occasional horseman.

The rolling sound of a fast-flowing creek grew louder and soon the travellers were beside what was normally a shallow rocky crossing. They stopped at the swollen creek and took in the approach that angled gently down the bank. On the other side the way out was a steep stretch of dangerous loose stones. It demanded determination from both horse and rider in a hard gallop from the water and up the challenging bank.

The three figures moved closer to the water. Only one, a woman, was mounted. The two men on foot were ill-prepared for the rough track and icy water crossing, their boots well worn, their apparel threadbare. One was leading a packhorse and both men were tethered by ropes to the lead horse and rider. They were not country men and they gazed at the water in dread.

'We'll never walk this flooded creek. It'll be shocking cold. And strong by the look of it,' muttered the younger of the two shackled men.

'It's for a hearty sailor at home in fierce water. Not for the likes of us,' agreed the older man.

The woman on horseback heard them. 'I hope you don't fancy yourselves as town gents. You two have been long enough on the land to rough your hands. We are crossing over this stream. We have a distance to travel before dark. Hold on to the ropes.' The scoffing and at the same time commanding tone did not invite argument.

The older of the two convicts who was leading the packhorse spoke in a subservient and hesitant voice. 'Ma'am, it really is dangerous. With respect, be careful. It could sweep away the unwary.'

'I am not unaware of dangers. The distance across is short if we act swiftly. Get down the bank. I will loosen the ropes.'

The woman deftly untied the two ropes that were knotted on the ear of her saddle and led to the shackles on the ankles of the two convicts assigned to her for the last six months of their sentences.

She was no beauty but a striking woman and any man could see she was not one to be trifled with. She rode side-saddle, as convention decreed, in a great swayback leather saddle, seated as comfortably as in an armchair. Her long black skirt was looped about her legs, her booted foot firmly in the stirrup. The scarlet jacket over her modest blouse was a vivid splash of colour in the grey and sodden scene. On her head she wore a cabbage-tree hat favoured by the men of the district. The woven brim shaded her face, her hair was coiled firmly beneath the plaited crown. She had no time or taste for fashionable bonnets. In her gloved hands she held reins and a whip.

'If you lose your footing keep your head up and kick strongly. Hang on to the rope and it will pull you across.'

The black stallion braced itself for the plunge through the creek. The horse and rider had forded flooded creeks before this day.

She nudged the black horse forward and it strode firmly, the water surging around its chest. Glancing behind, the woman saw the worried faces of the men as they waded carefully, the water at their armpits. One held the rope above his head as the packhorse gamely stepped through the current. The packhorse was strong and a handy swimmer if required. If it tripped it would be let free to make its own way through. Even a normally narrow channel such as this was not to be trusted when swollen and muddy from storms.

Before the woman's attention returned to the way ahead, the stallion stumbled as a submerged log rolled underfoot and suddenly they were in a deep hole where the current churned in a whirlpool. The horse was flung sideways, its rider wrenched from the saddle.

The two men and packhorse were on firmer ground and watched helplessly as the woman was swept away. The woman's horse, holding its head high, swam strongly till it found a footing. Slipping on stones it stepped into the shallows and charged up the steep bank, water streaming from the saddle, dragging the men in its wake. The packhorse's hooves clanged against stones and it too scrambled from the rushing water, the younger man clutching the reins, struggling to his feet after slipping on the bank.

Both men craned their necks to see what had happened

to their mistress but she was out of sight. They freed themselves from the ropes and stumbled along the creek edge, hanging on to trees until they saw a slash of red jammed into the roots of a tree toppled by the floodwaters. The woman was trying to drag herself free, but the waterlogged weight of her skirt and petticoats and the surging current kept pulling at her. The men looked at each other. Here was a chance to make away with two horses to freedom.

'We wouldn't get far, lad,' said the older man.

'I suppose it would go bad with us when we are so close to finishing our time,' the younger man whined reluctantly. 'What do we do?'

'Take the small axe from the packhorse. We can cut through this tangle. Get a rope we can throw out to her.'

The men worked quickly as the horses stood patiently on the bank, shaking their manes and flicking tails.

'We be getting to you, ma'am, hang on,' called the older man.

The woman's expression was grim, and although her arms were tiring as the water pulled at her clothing, her grip around the tree was firm and determined.

The older man threw the rope towards her and she caught it. He secured the other end to a nearby tree while the younger man used the axe to swiftly cut away a barrier of shrubs and saplings on the steep bank.

'Good lad. That's enough.' He gave an encouraging smile to the trapped woman. 'Right?' he called.

The woman hesitated before loosening her grip.

'It's strong, ma'am. Won't break. Hold tightly.'

Trusting herself into their care, she let go of the tree and was swiftly hauled in despite her waterlogged weight. She staggered up the bank and hastily made an effort to get to her feet and grasp at what dignity and authority remained to her. The men busied themselves with winding up the rope, stowing the axe in a pack saddle and wringing water from their clothes.

'That was fortunate. And quick thinking. I am grateful,' said the woman briskly. 'I must find a dry jacket. My skirt will dry as we ride.'

'We're moving on?' the young man asked in surprise.

The woman arched an eyebrow. 'Did you imagine we would camp at this miserable crossing just because we got wet? We are expected at Port Macquarie and we will be there on time.'

She went to the packhorse as the men exchanged a look of frustration.

'We should have left her. Gone on. Found someone and reported an accident,' said the younger man in a low and angry voice.

'You could live with yourself? I couldn't.'

'But surely she won't take us to be flogged? Not now?' The younger man's face was red with anger. And fear. His life had been dogged by ill fortune. Now for the first time having acted without self-interest it proved to him there was no gain in honesty or decency.

'It may go easy with us now,' answered the older man.

'And if not? Is she so hard a woman?'

'If not, it will be over and done with quick enough,' said the older man philosophically.

Seeing the woman returning in a dry jacket taken from the saddle pack the young man turned away, his face sullen. 'I suppose we have to be tied to the horses again?' He yanked at the rope.

'Do I have your oath to stay beside me? You can take turns on the packhorse. We must travel further to make camp before dark. Fetch the horses.'

She turned to the older man as the young fellow trudged to the horses. 'I will not forget what you have done this day. But I am obliged to do what must be done.'

The man's face was expressionless. 'Whatever you say, Miss Kelly.'

She swung into the saddle and watched him help the younger man on to the packhorse. 'Decide between you when to change over.'

She spurred the black stallion further up the slope, paused where the track began to level, and watched the packhorse pick its way towards her. The older man followed, leaning on a stout stick salvaged from the bush litter. The young man on the horse sat with shoulders slumped and his head bowed, angrily contemplating the punishment awaiting him at the penal centre that served the district.

They had indeed done wrong by their employer. Letting several unbranded cattle stray to be conveniently collected and 'bought' on the sly had seemed a quick and easy way to pocket some money. Cattle were often lost in the thickly timbered hills around Miss Kelly's unfenced property. But the purchaser was found out before he could brand the cattle and he wasted no time in pinpointing the culprits, pleading his own innocence. So in accordance with the regulations governing convict labour to free settlers the men were to be punished as the law stipulated.

But Miss Isabella Kelly was not about to put her men in the hands of the local magistrate, a man she knew despised her. She preferred to take them on a longer journey to Port Macquarie where they had been serving out their term before assignment. In 1840 there were no townships between her holdings at Mount George, well up the Manning River, and Port Macquarie on the Hastings River.

Eight days later the three returned the way they'd come. This time the creek crossing presented no challenge. The water had receded, the stream gurgled pleasantly and sparkled in the sunlight. The woman did not glance downstream where she had almost perished. It seemed to the men that she appeared not to recall that day, and rode on apparently more interested in checking her cattle on the remote rolling hills being cleared as part of her dream to become a great and rich settler in this vast and enthralling land.

Back at Port Macquarie the story of Isabella Kelly's accident and rescue by the convicts was being told with increasing embellishment. It was growing well beyond the version given by the young convict hauled before the court, who had smarted not only from the pain of the lashes received, but also from what he regarded as the injustice of the event.

There were many who shook their heads dismissively when they heard the story. The men in the colony over-whelmingly disliked Miss Isabella Kelly. To them she was wrong to meddle in the affairs of men. Settling the land and overseeing convicts was men's business. She might be a proud woman but she was bound to fall or fail. It was not right that a woman alone, with no kith or kin, an orphan from the old country, could better the men of the district with her cattle and horse breeding. She was an aloof and therefore mysterious figure who did not fit into the accepted ways of the new settlers.

But the legend she was to become was only beginning.

Sydney, 1998

Lara Langdon sat in the deep chair, hunched, trying to sink into the faded flower print as if she could disappear and escape what was happening around her. Hushed, concerned voices in another room. Cars arriving and leaving. A phone ringing.

Her daughter, sombre in black, came into the room looking concerned and tentative.

'Go away, Dani, please. Leave me. Just go,' declared Lara.

'Mum, you can't stay here. You feel terrible, I know, but you have to come to the funeral,' Dani pleaded gently. 'It'll be all right. I won't leave your side for a minute.' Her eyes were sad, her heartbreak obvious. She ached for her mother and knelt down by the chair, took her hands and gave a soft supportive squeeze.

Lara's mother, Dani's grandmother, Elizabeth, had died. Dani was trying to imagine how she would feel at the loss of her own mother, crouched there in the chair, and her heart constricted.

'Mum, people will think it very strange if you stay at home. At least come to the service. They'll think you didn't love her, respect her.'

'I've never cared what people thought. Nor did she.'

'Now that's not true. Elizabeth cared desperately what people thought of her. She just pretended she didn't.'

'Dani, you don't understand. I don't *do* funerals!' Lara's eyes blazed.

Dani almost smiled. She was glad that at last something had jolted her mother out of her inert state. But then she sighed. It was true. Lara had avoided funerals all her life. Bizarre really. She always had excuses, such as living overseas or being interstate, being bogged down in the demands of work, or faced with a domestic crisis.

If only people knew how fearful Lara was of this event. The bright, irrepressible, strong woman who had done so much. But Lara, Dani's mother, was unable to deal with death.

Dani remembered coming home during university holidays to find their cat lying by the front gate, killed by a swift hit from a passing car. Lara had fled inside. And it had been Dani who'd lifted the still, soft form, cradling the cat in her arms, singing and talking to their dead pet as she walked around the garden. When Gordon Langdon, her stepfather, arrived home the two of them buried the cat beneath a pretty shrub.

Lara had served dinner stony faced and never mentioned what had happened. But Dani knew she'd watched it all from an upstairs window.

Several times over the past year she'd tried to help her mother face up to the inevitable, that Elizabeth was fading fast. But Lara had always brushed her comments aside – 'Let's not get into that. I can't bear to think about it.'

Lara always had a way of deflecting the unpleasant. A flick of her hand, a twist of her head, avoiding eye contact and changing the subject with a light-hearted remark. But now Lara could not make this moment go away. She was unmoving, her eyes closed.

Dani wondered what special moments she was recalling. 'Mum, there'll be time to remember things . . . after,' she said softly.

Lara opened her eyes. 'I was wondering about that man who said he'd fix the verandah awning. He never called back, you know.'

Dani stared at her mother in shock, then stood up. 'Okay, enough of that, Mum. We have to go.' Gently but firmly she pulled Lara to her feet and steered her into the bedroom. 'Where are your shoes and jacket? And your bag.'

Lara stood meekly, her expression distant as if she was not participating in any of this. But when Dani pulled a dark blue blazer from her wardrobe, Lara shook her head, back in the present. 'No, not that one.' She took a black suede jacket off a hanger and shrugged it on, then with some haste stepped into her shoes. 'Let's go and get this over with then.' She strode outside to Dani's car.

Dani hadn't wanted to drive but everyone else had gone and she now had no choice.

They drove in silence for some time then Lara asked suddenly. 'Have you seen the will?'

'No. But I know what she wanted. Surprisingly she talked about it one time. We've arranged what she stipulated. I told you but I know you didn't take it in. It'll be okay, Mum.'

As her grandmother had requested, Dani arranged for native flowers, an Aussie poem, a few good old songs, her ashes to be scattered over a quiet backwater of Sydney's numerous waterways. Dani knew the spot Elizabeth described. She'd promised to see this was done ten years ago when she was only fifteen years old. It had been a difficult discussion, but Elizabeth persisted for she had seen a strength in her granddaughter like her own. Lara was soft, weak, in Elizabeth's eyes, too easily swayed by others. Dani had moral fibre and was fearless in standing up for herself. Elizabeth knew her granddaughter would see to her wishes.

Lara was one of those women who attracted attention, caught people's eye, made heads turn. In her youth it was because she was a very attractive woman. Later her appeal grew as she radiated a special quality in addition to her lovely looks. People were interested in her, asked who she was, wanted to meet her. There was, simply, something about Lara. Dani had long given up trying to understand what it was that drew people to her mother.

Dani herself was more than pretty, she was striking and emanated strength and personality. Though she didn't recognise that she had as much appeal as her mother but in a different way.

So it was Dani who greeted, thanked all who came, and physically and emotionally supported her forlorn and vague mother during the church service and the burial ceremony. Those attending saw the lost look in Lara's eyes, the way she turned to her daughter to answer questions and make decisions and how she hung back, seemingly disengaged from the proceedings. They felt sympathy for Lara, and all admired her daughter's poise, strength and charm. Lara was grateful that Dani had taken the reins.

Dani's husband pulled her briefly aside. 'What's happening? You driving your mother back to her place or ours?'

'Jeff, I'll take her home and stay with her. Can you pick up the baby and bring him over with all his gear? Don't forget anything. Call me before you leave to double check.'

'Dani, this is so inconvenient. Tim's just sleeping through, spending the night at your mother's will unsettle him.'

'Yes, it is inconvenient of my grandmother to die. But I am not leaving my mother alone. And I am not about to try and express milk.'

Jeff saw the dangerous glint in his wife's eyes. 'Lara's ex-husband is here. Gordon's being very nice. Offered to help any way he could.'

'I don't think my mother wants to deal with her ex right now. You take him out to dinner. Just get Timmy from the sitter. I'll see you at Mum's.'

Lara was waiting in the car. She didn't care where she went, she just wanted someone else to fix things. She thought of her cool white bedroom. Since her divorce it was always kept the way she wanted. Gordon was so untidy. She hated walking in and finding his clothes dropped on the floor or over a chair, papers or folders left on the bed, damp towels in a pile, water splashed on the bathroom mirror.

There had been so many homes. Images of houses Lara had lived in during her marriage spun through her mind.

America, Asia, outback Australia, Perth, Sydney. Before that, London in her single days. And as a small girl, there was Cedartown, by the river in a valley she hardly knew. It all seemed so long ago.

When Dani got in the car Lara shut down the fast-moving images of the past. 'Some people wore odd-looking outfits, didn't they?' Lara commented as they followed the last of the funeral cars back into the city traffic.

It was over and they were alone.

Lara's house was as it always was . . . clean, tidy, filled with flowers. The cat curled on its favourite cushion. Dani's baby son slept in his travel cot by her bed. She'd checked on her mother who was sleeping, having dutifully taken the prescribed sleeping pill. The suburb outside was quiet, the house calm.

Dani wondered if her husband Jeff was at home or out with Gordon Langdon, Lara's charming but dull second ex-husband. She rolled on her side. While she could never live at home with her mother again, it was nice to be under her roof. For so long Lara had provided a sanctuary and support for her, and been her friend. But a change in their relationship was taking place. Dani now felt the blanket of responsibility settle on her. She had a son to care for, and the mother-daughter role had shifted. And, she realised, quite clearly and calmly, that she also had to care for herself. Jeff wasn't there for her as she had always imagined a husband would be. She'd known this subconsciously during her pregnancy. If she'd thought a baby was going to fix her marriage she now knew differently. It was comforting to know that her mother would be there to help her through the inevitable tough times ahead.

Dani thought about how her grandmother, the feisty and determined Elizabeth, had always been supportive of her daughter Lara through the hard patches of life. And Lara had often talked about her grandmother Emily, Elizabeth's mother. Emily was another strong-willed woman, an English rose from London who'd sailed to Australia after the Great War to marry her soldier love. They'd settled in a little country town up the coast. Cedartown. It must have been hard on Emily after growing up near the centre of one of the world's great cities.

Dani had never been to Cedartown where her great-grandmother Emily, her grandmother Elizabeth and briefly her mother Lara had all lived. Perhaps she should visit Cedartown one day to see where their stories began. Perhaps. One day.

I

Sydney, 2006

Lara

LARA STOOD AT THE window looking at the drooping wet shrubs and plants. They needed the rain, Sydney's water supply had been critically low. But after nearly a week of solid downpour she was feeling housebound and bored. She felt her skin was growing mould. Come to think of it, she felt her whole life was stuck in mud.

One year ago Lara had quit her job as a television producer of documentaries and filmed segments for various programs churned out by one of the leading commercial networks. She'd turned sixty, been divorced from her second husband for nine years and so decided to travel and have a life with her new freedom.

Her career had been interesting in the beginning but in the last few years she felt like she had been treading water, remaking the same stories over and over. So she'd resigned and travelled overseas, visited friends around Australia and now she'd hit a wall and wondered what to do with the rest of her life. She was still employable and looked good for her age as she had so much time to devote to herself, revelling in gym, tennis and regular beauty and massage treatments, things she had no time for when she was working.

She'd never been a morning coffee with the girls type. She'd lasted three months in a book club. She'd slaved in her garden and there was now no room to plant another thing. She toyed with the idea of taking some further education courses. It still pained her that she'd never had the opportunity to go to university. Her widowed mother, Elizabeth, couldn't afford it in those days and Lara had dabbled in acting and modelling before getting a job on a fashion magazine. It had led to a bit of writing and helping out on fashion shoots. She'd shown a good eye for locations, unusual models, funky and different accessories and styling. She could see a story behind the superficial and was hired by a big film and media public relations firm that looked after the hot rock bands and movies in production. Finally she'd landed in television and quickly mastered video filming and editing. She had had offers to work in front of the cameras but had frozen, hating the idea of being on public show. That was a game for others to play, often under her direction.

Lara's first marriage to an American geologist, Joseph Moreland, Dani's father, had meant living abroad for a short time and then being posted to godforsaken places in the Australian outback. When he relocated to the United States to lecture at a college in South Dakota she decided she couldn't face the American way of life again. Even tinpot townships in the outback were preferable to suburban America: white clapboard house, identical to its neighbour's; emerald lawn clipped to even up every blade of perfect grass; the stars and stripes flying above the porch. They separated. Lara moved back to Australia with their ten-year-old daughter Dani, and then she finally found her feet in television.

When Dani moved out to go to university Lara had dashed into a second marriage to Gordon Langdon. However, Lara's TV job with its demanding hours and her husband's lack of work and ambition had seen the marriage wither.

The following years on her own had been calm and, looking back, fruitful. Occasionally the fear of growing old alone in a chair on the deck plagued Lara. She hoped one day there would be a lover or a companion who was secure in his own life without moving in on hers. She just wished that person would turn up. Life was pretty dull at present.

The front door to Lara's house opened and her daughter called down the hall.

'You there?' Dani's dog loped ahead of her woofing joyfully. This was its second home.

Lara's mood lifted instantly. Her daughter Dani's energy burst into the house like an electricity grid being switched on. Dani was super-charged and gave off sparks of enthusiasm and laughter and a torrent of chatter. Unless she was going through some drama or disaster and then there was a power surge of wails and despair, which often swamped Lara. Her daughter would dump a current upheaval on her and was cheered, comforted or advised, then sailed off feeling better but leaving Lara emotionally exhausted.

Dani came into the living room. 'Why are you in here moping at the window?'

'Hi, darling. I'm not moping exactly, just looking at the soggy crepe myrtle flowers and thinking that's how I feel. Wet bones and mould growing between my toes.'

'Not a good look, Mum. Come on, break out the teapot. I have news.'

Lara looked at the spark in her daughter's eyes. While she was a level-headed and beautiful thirty-three-year-old woman with a young son, there was a tension in the over-bright voice and expression that reminded Lara of Dani as a little girl about to break unpleasant news wrapped in throwaway lines.

'Okay, what have you done?'

'Jolly, go outside, off the sofa! Quiet!' Dani scooted the dog onto the covered patio.

'Don't let her back in with muddy feet.' Lara went into the kitchen to put the kettle on and Dani followed. 'So, what's the news?' She raised an eyebrow and gave her daughter a knowing look.

'Can't fool you, can I, Mum?' said Dani with a smile as she sat at the round table in the breakfast nook, normally a sunny corner looking out onto the flowers and shrubs in her mother's well-tended if overplanted garden. 'You know I've been talking about making a change, moving on with my life somehow? Well, I've stopped talking. I've quit my job. Finito. Out of there. I'm starting my real life.'

'Which is?' asked Lara as she arranged cups, milk and biscuits.

'To paint. Be a full-time artist. No more dabbling round the edges. If I don't give it a go now I'll never know how good I can be,' Dani said in a breathless rush.

'Fantastic! Good on you, darling. Earl Grey or Irish Breakfast?'

'Mum! What do I have to do to shock you?' laughed Dani, feeling relieved. Even though she and her mother were very close and spoke openly about almost everything in their lives and had developed a relationship that was now based more on friendship than mother-daughter roles, each occasionally reverted to type. 'I expected at least a few arrows. Like, how are you going to support yourself? How do you propose to launch yourself into the art world? Where are you going to do this messy painting business?'

'I imagine you've thought all that through being the Virgo you are. I'm not surprised. I know how difficult it's been and how frustrated you've been feeling about life in general. And I suppose graphic design must be restricting for a creative artist,' said Lara.

'So, do you want to know my plans?' asked Dani.

'Of course I do. How can I help? Where do I fit in?'

'You're unreal, Mum. Nice of you to offer, but I can manage my life and I want to do this on my own.' Dani felt slightly irked. Her mother had always been supportive even through the years she worked in the madness of television, which demanded so much of her time and attention. No wonder her mother's second marriage to Gordon had never worked out. Dani had no such excuse for the failure of her own marriage.

Lara saw the irritation flash across her daughter's face. Dani came across as a strong, occasionally opinionated young woman. But Lara knew there was still a needy and sometimes vulnerable young girl inside. A girl who was now a mother herself, whose life had gone down a path that was the opposite direction to what she really wanted. Lara had been able to help Dani through the stressful time of her divorce, was always there to care for eight-year-old Tim, even to help out financially. She was proud of how Dani had come through the break-up and recognised it was time for her to let Dani take control of her life again. Lara made a mental note to take a backward step.

'Sounds like you're taking control of your destiny without my help. So when do you get your last salary and do the goodbye lunch?'

'In two weeks. Then I have some holidays and sick

leave to use up. Most of the crew at the studio think I'm mad and I'll come a cropper. I suppose because none of them have the guts to give it a go. A few of the computer geeks don't see it as a big deal, art and their computer are the same thing to them.'

'And the others? Are they frustrated painters rather than designers of logos and websites or whatever it is they do?'

Dani watched her mother pour the tea into their favourite big mugs, yellow flowers on hers, blue flowers on Lara's. 'Hard to know really. Two of them have fine arts degrees and probably feel working in a graphic design studio isn't how they saw their art career going. Because I don't have an art degree they think I'm a bit off the planet and reckon I'll never make much money out of full-time painting. Like starving in a garret stuff.'

'You probably won't make much money.'

'I know that. It's not the object.'

Lara smiled. 'Good thing you and Jeff sold your house at the right time. Did your nest egg play a part in this jump off the cliff?'

'Of course. I have a son to look after. And child support doesn't mean I can really afford to stop work.'

'Jeff will probably think you're indulging yourself at his expense.'

'I don't care what he thinks. And we both lost out on the settlement. Fifty-fifty still had lots of holes in the final shakeout.'

'Like he picked out the valuable books and pictures?'

Dani took a deep breath to help control a rising sense of frustration. 'Mum, I don't want to go over that. I've moved on.'

Lara sipped her tea, thinking, Well, thank the lord for that then. Dani had gnashed her teeth for weeks over her ex-husband getting first pick of their supposedly mutually shared possessions. She changed tack. 'Do these people you've worked with for the past two years know you've drawn, sketched and painted since you could walk?'

'Of course not. The paper degree is all they care about. Anyway, I suppose they also had the art bug since they were old enough to pick up a pencil and doodle.'

Lara thought back to Dani's two-year-old efforts with finger painting and colouring in. At first she assumed it was motherly pride but by the time Dani was four Lara knew she had a definite talent. Dani would lie on the floor staring out the front door of their house in South Dakota sketching street scenes, people, dogs, cars in bold bright crayons or delicate detailed pencil. Lara still had most of her pictures tucked away. As Dani grew so her drawing and painting had blossomed.

'Do you have any regrets about not doing art at university?' asked Lara. Dani's academic choices had caused a bit of family debate. Deep down Lara had felt Dani should pursue and develop what was a God-given talent. Her father Joe had dismissed it as no way to get on in the world and argued that she should regard art as a 'hobby'. He urged her to concentrate on communications and journalism at university. Lara had ended up supporting the same line, as that's what she would have done, given the chance. Lara still harboured a desire to write 'something' some day.

'No . . . no regrets really,' sighed Dani. 'You hear stuff about academia cramping your natural style. I don't know. Anyway, all I want to do is fumble along on my own, explore a bit of the unknown, see what comes up. I've had enough of art schools, painting camps and life classes. It's not like I haven't had any instruction or experience,' she added defensively.

'Do you see yourself making a living from it though?'

'Mum, like I said, that's not why I've quit my job. For

once I can afford to take some time out to just paint and experiment. When the money runs out I'll see where I'm at. I'll just have to go back to work of some kind.'

'Maybe not,' said Lara brightly. 'It's a great idea.' She was trying to visualise space for a studio in Dani's tiny Paddington terrace house. 'So where will you paint?'

'I haven't decided. I do need something like a garage with good light. I'd like to do some big canvases. And as you know, painting is messy.'

Lara's house didn't have space, and it would be expensive to rent a studio. 'You can't very well move too far, what about Jeff's access to his son? . . . Something will turn up,' she added, deciding it was no time to be negative, but she foresaw problems taking Tim too far from his father.

Dani didn't answer. Sometimes her mother's positive and cheerful slant on life was annoying. Dani liked to plan everything and know what she was walking into and how she expected things to turn out. But for once she was doing something with no set plan in place. It was as if her long-suppressed talent had recklessly pushed its way to the forefront of her mind, making everything else seem irrelevant, unimportant. Painting was all she could think about. Now everywhere she looked she framed her interpretation of the scene as a finished picture. Her hands itched to hold a brush, she longed for the smell of oil paint, the feel of a stretched canvas, the sensation of losing herself in what she was doing with no sense of time or the world outside her art – just her and the gliding brush.

They finished their tea.

'I'd better get the Jolly Roger and dry her off. What are your plans for the rest of the day, Mum?'

'Oh, I'll go for my walk when it stops raining. I foolishly started a big project, the proverbial rainy day thing, and now it's going to take ages to finish,' said Lara putting the cups in the sink.

'What's that then?' asked Dani crossing into the dining room. 'Oh, I see what you mean.'

The long polished table was covered in shoe boxes, albums and loose photographs.

'All the family pictures I've been meaning to sort out since Mum died. So many I don't know who they are or where they were taken. The early years of my grandparents especially.'

'These aren't family pictures.' Dani studied a pile of sepia prints that looked like they'd once been framed. Each had a printed title under it. There were also yellowing newspaper clippings, piles of letters bundled together with rubber bands and string, and some old books, the one on the top titled *Peeps Into the Past*.

'Poppy, your great grandfather, was something of an archivist. He and Nana kept everything. Fascinating reading. Those photos came out of the old passenger trains that went up the North Coast. I remember taking the steam train to visit my grandparents every school holiday. Loved it, even though the smoke and soot penetrated every compartment. There was an old tin foot warmer for winter trips, a big bottle of water and a couple of glasses in a holder above the door, and photos like these on the wall under the luggage rack. The train got in to Cedartown in the early hours of the morning and Poppy was always there to meet me.'

Lara sighed with delight recollecting the detail. 'We'd hold hands walking across the dirt road to Cricklewood, their house, where a pot of tea was already brewing on the stove, and sometimes warm scones wrapped in a fresh tea towel. I loved those chats over the kitchen table before going to bed and seeing Nana later at breakfast. When I was older and working I'd sometimes just surprise them.

Walk in from the sleepout when they were getting up.' Lara smiled to herself and Dani saw they were warm and happy memories.

Lara had loved those school holiday breaks with her grandparents. Especially slowly waking to the smell of the wood flaring up in the fuel stove, the bang of the oven door as Poppy stored the toast he'd cooked over the fire on the end of a long fork made out of fencing wire. The bread was fluffy white, delivered daily on a horse-drawn baker's cart. They had an electric jug and a squat little electric toaster with drop down sides, but that first tea and toast in the morning Poppy made the old way. He brought the steaming tea to her bedside with a chunk of toast. The crust was singed crunchy, the middle soft with runny butter. The pleasure on her grandfather's face as she reached hungrily for the plate and sat up in bed to eat made her realise how much he enjoyed her visits. They'd chat about plans for the day, he'd tell her of something he'd spotted when he went to fetch the fresh milk.

The milkman had a horse-drawn dray loaded with milk urns and in the early morning hours the horse plodded along, stopping automatically at each house for the milk-man to pour milk into the clean billycan hung on the front gate. Lara loved it when the thick rich milk was allowed to sit so the cream could be scooped off to whip for Poppy's famous sponge cake, made to a recipe he said he got from a French soldier he helped at an army hospital during the Great War. Poppy had shown her how to make a sponge many times but all she remembered was him dropping scoops of butter into the mixture, reciting – 'Du beurre, du beurre, toujours du beurre.'

As she sipped her tea her grandfather would return to the kitchen and pour tea for her grandmother, who rarely arose from bed before getting a cuppa made exactly as she liked it. Eventually there'd be a defining clink when the empty cup was returned to its saucer, a signal her grandmother was getting up and required privacy. She would eventually appear in the kitchen in her best dressing gown with her hair neatly combed to greet Lara as she tucked into porridge soaked overnight and cooked by Poppy on top of the fuel stove.

As Lara recalled these precious memories, Dani browsed through the old photographs: *The Government Wharf at Cedartown. The Cedartown Brush. The Valley from The Mountain. Cattle on the Riverwood Flats. Bullock Team Bringing Cedar down the Mountain. The Cedar-Getters' Hut in the Forest.*

Dani spoke, bringing Lara back to the moment. 'Another world back in those days, Mum. Fascinating stuff.'

'The cedar went pretty quickly. The Cedartown Brush was just a pocket of rainforest on the river but you can see how it must have been all along the river once. In my day the Brush started to get overrun with vines and the canopy closed over. It was a dark and creepy place but I loved the excitement of going there. Can't imagine what's left now.' Lara paused, thinking back. 'Poppy always said the Brush was a real treasure. We have a picture of us standing in the buttress roots of a giant fig, probably hundreds of years old. When I went back with you as a baby on my first trip home from America, it was rundown, smothered in vines from the canopy to the ground and stank because millions of fruit bats had made it their home.' She laughed at the memory. 'I guess it's still a bat kingdom.'

Dani was only half listening. She was absorbed by the old pictures, particularly one taken from a hill looking down at neat dairy paddocks strung across rich alluvial flats to a fringe of trees on either side of the broad curving river. It evoked an atmosphere of complete tranquillity.

Slowly she shuffled through the pictures again, a strange sensation overcoming her.

The sepia image faded, replaced by a dense expanse of grey-green gums with towering straight trunks, and the prized 'red gold' cedars splashing their colour across the forested gullies and hillsides. Echoing down the nearest gully she heard the crack of a whip, and the sing-song language of a bullocky's devising as he urged his team of twenty bullocks down the mountain, hauling a great cedar log with a butt end as wide as a barn door. Metal jangled, wood creaked, the cattle snorted with heavy breaths.

At the cedar-getters' slab hut deep in the rainforest men paused for billy tea and damper as two possums roasted on the campfire. The men were pale skinned from spending so much time in the green gloom, sheltered from sun as they went about the dangerous business of felling the giants of the forest. Convivial company of other men, and the pleasure of beer, rum and women would come once they made their way to Riverwood when the job was done.

Another image, a raft of floating logs bumping downstream with the fast water from recent rains, heading for the sawmill. The logs had been held beside the upstream bank until the current was strong enough, and then all hands nudged them into the flowing river. The cedar-getters would travel ahead in case of log jams at bends or narrow sections of the stream. Men risked their lives, balancing on the logs, wielding axes and poles to free debris and keep the logs moving. And sometimes an unforeseen swirl of water would toss an unlucky bushman from the logs and into the river to be crushed between rolling tree trunks.

Along the river settler families watched the valuable flotsam pass on its journey to perhaps furnish elegant drawing rooms in England or rich merchants' homes in Sydney.

'Dani! Come back down to earth, please. What are you thinking?'

Dani blinked and combed her fingers through her hair as she gave a puzzled grin. 'Oh, I was just trying to imagine what it was like back then. Those men who worked in the rainforest, how they saw those big old trees as money, furniture, progress. I wonder what they'd think now it's all gone . . .'

'It's a way of life that's gone. Poppy used to tell me stories of the bullockies hauling logs and drovers bringing in mobs of cattle to the saleyards years ago. So many stories,' sighed Lara.

'It's stuff we never learned about at school in any detail,' said Dani. 'How long since you went back to Cedartown?'

'I haven't been to the valley for years and years. It probably hasn't changed much. Seems to have been bypassed. Always was a sleepy country town. Once the dairy and timber industry went there wasn't much left.'

'No tourism?'

'Don't think so! There's a nice river, pretty countryside, but nothing for tourists to do. Maybe camp a night, do a spot of fishing, drive up the mountain for a look-see and move on.'

'Sounds lovely. Are there people still around who knew our family? Would your grandparents' house still be there?'

'I haven't been there for years. Once Gordon and I stopped there when we were driving back to Sydney. He

27

wanted to see where my family roots were. He wasn't particularly impressed. We had a steak sandwich and a beer at one of the pubs and drove on.'

'But you've always painted such a warm, nostalgic picture of the place.'

Lara shrugged and turned away from the table laden with family memories. 'When I was a little girl it was special. Only because of my grandparents and it holds my earliest memories. I was born there. I left when I was five and went back for school holidays. Then less frequently. I wanted to travel in the wider world.'

Lara drew a breath and changed the subject. 'Come on, Jolly's sick of being out there. Look at the mess her nose has made on the glass. Though the weather does seem to be clearing up. Do you feel like a walk to clear the head?'

Dani resisted the urge to point out to her mother the change of subject was what her grandmother Elizabeth had done when she didn't want to talk about something. How it had always annoyed Lara and Dani. 'Can't, thanks. Got to run and collect Tim.'

Lara handed Dani an old towel in the laundry to wipe down the damp dog. They chatted and made arrangements to go to a movie later in the week. Dani kissed her mother at the door and halfway down the path to her car, she spun around.

'I've just decided. I'm going up to that valley to look around. It sounds like a place where I might find some ideas about the way ahead. I feel I have a connection with it.'

'It's four hours' drive! You can't commute!'

'I'll just go for a few weeks or so and use up my leave. Can Timmy stay with you?'

'Of course, darling. And Jolly too. I think it's a wild goose chase but if you want to get away that's the place to go.'

Dani settled the dog in the hatchback and gave a happy wave.

Lara watched the car turn the corner, then leaned on the gate, reflecting on the parting announcement. A few weeks in the valley. Silly idea. Dani would probably be back in three days. So why did she feel so unsettled about her daughter visiting the valley and town that held such long forgotten ties and emotions?

Lara returned to the dining room table and picked up a photo. It showed two young boys who looked to be twelve or thirteen, mugging towards the camera. The photographer holding a box camera at waist level was an unseen third person shadowed on the ground before them. The boys wore loose shorts, one had a vest knitted in a Fair Isle pattern over his short-sleeved shirt. They were barefoot with cheeky grins and gave the impression of being good friends or close brothers. She turned the photo over and written in pencil on the back was 'Clem and best friend, 1932'.

Cedartown, 1932

'Hey, Clem, you finished yet?'

'Yeah. Had to clean the milk shed. All done. So what're we going to do then?'

'Got some good green weed. Reckon the blackfish might be on.'

'You beauty. I'll get my rod.'

Carrying their fishing gear, the two boys walked across the dairy paddocks belonging to Clem's family, the Richards. It was a small farm by some North Coast standards but the rich alluvial floodplain provided lush grasses allowing his father to run more Jersey cows per paddock than farms further inland. The boys scrambled through the scrubby trees and undergrowth, following the track to their favourite spot on the river where there was a rough wooden landing jutting from the bank. Next to it an overhanging tree had a rope fastened to a high branch for the boys to swing out and drop into the river.

Late morning and the surface of the broad river was ruffled by a light breeze but the spring sun was warm.

'Good time for fishin' I reckon,' said Clem with authority. Within a couple of minutes of casting, his float gently sank and he gave the rod a sharp flick. 'Got him,' he hissed, then let out a gleeful shout. 'A beauty!' He landed a plate-sized blackfish. 'Beat you. First fish gets the prize,' he chanted, thinking of the extra Minties they had allocated for the prize.

'You've got a good rod,' grumbled Thommo. 'This thing of mine is too old.'

'No, it's not. Keith said that rod of your grandad's is special. Came from England, he reckons.'

'Do they have blackfish over there? Don't they go after trout and stuff?'

'Dunno. I'll ask.' In Clem's eyes his older brother Keith was an authority on just about everything. He didn't ask why Thommo was using his grandad's old rod when his family could've bought him a new one from Davidson's Store. Thommo's father was an electrician and had a small operation servicing homes and businesses. In addition Mr Thompson ran the picture shows screened in the Town Hall. To Clem the Thompsons seemed to be relatively well-off townies. Clem's family had been share farmers until two years ago when they'd got enough together through a small inheritance to buy the farm outright, but it was still a struggle to survive on the land. A lot of people in the town and valley were being hit hard by the long-running Depression and moving on.

For the two boys the Depression the grown-ups talked about was a distant abstract thing, marked mainly by drifting unemployed men looking for jobs, even for a day, or at least a handout of a bit of meat and some bread as they hiked along country roads and door-knocked in towns. The boys knew from overhearing conversations that many of the drifters had good educations and work backgrounds; men who had taught in schools, run offices, worked in factories and knew how to repair machinery. Some occasionally worked on the farm without pay for a time, happy just to have some food and a dry bed in the barn. However, government decree kept the unemployed on the move, and the whole tragedy was a complete puzzle to the boys.

The two boys had become close friends at Cedartown's small high school, which accommodated kids from all over the valley when they finished primary school at one-teacher bush schools. Occasionally Thommo would stay the night on a mattress made of corn sacks stuffed with hay in the sleepout that Clem shared with Kevin, his older, middle brother. Clem had his share of Saturday nights at Thommo's, where the mattress was kapok and on a real bed. Unlike their roaming days outdoors at Clem's farm, a visit to Thommo's meant unlimited time in the darkened Town Hall watching the serials and newsreels. They bonded strongly as mates. They lived for the moment. Their world was a small one.

For Clem and Thommo life during the Depression was as it had always been – school, working at home, and a lot of freedom to explore the district. Thommo helped clean and pack up the Town Hall after the picture shows and sometimes helped his father as projectionist, but, unlike Clem, he had no interest in electrical workings or engineering. Clem, the farm boy, was deeply interested in mechanics and had a natural gift for repairing most broken machinery. The mechanism for screening the films relied on a three-phase electric motor borrowed from a sawmill. Mr Thompson built the projection box where the operator also had to work the mechanism rigged up to open and close the curtains across the screen. Once the amplifier was in place they soundproofed the back wall of the hall with Cane-ite to give better sound. Clem was always trying to think up ways to improve the whole system.

Thommo was a keen member of the 1st Cedartown Boy Scouts where he learned camping and bushcraft skills. When he visited Clem at the farm he liked to show off his culinary skills, like whipping up a damper and cooking it in the coals of an open fire when they went bush for a day. It was too difficult for Clem to travel into town for the night meetings of the scouts and he envied Thommo's achievement badges he'd worked so hard to earn.

Thommo's parents, Frank and Vera, approved of his friendship with Clem. Even felt a bit sorry for him as they knew Walter Richards worked Clem and his brothers hard on their farm.

'Too bad young Clem can't get to scouts,' said Frank Thompson to his wife Vera. 'Any young fellow in the boy scouts is learning loyalty, honesty, courage at times of adversity. I loved my days as a scout master.'

When Clem mentioned the scouts to his father, Walter Richards brushed it aside. 'You have plenty to occupy yourself here. You'll learn more from me and your brothers. And besides, you don't have to be a boy scout to do someone a good deed every day. You can practise that at home.'

The boys spent much of their free time exploring the river in an old wooden dinghy, fishing, catching eels and yabbies. Sometimes they hitched a ride up the mountain range just out of town with a friendly driver of a timber jinker or cattle truck. At the top they had just enough time to scramble down a rough path beside a big waterfall to swim in the leech-infested surrounds at its base before getting the return ride back to town. But escapades like this were rare, usually reserved for the summer school holidays.

Clem was the outgoing and chatty one of the two boys and could generally talk one of his two brothers into getting the cows into the bails for the late afternoon milking if he and Thommo had planned a full-day adventure on the weekend. Being the youngest boy, Clem generally got his way. Though not as much as the youngest child, his sister Phyllis, who was five and the only one who could soften the normally hard lines on their father's face.

Clem's father, talked round by his mother, Nola, had come to accept Clem's friendship with Thommo. Walter Richards didn't approve of the boys skylarking in town. To his mind life was hard, no one gave you anything, you worked your way in this world. Clem sometimes wondered if there'd been a time in his father's life when he'd enjoyed himself, laughed, and did things just for fun. He was strict with all the family, quick to punish, and even Clem's brothers, with the physiques of men, cowered when Walter raised a fist. But Walter accepted Thommo's visits to the farm. Thommo enjoyed the space and freedom after the small house in town. He regularly cycled out from town, and was often at the Richards' table on Saturday nights. Clem's mother thought the boys were more suited to the other's home as Clem loved being in town and hanging round to watch Mr Thompson fiddle with the projection equipment.

Lara looked again at the names pencilled on the back of the photograph then put it down with others scattered around a shoe box of letters and clippings. She looked at the two boys smiling at the camera, and smiled back. Who were these boys? And whatever had become of them?

2

Dani

DANI DROVE OVER THE Sydney Harbour Bridge at dawn. Jolly the dog sat in the back seat amongst bags and baskets. Lara had tried to persuade her to leave the dog with her as finding somewhere to stay with a medium-sized, if happy, hound could be difficult.

As Dani headed up the near-empty F3 the dog settled down to sleep sensing it was going to be a long trip.

Dani stopped for a hasty breakfast at a highway servo and once the freeway ended she drove through small towns, past state forests and into the countryside. In the bright morning sun, crossing a shining river and seeing paddocks of beef and dairy cattle, some sheep and goats gave her the sense of moving into another world. She could feel her body relaxing as she realised she had no pressures of time or demands of duty. Her spirits lifted.

Reaching the bustling regional city of Hungerford, she crossed the bridge and glanced down at the attractive park and council chambers facing the river. She swung around and parked at the river's edge, letting Jolly run along the neatly tended embankment. They walked through the park admiring the flower beds, and a memorial of stone pillars carved with the names of all the local men who'd served in two world wars. Spotting a tearoom, she bought a paper cup of well-brewed tea poured from a huge teapot by a chatty lady who persuaded Dani she should try one of their rock cakes.

She sat on the river bank and shared the crumbly, old-fashioned, raisin-filled cake with Jolly. It was late morning, she had the rest of the day to drive the twelve kilometres into Cedartown and find somewhere to stay.

At the roundabout out of Hungerford she saw the sign to Cedartown via Riverwood. From what she'd seen on the map, Riverwood was a village on this side of the Oxley River, nine kilometres before Cedartown. In her great grandparents' day it was a bustling upriver township. 'Let's check out Riverwood village on the way, eh, Jolly.'

It was better than Dani had imagined. Wonderfully picturesque. She wanted to stop and start sketching the old buildings with their verandahs facing the river, the quaint main street along the river front with a small general store, a tiny post office, jacaranda trees carpeting the ground with mauve flowers and, on a corner, a delightfully renovated original house that had tables and chairs along the verandah, a front garden filled with roses, and glimpses of a courtyard at the back with tables and umbrellas. A sign proclaimed it to be the Nostalgia Cafe.

There was one couple seated at a table. A middle-aged man in a long white apron and striped T-shirt came to greet her with a smile. 'Good morning. Are you wanting morning tea or lunch, or just a cool drink?'

'I left Sydney at five-thirty this morning. We're ready for lunch.'

'We? A table for two . . .?' He glanced around.

'Actually it's me and the dog. Can I tie her in the shade in the garden?'

'Absolutely. I'll bring a dish of water. Would your dog fancy a small bite of something? Provided it's not a customer.' He laughed.

With Jolly settled on the grass under a tree with water in a pink china bowl, Dani read the menu, surprised at the selection of simple French-style dishes and carefully chosen wines.

'I'm George and my partner Claude is the chef. If you have questions, feel free.' He placed a bottle of mineral water and a goblet on the table.

'I'm impressed. This all sounds wonderful. Is Claude French?'

'Of course. Actually he was born in Australia, but we did the south of France thing, went back to his village, and his aunts and all the women taught him their special dishes. But we try to keep it fresh and simple. I can recommend the leek famiche or the salmon terrine.'

'I think the onion tart sounds wonderful. Especially if it's cooked by a French chef. I hadn't expected to find such culinary delights up here.'

'You'd be surprised what's happening in this area. People like us have run away from the city for the good life. There's a couple in Cedartown turning an old butcher's shop into a divine cheese factory. There's a venison and ostrich farm and in Hungerford the best German smallgoods maker you can imagine. Now, a little rocket and roasted beetroot salad on the side?'

'Why not. Don't know where I'll be eating tonight.'

'You're passing through, heading north or south?' George shook out the starched linen napkin and spread it on her lap.

'Actually, I've sort of arrived. My family came from Cedartown so I thought I'd come to the area and look around. Do you know any places that take dogs? Just for, say, a week.'

George poured water into her glass. 'Not sure about Cedartown. But why don't you stay here in Riverwood, it's only fifteen minutes to Cedars. And there's a farm, Chesterfield, down the road which has lovely cabins on the river on ninety acres. Dogs welcome.'

'Really? That sounds perfect. I'll call them. If I'm close by I can eat my way through your menu!'

'How about a few marinated olives and an excellent French olive oil with Claude's mini baguette to start?'

It was that easy. By the end of the meal George had arranged for her to drop in to see a cabin at Chesterfield five minutes away.

Again she was in for a surprise. Driving along the dirt track she came to paddocks with goats, a huge wooden shed that looked to be every man's dream and a large house surrounded by a verandah swathed in an old grape vine. It was a picture postcard. As she parked under the shade of trees a smiling woman came to meet her.

'You must be Dani. I'm Helen Moss. And this is . . .?' She patted the dog.

'Her kennel name is the Jolly Roger but we call her Jolly. She's very friendly and clean. I saw you have a border collie at the gate.'

'She's an old working dog put out to pasture. We also have a nosey little Jack Russell. I'm sure they'll all get on with your schnauzer. Would you like to see the cabin?'

As they walked around the house past a chook pen, a rabbit hutch and an aviary filled with tiny quail and doves,

Dani caught her breath at the panorama. The broad smooth river curved in front of the expanse of lawns fringed with trees at the water's edge. On the opposite bank were lush green river flats dotted with dairy cows. Farm roofs glinted in the sun. In the distance were the peaks of a small mountain range.

'This is stunning. Can you swim in the river?'

'There's a landing with an old dinghy if you want to fish, a kayak to paddle and, yes, it's good swimming when the tide is up. Though there's a pool on the other side of the main house. You're welcome to use it. We have three cabins tucked away so you're quite private. Only one is taken at the moment.'

The little A-frame one-bedroom wooden cottage with its tiny bull-nosed verandah was exactly what she needed.

'I'll take it,' Dani said immediately, then turned towards the big house where she had parked. 'That's your place?'

'Yes, it is. And we love it,' said Helen and went on to explain that it was built in the late nineteenth century for the first Presbyterian minister in the district. 'A lot of Scots came up this way in the early days. When we bought it the house had been modernised. We're trying to restore some of the old charm with antique furniture, polishing the original floorboards and uncovering the old fireplaces and walls and so on. My husband Barney and I are around if you need anything. Help yourself to vegies from the garden and eggs, of course. There's a local store but then you're only a few minutes from Cedartown and Hungerford.'

Dani put her bags and sketching materials in the cabin and with difficulty called Jolly away from the wooded area where she could smell wild rabbits and wallabies. 'Let's go stock up on provisions, some wine and other goodies, old girl. I might never leave this property.'

After shopping she watched the sun go down behind

the hills and the river turn a silken pewter splashed with rose gold. On the opposite bank the cows were trudging single file from the milking shed to their paddock. Sipping a glass of wine, an exhausted Jolly at her feet – she'd raced over every inch of the acreage led by the energetic Ratso the Jack Russell – Dani couldn't recall when she'd felt so at peace. This is what I need, time just for me, she decided. There was only patchy mobile phone reception at Chesterfield unless she walked to the top of the hill overlooking the dam. Dani decided to put off calling her mother and son till the next morning.

Helen and Barney Moss, who owned Chesterfield, took Dani under their wing without being intrusive.

Barney brought her a fish he'd caught for her dinner and offered to take her along the river in his small boat to show her his secret places. 'The landscape looks different from the river. You might find something to paint.'

Dani had been wandering about the property and the river bank making sketches. Helen invited her up to the big verandah to have a sundowner and Dani told her why she was in the area.

'What say I take you for a bit of a run tomorrow, show you some of the out-of-the-way spots? I have to deliver some leaflets,' said Helen.

'That would be nice . . . but I don't want to put you out.'

Helen, in her fifties, was short and stocky with bright blue eyes and a quick smile. Her hair was a peppered faded ginger, which Barney told Dani was not as fiery as it had once been.

'Though her tongue and temper are still hot,' he said with a grin. 'She gives them curry at those council meetings. A community activist is what they call her when they're being polite but she has a reputation as a bit of a bomb thrower.'

Helen was dismissive of the comments. 'He exaggerates everything. Look, I'd love to give you a bit of a tour. I'm delivering a newsletter to people who don't get into council meetings. And I wouldn't offer to take you if I didn't mean it. How's tomorrow afternoon suit?'

'Terrific. Thanks, Helen. I thought I'd drive over to Cedartown, go past my great-grandparents' old house. Mum is anxious to know what it's like. Got my camera to take photos for her.'

It was hot and in the middle of the day Cedartown looked deserted. Dani drove slowly along the residential streets where houses built in the fifties and sixties were unchanged. Some much older homes had been renovated and extended but all had small front verandahs, some screened by glass or wooden louvres or lattice. Roses flourished in neat front gardens. Brick dwellings dominated only in the newer areas opened up in the postwar boom years and were still proliferating into paddocks on the edge of town.

The main shopping street, Isabella Street, was wide and had fat Canary Island date palms down the centre with parking down the middle. She wondered if some of the old shops had been there when her great-grandparents moved in during the 1920s. She began to notice innovations. The gracious old stone bank was now a boutique B&B with a restaurant. There was a cafe, Convivia, serving organic food and juice next to the CWA meeting rooms. The two pubs were typical of old-style country hotels with wide verandahs, except now they boasted satellite TV and air conditioning. The main street encircled a broad sweep of public park that was dominated by an old Air Force Vampire jet mounted on a plinth, its nose aimed at the sky, giving the impression that it might just soar off at any moment. The cockpit and fuselage looked so small Dani wondered how one man, let alone a second, fitted inside.

Across the road and overlooking the park was the Services Club. Further up by the park boundary was a giant log mounted on concrete blocks. Dani imagined it was probably a memorial to the timber industry. The School of Arts (est. 1874) with iron lace verandah caught her approving eye, and a sign announcing it now housed the Cedartown Public Library. And a big wooden building with double shop-front windows advertised its new role as home of the Historical Society and Museum.

Dani led Jolly across the park and studied the museum's window displays of relics of early twentieth century life in the area. Or maybe even earlier, she thought, taking in a stiff wax model of a woman in ankle-length period costume standing next to a wooden washing mangle and a 'Kangaroo Butter Churner'. Old farming implements, saddles, gold-panning equipment and clay pipes were in the adjacent window. Judging from the layout and the faded gold letters above the door, this had probably been a large emporium in its heyday, selling just about anything anyone needed. Glancing inside she was amazed at the rows of packed display cases and standing exhibits. A sign announced that out the back there were farm equipment and horse buggies along with all manner of larger items. It would take a week to see everything in here, she decided, stepping inside simply to ask the man behind a table at the door the time.

'Two o'clock, dear. Plenty of time before we close.'

'Sorry, but I have to meet someone, I'll come back and spend a day here later in the week.' She went down the broad stone steps worn to a deep dip in the centre by the comings and goings over many decades of the people of Cedartown. I bet my great Nana and Poppy came in here, she mused.

Helen suggested they leave Jolly on her verandah with Ratso as it would be hot in the car and a few of the places they were going had cranky guard dogs or were in a national park.

Dani was glad they were in Helen's old station wagon as the back roads were dirt and gravel. She could hardly believe the beauty of the gullies and hills, and every so often a vista of the great river. She took photos of old houses and barns with rusting rooftops, some leaning precariously and partially covered with uncontrolled vines. She photographed a cow beneath a flowering fruit tree and a standing brick fireplace – all that remained of a simple farmhouse. The rolling landscape, its colours, the way the sunlight fell through the trees, the small hamlets, isolated community halls, a schoolhouse for a dozen kids, a lopsided old wooden shed, a rusting 1930s truck in a field, all excited her.

Occasionally they called into some of the newer homes or friends of Helen who'd charmingly 'fixed up' rundown farmhouses into farm stays or B&Bs.

'These places are lovely. I had no idea people came out here for holidays.'

'City families, wanting a taste of country living. Their kids haven't been near a cow or had the kind of freedom our kids took for granted,' said Helen. 'Tourism is an issue with council, we have to be careful how it's managed, what regulations are in place. More and more farmers are doing the farm stay as a very good sideline.'

'I can see I need longer than a week here. I could spend days in the historical society in Cedars,' said Dani. She'd taken to the local habit of abbreviating the town's name.

'Have you talked to Henry?' asked Helen as they headed into thick scrubby country on a dirt road.

'Who's he?'

'Henry Catchpole. Virtually runs the historical society, very big on family histories. In his seventies, probably knew your family. He's been here all his life apart from the war and his great-grandparents were pioneers.'

'Would he be useful?'

'I reckon. He knows everything that's happened in the valley and might give you some ideas of subjects and places to paint. He's very entertaining, tells a good yarn. He's been very helpful to me in sensitive issues with the council.'

Dani didn't answer as she looked around her. The scene was beautiful. The track wound down to a creek surrounded by ghost gums shedding their bark in hanging strips revealing silvery trunks mottled with faint mushroom-pink spots. The creek was clear, the stones beneath the water looked like they'd been artfully placed by a landscaper. On the other side of the creek the track was steep and sharp.

'Can we stop please, Helen? I'd love a photo of this place.'

Helen grinned. 'That's why I brought you here. This is pretty famous, or rather infamous. It's Kelly's Crossing. Goes back to the first settlers in the area.'

'Any relation to Ned?' asked Dani.

'Isabella was years before Ned. Apparently she was a pretty tough bird. A single woman who made a fortune in land, cattle, horses. There are stories of underhand dealings, that she befriended bushrangers, even slept with them, and flogged her convicts. There are stories about her riding around the country packing pistols on her hip. What's truth or legend, no one knows for sure.'

'Wow, if half of that is true, what a legend! What happened to her?'

'Not sure. Most people around here don't even know she existed.'

Dani stood at the edge of the dancing creek, sunlight

glinting on its surface. It was still and quiet and she could clearly imagine a woman riding across the creek, then spurring her horse up the steep bank.

'Fabulous spot,' she exclaimed. 'I keep getting visions of how it must have been here way back in Isabella Kelly's days.'

Helen, a pragmatic woman, surprised Dani. 'I had a feeling you'd relate to this place. A lot of things have happened at Kelly's Crossing over the years. Good and bad. Few people come here anymore.'

'What kind of things?'

'Ask Henry. He's got some bee in his bonnet about Kelly's Crossing.'

Dani kicked off her shoes and walked to the edge of the creek. The water was refreshingly cold. But there was something else that made her shiver. Dani had the feeling unhappy ghosts hovered here. She resolved nonetheless to come back to this place.

In a few days Dani was a regular at the Nostalgia Cafe, calling in for meals or a coffee and sometimes a glass of wine after walking Jolly at sunset. If they weren't busy Claude and George would join her and she gradually came to know their story. They also took a great interest in her 'doings', as George put it.

Claude was much younger than George, who was in his fifties, Claude barely thirty. They'd been together ten years as a couple. 'We make every day precious. Well, as much as we can when he's not in one of his moods,' grinned George. 'Chefs are very temperamental, you know.'

Getting out of the city to fresh air and a calmer lifestyle was the main reason they'd come to Riverwood and, although they had been there only eighteen months, they seemed to know everything about everyone in the area.

'Those boys love to gossip,' Helen told Dani. 'Don't tell them anything you don't want the world to know. They're worse than a pair of old women at a CWA tea.'

Dani arrived at the Nostalgia Cafe for lunch, left Jolly in her spot under the tree and saw at the side of the steps a boy sitting on the lawn with a selection of paintings spread before him. She stopped to admire the bright pictures of farm scenes and animals. Strong colours; firm, sure brush strokes and a few amusing touches jumped out at her. It seemed work too assured for the dark-eyed boy who gave her a winning smile.

'Are these yours?' asked Dani. 'They're very good.'

'Yep. Did them last week. I went to Jumbai to a friend's farm. That's what I saw.'

'Do you have art lessons? At school?' Or were you also born with the art bug, wondered Dani.

'Nah, I don't tell anyone at school I paint. I just do this for pocket money. My dad is an artist too.'

'I love the chook picture, how much?'

'Fifteen dollars,' he said firmly.

Dani handed over the money and picked up the board painted in thick acrylics of hens pecking in a backyard. 'What's your name? Where is your dad?'

'I'm Lennie, we live up the road, round that corner.'

'Well, thanks, Lennie. Hope you sell some more.'

'Saturdays are good here. If I don't, I'll pick fruit and sell that. I'm saving up for a scooter.'

Dani propped up the picture next to the verandah railing as she took her favourite table. George appeared and she told him about her trip around the district with Helen. Claude joined them, putting a fresh baguette and olive oil on the table.

The boys had never heard of Isabella Kelly or been to

the historical society museum in Cedartown. 'See, I told you we're not getting around and exploring enough,' said George to Claude.

'Darling, how're the painting plans coming along?' asked Claude, ignoring George. 'Are you going to make the valley famous?'

'No way. I'm just exploring options. Though it seems this part of the world hasn't been exposed in an artistic sense. When you think of artists claiming certain landscapes – Pro Hart and Broken Hill, Sid Nolan with Ned Kelly and Hill End, Arthur Boyd and the Shoalhaven, Hans Heysen and the Adelaide Hills, Norman Lindsay and bohemia, Albert Namatjira and the real outback . . .'

'Ah, there was an artist,' sighed George. 'And yet as an Aboriginal painter doing watercolours of the Northern Territory he was derided as selling out to whitemen's culture.'

'Until I saw those colours of the outback I didn't believe they were real,' said Claude.

'Max has told us a lot about him,' said George. 'Visiting Max is like doing a crash course in indigenous culture.'

'Who's Max?' asked Dani.

'Maxwell James. Lennie's dad. The kid who's selling paintings out the front. You haven't been to Maxwell's? That's the first place – after us – you should go!' exclaimed Claude. 'He's a terrific artist. Has his own gallery around the corner.'

'Really? I'd like to meet him. What's he like?'

'You'll like him,' said George. 'He's shy and gentle but pretty astute. Tunes into people right off. He sculpts, paints, carves and is one of the best didge players in the area. In his own way he's made a bit of a noise, well, spoken out in his mild way about issues concerning his people.'

'His people? You mean Aboriginal people? That's such a . . . parochial, well, condescending way of putting things,' Dani said gently. That explained Lennie's olive skin and dark curly hair.

'The ol' them and us. There's always been, and continues to be, a lot of strife between black and white in a country town. Same as gays. It's still an issue here,' said George. 'There's a mob of activist blackfellas and well-meaning do-good whitefellas – mainly women I might add – here. And they come at issues from opposite ends. Sometimes they actually meet in the middle or get together.'

'What sort of issues?'

'Ah, the usual. Everything. From health, community housing, unemployed youth to haranguing council over not flying the Aboriginal flag outside chambers.' George and Claude exchanged a shrug and a look. 'We keep out of it publicly. But I follow things closely.'

Dani gave them an amused but perceptive look. 'And what do you think is really the issue?'

'Old sores, an awareness things are being done better in other places. People here don't want to be seen as a racist country town but there are some types who hark back to the old days when attitudes – on both sides – were different.'

'It's beginning to change though,' added Claude. 'People like Max are good.' He nodded towards Lennie on the lawn. 'He's got great kids, they never ask for a handout.'

'Max is married to a very nice white girl. Sarah is a primary teacher and they have two boys. Len is ten and Julian fourteen,' added George.

'I'd like to meet Maxwell. In fact, I might wander up there after lunch.'

'You won't miss his place,' grinned Claude.

Dani turned down the short street with simple houses and pretty gardens. Spotting the gallery, her first impression was how kitsch. The mish-mash of bright colours, the dot-painted crazy-paving path, native animals sculpted from old tyres, wood and cement standing round the front garden. The water feature with cement lizards, wind chimes in trees, the rainbow serpent writhing over the gallery entrance, which was the garage next to the colourful house. A large sign announced this was the Long River Gallery.

Max ambled outside as Dani came through the gate. He was a handsome man. In his early forties, she guessed.

'Hi, I'm Dani. George and Claude suggested I drop by. So did your son. I own my first Leonard James.'

He laughed and shook her hand. 'Nice to meet you. Thanks for supporting him.'

'Is he following in your footsteps?'

'Not really, Len and Julian try to earn money any way they can. So long as they do their chores and homework I'm all for it. I'm not forking out eight hundred dollars for some fancy scooter.'

'Your place is quite amazing,' said Dani.

'It's different. Try to catch the tourists. They always like to take photos.'

'Tourists? You seem a bit off the beaten track, how do people find you?' asked Dani.

'Word of mouth, from the locals and of course the internet. I have a hot website.'

Dani laughed. 'I believe it. I'd like to look around. Is this all your work?'

'Mostly. There's stuff I do for the commercial side of things and stuff I do for me.'

'Ah, now that I can relate to.'

'You're an artist?'

'I've quit my job in Sydney as a graphic artist and I'm planning to paint full-time. Just to see what I can do.'

'That's the only way to know. Have you had any art training?' he asked with interest.

'Off and on all my life. I chose not to go to art school. I guess I didn't want to be told what to do and how to do it.

48

My father suggested communications and journalism and I got my BA but it's not what I want to do.'

They strolled into the art gallery and Max asked, 'Do you see yourself selling your work? Landscapes of places like this sell very well to tourists.' There was something noncommittal in his tone.

'Actually, no. I got a bit of money after my divorce so I don't want to feel I have to paint just to sell. Letting the market dictate what I do. I'm trying to find myself through my art. Not that I'm confused personally. Find my own style, I mean.'

'I understand perfectly,' said Max sounding relieved.

'These canvases are what I call potboilers, they sell real well.' He waved at small, neatly framed scenes of the area including a lot of seascapes and beach scenes. 'The coast is very spectacular, only thirty minutes' drive. And these are small versions of my large Dreaming ones.' He pointed at a collection of small, colourful Aboriginal paintings of styl-ised animals and subjects that looked more like abstracts. 'I have to cater to the market, I have a family and over-heads running this place. It's not just my paintings in here. I give space to other artists. But the big regional gallery in Hungerford is terrific.'

'I'll have to go and see what's in there.'

'They've got a fantastic director. A lady who was working as a curator in Canberra. In fact, there's a big exhibition opening tomorrow night. You should go. Sarah and I are going if you'd like to come with us. Are you stay-ing locally?'

'I'm at Chesterfield, ten minutes away. I'd love to go.'

'Ah, Helen and Barney. Nice people. How come you found this place? We try to keep it a bit of a secret.'

'My mother was born in Cedartown. My great-grandparents lived there.'

'Do you have other relatives still up here?' Maxwell had

a gentle soft voice and mild manner that contrasted with his looks, thought Dani. He was tall with broad shoulders, strong-looking. Handsome, too, with fine features, dark skin and thick curly hair. He sounded well educated and could obviously step between both cultures. George had told Dani that Max chose to identify as Aboriginal though his mother's family were half-caste, which was tougher than being dark skinned. But his wife Sarah's white family loved him and Max and Sarah were well liked in the area.

'No rellies left here. Which is a pity. I'd like to have some claim to the place,' said Dani, surprising herself.

'If you were born in the valley you belong here. There's a tree or a patch of ground where your spirit and Dreaming are. Maybe you should spend some time here, try to find that place.'

'That's a nice idea,' said Dani politely, thinking she had no desire to claim a connection with the town in the US where she'd been born. 'You must have roots deep in the soil here. I envy you.'

'If you follow the river from where it starts on the mountain all the way to the sea, you'll come to know the valley. And if you have a creative connection to it, you'll feel you belong, not just because of your great-grandparents.'

'I'd never thought of it like that. My grandmother talked a bit about growing up here but she moved away when my mother was young so I've never thought about having any connection here. I happened to see a photo at my mother's of the old days here, the early settlers, and that got me interested,' said Dani.

Max frowned. 'A lot of the early pioneers and settlers didn't understand the heart of the valley. They ripped out its guts, brought in strange animals, they fought my people, they changed it,' he said with quiet passion. 'But the land is forgiving. If you allow it, it can come back and embrace all of us. The river, that's the heart that pumps life through the valley. It's what we have to keep alive. That's the job I inherited from my people.'

'I wonder if my people and your people ever crossed paths?' said Dani to lighten the mood.

'Could be. My grandmother is still alive and in her nineties. What was your great-grandparents' name?'

'Williams. Harold and Emily,' said Dani. 'He worked for the railway. What about your family? Did they live in town?'

'Are you kidding? Blackfellas, even half-castes, were stuck out of town. Planters Field. Known as the blacks' camp in grandmother's day. Planters Field Aboriginal Housing Reserve. It's still a fringe community, but my family are scattered.'

'Being here has got me thinking about my family,' said Dani.

Max gave Dani a look as if he was deciding something. 'Come with me. I wonder about my family too.'

She followed him around the side of the house. There was an old log and some bleached and twisted branches that looked like snakes.

Max reached down to where some smooth stones were placed in a ring. He handed one to Dani. 'Feel that. An old cutting tool. Look how well it sits in your hand, see the sharp edge, how it fits with your fingers and thumb. Very effective too,' he said.

She took it and rolled it around in her hands and then, holding the stone, bent down and hit a boulder at the edge of the garden. It made a satisfying clink, a chip spun away. 'It does work well,' agreed Dani. 'How come you have this? It must be really old.' She handed it back to Max who turned it over in his hands, caressing it.

'Farmers dig them up occasionally and bring them to me. And I know where old ceremonial grounds are.' He paused and, almost wistfully, added, 'I wonder who made this, held this, worked with it. Perhaps one of my ancestors. It's from this area, as I am, and that links me very deeply with this valley.'

Dani was quiet a moment. 'So you were here first.' She looked Max in the eye, not rudely, or challengingly, but with a polite kind of defiance. 'I'd like to think I belong here too.'

Max replaced the primitive tool. 'That's why you've come back. You can't go forward until you know your past.'

Dani now slept through the strident dawn chorus of the bantam cockerels but on Friday morning Jolly's delighted barking woke her suddenly. The dog was pawing to get out onto the verandah and when Dani slid open the glass doors, she saw why. Two young children were romping in the dewy grass in their pyjamas. A boy had a large floppy-eared rabbit on a long length of string and it was sniffing around the bushes. An older girl had a young black Angora goat on a much stronger length of string.

'You're up early,' called Dani. 'Sun's not even up.' She pointed to the pale gold and pink streaks in the sky. A low mist hung over the river but she could smell and feel it was going to be a hot day.

'Sorry. We didn't know you had a dog. Will it chase our rabbit?' called the boy.

'Stupid, of course it will. Ratso does. All dogs chase them,' said the girl with the air of a smart young sister.

'I'll keep her inside. What are you doing with the animals?' asked Dani.

'Taking them for a walk. Our rabbit gets tired of being in the hutch,' said the girl.

'Even if it's a big one. Nan moves them round,' added the boy.

Dani had seen Helen move the rabbit hutch onto fresh grass. 'Helen is your nana?'

The children came closer to the verandah, looking up at Dani and the eager Jolly. The girl looked to be about six, the boy about eight, same as Tim.

'Yep. We're coming to live here with Nana and Pop,' he announced.

'Really? And what about your mum and dad?' Dani recalled Helen talking with pride about her daughter Angela, a teacher, and her lovely family.

'They're coming too, of course,' said the girl as if Dani had asked a very silly question.

At that moment Helen appeared around the side of the house in her dressing gown. 'My goodness, you little imps. I've told you not to go near the guests. Sorry, Dani. This is Toby and Tabatha, my daughter's kids.'

'No problem. They weren't to know Jolly was here. Do you want a cup of tea?'

'I'd better see to their porridge, thanks anyway. They've got a day off school and promised to help Pop in the shed. What about you?'

'Painting. Max has offered me space in his studio. Has an extra easel and the works. Very kind of him.'

'Great, so you'll transform one of your sketches into a big painting then?'

'That's the idea,' said Dani. She didn't tell Helen she was planning to paint the view of the river from the verandah as a gift for her. She'd wait and see how it turned out first. 'The kids say they're moving here.'

'Yes, we're so excited. Angela has got a job at the district school and her husband Tony is finishing his environmental degree. They're renovating the old cottage down the back of the property here. They'll help us run this place, and give us a breather occasionally. Can't remember the last proper holiday we had.'

'You came to Port last Christmas, Nana,' declared Tabatha.

'So we did.' Helen grinned at Dani. 'Barney and I looked after these two while Angela and Tony had a few days away. Some holiday!'

'They live at Port Macquarie?'

'For the last few years. Have a productive day, Dani. Come on, kids, you can groom the animals later.'

'We're putting them in the Cedartown Show next month,' explained Tabatha as they turned to follow Helen back to the big house.

Dani watched them go and suddenly missed her son. She hurried up the hill with her mobile and caught Tim before Lara took him to school.

'Why don't you come up here for the weekend, Tim? There's lots to do and I think you'll enjoy yourself.'

He sounded doubtful. 'Ma and I are doing stuff. Anyway, aren't you coming home soon?'

'Yes, but I want you to see this place. I might spend a bit more time here.'

'Why? You said you'd be gone a week or so. It'll be a week on Sunday. I miss Jolly.'

'And me too? What are you doing on the weekend?'

'Soccer practice,' he said quickly. The idea of a long drive to a strange place in the country held no appeal.

'Good luck, sweetie. Jolly is fine, she loves it here. Chases rabbits. Well, put Ma on and have a good day at school.'

'Hi, darling, what's up?' Lara sounded concerned.

'Nothing. Relax, Mum. I'm going to paint in a friend's studio. I was just talking to the grandkids of the woman who runs this place, the boy is Tim's age, and I thought you guys might like to drive up for the weekend.' Dani paused and when Lara didn't react went on, 'I'm thinking of staying on longer than planned. I feel I'm just getting organised. Would that be all right?'

'Of course. I'm glad you're feeling creative. But us rushing up there for two days . . . well, it doesn't seem worth it.' Lara sensed something in Dani's voice. 'School holidays soon. Maybe we could do something then.'

'Okay, you're sure Timmy isn't any trouble? There's all that driving him places and school stuff.'

'Nonsense, I'm loving it. Take care, darling, we have to dash to school.'

Lara meant what she said. In the past week she'd realised how empty her life had become since quitting her job. With the travel bug satisfied, she filled her days mainly with gardening and keeping the house immaculate. She was bored. Over the past week she'd become quite interested in some of Tim's schoolmates and their parents. Chatting with them at the school gate and sometimes over a coffee, she became more aware of the increasing problems and dramas many young couples were experiencing. How there was never enough time, or money, or solutions to job and family pressures. It seemed so different from when she was a child.

Lara had always felt isolated from the family life of her friends. There had only been her mother and her from when she was ten and tragedy had rocked their complacent, simple lives. Even so, comparing her childhood friends with those of her grandson, it seemed for all their material wealth, lavish homes and lifestyle, something was missing in these modern families. It wasn't just routine and discipline that was lacking, but there was a hollowness, a shallowness, a barely concealed desperation. Why did she now recall those distant childhood holidays with her grandparents with such nostalgia?

Lara supposed Dani's return to the country town where their family roots were had triggered her fond memories of another era, of time spent with her grandparents in the fifties when Australia was enjoying security and a postwar boom. A time when she felt loved and protected.

Lara's life with her mother Elizabeth was blighted by the shadow of tragedy, the fear of what could happen to change your life in a day, and the weighty knowledge that life was a struggle for her mother. Not just financially and emotionally. The bitter set to Elizabeth's mouth and the sad, often distrusting look in her eyes made Lara realise her mother was different, not like her friends' mothers. By contrast, at home at Cricklewood her relaxed grand-parents happily indulged her, and taught her to believe that beyond the confines of their small country town, and over the horizon, a huge world waited, a world where any-thing was possible.

Lara wondered how Dani felt about her childhood. She'd had only a brief time in the security of a complete family unit. Dani's relationship with her father was distant, emotionally as well as geographically, and his family was scattered around the USA. Lara hadn't ever talked in depth with Dani about growing up in a different country, or about Lara's divorce from Dani's father Joe, or about Lara's failed second marriage to Gordon. Yet Dani seemed well adjusted, even after her own divorce. Lara knew she and Dani were very close. Her grandson was happy. And so Lara never dwelt on past unhappiness if she could help it.

But she couldn't dispel the feeling that the ground was trembling beneath her firmly planted feet. There was a shadow of unfinished business in Lara's life and, she real-ised, it had all begun at Cricklewood, her grandparents' house. She looked at the dining room table covered in doc-uments, letters and photographs from the long-neglected family archives retrieved from the old house when her grandfather died. They now absorbed most of her spare time and were casting a web around her, of memories, nos-talgia and questions she should have asked long ago.

Lara took a deep breath. For an instant she wondered how Dani really felt about being near her great-grandparents' home but quickly she realised her daughter had no memories of Cricklewood. Lara had brought Dani home on her first visit back from America when she was eight months old. Lara took her baby home to Cricklewood to meet her grandfather. Emily had died a year before and it was a welcome diversion for Harold who was lonely, sharing Cricklewood and its memories with his little dog Rover.

Her mother Elizabeth had been very emotional and excited at seeing her first grandchild but she was working and unable to go with Lara and the baby to Cedartown. Lara was secretly glad. She wanted Poppy all to herself. When she got back to her mother in Sydney there was a lot of tension between them that was difficult to cope with, impossible to understand. Her mother refused to talk about whatever was making her so stand-offish after such a warm welcome a fortnight earlier. So Lara told Joe that she was coming back to America earlier than intended.

Life around Elizabeth was always drama filled, recalled Lara as she walked into the kitchen and switched off the murmuring radio. Thoughts of her mother and grandparents swirled in her head; places, incidents, people, feelings, confusing images of her childhood years.

Lara strode outdoors looking for something to do. Suddenly she envied Dani having a project, even if it was just an experiment for a week or so. I should go up there too. Make a pilgrimage to the ancestral homeland, she joked to herself. Why not? Lara swung back indoors feeling invigorated. She had plans to make.

3

Cedartown, 1928

Emily and Harold

'HAROLD, IT'S ALL FULL of trees! Bushes . . . my goodness, I hadn't remembered how . . . wild it is!'

'That's why it's called a bush block, Em. We looked at it over a year ago and it's not been touched.'

'Well, now it's ours. Every wretched weed and tree. Oh dear, it's going to be a big job clearing all this to build. Are you sure you can manage, dear?' Emily was having second thoughts about her planned trip to England and leaving her husband Harold to hold down his job as head porter at Cedartown Railway Station and to help construct a home. 'Perhaps I shouldn't spend the money. We'll need it for the building. They keep talking about bad times coming.'

Harry affectionately patted his wife's shoulder and lifted Mollie, their two-year-old daughter, from her arms. 'You've done a wonderful job managing the money and saving up and I know you've been looking forward to showing the girls off to the family back home.'

He gave the little girl a kiss on the cheek and smiled at the tiny determined figure of his wife beside him. Emily still looked as young and pretty as the day he'd proposed – her soft brown wavy hair parted on the side, her peaches and cream skin that she protected from the harsh Australian sun by always wearing a hat of some kind, her blue eyes and small, cupid's bow mouth. She was a dainty thing, and was often compared to Elizabeth Bowes-Lyon who married the Duke of York who later became King George VI.

But Harold had come to learn Emily had an iron will and feisty temper once riled. She was not a lady to be trifled with, to be short-changed or not treated in a manner she thought her due. She was firm with the girls, telling Harold he was too soft on them. He always gave in to her with a good natured, 'Whatever you say, Em.'

When she announced she'd saved up the fare for herself and the girls to travel – even if steerage class – to England, he'd been slightly surprised, but pleased she'd managed it. Yes, it had been a struggle but for six years Emily squirrelled away shillings of the housekeeping money, keeping it separate from what they'd put in the bank from Harold's pay packet to buy the block of land. She'd been frugal.

They were also lucky in that Harold was well liked by the farmers and business people whose produce and wares came through the railway goods shed where he worked. He often came home with little gifts of appreciation, particularly at Easter and Christmas. And they also frequently gave him damaged items that spilled from broken freight containers. Every time he shunted railway wagons out to the bacon factory and abattoirs on the southern edge of town he would check in with the shift boss and be given a parcel of saveloys, sausages or tender pork fillets. The manager of the butter factory on the other side of town also offered a billycan of cream or milk any time Harold helped out with freight shipments. These added luxuries were very welcome and cost no more than a smile and polite service.

'Remember, we won't have to pay any more rent to Mrs Moon while you're away,' added Harold to reassure his wife. 'I'm going to camp here and get cracking. In six months or so when you three come back it will all be nearly done.' He gave Mollie a playful nose nuzzle in the tummy and they both laughed.

'I'm afraid we couldn't manage in a tent,' said Emily. There was a touch of embarrassment in her voice. The idea of a nicely brought up London girl living under canvas would not be well received back in the old country where her father had a certain status in their essentially working-class community – he was in charge of furniture maintenance at Buckingham Palace. No, camping with children was out of the question. It was difficult enough in the two rooms they rented in the better part of town over the bridge.

It was now two years since they'd moved up the line from Lairwood to Cedartown to take advantage of Harold's promotion to head porter, but they had decided against another move, even if it meant Harold might miss being promoted to station master. They agreed it would be more practical and less disruptive to family life to settle in one place. So they'd bought the half-acre block of land for one hundred pounds and applied for a housing loan from the Government Savings Bank of New South Wales, which had a charter from the state government to facilitate the financing of houses in the country. The bank had a selection of house plans available for potential borrowers and the Williams had chosen plan number one hundred and twelve.

The house had big verandahs front and back, a wide

hallway with two bedrooms on one side, kitchen and living room on the other. The bathroom was at the end of the hall, but the sanitary pan toilet was well down the backyard. Emily had eliminated the two open fireplaces in the bedrooms, but retained the big open fireplace in the living room. It was a wooden house with an imposing brick wall on the front verandah. The roof was galvanised corrugated iron.

'And nor would I expect you to live rough in a tent. Come on, let's have a cup of tea to celebrate,' said Harold warmly. 'And you have to look at the plans and tell me if there are any more changes you want made.' He turned to check on their other daughter Elizabeth and spotted her down the back of the block poking a stick into a large ant bed. 'Hey, stop annoying those ants, Elizabeth,' he shouted, but without a hint of anger. 'They've got a right to live here, just like us. Come on, we're going now.'

Elizabeth, a pretty seven-year-old, threw the stick away and skipped up the bushy block to join the family as they began walking towards the nearby railway station. 'Where's our house going to be, Mummy?' she asked.

'It's going to be right here. Dad's going to build a lovely house for us to live in when we get back from England. See, there's a house being built down the road.' Emily was trying to visualise her own completed house fronted by a rose garden with a nicely painted paling fence and a shiny letterbox.

Suddenly there was a burst of laughter from the top of a nearby tree.

'Kookaburra,' announced Elizabeth. 'There are two of them with a nest in that tree near the ants' nest.'

'That's wonderful,' said Harold. 'Well, in that case I'll make sure that we don't cut down the tree so they can be there to laugh for you when you get back from England.'

'Thanks, Dad.'

Still holding Mollie, Harold took Elizabeth's hand and led them across to the railway station where he had his cubby hole office beside the big wooden goods shed. He'd miss his girls and he worried about the task he'd undertaken. His carpentry skills were basic but a mate who worked at Flanagan's Sawmill had promised to help him build a rough timber storage shed down the back of the block. The builder of the house would be recommended by the bank. He hoped Emily wouldn't make many more alterations to the basic plan.

Emily had already made a trip down to Newcastle – glad of the discount fare on the train – to choose several essential items for the new house. Her list included a sanitary pan cover costing twenty-four shillings and sixpence, a number two Bega stove with porcelain door for wood fuel at seven pounds nine shillings and threepence, and an Anti Splash bath with lion's claw feet at eight pounds three shillings.

Emily's most important request was that the house have a brass nameplate next to the front door and it be called 'Cricklewood' after the London suburb where she and her childhood sweetheart Harold had first met.

'First impressions are very important,' she declared.

As they walked across the railway line that divided the town, Harold was conscious they were settling on the side of the tracks where other battlers were making their homes. The well-to-do families lived closer to the river or in spacious homes near the centre of town. Nevertheless he felt a small stirring of pride knowing that he was providing a solid home for his devoted wife and daughters. He'd come to this country as a teenage lad with his dad and had never looked back or longed for the old country. Once his mother, brother and sisters had joined them they all considered Australia home. And he'd fought for his adopted country in the Great War.

Briefly thoughts of hardship and painful times flashed to his mind, but he resolutely pushed them away and began to whistle a cheerful song. Even after a decade, the war years sometimes encroached on his peace of mind, disturbed his sleep, or hit him with a deep sense of loss.

Emily glanced at her husband, wondering at the way he retreated behind that whistle, a song to which she knew no words, which put a distant light in his eyes and took him some place where she'd never been and would never know. She'd learned to keep her thoughts and questions to herself when he whistled like that. It had something to do with the war, which he rarely spoke about except to recount a humorous anecdote or tell of some cultural and seemingly trivial social event in France or Belgium, but he was a lovely storyteller and made everything sound interesting.

How lucky she was to have married the man she'd known since they were children in the crowded terraces of Cricklewood in North West London. He'd grown to a man in Australia, lean and handsome.

How delighted she'd been in 1916 when smartly uniformed Private Harold Williams arrived to visit while on leave from the Australian Imperial Force units that had been moved from Egypt to England. He was much taller than her five feet three inches, and was slim as a strong young tree. His hands had seen hard work but she admired his long fingers. He had a lovely smile and humorous blue-grey eyes that always seemed to spot the funny side of life. His dark brown hair refused to sit flat no matter how hard he tried to slick it down. She'd always thought him an attractive boy and now he'd become a handsome soldier indeed.

He was doing more field ambulance corps training before going into action in France. It touched her to learn that he'd kept in his pack her letters and a photo of her taken under a parasol at Brighton the previous summer. How she had worried when she didn't hear much from him during his early years in Australia, but she wrote to him frequently.

London, 2nd of March 1910
Dear Harold,
Thank you very much for your keepsake. I thought it was very good of you to send such an interesting book on Australian flowers and it arrived in perfect condition. They are different to what you would see here in London. I should like to see them in reality as they must be awfully pretty . . .

Would you like me to send you some books? I am as fond of them as ever and as I have got such a lot I will send you two every week, two will follow this letter.

The latest craze in London at the present time is the great number of picture palaces. You can hardly go from one street corner to another without coming across one of them, especially in the Walworth Road. They are places you can guess I never enter. Another craze is that of skating and we have several skating rinks in our neighbourhood. Up to the present I have never been to one but I look forward to that pleasure sometime or other. I suppose you know I have started work at a surgical instrument maker in Oxford Street and have been there just over twelve months.

It must be lonely for you out there if you don't make many friends, don't I wish I was out there. I've learned to play the piano by ear just a little, that reminds me, Cyril Bromley plays grand.

Dear Harold, do you ever think of the old times when we used to play together? I had a temper then and Harold I've still got it, I'm sorry to say. The girls at work call it my 'monkey'.

Well, I think I've told you all the news about
everybody and everything so I will now close with best
wishes, hoping you spend a happy Easter, and prosper-
ity and success in all your efforts.
From your old friend,
Emily.

How slowly the time had passed until November 1918
when Harry was back in England for two weeks' leave coin-
ciding with Armistice Day. They marked the visit, and his
birthday, with an evening concert at the London Palladium
and afterwards he took her to a charming little teahouse
in the theatre area for supper. It was there, at a table in a
quiet corner of the teahouse, that he reached across, took
her hands in his, and asked her to become his wife.

A week after the fleeting visit, Emily wrote to Harold
wishing him: *Health, wealth and happiness all the time.*
My thoughts will be always with you. I feel ever so pleased
we had such a nice evening last Wednesday.

Harold was back in France with his unit for Christmas
but this time he was spared the horrors of war. Emily sent
him a card that reflected their closeness, signing off: *From*
your sweetheart and pal with fondest love, Emily X.

The war had affected her family with the wounding of
Emily's brother Alf who had served in France with a British regiment. She treasured the embroidered card he sent
to her, spelling out in coloured stitching, 'Souvenir from
France'. His own souvenir was a severe leg wound that
kept him in a wheelchair for a long time.

Harold and Emily had only one more chance to be
together, for just a few days, before his battalion was sent
back to Australia.

The Australian government assisted with the passages
of brides and fiancées of Australian soldiers, allocating
berths for them on ships repatriating the Expeditionary

Force. These vessels with women and children as well as soldiers became known as Family Ships. Emily was eventually booked on the *Zealandic*, sailing on 27 March 1920.

Her departure that morning from the family home, and later from the railway station where the boat train left for Southampton, was highly emotional for everyone involved. Instructions from the Repatriation and Demobilisation Department of the AIF set out the ground rules for farewells:

It is not possible for this Department therefore to issue passes to persons other than passengers, and it is therefore advisable in the interest of all concerned that the final leave taking should be made at home or at the Railway Station. On no account will passengers' friends be allowed at the ship's side.

So Emily set out alone for a vast, near-empty country still emerging from the pioneering era on the other side of the world. It took great personal courage and no small sense of freedom and adventure. The Great War was over, the world was now apparently secure and, sustained by her love for the shy young man in the slouch hat, she was certain her life would be a happy one.

Dani

The sunset at Riverwood was an art show in itself. Dani would have been quite happy to spend the evening with a barbecued chop and a cold drink on the verandah before going to bed with a good book. But she knew Max and Sarah would soon be picking her up for the art show at the Hungerford Regional Art Gallery. So she dressed and when they arrived went out to meet them as they chatted with Barney and Helen.

Sarah was of fragile build with a sweet smile and soft pale gold hair. With the powerful build and dark good looks of Max they made a striking couple. But Dani saw straight away that the graceful Sarah had her own strength, she was no dandelion to disappear in a strong breeze but a woman who'd bend like a willow while firmly keeping to the spot.

'Let me know what the show's like, I'll pop in when I'm in town,' said Helen. 'Do you want us to let Jolly outside?'

'We had a big walk up the hill, she's had dinner and is very comfortable in her basket on the verandah, thanks, Helen. I don't think she'll go wandering after dark.'

Driving to Hungerford, Max filled Dani in on the Regional Art Gallery, how it had grown with council support and several arts grants. 'But it's really blossomed since Greta arrived as curator. She's been very innovative and given not just local artists exhibitions but painters and artisans from Canberra, Melbourne and Queensland.'

'But her main focus is local talent,' said Sarah. 'She's nurtured a lot of people. There's a woman who does beautiful ceramics and glass she found working in a shed on a farm, and a very eccentric and talented potter from Jumbai up on the mountain. They've sold pieces to galleries in Sydney.'

'I've heard Jumbai is an interesting place, once you cope with that drive up the mountain,' said Dani.

'Yeah, still remnants of the seventies hippy mob hanging out there, but it's now attracting artistic strays and some of the tree change set,' grinned Max. 'The farm scene is changing too I hear. Some biodynamic farming is happening, but I'm not sure what that means exactly.'

Sarah was more enthusiastic. 'It's a happening place,

but not everyone's cup of tea because of its remoteness. Sort of a sleepy hollow on top of a big hill, but hunt around and you'll find everything from classical musicians, to wild experimental bands, weavers and sculptors. It's a very vibrant community. Though there are rumours of a darker side to it,' she added.

'Sounds interesting. I'll have to make the effort even if it is a nerve-racking drive,' said Dani.

'There are no plans to improve the road, and the locals like it that way. Keeps out the tourists and bureaucrats,' said Max.

The gallery parking lot was full. Well-dressed people were threading their way through the cars and along the roadside into the front gardens of the gallery, which looked to be a restored and extended old home. Sculptures and installations from previous exhibitions were displayed on the lawns and along the verandah.

Inside there was a buzz and bright lights, a crush of laughing, chattering people, waiters circulating with trays of drinks. To Dani it had the stimulating atmosphere of a gallery show in Sydney. There were several display rooms and a long main area with standing works and walls ablaze with large, boldly executed, colourful canvases. In one section there were smaller prints and lithographs but the predominant works were the striking paintings captioned 'Dream Interpretations'.

Dani's initial impression was that none of the pictures had the subtlety and intricacy of Max's work. This was all show, it lacked soul. She whispered to Sarah, 'I'm glad they're not my dreams, more like nightmares. I wonder what the artist ate for dinner.'

Sarah smiled, 'I don't like to criticise another art-ist's work but I think he's indulged in a little too much Arcimboldo.'

When Dani raised a questioning eyebrow Max

explained, 'Sixteenth-century Italian artist who painted figures and portraits using creatures, food, flora and fauna as features. Very inventive if sometimes disturbing.'

'So what are your influences, Max?' asked Dani.

'Nature.' He indicated the outdoors. 'Certain places or images that I see and subconsciously file away. When I look at a landscape some of those impressions find their way onto the canvas. I don't paint a literal landscape. Well, you saw some of my work,' he said modestly. 'What about your influences?'

Dani was caught offguard. Max treated her as a serious artist. 'I suppose landscape, but more a sense of place. Places that mean something. I don't want to paint attractive "scenes". I have to feel a connection to it. Like there's something underneath. How it used to be. What it looks like after a fire, or a storm. What people, creatures, have passed through it. I can't explain really. It's a long time since someone has asked me anything like that. I've never really thought about what draws me to a subject.'

Max nodded. 'Very intuitive of you. It's how we think of country too. That we are interlinked, the land is a part of us, we share the same space, act upon each other. I see it as a layering process and we all return to the land eventually.'

Sarah nodded in agreement. 'It's not just an Aboriginal attitude. I feel it too. Your country calls you back, Max says.'

Max glanced around the room. 'There's Henry Catchpole, have you met him?' he asked, pointing at a spry-looking man with silver hair. 'His is one of the original families in the valley.'

'No, but Helen said I should meet him. He runs the local historical society, right?'

Henry, in his seventies, had impish blue eyes, a ready laugh, a firm handshake, held himself straight and looked her firmly in the eye. Dani guessed he had a military background.

'I hear you've come to explore your family roots. You're a Williams aren't you?'

'My great-grandparents. I've never thought of myself as being part of a . . . dynasty,' laughed Dani. 'I just came here on an impulse. I'm surprised you've heard about me.'

'Not much escapes Henry,' said Max. 'He's a walking encyclopaedia on valley history. Can tell you what your great-grandparents had for breakfast every day.'

'Hal Williams loved saveloys. Used to send young Lara up to the bacon factory for them,' replied Henry promptly.

Greta Handle, the gallery curator, stood on the small raised platform in front of a large canvas and called for everyone's attention through the microphone. She was statuesque, yet softly round. Her greying blonde hair sprang from the confines of a French roll. She radiated intelligence and an artistic sensibility, a hippy who'd joined the ranks of the bourgeoisie to conform but at the same time supported artistic rebels. She wore a loose emerald velvet jacket with touches of embroidery and a large chunky necklace of painted ceramic beads that looked like it had been specially made for her. She gave a short, articulate speech – a brief history of the artist and his work and an explanation of the theme of this exhibition. She then called on Councillor Patricia Catchpole to speak.

Henry's wife, an attractive woman in her late fifties, spoke succinctly about the role of art in the community and pledged continued council support for this important regional gallery. She then announced she had great pleasure introducing someone who was making a significant contribution to the region by giving a donation to the gallery and would be instrumental in assisting the growth of the shire.

'What's that mean?' said Max in a low voice to Sarah. 'Don't like the sound of that.'

Sarah shrugged.

'Ladies and gentlemen, please give a warm welcome to Mr Jason Moore.'

There was a murmur beneath the applause as a tall, dynamic man jumped up and kissed Patricia on the cheek, turning to give a dazzling smile to the audience.

'Has he just arrived from Sydney?' Dani asked Sarah. 'He looks like he's stepped out of a trendy cover spread for a yuppie magazine.'

Sarah shrugged again. 'I'm not up on the cool Sydney people. He's certainly got an air about him.'

Poised and self-confident, Jason Moore addressed the crowd in a warm and gentle tone that Dani felt was a bit of an act. She studied him without paying full attention to what he was saying. Mid to late thirties, well groomed, hair styled, clothes casually tailored and expensive labels she had no doubt. She felt Max stiffen beside her, so tuned into what Jason Moore was saying.

'I believe the time is ripe for this valley to become a landmark example of the transition between the old world and the new. Where fallow farms give way to a rich cornucopia of new opportunities, new lifestyles, new residents and a renewal of appreciation of what a special place this is. For years towns like this have been dying, productive farming dwindling, young people disappearing to cities far from their roots and families. That is no longer the future.

'As a statement of the commitment of the Genovese Foundation, founded by my family, to building the future of the Oxley River Shire, I would like to announce that – in addition to supporting the arts, such as this wonderful gallery – the foundation has plans to create a new and vibrant community.'

He paused. He had everyone's attention and the room was utterly silent.

'To that end a new township will be developed that will not only bring all manner of opportunities to the area, but we are dedicated to doing it right, learning from the past and consolidating a new future for a very special part of this shire. High on the list will be the development of an arts and cultural centre which we hope will spawn talent that may be displayed in a wonderful new space. So I therefore have great pleasure in declaring *Dreams and Means* open. Thank you.'

After a burst of polite applause there was a buzz of conversation about this startling announcement. It was clearly news to everyone.

Dani caught Henry Catchpole looking at his wife with a raised eyebrow. Patricia looked faintly smug. Being a councillor she would have known what a bombshell this news would be.

'Where is this new community going to be? Sounds like he's bought up big somewhere,' said Sarah.

'Here we go again,' grumbled Max. 'Another jackpot for the white mob with lots of dough. I'll talk to Henry and see what he knows.'

Sarah was engaged by a group of friends who swirled by and Dani was momentarily beached in the crowded room. She was relieved to spot Claude and George. As she threaded through the clusters of people, everyone was talking about Jason Moore's remarks. All interest in the paintings had evaporated.

Greta was surrounded, as was the ever-smiling Jason Moore. A newspaper photographer was snapping them both. A girl with a tray of empty glasses save for one champagne was negotiating her way back to the bar. Dani reached for the champagne at the same time as a large paw.

'Oh, sorry, do go ahead.' She looked at the owner of

the large hairy hand and saw ruddy cheeks, brown eyes behind glasses and a full bushy ginger beard.

'After you. They'll be around with another tray soon enough,' he said. 'I can recommend the food if it passes this way.'

'Quite an event,' said Dani conversationally. 'It seems that Mr Moore has dropped quite a bombshell. Do you know him?'

'Me? Not at all. I don't mix in society circles,' he said. 'Though I don't like the sound of his plan. Cultural centres and development means someone's trying to sugar coat a grab at making money out of this place. I'm glad I keep out of town and away from local politics.'

'So why are you here tonight?' asked Dani with a small smile.

He looked uncomfortable. As much from the apparently unaccustomed tie as her question. 'I'm just the artist. Greta insisted I be here.'

Dani felt sorry for him. 'Oh, congratulations, the show is fantastic. And such a roll up, I hope you sell a lot.'

'I dunno about that, these things bring out the freeloaders and social climbers. I didn't know that Moore bloke was going to make his announcement.' With relief he took a drink from a fresh tray as it was offered.

'I don't think most people knew, judging by the reaction. It did steal your thunder a bit. Why didn't you say a few words? I'd like to know about your paintings, how they make the transition from dreams to canvas,' said Dani warmly.

'I'm no good at talking and people aren't really interested. One woman asked me what the painting was called, like that explains it all. Didn't want to know where it came from. Unlike you. Do you paint?'

Dani hesitated then said firmly, 'Yes. I'm taking the plunge to paint full-time. See where it takes me.'

'Nice one. Wish I could just do my thing and not have to worry about feeding the family,' he said morosely.

'I have a son, I'm on my own. This is a bit of a gamble for me too,' she said, holding out her hand. 'Dani Henderson.'

'Thomas Banks.'

They juggled glasses to shake hands as Greta reached them, sounding slightly breathless.

'Excuse me, Tom, there's someone I want you to meet. A possible sale. Come along, time to sing for your supper.' She grinned apologetically at Dani.

Tom rolled his eyes. 'Excuse me.'

'Go ahead, I'll find my friends.' Dani turned away and bumped an elbow. 'Oops, sorry.'

She found she was staring at Jason Moore who had moved away from a group so they were both on their own. 'I hope I didn't splash bubbles on your jacket.' She eyed the crisp, pale blue linen.

'A few bubbles never hurt. Hello, I'm Jason Moore. Are you a local?' He shook her hand and his long tanned fingers felt smooth and unexpectedly strong.

'Er, no. Not really. I'm only visiting for a short time.'

'That's too bad, this is a lovely part of the country.' he smiled.

'So I gather. You must think so too. Your announcement made something of an impact. Where is your new community going to be?'

'If you're not a local, it's hard to explain. It's an area outside of Riverwood stretching into the lower slopes of the ranges. Known as Birimbal.'

'A big area presumably, is there anything on it now?' Dani wondered why she was suddenly so interested and, she realised, concerned. She hated the idea of suburban development encroaching on the unspoiled landscape. Places she wanted to paint.

'A few old farms. Not much really. Some crown land that's been released. While it sounds like it's out of the way it's quite accessible. In fact this land was the first to be settled in the old days and was the short route south to the big port for the settlers back then.'

Dani wrinkled her nose. 'Now that sounds familiar, I think Helen drove me around that area.'

'There's a place on it called Kelly's Crossing, it's a well-known little spot, that might locate it for your friends.' He drained his glass and put it on a tray presented by a hovering waitress, smiling, eyes glued to him.

Dani reacted with some heat. 'Yes, I know that place. Magical. Surely you're not going to build around there!' Her voice must have sounded as shocked as she felt.

'Not at all. Our idea is to preserve that magic while growing an area in the best possible way.'

'Growing.' She winced at the euphemism. 'You mean developing.'

His eyes sparked with what Dani momentarily thought of as a zealot's passion. 'What I mean is an archetypal concept of combining community with an appealing environment and the dream home ideal. Not in a rich man's sense but a home that encompasses all that is desirable with quality of life and the support network of a like-minded community,' he said. 'Home is not a house plonked on a bit of land. It's the whole package that is very rarely designed, planned or achieved.'

For a moment Dani was tongue-tied. 'Well, er . . . yes, I take your point,' she said, realising she'd struck a nerve and irritated him. 'But without knowing what you have in mind it still sounds a bit like a rural gated community.'

He sighed. 'I obviously have a long way to go in selling the idea. Why don't you come and see what I have in mind? Places like an unchanged Kelly's Crossing are an integral part of the concept.'

'I'm pleased to hear it.' Dani wasn't convinced. Whatever he called it, a housing estate, even a well-planned one, was still a hideous thing to build on the wonderful land she'd seen with Helen.

'Are you going to be in the area long?' he asked.

'I'm not sure. But I will be coming back here, so I do have an interest in its future,' she said with a tight smile, her words surprising herself.

He handed her his card. 'In that case, drop into my office in Hungerford any time and see what Genovese is planning.'

'Why Genovese?' She glanced at the card.

'I spent some time in Genoa studying architecture and design.' He looked at Dani. 'I know what you're thinking, that background is scarcely compatible with old dairy farms, mountains and a magnificent river. But sometimes ideas spring from unusual roots.' He gave her a brief smile as he was swept away by the photographer, a reporter and two women eager to talk to him.

After the show Henry and Patricia Catchpole invited Sarah, Max and Dani for coffee and a liqueur at a small tavern where the talk was all about Jason Moore and the Genovese Foundation.

In an aside Dani whispered to Max, 'I bet you're glad it wasn't your show. Talk about stealing thunder!'

'Yeah, poor Tom. He wasn't too happy. Mind you, he's a bit of a morose character. Good painter though.'

'I couldn't quite equate those turbulent out-there pictures with such a sombre, withdrawn man,' said Dani.

'Still waters. It's often hard to talk about your art,' said Max.

'So what did you think of the evening?' Henry Catchpole asked Dani.

'Very interesting. Why did Jason Moore open the show?' She glanced at Patricia. 'I mean, he's charming but why make the announcement that seemed to take everyone by surprise?'

Henry rolled his eyes. 'Good question. Politics. Can't keep it out of anything in this town.'

'That's true. When it's so sensitive an issue it's best to slide it in sideways on a social occasion rather than make a big public media announcement,' said Patricia.

'So the cultural centre in this new community is a bit of a sweetener,' said Max.

'I know what Jason has in mind, he's a visionary. It takes a while for people to get their heads around something revolutionary. Actually, it'll be quite something. The whole concept is amazing. If we're going to have development, progress, best to have forward thinking, and innovative and high-quality ideas,' said Patricia firmly.

'But how visionary? Really? Look at the beautiful pristine land that's going to be swallowed up in a new suburb, a whole town! Everyone's complaining about prime agricultural land going under roads and houses.' Dani's passion was fuelled by several wines and the liqueur. She wouldn't have picked the councillor as a woman to back a visionary concept. Patricia seemed too pragmatic. 'Jason Moore is a Sydney-slicker out to make his name and money and move on. What's he care about this valley?'

Henry patted Dani's hand. 'Steady on. If that was the case Patricia would have had his you-know-whats for breakfast. The Moores are long-time settlers in this area. In fact, they own most of the land. Been buying it up for generations.'

'They've been here almost as long as Henry's family,' interjected Patricia who seemed offended by Dani's criticism.

'Jason's great-grandfather was one of the first lawyers to set up in the valley. His grandfather expanded the business and his father continued it, taking on partners. He then went on to become a judge in Sydney. He moved there when Jason was a baby. So while the lad has had the old school tie upbringing in Sydney, his roots are here. I think he cares what happens here.'

'But he doesn't live here now,' persisted Dani.

'He does for the moment. He moved back a year ago when this all started,' said Patricia.

Sarah stifled a yawn. 'Why are we talking about this? I think we should be discussing Tom's show.'

'Ever the loyal artist's wife,' said Max fondly. 'Actually, we should make a move, our babysitter has to get up early. Do you mind, Dani?'

'Not at all. It's been a stimulating evening.'

Once they were out of town and on the road home, Dani asked Max. 'So, what do you think of Councillor Catchpole's ideas?'

'Patricia is okay. She's generally fairly balanced, for a politician. I can't complain as she is the one who led the campaign to have the Aboriginal flag flown outside the council chambers with all the other flags.'

'Surprisingly, there's been a lot of support from the locals,' added Sarah. 'Never thought I'd see blue-rinsed wasp grandmothers walking around with their shopping baskets wearing a ribbon to show they support flying the indigenous flag. Even had a TV crew from a current affairs show in Sydney up here.'

'The TV shock troops might be back if this development deal gets out of hand,' mused Dani. 'My mother worked in TV and I know what a feeding frenzy they'd turn it into.'

'It hasn't come to that yet as this is the first announcement, but we'll bear that in mind,' said Max calmly.

'Is Jason Moore married?' Dani wondered why she asked.

Max laughed. 'Every woman asks that. No. But he has a glamorous girlfriend. She lives in Sydney and he goes down there most weekends. She doesn't come to the sticks.'

'I rest my case,' said Dani, convinced her first impression of Jason Moore was right. 'Family roots in an area are no guarantee of sensitivity.'

There was silence in the car for a moment or two then Sarah turned to Dani in the back seat. 'Henry says he knew your family. Had a few anecdotes about your grandmother Elizabeth. I didn't know you had such long-time roots here too.'

'I don't think of it like that as I've never lived here. My mother was born in Cedartown, but left when she was little. I don't think she knows much about her parents' time. What did he tell you?'

'Something to do with the war years, Henry is such a military man. Apparently your grandmother was very beautiful. Said the only local falling out between the Yanks and the Aussies was over her.'

'Really? I hadn't heard that,' said Dani. 'She was beautiful.' It occurred to her that Lara had never relayed anything about her mother's youth. Possibly she didn't know the stories either.

As if reading her mind Sarah said, 'Maybe you – or your mother – should do some family research. Henry must know some of your family history.'

'I'm not so sure I'm all that interested in people I never knew,' answered Dani, thinking again what a small place the valley seemed to be. Everyone was either related or knew something about everyone else.

'That's where we blackfellas differ,' said Max quietly. 'That's not the advice I gave Dani.'

Dani was quiet a moment recalling Max telling her one can't go forward until the past is laid to rest. 'I don't think it's my journey. Maybe my mother needs to know her mother's story.'

'It's your story too, Dani,' said Max. 'Just as this is your country, your birthright. There's a reason you've stumbled back here. And it's not just to paint.'

Sarah added gently, 'If there's anything we can do to help you, just call on us.'

Dani took up Max's invitation to join him in his studio and they spent a compatible and productive morning painting together. Apart from art classes she'd always painted alone, regarding her art as a private journey leading her down a dim path until she found some light and reached a spot where the work began to come together. That pleased her.

With Max humming occasionally, the call of a bird outside, the scratch of brushes on canvas, she relaxed and lost her initial fear of producing something to show what she could do. Instead, as she explained to Max over a cup of tea, quietly provided on a tray with some cake made by Sarah, being with him in his studio felt like a casual and comfortable walk in the bush.

'That's because of what you're painting,' he said. 'You're capturing a place that's ideal for strolling, contemplating the play of light on the river, the sense of solitude. If you feel you're inhabiting your painting, that's good.'

Young Len popped in to say hello and gave a quick critical appraisal of Dani's work. 'Very nice. I know that spot. I like it. Maybe you could put in a pelican or a boat on the river.'

'Thanks, Len, I might do that. Are you going to join us, have a dabble?'

'Nope. I'll take my art gear to the market tomorrow. They sell better if people see you doing them.' He turned to his father. 'My mate knows this farmer who said we can pick his fruit and sell it. We're making a roadside stall.'

'Very good. Don't fall out of a tree.'

Len tweaked Jolly's ear as she lay in the sun in the doorway. 'Righto. See ya.'

'He's a great kid. My Tim is round his age. How's Len doing at school?'

'Middling. He's not a good reader. Likes to be doing his art or outside on the go. I wasn't a reader either, still aren't. Not like Sarah, she can get lost in a book for hours. S'pose Len takes after me a bit. Julian's like Sarah.'

'But you had your art,' said Dani. 'Maybe it's not as relaxing as reading, but it can be a good escape, don't you think?' She was recalling times when she was a teenager and there was a crisis in her life or she felt depressed and she found solace and relief in losing herself in a painting.

Max frowned. 'I had a tough time with my painting and schooling. I'm left handed and as a little kid the teacher used to force me to use my right hand. Banged my hand with the ruler if I used the left one, or else tied it to the chair. I used to cry and cry. Never fought back. I thought it was just something else because I was Aboriginal.'

Dani looked at the brush in Max's left hand. 'But they didn't stop you.'

He gave a triumphant grin. 'Nah, I learned to use my right as well.' He switched the brush to his right hand and kept painting. 'I'm ambidextrous. Can use two hands at once too.'

'How hard was it being a black kid in a country area like this?' asked Dani. Max must have started school in the late sixties when Aborigines had even further to go to achieve equality and acceptance.

'Some areas were better than others. Out in the bush where they'd been pushed off remote stations it was tough. Our mob here were scattered, we had stolen generations so we still don't know where a lot of them ended up. Sarah is trying to trace some of my family. But the immediate family, cousins and uncles and aunties, lived out at Planters Field, the reserve at the edge of town. Weren't allowed in the pictures or the swimming pool when we finally got one in town.'

'Terrible,' murmured Dani.

'But it wasn't all bad here. I had good schooling and was able to make something of myself. Married an educated pretty white girl. Wouldn't have happened in my parents' day. Well, it might have, but they'd never have been accepted in either society,' said Max. 'I've got mixed blood because of whitefellas taking Aboriginal girls out in the scrub. Very hard to trace all my rellies,' he added. 'It took a white man with guts to stick with his black missus and acknowledge paternity back then.'

Dani took a step back and, squinting slightly, looked at her painting. 'Family,' she said. 'My mother says there are always secrets, stuff you don't know, don't ask, and then suddenly it's too late.'

'That's for sure. Well, I'm taking a break. You're welcome to stay on as long as you like. I'll be in the gallery.'

'Thanks, Max. I will stay a bit longer. I'd like to see if I can finish it.'

'Don't rush it,' advised Max. 'Enjoy it.'

That evening Dani watched the sun set over the paddocks and river with a sense of achievement and pleasure. She'd finished the picture and while it had evolved differently from what she'd anticipated, she was pleased with it and hoped Helen and Barney would like it. She'd left it in Max's studio to dry and was keen to get going on another painting. Indeed, a series of scenes was forming in her head.

She went and poured herself a glass of wine. When she came back out onto the verandah the sun had set and the rich afterglow was reflected in the river. Ratso came racing across the lawn and Helen appeared and waved a bottle of wine.

'A post sundowner seeing the sun's already gone?'

'Of course. Come on up.' Dani went to fetch the cheese and biscuits she had laid in for these occasional pleasurable shared occasions.

'I'm exhausted, been full on with the kids today. The little ones, that is.' Helen settled back with her wine. 'How was your day?'

'Good. I loved sharing Max's studio. He made a few comments I found valuable and it felt comfortable. I didn't feel inhibited. I'm quite pleased with the picture I did.'

'Really, that's great. I'd love to see it.'

'Oh, you will,' smiled Dani. 'Now, Helen, is it possible for me to stay on a bit longer?'

'I was expecting this,' said Helen.

'Well, it's my mother. My being here has triggered her interest in the old days when she was a little girl in these parts.'

'She was born in Cedartown, you said?'

'Yes. She'll probably be on the doorstep of the old house in a flash. She lived there for her first few years and then came back for school holidays with her grandparents till she was grown up. So she has strong memories. But she's really never been back since Poppy – my great-grandfather – died.'

'Well, it will be a rich old trip down memory lane for her,' commented Helen. 'Will you all be okay sharing in here?'

'Of course.'

'Something nice about the idea of three generations of your family all visiting and discovering the past together, eh?'

'I guess so,' said Dani slowly. 'I still don't feel like I belong here in the way she does.'

'You haven't spent enough time here, explored enough. Go into the museum, it'll give you a bigger picture. You have to find your own connection with the place. Not that you have to of course, but I'm sure it would please your mother.'

'It's lovely being here, there's lots to paint, I've met some interesting people, but I can't see my association going beyond that. Mum seems to think I'll discover a sense of identity,' said Dani thoughtfully.

'It's not all old world around here. Angela and Tony asked me to let you know that they're off to an informal drinks buffet thing at a friend's house later tonight. Would you like to go? Barney and I are babysitting.'

'Oh, I don't think so . . .' responded Dani with hesitation.

'Why not? You should meet some younger people, get a different perspective on life in the valley,' insisted Helen. 'Go over and chat to them about it, they're doing the kids' dinner.'

Helen's daughter Angela and husband Tony were so pleasant and easy going and the sort of people she could relate to that Dani quickly accepted the invitation to go with them, if it was all right with the hosts.

'We told them we'd try to bring you along. It's quite a mix, some visitors, but mostly locals who are doing interesting things. No one over forty.' Tony grinned.

The gathering was at a magnificent house, elegant and expensive, on the river closer to Riverwood. The couple who lived there had fled Sydney's eastern suburbs and created a home that would be worth several million dollars in their former neighbourhood. The original nineteenth-century sandstone mansion, Riverview, had been restored and extended. It had a long verandah facing the river with lawns sweeping down to the banks lined with weeping willows. Fairy lights were strung in a huge Moreton Bay fig tree. Around the formal façade of the entrance long glass windows had undisturbed rural views and the interior was ultra modern and chic. For Dani's taste it was a little too minimalist with contemporary sculptures, abstract art, and retro Italian furniture of the 1970s.

The elegant setting, the bright young guests wandering between the candlelit dining room where a buffet was set to the courtyard with a bar and barbecue, and the comfortable seating along the verandah – it was scarcely what Dani thought of as the casual party described by Tony and Angela. But she was quickly introduced and everyone was relaxed, friendly and unpretentious. Several young couples had farms, or ran small or large business ventures – furniture making, luxury boat building, alpaca and Angora wool production, glass blowing.

Then she saw Jason Moore in very smart-casual city gear lounging on the verandah in an old-fashioned settler's chair, his legs rather incongruously flung over the extendable arms. He saw her coming through the doorway, waved and got up. Dani had been enjoying the social mixing, relishing the bright conversation. Now, as Jason came towards her with a smile, she felt herself bristling.

They exchanged greetings, he asked what she'd been doing and she was surprised that he remembered some of the details of their brief conversation at the art show, outside of their sparring over his new town project.

'So what are your plans?' he asked.

'Plans? I don't have any to speak of . . . just dabbling in a bit of painting, relaxing, talking to people.'

'No more exploring?'

'Not the kind you'd relate to. More internal stuff.' Dani didn't want the conversation to continue in this direction.

'Head stuff.'

She gave him a quizzical look. 'And how do you interpret that?'

'You paint, I design. I'm no artist on the page, but we both draw inspiration from a particular place, wouldn't you say?'

Dani was trying to fathom if he was having a dig at her, or if he was genuine, or if he had no understanding of what she did, or wanted to do. 'I'm not sure what you mean. As someone once said, "Please explain."'

He chuckled. 'I have to walk over the land – or, up here, ride. Get to know every bit of it, before I go away and sit down and draw the designs.'

'All on your own?' Dani was shocked.

'I modestly confess the initial concepts are mine,' he said. Then added, as if trying to change the subject, 'So what do you think of this house? Surprises a lot of people.'

Dani was glad to move into more general conversational territory. 'It's stunning. On the way here Tony told me a bit about Riverview. I think it's really clever how they've restored a nineteenth-century house and incorporated modern design and practical, elegant living, without destroying the ambiance of the original place.'

'I've always wondered what the first owner would think, coming back here tonight, for example,' said Jason.

Dani was immediately effusive. 'How could you not love it! There's just enough olde worlde charm inside, in the original façade and a subtle blending of modern extensions that marry really well with the old forms. Of course, sandstone is timeless.' She'd loved the beautiful sandstone exterior of the main building while in the formal living room one old sandstone wall was exposed and the massive fireplace still intact.

Jason looked pleased then uncomfortable. Dani couldn't read his expression for a moment. 'I'm glad you think so. Our hosts are very happy with how it all turned out.'

'That looks like Sydney sandstone in the wall. How did it get here?'

'In the old days practically everything sent to market from these parts went down the coast in Sydney-based ships. They often came up near empty and used sandstone as ballast. Dumped it over the side into the river before loading here.'

'Who designed this place?' asked Dani looking down the verandah and back into the softly lit comfortable rooms with walls of glass, soaring ceilings and wonderful display areas for the fine art pieces.

'I did.'

She blinked. Jason was staring at her, waiting for a reaction. She burst into laughter. 'Okay, you win. I'm surprised. And impressed.'

'I'm hurt you're surprised but happy you're impressed. Would you like to see how this place looked late last century? There are some pictures.'

She followed him inside as he led her to the intimate study where bookcases lined a wall. On a coffee table were several leather-bound books. He seemed very at home and opened one of the books to show her reproductions of old photos, drawings, plans and etchings.

Jason flipped through pages with some reverence, pointing out details on the original plan and building, comparing them with his own sketches and photos in the second book. 'It's a delicate marriage between the old and the new as you say. Just because it's old it's not necessarily good, tasteful or worthwhile keeping. Fortunately this house was well designed and thought out and, thankfully, survived.'

'So who was the clever person who created this originally? Not to detract from your work,' said Dani lightly. She had to admit though, she was knocked out by what he'd done.

'Ah, no one knows the real story,' he said.

Dani cocked her head. 'You know more than you're telling.' A thought struck her as she recalled his family connection with the area. 'Don't tell me it belonged to your family!'

'No, unfortunately. It was owned by the infamous Isabella Kelly. She built the first mansion in the valley above Kelly's Crossing before building this house here on the river.'

That name again, thought Dani. 'She sounds a cultured lady, not the rough, wild woman I've heard described.'

'Just rich. Money doesn't buy culture,' said Jason with a wry twist to his mouth. 'Well, there are rumours of course. We'll never know will we? And, besides, it's over and past.'

'But Kelly's Crossing is on your land. You owe her something!' said Dani with some heat. 'Aren't you curious?' She couldn't explain to him, or to herself, why she felt so strongly about the pioneer woman whose history drifted so tantalisingly around this valley.

'Now don't start earbashing me about sacred sites or something,' said Jason with a smile. But there was a withdrawn look in his eye.

They were both relieved when a couple joined them and they all headed to the buffet table. Dani didn't speak to him again but agreed with Angela and Tony on the way home that it had been an interesting evening.

4

Cedartown, 1932

'SO WHAT'RE WE DOING then? Clem spun the handlebars of his bike.

'Race ya down to the river?' suggested Thommo.

'Nah, we did that.' Clem didn't feel that secure on his hand-me-down bike. Thommo's newer bike, which Clem cared for, was oiled and polished so that it was in peak running order. 'Let's go up to the showground, see if there's any cattle in the yards.'

'Can we go and see your dad's friend at the bacon factory?' asked Clem. He'd been impressed at how a while back Thommo had scored some free saveloys and bacon bits from his dad's butcher mate at the abattoir.

'They'll be closed now. Let's go to the showground, ride round the show ring.'

The boys climbed through the cattleyards and sat on the slab railings, regaling each other with anecdotes, real and imagined, of the antics and risks taken by the stockmen, ringers and blacks riding wild bulls in shows they'd seen. Thommo harboured a dream to go up north one day and work on a station as a jackeroo and have real outback adventures.

'You won't make any money, you'll break a leg or something,' said the practical Clem. Being a farm boy he held no illusions about the romance of cattle and horses. 'I'd like to fix up cars like your dad's.' Frank Thompson had bought a 1932 Vauxhall sedan. Not like the old Bedford farm truck owned by Clem's father. 'I reckon one day everyone will own a motor car.'

'What about aeroplanes? Be mighty to go up in one, wouldn't it?' said Thommo wistfully.

They returned to their bikes and wheeled them across the grass, sliding them under the railing of the show ring where they proceeded to race around the dirt ring until exhausted.

'Gee, wonder if we can get some water. Let's try the kitchen behind the hall,' said Thommo.

They rode over to a cluster of timber buildings, one with a chimney, and Clem rattled its double wooden doors. 'Nope, locked. There might be a tap by the pavilion.'

'Just a tick, I'll go round the back,' said Thommo.

Clem waited, noticing it was getting late. They were under instructions to be back at Thommo's house before dark. A sudden rattling from inside the doors made him jump as Thommo flung back the bolt and pushed open a door.

'There's a broken window in the kitchen. No trouble getting in. Come an' look, it's full of stuff.'

'Do you reckon it's all right to be in here?' said Clem cautiously, but curiosity got the better of him. 'What kind of stuff?'

Thommo pulled out a chair to reach the shelf above the old sink where a large hot water urn and big teapot sat next to dozens of thick china cups. He handed Clem a metal canister. 'Biscuits. Are they any good? There's sugar and tea too.'

Clem tasted one of the broken biscuits in the bottom of the tin. 'All right. Just plain though.' He turned the tap on at the sink. 'Hope there aren't any frogs in it.' He held a cup under it and drank quickly.

Thommo was opening drawers and cupboards. 'Whacko, look at this!' He held out a leather pouch of tobacco and papers. 'Any matches? Need a match for a smoke, mate.'

'I know how to roll fags,' boasted Clem.

'Me too,' said Thommo, now poking around shelves by the stove and triumphantly holding up a box of matches.

They were inexperienced smokers and didn't know much about how to roll your own like their fathers did. But quickly enough they stuffed the stringy tobacco into the delicate paper, licked the side with gusto, stuck it down and lit up, puffing with bravado.

'What about a cup of tea, mate?' said Thommo with a sweeping gesture.

They found some candles and lit one, sticking it on a saucer while they boiled water in a saucepan and brewed black tea, toasting each other while brandishing their cigarettes like they'd seen in the picture shows. They dunked the biscuits in their tea and were chattering away when Clem glanced out the window.

'It's getting dark. We'd better go.'

Thommo took the tobacco packet and shoved it in his shorts pocket. 'Know just the place to hide this. We'd better go out the window.' He tossed his cigarette butt in the rubbish bin under the sink and climbed through the window.

Clem followed. 'Beaut idea comin' up here, Thommo.'

They grabbed their bikes but as they were about to ride

off Thommo issued a challenge. 'Dare you to ride through the graveyard.'

'What for?' asked Clem, glancing across to the cemetery adjoining the showground.

'Give you the tobacco and papers. And my silver American dollar.'

'What about you? I dare you back.'

'Nah, then it's not a dare. I'll ride round to the front gates and wait, you go through the cemetery from the back paddock. I'll watch you come down the middle bit near the Catholics.'

Clem didn't like the idea at all. He had a strong dislike of cemeteries, for some reason they scared him. And Thommo knew it. But he liked that fancy silver dollar someone had used to pay for a film ticket at the Town Hall. Thommo'd be watching out and if he rode really fast it'd be all right he told himself.

But as Clem pushed his bike under the sagging wire fence he almost turned back. Dark trees ringed sections of the cemetery. Further up the rise he could see the white headstones with urns and statuettes atop, the resting places of affluent Anglicans. As he rode he tried to feel bold and brave but there were too many shadows, rabbit and bandicoot holes, and scars of neglected graves that roughened the ride. Now the tiny squares around him, modestly marked, showed scattered beer bottles and mounds of ashes from after-dark binges. This area was known as the bottom-of-the-hill mob – where paupers and those of unknown faith and family were buried. He rode over twigs that had fallen off shade trees and the sound of them snapping set his mind whirling. He imagined he heard someone moaning, but it could have just been an owl hooting.

Clem put his head down and, feet jammed on the pedals, pumped as hard and fast as he could, the bike slithering and bumping over the ground, until he reached the gates near the gravel pathway between the Presbyterians and the Catholics.

He raced through the gates but Thommo wasn't there. Clem's fright turned to anger. He'd completed the dare and Thommo wasn't there to check. He started riding slowly down the road to town, catching his breath when he spotted, through the near darkness, Thommo racing towards him, stopping so suddenly he was thrown off balance.

'Is the bogeyman chasing you?' taunted Clem. 'You should go in there, it's really scary.'

'Aw, cripes, we're in trouble,' said Thommo breathlessly.

'For going in the hall? Who saw us? We didn't do anythin'. Just had a cuppa, and a smoke.'

'Shit, Clem, the fag end I threw in the bin must've still been alight. There's a bloody fire –'

'Fire! Where?' Clem felt a fist twist his guts.

Thommo turned and pointed. Shining through the darkness was an orange glow.

'Is that . . . the hall? Oh, strewth, what do we do?'

'Let's go. Get home and say nothing.' Thommo pulled the tobacco from his pocket and tossed it away.

'Wait. We're already late.' Clem remembered clearly Thommo tossing his butt under the sink. There must have been paper in the bin. 'Let's go up there, try to help put out the fire, or do something to help. The neighbours will have raised the alarm, that's for sure. We say we were messing around up here and saw the fire and came up for a look. I mean we would, wouldn't we?'

Thommo thought for a second, nodded and got back on his bike. 'Let's hope no one saw us at the showground.'

The hall was ablaze and a small crowd had gathered as some men wheeled out the water cart with pump and fire hoses that was stored at the showground. They soon had a futile spray of water disappearing in the flames.

Thommo began to relax, even feel a bit cocky. 'This is better than a bonfire, eh?' They moved closer but were waved back by the police constable who had arrived on his motorbike.

'Out of here, boys. Get along home now. This could get dangerous. The hall's a goner.'

The boys were quiet for a moment. 'How'd it start then?' asked Clem.

'Not too sure but we'll find out,' said the constable, giving them a hard look.

'We'd better get home for tea,' said Clem turning his bike around.

They passed more people on bikes and cars heading towards the fire as they rode back into town. They stowed their bikes in the shed and as they made their way into the house Thommo pulled at Clem's arm. 'You won't tell? I didn't mean it,' he said anxiously.

Clem wanted to tell Thommo that he should have been more careful. He had made very sure his butt was out, real dead. Thommo had been bloody careless, but instead he punched his friend affectionately. 'Don't worry, Thommo. We're mates. Mates stick together.'

'Promise, Clem. If my dad knew I'd been smoking he'd kill me.'

Vera Thompson called from the verandah. 'Come on, you boys, get inside. We've been worried about where you were, what you were up to. Now get in and wash for dinner.'

'I promise,' said Clem. 'Besides, if Mum and Dad knew, I'd never be allowed to stay with you again,' he whispered.

As the food was laid out on the table, Thommo excitedly told his parents about spotting the fire and going to see what was happening. 'And the policeman said the hall's a goner,' he added, now in the swing of the story.

'Tsk, tsk, what a shame,' said Vera Thompson. 'Sounds like it was started deliberately.'

'Probably one of the Abo kids,' said Frank Thompson as he loosened his braces and settled in his chair. 'They're a damned nuisance hanging around town. I watch 'em very carefully when they try to sneak into the films. What's for tea, love?'

That night in Thommo's bedroom the boys again agreed in whispers to keep quiet about the incident. 'We're mates,' reiterated Thommo fiercely. 'And mates don't snitch.'

It was the rule. And Clem never forgot it.

Dani

It was twilight and Dani had been looking for the back roads and shortcuts Helen had described but she wished she had a topographical map as her directions were confusing. She'd spent the day exploring and wasn't lost but realised she'd made a long circuit around the base of Bluey's Hill. So she wound back up through the patches of rainforest into lightly timbered country where the last of the daylight turned the gums to silver and the dirt road to muted rust pink. She hoped she'd be back at Chesterfield before nightfall as she veered past a fallen log partly obstructing the road. This was unfamiliar terrain and it seemed deserted and a little eerie. She hadn't passed any farmhouses or signs of habitation. The country was too rugged for grazing.

The shadows that striped the road swayed from a sudden breeze and appeared to come to life ahead of her. Instinctively she slowed, straining forward, her mind trying to make sense of what she was seeing. It was a creature striped like the shadows of tree limbs. Long legs, high haunches, a small head turned to face the oncoming car, a long rigid tail. Instantly Dani knew this was an animal unknown, unafraid, pausing in its eating of carrion in the dirt road. They stared at each other, the car was still moving slowly forward, until at its leisure and with a certain arrogance the animal sauntered from the side of the road to melt into the fringe of bush.

Dani swung the car across the road, throwing the headlights in the direction it had taken, hoping to catch another glimpse as she vainly tried to work out what it was. But in the instant her attention was diverted there came from the passenger side a blur of movement as a speeding grey mass was suddenly in front of the car and there was a resounding thud, a dark grey cloud blotting the bonnet. Something heavy had smashed the windscreen and bounced off the side door. Dani struggled with the careening vehicle, which plunged into the undergrowth coming to a stop amidst cracking timber.

She'd banged her head but knew she was all right, more scared and shocked than injured. Dani snapped her seatbelt and threw open the door, slipping on the grass and rocks. The car was tilted and she flung herself away, afraid it might roll on her.

In the glaring headlights in the fast-fading light she saw the dazed and injured big grey wallaby, and the buckled damage to her car. She turned, looking for the strange striped animal, but the bush was silent save for the twitching and scuffles of the injured wallaby trying to get to its feet. She was also aware of a wind, more than a breeze, that swirled around her, nudging her, prodding her forward into the bush.

She spun around against the wind, rejecting its thrust, and took a hesitant step towards the wallaby lying on its side, blood on its fur, large brown eyes accusing. Its feet were narrow, elegant, with long black-tipped claws. She knew she could not possibly lift it, yet she could not leave it there. The decision of what to do was taken from her as she leapt in fright when a man's voice called to her. 'Don't touch it. Keep back.'

Had he materialised from the bush or around the bend in the road? Dani shrank back at the unexpected sight of the figure of a man on foot striding towards her. What was he doing alone, so far from any farm, close on dark? Alarm bells rang and her mind began to race with what to do if he was to attack her, try to put her in the car and drive away with her. It was dented and the windscreen was shattered, but the car was undoubtedly driveable. She pressed herself against the car and, while staring at the hurrying man, reached in and slid the car keys from the ignition.

He stood over the wallaby.

As Dani saw him lift a rifle and point it at the animal, she cried out, 'Don't shoot the poor thing!'

'I would if I could. He looks buggered.'

Dani saw what appeared to be a gun was a stout stick. The man was nudging the animal, which flinched and struggled.

'Leave it alone. Oh, God, what do I do?' said Dani, now close to tears.

'You've done a good job on him. Too bad it wasn't the other thing.' The man crouched down in the headlights and Dani saw he was around her own age, well dressed.

'Other thing? Did you see it too?' she asked.

'The striped dog, panther, tiger, whatever. Yeah. Christ knows what it was.'

'I guess that's what distracted me. I was watching it and not the road, and the next thing the wallaby came out of nowhere. What was that animal?'

'Nothing I've ever seen or heard about. Not that I'm any expert.'

'Why are you out here then?' asked Dani bluntly.

He straightened and gave a crooked smile. 'Ah, on the prowl. Didn't you know this is haunted country?'

Dani's hand tightened on the key. Should she make a run and hope to lose him in the shadowy bush? Maybe if she left the car keys he'd drive away and leave her.

He gave a low laugh and reached out a hand as Dani shrank against the car. 'Sorry, didn't mean to frighten you. But I was getting spooked back there and when I saw that . . . thing, and then this wind hit and you crashed, it all seemed a bit weird.' He paused. 'I suppose my being out here seems a bit odd. He held up his other hand and Dani saw the petrol can. 'Out of juice. Damned stupid place to run out. Don't s'pose you've got any spare?'

Relief flooded through her but was instantly replaced with the thought this too could be a ruse. 'No. Unless you can siphon some out of my car.'

'Not easy without some tubing. My car is a couple of clicks back. Why don't we just take your car and I'll get a friend to bring me out tomorrow morning with fuel.'

Dani was still hesitant. The man seemed pleasant, had a nice voice, and friendly manner. Didn't all serial killers? 'What about the poor wallaby?' she stalled.

'If you don't mind the blood we can throw him in the back of your car and take him to the vet, or the wildlife people.' Dani wanted him to put the wallaby in her car and wait there till she sent someone back for him but she knew that made it obvious she didn't trust him.

He seemed to sense her hesitation and fear. 'Listen, it's getting dark. Please don't be nervous. My name is Roddy, I'm living in Riverwood, haven't been around here too long so I misjudged the distance. Really, I'm not a molester, predator or serial killer. Just a bloke who's pissed off at himself and longing to get home and have a beer.' He smiled disarmingly. 'Come on, let's do the right thing and take the poor bloody animal in for help. Unless you want to knock it on the head and put it out of its misery.'

'I couldn't do that! All right. I have an old blanket in the back for the dog, we can use that.'

'Stand back, they kick and scratch.' Deftly he flung the blanket over the distressed wallaby and, grunting, lifted it into the back of Dani's car. 'Do you want to drive? You know this road?'

'No. You drive. There's no windscreen.' She handed him the keys, deciding to trust him, and got in the passenger side, helping Roddy push out the last pieces of crazed and shattered windscreen.

'We'd better go slowly. You got a phone?'

'There's no reception out here. Who do you want to call?' she asked.

'The nearest WIRES or wildlife carer.'

'I'm sure the people where I'm staying can help,' said Dani, thinking of the capable Barney.

They drove in silence, Roddy concentrating on the road, the gushing wind hitting them in the face.

'Breezy eh?' Then he added, 'Did you notice the way that wind blew up when that animal appeared? I was walking thinking how still it was when that wind hit me and there was the dog . . . thing.'

'It was a weird dog. More like a tiger with a dog's face.'

'I reckon it looked like a thylacine.'

'The Tasmanian tiger? No one is going to believe us. They're extinct.'

'As soon as we get to civilisation we'll both draw what we saw and compare, okay?'

They didn't talk any more until Dani gave him directions to Chesterfield.

Barney saw them drive in and, noting the missing windscreen and bashed front fender, rushed out to meet them.

'Did you roll her? Or hit a roo?' he asked as Dani got out and found her knees were shaking.

'Wallaby. It's in the back. Can you help it, Barney? Oh, this is Roddy.' It was too hard to go into explanations.

Tabatha and Toby came running out and were dispatched by Barney to get first aid from Helen.

An hour later the wallaby had been given some rescue remedy drops by Helen and was laid on straw in an old chicken coop in the shed so it couldn't escape.

'Not that he's going far in that condition,' said Barney.

'Will he be all right, Pop?" asked Toby, who'd stayed close beside his grandfather holding the torch so he could work on the injured animal.

'Hard to say, mate. Shock could get him. Best to let him rest quietly. Don't say anything to Dani, she's pretty upset.'

'Who's that man Roddy?' asked Toby.

'Blowed if I know. Walked out of the bush at the right minute. Said his car ran out of petrol.'

'Pop, he says he and Dani saw a tiger. Or some weird animal. Are they kidding me?'

'What do you think?' asked Barney.

'They're drawing it. Let's go and see.'

Roddy and Dani sat in separate rooms while they did sketches of the animal they'd seen. The pictures were almost identical and Angela and Tony decided they were pulling everyone's leg. Roddy settled on the sofa, Tabatha curled beside him doing her best to beguile him. Barney handed him a glass of his home-brewed stout, and Helen sat down beside him offering a dish of olives. They all seemed entranced with this new friend Dani had found wandering in the bush.

Dani watched him as he laughed and exuded an easy charm. Roddy was an attractive man in an outdoorsy, boyish way and she suspected he knew it. He was perfectly at ease and no one seemed to think how they'd met the least bit odd. Tony offered to run Roddy out to collect his car the next morning as he was heading that way to inspect a fire trail that was due to be cut back.

When Angela called the children away for dinner, Roddy got to his feet. 'Could I call a taxi? It's not far to my place.'

'Are you sure you don't want to stay for dinner?' Helen's eyes sparkled and Dani could see she had already figured Roddy as a prospective beau for her.

'We'll run you home, no probs, forget spending money on a taxi,' said Barney.

'That's kind of you, but it's no trouble to get a cab if they'll run out from town,' began Roddy, smiling at Dani.

'By the time it gets here we'll have you home. Good thing for Dani you turned up when you did,' said Helen.

Dani was about to retort she could have got herself home even with the broken windshield but let it go. She shook his hand. 'Thanks for helping with the wallaby. And if you find out what it was we saw on the road, be sure and let me know.'

Before going to bed Dani took a torch and slipped out to the shed where the injured wallaby was lying, breathing evenly. She reached out and touched the top of its head, rubbing behind its ears. Then she heard a step and saw Barney.

'Just thought I'd check on him. That was a fair whack. Reckon he'll be all right though.'

'I feel terrible. I was just so distracted by that . . . whatever it was.'

'It's a funny one all right. Might be worth asking Max about it. Possibly a mutant, feral dog or something. Anyway, you made a new friend out of the episode, eh?'

'I don't know about that. I was really scared, Barney. But he seems okay.'

'He seems pretty taken with you.' Barney grinned. 'I reckon he'll be visiting us again. Even on the pretext of seeing to this fellow.' He shone the light on the wallaby. 'If he survives the night he'll have a decent old recuperation before he can go back home. Come on, time to hit the sack.'

The following morning Dani drove Angela's car to Cedartown while hers was being repaired. She crossed a low-level concrete bridge with hinged metal railings, which she guessed were designed for easy dropping during floods when a lot of old timber and fallen trees would be swept downriver. On both sides of the river the road running down to the bridge was winding and quite steep. Dani drove slowly imagining what it would be like getting safely across in stormy weather on a dark night and after a few beers. She instantly named it the Sober Bridge. The dark water appeared bottomless with a deceptively fast current below its glassy surface.

The historical society in Cedartown had a new window display that invited anyone passing to pause and consider taking a look inside. 'The Past Recreated' stated a sign near the doorway. But Henry Catchpole, the president, had assured Dani the real engine room of the society was out the back. Dani drove down a lane to the rear of the museum and parked by the low fence of the charming old house next door. She paused to admire the garden of roses and noticed the small sign on the gate, 'Rectory'. The cottage was set back a little from the edge of a high bank that provided a view of the river curving downstream towards Chesterfield. On the other side, neatly nestled in the sweeping curve of the river, was a beautiful expanse of neatly worked farmland and a bushy ridge. A few houses were scattered amongst the trees along the ridge, fine old homes built by early settlers who appreciated a good view, a view that was worth painting.

She walked to a doorway marked 'Private. Historical Society Staff', poked her head through the open door and was surprised to find so many 'staff' at work. Several big tables pushed together were covered in piles of newspapers, bulging folders, books and files. Half-a-dozen people sat around the tables absorbed in shuffling papers, reading and making notes. Three more worked at computers against one wall. The other walls were lined with floor-to-ceiling shelves packed with more reference material. Through an archway leading to the rear of the museum she spotted Henry who gave a big welcoming grin and waved her inside.

'Come in, come in. Welcome to the hysterical society, and say hello to some of the afflicted,' he quipped, then quickly ran through their names. Polite smiles of greeting went around the room. 'Mrs Henderson is a refugee from the big smoke for a few days, and wants to know a little more about our sanctuary,' explained Henry.

'Oh please, call me Dani.'

'I understand Dani also dabbles with paint, and if you're kind to her she might ask you to pose for a portrait.'

There was a little wave of laughter and one of the older women struck an exaggerated pose then announced, 'Great. I've always wanted to be hung in the Archibald.'

Henry gestured to a nearby tea tray. 'You're in time for a cuppa, Dani. Pot has just been brewed.'

'Have an Anzac, dear,' said another of the ladies, offering Dani a plate of homemade biscuits. 'Baked this morning.'

Over tea and biscuits the society members explained that they were mainly occupied searching for information to answer queries from all over the country, usually from people doing research into their family background. If anyone got bored with that, there was always a pile of freshly donated documents to be assessed and indexed.

'It beats doing gardening,' observed an elderly white-haired man, introduced earlier as Martin from the mountain. 'You never know when you're going to suddenly find a really delicious bit of historical gossip, some skeleton that raises an eyebrow.' He turned away.

'I think he just comes for the morning tea,' winked Henry.

After their tea Henry took Dani's arm. 'Come, I'll show you around and introduce you to some of the team working on the museum displays, then you can browse.'

Dani paused to look around the back room again. 'I'm amazed that there's so much going on behind the scenes, but then I've never been into history. Too busy living for the moment.'

'This is the nerve centre, these good folk give a day or two a week to help bring some order to the chaos. All the old newspapers are being put on computer. Not just Cedartown, but also the Hungerford rag and surviving editions of the old Riverwood newspaper.'

'Riverwood had a paper?' exclaimed Dani. 'It's a tiny village!'

'In fact it had the first newspaper in the district when Riverwood was the original settlement on the river. A big place then with the shipping coming into the wharf, there was a millet broom factory and six hotels. The paper was started by an American in 1866. Quite a colourful Yankee he was. Good writer too.'

'Amazing. What a great resource. Where are the original newspapers?'

'All in the vault.' Henry led her to a small air-conditioned room with shelves of leather-bound volumes of newspapers, and stacks of loose yellow-with-age papers and letters. He carefully took an old newspaper from one of the piles and opened it gingerly. 'See, they're falling apart. Don't know how much longer these can be preserved. Hence the need to transfer them all to computer.'

'What about photographs?'

'Thousands on the shelves here. Half of them are mysteries, we've no idea who the people are or where or when the pictures were taken. Families donate stuff and no one's ever bothered to write any info on the back. Still, at least people are more aware. I shudder to think what got dumped down wells or burned when the oldies passed on.'

Dani suddenly thought of the letters and photographs she'd seen on Lara's dining room table. 'My mum is going through stuff she got from her family who settled here yonks ago. She should give it to you guys.'

'Tell her to make sure she adds as much information about them as she can. I don't think we've got your family history in here yet.'

'I'm trying to get her to come up for a look around. It's ages since she's been in the area.'

'Great. Tell her that the morning tea is worthwhile. That might help,' said Henry with his irrepressible grin.

'So many queries from people from all over the place,' said Dani, looking at a batch of freshly opened letters that had come that day.

'And there's a pile of emails. Everyone's doing their family history,' sighed one of the ladies working quietly in a corner.

'I suppose technology has made it easier,' said Dani.

'Go on the Net and there's a maze of genealogical sites,' said Henry. 'But it's more than that. So many people today want to know about their connections with the past. Something they can cling on to, to give their life, and maybe society as a whole, some sense of continuity, a greater sense of meaning and purpose. The future seems so insecure these days, what with environmental concerns, wars and terrorism. The world's full of madmen.'

'Not like in your day, eh, Henry?' chuckled one of the men.

'Or yours, you old hippy,' rejoined Henry. 'Garth is doing a lot of research on one of our pioneers and is writing a book,' explained Henry.

As they moved back past the big work table one of the older ladies asked Dani, 'Do you have a family connection here, dear?'

'My great-grandparents. The Williamses. Harold and Emily,' said Dani.

The woman frowned slightly. Dani guessed she was in her seventies. 'So would you be related to Elizabeth Williams then?'

'My grandmother. Did you know her?' asked Dani. It hadn't occurred to her that there'd be people around who knew her mother's family.

'Oh, I've heard of the family. I was quite young at the time.' The woman turned away and busied herself at a filing cabinet.

'Come on, Dani, let's do the tour.' Henry led the way through a shed that had once been stables but now housed sulkies, farm implements and machinery, horse harnesses and saddles.

It struck Dani the woman had made an odd remark. What did she mean *She was young at the time*? At what time? It seemed a strange thing to say. Dani dismissed it as they came to a small cell that looked like an outdoor lavatory but she did a double take at the sign hanging on the solid wooden door: 'Jimmy Governor's Gaol'.

'The bushranger? He was kept in that?' she asked incredulously.

'Just for a night or two. He was captured around here, you know, wounded in a shoot-out. They kept him in this odd little cell because it was the only one at the police station until a boat came to take him down to Sydney. He was tried and hanged.'

Dani stepped inside the tiny cell which held a small iron cot. The windowless walls were of bare wood planks, the corrugated-iron roof unlined. 'It must have been freezing in winter and sweltering in summer.'

'When they replaced the old police station in 1909 the sergeant retired and took this cell to his place and used it as a fishing shack for years,' said Henry. 'We got it back when we opened the museum.'

Dani stepped into the shed where the farm displays were. The machinery didn't interest her much but she paused at the old stable stall that held rows of harnesses, saddles, branding irons, horse and cattle paraphernalia. There was one unusual saddle that caught her eye.

'That's a very old ladies' side-saddle,' explained Henry. 'All the go in those days of yore when it was considered unseemly for a lady to ride astride. This one is rather special.'

'Because it's old?'

'No, look here.' He lifted up a flap of the hand-stitched leather where Dani could just make out a symbol of a circle with what looked like an X in the centre.

'What's that stand for?'

'It's a brand. The K with an I through it is believed to be Isabella Kelly's brand. You heard of her?'

'Yes, by chance, and she sounds really fascinating.' Dani looked at the well-worn saddle with renewed interest.

'It was found in a shed on a very old property. It matches how her brand is described in some documents Garth has unearthed,' said Henry.

'Garth, who I just met in the archives?'

'Yep. He's a frustrated lawyer and thinks he's found a case worth digging into with Isabella Kelly. Not that it's going to achieve anything after all these years,' said Henry dismissively.

'I'd really like to talk to him. She interests me. Not sure why,' said Dani. 'What's Garth's story?'

'He's retired, a former librarian, bit of a pedant. That was his day job. He lived on a commune in the sixties and seventies and still plays a mean banjo. He lives up Dingo Creek and played in a band called the Dingoes years back. Then he stumbled over the Isabella Kelly story. Don't think he's got much to go on. It's all so long ago and Isabella had no family.'

'So if she has no descendants to tell her story, someone should put down the real story,' said Dani with conviction. She was thinking of Jason Moore and his dismissal of Kelly's Crossing and its connection with the controversial pioneer woman.

'You haven't lived in a country town, that's for sure,' said Henry. 'There's always gossip that's dragged up for decades. Myth becomes fact, secrets become casual banter. Even in my lifetime events that were considered shameful secrets in our family and never spoken about are now out in the open and the kids laugh at us about it. No big deal.'

'I bet there are still a lot of secrets out there,' said Dani.

'You're right, of course,' agreed Henry. 'Garth has been beavering away for years. He's very meticulous, and being a librarian helps. Why don't you have a chat with him?'

The next morning Garth and Dani were seated in the Convivia Cafe, a funky cafe with a small deli counter featuring freshly made goodies and a tiny store at the rear selling organic vegetables, many out of home gardens, honey, herbs and local dairy products. Garth slowly stirred his Chinese herbal tea, staring into the cup as if seeking enlightenment. He was in his sixties, pale blue eyes behind rimless glasses, thinning sandy hair, a light complexion best kept from the sun. The back of his hands had a scatter of ginger hairs and freckles. He wore a loose hand-knitted sweater made with more devotion than skill and his manner was modest, diffident, as if he was unsure why Dani was interested in his 'hobby'. She asked what had got him started on the Isabella Kelly story.

He looked up and shrugged. 'Oh, it's just one of those things. Maybe I'm a bit of a frustrated detective. In a literary sense,' he said modestly.

'But there must be something that intrigues you about this woman. Henry says you've done heaps of research.'

'Yes. I have,' he said with a little grin. 'Addicted, maybe.'

'Why?' persisted Dani gently.

He was quiet for a moment as if he'd never asked himself the question. 'I never married, you know.'

Dani had to force herself to appear relaxed, but his odd style of conversation had her tensing a little. 'Go on.'

'I was very attached to my mother and my sister,' he said.

Dani simply gave a little nod of understanding.

'So I suppose I'm a bit sensitive to the woman's viewpoint. I've been told I'm too objective for my own good. Always seeing the other person's side. And once I started looking at the legend, the myths, the innuendo, the conflicting stories about this woman, I had to find out the truth, if possible.'

'And have you?'

He didn't answer immediately. 'It's turned into a mammoth job. But as I'm retired I've been able to devote a lot of time to it. And I've come to feel I owe it to her. There's still a lot to uncover.'

'Are you sharing any of this? Do others know what you're finding out?'

He looked away, a slight frown creasing his forehead. 'Many people don't want to know the real story, they prefer the exaggerated myths. Why are you interested?' he countered, looking at her intently.

It was Dani's turn to contemplate her teacup. 'I don't know. It's just that since I arrived here almost everywhere I turn I come across a reference to Isabella Kelly. Is she the local icon, or scarlet woman?'

Garth looked surprised. 'That's unusual. That you've come across her. Mention her name and mostly you draw a blank. Old timers have a vague notion of this colourful, eccentric woman but I'm discovering that much of what they believe is wrong. Even a lot of references to her in the museum are wrong.'

'But the main street in Cedartown is called Isabella Street,' said Dani.

'It's not named for Isabella Kelly, more likely the wife of John Valentine Gorman who surveyed the town in 1843, naming the streets. He was about twenty-three years old and had married Isabella Johnston in 1841. Gorman made no definite statement, but she appears to have been the obvious reason for the naming,' said Garth.

'Would you share what you're finding out with me?' Dani asked before thinking it might put Garth on the spot.

'You're only visiting, why do you care?' he responded cautiously.

'I have a family connection here.' She hesitated then asked, 'Do you know Jason Moore? And the plans for a new town?' Straight away she knew she'd hit a bullseye. Garth's face twisted as if he had a stomach cramp.

'Property prices have been creeping up, this will push them higher. Good for some landholders, I suppose. I just hate to see that area become a satellite sprawl and good agricultural land go under cement and houses. I haven't seen the plans so I shouldn't criticise,' he said, trying to appear non judgmental. 'But I get a bit sensitive about anything to do with Isabella Kelly.'

'You're really swept up by her story aren't you,' persisted Dani softly.

Garth looked a little uncomfortable. 'She must have been very lonely most of her life. I don't like the idea that she had no one to help her, defend her in life or death.'

'She doesn't sound a wimp to me,' said Dani. 'She must have been pretty strong willed and independent. Or is that a myth too?' She found his preoccupation with the pioneer woman strange, even obsessive.

'Isabella was feisty, argumentative, litigious, God fearing and above all a lady with a strong moral and work ethic, from what I'm piecing together.'

'So what went wrong for her?' Dani thought he might be reading more into her attributes than he could possibly know from such a distance.

'She was naive, wanted to believe the best in people. And I think she was a bit of a snob. Impressed with people of "her class".'

'Garth, how do you know all this?' asked Dani.

'I've been going through the records, references and old newspapers in the museum. There's quite a lot of stuff really. It's been a slow process, particularly digging through the court records of her various cases where she was the plaintiff, the defendant or the victim. The verbatim court records of her actual words are very revealing. They aren't just cold statements. They seem to reflect something of her soul. I still have a lot more research to do in Sydney at the Mitchell Library.'

Dani was impressed. 'You *are* keen. What are you going to do with all this information? Is this an altruistic effort for posterity or a book or what? How do you plan to . . . vindicate this woman?'

'I'm putting it together as a manuscript. I'd like it to be published, just to set the record straight, bring some kind of justice . . . what's the word they use now? Closure . . . that's it, to her story. I haven't finished piecing it all together. There have been so many conflicting testimonies over the years.' His eyes were now bright with enthusiasm. 'My work also gives an in-depth portrait of the men of the district. And of course the development of this valley.'

Dani touched his arm. He was a little surprised but their eyes met and they both felt comfortable. 'Thanks for telling me about your pet project, Garth. I'm more fascinated with Isabella Kelly than ever now, so maybe I've got the same bug as you.'

He chuckled. 'Yes, she is infectious.'

'Would you let me read some of your book?'

'If you'd like to and are around for a bit. I hope the truth will come out one day. Now I have to leave, thank you for the morning tea. And good luck with your painting. If you ever want to paint landscapes you can't beat the views from Isabella's land. I'd be happy to show you around.'

'I've only seen Kelly's Crossing. When would you have time?'

'I'm in Cedartown twice a week. Any Thursday would be good for me. I'll bring what I've put together so far.'

'You can reach me at Chesterfield. Or here's my mobile number.' Dani scribbled it on a napkin and handed it to him.

He shook her hand and left the cafe.

Dani put on her sunglasses in the bright sunlight. Her mind was racing with all she'd seen in the museum and now hearing about Garth's search for Isabella. She gazed at the heritage buildings across the park, a scene unchanged for decades, still wrenching herself back into the present, when a voice hailed her.

'Morning, Dani. Enjoying the delights of downtown Cedartown? Hope you've been into the museum.' Jason Moore sauntered towards her with an easy smile, his eyes screened by trendy aviator glasses.

'Did that yesterday as a matter of fact. Very interesting, so much historical stuff. Wonderful it's being preserved,' she answered.

'Oh, there's miles of that old stuff around,' he answered airily.

'Really? Henry who runs the museum was telling me tons of memorabilia has been tossed out over the years.'

'Ah, they don't know where to look,' said Jason.

What a know-all you are, thought Dani. 'Well, maybe you could give them a few clues so they could rescue some of it,' she answered tartly.

He gave a dismissive grin. 'Ah, there's enough junk in that museum to keep tourists in there for a week. Besides, a lot of the old dears don't want to part with their family heirlooms. If you consider a butter churner and turn-of-the-century knick-knacks heirlooms. Hey, want to go for a coffee?'

'I've just had one, thanks. Anyway, what old dears are you talking about?' asked Dani.

'You thinking of making them an offer and flogging stuff off in Sydney? Many have tried before and failed.'

'Not everyone thinks in terms of ripping off old people and looking for a fast buck.'

'Steady on, I didn't mean it like that. We get the antique hunters cruising through here. Most people are awake to their family stuff being valuable. But there are old ducks out in the hills, still living as they've done since they were young women. Managing alone, now in their eighties and nineties still without electricity or water. They carry buckets from the outside tank, light the kerosene lamps, cook

113

with a fuel stove. Maybe that's what keeps them so fit and living so long.'

'I can't believe there are women doing that.'

He shrugged. 'Like I said, they're tough old birds. They have a choice I guess, but they're independent. Better than vegetating in a smelly old nursing home.'

'Surely there's a better choice than that!'

'Not unless you're wealthy, have a supportive family or qualify for social assistance. That's what I'm interested in developing for the future.'

'Really?' She was about to say she thought he was designing an expensive housing development. She reached Angela's ancient and muddy four-wheel drive and opened the door.

Jason looked surprised. 'This'll get you just about any-where you want to go,' he said.

I bet you drive an immaculate, expensive Range Rover with leather seats and a talking GPS, thought Dani. 'My car's in for repairs. I hit a wallaby in the scrub. Fortunately the wallaby is recovering but my car is in hospital.'

'Yeah, sunrise and sunset are the worst times. I've had a few near misses with wildlife. Well, nice to see you again.'

'Bye.' Dani got in the car. 'I have some shopping to do. My mother and son are coming for the weekend.'

It was nearing lunchtime when Dani heard Lara's car and she ran to greet her mother and Tim as the car pulled in beside the cabin.

Lara exclaimed at the view and setting while Tim and Jolly raced down to the river.

'It's stunning. How beautiful.' Lara had no recollection of such magnificent scenery.

'You see why I wanted to stay longer? I've painted this view for Barney and Helen. They've been so kind,' said Dani. 'In fact, they're doing a barbecue for us this evening.'

'Wonderful. So what are we doing this afternoon?' Despite driving from Sydney, Lara, as always, was full of energy.

'I've made tea, let's have that. But seeing it's years since you were in Cedartown you could cruise the old stomping grounds,' said Dani leading Lara onto the deck where she'd set out the tea things.

'I doubt Tim would be interested in Our Humble Origins tour,' said Lara.

'Probably not. Though he'd enjoy going through the Brush or fishing at the old Cedartown wharf. Looking at his great-great-grandparents' home wouldn't mean so much to him.' Seeing her mother's wistful face, Dani made a suggestion. 'What say we look around this area, have afternoon tea at Claude and George's cafe, see Max and his studio. Then tomorrow Tim and I can have time together and you can go into Cedartown and look around and we'll meet you there for lunch? The old bank is a boutique hotel with a fabulous restaurant. Enticed a smart Sydney chef up.'

Lara brightened. 'Sounds a good plan.'

As Dani expected, Lara was a big hit with her new friends. Claude and George liked her instantly and found they and Lara had mutual acquaintances in Sydney.

Max was out so Sarah escorted them around the gallery and told Dani to feel free to take Lara into Max's studio around the back. Lara was stunned by Max's work. 'It's sensational. Magical. Quite different. Awful how you immediately think of Aboriginal art as being traditional dot paintings.'

'Max is a fine artist. He just happens to be Aboriginal. He could be Croatian or Hindu. And I suppose some of those cultural influences might show in the art. What you paint comes from inside, not the outside,' said Dani. 'You might want to paint a scene or a person, but it's the process that goes on inside your head and your pot of creative juices that define how it is regurgitated onto the canvas.'

'Very graphic, darling. I understand exactly what you mean,' said Lara and they both laughed.

Lara admired Dani's painting of the river. 'It's beautiful. Are you sure you want to give it away?'

'Yes, and thanks for the compliment. I plan to do a lot more.'

As they walked to the car Lara said quietly. 'So you really like it here? You think you could settle into this painting thing for a bit?'

'Possibly.'

'If it's what you want to do, Dani, there are practical matters to be considered. I love having Tim with me. But it's hard for him. He wants his dog, his gear, and his routine. He wants you.'

'I know that, Mum. So do I. But I can't uproot him from school, his pals, all of that. Look, let's not jump the gun. You've just arrived. Let's enjoy being together in our home territory.' Dani turned the car for Chesterfield where they'd left Tim playing with Toby and Tabatha.

Helen and Barney were supervising the three children. Toby and Tim were riding on the small tractor driven by Helen as Barney slashed grass down near the river. Tabatha, with Jolly and Ratso nosing around her, was busily dragging branches from under a gum tree into a heap.

Helen hugged Lara in greeting. 'We've so been looking forward to you coming up. Dani is like one of the family now.'

'I hope Tim hasn't been any trouble.'

'They're all getting on like a house on fire. We're doing dinner while Angela and Tony finish work. Are there any vegetarians? Lots of chops, bangers, mashed spuds and salad. Kids' tucker,' said Helen.

'Sounds wonderful,' said Lara. 'Can I help?'

Lara and Helen headed towards the main house chatting easily. Dani smiled as she watched them walk across the lawn. Whether prince or pauper, Lara treated everyone equally without condescension or being sycophantic. She was just herself and people responded to her. However, Dani knew it hadn't always been like that.

Lara figured that now she'd 'mellowed' with age she didn't present a threat to anyone. Over the years many women, unfairly, regarded Lara – who was glamorous, interesting, holding down a tough job in a high-profile industry and between husbands – as the enemy. But here she was, still beautiful, bright, and brainy, thought Dani. Wasted in a way. She had thought it was a good idea when Lara announced she was getting out of the TV rat race, but it was time her mother replaced it with something else. Not a full-time professional job, but something other than being a retired, divorced grandmother.

Barney brought the slasher back up the hill and Tim and Toby ran to Dani. 'Barney says I can have a drive tomorrow, in the paddock, how about that!' Tim shouted gleefully.

'Great. You listen to what Barney tells you. Now, what can I do to help?'

'Everything's under control,' said Barney. 'How about we go fishing tomorrow morning before breakfast, Tim? Toby and Tabby have a good spot we'll show you. Get some blackfish for breakfast, eh?'

Dani looked at Tim's shining eyes and the awe Barney inspired. It hit her how her son missed having a grandfather around to teach him the things Toby and Tabatha knew. Helen and Barney's grandkids could milk a cow, care for animals, fish, handle a boat, ride their bikes through the bush, climb trees, and they knew about the wind and stars and tides.

Not that Tim's father could have passed on such skills. Jeff was an advertising executive, into the corporate buzz and material money-making dreams. His idea of entertaining his son was to take him to private previews of big hit movies suitable for kids his age, theme parks, a river cruise, fancy restaurants in the city.

As the twilight dwindled, Tabatha was showing Tim how to neatly stack more wood on the bonfire she'd assembled.

'So where am I sleeping?' asked Lara as the three of them returned to Dani's cabin after the welcoming barbecue and a few drinks.

'Tim and I'll take the futons in the loft, you and Jolly get the big bed,' said Dani.

'I don't mind scrambling up the ladder,' said Lara, looking at the loft area above the sitting room.

'I want to,' pleaded Tim.

'Okay. Do your teeth first,' said Dani and, as Tim disappeared into the bathroom, she gave her mother a hug. 'I'm so glad you're here.'

'Me too. I'm happy we can share all this. Tim seemed to have a good time this afternoon,' said Lara, shifting the focus as she suddenly felt she might cry.

'I don't think it's registered he hasn't seen a TV or a computer all day,' laughed Dani. 'Tab and Toby kept him on the run.'

'Especially Tabatha, she's going to challenge him a bit,' smiled Lara.

'These country kids seem very independent. Max's sons Len and Julian are the same,' said Dani.

'It might be good for Tim to experience a change in lifestyle, attitudes, values,' said Lara thoughtfully.

'That's a pretty drastic change, Mum.'

'It's up to you, Dani. If you're serious about spending time here, stretching yourself, experimenting with your creative muse, I'll help you any way I can. Tim can move in with me of course. But frankly I think it should be a journey you take together.'

'Yes, I miss him. I'd like him to experience a bit more of the outdoor country life, but I wonder how well he'd adapt.'

'Boys' stuff, you mean? He'd be fine,' said Lara with a smile, then added, 'Tim needs a granddad like Barney.'

'I've been thinking the same thing.' Dani leaned down and rubbed Jolly's ears. 'I'll talk to Helen and Barney, and Angela and Tony. See what advice they have.'

'You'll have to find a place to rent too. Ah, darling, go for it, I say. Tim is only eight, it's not like he's studying for Oxford. Yet.' She paused. 'But Dani, don't think everything up here is sweetness and light. This might be removed from the city but I reckon they have similar problems.'

'Why do you say that?' asked Dani.

'Oh, on the drive here the local radio news mentioned the tragic death of a young man up on the mountain. They think it was drug related.'

'There's no escape is there? Where *is* safe? I suppose such a thing wouldn't have happened in the old days. No drugs about then.'

Lara couldn't quite judge the tone in Dani's voice. 'There are dangers and temptations in any era. I'm not deluding myself,' she said carefully.

'Drugs are everywhere, Mum. But I don't think they're being shoved through the fence at the local primary school where Toby and Tabatha go.'

'I don't imagine that school even has a fence,' said Lara lightly. 'Let's not read too much into one boy's desperate gesture.'

Dani sighed. 'Mum, you always sail in and never worry about the problems. I like to look at all the pluses and minuses.'

Lara stood up and stretched. 'Sensible. Like your father. But you can do the equations till the cows come home and still trip over something unexpected. Or find reasons not to. Just do it! I'm off to bed, it's been a long but lovely day. Goodnight, sweetie.'

They gave each other a warm hug. 'Sleep well, Mum.'

Lara did not fall asleep immediately. She got up and stood at the window looking out at the curve of the silvery smooth river. She could hear the murmur of Dani and Tim talking in bed and the gentle snuffles of Jolly stretched across the foot of her bed. How peaceful it all is, she thought. Vivid memories of the calm quiet country nights she spent in her grandparents' house so long ago flooded back. Being close to where she was born and spent her early years was stirring deep emotions.

Once again she was a small girl curled on the narrow iron bed in the bedroom her mother Elizabeth had shared with her sister Mollie, where the sweetness of her grandmother's orange tree blossoms had perfumed the room.

Being where her mother had lived from babyhood to marriage evoked a confusion of feelings. Life never worked out the way you expected. Which is why – unlike Dani – she felt it pointless writing lists of pros and cons before making a decision. You might as well just jump in and deal with the issues, good and bad, as they came along.

Lara's instinct was telling her it would be a good thing for her daughter and grandson to stay here for a while. She hoped her grandparents and her mother were watching and approving.

5

Mount George, 1840

Isabella

ISABELLA PUT DOWN HER pen, blotted and folded the letter
addressed to the governor in Sydney, closed her wooden
writing box and leaned back in the curved leather chair.
Her lips were pursed in annoyance that this letter was
necessary. Landholders were entitled to apply for assigned
convict servants, but because she was a female, and a lone
female, her original application to the magistrate at Port
Macquarie had been referred to the governor and there
matters had stalled.

Miss Isabella Mary Kelly was not typical of women
settling in the young colony. She was a free settler, wealthy,
unmarried, and had a fiercely independent spirit. She was
firmly letting the governor know that she wanted some
action on the convict servant issue. The delay in resolving
the matter was not acceptable.

Isabella was a mature woman in her mid thirties who knew what she wanted and expected to be treated with the deference due to a lady of class and standing. This new home might not be the London establishment in which she had been raised but now she'd made the decision to be a landholder and breeder of cattle and horses in the colony, she was going to make it a success.

She went outside and gazed over the heavily timbered hills and river flats yet to be thoroughly cleared for grazing. Two years ago she had bought the 895 acres with the river as its southern boundary for five shillings an acre at a rather subdued auction at the Treasury Building in Sydney. She named the property Mount George after the youngest son of her guardian, Sir William Crowder, a justice of the London High Court. George had been like a younger brother to her, the closest she'd come to having a family.

Isabella, a poor Irish Catholic girl orphaned when she was only eight years old and taken in by Sir William, did not dwell on her humble origins, but nourished the love she had for the family who turned her life around. Even now, two years after establishing her fine dwelling in the bush, she still felt a strong surge of emotion as she scanned the vista that had so captivated her heart from the first day she rode on to the land.

She hadn't intended to settle in this wild country. She'd sailed from London, first class, on the barque *Sir James* for health reasons, a change of scene, and a touch of adventure that fitted well with her strong spirit. One of her travelling companions, the Reverend John Dunmore Lang, an evangelical Presbyterian minister, had impressed her. A Scot, he had been living in Australia for several years and, despite their differing religious persuasions, she saw he was a man of complex but passionate beliefs. He was devoted to his wife and family, and told Isabella of his dream that this unrestrained colony mature into 'a great Christian nation'.

He told Isabella New South Wales needed hard-working, God-fearing free settlers to make this vision a reality. She glimpsed the chance to make her life a really great adventure. The reverend was the first person to speak to her of the natives, believing the Aboriginal culture to be better adapted to life in Australia than that of Europeans.

Isabella believed breeding and background really mattered. She might be living in 'the wilderness' but she maintained rigidly high standards in her person, her home and her business. Mount George was about half-way between the Hunter Valley and the penal settlement of Port Macquarie to the north. The newly opened up land gave her a sense of peace, fulfilment and hope. It was her church, a place where she felt close to the Almighty who had created the beautifully blue distant mountain range, the great forests, and the tumbling streams that flowed into the big river rolling through her property. Isabella was known by other settlers as a plain, pragmatic, even stern woman. But few knew how the Australian bush stirred her spirit.

In the early morning she breathed deeply the scent of eucalyptus and wood smoke, and loved watching the misty dawn give way to blazing blue sky and sun. The animals fascinated her and, despite knowing of many dangers, she felt secure in this pristine environment. She had come readily to accept the dramatic weather changes, from torrential rain and flood to the searing heat of summer with dried grass, cracked ground and the pall of distant bushfires. She had no nostalgia for the land of her birth, the largely treeless and mossy green hills, the tiny potato fields, the network of small villages in what now seemed a toyland. Ireland's poverty had killed her parents and forced her out into the world an unformed, unknowing child. She had been fortunate to be led into the care of a wealthy family in London. Isabella firmly believed that providence had protected her.

And now it was up to her to forge her future. She felt this strange new land was calling to her to create a home here, to grasp the opportunities and optimism it offered, and to accept the challenges. Acquaintances in London, and indeed anyone who might remember her poor family and the young orphan girl, would scarcely believe she was embarking on a such a scheme as this.

She never doubted she could do it. For years people would wonder where she learned about horses and cattle. How did a woman, a single woman, imagine she was going to run an enterprise in the bush where there were so many obstacles? All Isabella knew, and trusted, were her own instincts, her strengths and limitations.

Having bought land and built a good home, staffed with four female servants still being schooled in keeping house the way she expected, Isabella rode south on an ill-formed track to Maitland, in the Hunter Valley, to buy cattle. She bought one hundred cows at six pounds each, one hundred calves, and hired four men to drive them to Mount George.

She was eventually assigned eight convicts to work for her, and she made it clear to them that they were not running the property, they were simply employees. She oversaw every aspect of their work, which raised eyebrows in every settlement that heard the stories of her pioneering methods. One of the convicts, Thomas Higgins, was appointed head man. While all the men were only six to twelve months off being given their ticket of leave, she sensed they would not be past theft or laziness.

With the extra workers and new cattle she soon needed more horses, so with two of the convicts on horseback she packed some supplies in the back of her dray and headed back to the Hunter Valley to buy them. It meant sleeping rough in the open for a few nights but a crude shelter of sacks stitched together and tied to a frame of saplings gave Isabella some protection and privacy. If it rained she tied tanned cow skins to the top of the saplings. She slept clothed beneath rough blankets, her saddlebag as a pillow. And, the men believed, a pistol close at hand.

'Good morning, Miss Kelly. I'm Charles Langley from Rich, Burt and Langley and I'm delighted to meet you at last.' The man raised his bushman's hat in polite greeting. 'Your letter to our company in Sydney indicated you're interested in purchasing some good-quality stock horses?' His words clearly signalled that he was aware of the eyebrow-raising stories in circulation about her.

'And good morning to you, sir. Yes, I am in need of good work horses and breeding stock. Your assistance would be appreciated.'

He gestured towards a rough log stool under a tree close to the spread of well-fenced stockyards in which horses were being assembled for the auction. 'Shall we sit for a while and discuss the detail of how we can work together, Miss Kelly?' He gave the log a perfunctory swipe with his hat, raising a little cloud of dust.

'Thank you, Mr Langley.'

'Now, do you want me to make the selection? I can assure you that I have had considerable experience both here and in England, though I must say that some interesting new breeds have been developed in New South Wales in recent years.'

'I will make the selection myself,' responded Isabella firmly, but gave a little wave of the hand and added, 'Naturally your opinion on prices would be welcome but I have a fair eye for a good horse. Certainly I expect your firm to handle the paperwork. If all goes well I am sure we can build quite a useful working relationship in the years ahead.'

Langley was delighted with her no-nonsense approach. He could also see how easily her unrestrained self-confidence would make most men in the bush feel rather uncomfortable. 'Very well, madam. Would you like to follow me and inspect the better quality horses? When you have decided, will you want me to do the bidding on your behalf?'

'Of course. But keep your eye on me as well as the other bidders. I may need to signal you from time to time.'

'Naturally, Miss Kelly.' Langley struggled to get his raised eyebrows back into place.

She stood well apart from the men inspecting the horses but looked intently as each horse was led around the inspection yard. 'The chestnut. That grey mare. The roan stallion. The black filly with its foal.'

Langley made notes including her whispered suggestions of potential price, and occasionally ventured a brief remark of approval.

By lunch time she had acquired all the horses she needed, most at prices that were within her budget. She got some extra pleasure from giving a nod of approval for Langley to bid substantially higher than agreed for a very good-looking stallion, probably the best horse on offer, which attracted strong bidding. She knew her little victory would be much talked about by the men at the pub in town that afternoon.

The owner of the property where the auction was held sought her out. 'Miss Kelly, it is an honour to meet you. I'm Charles Horton. My wife and I would like you to join us as our guest for dinner and perhaps stay in our modest home this evening.'

'Thank you, Mr Horton. I am adequately catered for at the lodgings in town and anxious to return to my property. My men and I have made arrangements to leave at daylight. I trust I can return your offer of hospitality should you be passing some time.'

'It is very likely. Your land is on the main route north and I travel that way from time to time.'

Isabella had indeed chosen her land well. The north-south trail up the coast ran through her property and crossed the rocky shallows of the creek not far from the house.

'I bid you a safe journey, Miss Kelly.' The cattleman tipped his hat and turned away. Isabella's attitude would give his wife more to chatter about. The women at the sale felt snubbed by Isabella Kelly and were scandalised at her travelling around the countryside with two scruffy convicts.

Isabella was unperturbed, more concerned with making sure the journey with her new stock went well. To help, she had Langley find her two dogs well trained in handling stock.

While the return journey was more challenging with the barely broken-in horses, all went well. She smiled broadly and gave a bold cheer when her homestead came in sight, a shout that was taken up with a wave of hats by the two men working the horses. Smoke was rising from the detached cookhouse, bedding hanging to air along a fence next to the kitchen garden in which two of the women were working. All seemed quiet at the piggery and stables, but there was a movement of some cattle in a nearby stockyard. Probably branding, mused Isabella.

The shouts from the riders, a cracking of whips and the barking of the dogs brought the women servants and several men from the outbuildings to welcome them home. She smiled to herself at the sight before her.

Isabella's house was certainly grand by local standards. The holdings in this part of the north coast were still pioneering ventures, so the big investment by Isabella in her house, and the vision she had, caused men to scratch their heads in amazement and envy. It had taken twenty-five thousand feet of milled timber to construct. The rooms were spacious and airy with eleven-foot ceilings and lined in rosewood, cedar and beech. They opened onto wide verandahs that ringed the house. She had brought out from England fine glassware and dining sets, good furniture, even a piano. She had big plans for Mount George, and for her new life.

Lara

Since her last visit was years ago, Lara drove slowly through Cedartown noting the changes, which she judged to be improvements. While the main street hadn't changed nor had some of the shopfronts, she liked the style of the organic cafes, the little art gallery and health food store. She tried but couldn't recall what had been on the far corner where a supermarket, garage and arcade of shops had been built. Maybe it had been the blacksmith's with its wide wooden swing doors, roaring forge and clanging anvil inside, the railing outside for tethering horses, and a tree stump worn to a comfortable dip and polished smooth by many resting backsides.

On walks into town Poppy often stopped to yarn awhile with the old smithy. Her grandfather had told her the blacksmith had been a bullocky hauling logs from the hills and had a special way with horses and many stories to tell. Lara had always hung back, afraid when the forge was going. The flying sparks and noise from the solidly built man in the leather apron with goggles who swung his hammer onto the anvil with such force held her back.

The old brick slipper factory was still there, thankfully unchanged though it appeared deserted. Lara pulled the car into the kerb and stopped. The gold brick building looked very retro with its fifties facade and she tried to remember if she'd ever gone inside. She did remember the pompoms shipped in huge cardboard boxes to the factory to be stitched onto the front of plaid, satin and felt ladies' slippers. She sometimes found the multicoloured silky balls in the goods shed after they had been unloaded from the train. Rats would chew the corners of the cartons and it was like Christmas if she was playing in the goods shed – a favourite space – and found loose pompoms spilled from a box. And more occasionally silky tassels that went on the ends of men's dressing gown cords.

Lara closed her eyes and was once again a little girl lost in the shadows of the huge wooden shed with its solid timber slabs weathered silver-grey, chinks between them slicing bright light into golden slivers. Sometimes fairy dust danced in these narrow sunbeams and Lara would twirl, arms arched above her head as she practised her pirouettes. In dim corners bulky items freighted by train for a farm or factory waited to be collected. Under the iron roof a lazy carpet snake occasionally draped itself over the tree trunk beams, having had its fill of rats and mice, which had scampered around the sacks of grain and chicken feed.

She could vividly recall the indefinable smell of the shed, and remember with pleasure those hours of innocent pleasure on Poppy's patch. Nana watched from the front verandah as Lara trotted from the house to deliver Poppy's morning tea – the billycan of fresh brew, a home-baked cake or biscuit. She'd hop down from the passenger platform and cross the double railway tracks and go up the ramp to Poppy's little office at the end of the goods shed where he kept meticulous records in neat handwriting.

Sometimes there were cattle trucks being unhitched from a freight train, which were filled with doe-eyed calves, fat cows and sleek steers. But best of all was going down the line with Poppy on his hand-pumped trolley as he checked the kerosene lamps in the signal boxes and dropped into the butter factory. Lara was allowed to climb the tiny ladder outside the big milk vat and look down into the rich swirling milk. Invariably they came home with the billycan full of the cream that Poppy would whip with the old handheld egg beater for one of his light-as-air sponge cakes.

So as Lara turned the car towards the railway station she felt a painful shock in her chest and caught her breath at the empty space where the huge goods shed once stood. There was only rough grassed ground littered with a few rusting train wheels, and a pile of rotting logs. It felt like part of her childhood had been ripped away. Even the old passenger platform opposite looked forlorn. The quaint waiting room and station master's office had gone. The hanging baskets and ferns and old seats were gone, just like the steam age itself. Now streamlined diesel-powered trains thundered through, rarely stopping.

It was nothing like it had been, and Lara's eyes filled with tears. How many years had it been? Fifty? That made her seem so old. And she wasn't! She was still filled with curiosity, energy, a desire for adventure, still wondering what was yet to come in her life. She was still a little girl who wanted the gnarled, sure grip of her grandfather's hand as their arms swung together walking back to Cricklewood.

Lara was dreading what might have happened to her grandparents' home as she drove onto the bridge above the railway lines. It used to be a wooden bridge with loose planks that rattled each time a car crossed. It had been a comforting, familiar sound throughout her life at Cricklewood.

There were still a lot of the old-style homes in the streets close to town and she could visualise how they could be beautifully restored. She wished that the newer, expensive-looking homes were built in the classic style of latticed verandahs, peaked roofs, interesting windows.

Lara held her breath as she swung right and glanced from the embankment road down at Short Street. The familiar roofline was there and as she got level and swung into the intersection of roads by the station, she let out her breath in a rush of delight.

Cricklewood was almost unchanged. It even had a fresh coat of paint in its original colours – dark burgundy, the trim picked out in cream and green. What was different was the garden. Nana's rose garden wasn't there, though there were flowers around the lawn and in the brick boxes on either side of the entrance and the window box of the main bedroom at the front. As she parked opposite she couldn't tell if the brass nameplate was by the main door. There was kerb and guttering, and the road was bitumen, unlike the rough grassy verge and dirt road she remembered. Through the side gates and down the back where the fence once divided the chooks from the garden was a large garage painted to match the house.

Her grandparents never owned a car but the new garage fitted in nicely. The front door was open, as were the side gates where a motor home was parked. She hesitated, thinking the occupants might have visitors, but she was now so drawn to the old house that she walked through the gate, closing it behind her, and stepped onto the verandah.

As she stood by the door she ran her fingers over the old brass nameplate with a tingle of pleasure, delighted that it was still in place. She remembered exactly how her grandmother had furnished the verandah, the wicker lounge with small table that always had a fresh embroidered cloth on it, the pot plants in their wooden stands, the canvas blind on the far end that was dropped when a southerly blew in with rain and sometimes hail.

Lara called out and when no one answered she rang the

doorbell. The twang of the brass ringer took her straight back to being a small child inside the hallway, hearing the doorbell and seeing a figure distorted behind the frosted glass panels of the door.

'Coming, one minute,' a voice echoed from the back, the kitchen or laundry perhaps.

'G'day. Can I help you?' The woman was round, smiling, in sweater and stretch pants. She had an accent Lara couldn't place.

Lara quickly explained the house had belonged to her grandparents and she was visiting the area after many years away.

'Oh, the Williams family, I've heard about them from the real estate agent who sold us the house ages ago. Great citizens of the old days from all accounts. Please, would you like to come inside?'

'I don't want to inconvenience you, but, yes, I'd love to if I may. I'm Lara Langdon.'

'It's no trouble. I am Kristian Clerk. We've made some changes of course but I think you'll find it nearly the same.'

Lara was instantly transported back to her childhood. But how much smaller it now seemed! She felt like Alice who'd grown tall while everything around her shrank. With Kristian's permission Lara opened the double doors with the panes of frosted glass that led into the front lounge room. How had her grandmother fitted all the lounge furniture, big bookcase, writing desk and even a piano in here?

The Clerks seemed to live simply without all the Victoriana clutter loved by Lara's grandmother. A gas heater stood in the open fireplace. Briefly Lara closed her eyes remembering the cosy winter nights after dinner with logs burning brightly in the fireplace, armchairs on either side, Nana knitting, Poppy with the newspaper, the big standing wireless tuned to the ABC. And vividly she recalled the wood box Poppy had made that sat to one side filled with kindling and chopped wood to add to the fire through the evening. What had happened to that old box? She used to sit on it, leaning against Poppy's chair, her head in a book.

Out in the kitchen, while her grandmother might not have liked the pastel-hued paint choice, she would quite likely have made the same improvements – an electric stove in the space where the wood-burning stove had been, a sink under the windows, a washing machine in the laundry in place of the wood-fired copper, the back verandah sleep-out glassed in and turned into an office.

Mr Clerk came up the back steps and Lara was introduced.

'Ah, so you are Lara. I always wondered if I would meet you one day. It is still there,' he smiled and pointed to the cracked cement slab at the base of the steps next to the new water tank.

Lara's baby footprint was still outlined in the cement where Poppy had pressed it and written her name.

The old tree with the swing had gone, the dunny down the back – the outhouse – appeared to be part of a large garden shed. She admired the vegetable bed and found the stumps where Poppy's special shed had stood.

'And what was this?' asked Mr Clerk pointing to a small slab of cement beside a tree stump.

'That was Nana's favourite jacaranda tree. Our dog is buried there,' said Lara quietly.

'Ah, I understand.'

'Would you like coffee, or tea?' asked Mrs Clerk gently.

'No, thank you, I really have to go. I can't thank you enough.'

'You're welcome, any time. Are you staying up here for long?'

'No . . . well, I'm not sure. My daughter has moved up to the valley. She's staying at Chesterfield for a little while. To paint.'

'Please, if she wishes to visit, she is welcome.' Mrs Clerk threw a questioning look at her husband.

'Thank you, Mrs Clerk. I'd like her to see where her great-grandparents settled. We'll phone you ahead to check of course.'

Mr Clerk was having trouble reading the signal from his wife so she turned to Lara. 'This might seem a little impromptu, but we are planning a trip in our motor home around Australia for several months. We have been looking for someone to rent this place . . . I don't know, but if your daughter is interested . . .'

Lara stared at her, her mind spinning. In her wildest imaginings she hadn't considered this possibility. 'Well, that's kind of you to offer. It would certainly be . . . an interesting experience for her. I'll suggest it.' She felt quite flustered but knew in her heart a house in town was not what Dani was after for her artistic escape.

'Please, think about it. There is no hurry. We have a friend coming in each week to keep things tidy and water the garden.'

Lara thanked them and said a hasty goodbye. She drove away, tears stinging her eyes. Suddenly the Clerks seemed to be intruders, she wished her grandparents were still alive, living in Cricklewood and there to offer her comfort and advice.

Lara was glad no one was around when she got back to the cottage at Chesterfield. She heard a boat on the river and the distant lowing of a cow. The tranquil scene of the river was soothing. But like the river there was a strong pull beneath the surface and Lara realised there was unfinished business here in the valley. She'd have to return.

Dani

There was no way Dani wanted to take up the Clerks' offer to house-sit Cricklewood. 'It's suburbia, Mum! Where would I paint? I didn't escape Sydney to stay in a country town backwater with neighbours watching my every move!' She also thought the idea of being in her great-grandparents' home a little creepy.

Lara shrugged easily. 'Just passing it on. I guess it doesn't have the same happy memories for you as it does for me.'

'Mum, I have *no* memories of this place,' Dani reminded her. 'I could just as easily be settling to paint in any other scenic part of the country. It's just coincidence I came here really. Besides, Helen says she knows of a place. More what I'm looking for even if it is a bit out of the way.'

'That's fine then, darling. Let me know how things work out.'

Dani shook her head. 'It seems such a weird thing to offer. She'd met you for what? Five minutes? Bizarre.'

'Not really, darling, when you think about it. It's rather a typical country gesture. If you're from a country town you always belong. People operate on trust and instinct more than in a city.'

'Nice of them, but not for me. And I don't want the responsibility of other people's stuff.'

Lara didn't answer, thinking how minimalist and simply furnished the Clerks' home was in comparison to her grandmother's knick-knacks, memorabilia and clutter.

'We'd better be going. Tim and I will call you when we get home.'

Dani hugged her son tightly as he and Lara prepared to drive back to Sydney. 'Have you had fun, sweetie?' she asked him.

'Yeah. Tab and Toby are nice. But when are you coming home, Mum?' he asked, looking worried. 'Have you got a boyfriend?'

'No, of course not. We've talked about this, Timmy. I have a different job now, I'm the boss and I have to spend time doing my paintings and I need space and quiet to do that. Next time Ma brings you up we can go fishing. It'll be fun, you'll see. The holidays aren't far away. Now be good and help Ma. I love you. More than anything in the world.'

Tim hugged her back but still looked dubious.

Lara gave Dani a quick kiss. 'He'll be fine. He reads the map for me. Looking for places to stop and eat. Talk to you tonight.'

Helen and Dani left the car at the old gate where a carved wooden plaque announced the property as The Vale. They stepped over the cattle grid, walked across overgrown paddocks, through a windbreak of eucalypts, peppercorn and pine trees.

'Now, as I said, it's nothing special, but it's secluded, lots of room and cheap,' said Helen leaning on a stick she'd picked up and panting slightly as they reached the crest.

Dani stopped and drew a deep breath as she looked into the hidden dip where a cottage nestled in the embrace of the rolling hills. Two horses stood at the edge of a broad dam and a large creek fringed with willows and paperbarks meandered through paddocks.

'It's not the river view that we have, but pretty. The

stream would get quite full with a good rain,' said Helen. 'It comes down from Little Mountain and ends up in the main river. Not sure what condition the house is in. You don't have to take it. I just thought –'

Dani cut in, 'Oh Helen, you don't have to make excuses, this place is stunning. Hard to believe we're only two ks off the main road. How old is it?'

'This house was built some years ago, I think the other farm cottages are falling down. It's part of a very old family farm, not sure what happened to the original homestead. The Vale has been rented before, off and on. Daresay it hasn't been cleaned or such. A solicitor in town handles the estate, which includes renting this place.'

'So long as it has good light and a place to paint,' said Dani. Now that she'd decided to stay awhile in the valley, finding a suitable place to rent had been her first priority. Lara had returned to Sydney with Tim who'd enjoyed the weekend enormously. Having playmates on a farm by the river had been great, but changing schools and living here might not be so appealing.

'There's a shed or old milk bails, I think. I only heard about it from people who rented here then came and stayed with us to be on the river.' Helen decided not to tell Dani that the family who came for a farm holiday had left The Vale early convinced there was something creepy, even haunted, about it.

Helen handed Dani the key and they went inside the cottage, which was dusty, musty and had the unmistakable smell of mice. Jolly romped ahead, nose to the ground seeking the source of the smells.

'Some of the verandah floorboards are a bit dodgy. But it's got a lot of potential,' commented Helen following Dani indoors. 'Not that you should have to spend money on a rental.'

'It's so cheap. What's a bit of white paint?' Dani ran

from room to room admiring the high ceilings, the exposed boards, the large windows, even a bay window with a window seat and French doors that opened from the bedrooms onto the verandah with sweeping views. There was a big open fire in a sitting room and while the kitchen had basic amenities there was a pot-bellied stove next to the old-style electric cooker. 'Do you think they'd mind if I tarted it up? I just love the layout.'

'I'm sure they won't give a hoot. The owner never comes near the place. But are you sure you want to take this on? You'd better check the outhouses.'

The old wooden bails had been upgraded from a milkshed to extra sleeping quarters. On one side was a sliding glass door looking towards the creek.

'The light, it's brilliant. Should be bright in here all day,' exclaimed Dani.

'It faces north,' said Helen, bending down to lift a section of the blotchy linoleum. 'Gawd, this must be fifty years old. You'd be better ripping it up and putting mats down on the floorboards.'

'They'll get splashed with paint. I rather like the bare look,' said Dani rubbing a foot over the coarse, broad-milled floorboards. 'I'll rip out the lino and do the boards with a limewash.' She stood there deciding where to put her easel. The room was empty save for a row of shelves on one wall which must have been used for clothing. A perfect place for her brushes and paints and rags and sketchbooks.

'So it's a yes then,' grinned Helen.

'You bet! Where do I sign?'

In the solicitor's office in town Dani signed a six-month lease. Mr Archer was courteous, formally old-fashioned. And curious.

'You're pretty isolated out there, that doesn't worry you?' he asked.

The image of the old cottage snug in the little gully sprang to Dani's mind. The place had no visible neighbours, no one would hear a call for assistance. The dirt road leading to the gate could possibly get boggy in a deluge of rain. Undoubtedly there'd be problems with all manner of creepy crawlies, snakes and wildlife on the prowl. It was totally unlike anywhere she'd ever lived. But she thought of the view . . . from every window in every room there was a vista of the paddocks, the creek, the distant mountain range, the beautiful stands of trees.

She smiled at the solicitor. 'Seclusion I think, rather than isolation. I'm sure I'll be fine. And hopefully I'll do a lot of creative work, and my son will settle in too.'

Helen didn't say anything but she wondered about Tim adjusting easily to such a place after being in a city. Maybe Lara would continue in her role of caring for Tim until Dani's six months were up.

The first person Dani told was Max. She found him arranging a display of carvings and artifacts.

'Hey, Max. Wow, they're great, who did them?'

'Local mob at Planters Field. They came to a course I teach at TAFE and then we started an art and crafts group in the community centre at Planters Field. Been good for keeping the young people out of trouble and the old people are passing on knowledge. What we sell goes back to the group.'

'Good on you, Max. I'm sure visitors will love these.' Dani picked up a carved and painted snake sitting next to a lizard.

'Hope so. Tourists always assume stuff like this has come from the desert or Arnhem land. We have just as much culture and history in this valley.'

Dani was surprised. 'It's not well known, I guess. What happens out at the Planters Field community? It sounds like they're still separated from the town. Like the old days . . . fringe dwellers.'

'Kind of, but there are services, Aboriginal housing, resources, a support network for kids who run wild, a women's refuge, that kind of thing. Council and other groups have beefed it up with new buildings. It's not like the outcast reserve it was in my grandmother's day.' He straightened up. 'So what have you been up to?'

'Oh, Max! That's why I came by. I have news – I've rented a house.'

'That's fantastic. A girl of action. Where is it?'

'Out of town on the road to Cedartown, a bit of a dirt road turn off, through an old gate, over a cattle grid past some trees and there's a lovely little valley with an old farmhouse that's still very, er, rustic. So it's pretty cheap.'

'I'm surprised. I thought you'd stay in town. But that's good. You need open spaces, let nature guide you. Have you got a good painting spot?'

'You bet. In fact, I was going to ask if you could come and have a look and help me set it up. There's old bails that have been converted to extra accommodation. Lots of light, perfect for a studio.'

'Be a pleasure. You can raid my surplus supplies too.'

'Oh, thanks.' Dani gave him a quick hug as Sarah came into the gallery.

'What's all the excitement?' she asked with a smile.

'Dani's rented a place out of town. On a property,' said Max.

'Really? That's terrific. But what about your son?' asked the practical Sarah, knowing what a big move it would be for an eight-year-old.

'Sarah, I haven't tackled that yet. I'm hoping the experience of being here will broaden him. I admire your boys and Tabatha and Toby so much . . . I'd love to see Tim learn a bit more about country life. Be more self-sufficient, not need the city stuff . . . you know.'

Dani hoped her voice wasn't trembling. She was scared that Tim would simply refuse or, if she insisted, he'd simply suffer and be resentful. In her heart she had a strange pull to see her son at home in this environment. Learn skills like chopping firewood, fishing, riding, roaming through the bush, camping out.

She looked from Sarah's slightly concerned and caring expression to the steady deep eyes of Max as he studied her. Dani wanted to ask Max to teach her son some of the knowledge he taught the Aboriginal kids. While she knew in her heart such things might not be useful in the career path Tim might choose or the life he might lead, she had a sense they were valuable lessons. Inwardly she smiled to herself imagining Tim visiting his dad in the city and regaling him with tales of bush exploits.

Max, sensitive as always, touched her hand. 'If Tim comes here, he will be part of our extended family. We'd be proud to have him join Len and Julian in some of our adventures. It will be good for him. Your instincts are right.'

Sarah nodded. 'Toby and Tabatha are good kids. They'll be mates for him. Angela and Tony, and Helen and Barney, are a great family. Kids need that sense of continuity, of grandparents, and an idea of where they belong, where they've come from.'

Max squeezed her shoulders. 'You've made a good decision, Dani. Now, when do we help with the moving in?'

'I'll have to make a visit to Sydney and pack up and rent my house, move my stuff. I'm going to do it quickly . . . before I get cold feet.'

*

Dani arrived in Sydney, rushing through Lara's door like a whirlwind. Lara took the news calmly, although her mind was spinning. She wasn't sure Dani was totally committed to the move but now she'd signed a lease, well, that was that.

'If you think this is right for you, darling, then I'm all for it. I just worry about Tim. When are you going to tell him?'

'I guess tonight. I can't hang about.'

'Dani, what if he is truly upset and against the whole idea?' asked Lara.

'Well, I know he's probably going to react badly because I haven't shown him the house and talked it through with him. But frankly it needs work before he sees it. I'm trying to make him see it's just a short-term experiment that will be enriching and valuable for us both. It's not the end of the world,' said Dani.

'No way, Mum! Why didn't you *ask* me?' cried Tim.

'I realise it's a sudden change. But you did have a good time when you stayed at Chesterfield –'

'That was a holiday! That's different. What about soccer? The comp season is coming up. What about my friends? What about school? In three weeks we have an excursion. Then it's the holidays. I'll stay here with Ma and then go up to your place. Just for the school break.'

He wheedled and complained, sulked and stormed off to his room.

Dani sat over a pot of tea with her mother.

'It's not surprising he's reacted like that,' said Lara. 'And, as we discussed, maybe he should stay here with me for the next few weeks, we've been having a great time while you've been up there. He's moved a heap of his stuff in anyway.'

'What do I do about my place?' Dani's dream of escape to artistic freedom was becoming very complicated.

'Honey, the school holidays are only a month or so away. And a friend of mine in Melbourne rang me a few days ago asking if I knew of a house to rent as her daughter is considering moving to Sydney and needs somewhere to stay to see how she likes it, if she can get work. She could rent your place. They're a lovely family.'

As always her mother had a solution. 'Okay, Mum, let's do that. But you're sure about looking after Tim? It's a full-time job.'

'I'm sure. But you consult your son.'

It was a short-term compromise. Dani sensed Tim was hoping she'd get the whole country art thing out of her system by the end of the holidays and they could go back to normal. And Dani realised she could get out of the six-month lease on the cottage at The Vale quite cheaply if she needed to. It was almost a peppercorn rent.

It was a wrench leaving Tim, especially when he looked close to tears. Lara dropped her arm around his shoulders and shot Dani a comforting message with her eyes.

'Look after Jolly, Mum,' said Tim tearfully.

'She loves it up there, all those rabbits to chase.' Dani hugged Lara. 'Thanks, Mum.'

Lara squeezed her arm. 'Do what you have to do, darling. I did.'

Dani thought about those words as she drove along the dawn-drenched highway. Her mother had been the one to leave her father and had made references to her own mother Elizabeth striking out on her own. Maybe it was a genetic flaw. Dani hoped she'd be able to feel settled and be in a stable and committed relationship one day. God, I sound like something in a women's magazine, she chided herself. She turned on the radio news to distract herself.

By the time she'd left the city and was considering

where to stop for breakfast, Dani felt her spirits lifting. She had a sense of severing, of a journey begun. Last time she'd headed north it had been on a whim, into the unknown. Now she was going towards a goal, a dream that had surfaced, if inconveniently. She would follow her mother's advice to trust her instinct and try not to feel guilty about it.

She began mentally to decorate and fix up the cottage at The Vale. And soon she was thinking about what she'd paint first. The possibilities were endless. Looking at the now familiar rural scenes flashing past, colours, brush-strokes and images of her vision of the hills, paddocks and towns came to her mind, and how she'd reinterpret landscapes and settings. And pushing to the forefront of her mind was the beautiful land around Kelly's Cross-ing, which could possibly disappear beneath Jason's new homes. That would be her first task, she decided, to cap-ture the landscape through the eyes of Isabella. The land Isabella had seen and been captivated by enough to settle and meet great challenges.

Helen had the cabins rented out and insisted Dani and Jolly stay in one of the spare bedrooms in the rambling main house as it would take Dani a few days to get set-tled. As agreed with the solicitor, the cottage would be furnished from 'old family memorabilia' stored in a barn on the property.

'I think I'll be buying a lot of paint and colourful throws to cover things,' said Dani.

'You never know, some of that "old memorabilia" could be valuable antiques,' laughed Helen.

'Not if it's been stored in a shed with rats and possums,' said Barney dryly. 'You'd be better off going to an auc-tion. Moxie's has one every Friday morning. A few dealers are starting to come from Sydney. You'll find a bargain or three, that's for sure.'

'Sounds fun. I'll go once I get an idea of what's going into the house.'

She dropped by the Nostalgia Cafe for a coffee and Claude and George were elated at her news.

'Can't wait to see it. How fabulous, you fell on your feet, girl,' said Claude.

'I did rather. Or maybe my spiritual friends would say it was all meant to be. I'm being led . . .'

'Bullshit,' declared George. 'I believe you make your own life. I threw everything up in Sydney to follow Claude to France, and look where we are now! A completely new life.'

'*Et nous ne regrettons rien*!' Claude touched his partner's hand.

George smiled at Dani. 'Never have regrets. Waste of energy. So, can we come to this auction thingy?'

'Love you to come. It's held at the back of the old butter factory in Cedartown. I'll let you know.'

Dani arranged with Max to go out to see The Vale and to set up her studio. They drove out in Max's old station wagon laden with the art supplies he was giving her.

'You are generous, Max, I suppose it seems silly to get the studio arranged before I even have a bed. But I'm waiting till the auction tomorrow.'

'Ah, this is all extra stuff from art classes I run at Planters Field. The group decided they didn't want formal whitey art classes. They started painting in the long grass.'

'Outdoors?'

'Yeah, sitting under a tree, using canvases and occasionally bark. One of the old men has taught the kids how to make brushes using hairs and twigs. They're starting to learn stories of their country.'

'Do their parents know the stories too?'

'Not many. So many were stolen generation, busted up from their relatives and land. Or they and their parents were made to live like white people – without any privileges. I'm the first in my family to get a good education, a job, and have a business.' He paused, 'I love Sarah and I can't imagine not being with her. But sometimes I worry what my old grannies and elders might have said about me marrying a white girl and becoming acceptable.'

'A foot in two camps. Is that why you work so hard for the local Aboriginal community?' asked Dani.

'Yeah. We still have a lot of problems. I need to keep that connection. I have mixed blood but I'm Aboriginal before anything else. I needed to know what my history is. We all do, Dani.'

She was silent, remembering Lara fumbling through the unknown photographs of her family. And what was she passing on to her son? She made up her mind that no matter how much Tim objected, six months or a year out of the city in the place where his maternal family had lived would give him a sense of continuity later in life wherever he settled.

'And do you know that history now?' she asked.

'Bits and pieces. Sometimes fragments come to me in dreams. I have one old aunty nearly ninety, she tells me things. Or explains what I dream. I've learned a lot from her.'

They clattered over the cattle grid at the entrance to The Vale and at the top of the rise Max stopped the car and turned the engine off. Late afternoon light slanted across the gully. There was a distant curl of smoke from someone burning off. The shadows of trees were elongated as if reaching out to engulf the small white cottage. The horses she'd seen were not around. There didn't appear to be any living creature in sight. All looked still, cold, quiet.

'Looks like I won't have any distractions out here,' said Dani lightly, trying to cover a trace of nervousness.

Max pointed to the tall scrubby grass close to the eucalyptus trees. 'See, there, by the trees. Two wallabies.'

'Oh, how sweet.'

'They've jumped the fence or part of it's down. Watch your dog, they can claw pretty good if cornered.' Max restarted the car but before putting it in gear he asked somewhat shyly, 'Dani, I thought I might do a little ceremony. Just to make it your home. Would that be all right?'

'Of course. What a lovely idea.' She didn't ask what he meant, figuring she'd find out.

Max stopped some distance from the house and they got out of the car. For once Jolly didn't race off, but stayed close to Dani, watching Max.

From the back seat he took a bunch of gum leaves and his didgeridoo.

They walked a few metres then Max stopped, speaking quietly. 'You stay here. I'll just go first. Ask permission.'

He crouched down and lit the gum tips and, as the fragrant smoke swirled above them, he put one hand on the ground and held the smoking leaves above his head as he softly chanted. The words were not very audible nor did Dani understand the language, but there was something respectful and gentle in Max's tone of voice. He then rose, placed the burning leaves on the ground and lifted his didge, balancing one end on his outstretched foot, and began to play. The shivery drone of the plaintive notes echoed across the gully, winding through the trees and fading towards the mountains. Jolly dropped to the ground, laying her nose on her paws.

When Max lifted his mouth from the didge, he stared into the distance as if listening. Then, after stamping on the leaves to be sure there were no sparks left, he came towards her, appearing deep in thought.

'So am I welcome? Cleansed? Safe?' she asked.

Max didn't answer for a minute. 'Strange, not sure what to make of it. A lot of voices, many spirits are here . . . Oh, don't worry, you're welcome,' he added, seeing the alarm on Dani's face. 'They'll look out for you. They're glad you have come. It will be fine. It seems you'll find what you've been looking for.'

He headed back to the car. 'Let's check out that studio of yours.'

Dani paused, gazing at the scene around her, the white cottage in the centre of the peaceful landscape. Safe. How many places were safe in this world? Awakening to sickening news, too often, of bombings, attacks and destructive accidents seemed another planet away from here. Had disaster and tragedy struck in this calm valley while generations had lived here, she wondered. Had the war years, the Depression, natural disasters touched the people who'd first settled in this part of the valley?

'Coming?' called Max holding the door open for her. And as she got in he closed the door and looked at her through the window. 'What were you thinking just now?'

'I was thinking this is a safe place. Or has this valley and the river seen its share of drama and trauma?'

'Indeed it has. There are sad stories buried in its soil. But you'll be safe here. The spirits are all around your cottage. They'll protect you.'

'Thanks. I'm glad.' She just hoped the spirits kept to themselves. She didn't want to confront any of them just the same.

'Someone's been here,' said Max as they drove in beside the house. He pointed to tyre marks in the grass.

'There were some roses in the front garden bed there too,' said Dani. 'I wonder if the solicitor came out to check. The owner doesn't live here.'

'You can put the key away, the door's unlocked,' said Max. 'Mostly how it is in the country. Or used to be. Vandals do roam around occasionally.'

There was a bigger surprise when they stepped inside.

'My God, it's been furnished!' exclaimed Dani.

They hurried through the house to find beds, a ward-robe, tables, kitchen dresser, wicker chairs along the verandah.

'It's old stuff, sturdy enough. Not exactly French-polished antiques though,' said Max with a man's practical eye.

'But, Max, it's fabulous. This is the real thing. I love it,' enthused Dani. 'Real and rustic.' She began calling the solicitor on her mobile.

'You'll probably have to go outside to get reception,' said Max. 'I'll take a look around.'

Dani raced out the door to stand on a small hillock close to the old clothesline held up by a wooden forked prop. When she returned she found Max in her 'studio'. 'He said it was stored up at the old house across the hill. I might as well make use of it. There's a caretaker who comes and goes.'

'Very handy. Now this is a great space, Dani. I reckon you should face towards that window when you work. Shall we bring in the stuff and see what goes where?'

Two hours later Dani and Max had arranged her studio with easel, boards, paints, rags, turps, brushes, jars, sketchbooks and several spotlights.

'Just one more thing,' said Max, going back to the car.

Dani went through the house again, visualising where she'd put the few personal items – books, rugs, ornaments, some photographs, china, linen and clothes – she'd brought with her. She looked at the stack of firewood by the pot-bellied stove and then saw on the old beechwood dining table the roses from the garden in a quaint crystal vase. She went back to the studio to find Max adjusting a large painting on the wall.

'I hope you don't think I'm intruding on your space, but I thought you might like this. It's a painting of the river flats near Riverwood.'

'Max, it's beautiful,' gasped Dani. 'I'm honoured to have the loan of one of your pictures. It will be my inspiration.'

'It's not on loan. I'd be happy to know you have it. You're part of this landscape now.'

Dani couldn't speak for a moment. 'Thank you, Max.' She hugged him. 'Let me buy you lunch at the Nostalgia.'

'There's certainly a lot of that around here,' smiled Max as Dani whistled for Jolly and closed the door, not bothering to lock it.

As the house disappeared from view in the gully and they turned onto the dirt road, Dani glanced back at the gate. The Vale, her new home. It was going to be fine. She just hoped she could live up to Max's expectations and produce good work.

Max was thoughtful as he drove. It was a great place for Dani, and he trusted the spirits there would protect her. For he had an unmistakable and uneasy sense that sadness lurked in the story of the land where The Vale now nestled.

6

Mount George, 1844

Isabella

ISABELLA UNHITCHED THE OLD mare from the dray, turned her loose and then lifted down the plants she'd collected from the wetlands and a thick pocket of littoral rainforest on her property, much of which she had yet to explore.

Labourers had built post-and-rail fences close to the homestead where the best brood mares and foals were kept and she was pleased with the progeny from her stallions and mares. She'd chosen well, even if she'd paid more than planned. The agent had been impressed and sought her opinion on several horses he had in mind for himself. He wondered where Miss Kelly had acquired her knowledge of horseflesh and assumed she must have come from a family of wealthy landowners in Ireland and England. He hoped he would continue to be hired by Miss Kelly when it came time to sell her young horses. Good animals were in strong demand from the British Army in India as well as in a fast-expanding Sydney town and other parts of the colony.

Isabella carefully laid the plants on damp sacks without disturbing the clumps of soil around the roots and marvelled at their unusual leaves, buds and seeds. Some looked like small creatures, others like works of art.

But she was most elated at discovering several carnivorous plants that trapped and ate insects and even devoured very tiny fish and tadpoles from the marshy wetlands.

She had first been alerted to these extraordinary plants by Lieutenant Benjamin Bynoe, a surgeon in the navy and amateur botanist, at a chance meeting in Sydney. At first she thought he was inventing the tale of plants that ate flesh, but when he produced his record books going back to his first voyage to the Galapagos with Charles Darwin on *The Beagle*, she had been convinced and intrigued. Isabella listened enrapt when he talked of his discoveries with Darwin in the Galapagos, devouring his knowledge. He was modest in recounting his exploits but Isabella was impressed and vowed when she had time and was properly established she would pursue further studies and research into the flora and fauna of her new land.

In the meantime she couldn't resist the urge to pick up plants that caught her eye. She had constructed a primitive greenhouse of bark and flour bags near the kitchen and had two convict girls collect used house water to pour on her plants. The girls thought it all a waste of time and effort but kept that to themselves. Very quickly Isabella had some success with the wild orchids, waxy epiphytes and ferns transplanted from the fringe of the dense and towering rainforest. She found it an eerie place and if it wasn't for the lure of strange and beautiful plants clinging to the bark of old trees, or growing in the deep litter of decaying leaves and between the high roots of the massive fig trees, she wouldn't have ventured into the forest.

Isabella far preferred the grassy open bushland with stands of eucalypts, beech and white mahogany. The acacias with their delicate golden balls of fluffy flowers, the deep red blooms of the flame trees and the she-oaks that rustled along the waterways delighted her eye.

She kept a meticulous diary with precise watercolour drawings of the plants she found and wrote notes describing their habitat. She wished she was a trained artist who could paint on a large scale and capture the vastness of this country. Her country. As far as she could see, even beyond the next mountain, she owned tracts of as yet undeveloped land. She had great dreams, but knew it would take time and careful planning to make those dreams a reality.

Isabella was deep in thought and out of sight in the plant house when she heard a commotion near the homestead kitchen. One of the servant girls was calling and distraught.

Rothwall, the overseer, was shouting. 'Where are they? Where are they? Damned gins. Should be shot, the lot of them!'

The girl broke into a wailing scream.

'Come on,' shouted Rothwall. 'Tell me where. Which woman is causing the trouble, has she been up here at the homestead?'

Isabella stepped from the plant shelter. 'What is this commotion about?' she called loudly as she went towards the arguing workers.

The servant girl ran to her, wringing her hands on her rough cloth pinafore. 'Madam, please, there is a native girl. She needs help. I went to their camp and it's terrible.' She burst into a flood of tears.

'You are expressly forbidden to go near any native camps,' snapped Isabella and turned her attention to the overseer who was carrying a musket. 'And you, Rothwall, what do you think you are doing with a weapon? Seeking another whipping at Port Macquarie?'

'Ma'am, with respect, I took it from the cook in order to protect your property. It seems there is some trouble with the blacks.' He proffered the gun and made a gesture of apology. 'I intended to protect this place.'

Isabella took the gun from the overseer and turned to the sobbing girl. 'Well, Hettie, what's going on? Speak quickly.'

The servant girl drew a breath and glanced fearfully at Rothwall. 'This black girl came to the kitchen garden and cried out. She made motions of a baby and was babbling in her tongue. So I ran and bade her show me.' She paused to swallow and take a deep breath. 'Down by the creek, o'er there near the crossing, she has given birth to an infant and two native men want to kill it. Or so it seemed, ma'am.'

'Please, Hettie, no more of this hysteria. Go back to your duties. I will handle this.' Isabella handed the musket to the girl. 'Put this back in the kitchen. Rothwall, follow me but do nothing without my instructions.' Once again Rothwall had overstepped the boundaries she set. She knew very well it irked him to be subservient to a woman. Isabella strode out in her boots, long skirt, cabbage tree hat tied down with a scarf, pulled her thick gloves from her hands and stuffed them in a pocket of her skirt as she set out. Behind her back Rothwall shook his fist at the girl as he followed Isabella.

Isabella could hear the wailing and men's voices as she approached the creek that led to Kelly's Crossing. A young Aboriginal woman, naked save for a small loincloth, was sitting next to a campfire, suckling a newborn baby. Two older women sat behind her, watching the confrontation between Florian Holmes, a convict labourer who worked for Isabella, and two Aboriginal men, elders of the tribe. One of the Aborigines was shaking a spear in the direction of the woman and baby, while Florian brandished a gun.

'Holmes! Step aside. Just what do you think you're doing?' demanded Isabella hurrying from the trees towards the group.

'Madam, these savages want to kill the child!'

'Put the gun on the ground, and tell those blacks to drop their spears at once.' Isabella knew Florian Holmes had learned a smattering of the local language.

Florian said a few words to the natives, who became less agitated and stared at Isabella sullenly as she approached the convict. 'What is the issue with the child?' asked Isabella.

Florian glanced at the woman and child and looked at his boots as he spoke. 'The child is sired by me, Miss Kelly. It is a boy and because of the light skin they want to send it away. Which I believe means to kill it. Noona says it is the custom as half-castes bring bad luck.'

Isabella recalled the pretty young gin hanging around the outhouses and kitchen hoping for food scraps and being curious. She was wilder than the native girls who'd been taken into the township to work as house girls for white people. Already there was talk of missionaries setting up places to convert and save the heathen women but Isabella was not sure that was a good idea. Her instinct was to let the natives keep to their customs, as long as they didn't get in her way. But she was angry that she had been so absorbed in recent months to have overlooked what some of her men were up to. Lust had caused the problem she now faced.

'Does Noonamaji wish to abide by their law? You certainly can't help the infant. It's probably best to allow their custom to prevail,' said Isabella.

'Let them have their way once and they'll try anything . . .' said Jack Rothwall in an angry undertone.

'Ma'am, Noona is a kind and pleasant-natured girl. I must defend her. And the child,' said Florian with some passion.

Isabella was surprised. Florian was still young, unschooled in the ways of the world. 'You owe this woman and child nothing, so learn from this unfortunate incident. Let matters be with the natives. I do not want conflict with the blacks on my property. I will overlook the "borrowing" of a weapon as you have been threatened by the blacks. Which you have brought on yourself. Return to your duties, Holmes,' she said firmly.

'Ma'am I cannot stand by and allow this – atrocity,' cried Florian Holmes.

'Disobey me again and you will be punished. Leave at once,' said Isabella sternly. 'You too, Rothwall.' She did not like the way the convict overseer was glowering at the two Aboriginal men.

Florian made a helpless gesture towards the girl who had been watching this exchange intently. On seeing him turn away, avoiding her, and walk to his horse, she began wailing. The Aboriginal elders, men and women, all began shouting, and the mother wailed louder.

Isabella too turned and walked away, Rothwall hastening to keep up with her. 'Madam, forgive me, but I fear this might cause trouble . . . among the other men. There is a lot of jealousy among the blacks over their women. If you'll forgive me saying so, the blacks will now consider their laws prevail over ours.'

'Then tell the men they should curb their desires and keep away from the blacks. Especially the women,' said Isabella curtly. She was annoyed at the whole episode, but particularly by her sudden feelings of remorse, and that she had allowed the native custom to upset her. Even from a distance the lithe black body of the young mother caressing her light-skinned baby had presented a beautiful tableau. And, she had to admit, Florian Holmes appeared to show genuine feelings of concern and attachment to the baby he'd fathered. Rothwall was another concern. He had been in brawls and drunken altercations in town and made no secret of his deep hatred of the natives.

A sense of ennui descended over the property, the convicts found tasks in sheds or on distant fences that kept them apart and sluggishly employed, away from Miss Kelly's steely eyes. The women went about their tasks without interest, whispering instead of shouting and laughing. It was an uneasy peace.

Late that afternoon the community magistrate, Mr George Rowley, passing through the area, stopped to pay his respects, and to discreetly observe how this unique pioneering lady was handling her staff and the property.

In the privacy of her sitting room after tea was brought in and the door closed, Isabella confided the details of the morning's fracas over the half-caste child. 'I am concerned that matters have not been easily concluded. The boy seems genuinely concerned about the welfare of the child and the mother, but Rothwall is a hothead and one day he may do something foolish. He would run every one of them off the place if he got a free hand,' said Isabella.

'It is becoming a common problem,' agreed Rowley. 'The attorney-general is aware of widespread instances of Aboriginal women being, ahem, detained against their will by white men . . .' he said delicately.

'No such arrangement was sanctioned here, I can assure you,' said Isabella quickly. 'Did not Governor Gipps issue a decree that anyone involved in such un-Christian acts would lose their licence and be prosecuted as illegal occupiers of crown land?'

'You are correct, Miss Kelly. The other issue is, unless

women are returned to their tribe, other members of their people could take aggressive action and revenge upon settlers. Even innocent ones. As you have done, keep this matter quiet. These situations must be dealt with by the natives in their own fashion. Unsavoury as the outcome might be.'

After a brief tour of the homestead facilities, Mr Rowley congratulated Isabella on the progress she was making and rode off, aiming to reach a small river settlement before sunset.

It seemed to Isabella all had indeed settled down. She took some of the men and moved a big mob of cattle to hilly, timbered country where the grass was rich. On her return after several days in the bush, she left the men to unsaddle the horses and walked along the side of the house where the struggling kitchen garden was planted near the well that tapped into a reliable underground stream. Nearby was a rough lean-to of bark and split timber where the sulky and harness gear was kept from the weather.

She paused on hearing the murmur of voices inside, then the delighted gurgle of an infant. From the entrance she saw, on a rough sacking bed behind the sulky, Florian Holmes kneeling beside Noona and tickling his baby son lying across her lap.

'Holmes! What is going on here? How long has that woman been here?' Isabella noted the coolamon cradle made from a curved piece of tree bark, a blanket, a billycan and enamel mugs, which indicated the mother and baby had been in residence for some time.

Florian scrambled to his feet. 'Please, Miss Kelly, it is just for a short while. I couldn't allow my child to be slaughtered.'

'That might be commendable in our society, but you are dabbling in native affairs, Mr Holmes, and putting all of us here at risk. You are breaking the law. I can be charged and thrown off my land, the blacks will retaliate.'

'No, no, Ma'am. They know Noona is with me. All will be well, I have –'

Isabella raised a hand in protest and interrupted his passionate speech. 'You cannot keep them here. They must leave.'

'If they leave, so must I,' he responded stubbornly. 'There will not be any payback from the tribe. Noona has been made an outcast. They made her leave the baby behind when they moved on. But that night she ran back to the campfire where she'd left the baby in the warm ashes. So she is free to make her own way in the world provided she does not seek to return to the tribe with the child.'

Isabella was momentarily stunned at this news. 'You are a young man, soon a free man, surely you can't mean to bind yourself to a native woman? You are very close to getting your ticket-of-leave. I'm sorry, I cannot condone their being here. I have put too much into this property. I have enemies in this valley and they will use any chance to bring me undone.'

Florian nodded miserably. He knew she was right. 'I don't want to cause you trouble, Miss Kelly. I will make some arrangements. In two weeks I can make my own way as a free man. Allow her to stay with the babe until then.'

'Who knows they are here?'

'Hettie. She's trustworthy.'

Isabella hesitated. Something about the earnest young man and the gentle girl with the beautiful baby touched her. She knew she should be running them off her land, reporting the young convict – sentenced for stealing bread for his grievously sick mother he'd told her – but he was a hard worker, good with horses, likeable and respectful. Unlike the other men. She had no doubt Hettie was passing along food scraps and felt protective towards them.

Hettie was a young girl, abandoned when her widowed father was jailed for drunken brawling in Sydney town.

'Two weeks. All right then, but no silly business and no talk later about your both sheltering here. Take your papers then and make your own way, though you will find it hard to get work with these two.'

'Thank you, Miss Kelly. We have a plan. Noona knows where there are some horses running wild, I'm going to catch and break them and sell them.'

Isabella raised an eyebrow. 'Be very sure they are wild horses and not runaways with brands.' She was curious as to where these horses might be but knew better than to ask. She glanced at the baby and at Noona's face, creased with a smile.

'Tankoo, miz,' Noona said.

'Noonamaji, what is the child called?' asked Isabella.

'Killy,' responded the mother.

'Kelly,' said Florian. 'Kelly Holmes.'

Isabella hastily turned on her heel and walked away, but suddenly stopped and looked back. 'Be careful, Florian,' she said softly and with feeling, then added, 'Especially of Rothwall.'

Dani

Dani tucked her sketchbook, charcoal and pencils under her arm and walked down to the river at Chesterfield. She had decided to sketch another aspect of the view before she moved out. It had been a frenetic time. She'd packed up her house in Sydney and rented it, and arranged for some things to go into storage, and her personal effects and favourite pieces of furniture to be freighted to The Vale. The independent-minded Tim had chosen the toys and books he wanted sent to Cedartown but made no commitment about staying there the six months Dani had suggested. He declared he would stay with her for the next school break and then decide. Lara was now gently supportive of the idea, which surprised Dani, but she was grateful.

Dani had completed several rough sketches as the sun began to set. She used oil pastels in bold sweeps to capture the colours melting across the sky. The water began to ripple as the wash of a small boat cleaved through the river close to the bank. The boat slowed and swung towards the pontoon where she was perched. She steadied herself wondering if Barney and Helen were expecting a visitor.

The engine was cut and a man gave a wave, 'How's it going?'

Dani studied the silhouette then recognised Roddy.

'I hope you're not running out of petrol,' she called.

'Cruising, no worries. Mind if I tie up?'

'If you like.' Dani scooped up her artwork and put it on the steadier wooden landing as he nosed in and jumped onto the floating pontoon. 'You coming to check on the wallaby?'

'Nope. I've come to see you,' he said as he secured the boat. 'Hi again, Dani. You know it occurred to me that you and I have shared an odd experience and we don't even know each other's last names. I thought I'd ask you out for a coffee, find out your life story. I hear you're a local once upon a time.'

'Not me, my mother.'

'Ah, my sources got confused.'

'And you? You're not a local,' judging by your knowledge of the area's geography, she thought.

Roddy sat down beside her on the pontoon. 'I had an aunt who lived here for a bit. Always talked about it. I've recently headed this way for business reasons. Don't know a heap of people under sixty so I thought you might be in the same boat. Hoped I could inveigle you into coming out for dinner.'

'In your boat?'

'We could motor down to Harrington Waters, anywhere you fancy.'

Dani hesitated, a dinner date sounded fun and he was personable. 'That would be lovely, but not tonight, another time. Or lunch,' she added.

'Lunch tomorrow then? You got a mobile number?' He wrote it down and then asked, 'How's the patient?'

'Barney says he'll live but he won't be jumping around for a bit.'

'Wow, what a sunset,' Roddy paused to admire the afterglow of the setting sun across the river. 'I can understand why you're giving the paint box a workout. Pretty place here but I guess you'll be glad to move. Get on with your new career.'

Dani bristled slightly. 'You seem to be well up on my moves.'

'Hey, small town. It takes some getting used to. Your friend Helen filled me in the other night. So when do you move to your new place?'

'Why do you ask?' Dani wondered if he knew about The Vale. Suddenly her privacy and security there seemed threatened.

'Sorry, don't mean to pry. I was talking to the boys at the Nostalgia Cafe, they told me you'd come up here to paint, and are renting some place in the country. I was going to offer to help you move your stuff if you have a lot of gear,' he said.

'That's kind of you,' said Dani, making a mental note to ask Claude and George to be more discreet. 'I have a truck bringing stuff up but getting it where I want it around the house might be difficult on my own. If I can call on you that would be great. Er, where are you living?' Dani realised she knew little about him. She'd have to find out what Helen had uncovered.

He whipped a card out of his wallet. 'Here's my number. I'll call you about lunch or dinner. Or both.'

'Thanks, Roddy. That would be nice. Be careful navigating home.'

'No worries. I've got night-vision goggles on board. See you soon, Dani, I hope.' He gave a wave as he jumped into his boat.

It wasn't till later that Dani glanced at the card he'd thrust into her hand. 'Rodney Sutherland. Investment and Corporate Consultancy.' Underneath was a logo that looked like a gas flame, a postal box address in Hungerford, an email address and a mobile phone number. I wonder exactly what his business is, thought Dani.

Helen was pleased to hear Roddy had come to visit Dani. 'He's fun, attractive, and on the lookout for opportunities I'd say. He's new to the area, was working in Western Australia in Margaret River setting up some project. He's keen to do something in this area. Loves it here, hates cities. He is single though. Got that much clear the other night.'

Dani ignored her big smile. 'He seems nice. Easy to be with and if he's willing to lend a lifting hand when I'm moving, I won't say no. But I'm not after a big-time relationship,' said Dani.

'Why not? Well, at least he might be useful for a roll in the hay now and again.'

'Helen!' laughed Dani. 'You're outrageous.'

'Come on, Dani, you're young and pretty, make the most of it. I dunno, you gen-Xers are a bit conservative compared to us baby boomers.'

*

'When can we come and see your house?' asked Tabatha skipping beside Dani. Toby, Ratso and Jolly were racing ahead as they took the food scraps to Pig, the fat old sow who had become a family pet as she was too old to breed or to turn into bacon.

'As soon as I fix it up with a few things of my own. I want to make it nice for Tim.'

'Is Tim going to stay here too? Come to our school?'

'I hope so, Tab, we'll see.'

'I hate it when grown-ups say that.'

'What?'

'We'll see. We'll see, we'll see,' she chanted and chased after her brother.

Dani smiled. She'd hated her mother saying it too. Well, she had time before Tim came up to stay, though she'd be down in Sydney before that. There were still some loose ends to tie up at the house, the last of her pot plants and odd things she'd stored at her mother's to retrieve.

The next morning Dani dropped in to the museum in Cedartown and found Patricia Catchpole heading for a coffee after leaving Henry at work.

'Come and join me, I'm keen to hear your plans. I gather you've decided to stay awhile. Excellent news,' said the councillor.

'Max James has been so helpful with the art side of things. Very encouraging as well as lending me a whole pile of equipment. I'll have the studio ready before the house!'

'It's an old place on a farm, right? Well, I wouldn't bother spending a heap of money on it if I were in your shoes,' advised Patricia.

'Just superficial stuff. I'm a nester I'm afraid, like to have things looking nice and my stuff around me,' said Dani. 'I'm hoping I can persuade my son to stay here for six months.'

'Mothers don't persuade, they just tell – this is what we're doing. End of story,' said Patricia firmly.

Dani merely laughed, but decided she wouldn't like to be on the opposite side of a debate in council with the forthright Patricia. 'He doesn't have much choice, other than staying with my mother, but that's not fair to her. So he'll have to make the best of it, though I'm hoping the country experience will be good for him.'

'So you're launching yourself as a full-time artist for six months. Then what?'

'I'm not making any plans. See what I produce, how I feel about things, the lifestyle and so on. I'll have to earn some money as I know art doesn't pay. Not the kind I plan to do.'

'Didn't you say you worked in a graphic design studio in Sydney?' asked Patricia, leaning forward.

'Yes, but I don't want to do that anymore.'

'Maybe not as a full-time job. But how about taking on one project and helping out with your artistic skills while you're here? We need talented people in the country. Pay the rent, get you out once a week,' said Patricia.

Dani drained her cappuccino. 'I could be interested. What is it exactly?'

'Marketing and creating a look, an image, for the new development Jason Moore is in charge of – the community at Birimbal.'

'That new housing development? I don't think so. He tells me it's different and sensitive and so on but, Patricia, it's still a housing estate whichever way you look at it. I hate the idea of it sprawling over that lovely land,' said Dani vehemently.

'I think you'd better trot along to see Jason at his office where the plans and models are. Let him explain. Remember I'm on council and we approved this. I don't want you going around believing we're a bunch of rednecks up here. I think you'll be impressed.'

Dani wondered just how innovative or cutting edge any development would be in such an out-of-the-way place. 'I'm sorry, Patricia, I didn't mean it like that. I've come to escape the city – the traffic, the malls, wall-to-wall suburbia, the crime . . . sadly, all the things sea-changers are generating to mess up a lot of coastal towns,' she added wryly.

'Don't we know it. Our shire includes the coast. The trouble is, Dani, how do you tell people the shutters are down, the gates are locked, don't come here? A few places have put population limits on their towns, but developers, and state governments, looking at the short term, see all this bush and crown land and think, perfect, we'll shove a town in there. The long-term view is that regional and northern New South Wales and southern Queensland is where all the population growth and investment will be.'

'And you think there's a way it can be done decently?'

'If there has to be economic growth, the dreaded P word – *progress* – then let's at least try and manage it. The finger in the dyke solution doesn't work.' Patricia stood up. 'Not everyone can opt out to a rural escape, try a new career, chill out, drop out of life for half a year. Call Jason and let me know what you think. We'd rather have people like you with us than against us, or, worse, on the fence.' She smiled warmly to soften their exchange. 'Come over to lunch next Sunday. I'll get an interesting group together.'

'Thanks, Patricia, I'd like that.'

Driving away, Dani couldn't help wondering if what Patricia had said applied to her. Opting out, escaping, dabbling, sitting on the fence. It didn't sound terribly serious. But for Dani, and Tim and Lara, this move was a huge upheaval. I have to make it mean something, have something to show for this big step, she thought. Dani made up her mind. She'd call Jason Moore tomorrow.

As if they'd been thinking the same thoughts, Lara phoned Dani at Helen's that evening.

'Hi, darling, what are you doing?' Her mother always asked that, or else, 'Where are you?' as the opener of most phone conversations.

'Feeding the dog. It's a beautiful sunset. What are you guys up to? How's Timmy?'

'We're great. He's doing his homework. Rushing it I fear because of some junk TV show. Such rubbish kids watch.'

Dani thought of Patricia. 'Don't let him watch rubbish, please Mum.'

'Makes me want to get back in the TV game and try to shake things up,' declared Lara.

'You're not serious. TV has changed since your day, not for the better, I agree. But maybe you should think of doing something with your time.'

There was a brief hesitation before Lara spoke. 'I've thought about that. And made a decision. I've decided to tackle the family history.'

'Fantastic! You've got all that stuff on the dining room table to work on, and you can get on the Net and see what it reveals about the distant past. There's plenty to start on. Sounds good, Mum.'

'Well, that's not exactly how I plan to do it. There are so many unanswered questions, big holes in our recent family history that have got me really intrigued . . . curious. I'd like to find the answers. I hadn't planned on tracing the family tree back to the Huguenots on the Williams' side, or anything like that.'

Dani began to get a feeling that her mother was about to drop a bomb. 'So what *are* you planning to do?'

'I thought I'd move up there too. Not with you, of

course, but find a place to rent while I dig around. There are probably oldies up there who knew my Nana and Poppy . . . I could still help out with Tim. Might make it easier for him to settle in knowing he doesn't have the option of staying down here with me . . .'

Dani was in shock and slightly annoyed. She adored her mother but just as she was striking out on her own adventure here comes Lara galloping over the horizon. 'Mum, I'm a bit surprised. How long do you plan on staying? What about your house? I mean, I suppose you could stay with me at The Vale when it's fixed up . . .'

'No, darling, I wouldn't dream of that. You do your thing. At first I thought I might wait until you decide what you want to do in six months' time, but I'm nervous some of the old folk might drop off the perch and take information with them. I'd prefer to find a little place in town. Or maybe ask Helen if she'd consider renting one of her cabins to me for a month or so.'

Dani felt faintly relieved. A month wasn't so long and her mother was being sensitive to her desire to be alone to paint, explore a new lifestyle and rethink her future. With the initial tension gone, she reflected that they enjoyed each other's company. It was just a matter of making it clear that she needed her own space. Cedartown was a small place. 'I'll ask Helen. Just when did you think you'd make the move? I mean Tim's school doesn't break up for a bit.'

'Of course we'll wait till then. But I might come up for a couple of days soon and settle my accommodation.' Lara was aware of Dani's feelings and did feel a pang of guilt at moving in on her new-found space and freedom.

'Lovely. Though I'll be a bit busy getting my place set up . . .' began Dani.

'Darling, you do what you have to . . . I'll sort things out. I'll call your friend Henry at the museum and start the ball rolling.'

'Yes, Henry will be a goldmine of info for you. Well, let me know how you go. Put Timmy on, take care.' Dani chatted to her son, listened to his news and told him more about The Vale.

'Sounds cool, Mum. Do you think I could bring my mate Justin when Ma brings me up next?'

'Of course you can! Great idea. But I'll call his parents to be sure they're okay about it.'

Dani made an appointment to see Jason Moore at his office in Hungerford, a little unsure about working on his project. The idea of collaborating with the smooth charmer from Sydney didn't appeal to her. She was getting used to and loving the more upfront, down-to-earth, dry-humoured, unpretentious locals. But Patricia had insisted that she at least meet with him.

Dani parked in the main street and got cash from the ATM, browsed in a bookstore and bought wine in the rather quaint bottle shop that had once been some sort of church building, but decided against tackling the large supermarket. She preferred shopping in Cedartown with its smaller providers and local produce, much of it organic.

Then she spotted an antique shop painted lavender called Isadora's. It was filled with tasteful treasures. Dani lingered over the estate jewellery wondering who had owned the beautiful pieces. But it was the back room filled with memorabilia of more gracious times that charmed her.

The owner introduced himself. 'I'm Barry, are you looking for anything special?'

'Well, everything in here seems special,' said Dani. 'Where on earth do you find these things? I just love that art deco lamp.' She pointed to a lithe bronze figure holding a crystal globe. 'Reminds me of the dancer Isadora Duncan. Is that where the name of the shop came from?'

'I'm not sure, you'll have to ask Maree, my partner.

We poke around the sales here and there but you'd be surprised what treasures are sitting in old farmhouses. Though now families are more savvy about the value of deceased estates.'

Dani paused and ran her fingers over a wooden box with an engraved brass clasp. It opened to reveal a writing box with a raised surface for the paper, an inkwell, grooves for pens or quills, small slot holders lined in velvet and a tiny inlaid mirror. 'How gorgeous. I love this.'

'It's old and, look here, a secret compartment.' Barry showed her how a brass handle unfolded from the side. 'For carrying. Nifty, eh? It's early to mid nineteenth century.'

'It would be lovely to carry all my sketching things,' Dani sighed as she glanced at the price tag. 'I'll have to think about this, save up. Or sell a painting.' She smiled and fingered the clasp. 'There are initials – WC. I wonder who he, or she, was.'

'I try to find the provenance of a piece as best I can, but the owner of this box is a mystery. It was made in England and presumably brought out by pioneers. I wonder what letters were penned on it about their new life,' mused Barry.

'Well, you certainly have wonderful things,' said Dani.

'Pop in again, we get new bits regularly. Are you living around here?'

'I'm staying out of Cedartown for a few months. I'll definitely check you out again. I'm Dani by the way.'

'Look forward to seeing you again, Dani.'

Dani found Jason Moore's office tucked away in a side street of the CBD where a row of old-style homes had been converted into offices and rooms for a vet, a solicitor, and several medical practitioners. She opened the door and was greeted by a woman in her seventies with a neat cap of curled, blue-rinsed hair, a shirt fastened at her throat with a cameo brooch.

'Good morning, you must be Dani Henderson. Please take a seat. Can I get you anything? Tea?'

'Please don't go to any trouble. I'm fine.' Dani wondered if the bustling lady was Jason's mother, or an elderly aunt. She appeared very efficient in her pleated skirt and sensible shoes as she disappeared down the narrow hallway.

The small reception area was unadorned apart from a flower arrangement tucked into a hollowed, weathered fence post with a glass vase inside. Several recent glossy architectural and art magazines were spread on the small table next to the sofa and chair. The woman who'd greeted her had a desk, computer and phone behind a white bamboo partition.

The woman returned and sat down at her desk as Jason appeared, hand outstretched with a welcoming smile. 'Thanks for coming in, Dani. Lovely to see you again. I'm so pleased Patricia twisted your arm.'

'Oh, she didn't have to twist too hard,' lied Dani, wondering with suspicion exactly what Patricia and Jason had talked about. 'I'm very curious about your plans.'

'This is Miss Lawrence, my right hand. Come in. Would you care for coffee or tea?'

Dani returned Miss Lawrence's nod. 'I'm fine, thank you.'

She followed Jason along the hall. One side was glass and revealed two rooms that had been made into one, with a conference table, flat-screen TV and white board.

'This was obviously an old house,' said Dani. 'I love how the whole street has taken on a new lease of life.'

'They were little houses dairy farmers retired to from the land. They were going to be bulldozed but I managed to persuade Patricia this would be a better way to go so she swung the council. High-rise commercial buildings are on the horizon but, as I thought, doctors, solicitors and so on were quick to move into these places.'

171

Never a man to miss an opportunity, surmised Dani. She bet he had already reserved an office in whatever new high-rise office block was being mooted in the town.

Jason held open a door. 'Please, this way. Before I show you the presentation, can we chat a bit?' He spoke earnestly, leaning forward and locking his eyes on her. 'The man behind this whole project is a visionary in my book, which is why I agreed to come on board.'

'Oh, who's that?'

'A very big developer, well, entrepreneur, dabbles in all kinds of projects. Especially environmental and energy ones.'

'Like? I mean, would I know him?'

'I doubt it. He's very low key. Selling this concept is my job as well as helping create the vision.'

'And what vision is that exactly?' Dani hated nebulous ideas that masqueraded under 'the vision' thing. Trying not to sound as facetious as she felt, she asked, 'And what is the mission statement for this project?'

Jason flinched but ploughed on, ignoring the barb. 'The fact is, people are moving away from cities in droves, so if what they're looking for are homes, amenities, lifestyle, beauty, tranquillity, isn't it better to provide that in an organic, sustainable, integrated and creative way? We want people to inhabit the existing landscape rather than impose themselves on it.'

'That's a nice philosophy,' admitted Dani. 'What's the reality?'

'It seems the reality is that the world is going to run out of fuel and we must make provision to change how we live,' answered Jason. 'That means, frankly, fewer people, and living in a place where, if needs be, people are self-reliant, self-empowered, in a community that cares for them as they care for it.'

'So who is going to start that ball rolling?' quizzed Dani.

'A developer prepared to look at the whole concept as a community and be sensitive and clever in working each home into a suitable position so that it has light, sun, and privacy while leaving as much bushland and trees as possible.'

'By sustainable do you mean solar power, compost toilets and water tanks? It does sound a bit like an expensive hippy commune,' she said lightly.

His earnestness melted as he conceded her point. 'Well, sometimes those alternative ideas from the seventies were the forerunners of this so-called new thinking. Because we have modern technology to help create an innovative community we can use green power, and we can safely recycle water and sewage. We still have to educate people, change their taste, if we're to get away from pretentious energy-wasting homes.'

'That's a big call. Aussie culture is very much about a family house on the quarter-acre block, water views, all the trimmings. Two cars in the garage, a boat, a holiday shack. You can't deny people's aspirations, it's what everyone works for,' said Dani.

'I'm not against people wanting the security and pleasure of a home they've worked for. Here we can have a variety of homes that don't shriek my place is more expensive, bigger, better than yours. They're designed to take advantage of their position, north facing, open to breezes and light, with views as well. What people create within their home and garden is their expression of who they are,' said Jason. 'We believe that the whole design is a gift to future generations.'

'Why not just leave the unspoiled bushland as a gift to future generations?' said Dani evenly.

He sighed and made a gesture that made Dani feel as

though he thought she was a simple child. 'People have to live somewhere, Dani. Our cities are exploding and councils see growth as a means to prosperity. And, frankly, if we don't do it someone else will. Perhaps with no sensitivity but as it's been done in the past. The slash-and-burn approach. Raze the land, cram in houses, start from scratch and eradicate any reminder of how it was before.'

'Okay. So we have all these beautiful, environmentally sensitive homes in a bushland setting. What about amenities? I mean, we're talking about a huge area,' asked Dani.

'I'll show you the layout in the boardroom shortly. Essentially it's what we call cluster communities.' Jason was keen to move on. 'There's a pattern to the layout that links homes without appearing intrusive. There's a central arrival area with parking, a network of paths for bikes and walkers, a community pool, a gym and sports facility with soccer and footy field, a skateboard park and tennis courts. At the river there's a small landing and a boathouse. There's one general store for convenience foods. Lots of places where people can sit in the sun, walk around, meet each other. A place that encourages social interaction yet gives an overall sense of privacy and being part of the natural setting.' He paused. 'If it sounds like a big sales pitch, you're right, but we are trying to do something special.'

Dani was determined not to be swayed but she thought it sounded like the sort of place Tim would love. How remote and lonely would he find her cottage at The Vale? 'It sounds so big though. Intrusive. What does the council think?'

'It took some involved and lengthy show-and-tells,' admitted Jason. 'They of course were concerned about the infrastructure but glad to have more growth in the area. There's a sewage-recycling plant, and wind and solar power designed to return energy to the main grid. And power and telephone lines are all underground. Wherever possible we've kept things as unobtrusive as possible.'

'It sounds expensive. Is this going to be a place for only those who can afford it? It's still in reach of Sydney so you'll have a bunch of yuppie weekenders who price everyone else out and have no commitment to the area.'

'Some, perhaps. Hopefully people who choose to live in this type of a setting will appreciate and care for it. There's a tiered system of larger homes to modest places for the downshifters. Some areas are set aside for small farms as well.'

'But the whole thing is geared to people who can afford to sell in the city and move into this community,' said Dani. 'What happens to the people already living here with no big asset to sell? Where do they go when they want to downsize?'

Jason paused and spread his arms. 'That's the conundrum isn't it? They either stay where they are, move further away, or move to a home unit. Not the best options, I admit.'

'There's a challenge for you then,' said Dani quietly. 'Maybe stage two could address the local people. Farmers who want to get off the land as they age. Have you considered people other than tree-changers, young families, retirees from the city and baby boomers?'

'We have. There are some townhouses that might suit young people and compact one-level homes, which we call support houses, designed for older people who want to stay in their home but have a safety net around them dotted through the community.'

'That's a good idea,' said Dani. 'Baby boomers aren't going to slink off into the twilight in existing retirement homes.' Dani had never thought about where her mother might end up. 'I like the idea that they are still part of a community.'

'It's what we have to get back to – looking after each other but still being able to shut the door and be in our own space. The proverbial hearth and home is at the core of our civilisation whether it be a small fire in a cave, a pot-bellied stove or under-floor heating. Shelter, warmth, food, a place to be cool in summer whether it be lying under a tree on the river bank or catching the breeze on your verandah or courtyard.' He leaned back, waiting for her reaction. Dani could tell he'd delivered this spiel before now.

'It's a lot to take in,' she said slowly. 'So where do you see me fitting in to this scenario?'

'The land is country that originally belonged to Isabella Kelly and it occurred to me that the connection gave us a local identity to help market and brand the community. However, there's been a lot of resistance to the idea of attaching the name of an infamous, scandalous woman to the project.'

'How ridiculous! She sounds colourful. I'm intrigued by the conflicting stories I'm hearing about her.'

He pounced. 'Then perhaps you could undertake a bit more research to find out about her. In addition to photographs of the landscape I thought a series of paintings might set this project apart. We'd like you to paint the country, and any other conceptual ideas you have, and somehow involve Isabella. We'll put you on a retainer to see what you come up with and then commission work from that.'

Dani was floored, it was a great offer, albeit challenging. 'You've never seen my art, and who passes judgment on my work? You? The mysterious entrepreneur?'

'Partly. Mainly it will be the man who is primarily funding the project.' He stood up, indicating a tray with glasses and bottled water. 'Some cold water?'

She nodded. Dani was quietly thinking through the

offer as Jason filled two glasses. The money would be very helpful, but would this take her away from what she hoped to do with her art? She'd quit her job to move away from what she'd done previously.

Jason broke into her thoughts. 'By the way, Maxwell James thinks you'd be the right person for the job because of your graphic design and advertising background. But we want creative work not just commercial art.'

Dani was surprised and somewhat reassured at the mention of Max's name. She'd find out what he knew about all this. And Jason Moore.

Jason gestured to the boardroom. 'While you're mulling it over come and see the plans, architectural drawings and specifications.'

After another exhausting session that left her head spinning, Dani told Jason she'd have to think about it. It was a big step to go back to working for somebody after having made the great leap to freedom. And while on the surface the whole idea sounded attractive and innovative, Jason Moore came across as too citified, too much the big-time smoothie fronting for some shadowy billionaire businessman. It was not the kind of project, or person, she had expected to come across in a quiet backwater. Or maybe that's precisely why these developers had chosen this beautiful river valley. She'd hate to be part of a scheme that spoiled this place. She thought of her great-grandparents. What would they think standing in her shoes right now?

Dani declined Jason's lunch invitation, thanked him, and only began to relax when she got onto the long, quiet bushy road from Cedartown out through Birimbal, the route to Kelly's Crossing, where she stopped.

Standing by the splashing clear stream, hearing the call of a whip bird, Dani tried to imagine this being the backyard of homes nestled amongst trees on the hills and in the gullies. She recalled how her mother had talked so nostalgically of the bush and countryside she had experienced in nearby Cedartown when she was a child, and, while they couldn't go back to that safe and innocent time, perhaps Jason was right. If there had to be building in the bush this project could show the way, creating a place to be enjoyed while retaining the natural landscape and some remnants of the original setting. And, if done well and sensitively, it might alter how everyone thought about progress, development, change.

He hadn't mentioned the proposed cultural centre. She still had a lot of questions. But it would be challenging to be part of a staggeringly big new project like this, though it wasn't where she saw her life heading. But then again, she would have an opportunity to paint what she saw as the statement of what this was all about – the present meeting the past to combine and merge rather than to subjugate it. She needed to talk to Max.

7

Mount George, 1845

Isabella

THE VISITOR DID NOT announce himself in the usual way, by riding slowly to the homestead, dismounting in front, calling a greeting, making his arrival known to the servants about the yards. Instead he galloped straight to the front entrance, swinging from the saddle, shouting to a native working in the garden to take his horse. The Aborigine moved slowly, and the visitor flushed with anger.

'Come on, man, move. Move!' he shouted, thrusting the reins at the native, and strode up the front steps, flicking off his broad-brimmed hat and running a hand through his sweaty hair. He spotted Hettie coming to the door along the central hallway. 'Fetch your mistress.'

Hettie looked past the man, wondering what emergency called for such haste. 'Is there something the matter, sir?'

'That is my concern. Show me to the drawing room. Tell Miss Kelly Mr Flett has arrived.'

He seemed to know where the drawing room was without Hettie's guidance so she fled to the plant house calling, 'Miss Kelly, a visitor. In the drawing room. Mr Flett.'

Isabella put down the native orchid she'd been potting and pulled off her gloves and work apron. 'Have Lola prepare him refreshments. Run and tell Florian to keep Noona and the child quiet and out of sight.'

'Master Florian is far away. Noona is in the wash house.'

'Then tell her to keep the child with her and remain indoors.'

The last thing Isabella wanted was the Community Magistrate to know she was harbouring a half-caste child. Without any formal acknowledgment Isabella had allowed more than two weeks to pass since her ultimatum to Florian, Noona and their child. She'd closed her eyes and busied herself about her property. Florian was a valuable worker and Noona was proving to be a quick learner around the house. She could imagine the pleasure it would give Henry Flett to charge her for allowing one of her white servants to fraternise with a black on her property.

Isabella did not like her wealthy neighbour whom she regarded as filled with self-importance and lofty ambitions. Each time she'd brought a dispute with one of her servants before the court Flett had ruled against her or dismissed the case. Indeed there were so many occasions when Flett had been hostile to her court applications that several of the servants, when arguing with their mistress, would threaten, 'I will take you before Mr Flett.'

It still rankled Isabella that a high-quality side-saddle sent out from England arrived when she was away from the district. It was left with a storekeeper who let anyone borrow it. When Isabella finally retrieved the saddle she found it damaged and roughly repaired. She had summonsed the storekeeper for ten pounds, the cost of the saddle, in the small debts court. But on the day of the hearing the river was in flood and she couldn't cross. Flett dismissed her claim on the grounds she did not attend the hearing.

In keeping with her upbringing and not wishing to make more of an enemy of Henry Flett, Isabella remained courteous and civil, but cool. 'Good morning, Mr Flett. Forgive my delay, I was occupied with my plants which required me to tidy myself.' She indicated to him to be seated as he'd risen to greet her.

'I did not expect the lady of the house to soil her hands,' he said with an attempt at levity.

'I'm sure you are aware running a large property cannot be totally left to assigned staff.'

Mr Flett avoided soiling his hands, preferring to work from his large cedar desk. 'I have an excellent manager and overseer. If I may say so, Miss Kelly, it is unusual, indeed unseemly, for a lady like yourself to be involved in such matters. Although you have so far made a grand success of your holdings.'

'Thank you, Mr Flett,' said Isabella, ignoring his condescending tone. She knew very well what the men in the district thought of her activities. Most were envious of her success. 'And is this a neighbourly call or a business matter?' she asked pointedly. Henry Flett did not make social calls on Isabella Kelly. While the activities of each was known to the other, and settlers could call upon their neighbours in times of trouble, Henry Flett would not be the first person to whom Isabella would turn.

Isabella poured the tea the maidservant placed beside her and passed the fine bone-china cup to Henry Flett.

'Thank you. It is pleasant to have a lady attend to these courtesies of refinement,' he observed.

Isabella sipped her tea and waited.

'You ask the nature of my call. Well, it is social and business, dear lady.'

Isabella winced at the endearment, which sounded false and insincere. 'And that is?'

Flett adopted her no-nonsense approach. 'I have done exceedingly well since my arrival in the colony. I intend to rise to greater heights in the public domain and have bold plans for my lands at Tarree.'

'I wish you well in your endeavours.'

'Thank you. A man of my stature does have obligations and as one looks to the future, a family with a wife of standing would enhance my ambitions.'

Isabella put down her cup and folded her hands in her lap, affecting a calm demeanour. Inwardly a small fury was brewing as she now glimpsed the reason for his call.

Flett noted her prim posture, which he took for acquiescence, and ploughed on with a hearty bluster. 'Therefore, Miss Kelly, I thought it mutually advantageous for us to become man and wife. I hope you will consider my proposal favourably.' He drank the rest of his tea without pause, replaced the cup in its saucer and waited for her reply, a satisfied smile lurking beneath his moustache.

Isabella fought to control her temper and her urge to laugh. The man was preposterous. As if she didn't see very well the reason for this offer of marriage. It would indeed benefit him. Once they were married everything she possessed would convert to his ownership – married women being deemed incapable of managing their own money and affairs.

'I am indeed surprised, Mr Flett, as you must surely understand. And I thank you. But I am afraid it is out of the question. I cannot and will not countenance marriage.' She paused, seeing the shock on his face followed by a flush of red. More gently she added, 'Surely you, as a landholder, can appreciate my attachment to my land and all that I have achieved. By merging our holdings I fear I would have no control or decision in the future of my own properties.'

Flett could not argue with this and knew Isabella was aware of the motive for his proposal. 'Madam, in truth you would do better and have more protection as my wife than as a sole woman property owner in this valley.'

'Then I must suffer the consequences and try my best to manage my affairs – as I have been doing, sir.'

Henry Flett rose, picking up his hat. 'Very well, madam.' He gave her a stern look as if admonishing a child. 'I would not want anyone to know of our discussion.'

'Nor I, Mr Flett,' retorted Isabella.

He strode from the room, turning at the doorway. 'If any word of this conversation is ever known outside this room you will have an enemy for life.'

Isabella, though short of stature, drew herself up, smoothing her full skirt that did little to shroud her dumpy figure. 'As much as you, Mr Flett, I want nothing to be known of what has passed between us this day. I bid you good morning.'

He didn't answer but strode from the house, shouted for his horse, then rode off as briskly as he arrived. He never looked back, his mind struggling to come to terms with the spirited rejection handed out to him by this woman. Well, he rationalised, at least he would not have to put up with that arrogant, insufferable, plain-faced woman as his wife. The fact she was not attractive irked him even more. She should have been grateful for the opportunity of being attached to a fine specimen of a man such as himself. The plans he'd made for their conjoined holdings faded in the heat of anger generated by the wound to his ego.

'She will regret this day,' he swore to himself.

Isabella was also shaken and disturbed by the encounter. Henry Flett had always challenged and confronted her, ever unsympathetic to her requests. She would have to be careful, he would be a formidable enemy now.

Lara

Lara could move as swiftly and impulsively as Dani. She had called the Clerks and made arrangements to stay at Cricklewood for a month with an option to stay month by month after that. If Tim wanted to, he could stay with Lara in town where it would be easier for him to get to school and go to The Vale to be with his mother on weekends.

Tim couldn't understand the sudden upheaval in his life. First his mother had rented their city house and shifted to the country to paint. It was okay staying with his grandma Lara as he still saw his friends and continued his regular routine. But now Ma wanted to go to the country and stay in some old family house that didn't sound like fun at all. Not like the farm where Toby and Tabatha lived. He hoped he could spend time with them. Even though Barney had promised to let him drive the quad bike around Chesterfield, Tim hoped this uncertainty would all be over and done with soon and they could go back to how life had been before.

He was so cross with his mother and grandmother he wished he could go and stay with his dad. His dad's life seemed appealing for a change. His father thought his mother's move was 'irresponsible' but he hadn't offered to keep Tim with him. He worked late, travelled a lot and tended to leave Tim to his own devices with DVDs, or supervised outings with sons of his friends. Sometimes they'd go to a movie but there'd been too many outings to museums, the aquarium, the zoo, and even the art gallery, which Tim found boring. He'd done those on school excursions.

Some of his mates envied him going to the country, others felt sorry for him, but none of them really understood. They lived in units, suburban homes or inner-city terraces and couldn't imagine living in a place like Cedartown. He tried to play up the adventures of fishing and racing the boat down the river, riding on the tractor, hunting rabbits with Jolly and Ratso, feeding the animals, making bonfires, all the things he did with Toby and Tabatha which made a day pass before you knew it. But they just didn't get it.

Tim loved his computer, the plasma TV at his dad's, but at Chesterfield he didn't miss these at all. The trouble was he didn't want to choose one life over the other. And he had no say in what happened in his life. He'd long ago learned that digging in his heels, refusing to do something or throwing a tantrum didn't work in his family. He'd seen friends get their way with these tactics but he didn't, not with his mother and grandmother.

Tim was staying with his pal Justin while Lara made a quick mid-week trip to Cedartown to see the Clerks and get the rundown on living in the house. On the way Lara wished she'd caught the train. Stress free, scenic, sentimental. Every time Lara thought of train travel she thought of childhood train trips to Cricklewood. Uncomfortable, stiff, upright dark green leather seats. The cold carriage with a travelling rug to keep her snug in winter, and in summer the stifling heat and fine ash that blew in from the steam loco with the thick hot air.

Wreathed in nostalgia those youthful journeys seemed wonderful, as did each day she'd spent in the cocoon of Cricklewood. She tried to recall days, moments, memories of distress or hurt or unhappiness. Dani told her to take off the rose-hued glasses when Lara talked of her early childhood. But in truth Lara couldn't recall anything back then that caused her pain or anger. She remembered the shock of a bee sting and her grandmother's ministrations with the Reckitts blue bag used for rinsing the wash. She remembered the famous walk with Poppy in the nearby bush where her toddler's legs gave out and she sat to rest on a convenient mound that exploded to life beneath her bottom with angry green ants nipping and pinching. Poppy carried her home talking of the wonderful structure that was inside the dirt mound, making it sound a palatial labyrinth so she almost forgot the stinging pain.

In this quest to fill the gaps in her past that she'd never questioned till now, it occurred to Lara that her outer life had come to a standstill, but in her mind and heart she was travelling with increasing emotional speed to places where innocence had become experience and knowingness.

Lara's hands rested easily on the steering wheel as she drove sedately north, but around her the sounds of childhood called to the rhythm of the steam train's metal wheels spinning over the joints of the railway track. *Come back again, come back again* . . . The sound of steam trains echoed throughout her childhood. They carried her through tunnels where remembrance was blurred and forgotten, then whistled into sunshine. Fragments of the past were reassembled by the familiar. The highway and anonymous cars were in her vision and she was alert to respond as required to the traffic about her. But in her mind's eye she was revisiting her own childhood.

Lara could recall every toy she'd owned and loved. They were few and precious. It was not a childhood brimming with a superficial glut of gimmicks, commercial merchandise, expensive high-tech electronics. Would she be the same woman if she had been exposed to what she saw advertised for kids today, she wondered. How she'd loved the woolly blue koala she'd hugged and lugged everywhere. A simple wooden train, the favourite books read to her by Elizabeth in bed each night. The gift of being able to read by herself and long-anticipated new books that came only at birthdays and Christmas. But most of all – the dolls' house.

She saw again the blue roof, the cream windows framed by postage stamp curtains, the wonder of how other homes could be so different from what she knew. Her dolls' house had an upstairs floor, a chimney, flower-patterned wallpaper, paintings in gold frames on walls, lights that looked like birthday candles. A room where walls of bookshelves were filled with a lifetime of reading. The ritual slipping of two hooks that swung open the rear wall gave her access and the power to orchestrate the lives of those within. The tiny figures of a created family became more real than her own.

So many memories swirled in her head. Lara tried to focus her recollections, to give the flashbacks some solid foundation of family, of continuity, a sense of her mother's family history as she knew it.

Emily and Harold Williams moved to Cedartown and built Cricklewood in the 1920s. Her mother Elizabeth was born in 1921 and then her Aunt Mollie five years later. Elizabeth married during the Second World War. According to Mollie, it was 'to escape the narrow prejudices and limited horizon of a small town'.

In later years Mollie told her niece Lara that the marriage was a disaster as there'd been some scandal and Elizabeth found herself trapped. And after the war Elizabeth was left alone with her parents at Cricklewood with a baby girl – Lara.

A few years later Elizabeth married a wonderful man, Charlie Jenkins, a country boy from a farm outside Cedartown, and they moved to Sydney. Charlie became the only father Lara knew and loved until his untimely death when she was ten. After that Poppy, her grandfather, became the most important man in her life until she married.

It was a sketchy story with many gaps and inconsistencies. But Lara was busy with her own life and paid little heed to past history. Occasionally a question arose but Elizabeth was vague and unforthcoming, so Lara, recognising it pained her mother to speak of the past, let it go. Elizabeth said the war years brought back bad memories, though she sometimes watched the coverage of the Anzac Day parade, until Charlie's old battalion passed, before switching off the TV coverage of the annual national homage to war veterans.

Lara had always accepted and acknowledged Charlie as her father and, despite the mystery of her real father, she never had any curiosity about who he was. Mollie recalled him as a handsome larrikin who seemed to Elizabeth the best bet to make a life away from a farm or country town.

There had been moments – a doctor asking about her father's medical history, friends staring at her newborn Dani enquiring which side of the family she looked like – when it hit Lara there was an unknown factor in her life. Now she was sad, and slightly ashamed, that she had never pursued the other half of her history.

Perhaps things did happen for a reason. Dani's desire to visit the valley, Lara's own growing sense of emptiness in her life seemed significant pointers. This time she really wanted to visit Cricklewood, to wander through the rooms she recalled from babyhood anecdotes and first childhood experiences.

*

Dani

Dani had agreed to go to the monthly antique and collectables fair in Cedartown with Roddy who was curious to see what was on offer. He'd helped Dani, dragging a sofa from room to room until she found the right spot. Now she knew what she needed, or would like, to make The Vale 'homey'. The floor painting and DIY stuff would be a gradual process.

Roddy picked her up in his large old green Mercedes, which was in immaculate condition. Dani hoped he had plenty of petrol.

'Let's hope we don't find any large cumbersome items,' she said.

'Plenty of room, or we can collect them later if we do.'

She sank back in the leather seats and ran her fingertips over the walnut dashboard. 'What a lovely old car.'

'It's a classic, runs like a train, can't beat those Germans. She does get a bit arthritic at times, as old ladies do,' he said. 'I'm saving up for a new Maybach 62, but it's going to cost over six hundred and fifty thousand dollars.'

'I'm not into cars. So, are you looking for anything special?' asked Dani. It occurred to her she had no idea where Roddy lived, his lifestyle or work. Though he always seemed to have plenty of free time.

'Not really. I've moved and I'm renting a place over at the beach. Holiday Point. New apartment. It comes with everything. Decided I like walking out the door for a surf,' said Roddy.

'Sounds nice. What about work?' asked Dani lightly. 'What does Rodney Sutherland Investment Consultancy actually do?'

'I'm cruising a bit at the moment. Looking for opportunities. I needed a break. I had a big deal happening in

WA with a vineyard takeover. Couple of things in Perth. Nice city if you haven't been there.'

'Riverwood, Holiday Point . . . a long way from big-city deals,' commented Dani. 'You said your aunt lived here for a while. Is that your connection to this valley?'

'Sort of, but that's not why I came. There's a lot of money floating around this area. Birimbal development, talk of new energy sources, maybe a dam, plantations. I have people who need to invest capital for tax purposes, delayed profits, make a bit of a detour from the tax commissioner for a bit.'

'Really? I hadn't thought of this sleepy area as a hot spot for tax relief. A dam? Where?'

'Somewhere up the mountain, there's a massive flow of water over those falls. It was just an idea being mooted but it's all pointing at increasing development. I'm just looking for the right project for my clients.'

'That's awful. I thought Jason Moore's scheme was bad enough. I was hoping this valley would remain a secret.'

'Big ask these days with so many people downshifting, and that includes people our age, not just baby boomers, greenies and hippies. People who are choosing a balanced life rather than slogging away to pay a mortgage with no quality of life. Mind you, there's probably more down-shifters in the cities than in the country.'

'I can relate to that. What about you? Have you been married? Do you have kids, a mortgage? asked Dani.

'Hell, no. I'm not ready to downshift, I'm still in wealth-creation mode,' he answered. 'Now, do we have a list of stuff you want? And are you bidding or shall I? I'm good at auctions.'

'I'll have a go. I know my budget,' said Dani.

There was quite a crowd browsing through the items spread about on the grass and inside the big shed that had once been the stables for Moxie's Emporium. Roddy and Dani went in different directions, agreeing to meet by the tea stand in half an hour. She recognised Greta from the art gallery who introduced her husband.

'How are you settling in, Dani? Started painting yet?'

'I have, as a matter of fact. I had the studio set up before the cottage. That's why I'm looking for a few more furnishing bits. Max James has been really helpful, loaning me art supplies.'

'Excellent. We're after more prosaic items – farm machinery, horse things. Enjoy the day.'

Dani was quietly amused to spot the artist Thomas whom she'd met at his showing at Greta's gallery. He was pawing through a pile of old pictures and photographs.

'Hello. I met you at your show,' smiled Dani.

'Oh, yes. Right,' he mumbled, obviously not recalling her at all.

'Sad isn't it, to see these old family photographs being tossed out,' she said, picking up a large framed wedding portrait of the 1920s.

'Not many are interested in the old days, that's for sure. I'm just looking for frames. Saves a few bob and some people like the old carved ones. Fix them up, they look good,' he said glumly.

'I can't imagine your work going into frames like these,' said Dani, thinking of the nightmarish modern paintings he'd exhibited.

'Ah, that's my real art. Doesn't sell much. So I do "rural landscapes" and frame them in these for the tourist market. Soul-destroying, but a man's gotta eat.'

'How depressing. I've moved up here to try and discover my real art, gave away my usual job,' said Dani a little bleakly.

Thomas straightened up. 'You're mad, love. Or hope you've got a rich boyfriend. Art's a tough mistress.'

'Why don't you give it away then? Do something else to earn money?' asked Dani mischievously.

Thomas studied her for a moment, a bit of a smile breaking out above the ginger beard. 'Then I'd *really* be miserable!'

He drifted away and Dani couldn't help wondering what it would be like married to such a dark-spirited man. Jeff, her ex-husband, had been moody and when what she called the black dog times struck he cast a pall over the house. It was one of the first things Tim had confided to her after the break-up that 'without dad around all the time they had more fun and laughed a lot'.

Dani was fascinated with the wares for auction – junk, quality pieces of furniture, memorabilia, practical farm stuff, boxes of 'deceased estate' items jumbled together in cartons as job lots.

'Bit like a lucky dip these things,' said a voice beside her as she thumbed through books and knick-knacks in one box. She turned around to see Barry from Isadora's.

'Hi, Barry. You looking for treasures for the shop?'

'Never know what you'll find. We just enjoy the atmosphere. This is Maree, my partner,' he said, introducing a pretty woman with a cloud of curly hair wearing interesting antique jewellery.

'Wow, I love your necklace,' said Dani admiring the heavy silver locket set with pearls and amethysts. 'Is that from Isadora's?'

'Maree grabs things she likes before they get a chance to get into the stock,' smiled Barry. 'Have you found anything of interest?'

'A big wooden box for firewood that will look nice by the fireplace. And I could go mad over some of the furniture but my place is pretty well furnished with big pieces. I need boring things like kitchen utensils.'

'There's a canteen of lovely old bone-handled cutlery

over there,' said Maree. 'A bit of elbow grease will bring the silver up wonderfully.'

'Treasure hunting?' came a voice behind Dani and she turned to find Jason Moore standing there with a large smile. He was dressed in jeans and a white T-shirt and to her surprise had a white Maltese terrier on a leash.

'This is a popular place, I think I've met everyone I know in the district,' said Dani. 'Jason, this is Barry and Maree . . .'

'Yes, we know each other. I'm in Isadora's a lot.' Jason shook hands with Barry as Maree stooped to pat the dog.

'What a sweetie, what's her name?' she asked.

'Sugar. She's not mine, belongs to my girlfriend,' said Jason.

Dani recalled the Nostalgia boys telling her Jason had a chic Sydney girlfriend who didn't care much for the country. 'Oh, is she here too?'

'No. She's overseas, I'm dogsitting. So, what've you found?'

'You should bid for some of those boxes,' said Maree, pointing to the jumble in the deceased estate 'lucky dips'. 'They go for a few bucks and you always find at least one thing you want to keep.'

'Then you bring them back in for the next auction,' grinned Barry.

'I'll have a look. I'm always after old books,' said Jason.

'We'll be off, nice to see you again. And we still have your writing box in the shop, Dani,' said Barry.

'I'm still saving up!'

'Don't worry. It's not the sort of thing that will sell in a hurry.'

Barry gave a little wave and Maree said, 'See you later maybe,' and moved on to continue browsing.

Jason fell into step beside Dani. 'I'm told there are

some good buys today. I spotted a Sydney dealer. You after anything special?'

'Just odds and ends for my house. What about you?' Dani hoped he didn't press her as to whether she'd made a decision about the job.

'I was a bit bored and everyone kept telling me I'd enjoy this. I've found a couple of things I might bid on. Fancy lunch after the auction?'

Dani glanced around wondering where Roddy was. 'Oh, thanks, but I can't. I'm with a friend. I'm still getting settled and my mother and son are due soon. So I haven't . . .'

'No rush, Dani. Call me any time.' He gave a wave and strolled away, the little dog obediently trotting at heel.

She watched him go, thinking for the first time she'd seen a more relaxed side to the man she considered so – how did she think of Jason Moore? He was a mass of contradictions, seemingly slick, superficial, ambitious, and at the same time passionate about how people and the environment were to survive successfully in the future. Now she'd seen a more casual side to him, a man obviously a bit lonely, willing to care for a spoiled lap dog while his girlfriend jetted overseas.

'Hey, let's get a coffee and get ready for the auction. Plan our strategy.' Roddy bowled up with a sheet of paper with several items ticked off.

To Dani's surprise, Henry Catchpole was the auctioneer, with a strong voice and rapid-fire calling of bids. She decided to let Roddy do her bidding as it all went so fast. He left his bids till the last minute, managing to close out others so Dani came home with the cutlery canteen; large glass jars from a long-closed sweet shop; a good quality Persian carpet, if threadbare in patches; the firewood box; several big carved wooden picture frames; and two boxes of 'assorted materials' from a deceased estate. And all at what she considered to be bargain prices.

Roddy took her to lunch at the waterfront restaurant in the Harrington Waters estate where lavish homes overlooked the river. It reminded Dani of the Gold Coast. She thought back to Riverview, the house on the river Jason Moore had renovated. She wished there were more modest versions of houses like that. She tried to describe it to Roddy but it was obvious that his taste differed. He liked lots of glass and luxury-plus with a golf course or beach at the doorstep.

'You should see some of the places in Perth and down the WA coast, absolute stunners. There's a lot of money over there.'

'And people pour a million or more into their homes?' asked Dani recalling pictures of some of Perth's extravagant waterside homes. 'I think we're going in the wrong direction. I'd rather live more modestly, have a nice lifestyle, be energy efficient and environmentally friendly and spend my cash on fabulous holidays somewhere!'

'Your friend's place, a converted historic mansion, sounds a bit pricey,' countered Roddy. 'And you, watch out, some of the greenies could attack you for having a polluting wood fire to heat your house.' He sipped his wine. 'I say, why not have it all – the big home, a nice boat like one of those cruisers out there and the five-star vacation.'

'I see where your priorities are,' said Dani with a smile to mask her disagreement. 'I can't afford that lifestyle. I have to work. In fact, I've been offered a job, and I'm in two minds about what to do.' She was suddenly glad to have someone to talk it over with. She'd held off telling Lara, not wanting to distract her until she arrived and had finalised renting Cricklewood.

Roddy appeared to listen attentively, but it seemed to Dani his mind was elsewhere.

She paused after giving a sketchy outline of Jason's job offer. 'So, what do you think? Have you heard much about this Birimbal development? I just wonder if it's going to live up to all the hype and dreams.'

'I know about it. Solid money behind it. Of course, they've got to sell the idea to the punters. But long term, what do you care? Take the money, an opportunity to do your painting thing. What've you got to lose except putting in a bit of time?'

'I know, it's just hard for me to be detached about anything I do. If I get into a job it's boots and all, a hundred and fifty per cent.'

'Ah, life's too short, Dani. Remember, you came up here to chill. Now you've got your mother, your kid, a job here . . . What's different?'

He had a point. 'But it is the lifestyle, less stress, the countryside is so calming . . . and I have a painting project that can challenge me as an artist as well as professionally. I'm so intrigued by Isabella . . .'

'So who's this dame? What did she do?' His attention was back with Dani.

She gave him the rudiments of what she knew about Isabella, 'Colourful, controversial, a colonial wild woman by all accounts. Though Garth reckons a lot is urban myth but the locals like it that way.'

'Who's Garth?'

'He's been researching the real story for ages, which isn't as colourful but there are a lot of skeletons rattling around and maybe she wasn't the villain everyone likes to think. Garth is retired and works at the historical society in Cedartown each week. He's dedicating his life to getting her story out there.'

'And the outfit behind the Birimbal development are

trying to link her to their project?'

'Well, it is on some of her original land. You heard of Kelly's Crossing?'

Roddy shook his head and looked thoughtful. 'Sounds interesting.'

'So the appeal of this job offer is really Isabella. I like the idea of her coming back to life through her land. If it has to be developed and built on, this at least might be something she'd approve of,' said Dani.

'So you're going for it?'

'I am. I've just decided. I'll take the job.'

Roddy raised his glass. 'Here's to you. And to Isabella – may her story finally be told.'

Lara drove into Cedartown, had a delicious sandwich and coffee at the Cheese Factory deli, and then went to see the Clerks at Cricklewood. Mrs Clerk was very organised with a typed list of information – contact numbers for electrician, plumber, and local stores, and details on the running of the house.

'It's pretty straightforward and there's always Mrs Sanderson down the road. She comes in to water the garden and so on if there's no one here. Let her know when you need her. She cleans as well if you like,' said Kristian Clerk.

'Wonderful. Can you show me round the garden routine and the chooks?' asked Lara.

Afterwards they had a cup of tea on the back verandah and Lara then excused herself as she'd driven straight through from Sydney. 'I want to get over and see my daughter's new place before dark. She's in the scrub somewhere but seems happy enough. I think young Tim will be staying here with me on schooldays if that's all right.'

'Wonderful. Our grandkids love staying here. The river and the Brush are just down the road and of course they can walk into town and go to the movies.'

The two women embraced warmly. 'Enjoy your trip, and please don't worry about anything here,' said Lara.

'We won't. You enjoy the memories,' said Richard Clerk.

As Lara drove away she realised she'd been so busy taking in all the details that she hadn't felt as emotional as on her first visit. She was looking forward to the break and the little adventure it would be playing detective and returning to the happy days of her childhood.

'Darling, this is so sweet. Look at the lovely old furniture. This isn't exactly as rustic as I'd imagined.' Lara ran her hands over the polished cedar dining table.

'Come and see my bedroom and the studio. I need your help with how to dress them up,' said Dani, pleased that her mother liked The Vale.

Lara took one look at the original floorboards underneath the old linoleum. 'If you spent the money sanding and polishing, these would come up a treat.'

'Well, I'm not spending that kind of money. What else can I do? I've bought one good rug at the auction.'

'Darling, we can scrub it back and slap white paint, or limewash over the boards in no time. Maybe do the walls as well. Couple of rollers, sponges and white paint and it'll look divine. Nice and fresh and you can put anything with it. We can do it, it'd be a project for the next couple of days. Once you get the hang of it you can finish it off. Don't you have some friends who could come and help? A painting party?'

Dani laughed. 'Typical of you, Mum. All right, we'll give it a bash. Sit down and relax and give me a list of what to get. I have to go into town so I'll pick things up and we can make an early start tomorrow.'

'I bet Barney has everything we need,' suggested Lara.

'I'll give him a call and tell him what we plan to do. I'll get the paint, rollers and a picnic. He just might have wire brushes, and something to pull the tacks and nails out with,' said Dani.

Within fifteen minutes Dani was off the phone and triumphant. 'No worries, to quote Barney.'

'What sweeties they are,' said Lara. 'So, it's all settled. I'll stay another day, I'm sure that's fine with Justin's mum.'

'Barney will be over tomorrow morning with most of what we need – he says to get primer and paint. Helen, Angela, Tony and the kids will be over too as it's Saturday. We'll have a working bee with anyone else you can think of . . . though I do hate to ask people I hardly know,' said Dani.

'Nonsense. This is a great way to get to know people better,' said Lara. 'What about the boys from the Nostalgia Cafe? They could come after lunch, and Max and the boys – it'll be fun. I'll make a picnic lunch – chilli con carne, French bread and salad. Easy. I'd better come and help with the grocery shopping.'

'No, Mum. Add things to my list. You rest . . . you're going to be busy tomorrow,' said Dani.

They had a simple dinner and sat outside with a glass of wine watching the day fade beyond the hills. Crickets chirped, a frog's call reverberated from a pipe or gutter near the water tank, birds murmured and squabbled as they settled in the trees around the house.

'Peaceful, isn't it?' said Dani.

'It is that, for sure. But you are a bit . . . cut off out here. You've been such a city gal. You're not nervous?' asked Lara with a slight frown.

'That's the whole idea . . . to step outside my comfort zone. And it's not forever. If I get the heebie-jeebies I'll move.'

Lara didn't want to mention things one thought about in the city – locking doors, rapists, thieves, dubious strangers, the lack of security. 'What if you fall, the dog gets bitten by a snake?'

'Mum! Please. There is a woman living over the hill – haven't met her yet, but I'll get her number. Town is ten minutes' drive. Quicker than getting to the vet in Paddington.'

'I suppose so.' Lara cheered up. 'I'm wondering how I'm going to feel my first night alone in Cricklewood. And I must arrange to meet Henry Catchpole at the museum. And we'd better talk to the school about Tim. There's a lot to do . . .'

'I've taken a job,' blurted Dani.

'What? With that development guy? Dani, honey, if you need the money, let me help. You came here to *paint* . . .'

'That's part of the job.' Dani poured them another wine and tried to explain all that Jason had told her with the same enthusiasm.

Lara listened, trying to visualise contemporary eco homes in a bush setting, dotted over the hills where once bullock drays, wild cattle and bushrangers had roamed. What would Harold and Emily think? 'Interesting. You know, I think my grandparents would approve. If change has to come, let it be gentle. I imagine your Isabella would be pleased that they're not ripping the guts out of her country.'

'Yeah, I suppose. I can't help thinking there's still unfinished business to do with her land, with Kelly's Crossing especially. I'm due for another meeting with Garth. He's back from the Mitchell Library in Sydney.'

Lara stretched and yawned. 'Tell her story in your

pictures. Nice idea. Well, I'm off to bed. Hope I can sleep in all this silence.' Lara dropped a kiss on top of Dani's head.

'Thanks for your help, Mum.'

'It'll be fun.' Lara turned. 'You sure you don't mind me encroaching on your haven? If I'm in town, we're not exactly on top of each other.'

'Not at all, Mum. I'm glad you and Timmy will be close. I won't feel so . . . secluded.' Dani smiled and meant it. They hugged each other, glad to see things settled.

Cedartown, 1934

Thommo stirred, and the straw stuffed in the cretonne-covered sack that served as a mattress rustled. Clem was trying to be quiet as he pulled on his gum boots and fumbled for a shirt in the dark. He padded out to help with the milking while Thommo pretended to sleep on. It wasn't quite dawn and even though it was summer the early mornings were brisk. So if Thommo went with Clem he'd be obliged to help. He didn't know how to milk and Clem's dad was very particular about the cleaning up afterwards. All that washing and sterilising. Thommo hated dairy cows. He much preferred cattle as an anonymous carcass hanging in the cold room at the back of the butcher's shop where he worked after school. He was getting to recognise the different cuts and had learned respect for the men wielding the flashing knives carried in a leather pouch strapped across their blue-striped aprons. He closed his eyes. After breakfast he'd help Clem with his other chores and then they'd have the day to themselves. Maybe play with Clem's billycart or the crystal radio set Clem had made.

The boys carried their plates to the washing-up tub where Phyllis was washing up the breakfast dishes. Thommo liked Clem's little sister and enjoyed teasing her. Clem's older brother Keith was out in a paddock cutting hay while his dad sowed a new crop of corn for the six big sows who gave birth to as many as three dozen piglets every six months or so. The more hands to help the better. Clem's mother and sister were in charge of the dairy, separating the milk and cream, making butter for their own use. The boys helped Phyllis and their mother with milking the thirty cows, taking the cream in ten-gallon tins on the horse-drawn slide down to the siding where the railway line passed the farm gate. It was collected by the goods train and taken into the butter factory in Cedartown.

'Had enough to eat?' asked Clem's mother, sprinkling flour on the board where she was kneading bread dough.

'You bet. Yes, thank you,' Thommo corrected himself with an instant change of tone. Eggs, bacon, tomatoes and onions all home grown. Bloody beautiful, he wanted to say out loud, but simply gave her a big smile.

No wonder the swaggies wandering through the country liked to check out the farms. They usually scored a full tucker bag for the track ahead. And later, around camp-fires, the roaming unemployed would swap stories about their luck, where the good farms were that might need more wood chopping, a bit of labouring in paddocks or bush, or helping the missus smarten up the vegie garden so they could earn at least a feed. And where there were folk who were happy enough just to hand over food in a paper bag and send them on their way.

'What're you doing today, Clem?' asked Phyllis.

'Dunno. We'll think of something.'

'You make sure you get back here before dark. I've

made you a bag of sandwiches.' Clem's mother knew she wouldn't see hide nor hair of the boys for the rest of the day.

'Thanks, mum. Hooroo.' Clem and Thommo sprinted from the verandah.

Because it was Christmas holidays with no school and his mate Thommo visiting, jobs around the farm were quickly done.

The family didn't get a holiday away from the farm unless they could pay someone to look after the cows. And in these years money was scarce.

But it was holiday enough for Clem to stay in town with Thommo, going to the pictures Thommo's dad screened in the Town Hall for free, wandering round the park, the showground, the river and the Brush. And Thommo, being an only child, enjoyed spending time on the farm with Clem's big family. There never seemed enough hours in the day for all the things they planned to do.

There was a rough tennis court at the side of the house where Clem and Thommo had a hit and a giggle with Phyllis. Sometimes they'd double up on the Clydesdale horse and plod down to the river through the pumpkin patch and go for a fish or a swim. Occasionally Clem's dad would take them out to shoot a rabbit. He'd taught them how to use the small-calibre rifle by shooting at tins hung on a fence. When adventuring around the property they usually carried their shanghais, mostly for fun target competitions but sometimes they gave rabbits a scare. They made shanghais using bush hardwood for the handles and cutting rubber strings from old truck or car inner tubes. Leather shoe tongues held the small stones used as ammunition. Clem's mother was a dab hand with her shanghai, using it to scare off birds after her new chickens and eggs.

In town the boys always managed to get together with a gang of Thommo's mates for a game of cricket or to borrow a boat to row as far as they dared down the river from the wharf by the Brush. Other times they'd sneak into the big railway goods shed and hope Mr Williams didn't catch them. Sometimes they saw Elizabeth and Mollie Williams playing around the station. The girls considered it 'their patch' as their father was in charge of all the freight.

The boys thought the Williams girls were a bit uppity, not like Clem's sister Phyllis. Elizabeth was about the same age as Clem and Thommo, Mollie being just nine was shy and quieter. Both girls were very pretty and Elizabeth was now aware of her effect on boys, who generally teased, shouted, giggled or whispered to their mates and laughed loudly. Elizabeth ignored them, held her head high and marched home from school across the railway bridge with Mollie in tow. Emily had forbidden them from taking the shortcut through the railway yards where she knew the boys hung around. Elizabeth had a sneaking suspicion that her mother Emily watched their progress home from behind the lace curtains of Cricklewood's front room.

The boys were wearing khaki shorts, well patched, old shirts with scruffy collars and sleeves torn off at the shoulders, and equally well-worn straw hats. Clem had their lunch in a calico flour bag knotted to his belt. They were walking along the railway line beyond the farm gates, each balancing on the metal track. Thommo was counting the sleepers.

'Let's go fishing down at the point,' suggested Clem.

'How we gonna get down there? Too far. What's wrong with the river down on the flat where your dad's been planting?' asked Thommo.

'The ten o'clock cattle train comes along here and stops at the railway cattleyards. We could hitch a ride. Hide in one of the wagons,' suggested Clem.

A grin split Thommo's face. 'Ya reckon? And how do we get off?'

'It slows down going round that hill just before it swings away from the coast. I heard Keith and his mate Reg talking 'bout how they done it. The swaggies ride them all the time. Even get in with the cattle.'

'Let's grab the fishing rods. We can get worms down at the beach.'

They made a dash back to the shed behind the farmhouse imagining the whoppers they were going to land.

Thommo had a sudden thought. 'And how do we get back home this arvo? Your mum said we had to be back before dark.'

'Something will turn up.' Clem quoted his father's favourite phrase. 'Anyway, Dad knows Mr Geary who runs the store down there. He comes up to buy ham from Mum for Christmas.'

As they waited in the shade of some trees near the cattleyards, neither of them wanted to admit they were nervous. But it turned out to be easier than they thought. The pens were full of complaining cattle and they soon heard the whistle of the approaching train. Two men jumped to open the race that led to the chute where the cattle were herded into the cattle trucks. Everyone was busy and took no notice of two young boys hanging near the yards.

As the reluctant cattle made their way, single file, into the trucks with covered grates, the boys slipped around to the tail of the train and clambered up into the guard's van.

'What happens if the guard gets in here?' asked Thommo.

'I've watched lots of times. He stays up front with the driver on this run. If he finds us all he can do is chuck us out,' said Clem philosophically.

They waited while the cattle were loaded, the driver, guard and roustabout at the yards enjoying a quick smoke before the driver and guard swung up into the engine.

It was hot, but there was a pile of empty wheat sacks to sit on as the train rolled along the river flats, then slowed on some rising grades as it swung inland for a mile or so before turning towards the inlet where the river met the sea. They'd left the sliding door to the van open and puffs of steam from the engine floated past. Clem made frequent scans out the door as they went along, and eventually spotted the section where he knew another uphill climb to the sharp bend around the point would slow the train to a crawl.

'Get ready, mate. Jump time coming up,' he shouted excitedly.

The old steam train slowed to a walking pace and Clem called out, 'Right, throw the rods out and get down.' In a flash he'd turned, climbed down the metal ladder and jumped onto the rough verge.

Thommo followed him out the door, clinging to the metal ladder, then dropped, executing a bit of a somersault before regaining his balance and racing back for their fishing rods.

It was one of those days that burn bright in childhood memory. They hauled sand worms from the beach, and cracked open oysters with Thommo's penknife, eating some and saving some for bait. They found heaps of sea shells, putting special ones in their pockets. A dead fish washed up on the shore was added to the bait then they settled themselves along the sea wall, casting into the swirl of water rushing into the bar between river and sea. Sometimes they sat in silence willing a big'un onto their hook. When they talked it was in the casual shorthand of good friends.

'You staying at the butcher shop then?'

'S'pose so. Dad says it's a good trade.'

'Wish I could get a job in town.'

'Jeez, Clem, you can't leave the farm. Can ya?'

'Mr Henry at school says I have an . . . aptitude . . . for engineering.'

'You mean like engine driving, fixing cars and stuff?' asked Thommo. 'Sounds hard. I'll be glad to get out of school next year.'

'Me too. Could I get a job with your dad? Running the projector or something?'

'We can ask him. He knows everyone in town.' Thommo concentrated on his fishing. Making plans for the future seemed too hard on such a nice day.

They caught several beautiful silver bream in the main stream, good-sized leatherjackets near the rocks and a few fat mullet that Clem laughingly said 'Seemed to be wagging school.' The really big school of mullet that came along tantalisingly ignored all bait and the bread-crust burley. The boys shouted at them, and laughed about the frustration they felt, wishing they had a net. Then Clem had a bite and a run that nearly broke his rod and pulled him off the wall. A big jewfish or perhaps even a shark that got away.

They put the fish in the calico bag that had held their lunch and wandered around to the boatshed where Mr Geary had a bit of a shop and Clem introduced himself and asked if he could have some spare ice from the chest where Mr Geary kept bait for the local fishermen.

'You boys on your own then? Out for a day fishing, eh?'

'Yep. Look what we caught.' Clem opened the bag.

'Very good. Fish dinner then. Say, how'd you boys get down here from your place, Clem?' asked Mr Geary.

'Ah, we got a ride,' answered Thommo quickly.

'Not sure how we're getting back home,' added Clem.

Mr Geary nodded. 'Well now, don't know there's anyone with a vehicle around. You should've ridden your horse down, Clem.'

'If we can have some ice we'll walk, thanks, Mr Geary,' said Clem.

'Hang about, lads, I've had a thought. The cream boat should've finished its run and be heading back upriver to the co-op. Maybe you can get a ride. I'll go and talk to Neville the boat driver.'

And so as perfect an end to a day they'd long remember, the two boys perched on the deck of the *Surprise* as Captain Nev motored back along the waterways. He indicated where the channels and the mudbanks were near the islands, pointing out the farms and jetties where he'd collected the full milk cans before dawn that morning. In the waning afternoon the water was still, cormorants and pelicans posing like statues at the water's edge. He told them of days when fog and mist obscured the river, when it raged from floodwaters and sank to dangerous shallows in the harsh dry summers. The cream boat driver knew everyone on the river from oyster farmers and fishermen to the dairy farmers and workers in the waterside villages. They all used the river.

Soon the landscape was familiar: cattle grazing along the river flats, the banks rising up to the paddocks of neighbouring farms. The cream boat nosed in to the jetty nearest Clem's home and the boys jumped ashore leaving behind the biggest bream for Captain Neville's tea.

As they came up the hill from the river they waved to Clem's dad following the old plough towed by George, the Clydesdale, back to the barn. The cows were walking single file from the bails after milking and Keith was cleaning up. At the back of the house they could smell just-baked bread and a gramma pie cooling for supper. Phyllis and Kevin were playing Ludo and Clem's mother was darning socks. Proudly the boys displayed their fish, declaring it had been a bonza day. One of the best.

In years to come as heavy artillery fired around them, Clem would call to Thommo and remind him of this day. A day when the world was a very different place.

8

Lara

THE PAINTING PARTY AT The Vale was a huge success. As well as the gang from Chesterfield, George and Claude popped in between meal times at the Nostalgia Cafe bearing food and advising on decor. Max came with the two boys, leaving Sarah in charge of the gallery. While Max got to work with a large wire brush, Len and his brother Julian started painting a mural on the water tank of a serpent coiling around the rungs. Roddy was assigned the job of applying paint stripper, carefully following Barney's instructions. Jolly and Ratso managed to walk in the paint, leaving a trail of dog footprints which Dani decided to leave as an extra feature in the hallway.

Lunch was eaten as a picnic at the old table on the sheltered patio and by sunset the job was done.

Dani raised her glass in a toast. 'To everyone, thank you all so much. My house is transformed! Cheers.'

'It's been fun. When's the housewarming?' joked Barney.

'Isn't this it?' asked Max. 'Too many parties.'

'You can say that again,' said Lara. 'We're invited to Councillor Catchpole's house tomorrow. I hope this paint will come off my hands and face by then.'

'Turps,' recommended Max. 'Well, you've no excuse not to get to work now, Dani.'

'I'm starting as soon as Mum leaves. In fact, I have a series to start on that's going to be a bit of a challenge.' She hadn't told Max about her job yet. She wanted to sit quietly with the thoughtful artist and talk through her ideas. Max had a way of helping her focus and clarify her thoughts.

'Why don't you come over to our place for a barbecue dinner tonight,' suggested Helen. 'Barney caught a couple of crabs in the trap and there are the blackfish Toby caught. Everyone's invited.'

Lara was ready for a bath to ease her aching arms and back and a relaxing drink at her cabin at Chesterfield. 'Sounds great. Do you want to stay the night with me, Dani? The paint smell is a bit strong in here.'

'You're right. I'll clean up and see you at Chesterfield. Are you coming, Roddy?'

'I'll help you tidy up but I can't do dinner. Have to see a guy.'

Roddy was the last to leave. 'You pleased with the job? Probably wouldn't make a home decor magazine but it's certainly fresher looking, eh?'

'I disagree, I think it has potential to make a very nice rustic spread when I'm finished. It's what's called shabby chic.'

'Whatever you say. I'm a modern minimalist. Anyway,

you look chic. Or cute.' He brushed a strand of her paint-splattered hair.

'I think it should be shabby actually,' she laughed, indicating the old T-shirt and torn jeans she'd chosen as painting gear. She wasn't feeling at all attractive, it had been a long, hard day.

But Roddy didn't seem to think so. His hand still rested on her hair. He touched her cheek and leaned forward to kiss the top of her nose. Dani closed her eyes, overcome at the tender gesture. His lips brushed hers and he drew her close to his chest.

Dani returned his kiss but then pulled away in some confusion, smoothing her hair. 'Oh, you took me by surprise . . .'

'A nice one, I hope.' Roddy looked at her expectantly.

Dani was flustered. It had been a long time since she'd kissed a man. After her divorce she'd had a few dates but had felt no attraction to any of the men. Roddy had caught her unexpectedly. 'Oh, of course, Roddy, but right at the minute . . . I'm not ready for this.'

He misinterpreted her remark. 'You look good to me. But, hey, I know you're going out to dinner.' He leaned over and kissed her lightly again. 'I just couldn't resist. I'll phone you in the next few days, okay?'

'Sure. And thanks so much for helping out today.'

'No worries. I'm not the handyman type, it was an interesting experience. Come over to my place at the beach soon and we'll have a bite.'

Dani watched him drive away as Jolly nudged her leg looking for attention and her dinner. She rubbed the dog's ears. She felt vague stirrings of long-suppressed feelings but didn't think she was ready to plunge into a relationship. And she knew so little about Roddy. Maybe Helen was right . . . she smiled to herself. Roddy was attractive, healthy, co-operative and unattached. What could be the harm? She hummed to herself as she prepared the dog's food.

'Just a small one, Jolly. You'll get a lot of leftovers at the barbie.'

At Chesterfield, Dani drew Max to one side and asked what he thought about Jason's job offer.

'I don't know him well, I met him for the first time at Thomas's art show in Hungerford. But he's come around to the gallery a few times, brought visitors and bought a few pieces. He's interested in some of the local history, asked what I knew about Isabella Kelly, which isn't much. Then he mentioned you.'

'And you thought I was capable of doing what he wanted? Why didn't he ask you to do the pictures for the development?' asked Dani.

'Ooh, not my cup of tea,' said Max hastily. 'I can't paint to order, never worked in that kind of commercial way.'

'That's what I'm trying to get away from. I'll turn it down.'

'Now hang on, Dani, there's more to this than that,' said Max gently. 'For a start, the money will help you out, I'm sure. And it's a means of exploring the landscape, scratching below the surface and . . .' He paused, trying to frame his words, 'and I think it's important you make contact with Isabella. You're a woman, I think she'd prefer that. I sense her restless spirit hovering in this valley and there's a story beneath the mythology. Remember what we talked about, the story beneath the paint on the surface? It will be an artistic challenge.'

Dani was thoughtful. 'The idea is clever – coming up with a line of pictures to give some link and history to his project through Isabella. So you think I should take up his offer?'

Max simply smiled at her, and waited.

Dani knew he wasn't going to say any more on the subject. 'I'll think about it. Let's get a sausage.'

On Sunday at Patricia and Henry Catchpole's house Lara felt she could have been in middle-class Melbourne. It was only when she looked out the windows and saw the expanse of paddocks, gum trees and distant hills that she was aware she was on a farm some distance out of town.

Patricia told Lara that Henry, 'Ran enough head of good cattle to make a few bob and keep him out of mischief.' He was usually out of the house at sunrise checking on the livestock and fences. 'Or else he's pottering in his shed or with the historical society mob at the museum.' She smiled fondly. 'He works quite hard for seventy plus.'

'Maybe that's what keeps him so fit and spry,' said Lara. Looking around at the Sunday lunch Patricia had set out for twenty people she added, 'You've gone to a lot of trouble. And your house is lovely.'

Patricia glanced appreciatively at the rosewood furniture, the crystal and cut-glass ornaments, vases, candlesticks, gleaming silver, lace, linen, and piles of framed photographs on side tables and on top of china cabinets. 'We do have a lot of stuff. Henry and I got together twelve years ago, both of us had raised a family and I had a houseful of things so when I moved up here to his place we added that extra deck and family room.' She pointed to where guests were spilling outside to the barbecue area. 'Now, there are some people you should meet. Dani has already made quite a few friends. But I want you to meet Carter Lloyd.' Leading Lara through the throng she explained, 'Carter is the regional head of the National Parks and Wildlife. Started in forestry interestingly enough, went from cutting down trees to hugging them . . . so to speak.'

'Is he a local?'

'Is now. Came up here when he was widowed and worked with the group that regenerated the Brush. Have you seen what they've done?'

'It's amazing. I remember the Brush as a dark, creepy place, vines smothering the old trees, full of flying foxes and it stank. It wasn't a big tourist attraction when my grandfather took me there.'

Lara had taken a brief walk through the Brush after she'd arrived. She strolled along the new wooden pathway through the cleared undergrowth and neatly labelled trees. It was a tourist attraction and without the smothering canopy of vines the Brush was lighter, airier, cleaner but for Lara it had lost the spooky, smelly magic she remembered.

'Get Carter to tell you what they did to save the Brush . . . they pioneered a rainforest regeneration method that's recognised and followed all over the world. When you settle in up here you'll have to take your grandson through. It's a popular school project.'

'I'm going back to Sydney to pack up a few things. I've arranged to rent my grandparents' old house in Cedartown from the Clerks. Very serendipitous, can you believe it?' said Lara.

'Serendipitous? Now that's a word I like to hear.' The man Patricia had led her to gave a big smile.

'Carter, this is Lara Langdon. She'll be living up this way for a month or so.'

'How do you do?' Lara shook his hand noting his warm smile and deep blue eyes. He had unruly curling hair speckled with grey and was a solid build. She could imagine him doing something powerful like whacking down trees, but his voice and manner were gentle.

'I haven't had the pleasure of meeting your daughter yet. Henry and Patricia tell me she's an artist?' he said as Patricia excused herself. Her strategy at parties was to make one formal introduction and then everyone was on their own.

'That's the plan. The reason she moved up here,' said Lara.

'And you? Why are you only visiting for a month? It will take you more than a month to explore the area.'

'Oh, it's a long story.' Lara was evasive. This was a social occasion. It was all too hard to explain. She wasn't sure why she was continuing this search that drew her to the valley.

'Sorry, didn't mean to pry. But you did mention something serendipitous . . .'

Lara smiled and relaxed. 'Well, I was born here. Moved away when I was young and now I'm suddenly seeking answers to a few questions in the family history. And strangely enough my grandparents' old home is available to rent, well, house-sit at least.'

'Ah, not so strange. I'd take that as a good omen. Then you probably know the valley better than me.'

'I doubt that. We lived in town. But what brought you here originally, the Brush?'

'Can I replenish your drink? Why don't we sit down?' he suggested.

'Is it that long a story?' she laughed. But Lara was glad to sit down. She could see Dani with Angela, Tony and several other young people. She noticed a handsome man to one side watching Dani.

While Carter went to get the drinks a woman sat down beside Lara. 'Hello. I'm Natasha. I've been talking to Henry. He says you're doing your family history.'

'Not quite. Well, I'll see. It's strange being back in a place you only remember from childhood,' said Lara.

'Oh, my. You're lucky.' Natasha paused as Carter refilled Lara's glass and proffered the bottle to Natasha. 'Thanks, no, I don't drink.'

'Natasha, this is Carter,' said Lara.

'Sorry, have I taken your seat here?' asked Natasha.

'Not at all, I'm acting bartender,' said Carter diplomatically, giving Lara a look that said, we'll catch up later.

'You didn't grow up here then?' said Lara to the woman who was slim and dark, probably about sixty. 'Actually, with your name and looks you could be a ballerina.'

'I am of Russian ancestry. I came here as a kid. I've been doing my family history . . . only recently though.'

There was something in her voice and demeanour that suggested to Lara a sense of pain. 'It's a shame we only start to ask questions at this stage of our life isn't it?' Lara's intuitive response hit a nerve in the woman beside her.

'Oh God, if only I'd known sooner. I always had a sense there was a family secret. But growing up here, the war, events in Russia, it was all in the past. My mother died quite suddenly when she was in her fifties and it wasn't till my father . . . well, the man I thought was my father, was dying that he told me he was my stepfather. That my father had died when I was a baby. It was such a shock. And what was so awful was that I was *relieved*. I always felt so guilty that I never felt close to him.'

'News like that must be hard to take in,' said Lara quietly, a little stunned at Natasha's vehemence.

'Trust your instinct. I went back to Russia and started searching. I didn't even know my real father's name! No one would tell me anything. I found an old aunt, well, step-aunt, and she quite matter-of-factly told me what she knew.' Natasha drew a breath, 'And that was, my stepfather *killed* my father. Shot him during the Stalinist purges or something.' She shook her head. 'How could my mother marry the man who killed the father of her child? It haunts me. Mostly because I can't track down any paperwork, it's all gone.'

When Lara didn't answer, but just sat there looking at

217

the distressed woman, Natasha took her hand. 'I'm sixty years old and I feel like a little girl who's lost her daddy. Family secrets, be prepared. Everyone has them.'

'I suppose there are always surprises in a family,' Lara said carefully. Looking around she saw Carter watching and when he saw her pleading expression he came towards her.

'Back again. Can I steal Lara? I'd like to introduce her to someone.'

'Of course.' Natasha rose. 'Sorry to monopolise you.' She squeezed Lara's hand. 'Good luck.'

As they reached a far corner of the patio, Lara drew a breath. 'Phew, thanks for that.'

'You looked a little desperate.'

'Poor woman. She was a bit intense.'

Dani suddenly appeared at Lara's side. 'You okay?'

'Fine, darling. This is Carter Lloyd, my daughter Danielle. I just had a woman pour out some of her deep family secrets,' explained Lara.

Dani looked at Carter. 'That's my mother. As soon as people meet her, they pour out their life story.'

Carter laughed. 'I was just about to do the same thing. Now, I've heard a bit about you. What are you going to be painting while you're here? Plenty of great scenery in our valley.'

'I'm looking at some of Isabella Kelly's country,' said Dani neutrally.

'Pretty country. Shame it's going to be built on.'

'What do you know about it? Do you know Jason Moore and his development?' asked Dani, curious about his reaction.

'No, I don't, though Patricia said she invited him today, so I'm looking forward to a chat,' said Carter. 'If the deed has to be done, well, at least it's sounding as sensitive as these things can be. I'm only going on what Patricia told me,' he added.

Dani continued before Lara could mention Dani would be working for Jason. 'Do you know Isabella's country well?' she asked.

'Carter is the head of National Parks and Wildlife,' interjected Lara.

'Oh, I'm just one of many,' said Carter. 'But, yes, I know the area quite well. What are you after? I know where there's an ancient red cedar that somehow escaped the old timbermen. And some of us eager axemen later on.'

'I don't know how the cedar-getters got in to find those trees when they were in such thick and rugged country,' said Lara.

'When the cedar leaves turn red after winter it's a dead giveaway. Getting the logs out was the hardest,' said Carter.

'You were cutting down trees?' asked Dani.

Carter nodded. 'I grew up in a rural city built on wheat and sheep, conservation wasn't known then. I heard about a scholarship with the Forestry Commission and as I was a Queen's scout, liked hiking and the bush, I thought getting a tertiary education at the Forestry Commission's expense, being indentured and working as a field officer in the bush, sounded pretty good. Bring it on! A young man's adventure. So, yes, I did my share of ringbarking trees while I was working with the logging crew.'

'Before all the save the rainforest protests?' asked Lara.

'When the first greenies appeared and started having a go at us we thought they should be shot. We were the professionals.' He laughed heartily.

'So what converted you?' asked Lara. 'I assume you're of a different mind now.'

'I was sent out to work logging, wood chipping, mowing down rainforest species for veneer, but I was in areas worked over before. Then I was sent to open up Bearing

Tops and I was exposed to beautiful virgin bush and it struck me stuff like that wasn't easily renewable. And with the start of the protest movement I began to pay a bit more attention to what the National Parks was doing.' He paused. 'Forestry had no plans for the future, for sustainability, for preserving Aboriginal artifacts, animal habitats, providing tourist facilities while still supplying timber.' He shrugged. 'I started to look at things differently. In short, I defected.'

'So why is there still such controversy?' asked Dani.

'Blame politicians and industry. They've reduced the amount of land for logging but not the quotas. When people find out what's really happening in New South Wales it'll be too late. And the sad thing is we're all too scared to speak out in public. Job security, families and so on.'

'But that's shocking,' exclaimed Lara.

'That's life now, unless a whistleblower speaks up,' said Dani while spotting Jason Moore smiling at her. She quickly excused herself. 'Oops. Someone I must see, excuse me.' She left Carter and her mother settling themselves at one of the tables laden with snacks. Dani could see her mother had her old TV news documentary hat on as she and Carter continued their discussion in earnest.

Jason greeted Dani warmly. 'You've been quite the social butterfly. You seem to know a lot of people.'

Dani knew he'd been trying to catch her eye. 'People are so friendly and hospitable, don't you think?' she said, noticing Jason didn't have his girlfriend's dog with him this time.

'It is a sociable community, but there's still networking of a kind going on,' he said glancing around. 'It's just more down to earth than in a city. It's not about name-dropping, real estate prices, parties or sport, but cattle prices, who's found a good fishing spot, who needs a hand doing something, who's got something to sell. Country life,' he said.

She couldn't tell if he was being facetious or if it was a casual observation. 'Not like Sydney society. Do you miss it?'

'Not at all. Do you?'

'I was never part of it to any great extent,' said Dani. 'It was more my husband's scene.'

'Same here. I have to read the Sunday social pages to find out what my girlfriend has been up to during the week. So, have you come to a decision? Or do you want to discuss the job tomorrow?'

They were standing apart from the main group clustered around the barbecue where Henry was serving his home-grown meat.

'I've thought about it, carefully, as I did have a lot of reservations. And I've decided that, yes, I would like the job.'

Before she could go on, he grasped her hand, pumping it enthusiastically. 'Great! I'm really pleased, Dani. I think you'll get a lot out of it. I hope you will. What I mean is, that you'll get involved, your paintings will get exposure, I feel sure this is going to work positively for both of us. Can you come in tomorrow?'

Dani was a bit taken aback at his robust enthusiasm. 'Ah, yes, I will. I still have a lot of questions and I need to walk over some of the land. By the way, do you know Carter Lloyd?'

'I know of him, we've been dealing with his local deputy. I'd like to meet him, he's a bit of a legend. You *have* been making inroads into the local community.'

Dani had to smile to herself. 'Like you said, this is a sociable community. And everyone knows about Birimbal and has an interest in what you're doing.'

'That'd be right,' he admitted. 'Well, we can discuss this tomorrow. Round nineish?' He glanced around once more. 'Are you here with friends?'

'My mother. She's been up for a few days. I'd better go and see how she's doing.' Dani excused herself before Jason Moore could ask to meet Lara. For some reason she was uncomfortable at the idea. She looked around and spotted Garth from the historical society talking to Henry.

Henry lifted his arm, signalling to her. Dani picked up a plate to get her food.

'Try a steak, Dani, you won't need a knife, tender as butter.' Henry slapped a piece of meat on her plate. 'Salad and you-name-it on the table. A spud and a sausage too?'

'No, thanks, this looks wonderful. Hello, Garth. How are things?'

'Pretty good. We were just talking about you. And Isabella. Thanks, Henry.' Garth picked up his wine glass as Henry added an extra sausage to his plate. 'Trimmings?'

'Yes, please.' Dani followed Garth to the table where there were salads, crusty bread and condiments. 'How are things coming along with your book?'

'Good. Interesting. I met a friend of yours, which has been great.' He put a dollop of mustard on his plate, butter and sour cream on his baked potato.

'Really? Who was that?' asked Dani.

'Rodney Sutherland. He's very impressive, isn't he? Really keen on Isabella. If this all takes off, it will so help my book. Thanks very much, Dani.'

Dani busied herself with piling salad on her plate. 'Well, I mentioned Isabella to him . . .' She was trying to recall what she'd said. She must have mentioned Garth's name but not for any specific reason. 'What's his interest in her?'

Garth looked at Dani with bright eyes, the most animated she'd ever seen him. 'He's got a plan. He reckons Isabella could put this whole area on the map. Reckons he'll buy my book too.'

'We'll all buy your book, Garth,' said Dani. 'In fact, I was hoping to talk through some more detail with you.'

Garth found a seat and settled his plate on his lap. Dani sat beside him. 'I can't believe after all these years of no one caring about her she's going to be known all over the country. Hopefully,' he added, biting into his steak.

Dani busied herself with her food, wondering how Garth thought his book was going to do that. 'Well, the Birimbal development will certainly help. Jason wants everyone to know they're moving into Isabella Kelly country. It's a big challenge for me to try to visualise and reinterpret those times,' said Dani.

'So are you going to be working with Rodney too?' asked Garth.

Dani put down her fork. 'I'm not sure what you mean, Garth. What work is that? What exactly has Roddy told you?'

Garth looked flustered. 'I hope I'm not talking out of turn. I mean, you told him about Isabella's story, he said you were friends. So I gave him my manuscript to read even though it's not quite finished and he got very excited and said he'd go straight down to Sydney and get things moving. Said he had all the right contacts and everything. I really don't know about these things.'

'What things? What is Roddy planning?' asked Dani patiently.

'The picture. A film. About Isabella.'

Dani stared at him, speechless. 'A movie?' Her mind started to race. It was a brilliant idea. If they could make a couple of movies about Ned Kelly, she thought, Isabella was a natural. But why hadn't Roddy mentioned this to her yesterday when they were working together at her house? 'And he knows about film making? Financing, I suppose. But there's no script written.'

'That's what I mean about my book! He's taken it. To

sell for the film,' Garth's usual taciturn manner came close to sparkling.

'Garth, you didn't just hand it over! I mean, are you having a contract or some agreement drawn up? Not that I imagine Roddy would do the wrong thing of course.' Dani was remembering all the horror stories Lara had told her of film and television deals where people got ripped off.

'He sees it as a thing that can involve the whole town. Put us on the map, specially for tourism. He's very excited,' said Garth.

So excited he didn't mention it to me, thought Dani. 'It is a good idea, but Australian films and TV haven't been setting the world on fire lately. So what's the next move?'

'I have to finish the book. I'm still searching for the end . . . what happened.' He stopped, looking away, his cheeriness dissipating. 'It's frustrating trying to wrap up all the facts and get it right. But he said he had enough to sell the idea.'

'I hope he's selling your version and not what seems to be the popular misconceptions,' said Dani. 'You know how the media likes to hype up the sensational side of a story.'

Garth looked shocked. 'Oh, no, he assured me he'd stick to my book.'

'Adapt it? Then he should be paying you for the film rights, Garth. He can't just take it and shop it around on spec,' said Dani, knowing it was exactly what Lara would say. 'Perhaps you'd better chat to my mum over there. She used to work in TV.'

'To be fair to Rodney he's only just got the manuscript, let's see what he has to say when he gets back from Sydney,' suggested Garth.

'That's fair enough,' said Dani, faintly annoyed that Rodney hadn't mentioned Garth or his trip to Sydney.

'Perhaps the three of us can get together and see that we are telling the same story. Jason Moore is using Isabella as the symbol of the Birimbal development and I'm going to do a series of paintings about her. To go in the promotional material, and maybe to be hung somewhere.'

'That's great,' said Garth. 'But what are you going to paint? There's only one photo of her in existence.'

'What do you think Isabella would want?' asked Dani quietly.

'Oh, her land. Her country. Birimbal is part of that. Have you met Carter Lloyd? He thinks he knows where the original homestead was, where so much happened. That's where I'd start,' said Garth firmly.

'And Kelly's Crossing?' The mysterious stream and its haunted setting came back to Dani.

'Of course,' agreed Garth. 'That's what I want to do with my book, and now with your pictures and a film, people will know what Isabella was all about.'

'Maybe we should lobby Carter to get National Parks to put a plaque there, naming it Isabella Kelly Crossing.' Dani was half serious.

'That would be wonderful. When I started this research years ago I never thought anyone would take any notice. I just felt it should be done,' said Garth looking quite overwhelmed.

'I think people are going to take notice,' said Dani standing up. 'Garth, could I read your manuscript, please?' She hadn't followed up when he'd first told her about it.

'I'd love you to. But Rodney has my only spare. It costs a lot to print it out, would you mind waiting till he comes back?'

'Of course. I'll be speaking to him. I'll ask Roddy to run me off a copy,' said Dani. 'Excuse me, I'd better go see my mum.'

Lara and Carter Lloyd were finishing their lunch. Lara was looking very animated as Carter finished recounting an anecdote.

'Had something to eat? The steaks are fabulous,' said Lara. 'You must hear some of Carter's great stories.'

'I've been hearing about you from Garth and he tells me you have an idea where Isabella's original home was, Carter. Could you show me where?' asked Dani.

'Ah, not as simple as that though I'm happy to oblige. It's just a hunch based on some old documents Garth unearthed. It's a bit of a hike if you're up for that. And I'd want to take Max with me.'

'In case we get lost?' said Dani.

'Think he'd be the first to admit he's no tracker. But I get a bit superstitious. I dunno, I sometimes feel I'm trespassing so if we have an elder with us . . . it can help,' said Carter seriously.

'Really? But if it's on the Birimbal development, then that is trespassing, isn't it?' asked Lara.

'I'm sure Jason won't mind, I'm doing research,' said Dani.

Carter still looked serious. 'Lot of ghosts up in that country if you ask me. So what else has Garth told you?'

'Someone is interested in turning his book into a movie,' said Dani.

Carter was instantly dismissive. 'That'll be a dud. Garth is sticking to the facts too much, keeps knocking back the legend. Who wants to know the boring reality? Bring on the wild stories. Who cares if they're true or not? She's become larger than life, a lot more exciting than the stitched-up spinster she was.'

Lara burst out laughing. 'Well, from a commercial point of view, you're right. Films always stretch the truth.'

Dani felt slightly aggrieved. 'I think that's unfair. That's the whole point of Garth's research and book – to disprove the myths about her being such a hard and difficult woman. Maybe she was, but maybe she had reason to be like that.'

'Darling, if Isabella is going to be the face of this big new project hadn't they better be sure she's the sort of woman people want to be associated with?' asked Lara reasonably. 'I mean, I wouldn't want to buy into an estate named after a murderess or whatever.'

'Mum, it's not an estate, per se. That's another sales aspect they have to get across. It's a totally new development concept and lifestyle. It's called TND – traditional neighbourhood design.'

Carter nodded. 'From the little I know it seems they're trying to develop this concept in a very eco-friendly fashion. Hamlets linked within walking distance between villages with green space. Even small farms. Makes a lot of sense.'

'Would you like to meet Jason?' asked Dani. 'Hear it from the horse's mouth?'

'I'm reluctant to leave your charming mother but, yes, the future of our area always concerns me.' He turned to Lara. 'See you when you move up and settle in.'

Dani introduced Jason to Carter and joined her mother who was with the Catchpoles.

'I was just thanking Patricia and Henry for a wonderful lunch. So many interesting people,' said Lara.

Patricia smiled. 'A lot of people in the city and elsewhere think we're a bit behind the times in this valley. Actually, I find there are more stimulating people and ideas here than anywhere else I've lived.'

'Well, I've heard a few interesting ideas today,' said Lara. 'From the future of forestry to a film.'

'Film? What's that about?' asked Henry.

'Someone is thinking of making a movie about Isabella Kelly,' said Lara.

Patricia's eyebrows shot up. 'Really? First I've heard of it. Who would that be?'

'One of Dani's new friends,' said Lara.

They all stared at Dani.

'Well, I don't know for sure. Garth has had some interest in his book from a guy I met up here. I don't know much at all,' said Dani, hoping she wasn't doing Roddy a disservice.

'Find out!' declared Patricia. 'Council would be most interested. If it's a high-profile project it could be of great value to the community.'

'If it's done properly and not like some of the stupid flicks that have been made,' commented Henry.

'I'll find out and let you know,' said Dani, anxious to change the subject. 'And some other news is – I've taken a position with Jason Moore to do some artwork for his development. Help pay the rent.'

'It's to do with Isabella too,' added Lara.

Henry looked at his wife. 'Well, I'll be blowed. Couldn't give away a dollar with Isabella Kelly's face on it, now everyone's getting in on the act.'

'We'll see, dear,' said Patricia. 'Before anyone marches in and cashes in on our local identity, council will want to know just how they plan to exploit her.'

Henry looked at Dani and winked. He knew the signs. His wife would want to be in the loop on these new developments. 'Can't stop enterprising people trying to make a quid.'

'I'm not sure we want the valley to be known as Isabella Kelly Country,' mused Patricia. 'No one has a good word to say about her.'

'Ned Kelly was a thieving, murdering bushranger and everybody loves him. A local hero in his part of the world,' said Henry.

'Let's wait and see what Garth finds out and if a film is

going to happen,' said Dani. 'The idea is Rodney Sutherland's. He's new to the area. I'd like you to meet him.'

'Absolutely. Bring him round for a drink,' said Patricia. 'Now just one small favour, a reporter for *The Chronicle* newspaper is here, and I thought it might be nice for her to do a photo and bit about you and your mother moving back here, albeit temporarily. Would you mind, Lara? Dani?'

'I can't tell her much. You better do the talking, Mum,' said Dani.

After sharing a very early breakfast at Chesterfield with her mother who wanted to be on the road back to Sydney by sunrise, Dani headed to The Vale to get ready to go in and see Jason Moore and be briefed a little more about her job.

As she drove through the gates she caught a glimpse of a distant figure on the other side of the creek. She stopped and saw a woman in a bright yellow dress and straw hat. She was too far away for Dani to make out who it was and, as she wondered what she was doing, she saw a horse come from the nearby stand of trees and trot to the woman. The woman stopped to fondle the horse before continuing to walk around the bend of the creek and out of sight, the horse following her. Probably my neighbour on this property, thought Dani. I must get her phone number from the solicitor and make contact.

Standing in her freshly painted bedroom, Dani contemplated her meagre wardrobe. She hadn't planned on rejoining the workforce so she didn't have suitable clothes. She finally chose a cotton skirt and T-shirt, which she dressed up with an elaborate carved necklace, sandals and a cotton sweater knotted over her shoulders. She threw her sketchbook and a notebook into her leather shoulder bag, applied minimum make up, sprayed on a tangy citrus perfume – Je Reviens – and felt ready.

Jason Moore smiled at her approvingly as he walked from his office. 'You look ready to get going. You've met Miss Lawrence, my secretary.' Dani smiled at the prim older woman. 'Come and meet the other two team members here. The rest are in Sydney but they'll be coming up and down as required.'

He introduced Fred Lansdowne, the project manager in charge of construction and liaising with local contractors; and Tony Bartholemew, who was overseeing the clearing and laying of infrastructure like water and sewerage.

Jason asked Tony to outline the environmentally friendly concepts of the development.

'We've got a complicated reticulation system with used domestic water being recycled onto gardens, and a sophisticated version of bio-cycle and composting toilets,' he began.

'Compost toilets?' said Dani. 'You don't mean those dry loos you find in national parks?'

'Not quite. In the house you flush your fancy loo as normal. But the waste goes through a special fast-drying system to reduce it to a non-smelly dry compost that is diluted with the grey water and recycled. Goes out on the garden as close to potable water as you can get,' said Fred.

'Remember, the power is environmentally friendly,' said Jason. 'Eventually we'll look at hydrogen fuel cells producing power.'

Dani shook her head. 'Too much info. Point me at the design side.'

Jason laughed. 'Wait till you meet Kate, our coordinating architect. She speaks your language.'

'I thought you'd done the design concepts?' said Dani.

'I have. But it's big-picture stuff. Kate interprets it into specifics, structural designs with mathematical precision. How it can physically be built from my scribbles. Now we need you to add another layer.'

'For the layperson you mean? The finished picture and its inspiration,' suggested Dani.

'You got it in a nutshell,' said Jason. 'When we go to sell the development at an evening dinner or a roadshow event, we want to show customers where it all began.'

'With Isabella,' said Dani softly.

'Over to you, Dani,' said Jason.

Dani was thoughtful and debated whether to raise the subject of the film. She hadn't heard from Roddy and Garth could be misinterpreting things. If Roddy didn't make the movie happen, now that the idea was out there, floating in the universe, someone else might do it. In the end she made a casual remark. 'There's a rumour of Isabella's story being turned into a movie.'

Jason was immediately alert. 'Really? Who? What sort of film? This could be good for us, or a negative if it's not done well. What do you know, Dani?'

'Not much. Yet. But I'll probably know more soon and I'll let you know. So what do you want me to tackle first?'

Jason was businesslike. 'We need images of the landscape, how it might have looked in her day, what she might have done with the land, how that links in with what we're doing. Including images of Isabella.'

'I'll have to imagine all that. In the one and only picture of her she was a rather plain and dumpy lady.'

'But look what she achieved. Make her interesting, Dani. Make us want to like and admire her. What inspired her to live here and love this valley?' Jason spoke intensely, then paused. 'That's about as detailed a brief as I can give you. We'll need some images for brochures, website, PR and the original art as big paintings that could hang in the central building.'

Dani had been writing in her notebook. 'Well, that's clear enough. What's my deadline? I'll show you rough sketches as I go along before I start on big oil paintings.'

'Very sensible. I'm available whenever you need me. In fact I'd like to be a sounding board,' said Jason, 'no matter how rough your first ideas may be. You can have a desk and a bit of space in here.'

'I think I'd prefer to work in my studio. But it would be good to get feedback as I go along,' said Dani.

She thanked Fred and Tony and shook Jason's hand. 'I'll be in touch.'

'Before you go, Dani.' Jason led her from the small meeting room, 'I have set a space aside for you. And I have a token gift. A kind of welcome to the group.'

'A gift?'

'It might come in handy.' Jason walked down the hall-way to a room fitted out simply with a desk, a couple of chairs, a phone and a filing cabinet. Sitting on the desk was a bulky parcel wrapped in purple paper. 'Take it home to your studio.'

'I'm rather embarrassed at a gift on my first day,' said Dani.

'It's not a gift then. It's a bribe. To keep you inspired,' said Jason lightly.

Dani tore off the paper and gasped at seeing the antique writing box she'd admired in Isadora's. 'Oh my god. How did you know?'

'I heard you and Barry talk about it at the auction. I popped in and we both thought it had your name on it.'

'Not my name. Someone called WC. I wonder . . . It's just lovely. And, yes, it will be useful.' Dani felt uncomfortable at the gesture but she was thrilled with the gift.

She ran her fingers over it. 'I can't help wondering who it belonged to. I'll treasure it. Thank you, Jason.'

'My pleasure. Barry and I like to think that even though it's not her initials, it's the sort of thing Isabella might have used.'

Mount George, 1845

Isabella

The candle had burned low. Isabella pored again over the large documents spread on the table. She studied the neatly lined configurations, seeing not just the outlines of squares and rectangles but the beautiful bushy blocks of Birimbal estate. It was a bold concept to develop a new town on part of her extensive holdings, a chance for new settlers to establish small farms and town-based businesses in a valley rich with potential, as she had already proved.

On a separate piece of paper she read again the advertisement that she'd placed in the *Australian* newspaper in Sydney several months before to which there'd been no response.

A most splendid portion of Miss Kelly's estate, situated at the crossing place of the Route from Maitland, Port Stephens, New England, to Port Macquarie, having a portion cleared on the River, and now subdivided into allotments of one half-acre each, more or less, comprising one thousand acres of fine land on the banks of the River and Creeks thereof rising to the Hill, all described, staked out, and charted as Georgetown.

Very little has been made known yet as to the importance of this River, its splendid waters, alluvial flats,

*agricultural qualities and pastoral commands of country,
whether as to sheep, cattle, stock of any kind . . . The Timber is stated as the finest growth and description as cedar,
flooded and other gums, oaks, barks, corkwood, fig, hick-
ory black, variegated satin, and other woods. The Water
is abundant and pure . . . the situation is, of all others, the
most important resting place for the traveller on his route
to or from Port Macquarie . . . The soil here will produce
any grain or vegetable . . .*

She skimmed through the advertisement, which
described the streets laid out and named Isabella, Gipps,
Church and George. The advertisement also mentioned the
proposed George Inn, which was Isabella's existing house.
She planned to add upstairs rooms for accommodation
when a licence was granted. If the sale of her township
was a success she had designs to build a grand mansion.

Isabella had had no doubt her plan would succeed as
her property was on the main route north. The township
she envisaged was located on either side of the route
through Kelly's Crossing. The soil was of good quality
and she had already proved what strong cattle and sound
horses could be bred here. And while her own impressive
home was an example that owners could aspire to build,
there were several sturdy slab huts belonging to workers
that she saw as the start of a small community. But not
one block had sold.

Her solicitor consoled her as best he could, pointing
out her land was so isolated. And as shipping could travel
no further up river than Cedartown the upper-valley hill
communities like her proposed Birimbal were being left
behind.

One of Isabella's neighbours, Mr Andrews, visiting on
a journey south, commiserated. 'It was a brave plan, Miss
Kelly, but the river trade has beaten you I'm afraid. The

days when we were all dependent on bullock drays are over. The future is on the river and more ships are crossing the bar every month. I'm thinking of building a ship to get into the trade.'

'It would be a big undertaking,' said Isabella, thinking of the river land she'd purchased some time ago but had left undeveloped while she had worked on creating her dream town. With more boats now serving the communities downstream maybe she should move her energy and finances to that area.

'I'm fortunate to have an assigned servant who was a shipwright in the old country, so plan to avail myself of his skills. Perhaps you might like to be a partner?'

Isabella declined politely, and made plans to revisit the riverside property she had purchased as soon as possible.

With characteristic initiative Isabella acted quickly. Now that Florian had his ticket-of-leave Isabella installed him with Noona and child on the property down by the river and declared she intended to build a large riverfront home in the future. She'd moved some cattle down to the river flats in Florian's care.

She missed having Florian and Noona's help at Birimbal and while she had no doubt it was local knowledge that one of her employees was cohabiting with a native woman, she didn't want to invite any more attention than was necessary. So she made do with the assigned servants despite several being troublesome.

In particular one called John Hendon was lazy and careless. In Dungog Isabella took out a complaint against him before the magistrates for neglect of duty. Their decision was that for punishment Hendon work for two months on the treadmill in Sydney and then be returned to her.

Returning home from Dungog after this episode Isabella broke her journey and stayed overnight with distant neighbours, the Ralstons. Mrs Ralston, a timid woman socially, busied herself with preparing supper for her husband, three daughters and their visitor.

Isabella sat in the drawing room repeating the charges she'd made against Hendon. 'He was very careless and lost me thirteen head of cattle which were in his charge. I gave him time to find them and he did not. Last May I had him take some pigs to Gangy and he lost some of them. Including the best of the lot. His conduct has been insolent as well. Although reluctant to go to court I could not allow his conduct to pass.'

Mr Ralston agreed. 'Indeed, Miss Kelly. They are an unreliable lot. One trusts that the punishment will bring about some change.'

They spoke more on matters of farming before being ushered into the meal.

The Ralston girls would long talk of the night Miss Kelly stayed in their modest home. The girls were in one bed, Isabella in the other. She slept fully clothed, her dog on the floor beside the bed guarding her. The girls believed she carried a pistol and they made a special effort not to disturb Miss Isabella Kelly or her large dog.

On her return home Isabella was busy and all ran smoothly for several weeks. As far as Isabella was concerned the complaint against Hendon had been dealt with, so she was shocked to learn that Hendon had been paroled after one month with a ticket-of-leave, a privilege which was only granted to prisoners with no convictions, even though he was one of her assigned servants. No one had notified her that he'd been released, moreover that he was residing in the district. He obviously had influence or friends in high places.

Isabella sent her trusted female servant, Hettie, to work with Florian and the growing cattle herd on her land by the river. The newly assigned female servant, Mary, was less satisfactory but Isabella hoped she would improve. She had also taken in an orphan boy, Frank, twelve years of age, to milk the twelve cows and mind the cattle and horses. Frank, who far preferred working for Miss Kelly than being at orphan school, was loyal and had taken a great fancy to the working bullocks Bluey, Roger, Gilbert and, in particular, Merryman – a bullock with twisted horns, one curving up, one curving down.

One afternoon as Frank was lying on the grass watching a small herd of cattle graze he heard a commotion and saw a man he recognised as Hendon and another horseman driving four of Isabella's bullocks with the aid of some dogs. There were also two smaller bullocks he hadn't seen before being herded by Hendon and his mate.

Frank watched, then decided to follow them, keeping well hidden. When they kept going after passing the marked trees that identified the boundary of Miss Kelly's land, Frank knew they were up to mischief and headed back to the homestead, returning the cattle to the home paddock. He found Isabella and told her what he'd seen.

She could barely control her fury. 'Fetch my horse, Frank.'

'Sultan is stabled for the night, Miss Kelly,' said the boy, surprised she'd ride out at this late hour.

'No matter. There is a good moon.' Isabella began making preparations.

Warmly dressed with a jacket over her riding habit, a hefty stockwhip, a waterbag, damper and knife, Isabella galloped away from the stables, the black horse revelling in the bright moonlight and crisp night air. She followed Frank's directions and realised the route led past her neighbour Jack Fletcher's property. While they did not meet socially, they knew each other. Lantern light could be seen in the slab house belonging to Fletcher and a log smouldered, glowing red, near a fenced yard.

At her approach dogs barked and two figures, one holding a lantern, came outside.

'Who goes there?'

'Your neighbour, Mr Fletcher.'

'Miss Kelly?' He sounded surprised, holding the light aloft to see her mounted on the large black horse. 'Is there trouble?'

'I hope not. Four of my working bullocks have been taken this way this afternoon. What do you know about this?' Isabella got straight to the point.

'I trust I am not being accused of any dealing in this matter,' said Fletcher irritably. There had been skirmishes between them over straying cattle before this evening.

'My boy saw the convict Hendon with them. He is a scoundrel who should be in gaol. Have any of your men seen bullocks being driven near here?'

'The hour is late, Miss Kelly.' Fletcher's tone was curt and he made no offer to invite her inside. Nor did Isabella make any move to dismount. 'I can offer no assistance in this matter. If I find stray bullocks in my herd I shall notify you.'

'I do not expect Hendon delivered them here, but as they have been seen on your land and if any of your men are implicated, I will not hesitate to press charges.'

'I cannot be responsible for men who pass through my land with or without stolen property, Miss Kelly,' snapped Fletcher.

The other man stayed behind in the shadows and Isabella could not recognise him. She gathered the reins.

'They cannot have moved too swiftly from here. Good evening, gentlemen.'

They watched her ride away, a woman alone in the night, determined to recover her property.

'Those men are done for. She'll track them,' said the man in the shadows.

'She knows this country and I doubt Hendon has

moved too far. He holds a grudge against her even though the magistrates reduced his sentence,' said Fletcher, lowering the light and going indoors.

'She has few supporters on the bench in Dungog I hear.'

'Nor hereabouts,' muttered Fletcher. 'A woman has no business lording it over her neighbours like she does. She will come undone, have no doubt.'

Isabella rode some distance from the Fletcher homestead before stopping to take some deep breaths and decide on her next move. She looked at the dark bush all around and up at the great sky filled with stars. She had acted impulsively, in anger, without careful planning. She turned Sultan for home.

On hearing her arrival young Frank, who slept in a shelter next to the stable, came with a lantern.

'Do I unsaddle him, Miss Kelly?' he asked as she swung to the ground.

'No. I'm going out again. Get Pepper. I need a few supplies.' She hurried to the house as Frank went to find Pepper, the best dog Isabella owned for working the cattle.

Within the hour she was back on Sultan, her saddlebag strapped behind her, Pepper trotting ahead to find the trail of the missing bullocks. He was quick to find it and set off confidently. The thieves would be camped for the night and she hoped to catch up with them.

Several hours later Pepper was still following the trail. They'd swung through Fletcher's property and into an adjoining gully so it was most likely that Fletcher or some of his men had seen the bullocks and Hendon and would not admit it. Fletcher was no friend to her and would never admit to any involvement with Hendon. Isabella was weary and she felt it safer to snatch a few hours' rest and move out again at first light. They had set a fair pace and Sultan was glad to be hobbled. She tied Pepper to the tree and he settled down, nose on his paws. Isabella spread a sturdy canvas on the ground close by Pepper, used her saddle pack as a pillow, and covered herself with a blanket. She slipped her revolver under the pack.

Close to dawn she set off again and noticed by Pepper's tail and excited sniffing that they must be getting close. In the early light it was easy to see the grass and low scrub trampled by the cattle. They were headed toward heavily timbered ranges where it would be difficult to find them. But Isabella was in luck. She heard the grunt and deep bellow of cattle stirring. She dismounted and, leading Sultan, made her way cautiously down a slope, softly calling Pepper to stay back.

Suddenly she could see them. The men were stirring. Hendon, a rug thrown over his shoulders, was poking the embers of the night fire. He hadn't yet put on his boots. The four bullocks and the two smaller ones they'd been using to lead hers were held in a rough but sturdy sapling yard. This looked to be a well-established campsite.

Cattle theft was becoming a big problem all over the colony because of the rising demand in Sydney for beef and bullocks to pull drays as more settlers arrived. Isabella wondered how many other landholders in the area had had some of their stock stolen and driven into this yard.

The men moved away from their blankets and saddlebags.

Isabella strode into the open. 'Good morning. I have come for my cattle.'

The men spun around and froze as they saw the Colt revolver Isabella pointed at them.

'These animals were purchased. A legitimate sale,' blustered Hendon.

'I know you, Hendon, and what your word is worth. Drop the railing of the pen,' Isabella commanded.

'We have documents that prove we own these animals. You are stealing from men who have done business.'

'I branded those four big bullocks. There has been no sale. Your release from bondage was luck that you never deserved, and this shows just what kind of a man you are. Now get over there and drop the rails of the yard. Move! Drop the rails.'

Hendon stiffened and tried to find the courage to speak what he felt about the woman who had dominated his life for the past few years of servitude. He hated her with intense passion. But he couldn't say aloud what he heard in his head while she pointed a gun at him.

The two men exchanged a quick glance and Hendon's offsider made a sudden lunge towards their swags but stopped as a bullet raised dust near his feet.

'No more nonsense,' snapped Isabella. 'I have others close behind. All I want is my property.'

'Do it,' said Hendon. 'She would kill us given the chance.' As the man moved to the pen Hendon snarled at her, 'Take your beasts. But do not try and bring us before any bench. Your word will not match ours.'

Isabella didn't answer, with the cocked gun still aimed at Hendon she walked to their swags, collected a rifle from one and a pistol in a holster hooked over a saddle. She whistled Pepper who went straight into the pen, snapping at the heels of the bullocks, driving them out at a lumbering trot back the way they'd come during the night. The two smaller bullocks stood docilely by. They had worked with strange cattle many times before. Their job was done.

'If we both rush at her . . .' whispered the second man to Hendon.

He shook his head. 'I know her. She will not be believed. We have witnesses to the sale, do we not?' Hendon gave Isabella a look that was close to a smirk. The other man still looked confused, nervous and flustered.

The bullocks were out of sight, Pepper's sharp bark fading. The men's horses were unsaddled, hobbled some distance from their campfire. Isabella gave a short whistle and Sultan trotted to her.

'Move down to the water and sit down for a while.' She fired another shot that whistled over their heads. They obeyed her instantly.

When the men were squatting in the creek Isabella pushed their guns under a strap on the pack and pulled herself into the saddle. Sultan followed the bullocks at a swift pace and they were soon well clear of the two angry, swearing men who knew it was pointless to go after her.

'What do we do about the delivery?'

Hendon shrugged. 'There are other cattle we can get, don't worry. We won't be short of the number we promised.' He gazed up the hillside where Isabella had disappeared and cursed her again. 'One day I will get revenge for this, Miss Kelly. And I am not the only one you'll regret crossing.'

In the cheerfulness of the bright morning Isabella allowed the warm sun to soothe her anger. Men such as Hendon were opportunists with no scruples, but it was painful that neighbours such as Fletcher were prepared to align themselves with thieves and not join forces with law-abiding landowners to make their valley stronger. And, she recognised once more, there were men who were civil to her face but swift to take advantage of her given the chance.

A chorus of bird calls caught her attention and she let the beauty of the bush wash away the ugliness of the men she had just outwitted. The gum trees were losing their bark revealing silvery pink patches. Tree orchids hung from the branches, and a wallaby returning late from its foraging bounced through dappled light. By the time she reached her homestead the hours in the tranquil bush had restored her spirits.

9

Cedartown, 1938

EMILY WILLIAMS SAT AT her Singer treadle sewing machine, blue cotton voile bunched around her knees. The fabric had been a purchase from Mr Kahn, the hawker who came around every three months with his small horse-drawn wagon filled with all manner of delights, treasures and practical household items: sewing supplies, pretty soaps, feather dusters, brooms, pegs, bolts of material, potions and lotions. The roll of blue fabric was just enough to make a dress for Elizabeth, a nice blouse for herself and a few squares to add to her ongoing patchwork quilt.

Elizabeth called from her bedroom. 'Is it ready, Mum?'

'Nearly,' she shouted back, then muttered to herself, 'I do hate the idea of a machined hem. It should be hand stitched and you'd never see it.' Emily was normally very fastidious about sewing. She had worked as a dressmaker's apprentice in a small exclusive shop in London that occasionally had royal commissions. She prided herself on turning out her family in smart, well-made clothes even when quality materials and trimmings were hard to come by.

Elizabeth appeared on the back verandah in her slip. Emily lifted the needle foot, pulled the dress away and bit off the cotton thread. 'Doesn't look so frumpy now.'

'Thanks, Mum. I'll be ready in a tick.'

'Where's Mollie?'

'She's ready. She's with Dad putting the picnic things in the laundry basket.'

Emily patted her hair. 'I'd better put some powder on, the Gordons will be here any minute. Don't forget the blanket, Harold,' she called out.

Harold winked at his younger daughter. 'Anyone would think the king was coming to this shindig.'

'Well, it is Empire Day, Dad. Queen Victoria's birthday. We learned about it in school yesterday,' answered twelve-year-old Mollie.

'What else went on? Not a lot of schoolwork it seems. And a half-day holiday,' smiled her father.

'They raised the flag and we sang "Here's to the Red White and Blue". I was in the school procession and Mr Blake gave a speech. The boys got to throw their hats in the air. Andy Gordon said they're having a bonfire tonight.'

'Sounds like you've already done a lot of celebrating, what with the picnic and events about to start. Ask your mother if you can peep over the back fence at the fireworks.'

The Gordons lived on one side of Cricklewood and the three Gordon boys had been building a giant bonfire for weeks. It was at the edge of the small creek that ran behind the houses. Cows that people left there to graze had been taken elsewhere and neighbours were alerted to lock up their dogs as there'd be firecrackers going off.

Emily appeared in her straw hat with bright red berries

on the side. She smoothed the collar of Mollie's dress and cast a critical eye at her husband, who quickly stood to attention.

'Harold, not that cardigan, put your proper jacket on. And don't forget your hat,' she fussed.

'Mum, he never goes outside without his hat,' laughed Mollie.

There was a toot at the gate as the Gordons pulled up in their car followed by the boys with a horse-drawn sulky. The picnic supplies, pillows, blanket and a parasol were stacked around the feet of Mollie and the three Gordon boys. Emily was helped into the back seat of the car.

'Where's Elizabeth? Come on!'

Elizabeth came out the front door and slammed it shut, holding onto her dark blue felt hat with its small feather trim and her mother's good leather handbag she'd borrowed. Her new blue dress showed off a glimpse of slim calf, ankles and her best shoes . . . tan suede brogues with perforated detail around the laces and a small chunky heel. At seventeen she looked very grown up with her wavy brown hair coiled at the nape of her neck and a touch of powder and lipstick.

The three boys in the sulky let out good-natured wolf whistles as she squeezed in beside her parents in the back seat of the car, carefully smoothing the folds of her dress.

The Cedartown Park was crowded. Families and groups had staked their positions on the grass ringing the bandstand decorated with Union Jacks. The school brass band had already marched into the park and were playing patriotic songs. To one side a tug-o'-war rope was being tested by energetic teams of boys and girls, and there was much enthusiasm for the three-legged, sack and egg-and-spoon races.

Thommo's parents were seated near Clem's mother and the Richards kids. Clem's father refused to go into town 'for a lot of silly folderol', but Nola Richards looked forward to this outing as it was one of the rare opportunities for her to get off the farm – even if she did have to rise earlier than usual to get her household and farm tasks done, prepare the picnic and press the boys' shirts with the heavy flat iron heated on top of the fuel stove.

'How are you, Mrs Richards?' asked Thommo's father.

'Doing nicely, thanks, Mr Thompson.'

'We so enjoy having Clem around more often,' said Vera Thompson with a warm smile. 'He's a great help to Frank now we've built the picture theatre. So much nicer than showing films in the Town Hall.'

'Clem's a whiz with engineering things if you ask me. Must be a big help with the machinery on your farm,' said Frank Thompson.

Since leaving school, Clem had been working part-time for Thommo's dad, occasionally running the projector for night screenings at the new Liberty Picture Show to give the Thompsons a night off. And he had proved to be a great asset at repairing the old projector from the Town Hall.

Thommo had convinced his father that he knew so little about the mechanics of the projector he should learn a trade rather than help him with the picture show. He suggested his father give the job to Clem.

Clem generally stayed the night with Thommo before cycling back to the farm to do his share of work there. He squirrelled away the money he earned from his job at the Liberty as there was no pay for his work on the farm. His father made it clear he was lucky to have a roof, a bed and food in front of him.

Thommo was learning a trade with Mr Hinton, the butcher. But the two boys, such close mates, still made time for Sunday excursions together. When they had a free

Saturday night they went to one of the local dances or concerts. At first they'd felt shy and awkward around girls, but as they were both handsome and cheerful they soon found they had no trouble attracting attention from the young ladies – even those carefully chaperoned.

The Williams family settled close by. Emily nodded politely. 'Such a nice day for a picnic, Mrs Richards.'

'Indeed. My goodness, Mollie is growing up isn't she?'

Emily glanced at Mollie spreading a rug to sit on. Elizabeth was nowhere to be seen. Harold had also gone to find his friends. 'Mollie passed her latest piano examination last week. And your family?'

'Keeping busy. Always a lot to do on a farm.'

'Yes. Well, I'd better go to the tea tent, we CWA ladies are on duty,' said Emily rather pointedly. 'See you later, I'm sure.'

'Nice to see you, Mrs Williams. Say hello to Harold. Haven't seen him since we collected some spare parts for our tractor.'

Emily excused herself, telling Mollie to mind their spot and picnic things as she went to see when she was needed on duty in the tea tent. Emily had little time for Clem's mother, Nola Richards. The hard-working farm wife had no refinement in Emily's eyes. And it was a shame Mrs Richards didn't attend the Country Women's Association meetings; after all, the whole idea was that women help each other and the Richards had been very glad of the help from the CWA after the last drought.

But Nola Richards was in good spirits and ignored the snub from Emily Williams. She settled back, fanning herself with her cotton hat, to watch the fun and games. Looking round she saw her son Clem with Thommo, inseparable as always, talking in a group under a tree. One of the girls looked to be Elizabeth Williams. Pretty as a picture, but she knew it too.

Eleven-year-old Phyllis came racing towards Nola Richards. 'Mum, Mum, our Keith and Kev are in the tug-o'-war.' She yanked at her mother's arm.

'Hold your horses. Someone has to watch our things. I can see from here.'

'No, come close. Cheer them on,' wailed Phyllis. Then, spotting Mollie, she called, 'You coming to watch the tug-o'-war, Mollie?'

Mollie smoothed her skirt, sticking out her legs to show off her new socks with the frill around the top. 'I have to stay here and look after our lunch.'

'Then watch ours too,' exclaimed Phyllis and dragged her mother to her feet.

'Would you mind, Mollie?'

Mollie nodded. 'Yes, Mrs Richards. I'll do that.'

Nola walked to Mollie and leant down, patting the bow in her hair. 'You do look very pretty. Thank you so much.'

Phyllis raced ahead of her mother calling to her big brothers.

'Look at Mum,' said Clem, watching from under the tree. 'She loves all the games. She'd be in the races like a shot.'

Elizabeth gazed at the plump woman in the faded floral frock that barely buttoned across her expansive chest. Mrs Richards had loose curls of hair blowing free under her hat, she looked flushed, and her robust laughter was loud as Phyllis dragged her mother to the starting line.

'Your mother isn't going in the sack race, surely?' Elizabeth said to Clem.

'She'd give it a go but she's over the age limit, I reckon.'

'Good on yer, Mum!' shouted Phyllis as Nola Richards put an egg in a spoon and ran a few paces to show a youngster how it was done.

'So what's happening tonight? Are you going to the fireworks?' said Elizabeth to the group, but her eyes flicked over at Clem.

'The Gordon boys are doing the bonfire. They've got crackers from the Chinaman,' said Thommo.

'That's kid's stuff,' sniffed Elizabeth. She'd grown up next to the Gordon boys who were almost like cousins. She and Mollie were in and out of their house, just as the boys were at home in the Williamses' backyard or on their back verandah. Emily was strict about not allowing the boys to tramp through the house.

'There's supposed to be rockets over the river when it gets dark,' volunteered Cynthia Joyce, Elizabeth's friend from the bank. Elizabeth had a job at the local auctioneer and stock and station agency next door to the bank, and the two girls had become friendly and shared lunchtimes in the park.

'Let's go, it'll be fun,' said Elizabeth, then turned to the boys. 'You both coming to the fireworks?'

The boys looked at each other and shrugged. 'S'pose so,' said Clem. 'I'll stay the night with you Thommo.'

'Righto. Hey, they're starting the ceremony. C'mon.'

The group hurried to where the crowd was gathering at the bandstand to watch the arrival of the special guests. Seated on chairs were the mayor wearing his insignia; Mrs Mallory from the Red Cross Committee; Mr Higgins, the school principal; and Major General Jones who had been a hero in the Great War and was invited to such occasions to wear his medals and present prizes.

Everyone rose as the band played 'God Save the King' and then, as the Union Jack was run up the flagpole by the boy scouts, everyone sang 'Rule Britannia'.

The formal speech fell to the mayor, who had a booming voice and was never at a loss for words. Or, as Harold hissed to Emily, 'There's a man that can talk underwater with a mouthful of toffee.' Emily nudged him as Mollie giggled behind her hand.

'Ladies and gentlemen, boys and girls, once again we come together to celebrate Empire Day and commemorate the British Empire on whose lands and dominions throughout the world the sun never sets. Storm clouds are gathering in Europe and our empire could well be facing dark days ahead. So let us salute the king and empire and show our patriotism.'

He paused dramatically, and Emily whispered to Harold, 'Does he mean war might break out?'

'Let's pray not. Though if the stories from Europe are accurate, it's very troubling,' said Harold.

'If there's a stoush, mate, we'll show them what we're made of,' added a man with a strong Scottish accent standing beside Harold.

The mayor went on to thank everyone involved in this fine occasion and called on General Jones to present prizes to students who had turned in the best essays on 'What the Empire Means to Me'. But Harold wasn't listening. He glanced around to spot the young men, the Gordon boys, the Richards boys, young Thommo and Clem standing next to Elizabeth and Cynthia. They looked carefree, innocent and happy. As he had once been, when marching off to war seemed a high adventure. Yes, when called upon Australians would rally to support the mother country. But at what cost?

There was another song, three cheers for the king and everyone dispersed to enjoy their picnic hampers or get a sandwich from the CWA stall. Later there was a dancing display by the primary school children, more races, and novelty competitions involving eggs, buckets of water, horseshoes, and cricket bats bashing tennis balls all over the place. Then there was a 'tired but happy' exodus of families bound for dinner tables and backyard bonfires, though many began to make their way to the river for the twilight fireworks.

There was a discussion between the Williamses and the Gordons and it was agreed that the older children could stay at the river and walk back home – a fifteen-minute stroll. The younger children were to go home and change, have supper then join in the neighbourhood bonfire in the Gordons' backyard.

Clem, Thommo, Elizabeth and Cynthia found themselves paired off as they headed down to the river to find a good spot to watch the rockets go off. The girls walked in front, the two mates hung back talking in low voices.

'Go on, I dare you, Clem.'

'Nah, too many people around.'

'You're scared. A gutless wonder. You and all your talk about girls at the pictures,' niggled Thommo.

'What if she says something to her parents? I'll get shot.'

'She won't if she likes it.'

'What about you and Cynthia? I will if you will,' declared Clem with sudden firmness.

'Righto. You're on.'

'How am I going to know if you do it? And same for me. The girls won't kiss if someone else is watching.'

'Scout's honour,' said Thommo holding up three fingers in a mock salute. 'We tell the truth.'

They emerged from a patch of rainforest onto a wide open grassed area beside the river. 'Cripes, look at all the people,' said Clem.

'Wait till it gets dark. No sweat then.'

They gathered around the Cedartown wharf waiting for the last light to fade so it was dark enough for Mr Holland, the blacksmith, and his handful of helpers to set off the sky rockets from bottles strategically placed along the bank. There'd been a small display of catherine wheels, jumping jacks, basket bombs and double bungers, while children twirled sparklers and let off strings of tom thumb crackers.

Elizabeth sat close to Clem. She'd given her hat to her mother to take home and undone the neat coil of her hair so it fell loose about her shoulders. Clem thought she looked prettier than ever. His hand edged towards hers on the grass.

'So what'd you think of today?' he asked quietly.

'Same as last year. Did your family have a good time?'

'You bet. Mum doesn't get out to things too much. Dad's pretty strict about gallivanting around, as he calls it. Not with me but.' He casually covered her hand with his.

'Are you the favourite?' she teased.

'Nah. I stand up to him. I sometimes got beltings for it when I was a kid, but I do my share around the farm, so he lets me get away to town when I work at the Liberty.'

'You don't like being on the farm?' asked Elizabeth. She knew most of the boys from farm families would end up farming.

'I like the idea of city life. Not that I've ever been to a real big city. I want to get enough money and work down south,' said Clem firmly, pleased she hadn't taken her hand away.

Elizabeth sighed and leaned her shoulder against Clem's arm. 'Me too. I hate it here. I'm learning bookkeeping and hope to get work in Hungerford next year.'

'Mr Thompson told me I should go for some training at the motor shop in Hungerford. I'm pretty good with engines,' said Clem trying not to sound like he was boasting. Elizabeth smelled nice and he was itching to put his arm around her shoulders.

They were silent a minute watching Cynthia and Thommo skylarking with several of their friends.

Then Elizabeth said, 'What the mayor said, about dark days and all that. My father thinks there could be a war.'

'Ah, I dunno about that,' said Clem, a little surprised at her concern. It all seemed a long way from the wharf at Cedartown. 'Hey, it's getting darker. Won't be long before the show starts.'

Elizabeth ignored his remark. 'Dad says if England goes to war then we'd have to help too. Would you go and fight?' She turned to look at him and Clem nearly leaned forward to kiss her but thought better of it with so many people around and it not yet really dark.

'Strewth, yes,' he enthused, even though it was the first time the idea had been put to him. 'You bet. Like a shot. Get me off the farm for sure!'

There was a chorus of shouts as the first rocket whizzed into the sky flaring pink and green stars that drifted down towards a reflected display on the river surface. More and more rockets soared up with a chorus of explosions that brought screams of delight from the crowd. And then a wall of spinning, sparkling fireworks hanging on the old wharf shed provided a stunning side-show while more rockets were readied for a grand finale high over the river.

The sudden silence and darkness that came as the show ended was broken by a roar of applause.

The crowd broke up, most keen to get home for more food and backyard fireworks. But there were dawdlers, some older blokes who settled down for a few bottles of beer before calling it a night, and some younger folk who just wanted a bit longer together away from adult scrutiny.

Clem and Elizabeth sat talking about work and future social events until Thommo and Cynthia came up hand in hand. Thommo was waving a red, white and blue balloon he had picked up and he marked their arrival by letting it go, giving a silly salute as it rose into the night sky.

'You're a clown,' giggled Cynthia.

The foursome walked up the dirt road lit by the rising

moon and as they came opposite the great stand of the Brush, Thommo, on cue as Clem had prompted him, nudged Clem in the back.

'Hey, dare you to go into the big fig tree. The Abos reckon there's spirits, ghosts, in there at night.'

'Yuk. It's full of flying foxes. And it smells,' said Cynthia dismissively.

'The bats are all out hunting. You been in there?' Clem asked Elizabeth.

To his surprise she said coolly, 'Of course. Lots of times with my dad. Not at night though.'

'Go on then, I dare you,' laughed Cynthia. 'Bring back a fig leaf!'

'Or wear it,' giggled Thommo.

Clem grabbed Elizabeth's hand. 'Righto, here we go. Come on, let's show them.'

Laughing, they took the rough track into the rainforest and almost at once were plunged into darkness under the forest canopy. They paused for a moment to let their eyes adjust.

'This is spooky,' whispered Elizabeth, gripping his hand.

From his pocket Clem pulled a small torch that he used to show people to their seats in the picture show. 'This'll help, come on.' They walked as quietly as they could. 'Those noises, nothing really, just little night animals and stuff,' he said to reassure them both.

They reached the towering old tree and stopped, staring up through the black maze of branches and loops of aerial roots to the moonlit sky.

'Dad reckons this was here two hundred years ago,' said Elizabeth. She turned to look at him and Clem grabbed his chance, leaning over and kissing her quickly.

He wasn't prepared for Elizabeth to wrap her arms around him and kiss him back but he held her tightly, the beam of torch wavering across the giant buttress roots. They were conscious of nothing but their lips and quickening hearts.

Suddenly there was a loud noise, like someone or something, crashing through the undergrowth near the huge wall-like buttress roots of the tree. Elizabeth screamed and broke away from Clem.

'S'all right, it's okay,' shouted Clem, waving the torch around, but for Elizabeth that only made the scene more grotesque and she screamed again. Clem grabbed her around the shoulders.

'Was it a ghost?' Elizabeth was scared.

'It's all right, probably a wallaby or something. Let's get out of here anyway.' Clem felt shaky, unsure of just what they'd heard.

Soon they were laughing about it with Thommo and Cynthia. It would be a good story to be embellished later.

Elizabeth held on to Clem's hand all the way to Cynthia's house and then to Cricklewood. 'I'd better go round the back,' she said. 'See you, Thommo.'

'Yeah, righto.' Thommo hung back at the front gate as Clem led Elizabeth through Emily's front rose garden.

'Jeez, you took long enough,' complained Thommo when Clem returned close to ten minutes later. 'So did ya?'

'Yeah. She kissed me too. What about you and Cynthia?'

'Nah. I didn't feel like it. Not my sort,' said Thommo dismissively. 'Girls, they always scream and muck up. So what're we doing tomorrow then?' he asked briskly, wanting to move away from the topic of girls.

Clem touched his lips, recalling the surprising softness of Elizabeth's mouth, and was reluctant to interrupt the surge of delight that he felt sweeping through his whole body. But he forced himself to reply to Thommo. 'Have to go home and help with the milking and the pigs early tomorrow. Want to play cards tonight? Your call.'

'S'pose so,' said Thommo, glad his mate was thinking about things they both liked. 'Or maybe dominoes, eh?'

Dani

Dani was absorbed in putting down the foundation of a painting, with a Bartók concerto playing loudly. It was wonderful not to have neighbours so she was surrounding herself with sound. She was trying to capture the sheen on the surface of the river in a particular light, so she was applying the paint in thin layers to give a translucent, film-like quality. As she stood back from the easel she became aware her phone was ringing.

'Are you working? Am I interrupting?'

'Roddy! Hello, stranger.' It had been at least ten days since she'd heard from him.

'Yeah, sorry about that. I got tied up in a few business deals. Once I get involved I kinda zone out of the real world. Like you when you paint, I guess.'

'I have answered the phone though,' retorted Dani. 'So what's happening down there in Sydney?'

'I'm in New Zealand. Quite a few things are moving along. I'll be back up there next week. Hey, didn't you mention you know someone on the council there?'

Straight to the chase, thought Dani. 'Yes, I do. Why?'

'This project needs some local support –' he began.

'Would this project be the Isabella movie,' cut in Dani, tired of his obfuscation.

Roddy laughed easily. 'Touché! You've spoiled my surprise. Yeah, what do you think, she's a natural, eh?'

'Yes. That's why I'm painting her for the Birimbal development,' she reminded him.

'Great, the more the merrier, cross promotion. Who leaked the news?'

'It's not public knowledge . . . yet, it was just a rumour. Is it really going to happen?' Dani hoped Garth would get a good deal for his manuscript if Roddy was serious.

'Doing my best, babe, talking to the money men, got to get a creative heavyweight interested. Turns out they're both here in Wellington.'

'What kind of creative heavyweight?' she asked.

'A director, famous old guy. What's the word – an *auteur* – that's it. Russell Franks, ever heard of him?'

'Of course I have. He made some brilliant films but he'd be getting on, wouldn't he? I thought he was English.'

'He is. Been living here in Wellington on and off for years, he's seventy. Made a big TV series recently in the UK. He loves Isabella. He's going to draft a script treatment.'

Dani was a bit stunned. 'Well, you don't waste any time when you get an idea. I assume Garth is getting paid?' she said none too subtly.

'I'm coming back to see him – and you I hope – in a few days. I'd like to get the council on side to help with infrastructure. This film will put the valley on the tourist map, all kinds of opportunities. So don't say much. We'll make a big announcement, get media coverage once the ink has dried. Call you when I'm back.'

Dani called Lara. 'I don't know what to think about this. I guess I'm feeling a bit jealous. I feel so connected to Isabella, I'd hate to see her ripped off again.'

'I have to say it's a damned good movie idea,' said Lara thoughtfully. 'And Russell Franks, he's got a pretty amazing track record. Hope he's not past it.'

'Roddy said he'd just done some big series in the UK.'

'That rings a bell. Look, darling, if it happens, and God

knows how easily these things fall over, then it's a bonus. Have you told Jason Moore?'

'Not definitely,' said Dani slowly. 'It was only a rumour from Garth and it all seemed a bit unlikely . . . well, sudden. But Roddy is going for it, hammer and tongs. So now I think I should tell Jason it's happening.'

'Perhaps I should talk to Roddy and see if I can get involved,' said Lara suddenly. 'Do the "making of doco" or something. Maybe that's why I've come back here!' said Lara with a laugh, but Dani could tell she was serious.

'Just wait, Mum. He'll be here in a few days so we'll talk to him then.'

Dani sat at the bare desk in 'her' office as Jason leaned back in a chair, his hands clasped thoughtfully under his chin. 'Why don't I like the idea?' he said, as much to himself as to Dani.

'I felt the same, a proprietary thing, I think. But won't it be good publicity for Birimbal?'

'Possibly. If the film is any good. But that could be a year or more away. We should cash in on the fact it's going to be made as it gets people familiar with the location. Our big aim is to make people understand what kind of a project we're setting up.' He paused. 'Getting Russell Franks is a bit of a coup though. Who would play Isabella?'

They amused themselves for a few moments running through names of the world's top actresses.

'I assume your friend plans to film here in the valley and not in California or someplace,' said Jason.

'Here definitely. That's why he wants council help,' said Dani.

'Has he asked you to help him in any way? Could divide your focus a bit,' said Jason straightening and giving her a direct stare.

'No way. My mother is keen though. She worked in TV.' Dani wanted to get off the subject of Roddy. She'd alerted Jason, it was up to him and his company to decide what to do, if anything, about the Isabella movie. 'I've started painting but I'm hoping Carter Lloyd will set a date to take me out to Isabella's original home site. He's such a busy man.'

'I'd like to come along. I know the country but not its history,' said Jason. 'Let me know. Carter is a pretty impressive man, knowledgeable and very charismatic. Maybe he should be in the movie!' He escorted her to the door. 'Nice bit in the paper about you and your mother returning to find your family roots.'

'That's my mother's idea. My escape to the country to find my artistic soul seems to have set off a chain of events,' said Dani.

Jason opened the door into the reception area where Miss Lawrence sat at her desk busily typing at her computer. 'Anything to do with family history can be a can of worms,' he said quietly. 'Let's not go there. Keep me posted about the trek to find Isabella's home.'

Roddy arrived unannounced on Dani's doorstep, which irritated her. He quickly smoothed her ruffled feathers by giving her a hug, waving a bottle of expensive champagne and holding up crossed fingers.

'We're that close to signing off.'

'Does that mean money? Going public? What's your next move?' she asked.

'Courting council,' he answered promptly. 'I've got the location manager coming up to do a recce for suitable spots to film. We'll have to build Isabella's house, find sulkies and drays. That museum is a resource goldmine.'

'So you need permission to do all this stuff?' Dani was

beginning to understand why he was so keen to get Patricia behind the plan.

'I want the whole district to get involved. Maybe we'll build a small period township and make Isabella's house solid, not a mock-up, turn it into a B&B later. The whole thing will be a big tourist drawcard. The movie will bring bucks to town . . . a hundred crew and cast have to be housed and fed for a couple of months. Too bad the Birimbal development won't be finished . . .'

'That's residential housing, of a very special kind, not the sort of thing for short-term lease,' said Dani quickly. 'That was one of the criteria for the village homes. But I'm happy to introduce you to Patricia.'

'Do it informally, have us over for coffee so I can pitch the whole thing so she can go in to bat for me in council,' he said.

Dani knew Roddy would be turning on all his persuasive charm with his silver tongue. But she reckoned Patricia was a practical woman who wouldn't be easily swayed. 'It seems a win-win situation for the area so I'm sure the council will be supportive.'

'I'm hoping they'll stump up some money, perhaps do a few targeted, exclusive fundraising events from those businesses who'll benefit most,' said Roddy.

'Ah, that's different. I have no idea about that,' said Dani.

'I've done some homework. The council is pretty cashed up and they have a budget for tourism and I believe a theme park was mentioned at one stage . . .' he stopped. 'I won't bore you with all this. Come on, I thought we'd share the champagne and I'd take you out to the beach for a swim and lunch.' He leapt up and gave her a quick kiss.

'Let me tidy up my stuff in the studio. God, I'm hopeless, aren't I? I was going to finish that picture this afternoon,' she chided herself.

'You'll feel refreshed and inspired. Shall we take the champagne with us?'

'Let's go,' laughed Dani.

Dani didn't get home till dark and probably wouldn't have returned from Roddy's glamorous penthouse apartment at the beach if she hadn't had to feed Jolly. It had been a lazy afternoon – they'd gone to the beach for a surf, returned and shared the champagne, though Dani noticed the expensive bottle had been returned to the wine rack and he'd opened a mediocre bottle from the refrigerator. But they'd brought back gourmet deli food from the cafe at the beach, eaten on his balcony, then, after the champagne, Roddy opened a bottle of chilled white wine. So it seemed quite natural that he kissed her and led her into the shaded bedroom with ice-white linen and a pristine ensuite. There was nothing personal in the place that she could see, other than papers and files on a desk.

She recalled what Helen had said about Roddy being good for a fling and she grinned to herself. The sex had been nice, and it was good to feel attractive and have someone to share things with. Not that Roddy was interested in what she was doing.

She missed her son. She hoped Tim would adjust quickly when he made the move to Cedartown with Lara. She'd have to cool the relationship with Roddy when Timmy was around. She'd introduce Roddy slowly and casually to her son. Nevertheless, she'd been intrigued listening to Roddy's extensive plans for the Isabella movie which, if his whole scheme built around the film came off, would be an enormous undertaking for the town.

The following week Helen and Barney insisted on hosting a barbecue picnic at Chesterfield as an official welcome to Lara and Tim. The weather was warm enough for the kids to head to the river for a swim while the adults lounged around the pool after lunch. Max and Sarah had brought along Les White who'd be Tim's teacher. Angela and Tony had invited another couple who had children at school with Toby and Tabatha so Tim would know a small group when he started the following week at Cedartown Primary School.

Dani began to relax as she watched Tim, Toby, Tabatha, Max's sons Lennie and Julian, and the other kids race to the river with the dogs while Barney towed his boat behind the tractor down to the landing, promising the kids a spin up the river later. It was a relief to her as Tim's initial reaction to The Vale hadn't been overly enthusiastic.

'We're in the country, Mum! Like waaaay out! Who am I going to play with? What am I going to do? How early do I have to get up for school?'

He'd deliberately found fault with almost everything, but Dani held her tongue and her temper. 'This house is so old! What happens if something goes wrong? We're all alone here. Toby told me there're snakes out here.'

'There are snakes at Chesterfield too. Wear shoes and keep your eyes open,' said Dani calmly. Though she had exactly the same fears as Tim, she wasn't going to show it.

At least Tim's first few days at school went smoothly. She was so grateful that Toby had taken him under his wing, being in the same class. After her freedom at The Vale she was still adjusting to the routine of driving Tim into school and picking him up at Chesterfield in the late afternoon.

To give Dani a bit more time for work, Tim went home with Tabatha and Toby. Helen made them afternoon tea and they hung out with Barney in his massive shed where a horde of guinea pigs had escaped and made it home. Tim helped Toby with his chores of feeding Pig, the old sow, checking the chickens and ducks, playing with the wallaby which had recovered but refused to leave, or picking beans and other vegetables. Tim always had a parcel of produce or homemade biscuits from Helen when he got in the car to go home.

Lara was staying with Barney and Helen at Chesterfield for a week as the Clerks had arranged for some roof repair work to be done at Cricklewood before she moved in.

Dani had worked out a sequence of pictures to paint that she believed would reflect the beauty and spirit of some of Isabella's country. There were still gaps in the whole story as she was waiting to read Garth's manuscript, which Roddy had promised to lend her. She gathered her sketches together and called out to Tim.

'I have to go into the office in town, do you want to come in after school and meet Jason Moore and see where I'm working?'

To Dani's surprise Tim was rather intrigued with the project models so Jason set him up at a computer to take a virtual walk through Birimbal village.

'When is it going to be ready? It looks so cool, I'd like to live there,' said Tim to Jason, with a pointed glance at his mother. 'Look, Mum, you can ride a bike everywhere and there are little pocket parks all around, as well as the big park. There's a dam and a lagoon and what's this bridge thing?'

'That's a walkway with a viewing platform for people to sit and watch the wildlife on the wetlands around the lagoon and the natural bushland. Birds and wallabies and whatever lives there,' explained Jason. 'Every little neighbourhood is linked by foot and cycle paths with lots of trees and landscaping. Even the animals have their own vegetation pathways between the various stands of bushland so plants and animals aren't displaced.'

'Is that where stormwater is being integrated as well as making some areas more private with the bushland corridors?' asked Dani.

Jason nodded. 'And on the outskirts of each village there are small farmlets. Either for hobby farms or people wanting to sell their produce.'

'Where do the cars go?' asked Tim peering at the houses set back from the roadside with large front gardens.

'The garages are at the back of the homes with alleyways for services,' said Dani. 'I've always thought the idea of having the garage lumped at the front of the house such an eyesore.'

They left Tim playing with the scale model of the village set out on a long glass table in the boardroom as Dani went through a series of sketches she'd made of Isabella's country with Jason.

'I've done Kelly's Crossing – as I've been there. The river, the view from the lookout over the river and valley, plus that beautiful house you renovated, or re-designed, on the river,' said Dani showing him her pen and ink and watercolour roughs. 'Carter says he can take us up to the original home site next Tuesday. Wear strong shoes.'

'These look great, Dani. I'll be there. Maybe Ginny will want to come too. My girlfriend,' he explained. 'She's coming up for a week.'

'I'm sure that'll be fine with Carter,' said Dani, but she was put out as she wanted to have Max and Carter explain the significance of the area and she didn't want it to be a touristy hike.

That night Dani tacked her sketches on the studio walls and studied them. Looking at the landscapes she really felt as if she was sitting by a little creek in the middle of the timbered hills in the lowlands of the valley. It was a place where she felt embraced and protected by the distant high green ridge edging the sky. She felt satisfied as much by the familiar country as the artistic interpretation. She imagined not a lot had changed since Isabella's time. More farmhouses, cleared and fenced land, but the majesty and beauty of the area were still there. She wished she could summon up the ghost of Isabella to talk to her. What had happened to her? What had Garth unearthed?

She hadn't heard from Roddy since their lazy day of lovemaking at the beach. She hoped it was because he was busy with the film project and not because she'd told him her son had moved in with her.

The days were getting longer and so late one afternoon when Tim came out of his room complaining that the computer had crashed again – 'It's the stupid electricity out here' – Dani suggested he go outside and explore.

'Go down to the creek, Barney says there are eels in there.'

'What would I do with them?'

'Kids catch them for fun and let them go. Some people used to eat them in the old days, I think.'

'Yuk. Mum, how come we don't eat stuff like Ma and Helen cook? Roast things, puddings, barbecued fish and sausages.'

'What's wrong with stir fry and the lovely quiches I get from Claude?' asked Dani, stopping what she was doing to stare at him.

'Aw, nothing. But it's restaurant food, like Dad gets.'

'My, you are acclimatising to country home-style cooking,' she remarked. 'Next you'll want a cow so we can milk it for breakfast.'

Tim gave her a disgusted look and wandered out of the house.

It wasn't till Dani realised it was almost dark that she wondered where Tim was and rushed outside calling him. Then she heard a faint 'cooee' echoing from the creek. It didn't sound like Tim. Would he even know how to send a cooee call? She hurried in the fading light and could see figures across the creek in the paddock.

'Tim? Tim? Are you there? Are you all right?'

'Over here, Mum. Come on over. Cross where the rocks are, it's shallow,' shouted Tim.

Relieved, she got to the edge of the stream and peered across to where Tim was standing with a person she couldn't recognise and two horses.

'What are you doing?' she called. 'Wait, I'll take my shoes off.'

'Mind how you go, there are sharp rocks,' came a woman's voice.

The water came to Dani's mid calves, drenching the bottom of the cotton pants which she'd hoisted up her legs, as she made her way gingerly across the creek.

'Mum, this is Kerry. She lives over the hill and these are her horses. Aren't they cool? I've been playing with them.'

Dani reached out to shake hands. The woman was small, wearing trousers, a baggy shirt and a battered straw hat. Her features were hard to see in detail, but she looked to be in her forties, maybe older. 'Ah, my neighbour, how nice to meet you at last.'

She nodded and seemed uncomfortable but Dani realised it was more shyness. 'Er, yes. Are you settled in over there all right? Need anything at all?'

'No, thanks, we're very comfortable.' Dani suddenly remembered the furniture and the vase of flowers. 'I'm very grateful for the furniture, it's lovely. Would you like to come over for a cup of tea sometime?'

'Busy with the farm at present, thanks. Your lad here, he likes the horses. Told him he could give them a carrot or apple. Quiet old things.'

'Can you ride them?' asked Tim.

'Did once. Jumpers. Followed the circuit,' she said and gave the horses a fond look. 'Not any more. Well, best be going.'

'Thanks, Kerry,' said Tim. 'See you round.'

The woman gave a nod and walked away into the near darkness.

Dani noticed she had a limp. 'What a strange woman. Talks in shorthand.'

'She wasn't like that with me, Mum. Told me a lot of stuff. About the horses – Juniper and Bomber – she won cups and ribbons in shows. Wanted to go in the Olympics but had an accident. Can we get carrots and apples for them, please, Mum?'

Dani thought Tim's interest in the horses would fade. But he was down whistling them before school and when he got home. The horses didn't cross the creek but came trotting from the trees at Tim's whistle and soon began to wait for him each sunset.

She told Claude and George of Tim's new passion when she next called by the Nostalgia Cafe to pick up her weekly order of quiche and lemon custard flan.

'Well, darling, he must have riding lessons then,' said George. 'Always comes in handy if you can handle a horse.'

'Don't tell me you ride,' said Dani.

'He certainly does,' said Claude. 'He looks divine in all that sexy polo gear. I watched him play with the social set.'

'I don't think Tim is going to get to the polo stage. Well, not for some time,' said Dani.

'Who owns the horses?' asked George. 'I'd love to ride again. Such beautiful countryside.'

'They live in my neighbour's paddock, think they're retired racehorses out to pasture. I've just met her – Kerry Smith, ever heard of her?' The boys were such gossips and interested in everyone in the district, Dani figured they'd know of her.

'Kerry Smith, I've heard of her 'cause of the horsey thing,' said George immediately. 'Bit of a recluse apparently.

Did a lot of show jumping and married a horse trainer and lived in Sydney. Her husband was killed in some nasty accident. I'm fuzzy on the details. She's related to the original family who own your place and I think they let her live here quietly. Think she went a bit nutty after the whole nightmare.'

'Well, who wouldn't,' added Claude.

'If she's a bit off the planet is Tim safe with her? They seemed to hit it off,' worried Dani.

'She's probably more comfortable with kids than adults. I wouldn't worry about it, darl.'

'It's nice for him to have an outside interest like that,' added Claude.

'Yes, it does keep him away from the computer,' said Dani watching Claude tie up the box with the quiche and flan inside. 'By the way, Tim is complaining I'm feeding him restaurant food. He wants barbecued bangers.'

Claude shuddered. 'Oh no, we have to raise his level of food appreciation above that. Send him round to my kitchen to learn how to cook.'

'Seriously, would he like that?' said George. 'What about a job on Saturdays helping out in a simple way, like peeling some carrots? We'll pay him and it just might get him to understand what good food is all about.'

Such an idea had never occurred to Dani. 'He shows no interest in food at home, other than eating it. But for money . . . who knows? Thank you both for offering. I'll suggest it.'

Dani mentioned Tim's fascination with the two horses to her mother and Lara was immediately enthusiastic.

'Riding lessons, that's the shot. Be good for him, give him an interest of his own instead of tagging along with the others all the time.'

'I can't afford riding lessons!'

'I'll shout him. Goodness, this is the country, not snooty

Centennial Park Stables. Must be any number of people who give lessons. What about the woman who owns the horses? She sounds experienced,' said Lara.

'Mum, she's weird. Gave me the creeps. And I'm not letting Tim on a thoroughbred show jumper. And don't mention it to Tim. I don't want to get his hopes up.'

'Maybe when I move into Cricklewood on Friday I can ask around. Perhaps Tim could stay a night or two with me in town after school.'

'We'll see.' But Dani was tempted. It would be good for Tim to play with schoolmates after school, join a soccer team or whatever. And a night or two to herself would be nice. Roddy flashed into her thoughts. She'd made the introduction to Patricia Catchpole and he'd called Dani to thank her, saying he was going to be busy planning a presentation to the council and he'd see her soon. Dani said that would be nice, but she wasn't that anxious for another date. Just knowing he was around was pleasant but she was enjoying her son and time alone with her painting.

And she was really looking forward to the expedition into the foothills of the valley to find Isabella's original home site. Like her mother, she'd be digging into the past.

10

Mount George, 1846

Isabella

IT WAS MIDDAY AND Isabella was having her lunch served by Mary, a servant so inept Isabella had dismissed her once already. With no other good help available Isabella had been forced to rehire her. The meal was unexpectedly disrupted by the distant sound of livestock.

'What's that noise?' Isabella, clearly annoyed, got up from the table.

'Sounds like sheep.' Mary glanced through the window but could see nothing.

'Come with me, we'd better see what it is.'

Isabella had frequent problems with people moving stock through her property as the main stream crossing in the area was on her land. Several times some of her horses had gone missing. As there'd been no rain for some time, she was in no mood to let travellers take advantage of what grass she was nursing to feed her own cattle.

The two women walked briskly to the top of a small hill behind the house and looked out on a vast spread of cleared grazing country.

'Oh, Miss Kelly, just look at that,' exclaimed Mary.

Isabella folded her arms and scowled. A huge herd of sheep were spread over her property. 'Right,' she snapped. 'I'll get a horse, you put away lunch and get the dogs.'

Over the next hour Isabella and Edward, one of her stockmen, rounded up about six hundred sheep and moved them to her stockyards. As they paused to drink from water bags carried to them by Mary, a young shepherd arrived at the yard.

'Who is your master?' demanded Isabella, making no attempt to disguise her anger.

'These sheep are owned by Mr Rowley over there. Mr Brisbane, his overseer, told me to rest here awhile.'

'Did he indeed. We'll see about that. Now you can help us put the last of them in the yard and then I'll deal with who said what and who owns what.'

Isabella watched as they struggled to round up the last of the herd when a horseman came galloping across the home paddock and headed straight at Isabella, pulling up his horse with a vicious jerk with only a few yards to spare. It looked as though he was going to ride right over Isabella and she stumbled, hampered by her long skirt, but quickly struggled to regain composure.

The horseman, red faced and angry, shook his fist. 'And what are you about, madam?'

'You are Brisbane, the overseer, I take it?' said Isabella coldly. 'These animals are eating my feed. I'm impounding them and charging you two pence a head for their release.'

'Never. These sheep belong to your neighbour and you

have moved them from his land,' protested the overseer who jumped from his horse, barely holding his temper in check.

'That is not so. His land begins on the other side of the gully. The sheep had crossed onto my property. I am within my rights to demand payment for their feed.'

The overseer ignored her, strode to the yard and began pulling down the rails to release the sheep.

'Edward, get those rails up again,' called Isabella.

Her worker began lifting the rails but Brisbane slammed them down once more. The two men argued, and almost came to blows. Mary had edged a short distance away, looking concerned. Isabella hurried into the house and returned with a lock and chain.

'Here, Edward, chain the gate,' said Isabella. At that moment, her neighbour George Rowley, who owned the sheep, rode up demanding to know what was going on with his sheep and his overseer.

'I am impounding your sheep for grazing unlawfully on my land,' shouted Isabella.

'You have no right! Don't be so insufferable, woman. Brisbane, drop those rails,' exploded Rowley.

There was a scuffle between Rowley, Brisbane and Edward and when Isabella stepped in to break up the fighting, she could smell the liquor on Brisbane's breath. Brisbane turned on her, grabbing her by the neck, twisting her and kicking her in the back, eventually knocking her down.

Edward, battered and frightened, fled as Brisbane picked up a rock and threw it at him. The young shepherd took fright and bolted too. Mary began backing away towards the house. Isabella struggled to her feet, shouting at the two men, pulling at Rowley's jacket as he and Brisbane dropped the rails and the frightened sheep began to stream out of the yard.

Brisbane, incensed and furious, lifted his stockwhip and lashed out at Isabella, the handle of the whip striking the side of her face, drawing blood. She turned to run to the house when for good measure Brisbane flicked the whip, hitting her arms and shoulders.

After Brisbane and Rowley left with the sheep, Isabella bathed her face and tried to cool her anger as she examined the red welts around her neck, arms and shoulders. She summoned Mary who stood sullenly in the doorway.

'You saw what happened Mary?'

The girl nodded.

'Do you know where Rowley's shepherd might be?'

'No, ma'am.'

'I am going to swear out an arrest warrant for Brisbane and Rowley and I will require you and Edward to give a deposition about what you saw.'

'Yes, ma'am.'

Since Rowley was also the local magistrate, Isabella had no choice but to travel further out of the district in order to lodge her complaint against her neighbour. It would be several weeks before the case could be heard.

Just before the hearing, as Edward was driving a mob of Isabella's cattle along the public road, the overseer Brisbane rode towards him and pulled him up.

'Ho, you there. You still working for that witch of a woman?'

'I am employed by Miss Kelly,' Edward answered.

'And these be her cattle?' asked Brisbane.

'I am moving them along a public thoroughfare,' replied Edward cautiously.

The overseer gave a strained smile. 'And fine-looking cattle they are too. So, would you care to come and take some refreshment at my home?'

'Thank you, sir, but no. I will keep about my business.' Edward had the feeling Brisbane might want to talk about the forthcoming court case in which he would be giving evidence against the overseer and his employer, Rowley. As Edward turned his horse, Brisbane gave a sharp whistle and short command to his dogs, setting them among Isabella's cattle which, taking fright, bolted, scattering in all directions.

'Well, now, look at that,' said Brisbane with a malicious smirk. 'You should control your cattle better. Miss Kelly won't be pleased with you.'

Isabella travelled alone to the committal hearing and sat in the small courtroom, tightlipped, listening to the evidence. The shepherd had little to say other than he was obeying Brisbane's instructions and had run away when the argument between Brisbane and Edward broke out.

Brisbane testified that when he found Miss Kelly impounding the sheep, he offered to pay generously for any damage they had done but she became abusive and had struck him with a stick. He didn't look at Isabella who was clearly outraged by his blatant lie.

When Isabella took the stand, she was composed and calm, stating that the sheep most definitely had strayed onto her property and she had every right to impound them. Rowley's sheep had been trespassing and destroying her property regularly for several years. She denied that she had struck Brisbane who had been abusive and, she believed, intoxicated. He had beaten her with his stockwhip and Rowley had looked on. No one came to her aid. Here she shot an accusing glance at Mary.

Edward backed up his mistress's story to the point where he'd run away when Brisbane had struck Miss Kelly, after which he saw nothing else.

Rowley admitted he had arrived late on the scene. Under cross-examination he maintained that Isabella Kelly's testimony was unreliable because she'd already been before him several years ago over an outstanding bill, which she refused to pay. Although Isabella rose out of her seat to justify the unpaid bill, she was refused permission to speak.

Mary took the stand, head lowered, avoiding Isabella's eyes. Mary had left Isabella's employ right after the incident with the sheep saying she was getting married. Although this left Isabella short-handed she was glad to see the back of the inept servant. Mary told the magistrate that they had heard sheep and went out and found them coming from across the gully from Mr Rowley's land. She saw Miss Kelly and Edward impound the sheep and when Mr Brisbane arrived he had put his hand gently on Miss Kelly's shoulder and begged her to release the sheep. Miss Kelly struck him. Mary denied emphatically she'd seen any attack on Miss Kelly.

The judge summed up and the jury retired to consider the verdict, emerging swiftly to find the two men, Rowley and Brisbane, guilty of allowing their sheep to stray, but not guilty of attacking Isabella. They were given a three-month sentence and a large fine.

Isabella felt genuinely sorry for Mrs Rowley and over the next few weeks she sent Edward several times to see if she needed any help. Her offers were refused but Mrs Rowley did petition the court for a reduction of her husband's sentence. A month later the court released Rowley. After Brisbane was released from gaol, he married Mary the following month.

These events only cemented the idea in Isabella's mind that she should move from the mountain to her property at the river away from troublesome neighbours who so blatantly lied and cheated her.

Florian and Noona had a second child, a little girl, and were managing her river property very well. Frank, the teenage orphan boy, had become attached to Florian's family. They had, as Isabella instructed, stockpiled a lot of fine cedar which Isabella planned to use to build a home. She would keep the grand house at Mount George in the hope that her dream of establishing a township would come to fruition. Occasionally her thoughts strayed to her guardian's son George Crowder back in London but she never dared write in her letters her desire that one day he would come to New South Wales and establish himself in the valley.

Isabella packed basic goods to take with her in the dray to the temporary river house. She'd sent a message ahead to notify Florian she was coming for an extended visit, and had Edward and another hand round up the best of her cattle on the mountain property to sell through an agent, leaving a small herd behind. The money raised would finance her new home at the river. She was aware that splitting her business between the two properties would be inconvenient, but she saw no other way out of the predicament aggravated by the court case. The staff had been drastically reduced. Mary had not been replaced and Isabella managed without any female help.

After checking out the loaded dray with her two best horses tied behind, Isabella took her writing box filled with important papers from her desk. She was very attached to the beautiful walnut box that her guardian, Sir William Crowder, had given her as a parting gift when she sailed from England. His initials were etched on the sterling silver clasp. She tucked it among her belongings, which included a large box of precious plants wrapped in wet sacking. Ensuring the house was secure, she padlocked the gates and set out on the track to the public trail that would take her thirty-two miles down to her other property close to the main river.

After the thickly timbered country of Mount George with its relatively narrow vistas across the ranges, she was delighted with the change of scene that greeted her on the second day on the creaking dray behind the steady tread of the horses. On a low hill she stopped to admire the sweep of the calm river with the lush flats fringed with narrow stands of silky oaks, eucalypts and paperbarks where her cattle grazed. The scene was idyllic, the glint on the water calming. The openness gave her a sense of freedom. At Mount George, even on good days, she never totally dispelled a nagging feeling of confinement or the sense she was being watched from the trees. She took several deep breaths, smiled with a sense of relief, and release, then urged her horses towards the rustic comfort of her river home.

Florian and Hettie, her loyal servants who'd been sent from Mount George to work at the river, were full of welcoming smiles. Noona hung in the background holding her new baby daughter cradled in a bark coolamon as Kelly, their little boy, ran towards Isabella, interested in all that was going on.

The small and almost primitive homestead cottage had spawned several simple bark shacks nearby since her last visit, and there was now a large bark roofed shelter that served as a communal dining area with a campfire and pit for cooking. Florian and Baldy, a ticket-of-leave employed by Isabella, quickly settled the horses in the rough bush stables and unloaded her belongings.

Hettie smiled to herself as she unloaded Isabella's orchids and some other strange plants. Obviously the mistress was going to put down roots for a while. She was pleased that Isabella's arrival coincided with her preparation of a fresh stew pot, loaded with vegetables from their well-fenced and thriving garden.

In the ensuing weeks Isabella made the best of the simple and spartan domestic facilities on the farm. Any inconvenience was forgotten as she worked on plans for her new home, sometimes discussing the detail with Hettie, who was thrilled at being involved in such an exciting and unexpected development.

She made a trip to Sydney by boat from Port Macquarie to arrange for construction of the home on the river using a bold combination of Sydney-basin sandstone, convict bricks and local cedar. While it wouldn't be on the scale of her Mount George mansion, she wanted it to be a comfortable home.

Life had settled into a smooth routine. Hettie organised the domestic duties and Noona was proving to be an able assistant with the laundry, gardening and other chores. Occasionally Noona prepared bush food she'd caught, roasting a large goanna or a wallaby in a fire pit in the ground covered by green branches. Florian had an Aboriginal stockman to help with the enlarged cattle herd, branding and mustering.

Hettie's new husband, Richard Ball, had been working in Sydney as an apprenticed clerk. When he returned Isabella promptly hired him to handle her paperwork and deal with her agents who she believed cheated her on occasion when she wasn't present at cattle sales.

After some months she set out to return to Mount George. She needed to restock and check on the pastures. She had sent word to Edward of her visit and asked him to go bush and muster her cattle. For the first time in a long while Isabella was feeling cheerful about returning to Mount George. She believed she had control of her destiny. Her dream of becoming a successful landholder, horse and cattle breeder had been achieved. She was still determined, when the time was right, to build a township and ensure her legacy lived on. Isabella Kelly would make her mark and not be forgotten.

There were few to witness a meeting one subsequent chilly night when five men gathered at the house of one of the leading figures in the district. Their evening meal had been most satisfying, the wife of the host had withdrawn and the men settled down to cigars, port and the business at hand. At dawn the men mounted their horses and rode their separate ways, collars turned up against the cold air, hats pulled low. Only cattle standing motionless in the dewy paddocks watched their quiet departure.

When Isabella eventually wove up the track to her mountain property, she had an odd sense of foreboding. There had been a good shower of rain that morning, yet the moisture-enriched bush air she loved to breathe had developed a strangeness, no, a foulness, that made her frown. An odd smell. Something burning? There were no signs of any recent bushfires.

She broke through the thicket with a smile, ready to look down on her magnificent home. But it wasn't there any more. Where her home had stood, the finest in the region, were the blackened remains of the building. Two chimneys stood amid the charred beams, tumbled stones, burned fine furniture, fixtures, chandeliers, clothes, possessions brought from England. All around was untouched. The outbuildings and stockyards were still there, but there were no animals, no movement, no sense of habitation.

She halted the horses and stood in dismay, then collapsed back into the seat of the dray and began to sob, trying to comprehend the nightmarish vision. This was no accident of nature. What cut her most, above the shattering loss, was the immediate knowledge that this had been deliberate destruction. Someone, or some people, hated her enough to destroy her mark upon the land. All that was precious to her. It was a heartless, vindictive, malicious act that almost caused her to faint.

Isabella's sadness at her loss turned to determination that something must be done to find the culprit. Or culprits. In spite of his gaol sentence Rowley was still the resident magistrate and the only person with authority over the local constable to launch an investigation. Rowley refused, taking little interest in Isabella's 'unfortunate accident'.

So Isabella journeyed to Port Macquarie to see the police magistrate. But when she complained about Rowley's inaction, the police magistrate was offhand and not prepared to pursue the matter, which angered Isabella, though it didn't surprise her, knowing that the police magistrate was a friend of Rowley's.

'Then I will find out who is responsible myself,' snapped Isabella.

The aide to the police magistrate shook his head. 'I would not like to be in your shoes, Miss Kelly. The police magistrate is a vindictive man.'

Nevertheless Isabella decided to show them she would not be intimidated or bullied. She would build a small slab cottage at Mount George and live there, in some discomfort, while her home at the river was being constructed. 'I will not be chased from my land,' she promised herself. 'I will show these men I am stronger than they think.'

Lara

Dani and Lara sat on the front verandah of Cricklewood enjoying afternoon tea. There was a faint breeze and the late sunshine caught the cheerful bright red geraniums in the brick boxes on either side of the front steps.

Dani put the blue and white delft china cup in the saucer beside the plate of lemon drop cakes Kristian Clerk had left for them. 'If I had the talent of Margaret Olley I'd put the cup and the biscuits by those geraniums and paint it. I love how she paints what's around her. So, do you feel settled in?'

'I didn't have much to unpack. Kristian left everything so orderly. But it does feel . . . nostalgic. I used to sit out here with Nana and Poppy. Nana would put her feet up on the wicker chaise, tea things on a tray with doilies. All that's missing is the occasional steam train,' said Lara.

'Where are you going to start with the great family search?' asked Dani. 'I mean, what are you trying to find out?'

'I wish I'd talked more with my grandparents about the family's past,' sighed Lara, avoiding the last question. 'And my mother. I wish she'd kept a diary. It'd make everything so much easier.'

'You can talk! You don't keep a diary either. I keep sketches, I suppose that's something,' said Dani. 'I've got notebooks filled with drawings of places I've been, people I've spotted on a bus or something. It's hard to paint from memory without a reference. Anyway, you haven't gone through all those old letters. You don't know what you'll find there.'

'That's where I'm starting. Plus, going to the historical society. When he was young Henry knew my grandfather, it's a link. What about you and Isabella? How's that coming along?'

'Carter has come good on his offer to take me and Max out to where she first settled. I want to see the views she saw, walk over the land she walked.'

'Is that where the Birimbal development is going to be?'

'Partly. They haven't done much work on the hilly part where she planned Georgetown. They've started on the land closer to the river. Apparently some of her original land, where the home was, is owned by a company.'

'Are you taking photographs? I'd like to see it. Sounds too much of a hike for me,' said Lara.

'Yes, but I'll also sketch it. I'm not painting realistic

imagery, otherwise a photo would do.' Dani gathered up the tea things. 'Well, Mum, I'd better go and get Tim, school will be out. I hope he's settling in okay.'

'It's only been two weeks, don't fret, he'll be fine,' said Lara.

'You always put a positive spin on things. He was fine the first few days but the reality has hit. He's moody and miserable,' said Dani.

'He's got friends – Toby, Tabatha, Len, aren't they looking out for him?'

'They're not all in the same class. And being out at The Vale he's feeling isolated. Though Toby and Tab are coming to spend the weekend as Angela and Tony are going to a wedding somewhere.'

Lara changed the subject. 'So how's the movie coming along? And the Roddy relationship?'

'Nothing to report on Roddy. He's nice, Mum, but he's busy, this movie thing seems to be taking off. He won Patricia over and she had him address the council and they're all for it.'

'Why wouldn't they be?' said Lara.

'It's not that simple, Roddy wants them to put in some money. Help with building the infrastructure and in return they get to keep it as a permanent tourist attraction.'

'Good idea. He's quite the wheeler-dealer. He'll be a good executive producer,' said Lara dryly.

Dani went indoors. The house needed a few skylights, she decided, it was too dark, too many doors. Lara had explained each room could be closed off for warmth. There was a smell she couldn't put her finger on, an old smell. Floor wax, wood smoke, it wasn't unpleasant, but unlike The Vale, which didn't feel lived in, Cricklewood was crammed with past lives and memories. Especially for Lara. Dani hoped her mother would be all right here alone. Maybe Tim should stay with her mother during the week and be closer to school friends. She didn't dare raise that with him just yet.

When her daughter had driven off to collect her son and return home, Lara made yet another walk through the garden of Cricklewood, hosing the flowers and small vegie patch, remembering the perfume of the orange trees. She ate dinner at the kitchen table, listening to the radio, then went along the hallway to the lounge where lamplight glowed through the frosted glass doors. As her fingers closed around the metal door handle it felt just the same as it had from the time she could reach it.

The room was softly lit and cosy. She decided against turning on the television – how out of place it looked in the still old-fashioned room – and pulled up the coffee table in front of the lounge where she'd stacked the boxes and folders of letters and photographs she'd brought from Sydney. Where to begin?

The first box she opened was full of photographs, some loose, some in envelopes, many in albums. Photographs of people, places, events. Men with rolled up sleeves in front of a tractor, a dray, a 1930s' car. Formal functions, parties and weddings, and casual pictures taken for no apparent special reason. Yet these casual shots were intriguing – someone having a haircut in the garden, a sheet over their shoulders, a smiling woman waving scissors. Kids at the beach, in a rowboat on a river. A baby in a white cane pram; a haul of watermelons from the garden; a pet dog and girl, whose hair was styled like Joan Crawford, posing with a cumbersome 1940s' bicycle. Lara hoped she would be able to put names and stories to them eventually.

At the bottom of a box of letters she found a small parcel wrapped in brown paper and tied with string. She unwrapped it to reveal an old leather belt with a tarnished metal buckle featuring the words 'Gott Mit Uns' embossed over a crown. Had her grandfather taken this from a dead

German soldier as he groped around in the dark slush of no-man's-land? Thinking of all that suffering she pulled a letter from an envelope on Buckingham Palace letterhead and read:

The Queen and I wish you God-speed, and a safe return to your homes and dear ones.

A grateful Mother Country is proud of your splen-did services characterised by unsurpassed devotion and courage.

George R.I.

Was it all worth it? Lara wondered.

And then she came across a photo of her grandparents, sitting in the same room, on either side of the fireplace. A bit posed perhaps but just as she always remembered them. Nana with her knitting, Poppy with the newspaper, logs burning brightly in the fire. She glanced at the fireplace where an electric heater now stood on the whitewashed bricks. If she lived here she'd put an old grate back and burn wood. It was a double fireplace, its chimney shared with the kitchen where the wood-burning stove had been. She'd put an Aga range in there and the electric stove in another part of the kitchen.

Lara chided herself. Ridiculous, she was only housesitting for a month or so, she shouldn't feel so pro-prietary. She began to read the letters at random.

Had she fallen asleep? Was that a clock chiming some-where in the house? Lara stirred and lifted her head from the back of the sofa. It sounded just like her grandmother's clock on the mantelpiece above the fire. Except it was no longer there. A letter slid off her lap. Lara bent to retrieve it. She knew it was late. As her hands touched the blue aerogram, she froze, overcome with the feeling someone else was in the room.

She leapt to her feet. The French doors onto the front verandah were closed. She knew she'd shut up the house after dinner. As she stared at the glass doors she remembered her grandmother had lace curtains fitted to them. It seemed everywhere she turned in this house she found a memory. But as her heartbeat began to steady something in the dark to the side of the hall door caught her attention.

The figure of a man was watching her. Before she could move or make a sound, she took in everything about him with the speed of a camera shutter. Then he was gone. Lara expelled her breath, unaware she'd been holding it. Had she really seen him, had someone been there? Who was he?

'I am not seeing ghosts,' she said aloud, firmly, but hurried from the room, shutting the doors to the hallway, leaving the lights on. In the kitchen she poured herself a glass of red wine and sat at the table. She was strangely calm. Whoever he was he was a benevolent spirit, she decided. She closed her eyes and recalled the image impressed in her mind from that one instant. Young, early twenties. Fair haired, light hazel eyes, slight build. He was half smiling. A gentle face. He looked . . . nice. He was wearing khaki, a military uniform of some kind.

Lara got up. Kristian's cuckoo clock pointed to five past two. That wasn't the clock she'd heard chime. Lara rubbed her eyes feeling utterly exhausted. She went straight to bed in the guest room, the room her mother and her sister Mollie had shared as kids, and fell fully clothed into bed, pulling the cover over her, leaving the bedside light on and her book untouched.

When she awoke she knew she'd slept without moving, and felt stiff and ravenous. Sun streamed into the room, she heard a rooster crowing down the road, there was dew on the grass. No need to go to the dunny down the back garden now there was inside plumbing. All that was missing from the familiar childhood mornings was the smell of toast.

Dani rang to see what her plans were for the day. 'How'd you sleep in the old house?'

'Like a log. I fell asleep in the lounge room. Woke up and saw a ghost,' said Lara cheerfully.

'What!' shrieked Dani. 'Who? Not your grandparents?'

'Some bloke. A soldier. No idea who he was. Don't think he belongs here. I'm tucking in to bacon and eggs and after I'm cleaned up I'll get a few more groceries and go to the historical society.'

'You seem very calm,' said Dani. 'I'd be packing and moving out. You can come here, Mum.'

'Nonsense, it's fine. Over-active imagination from reading letters and looking at photos.'

'Call me if it happens again. Middle of the night, whenever. I'll come and get you,' said Dani firmly.

Henry greeted Lara warmly. 'You picked the right day to visit our museum. All the troops are here. Tuesdays and Thursdays.' He introduced Lara to the group working in the backroom and archives.

'Ah, your daughter was in here a few weeks back. Mentioned you might be doing some family research. The Williamses, right?' A smiling grey-haired woman leant across the littered table to shake Lara's hand. 'I'm Ellen Brooker.'

'Yes, did you know them? Are you a local?' She looked to be Henry's age so it was possible, surmised Lara.

'No. I'm a recent arrival. Haven't come across them in my filing.' She indicated the piles of folders.

'Don't think we have your gang in here,' said Henry. 'I'd remember if the old fellow had brought in something.'

'My grandfather served in the First World War with a lot of blokes from the Newcastle area. He came up here after he married. He proposed to my grandmother when he was on leave in England just before being shipped back to Oz,' said Lara.

'Are you going to look at all the family, like the kids they brought up here, back in your mother's day?' asked another of the men at the table sorting through files.

'Yes, I'm trying to fill in a few gaps in recent history,' said Lara easily. 'Who knows, I hear you can get hooked on this genealogy stuff. I might end up going back centuries.'

'Many do, many do,' said Henry. 'Can I treat you to a cappuccino across the road?'

Settled with their coffee in a quiet corner of the cafe Henry looked puzzled. 'I'm intrigued that Harold served in the Great War and apparently never acknowledged it publicly. Must have taken a toll on him, post-traumatic stress thing. There are some very moving stories in letters in the museum. Stuff the blokes wrote, or their loved ones left behind.'

'I don't think there was any scandal, that he was ashamed or that he did anything wrong,' said Lara quickly. 'I think he just got on with things, put the war behind him.'

'He was a decent man all right. Everybody liked Harold. Your grandmother, she was a bit more . . . conservative. Don't think I ever said more than "Good morning, Mrs Williams" to her.' He stirred his coffee. 'Odd that, how he put the war behind him. So many of them had bad memories, guess they didn't feel there was anything to celebrate.'

Lara was thoughtful, remembering the many walks with her grandfather when he'd tell her stories about all sorts of little incidents in his life from boyhood days in North West London to settling down as a married man in the valley. 'He used to tell me amusing anecdotes about the war, not often, mind you, about escapades with his mates and the like. He never mentioned bad times.' Lara opened her shoulder bag and found an old brown envelope. From it she extracted a postcard. 'I found this yesterday among the old family papers.'

Henry took the postcard. It featured in colour the flags of Britain and her European allies in the war, and the words 'To MY Boy Who is doing HIS DUTY to His King, Country and to us AT HOME.' On the back was a brief message congratulating him on his twenty-first birthday.

'Touching stuff,' said Henry and handed it back.

Lara gave him a one-page letter, yellow with age, and a little torn around the edges. 'So is this. I cried after reading it.'

The letter was from her great-grandfather to his son written in November 1915.

Dear Harold,
Just a few lines as I see by your last letter that you are likely to be sailing in a few days. I hope that you will be happy and that you have a good voyage wherever you go. Always do the best you can and be obeying the officers at the same time look after yourself. Let us know whenever you can where you are and don't spend your money foolishly because it will be handy to you when you get back.

Next week will be Christmas so I must wish you a Merry Christmas and Happy New Year and if I don't hear from you before you go I wish you good luck and a safe return. Goodbye and God bless you.

Your affectionate Father.

Henry put the letter on the table and gave a nod of understanding. 'Where did his unit end up?'

'In Flanders on the Western Front. He was with the 56th Battalion. I found his discharge papers. Did a lot of work as a stretcher bearer apparently.'

'Flanders, eh? He would have had a rough time.'

*

288

Péronne, 1917

Harold

It was the silence that got to him. After so much noise.

He'd never forget the first time he went into the trenches in France and experienced shellfire: the splintering of the duckboards and trench breastworks, the exploding shells that almost concussed them with sound, sending them numb, the smell of explosives and death. He'd had to climb through the shattered trench littered with the bodies of the men of his brave battalion who'd been waiting for zero hour to go over the top at six pm, only to be hit by heavy bursts from the deadly German 5.9s. The men had fought through the night to establish a defensive line where they'd been told there was a German support trench. It didn't exist and bungled information from above, along with no backup from the Tommies, had seen countless die consolidating no more than a ditch.

Harold hated fighting. But not one to shirk his duty he had enlisted in the medical unit and was proud of the red cross emblazoned on his uniform sleeve. He was serving as a stretcher bearer with Scooter Munro, a raw-boned, big bush lad from inland wheat country. Harold and the football-mad Scooter had formed a bond, forged in the gut-wrenching work of retrieving the wounded, dragging back the dead.

In the pre dawn, sudden silence, the field fell quiet as if both sides were exhausted. The dead were hard to look at but through the day it had been harder to watch the wounded attempting to drag themselves back towards the parapets and being picked off by snipers. Some were left to wait in the thirsty sun with flies crawling in wounds, minds tormented. An Australian officer and an NCO had crossed under a white flag and asked a German officer for permission to bring them in. The answer from the rear command had been no.

With nightfall the stretcher bearers had gone out to recover the wounded, guided by calls and moans. Now fog, dust and smoke shrouded no-man's-land between them and the Germans who were well dug in and familiar with the landscape dividing them. Ghostly images of crumpled bodies scattered in the mud began to filter through the haze. The haunted faces around Harold showed the ordeal they'd been through.

And then came a cry for a stretcher bearer: 'Over here, over here, New South Wales! Stretcher bearer!'

Harold and Scooter leapt up, despite their exhaustion, and climbed onto the fire-step of the trench for a squint over the parapet across the dark and battered landscape.

'We missed one, Scooter.' Harold bent down and grabbed a stretcher.

'Heard that before, mate. We'd better be quick and get back before first light and the fog goes.'

Following the calls, they soon found a wounded soldier squirming slowly over the soaking, pitted ground, his badly injured comrade slung across his shoulders.

'Get me cobber in, he's bad.'

As they lifted the man's cobber from his back and laid him on the stretcher, Scooter urged the wounded soldier to climb aboard. 'Me and Harold here, we'll get you both in.'

'Too cramped. He's got a bad hit in the gut. Take him, I'll make me own way.' Determinedly he began to crawl, dragging his bloodied, splintered leg.

'We'll come back for you, it'll be quicker than carrying two,' said Scooter. Bent low they scrambled back to the trench where willing hands were waiting to take the unconscious soldier.

'Another stretcher,' demanded Harold. 'Got to get his mate now.'

They had almost reached the wounded man when a breath of wind lifted the veil of mist and a German sniper opened fire on them.

'To your left, man. A shell hole,' shouted Harold.

He rolled out of sight and for a while there was an eerie silence. Then to Harold's relief they heard a burst of coughing and spitting followed by a throaty, 'Toss me some water, matey.'

They threw a water bottle into the hole and ducked low as more shots came from the German trenches. The sky became lighter.

It hurt Harold but he had to shout, 'Hang on, mate, we'll be back tonight. Too risky to try to carry you out now.'

Scooter led the belly-down retreat through the mud as he and Harold headed to the safety of the trench.

During that long day between bouts of shelling they'd hear the digger whistling to himself to let them know he was still alive and to keep up his spirit. That night as soon as it was considered reasonably safe to go over the top, Harold and Scooter crawled to him.

As they loaded him onto the stretcher, he grabbed Harold's wrist and said weakly, 'Tell me mum I did all right. Don't let me cobbers forget me, eh?' And he began to whistle softly a tune that had become popular among the troops – 'Mademoiselle from Armentières'. As they lowered him into the trench the whistle slowly faded with his last breath.

It was a tune Harold never forgot. After the war he found himself whistling the same notes in times of sadness, stress or when, unbidden, moments and fragments of the war came back to him as vividly as yesterday.

Harold never talked of what he'd seen. Of popping eyes staring out from blackened frightened faces, the caked mud and blood like a second skin, boots tramping over faces of dead comrades, bodies alive but beyond repair, the demented cries for a mother, the confusion, the waste of men, the dispirited and the pitiful. Gone was the gaiety, the buoyed confidence of brothers in arms.

Instead he talked to family and close friends of the mateship, the pride they took in their unit which bonded them one to another. The self pride, the camaraderie, sportsmanship and the knowledge they felt they were fighting for their country – Australia – just as much as if they'd been in trenches around Sydney. And he talked of the humour.

Lara

Lara smiled as she recalled funny anecdotes of the 'inno-cents abroad' recounted by her grandfather. It suddenly occurred to her she knew more about her grandfather's war than her mother's war years.

'So you would've known my mother then?' she said to Henry.

'Not really, I was a good ten years younger than her. I remember seeing her and Mollie around, they were pretty girls.' He stirred his cup, 'There are people around from those days, it might be worth talking to them. If you really want to scratch old scars.'

'Really? Like who?' Lara reached in her bag for a note-book as Henry began to reel off names of old families and schoolfriends from her mother's and grandparents' day.

'Don't you have any family relations left round these parts?' asked Henry curiously. 'Your Aunt Mollie lived overseas and your mum married a soldier, didn't she? One of the local lads?'

'What do you know about her marriage?' asked Lara.

'Nothing, I was not much more than a kid. I was more interested in hanging round the army camp out of Cedartown. Used to cycle out there to see the boys from town, cadge a ride on a motorbike, watch them do field exercises in the paddocks. Was a bit of a lark. So where'd your father serve?'

'Ah, that's a tricky question. I'm not sure.' Lara hesitated and in a sudden impulse decided to confide in Henry.

'Mum married during the war, a year before the war ended, but the marriage didn't work out, and the only father I ever knew was my stepfather Charlie Jenkins. Sadly he was killed when I was ten. Frankly all I know about my birth father is his name.'

'I knew the Jenkins family. The town was shocked when Charlie died. So you want to know more? After all this time?' Henry raised an eyebrow.

'I think I do. I suppose it's at the core of this search I'm embarking on.'

'What's his name? Is he still alive? He might still be around.'

'No idea. From my mother's refusal to discuss him, I don't think it was a friendly parting. The name of my father on my birth certificate is Clem Wallace Richards. Mum always used the name Jenkins.'

'Sure to be someone around who might remember him, or the family. Sort of rings a bell,' said Henry glancing at his watch. 'I have to get going, a family are bringing in some memorabilia for the museum. It's always a bit hard for them, parting with family stuff.'

'I'll come over with you. I haven't had a chance to go through the museum properly,' said Lara.

'Ah, you need a week to do that,' said Henry.

Henry was right, decided Lara. So many stories in there, so much that was familiar, interesting, and sad. How times had changed. But it was the women's stories that captivated her. How hard they'd worked, often in very simple, indeed, primitive conditions, yet they'd held the family together, made attempts to make their humble homes cosy and comfortable even if it was only gum tips in a jar on the rough timber table, a newspaper cut into a frill to line a shelf, a struggling garden.

She poked her head into the busy staff area of the historical society. 'Thanks, Henry, I'm a bit overwhelmed. I'll come back another day. Nice to meet you all.' She gave a wave and headed out the back door.

'Good luck with your family search. I'll put out the word re the Richards family.'

'Thanks, Henry. Bye.'

Back at Cricklewood Lara settled in a bentwood rocking chair on the front verandah with a pot of tea, a sandwich, a pile of family letters and assorted newspaper clippings. She spread the clippings across a card table she had put up beside the chair and was startled by the first to catch her eye. It was a page from a magazine called *Aussie* and it carried a 1918 date line. In one column was a poem, by Anonymous, titled 'Stretcher Bearers'.

'My God, what an extraordinary coincidence,' she said aloud to herself, then read:

Stretcher Bearers Stretcher Bearers!
Seeking in the rain
Out among the flying death
For those who lie in pain,
Bringing in the wounded men
Then out to seek again.

Out amongst the tangled wire
(Where they thickest fell)
Snatching back the threads of life

From out the jaws of hell;
Out amongst machine-gun sweep
And the blast of shatt'ring shell.

For you no mad, exciting charge,
No swift, exultant flight,
But just an endless plodding on
Through the shuddering night;
Making 'neath a star-shell's gleam
Where ere a face shines white.

Stretcher Bearers! Stretcher Bearers!
To you all praise be due,
Who ne'er shirked the issue yet
When there was work to do.
We who've seen and know your worth
All touch our hats to you.

How she wished she'd asked her grandfather more
questions. Perhaps in his last lonely years after Emily died
he might have shared some of the pain. She recalled him
finally joining the Cedartown Services Club – which surprised her as he'd never set foot inside in all the previous
years. He'd modestly produced his demobilisation papers
to 'prove' he'd served. And each Friday he popped in for a
hot lunch and a yarn with the locals.

Wrapped in tissue paper was a gold medallion presented
to Harold Williams in 1919 by the Horseshoe Bend Ladies
Welcome Home Committee. The words 'Welcome Home'
were inscribed in a horseshoe under a royal crown. The
newspaper report he'd kept noted that the medallion was
presented to fourteen returned servicemen on the night by
the mayor, Major Cracknell. The major was quoted: 'All
they thought of was to do their duty for their country and
the Empire, and that they did.' Lara almost smiled at the

major's final comment, in which he conceded that some of them 'might not be in the same state of health as when they went away'.

There was one photo that brought back a vivid memory for Lara. It showed her grandfather marching in the one and only Anzac Day march he ever attended. It was in 1966 in Sydney and Elizabeth and Lara had gone to watch. How he'd chuckled at the resulting photo and asked Lara what was so surprising about it.

'That you're all in step after all those years,' she'd laughed.

That had been a wonderful visit with him. She'd started working and they'd had a special day out in the city together. She sighed as she put the photo to one side and started to read the letters.

At four o'clock Dani and Tim appeared. Lara quickly put the letters back in the box.

'Hi, Ma, what are you reading?' Tim bounded up the front steps.

'Oh, lots of old family letters. Some from your great-great-grandparents. Written right here in this house.' She returned his hug.

'We've registered for the local soccer team,' said Dani, giving her mother a look that said this was a positive step.

'Fantastic. What else have you been up to?'

'Oh, the usual school stuff. It's different.' Tim gave a small shrug and didn't look too impressed.

'Can I get some eggs, Mum?' Lara nodded and, as Dani headed down to the garden, Tim squeezed into the chair beside his grandmother.

'Ma, you know what? There's horses across the creek at The Vale. I really like them.'

'Horses? How wonderful.'

'Ma . . .'

'Yes, sweetie?'

'Do you think I could have riding lessons? Then maybe I could ride round the paddocks. Tabatha can ride.'

Lara had been waiting for this opportunity to give Tim an interest that would help settle him into this new environment and make life very different from what he'd had back in Sydney.

'You bet. But we'll have to check with your mother, and you can't just jump on a horse you don't know. I'd love you to have proper lessons. There must be someone here giving lessons. I'll look into it.' Lara paused.

'Thanks, Ma. You're just the best.' He planted a kiss on her cheek and they hugged each other.

'Thanks, Timmy. I love kisses and hugs like that.' Lara knew boys Tim's age were not always demonstrative. 'Now there's something else. We're all up here for a while doing our own thing and I reckon it would be good for you, for your mum and especially for me, if you stayed a couple of nights each week here with me at Cricklewood. You'd be in town away from that bush cabin your mother loves, it'd give you a chance to see your school friends and do things, like riding lessons.' She reached out and took the boy's hand. 'Well?'

Tim seemed relieved and grasped at the straw his grandmother offered. 'Cool, Ma. If I stayed here in the week I could go to extra footy practice, and I was thinking of joining the band, and stuff. But it's all after school and that's hard for Mum to come in and get me when it's late.' He went on in a rush, 'I can spend some time with Toby and Tab . . . and I can see Mum on weekends . . .' Suddenly it seemed to be Tim's idea and he was trying to persuade Lara.

She stifled a smile. 'Gee whiz, Tim . . . that's an interesting idea. I'd love to have some company during the week . . . and your mum is so into her painting she might like a bit of freedom from her usual routine.'

They squeezed hands in agreement.

'Ma, it's hard here. I miss my friends back home. We email but . . .'

'But there're other things, different things,' suggested Lara quietly.

'Yeah. So I might as well do things like horse riding,' he chuckled.

'Okay. You're on. A few formal lessons before you hit the paddocks with Tab.'

Dani came back with a carton of eggs and some spinach, and gathered up her bag. 'Righto, let's hit the road.'

Tim got up, looking a little smug. 'Me and Ma have worked out something. Is it okay if I stay a couple of nights a week here with her? I have stuff at school . . . and . . . I'm starting riding lessons.'

Dani gave her mother a surprised look, how did she work all this out in ten minutes? 'Wow! What's brought this on? You have two homes here . . . your town house and your country house . . . you can come and go so long as school work doesn't suffer.'

'We have to sort out the riding lessons if you approve. Tim says he's made friends with horses across the creek at The Vale,' said Lara.

'Kerry's horses. She lives over the creek. I told you about her. Well, let's head off. We'll talk about this more shall we, Tim?' Dani threw her mother a relieved look. 'Horse riding, now, that's something different. Wait till you tell Tab and Toby. And Justin down in Sydney.'

A few days later and feeling very settled, Lara set out before breakfast for an energetic walk down the road, over the bridge across Cedar Creek, up past the old timber mill that now made mainly plywood and veneers, then through a stand of old gum trees to relatively new streets filled with comfortable homes. It was an area that had been only bush when she'd walked here so often with Poppy.

Mid morning she was ready to do some shopping, and to see if Henry was at the museum and show him the stretcher bearer poem. She opened the mail box at the gate and took out some letters for the Clerks. There was an envelope addressed to her with no stamp, just Lara's name on the front. An invitation someone had dropped in perhaps, she thought, as she opened it. She unfolded the single page and was surprised to see it carried only one short sentence in bold letters.

'What the hell does this mean?' gasped Lara, and read again . . .

Don't go digging up the past . . . it could lead to something very unpleasant. Be content with what you know, and what you have.

Suddenly the morning was no longer bright and sunny.

11

Dani

EVEN THOUGH THEY'D ARRANGED to start their bushwalk at eight in the morning, it was already very warm and Dani knew it was going to be a stinker of a day. Carter had urged everyone to be on time at the rendezvous point, but running late and the last to arrive in a rush was Jason and his girlfriend in her new sportscar. Dani was instantly irritated by Genevieve, 'Do call me Ginny if you wish', who had brought along her white Maltese terrier. Dani recalled Jason dogsitting the small, curly-haired dog with hair falling over its eyes and a mincing trot.

'Is that thing going to last the distance?' asked Carter, eyeing the dog. 'It's a fair hike. Be a good breakfast for a snake.'

'What! Snakes? We're not going to see a snake are

we?' Ginny sounded faintly accusing, as if this was a detail overlooked by Jason.

'Hopefully you'll see it before it sees you. It *is* the bloody bush,' said Carter.

'A snake will take off before we get near it,' said Max gently. 'It'll feel the vibrations. Most aren't really aggressive. Stay in the middle of the group.'

'We're in their territory. Out of your comfort zone, I assume,' said Carter with a slight smile.

'As you'd be in mine, I suppose,' retorted Ginny with undisguised sarcasm.

Dani could see Carter was not swayed by Ginny's sleek blonde looks, and she in turn was not intimidated by the older man with the strong personality who was in charge for the day. She quickly realised Ginny was shrewd and smart. From what Jason had mentioned, Ginny had a successful modelling career, travelled a lot and, by the understated couture label and the discreet classy jewellery, must earn considerable money. Or she came from a moneyed background. It was subtle: the educated voice, the soft and natural make-up that took effort to achieve, the loose fall of beautiful hair aided by the scissors of a master hair stylist.

By contrast, Dani had become so absorbed in her new life in the valley that each morning she twisted her hair into a knot and usually threw on un-ironed clothes for whatever she was doing in the studio. Her hands hadn't seen a manicure in months.

'Don't worry about Sugar, we can sling her in the backpack if the going gets too rough,' said Jason.

'Fortunately it's not a national park, so the dog really isn't a problem,' added Max, giving the dog a quick pat to help ease the tension.

They each carried water and Dani had asked the boys at the Nostalgia Cafe to make interesting sandwiches and snacks for their lunch, which Carter insisted on carrying in his large backpack. Dani had a sketchpad and camera in hers. As did Max. She assumed Jason was interested in the history of the land he was developing but Ginny was just having a novel day out, she surmised. At least she had a hat and sensible shoes. Designer trainers, of course.

They set out from the picnic reserve at the edge of the river where they'd left the cars and crossed over the low stone causeway. Within minutes they were climbing uphill into lightly timbered country. They walked single file with Carter in the lead wearing shorts, hiking boots, a battered army hat and a shirt with the National Parks and Wildlife emblem. Max was at the rear, moving gently like a silent shadow, glancing around the bush and sometimes pausing briefly to look up into the tree tops. There were a few comments exchanged but as the way became steeper they all concentrated on following where Carter led, as there was no real track. He'd been through here before so knew where to point out some natural features.

'Look at that stump. Huge bloody Australian red cedar, must've yielded a hell of a lot of timber for the old-time cabinet makers,' said Carter.

'How long ago would it have been logged?' asked Jason.

'A hundred years ago, I reckon. And it would have been hundreds of years old,' said Carter, running his hand over the wide flat top of the stump. 'They would have used a big cross-cut saw and a lot of muscle to get it down.'

'A slice of timber that big would make a great top for a dining table,' commented Jason. 'Be hard to get anything like it today.'

Dani took off her backpack and got out her camera. 'I want a picture of that stump, it's like . . . well, a memorial, I suppose, to a lost era. Go ahead, I'll catch up,' she added as the others began to move on.

'I'll wait for you if they get too far ahead,' said Max

who could understand why she wanted a picture of the old weathered stump with its partly exposed labyrinthine root system hinting at the strength and power that had once anchored a mighty tree through decades of storms.

While Dani was absorbed in trying to capture the play of light and shadow there was a gust of wind, a rustle of grass, and she turned, curious. With the camera to her eye, she instinctively pressed the shutter. In the undergrowth of grass and scrubby small saplings, there was a creature – yellow eyes, stripes, a flash of a small head and a long tail. Dani snapped again and then it was gone. She lowered the camera, wondering if she'd really seen the same creature a second time, or was it an illusion of the dappled light? Then she heard the crack of a twig and movement as it raced away from her.

Dani felt shaky. She knew it was no common creature and she remembered the strange dog-like animal she'd glimpsed on the road when she'd driven into the valley and met Roddy. Possibly not far from here. Had she captured a picture of the phantom beast?

'Come on, Dani,' Max had walked back to get her. 'The others are pushing on. We have a long way to go.'

'Yes. Yes, I just got carried away.' She hurried to Max.

'What happened? You look like you've seen a ghost.' But the softly spoken Aboriginal artist wasn't joking. He studied her face. 'Well . . .?'

'Max . . . when I first came up here and drove into this valley, I saw an animal . . . like nothing I've ever seen. Of course, no one believed me, made all kinds of suggestions and jokes, so I shut up. But I'm pretty sure I just saw the same . . . thing.'

Max gave a nod of understanding. 'I've heard stories . . .'

'And what do they say?' asked Dani as they walked to join the others.

303

'Depends on who is talking. Some will say that it's a feral born of wild dogs and whiteman's animals, a mutant, a genetic freak. Or that it's the guardian of its spiritual country, created from the Dreamtime. Take your pick.'

'I'll opt for the Dreamtime wanderer,' said Dani with a little smile. 'My imagination must be running wild.'

'I would suggest you keep it to yourself. These kind of stories have a way of getting out of hand, bringing in media, hunters, who knows,' said Max. 'This is private land, part of which will be homes to families. The idea there is a wild creature roaming, mythical or not, could be a problem.'

'Max, I might have a photo of it!' How could she not have checked? Stopping, she held the camera to view the digital images.

It was there. Half hidden, shot at an angle, but no mistaking the shape of its head, haunches and long tail. Branches obscured its body so it was hard to judge its width. The stripes could have been shadows, but it was similar to the animal Dani had seen on the road. She flipped to the second picture but the animal was not in the frame.

'Could it be the same one I saw a while back or another one?' she wondered.

'Something tells me it's the same one, the area you describe is close to here.' Max handed the camera back to Dani after studying the picture. 'You could sell that for a lot of money. You could put Jason's development on the map. But Dani, I sense it would bring trouble. There is something bad, evil, connected to it.'

Dani stared at him. There was concern in his dark eyes. It troubled her. 'What should I do?' she asked in a small voice.

'I say erase it. Say nothing. But remember it – and paint it.'

Max was right, this could fetch money, notoriety, publicity for Jason's whole development. And suddenly Dani could see where that could lead. She looked around her at the hillside of trees and in the distance the ranges and gullies and unseen pastures where villages would flourish among the natural bushland and landscaping. It was so peaceful.

Dani glanced down at the image. She almost imagined she could see something in that glint of a yellow eye. Her thumb hovered over the button where a message box flashed. 'Erase?'.

They soon caught up with the others who had stopped for a drink, a breather, and to admire the view from the crest of the hill. Sugar was comfortably ensconced in Jason's backpack, head and front paws poking out, looking smug.

'I don't imagine this view has changed much since Isabella's day,' said Jason.

'She wouldn't have cleared so much land,' said Max looking at the expanse of pasture dotted with stands of trees.

'It's so orderly, look at the lines of trees, kind of like spokes of a wheel,' said Ginny with a wave of both arms.

'That's stage-one village. Those will be tree-lined streets. We left as many trees as we could, then landscaped and planted more,' said Jason with pride. 'Now the masterplan has got the nod, we're just waiting for the green light on detailed design drawings and then development approval from the council.'

'God, who'd want to live in the middle of this wilderness,' said Ginny. 'I thought you said it was linked to towns. I rather expected to see . . . well, some civilisation.'

There was a chuckle around the group and Jason reassured her. 'It's not remote. Some people just want a modest rural setting for their future home, and look how beautiful it is. There will be everything you need right down there eventually.'

'And over that rise is Riverwood,' added Max.

'Where we had lunch at that Nostalgia place?' said Ginny, 'That's not a town.'

'Well, there's no shopping mall, that's for sure,' said Carter with a grin.

'I don't go to malls,' said Ginny coldly.

'No, you go to Europe,' said Jason giving her a peck on the cheek.

As everyone grinned Carter winked at Jason. 'Reckon you'd better get into the Sydney property market.'

'Done that. Where're we having lunch?' said Jason, adjusting the dog in the backpack.

'I could murder one of Claude's sangers,' said Dani lightly, trying to ease the tension. She wondered what Ginny thought of the food at the Nostalgia Cafe. She seemed hard to please.

They stopped for morning tea in a shady clearing beneath some trees. Carter kicked a log to make sure there was nothing inside, then, with a flourish, pretended to dust it off for Ginny. She ignored the gesture and sat on the grass, her legs folded.

'What's left of Isabella's property?' asked Dani.

'Not much, as you'll see. I've only just been able to identify the location through some old survey papers National Parks found. They show existing properties in the 1840s and '50s,' said Carter.

'There weren't many of them back then,' said Jason. 'The settlers had to rely a lot on neighbours, help each other as much as possible. No roads, just a public track which could be miles from their home.' He glanced at Ginny hoping she wasn't going to make some comment about the area still appearing isolated.

'True enough,' said Carter, 'And that was the cross Isabella had to bear. Most of her neighbours became her enemies.'

'Seriously? Was she that bad a person?' said Dani.

'She was successful and that pissed the men off,' explained Carter while passing the cake. 'Must have been a tough old bird.'

Dani turned to Max who'd been silent, sipping his mug of coffee from the big Thermos. 'What do you think, Max?'

'By all accounts she had problems from the start. Any normal wealthy, civilised, single woman would've given up. I have the feeling she must have felt very strongly about this land to fight so hard to stay here,' he said quietly.

'Perhaps she had no choice,' said Jason thoughtfully. 'Wasn't she an orphan, no family to go back to? If she wanted to breed horses and cattle, I can't imagine her in a drawing room in Sydney.'

Carter nodded. 'Her guardian William Crowder had probably dropped off the perch. Max is right, the bush gets you. I remember when I first started working in the scrub. Spend time alone out here and it sneaks up on you.'

Jason glanced at Ginny. 'Do you reckon you could live on a property, a nice modern house, sweeping vistas over the river, ride the hills in the misty morn?'

Dani, like Ginny, couldn't tell if he was joking, being facetious or meant it. Was he hinting at a future life in the valley rather than Sydney?

'I don't ride and don't intend to,' said Ginny, standing up. 'God, it's hot, let's get going to the river or stream you told me about.'

Everyone got up. 'You bet, Kelly's Crossing for lunch,' said Carter. 'After calling in on Isabella.'

They continued across country, strung out, Carter in front, then Jason and Ginny now leading Sugar on her leash. They walked close together in deep discussion. Max and Dani brought up the rear, pausing to snap photographs or for Max to point out an interesting plant, an orchid or staghorn far up in a tree, a bird's nest or a hole in a tree providing shelter to some nocturnal animal.

Dani's mind was clicking over with ideas. The intimacy of the close-up images, the detail, was just as important as the grand views. She was especially taken with the orchids and some unusual carnivorous plants Max showed her. She could visualise them in paint on canvas. When Dani and Max caught up with the group, they were examining a well-weathered fence post made from a whole tree trunk or big branch. Nearby, indicating the fence line, was another smaller post of the same vintage made from a split log.

Max ran his hand over the grey post. 'A paddock corner gate post,' he said. 'Been there a long time.'

'It looks tired, doesn't it?' said Dani. 'Like, I'm sick of standing up here for a century or more.'

'So this was an outer paddock?' asked Jason. He looked around but there was nothing else indicating someone had lived here or worked this piece of land.

'I reckon it was the entrance,' explained Carter, 'These would have been the home paddocks. The house site is about a couple of clicks away.'

They set off with enthusiasm, except Ginny who muttered to Jason, 'What's so interesting about an old post?'

He thought a minute then answered, 'It's old.'

'She must have planted these trees. They're in a line,' said Max indicating the row of old beech trees with occasional gaps like missing teeth.

'Yeah, I thought that too. But look at this one here,' added Carter as they came around a small outcrop of rock. There was a magnificent old strangler fig tree with a huge heavy canopy of drooping branches, a tangle of aerial roots seeming to hold it upright. 'Get a load of this,' Carter added with delight, and pointed to markings high on the sturdy trunk. There was no mistaking the burned initials – IMK – and beneath it her brand, the same as on the side-saddle in the museum.

'I feel all tingly,' said Dani. 'Did Isabella come out here and do this, or one of her workers I wonder?'

'They must have been branding cattle in a yard here. You'd need a fire to have the branding iron hot enough to do that,' said Carter.

'A woman wouldn't be branding cattle back then,' said Ginny dismissively.

'Sounds like Isabella did,' said Jason. 'What a woman.'

Carter agreed. 'Yes, she did a lot of her own stock work from mustering, to branding and taking them to the sales. There are plenty of mentions of her in pioneers' letters and reminiscences.'

'Well, where's the house?' asked Ginny, bored with the tree, though Max and Dani were taking photographs.

'Ain't much to see,' said Carter. 'Buggers burned it down. That must have hurt.'

Jason took up the story. 'Her neighbours did it. They didn't like her, so when she was away they burned down her house and it was a showpiece in those days – had chandeliers and even a piano.'

Ginny was impressed. 'Really. Sounds like she had a touch of class.'

'Indeed. In those days most settlers lived in primitive slab huts with only the basics,' added Carter.

'She seems to have had a lot of bad luck,' commented Ginny.

'Locals probably said bad management. Or in today's parlance, bad karma. She had a lot of enemies, that's for sure,' said Jason.

'Do you think she's the right character to associate with your development?' asked Ginny with a raised eyebrow.

'I've been down that track,' said Jason.

'We haven't heard the whole story,' said Dani quickly.

'There's a historian writing her life story after doing incredible research.'

'Well, good or bad, I don't see some long-gone, forgotten pioneer woman selling your homes, Jason.' Ginny had the last word.

Jason shrugged. 'Who knows? Hopefully Dani will create interest and revitalise the story of Isabella through her art. People won't be buying just a piece of land – they'll be living with a part of history.'

'I see it,' shouted Max who had wandered away from the group and up a small rise in the land. 'Over here. The house.'

Ginny looked where he was pointing and back to Carter waiting for an explanation.

'There, see the big old pepper tree to the left, and that big brown pile of bricks, that's what's left of a chimney stack.'

'And there's another one,' said Dani. 'Must have been a big house. Convict-made bricks probably.'

'Imagine we're standing in the driveway, well, a tree-lined track worn bare by horses, cattle, drays, wagons and sulkies,' said Carter. 'And on that rise we see the gracious homestead of Miss Isabella Kelly – two storeys, a verandah covered in vines and ferns, a garden, enclosed yards, stables and out dwellings.'

Dani picked up the story. 'It's early evening, lights shine through the windows and there is the sound of piano music.'

'Did she play the piano?' asked Jason.

'She owned one, we know that. And she was a refined lady, well brought up, as they say, by her English guardian Sir William Crowder. She knew French, so she most likely learned music,' Carter said.

'I can't see a woman who chose to live out here, brand cattle and do a man's job, caring much about the social graces,' observed Ginny, but she failed to break the spell that transported the others.

'And down at the fringe of the bush is the single light of a campfire where the Aboriginal stockman and his family eat, knowing their people, their relatives are somewhere out there still,' said Max with a small smile.

'Let's go and see what else is there,' said Carter striding ahead.

Dani was thoughtful as they headed towards the lonely ruin. Ginny stopped while Sugar sniffed at a bush and Dani caught up to Jason. 'Did you hear Carter say Isabella's guardian was William Crowder?'

'Yeah, I guess so. Why?'

'His initials would be WC . . . that's what's engraved on the clasp of the writing box you gave me!'

Jason stopped. 'Hey . . . do you think? Could be, eh?' He broke into a big smile. 'Barry at Isadora's was convinced it could have belonged to her. Well, let's decide it is. I knew it was special.'

'What's special?' asked Ginny joining them.

Before Dani could say anything, Jason explained. 'I gave Dani a writing box for her art things . . . it's old, English, and has the initials WC on it. Now we think it belonged to Isabella's guardian, William Crowder. It'd be the sort of thing you'd give someone travelling abroad then, wouldn't it?'

'I really wouldn't know,' said Ginny tightly. 'An interesting gift. Was it for a special occasion?'

Dani stood there thinking Ginny looked like a coiled spring.

Jason seemed unaware and went on cheerily, 'Ah, it was more a bribe. I was trying to convince Dani to work for us. She was against this whole idea – until she saw what we're doing.'

'Really. Perhaps you'll have to try and convince me

about this whole idea. No wonder you want to spend so much time up here.'

'Ah, excuse me, I'll join the others, they seem to have found something else.' Dani hurried away leaving Jason and Ginny facing each other, Jason beginning to realise Ginny was mad as hell and perhaps he'd put his foot in his mouth. Despite his sophistication, charm and manners, Dani saw Ginny had him twisted round her finger.

They prowled between the exotic trees that had propagated around the house site and the remains of the chimneys, as well as some low mounds of buried ruins covered by scrub.

'It's a bit like an archaeological dig,' said Carter. 'The trees are a big giveaway. Settlers always planted a pepper tree.'

Dani was trying to imagine Isabella's grand home. 'I wish I knew what it looked like so I could paint it. Be a nice comparison with the new homes.'

Max had his sketchbook out. 'I like it how it is. A clue that someone once tamed this land but it's been reclaimed by nature. I'm trying to see below the surface. Think of the layers, Dani. You paint the original landscape, then that's wiped away and rebuilt with the pioneer dwellings. That's wiped out by fire, and nature takes over again, slowly but inevitably. You don't paint what you see on the surface, you paint knowing all that has gone before.'

Dani smiled with understanding. That was what gave Max's paintings such depth and drew you in. You sensed there was more happening beneath the surface. 'Yes, Max, I know what you're saying. There's always another story beneath the surface of a good painting.'

'In life too,' added Max.

'A lot of artists and poets have been inspired by this country,' said Carter. 'The first explorers and artists painted the rainforests, or the jungle as they called it. It was only later with settlement that the eucalyptus became the icon and they pictured more benign rural scenes.'

'Except for blackfella spearings and massacres and the loneliness of pioneer life,' said Dani. 'Like that McCubbin painting of the couple burying their child in the bush.'

Jason joined them, Ginny and the dog trailing behind. Dani could see Ginny looked annoyed and Jason spoke with ill-disguised tension. 'Worth the walk I suppose. Not that much to see.' He picked up a stick and poked it through the undergrowth around the bricks. 'Might take one home for a doorstop,' he muttered.

'Be careful not to upset a snake,' said Carter.

Ginny grabbed the dog and held it as she watched the others wandering around the site.

'Here's something interesting,' said Max. Sheltering under a tangle of growth he found what looked to be a stump and a pile of carefully stacked stones.

'Is it a wall?' asked Dani.

'Look at the plants. These are from the rainforest – orchids and some kind of succulents. They've grown from plants brought here.'

'Looks like a rockery,' said Jason. 'Perhaps Isabella was a bit of a collector.'

'She probably just liked pretty plants,' said Dani. 'Like any woman.'

'Well, you'll never know, will you,' said Ginny who sounded bored and fed up with the whole expedition.

Dani smiled at Carter. 'Thanks for bringing us here, I feel I know her so much better. Just looking at the view she saw every morning means a lot.'

'Right, lunch and back to the cars.' Carter strode ahead.

It was a relief to cool off at Kelly's Crossing. They perched on rocks and put their feet in the clear water. Ginny and Jason sat on the bank of the stream feeding the dog crusts from their sandwiches.

'Why don't you get a plaque put up here to honour Isabella? Something that tells people about her?' Dani said to Carter.

'I'm working on it,' he said. 'This place has a bit of history, right Max?'

'Yeah, so I've heard. My people think it's a bad place. I've been meaning to ask my mother about it. She got a lot of stories from my grandfather. Once she found him.'

'What sort of bad things?' asked Ginny. 'This place gives me the creeps.'

'You haven't liked anywhere much have you?' said Jason in a neutral voice.

'Why should I? I've no interest in some woman from ages ago. I think it's weird. And I'm certainly not going to be living up here. You seem to have your own friends and a different life here, Jason.'

'Perhaps I do. And it's not just for business reasons I'm committed here, Ginny. It doesn't matter where you come from, it's where you see your future.'

This sounded like a conversation they'd had before.

Max broke in gently. 'I think where you come from does count. What about you, Ginny, where are your roots?'

Dani knew what Max was trying to say but unknowingly he hit a tender nerve in Ginny's psyche.

'Where I come from, my background, is none of your business,' she snapped at Max. 'I'm not asking you about your family history.'

'Maybe you should,' said Carter easily. 'It's quite a story.'

Dani gave Max a querying look. All she knew was he'd grown up in Planters Field, his parents were of mixed blood and he'd married Sarah, a white girl, and they had two lovely children. 'So what is the story, Max?' she asked.

'We lost some relatives in the stolen generation that

we didn't even know we had. My family have always been here in this valley.'

'Really? How interesting!' exclaimed Dani. But before she could ask more questions Ginny stood up.

'Well, I'm not interested,' she snapped. 'I'm getting another cup of tea.'

'That's your trouble,' said Jason tersely. 'You're not interested in anyone but yourself. And I'd never realised till now just to what degree.'

'Settle down, you two,' said Carter calmly. 'Don't spoil a nice day. Sort things out when you get back.'

'I'm going now.' Ginny gathered her things.

'Calm down, Ginny. This isn't Sydney, you can't hail a cab. Go for a walk, cool down, we're nearly ready to go,' said Carter. 'Anyone want anything else to eat? Good tucker, Dani, tell Claude thanks.'

Ginny headed for the small fire that had been set up in a cleared spot back from the creek bank, but Sugar ran off when she dropped the lead to reach for the billycan of tea. She gave chase. The next moment they heard a shriek from Ginny and everyone jumped up.

Carter was first up the track, shouting 'Whatever it is, don't move.'

They found Ginny standing in the middle of the track clutching the dog. Standing in front of her, blocking the path, was an enormous goanna well over a metre and a half long. At the sudden appearance of more people the goanna panicked and ran at Ginny, who dropped Sugar. The goanna jumped up onto Ginny's shoulders, scrambling with its claws, ripping her blouse. Carter and Max grabbed its tail and snout and shouted at Ginny to keep still as they unhooked the goanna and put it on the ground where it marched calmly into the undergrowth with its head held high, dignity merely ruffled. Dani picked up Sugar.

Ginny was sobbing, dabbing at the scratches on her legs, arms and shoulders.

'Oh my God, it's ripped me to pieces. Is it poisonous? I'll have to get a shot.'

'You'll be right, love,' said Carter soothingly. 'Come on down to the creek and rinse yourself off. Bloody lucky it didn't get to your head and scratch your face. Poor thing thought you were a tree.'

Ginny shuddered, and Jason put his arm around her shoulders.

'Ouch, that hurts, don't touch me,' screamed Ginny. She and Sugar stomped to the creek.

'Sorry about that, maybe I shouldn't have brought Ginny. Hiking and the bush is not her scene,' said Jason apologetically.

'Don't worry about it, mate,' said Carter.

'Strike one for the spirits,' Max whispered to Dani and they exchanged a quick smile as they followed the others back to the creek.

Dani related the story to Lara and Tim that night and they fell about with laughter as Dani imitated the wild dance of Ginny with the goanna clinging to her shoulders like some live accessory.

'Poor Jason. She's probably still giving him heaps,' said Dani.

'So the trip was worth it then?' asked Lara collapsing into a chair.

'God yes. I really feel I'm getting closer and closer to Isabella. I wouldn't be surprised if she walked into my studio one day,' said Dani, wiping away the tears. 'But it was worth it to see that stuck-up Ginny come so unstuck!'

Dani was deep in thought as she worked on her first sketches after their hike to Mount George. When the phone rang she debated leaving the studio but then made a run for it.

'Hey, gorgeous, how're you travelling?'

'Hi, Roddy. Good. What's happening?'

'A lot. Shall I come over and tell you all about it? How about lunch at your local cafe?'

'I'll meet you there once I scrape the oil paint off.'

'I'm happy to pick you up, make an afternoon of it, if you like.' His voice held a buttery invitation.

'Can't today, have to collect Tim after school. Mondays to Thursdays are good though, he's generally with my mum or at a friend's place.'

'Mmm, can't think too far ahead at the moment. See you at the Nostalgia Cafe round twelve-thirty then.'

When Dani arrived at the cafe, Roddy was ensconced at a table with Claude and George hovering, hanging on every word. Roddy rose and gave her a quick kiss on the cheek.

'Hi, boys, has Roddy filled you in?' she asked as the others gave her a hug and a peck.

'Dani, it's too exciting. We're planning the premiere . . . an exclusive screening down the road at the Riverwood Terrace,' said Claude.

Dani laughed. 'That would be exclusive. Have you been inside our village cinema?' she asked Roddy.

'I've never noticed one,' he said looking puzzled.

'A friend of ours set it up in his darling heritage house near the river,' said George. 'Canapés and drinkies on the lawn under the trees – BYO – the screening room is a proper little cinema with a big old projector, plush seats red velvet curtain, the lot.'

'It seats thirty-five people,' added Claude. 'And the house is filled with movie memorabilia. He bought stuff from every old cinema that closed in Sydney and Melbourne when multiplexes came in.'

'We'll see,' said Roddy cautiously, failing to see

the humour in the suggestion. 'I have quite large plans actually.'

Over lunch Roddy outlined his ideas, starting with the first step – the media launch.

'Why are you doing it here and not in Sydney?' asked Dani.

'It'll get picked up for the national press. But initially I need the support of the locals – plus I'm offering them the opportunity to be first to invest. As a way of saying thank you to the town.'

'But where's the big money coming from? I mean, what's the budget for this film?' asked Dani, practically.

'Depends on the star names of course. The bigger the name the bigger the price tag. Thirty mill with a middle-of-the-road name should do the trick.'

'And Russell Franks directing. He's discovered a lot of stars, why not go for an unknown?' asked Dani.

'The banks and investors want a sure thing. And that means a big name.'

Dani dug into her salad and decided this was out of her field. Lara with her TV production background would be more on top of the budget and feasibility details. 'So what's happening for the media launch?'

'Need somewhere very smart for a flash cocktail party. Does your boss have access to a mansion or big restaurant on the water perhaps?'

Dani was not about to involve Jason. 'I've no idea. Would this be a paid-for event?'

'Christ no. Contra. We'll show the joint in the film, all the media will mention it, you know how these things work. Product placement, cars, accommodation – all free in exchange for publicity.'

'But, Roddy, isn't it a *period* film?'

He winked. 'There's ways around those things. Star

power, premiere, promotional things. And God knows what Russell will do with the script. You know what a wild thinker he is.'

'Not really. I just know his name, and that some of his films were a bit way out, over the top. Fellini meets Tarantino type thing. Aren't you using Garth's manuscript about Isabella to base the script on?' Dani was beginning to think Roddy was stretching things a bit.

'Cinematic licence. Don't worry, he'll get a big credit, a plug for his book. Maybe he could put a still from the film on the cover.'

'He hasn't got a publisher yet. He's still fiddling with the end. I think money is holding him back, he needs to go to Sydney to do more research. A film-option payment would help,' said Dani pointedly.

'Let me worry about that. Now, I need your help with some visuals for the launch. How many paintings have you finished?'

'Roddy! I'm still in the rough stage, laying down out-lines, ideas. And you can't have them just for the asking. They've been commissioned by Jason to launch *his* development project. Not to raise money for a film.' Dani was getting worried at Roddy's presumptuous attitude.

'Come on! It's cross promotion. The movie will put his whole bloody development on the map.'

'Well, the Isabella component is only a small part of it really, just an associated image, it's not the selling point.' Dani back-pedalled.

'Whatever. But c'mon, sweetie, couldn't you whip up something for me? We need a visual for the launch.'

'There's only one photo of her in existence, copy that from the museum. Mind you, she's a plain old duck.'

'Shit. Hey, why don't we dress you up in the period frock and hat, whatever, and pose you down by Kelly's Crossing?'

Dani burst out laughing. 'Side-saddle on a horse I suppose!'

'Yeah, terrific idea. Come on. We're making this a splashy launch. Russell Franks will be there. The locals can't believe such a world-famous movie icon is coming to this town.'

'You're bringing him over from New Zealand? Who's paying for this launch – if you don't mind me asking? Have you got the thirty million?' If Roddy was putting up some of his own money he must really have faith in the deal.

'I've got the seed money to get the ball rolling. I told you, there's a guy in New Zealand doing the distribution deals and guarantees. I really want the town and district to get behind this.'

'Well, if you've won over the council that's half the battle,' said Dani. 'I'm glad Patricia was helpful.'

'We're not totally there yet, that's why I want this launch to swing the naysayers on council my way. Get the public behind it and have them put their hand in their pockets. Claude and George say they're in. Eventually everyone will see the benefits and get starstruck. Even after the film has come and gone, the town inherits the flow-on, tourists, fame. Win-win.'

'Fabulous,' said Dani, feeling his enthusiasm. But she couldn't help wondering what her mother would say about it.

Lara was cautiously optimistic. 'It could be good. Isabella is a great character, beautiful location, with an interesting director and a star . . . could work.'

'Wouldn't it be better as a TV miniseries?' asked Dani.

'Another bush-and-crinoline saga? Haven't we done those to death?' said Lara. 'Be interesting to see what

Russell Franks does with it . . . Mad characters and music, arty photography, violence, humour . . . God, he could spin it off into any direction.'

'The trouble is, what if the film is a dud, or people hate it? And Isabella? Could backfire,' said Dani thoughtfully.

'Don't panic just yet, wait until the film is actually made. And if it gets made, well, hats off to Roddy,' said Lara. 'People have no idea how hard it is to get a movie up. Like everyone thinks they can write a book.'

Dani heard the self-deprecating note in her mother's voice. 'C'mon, Mum, you know you can write. Forget doing a script for a documentary. Maybe it's time to dream up a book idea. Use your own experiences.'

'I'm not writing my life story,' declared Lara. But Dani had touched a soft spot. Lara had always harboured a desire to write.

'Maybe not, but what about your family? Could be there's a story in that lot, way back? Keep digging. You don't know what might turn up,' suggested Dani.

'We'll see,' said Lara. And although the subject was put to one side she sensed that there were secrets waiting to be uncovered in her vaguely explored family history.

Dani took a selection of sketches into the office and Jason and some of the other staffers discussed which ones they liked before making a final selection.

'These look like winners,' Jason said with a smile, gathering up the approved sketches. 'Okay, go ahead, Dani. Now the hard work starts.'

'No worries. Thanks.' Dani decided not to mention Roddy's request for one of her paintings to promote his film.

'How is your son settling in?'

Dani knew it was merely a polite comment, but answered, 'So-so. After school is a bit of a problem out at The Vale, so he's spending time with my mother and friends most afternoons and I collect him later. Gives me a bit more uninterrupted work time.'

'Is he into any sports?'

'Yes, but at the moment he's got a bee in his bonnet about learning to ride. I guess for a city boy it's an appealing novelty.' She picked up her bag and sketches. 'Okay, I'll be going.'

'Hang on, Dani. Look, I love riding and I reckon some time on a horse would be good for Tim. There's a terrific young woman who runs a small equestrian centre in town. I'm happy to set it up for him.' Seeing Dani's hesitation he quickly added, 'Mardi is experienced, he'd be safe and her charges are reasonable. Be a good opportunity.'

Jason's enthusiasm surprised her. 'Well, my mother has agreed to pay for lessons, I suppose it's one way to find out if he likes it or not,' she said.

Jason wrote a name and number on a bit of paper and handed it to her. 'I'll phone her later today so Mardi will know who you are when you call.'

Dani and Tim's lives settled into a routine in the valley with Tim staying Monday to Friday at Cricklewood with Lara, and Friday night till Monday morning with Dani. He started riding lessons with Mardi, a cheerful young woman who handled new riders with firm and calm instructions. She soon had Tim sitting comfortably in the saddle and quickly gaining confidence with exercises in a large outdoor yard near the stables.

Lara found herself increasingly fascinated digging into the family past, and spent more and more time at the historical society going through records and newspapers. She even began calling on and chatting with people around town who remembered her grandparents.

But occasionally she sensed some of the oldies were a bit reluctant to open up and talk freely. They were inevitably polite, but sometimes evasive and vague. And Lara was convinced it wasn't just the result of a fading memory. She had the impression they were holding back, being cautious, as if there was something they didn't want to talk about.

Lara ran into Carter at the local produce shop and he took her for a coffee and they passed a pleasant hour chatting about their careers and travels. He mentioned their hike to Isabella's original home and they laughed at the goanna streaking up Ginny. Lara told him a little about her detective work into her family history and was tempted to tell him about the strange message in the letter that had been dropped into her mailbox. She hadn't told anyone because it seemed so absurd, a bit of dramatic nonsense. She enjoyed Carter's company and, being of a similar age, they found it easy to relate to each other.

By contrast, Dani found Roddy was like a perpetual whirlwind. He made another dash to New Zealand, a trip to Sydney to see his lawyer and organised for Russell Franks to be flown over for the media launch, as well as hiring a PR firm to handle the press and promotional side of the film. He stopped by The Vale mid week for a home-cooked dinner and stayed the night. He talked all evening about the film deal rather than the creative aspects and didn't ask to see Dani's paintings, which she was rather glad about.

'Garth is excited that Isabella is finally going to be recognised up there on the big screen,' said Dani.

'I hope he realises it's not going to be word-for-word from his book. The director needs freedom to move,' said Roddy. 'I've been talking to a developer from down south who's keen to work with the set construction so it becomes a permanent site. He's talking with the council about the land for that. Patricia reckons the council is getting more and more enthused about the film project. Everyone can see a way to make a buck. Even had restaurant and food people lobby to get the catering contract.'

'Claude and George might be interested in that,' said Dani.

'Tell them to give me a call. Best deal gets the gig.'

'But it really is a long way off happening, isn't it?'

'Yeah, in a way. But by normal industry standards we're moving pretty quickly with this one. There's something about it that makes everyone want to get on board real fast.'

'The mystery that is the magic of Isabella, eh?'

'Spot on, kid. Spot on.'

Angela and Tony had rung earlier to invite Dani to another party with their friends at Riverview, the beautiful house on the river that Jason had renovated. They suggested she bring Roddy along. When she mentioned it over the second coffee, he accepted immediately.

'Great idea. I can do a bit of networking. Classy place, huh? So they have money?'

'I have no idea, Roddy. You're not going around with a hat asking people to invest in the film are you?' Dani was only half joking.

He lifted his shoulders. 'People love the idea of being in showbiz. Anyway, it's a good tax lurk.'

Roddy was discreet but he managed to generate quite a buzz at the party and always seemed to have a group around him.

Barney and Helen took Dani aside.

'So what do you think about this film? Be wonderful to see Isabella's real story told,' said Helen.

'I gather it'll be pumped up a bit . . . you know, with all the colour and controversy,' said Dani.

Helen wrinkled her nose. 'You mean all the horse shit, 'scuse me.'

'Well, it does make it more interesting, more action,' interjected Barney. 'That's what movies do. The main thing is that it's a big hit so we all get a share.'

'You're investing?' asked Dani in surprise.

'Why not? Got to support the local scene. We all stand to benefit. Think of the tourists who'll come here,' grinned Barney.

'Be careful, I wouldn't sink my life savings into a film,' said Dani worriedly.

'Nah, not that silly. But, like the lottery, you gotta be in it to win it,' laughed Helen.

Dani was shocked that on the strength of the local grapevine people were prepared to part with their hard-earned cash to be part of Roddy's Isabella bandwagon.

'Wait and see how the media launch goes,' suggested Dani.

During the evening several other locals approached her about the chance to get in on the ground floor with the movie before it went public. She wished they wouldn't ask her opinion as she had no idea whether the film would work and be successful, and she felt vaguely responsible.

She found Roddy and pulled him to one side. 'I have to get up early tomorrow morning. I promised Tim we'd go to the beach first thing. He's sleeping over with Len at Max and Sarah's.'

'Oh, too bad. Party's really starting to jump. I'll drive you home, come on.'

'I can get a cab . . .'

'It'll take forever. Are you ready?'

'Er, yes, I'll just say goodnight to our hosts and Ange and Tony.'

As she threaded her way through the big living room to the terrace a few people stopped Dani to say how exciting it was about the movie and her scintillating boyfriend. 'Just a friend,' she said lightly.

Roddy drove Dani home, followed her inside and poured them a nightcap.

'A successful party. What did you think?' he asked, putting his feet up on the coffee table.

'Yes, I really like Ange and Tony's friends. And that fabulous house.'

'Yeah, I got a lot of interest. A few definite bites. Now, they approached me, I wasn't out there touting,' he added.

'I just worry about people being prepared to put up their money at this early stage,' said Dani.

'Honey, that's how you make a killing. Get in early. And without investment there's no budget to make the damn thing.' He saw her expression didn't change and he swallowed the last of his drink and took her hand. 'C'mon, let's go to bed. You need a cuddle.'

Dani didn't protest. Roddy's charm and personality overpowered her. She was worried about the whole Isabella film project, her work, the diametrically opposed views of Jason and Roddy, her future. 'I'm just wondering what the hell I'm doing here,' she said.

'Yeah, this place is a bit rundown and bloody isolated,' said Roddy, misreading her comment. 'Come on, guarantee you'll forget where we are in three minutes flat.' He gave a cheeky grin and led her into the bedroom. Dani followed willingly. But as Roddy slipped her clothes from her body she suddenly wondered how Isabella had managed on her own with no physical comfort from a man. She must have been a strong woman. And a lonely one.

The invitations and press release for the official media launch announcement of *Isabella* caused a stir in the valley. Gossip, rumour and tantalising snippets in the local rag

326

now seemed to be backed by action and serious financial substance, and it had everyone talking. The local newspaper and radio interviewed Roddy who said the details about the film would be revealed at the launch. He managed to put the spotlight on the financial opportunities it offered to local investors and business people.

'You look stunning, Mum!'

Lara smiled while Dani did a twirl in her sparkly top and short white skirt that showed off her long tanned legs. They'd both shopped in Hungerford's small shopping mall and been pleased at finding new outfits and accessories to wear to the launch.

'You look terrific too, darling. Do you think we'll measure up to Roddy's expectations?' asked Lara. 'Sounds like he's going all out for this film.'

'I hadn't planned on going to a red-carpet function while I was up here,' said Dani.

Roddy had told Dani the function would be upmarket and that Roz, the PR whiz, was doing a brilliant job. But Dani got a bit bored every time she saw Roddy and every conversation focused on the film. She'd been busy painting in her studio after a session with Max about how to prime and mount her canvases before starting work. She was very conscious that these paintings would have a life of their own when they left her hands and she hoped they'd spark interest in the history of Jason's Birimbal development.

Tim enjoyed staying with Lara during the week and his riding lessons were working out very well. Jason seemed to have taken an interest in Tim's riding. He had developed a routine that enabled him to drop by when Tim was having a lesson. Tim told Dani that Mardi, his riding instructor, was a friend of Jason's and that he'd given her the horses for the school.

'That was generous of him,' said Dani. 'Does Jason ride there?'

'Sometimes. He's so good. He says one day we can go riding on Kerry's horses.'

'Did he indeed. You'll have to have a few more lessons before taking off for the hills,' said Dani, making a note to speak to Jason about this.

Tim, dressed up for the media launch, had tried to adopt a nonchalant air but was pleased when Dani and Lara broke into applause at his appearance in the trendy pants, new shirt and casual jacket he'd chosen on their shopping spree.

'So what's this place Roddy's chosen?' asked Lara as they drove away from Cricklewood.

'Some private garden that's pretty special. The owner rarely lets it be used as he doesn't want it trashed with weddings or the like. Roddy charmed him into agreeing to the launch,' said Dani.

They followed the map printed on the back of the invitation featuring a photograph of Isabella Kelly with the line – 'Rod Sutherland Productions Presents . . . *Isabella*, the Movie'. There was a number on a post on a little-used road behind Riverwood with coloured lights around the trees as the only indication this was the setting for the film party launch.

Lara drove cautiously along the bush track and then they came to a long gravel driveway with lanterns and flame torches. Guests were heading along a terrace with a low stone wall marked with massive urns filled with flowering shrubs. 'God, I hope it's not a hike, I shouldn't have worn high heels,' said Lara.

'Wow,' said Tim.

'You said it, Tim,' said Dani as they looked down at the scene below.

Along the broad path that curved down to a level lawn where a marquee strung with lights was erected there was a dry stone wall topped with carved statues. Most guests were standing or sitting at small white tables and chairs on the lush lawn enjoying the sunset over the river. A quartet played background music as waiters in white jackets circulated with trays of food and drinks. The lawn appeared to be an oasis in the centre of the gardens, which radiated in colourful sections of trees, shrubberies, flower beds, archways and trellised canopies. A fountain and reflecting pond lit by pink lights was at the far end of the lawn.

Roddy was wearing a white linen jacket and dark blue pants, a red silk handkerchief in his top pocket. Dani noticed he was wearing a heavy gold chain and watch she'd never seen before. An attractive woman with hair highlighted in different shades of red was beside him. She wore a short red dress and large sparkling earrings. Dani assumed her shoes and dress were from a very hip Sydney designer.

Roddy gave Dani a kiss and introduced Dani, Lara and Tim to, 'Roz, our marketing and public relations director.'

They chatted for a moment about the stunning setting and as another group came in behind them, Roz ushered them on, pointing to a waiter. 'Do help yourselves . . .'

'Where's the movie director?' hissed Dani over her shoulder but Roddy gave a wink and lifted crossed fingers.

'What's that mean?' whispered Lara. 'He's a no-show or he's dropped out of the deal?'

'Guess we'll find out,' said Dani, and, looked around at the guests. 'There are so many people here I've never seen before.'

'There's Toby, Tab, Lennie and Julian, see you later.' Tim shot off to where the kids were gathered at the entrance of the marquee.

Dani was pleased to find some familiar faces, so many of the people she now regarded as good friends – Helen and Barney with Angela and Tony, Max and Sarah, Claude and George, Patricia and Henry Catchpole. She recognised a few parents from Tim's school and then she spotted Jason, though she didn't see Ginny. Lara had been drawn aside by Carter Lloyd and then Dani heard her name and turned to see Greta, the director of the art gallery.

'This is quite an event,' said Greta. 'Certainly will put the valley on the international map. I'll have to see if the art gallery can be involved, sponsor the local premiere or something.'

'That's a long way off,' said Dani.

'Things are certainly moving along. My husband is keen to invest. And it makes your subject very timely. How's the painting coming along?' she asked with genuine interest.

'Slowly. I'm feeling my way. But I'm enjoying it and I feel I have a clearer idea of what I'm doing,' said Dani. 'Max has been so helpful.'

'He's a generous spirit. And a fantastic artist.'

'He's very modest. I think his work is amazing. Don't you think he'd sell well in Sydney or overseas?' said Dani.

Greta smiled and leaned closer. 'Funny you say that,' she said in a stage whisper. 'There's a major dealer coming through on his way north. I've known him for years. He's scouting for a big New York gallery, I want him to see Max's stuff. I haven't told Max yet. I'll just spring it on him. He is very self critical and hides work he doesn't think is good enough.'

'I know what you mean,' said Dani slowly. 'It's not that he's a perfectionist but with his paintings he's always striving for something that's just out of reach. Does Sarah know?'

'I'll tell her closer to the time. Keep painting, Dani. Don't try to make every picture perfect, the more you do the more you learn, I'm sure you know that. Well, I'm off to look around these gardens before it's dark. I hear the roses are unbelievable.'

Dani watched Greta disappear and thought again what a nice woman she was. She hoped something would come of the art dealer's visit for Max.

'Evening, Dani. Do you have a drink?' Jason signalled one of the hovering waiters.

'Not yet. Been chatting.'

Jason's glance flicked to Roddy and Roz welcoming guests. 'So are there going to be any big surprises tonight?'

'I have no idea. I kind of tuned out of the details,' she said. 'I just hope the movie works.'

Jason gave her an amused look as she took a glass of champagne. 'You mean it's not signed in blood? I wouldn't be hosting an event like this on the off-chance.'

Dani didn't want to be disloyal to Roddy, nor did she want Jason to think she was distracted from her work – which he was paying for. 'This is all part of it, I gather. Like your plans, things go in stages. Before people invest money in a film or a new lifestyle they want to know what it's all about, what bang they get for their buck.'

'Well, I'm not putting any bucks into this scheme,' said Jason firmly.

'You're not a moviegoer?' said Dani. She hoped Jason didn't spread his pessimism around.

'Love 'em. Never been a fan of Frank's work though. And to be honest he seems a bit past it. Living off a few controversial flicks in the seventies and eighties. They must be paying him heaps. But his work doesn't seem suited to an Aussie bush flick,' Jason said.

'You're such a cynic.' But privately she agreed with him.

Guests were being ushered to stand to one side of the wide gravel path that wound up from the river through an avenue of trees across the centre of the lawn, past the marquee and up the hill. Obviously from the attendants stationed along the path someone was going to make an entrance. Everybody looked expectantly towards the floodlit trees at the edge of the lawn.

Dani spotted Garth and stood beside him. 'This is all because of your book,' she said quietly.

'Oh, I wouldn't say that. Sooner or later others would have discovered Isabella.'

'Have you talked to Russell Franks about the script?'

'Oh, I'm sure the great man has his own ideas. I've just put down the basic facts.'

'But, Garth, Roddy used your book as the inspiration, I hope you have a deal sorted out,' said Dani.

'Oh, my, yes. A wonderful contract. Nothing happens till the film is completed of course.'

'So nothing upfront? Option payment or anything?' asked Dani, realising that he hadn't seen a penny yet.

'Don't worry, Dani. I'm sure everything will come together. It'll be wonderful publicity for my book when it's done and published,' said Garth.

Dani hoped Garth was right. Some people just had no business sense. Especially creative types. She suddenly wondered which camp she was in. She was generally pretty smart about business deals but if it was one of her paintings that was going to get big public exposure, would she hold it back waiting for money upfront, or put it out there and trust, as Garth was doing?

'I'm sure it will,' she said trying to sound enthusiastic.

Over the public address system in the marquee came Roddy's voice. 'Ladies and gentlemen . . . Please stand clear . . . and raise your glasses to toast . . . Miss Isabella Mary Kelly!'

There was a loud chorus of music, rather reminiscent of the theme from *The Man from Snowy River*, and the sound of galloping hooves as out of the trees came a huge black horse and, mounted side-saddle, a woman dressed in period clothes, her long black skirt looped up showing her foot in the stirrups. She wore a bonnet and high-collared blouse, and in her gloved hands she brandished a stock whip. She reined in the horse, which pranced, its neck arched, tail swishing. The crowd gasped to see her pull a pistol from a holster by the saddle. She fired a shot in the air, kicked the horse into a fast canter and charged along the pathway to the cheers of the crowd.

'I hope that was a blank,' said Dani leaning close to shout in Jason's ear. 'She seemed to know what she was doing.'

'That was your son's riding instructor,' said Jason with a laugh. 'Mardi might be in the movie!'

Before Dani could answer, there was a clatter and another horse trotted from the trees drawing a highly polished sulky with a white-haired man sitting beside the driver. He wore a rainbow silk scarf with a high-necked, full-sleeved pirate-style shirt. He waved to the crowd as if he were royalty. The driver, also in period costume, pulled up in the centre of the pathway and Roz stepped forward to help the older man from the sulky.

As he awkwardly stood up Roddy announced, 'Please welcome internationally famous, award-winning film director – Mr Russell Franks!'

There was enthusiastic applause as photographers and a TV film crew crowded in to record the arrival of the eminent director.

Everyone was ushered into the marquee where there was a podium and large posters for *Isabella* as if it was a finished movie. Other flyers had slogans: 'Great invest-ment opportunity', 'Will put the valley on the international tourist map', 'There's never been a woman like Isabella', 'Russell Franks and Isabella – a marriage made in heaven, and the valley!' There were rows of neat white chairs which quickly filled so the rest of the guests clustered around the sides and rear of the marquee. Dani found a seat next to Lara and Carter. Tim and his friends sat cross-legged on the strip of carpet at the front.

At the microphone Roz called for the audience's attention and introduced herself. She then went on: 'As the promotion and public relations director for Sutherland Films, it is my pleasure to introduce the executive producer who has pulled so much together in such a short time and will undoubtedly be recognised as the man who brought the Australian film industry into the international arena in the twenty-first century – Mr Rodney Sutherland.'

Rodney rose from his seat beside Russell Franks who was facing the audience and beaming. The director held a large glass of red wine and had his legs stretched in front of him showing a pair of hand-painted multi-coloured cowboy boots.

Roddy quickly launched into the thrust of his speech. 'As many of you may know, making a big-budget, quality, international film is no easy undertaking and there are always unknown variables. However, there are certain ingredients that can give a project some insurance and potential for success. They are: a great story and characters – and there can be no more intriguing and colourful character than Isabella Kelly – star actresses are going to kill to play her; and a brilliant director – and here we have not only a man of huge renown but an auteur, a man who puts his own stamp on a movie from writing the screenplay to interpreting the visual story on the screen. Russell Franks is at the peak of his career and believes *Isabella* will be the film for which he will be remembered.'

Here Roddy gestured to Russell Franks who rose to his feet, rather shakily it seemed to Dani, and lifted his glass to the crowd to acknowledge the smattering of applause. Roz was at his side and gently eased him back into his seat. Dani and Lara exchanged a glance.

Roddy continued. 'But what makes Isabella even more special is this is an Australian story, as yet untold, set in God's own country, which will capture the hearts of the world. With top actors, an Aussie Oscar-winning cinematographer and your help we will make this an Australian-backed feature film where the profits come back to us, to this community, to every mum and dad who wants to have a flutter and pocket the profit. The rewards won't go to some Hollywood studio.' Roddy was almost shouting with enthusiasm and there was more applause.

'He's good, isn't he?' Lara said to Dani.

'I guess you have to be a bit of a salesman with a silver tongue to get something like this up and running,' said Dani non-committally.

Roddy pointed out the advantages of investing in and supporting the film for the benefits it would bring to the valley and, as he wrapped up his speech, four attractive girls circulated through the crowd handing out glossy coloured brochures with details of the film, how to invest, an application form, and pictures of the proposed movie set of Isabella's house, the George Inn, stables and a court-house which would all be left intact as a tourist attraction for the use of the town.

With the formalities over, people milled around as hot food and more drinks appeared. A knot of fans gathered around Russell Franks who was proclaiming that his Isa-bella might well be found here in the valley – a search to rival that of discovering Scarlett in *Gone With the Wind*. Roz was glued to his side taking business cards and mak-ing notes. There was talk of the money that would flow into the town as business people began to grasp the scale of having at least a hundred cast, crew and technical sup-port in the area for several months.

Roddy made a point of introducing Dani to the great director.

Russell Franks held her hand in a moist clasp, a glass of red wine in the other, and gazed into her eyes. 'Ah, Rodney's friend, the artist. You look like a creative person. And how have you found Isabella?' His cultured English accent was warm and honey toned. He didn't sound pompous and Dani could well imagine him coaxing a fine performance from actors.

'We know so little about her. She's something of an enigma. I'm curious about the story you'll tell.'

'Ah, my dear, she will tell her own story. A delicate young girl taming the wilderness, outwitting men who wish to tame her also.'

Dani blinked. 'Isabella was in her thirties, I believe, when she came here. True, she had battles with the local property owners –'

Franks cut her off with a wave of his hand. 'Fragility, the English rose in the wildness of the forest. A free spirit who conquers man and beast, so many elements to play with. Rodney has found a gem. He is most inspiring. A magnificent entrepreneur.' He took a mouthful of wine.

'Have you finished the script?' asked Dani, wondering if Roddy would let her read what sounded like a bizarre distortion of Isabella's life.

'A work in progress, my dear. I like my actors to improvise. There's something on paper of course. Roddy's money bag needed a token before handing over a small down-payment.'

Franks chuckled as Roddy explained, 'The financier in New Zealand has an outline of the script. Loved the whole idea, hence the seed money.'

'But you still have to raise the rest,' said Dani.

'Reason for this shindig,' said Roddy. 'Well, we'd better circulate.'

Later Jason joined Dani. 'So? What do you think?'

'Interesting. Though I'm wondering why Franks has

336

moved to New Zealand if he's such a big name in the UK and Europe,' said Dani.

'He's still a star in the antipodes. He seems to think he's going to do for the valley what Peter Jackson did for New Zealand with *The Lord of the Rings* trilogy.' When Dani didn't comment Jason asked, 'Are you okay for a ride home?'

'Yes, thanks,' replied Dani. She wanted to get away from Jason and his less-than-enthusiastic slant on Roddy's launch.

Helen and Barney wanted Dani, Lara and Tim to go back for a coffee at Chesterfield but Dani was suddenly tired. 'Thanks, guys, I think I'll crash at Cricklewood with Mum and Tim.'

Tim was very excited about the whole evening. His riding teacher had made a big impact, he and the gang had explored the gardens. 'Len said people are going to be paid to dress up and be extras in the film. Roddy said I could ride in a scene,' he bubbled on.

'Well, you've got plenty of time to improve your riding skills, it'll be months before they start filming,' said Dani, exchanging a look with her mother.

'I do hope it comes off. For everyone's sake,' said Lara quietly.

At Cricklewood's gate, the lights shone through the French doors onto the verandah, a waft of a flower perfume drifted on the breeze.

'I'll bunk down in the sleep-out next to the office, if that's okay, Mum,' said Dani. 'Did you get enough to eat, Tim?'

'I didn't like some of those fancy things. I could go a peanut butter sandwich.'

'And a cup of tea. You coming, Mum?'

Lara was standing by the gate as Dani and Tim waited by the front door. She'd noticed something sticking out of the letterbox. Lara's heart skipped a beat as she saw the handwritten envelope addressed to her. She crumpled it in her hand. 'Coming. Tea sounds a good idea.'

Dani and Tim were sound asleep before Lara got out of bed and opened the letter.

Don't believe the stories you hear. Stop prying and asking questions from those who don't know the truth. Let sleeping dogs lie, you'll regret you ever started this. Go home before you get hurt.

Lara dropped the letter as though it was contaminated. She sat on the edge of the bed shivering. Who knew that she'd been visiting people who'd known her family 'for sentimental reasons', talking over cups of tea, skirting the real subject? What did the note mean about getting hurt? That what she might find out would hurt her emotionally or did it mean she might get hurt physically, be prevented from finding out the truth? She couldn't ignore the notes anymore.

Lara switched out the light and stood at the window in the darkness. Was someone out there watching her? A car rolled over the railway bridge, a smooth sound. She remembered the bridge being wooden with a loose plank that clunked every time a car passed over it. And as if the years were racing to catch up with her, a train approached, but it sped through Cedartown without pausing. A blur of lights, a hum of steel wheels, and it was gone. The night was silent once more.

'I'll have to tell Dani about the letters,' said Lara with a resigned sigh.

But sleep did not come easily to her as she lay in her grandparents' bedroom.

12

Cedartown, 1940

IT WAS CHILLY, DAWN a long way off. White frost iced the ground around the railway platform. The passenger train steamed into the dark station where a light glowed in the station master's office and one dim light hung outside the waiting room. A hiss of white steam puffed into the night air as the train rolled to a stop. The station master took the incoming mail bags from the guard in his van at the rear of the train and tossed a couple on board for Broadmeadow and Sydney.

Towards the end of the train a carriage door slammed and two figures stumbled onto the platform. The station master eyed the men, who were laughing and staggering as they shouldered their big kit bags. He waved a green signal light to the engine driver which was acknowledged with a short sharp blast of the whistle, and more hissing of steam and belching of smoke. Then a creaking rattle travelled along every carriage as the wheels turned and tightened the couplings. The train rolled out of the station, under the wooden bridge, heading south, drawn blinds obscuring sleeping passengers.

The two soldiers were intoxicated but the station master, while frowning, tried to be tolerant and helpful. He recognised Clem Richards.

'Well, you two are a sorry sight. Been a boozy trip, eh? Where are you off to at this hour of the morning, Clem?' There was nobody waiting to meet them.

'Don't worry, Mr Jackson. We'll sleep in the waiting room till the sun comes up,' grinned Clem.

'Oh no, you won't, I'm locking up. And there're no taxis.'

'We can walk to my place,' said Thommo.

'Your mum doesn't know you're here. Too early for her to be woken up, I reckon,' said Clem.

'Say, why don't we go over the road to the Williamses'. Wake Elizabeth up. You can surprise her, give her a cuddle,' said Thommo, his words slurred.

'I wouldn't recommend that,' said the station master. 'Harry Williams will have your balls on toast if he finds you two mugs at his place and plastered to boot. You can doss down on the seats in the waiting room, but be gone before anyone turns up in the morning.'

Thommo gave a sloppy salute. 'Righto, cobber. Thank you, sir. Many thanks, sir.'

'It's a surprise visit. We got two weeks' leave from training camp,' explained Clem.

'Save your surprises till you're sober and the sun's up. I'm off home to my warm bed.' He locked his office door and glanced in the waiting room. 'You can light the coal fire in the grate there if you like. The heater was on for a bit. Keep the door closed and your boots on and you should be all right.'

Clem eyed the benches. 'Which one do you want?'

Thommo threw his kit bag on the closest seat and curled up using it as a pillow, hugging his thick great coat around him. 'Bugger lighting the fire, let's get some shut-eye, mate.'

'Any beer left?'

'Nah, finished the last bottle 'round Kendall. I'm going to dream about breakfast. S'pose you'll be dreaming about your girl, eh?'

Clem closed his eyes. 'Yeah. I might pop round and see if her old man will let me in for breakfast. He's a good bloke.'

'We're still going to have a bit of a muck-up, you and me, though. Right, mate?' asked Thommo, who didn't have a girlfriend and knew how possessive Elizabeth could be with her boyfriend Clem.

'You bet. We'll think about it all the time we're over there,' agreed Clem sleepily.

As they sank into sleep a truck rattled over the wooden railway bridge, a few loose planks making heavy clunks. Neither man stirred. Nor did Elizabeth or Mollie sleeping soundly in their bedroom across the road at Cricklewood. The rattle of the old bridge was as familiar to them as the magpie that sang in the mulberry tree every morning.

Clem changed his mind about fronting up at the Williamses' house when the noise of the milk trucks going to the butter factory woke them. He was stiff with a sore head, and they looked filthy and dishevelled after having travelled for the last three days. He knew the Williamses wouldn't be impressed.

'Come to my place. Mum'll be all right,' said Thommo. 'Won't be the first time I walked in at breakfast time.'

'What about your dad?' asked Clem, thinking his own father would probably give him a backhander. As long as he could continue to stand on his own two feet Walter Richards considered himself strong enough to take a swing at any of his three strapping sons.

'My old man likes you. He'll be jake. I could eat a horse. Let's go.' Thommo hoisted his bag on his shoulder.

Vera and Frank Thompson fussed over the two boys, treating the twenty-year-olds like youngsters, delighted to see them after months away.

'You look so . . . grown up.' Thommo's mother tightened the belt on her dressing gown. 'I can't bear the thought that you'll be going over there, fighting . . .'

'We're soldiers, Mum! That's what we're being trained to do.'

'But we're looking forward to this time off,' said Clem to diffuse the emotion. He added with a cheeky grin, 'Go round and skite a bit to old pals.'

'I suppose you'll be seeing a lot of Elizabeth Williams,' said Thommo's father.

'Yeah. She's been writing me lots of beaut letters. But Thommo and me still plan to have a bit of fun and games,' said Clem giving Thommo a wink.

'Now don't you do anything silly. Some of the stories we hear about the boys in uniform around the district would curl your toes,' said Vera.

'Mind you, they're not all local boys,' added Frank. 'There's now an army camp out of Riverwood a bit. The kids ride their bikes out there at weekends for a stickybeak. The girls are flattered by the blokes wanting to chat to them all the time.'

'Most of them seem nice enough, the girls certainly think so. Gives the local boys a bit of competition,' said Vera.

'What are your plans this morning? Want a lift out to your place, Clem?'

'That's kind of you, thanks, Mr Thompson. You can drop me by the farm gate,' said Clem. He was never sure how his father was going to react. Walter was a rough old bloke. 'Got to keep 'em in line,' he said in justification whenever his wife chided him about being too strict on the boys, belting them for the slightest mistake. Clem had been first to enlist, Kevin had followed a few weeks later. Keith, being the eldest of three sons, was told by the recruiting officer he was not eligible due to feet and knee problems. They preferred not to take all the sons from one family and Keith was needed to work on the farm with his father.

'Call me Frank now, Clem. No more "Mister" stuff. You're going off to do a man's job.' They awkwardly shook hands.

Clem was a slight, bowed figure as he walked the track leading to the farmhouse, his canvas kit bag a bit heavier with the few bottles of beer he'd bought in town to share with his brothers and father. In a far paddock one of them was ploughing with their old draught horse. A haze of dust churned behind the figures in the morning sun. He wondered where Kevin was. He'd joined the navy and was probably still learning the ropes.

Everything around the farm was familiar and yet different. He looked about with new eyes. This was his home but he saw no future here. He was finished with the endless morning and afternoon processions of plodding cows, the memories of milking on cold mornings before school, of cleaning the bails, chopping wood or whatever task his father demanded after school before being called in to tea and then falling asleep over his homework. He could never recall praise or thanks, only criticism, hard whacks and shouted commands. Unlike Thommo, Clem had slipped easily into the tough and disciplined regimen of the army. He liked the order, the knowledge of what he had to do, how to do it, and then doing it well.

Elizabeth had been working in the big stock and station agency that handled all the cattle sales that went through Cedartown for years now. He suddenly remembered the fire at the showground cattleyards when they were kids.

It'd been Thommo's fault, but he'd never let on to anyone. But now Clem was a bit worried about Thommo being in the same infantry unit with him. Thommo was the proverbial loose cannon and wasn't taking well to the discipline of the army. As a mate Clem felt responsible for helping him stay out of trouble, but it wasn't easy.

The farmhouse came into view. It looked run-down, with the clutter of equipment, a neglected dray, milk urns, a broken table, rolls of wire and old tyres piled around. Washing sagged on a line with the appearance of always having been there. Nola was constantly hanging out washing.

After the neatness and order of the army camp the messy display offended Clem. It was how it had always been. This was his home but already after a few months in the army he felt removed. He didn't belong here anymore. Talking to other young men about plans 'after the war was won' broadened his vision of the opportunities that were his for the taking if he made an effort.

The letters from Elizabeth who was 'saving every penny to get out of Cedartown' reinforced his determination to not live back here. He knew Keith would never leave the farm and valley, and it gave him a sense of relief. Maybe Kevin would get other ideas after being in the navy. His sister Phyllis, just thirteen, might eventually marry someone with their own farm or her husband might move in here.

Times were still tough; they hadn't really got over the hardship of the Depression years, and now everyone had to put up with wartime shortages, rationing and restrictions. Clem was pleased he'd been able to save money from his pay to slip to his mother. He couldn't recall ever giving her a proper present. Doing some special job around the house she wanted done had been all she'd ever asked for a birthday or Christmas. One year he had fixed the old cuckoo clock that she had got from her mother. How Nola treasured it.

He couldn't remember his father ever giving her anything. Well, there was the time he gave her the wood-fired copper where she boiled the clothes on wash days. It had been Kevin's job to keep a pile of twigs and kindling ready to light the fire on those days, usually every Monday. The copper had been a luxury after the days when the children were babies and toddlers and Nola had boiled the washing in kerosene drums on an open fire down by the creek, spreading it on the grass to dry enough to carry home. There they were hung out to finish drying on an old wire line propped up with a forked stick. It was still hard physical work lifting and hanging the clothes and Clem wondered if his mother might have preferred the time on her own down at the creek surrounded by the pretty paddocks and the calm company of cows.

His thoughts turned to Elizabeth. He couldn't imagine her doing the washing at a creek or in a wood-fired copper. She was a modern young woman, worked in an office and had soft hands with painted nails. He smiled to himself thinking of the pretty bracelet he'd bought for her. Real gold too.

He and Thommo had gone into a pawn shop when Thommo needed money after gambling and had sold his watch. He didn't want to borrow the money from Clem. There Clem had spotted the thin chain bracelet with a small heart dangling from the clasp. It was the first frivolous thing he'd ever bought and he hoped Elizabeth would like it.

He wanted to show his mother but didn't want to hurt her feelings because he hadn't bought her something special, just for herself. He'd never seen her wear any jewellery other than a modest crystal brooch and her plain gold wedding band. Had his father ever given her a personal gift?

Had there ever been tenderness, laughter over silly things or shared tears between them? Sex seemed to be a silent secret event behind their closed bedroom door.

He grinned as his thoughts turned to sex. He'd learned a lot more about that since joining the army. A lot more than the farmyard and schoolyard had taught him while growing up. The subject of sex had never been mentioned to the boys by their parents.

While away at army camp it had been Thommo who'd decided they should visit a house where you paid for sex. 'The women will do anything, mate. Honest,' enthused Thommo with the authority of experience.

But it had been an unsatisfactory experience for Clem. He was too drunk to respond well to the enticements the girl offered, and he swore he'd never do it again. 'Save your money, mate,' he advised Thommo as they staggered out.

Within a day Clem slipped back into the farm routine. His mother gave him a teary and loving welcome home; his father shook his hand effusively. Before lunch the copper was lit and most of the clothes from the kit bag were being boiled.

Back in his work clothes, jumping to directions from his father, Clem felt he'd never been away. But he was a reluctant worker knowing Thommo was waiting for him in town. By now Elizabeth would know he was back home – Thommo would have been round to see the Gordons next door. Two of their boys had joined up. They'd no doubt shout the news over the fence to everyone at Cricklewood that Clem was back on leave.

So Clem worked hard and fast, making a list of things that needed repairing. He talked to Keith about the prospects of the farm during these hard times. His older brother was quiet and stolid, a hard worker from before sunrise to teatime when he put his head down and chewed steadily through the evening meal before taking his dish to the kitchen sink.

Neither Keith nor his father spoke during mealtimes. That was how it had always been at the table. Only Nola broke the solemn silence, asking someone to pass a plate or the sauce, or offering more food or volunteering some gossip or news she'd heard on the radio. Her remarks were usually received with little more than a grunt from the old man, though Clem and Kevin tried to show some interest in the minutiae of their mother's life. If Phyllis spoke up and tried to be part of the conversation, her father would glare and remind her that girls were seen and not heard, so she suffered through each meal.

Clem found he missed the raucous meal times with his army mates and the sad realisation came to him that he really had little in common with his family, nothing to share.

On the afternoon of his second day home Clem took the farm truck and drove into town to collect spare parts, feed, seed, and 'do some stuff'. First stop was the stock and station agency where Elizabeth worked. Looking through the cursive gold lettering on the glass window he could see Elizabeth behind a desk next to the partitioned office of George Forde, the auctioneer and owner.

Donald, Forde's offsider, had a smaller office at the back in a big shed where they stored produce, feed, spare parts for machinery and farm vehicles, horse needs including harnesses of all kinds, a wide range of tools and fertilisers and chemicals. There was a loading dock off the back lane and there was nearly always a farmer or two rolling a smoke and having a yarn with Donald, sometimes over a cuppa, about the war, the weather, crops and livestock. George Forde maintained Donald knew everything everyone was doing before they did it, and way before *The Chronicle* newspaper got onto it.

Clem stepped inside. 'Got any good calves for sale, love?'

Elizabeth looked up, her face flushing with pleasure. She gave a cheeky shrug. 'Thought you'd had enough of cows. About time you came to town.'

Clem quietly shut the door and glanced at Forde's office. 'Boss in?'

Elizabeth shook her head and patted her hair that was rolled in a coil at the nape of her neck. 'Donald's out the back.'

'Give us a kiss then.' Clem reached for her.

'Not in here, Clem –' Elizabeth started but he grabbed her, drew her to him, crushing his mouth on hers.

'Mmm. You smell good. Feel good too.' He patted her backside.

'You're terrible, but I like it,' she giggled. 'It's good to see you.' She eyed the striking young man in uniform, noting his highly polished army boots. 'I'm glad you wore your uniform to impress me.' She squeezed his hands. On an earlier leave he'd given her a copy of the formal picture of him in uniform. Elizabeth hid the photograph under her pillow and kissed the picture of the handsome figure in his army khakis and slouch hat with the rising sun badge on the side.

'What time do you knock off? Reckon you could get an early mark? I got to be back for milking.'

'Oh, blow those cows.' She glanced at the old Victorian-era pendulum clock in a carved wooden case on the wall. 'I could ask Donald if he'd mind sitting in here for a bit to get the telephone and so on. Mr Forde is out looking at a clearing sale he's doing on Friday.'

'I'll go ask Don. Man to man,' winked Clem. 'We could take a stroll down to the river.'

Donald was wiry and tanned, a cigarette constantly stuck to his lip. He was dressed in his uniform of navy work shirt and old pants held up by a plaited leather belt he'd made himself when he was a stockman.

'G'day, Donald. I just popped in to see Elizabeth. Been away at training camp.'

'Good on you, Clem. So how're you finding it? Them sergeants giving you a hard time?'

'It's not too bad, if you toe the line. Tucker's good. Nice fellows. Thommo is in the same unit as me.'

'How's your dad managing without you? Bet Frank Thompson misses you about the picture show too. Still handy with a spanner? Thought you'd go in with the engineers.'

'Infantry suits me. Might do a course through the army later but. Learn a good trade. After we get back from knocking off a few Jerries.'

'When do you boys ship out?'

'They don't tell us much. Got to be back in camp in a week or so.'

Donald broke the burning end off his cigarette, stamped on it and tucked the rest behind his ear. 'S'pose you'll be wanting to spend some time with Elizabeth?'

'Yeah. Do you think she could have a short break now? I can't stay long in town.'

'George has gone for the day. I'll sit in there and read the newspaper for half an hour.' He gave Clem a quick grin and a wink.

'Thanks, mate.'

Hand in hand Clem and Elizabeth wandered down the dusty road that wound past the Brush to the river. Apart from an old man fishing from the unused wharf they were alone. The tangle of remnant rainforest that stretched to the river was smothered in rampant vines dotted with the purply blue flowers of morning glory. They walked through the roughly cleared patch of grass by the wharf that was used for weekend picnics, and where some anglers pushed their wooden rowing boats into the river.

'Hey, remember the Empire Day fireworks when Thommo dared us to go into the Brush?' grinned Clem.

'First time you kissed me,' said Elizabeth.

'I thought you kissed me!'

'Well, you've made up for it,' she laughed.

Clem stopped and pulled her to him and kissed her long and hard.

Elizabeth pulled away, touching her lipstick-smudged lips and smoothing her hair. 'Clem Richards! In the middle of the road where everyone can see!'

'What everyone? C'mon, Elizabeth. I'm going to starve for you while I'm away.'

She gave him a quick peck and they continued walking. 'Are you scared?' she asked after a pause.

'About whipping the Jerries? I don't think so. Me and Thommo and the boys from the 13th Battalion will get in there and do the job.'

'I'll keep writing to you. Tell you what's going on.' Her hand tightened around his.

Clem felt a sudden rush of insecurity, wondering just what would be waiting for him 'over there', and for a moment he doubted Thommo's exhortations of it all being a great adventure. They walked in silence to the river and he led her to the hand-hewn seat an old timber worker had made from a fallen tree. She leaned her head on his shoulder as he held her close. The fisherman wound in his line and began packing tackle in a small basket.

'How much time have you got? Why do you have to work at the farm? Can't your brother do it? You and Kevin are enlisted men,' said Elizabeth.

'You don't know my father,' said Clem. Elizabeth had never been invited to his house for a meal and Clem hadn't given his family any clue that he was serious about her. She was just one of the home-town girls they all knew to nod hello to, just as they greeted Harold and Emily Williams in the street in the same polite but distant manner. 'He's a hard man. He doesn't know how to be anything else. I feel sorry for Mum, all she does is work and look after us boys and Phyllis. She'll miss Kev and me. Keith's the quiet one. At least he and Dad seem to get on so just as well he's staying behind.'

'What you said in your letters, about not going back to the farm, did you mean it?' asked Elizabeth snuggling closer to him.

'Bloody oath, 'scuse me. I reckon I can get a job fixing motors. And I don't mean just cars. Thommo's dad knows a fellow down in Sydney with an engineering factory, said he'll get me in there any time I want.'

'That's what I'm doing. Moving to Sydney. I'm saving up. I'm not staying in Cedartown forever,' said Elizabeth firmly.

'So, what say we go south together, eh?' joked Clem.

'Oh, yeah, and when would that be?' Elizabeth spoke lightly with a smile but he felt the tension in her.

'Let's hope this war thing is over quick. You wait for me, okay? Don't you have nothing to do with any other blokes.'

Elizabeth straightened up. 'Well, it's not like we're engaged or anything, Clem Richards.'

'Aw c'mon, Elizabeth . . .' he leaned over and kissed her cheek. 'I brought you something.'

She turned to him, her eyes shining. 'A present?'

'Yeah, give us a kiss, a proper one.'

She wound her arms around him and they kissed long and hard, oblivious to the fisherman walking back up the road.

'Crikey, you know how to kiss all right,' breathed Clem. 'Just as well it's daylight or I'd throw you in the bushes and jump on you.'

'So where's my present? I'll have to be getting back to the office.'

Clem pulled the small velvet bag from his trouser pocket. 'Hope you like it.'

Elizabeth untied the ribbon, trying to hide her disappointment it wasn't a small box that might contain a ring. She pulled out the fine gold bracelet.

'You like it? Here, let me help put it on you.' He slipped it on her wrist and fumbled with the clasp.

'It's pretty.' Elizabeth jiggled the little heart locket.

'That's my heart, you can carry it around while I'm gone,' said Clem, his voice choking up.

Elizabeth looked at him, her eyes wet with tears. 'I'll miss you, be careful over there.'

'Ah, Thommo will watch out for me.' He paused, and stroked the bracelet on her wrist. 'Elizabeth, you're my girl. You and me, we've always liked each other.'

'Oh Clem,' sighed Elizabeth. 'I really love you.' They kissed, more tenderly than passionately.

'Then you'll wait for me. And when I come back, we'll . . . get married. Try our luck in Sydney, eh?' whispered Clem.

Elizabeth hugged him. 'Oh yes, Clem. You bet.' She drew away from his embrace. 'So can I tell people we're engaged?'

Clem blinked. The vague idea of a future with Elizabeth, trying their luck in the big smoke, hadn't quite settled in his mind as a direct proposal of marriage. 'Ah, well, just between us. I wouldn't say anything to the parents. They're upset enough about us going away.'

'So where're you going?'

'Blowed if we know. Somewhere foreign. Exotic.' Clem was glad to change the subject.

Elizabeth stood up. 'C'mon, let's go back. So when am I going to see you? There's a dance on tomorrow night.

And Mum and Dad thought they'd like to have a bit of a party for the Gordon boys and friends. Supper and a sing song, you know what Mum's like.'

'Sounds good. Thommo and me will be there.'

He waved goodbye through the glass shopfront as Elizabeth settled at her desk. Behind her Donald gave Clem a thumbs up as he headed back out to the loading bay.

'So does this mean you're engaged then?' asked Mollie as she admired Elizabeth's bracelet that night. 'Where's the ring?'

'He'll get one. We don't want anyone to know. It's a secret,' said Elizabeth, suddenly deciding not to break the news until she had a ring to flash. Her sister always cut straight to the heart of a matter.

'Why?' asked Mollie.

'Because everyone is upset at the boys leaving and the war and everything.'

'So wouldn't it be nice before he goes, to, you know, have a ring and everything? What if he gets killed?'

'Mollie! That's a horrible thing to say.' Elizabeth stared at her sister. The cold brutality of the statement brought home the possibility that had hovered at the periphery of her mind. 'I try not to think about that. Anyway, he mightn't ever leave Australia.'

'That's not what Dad thinks.' Mollie gave the know-it-all look of a fifteen year old. 'So, is he a good kisser?'

Elizabeth relaxed and threw a cushion from the chair at Mollie. 'Yes, if you must know. Now don't you say anything to Mum and Dad.'

For Clem the days became increasingly busy. He worked around the farm doing jobs for his dad and tried to spend time with his mother, but he spent more and more time in town. He wanted to see Elizabeth every day, and there was Thommo. He always had a plan, a beer at the pub where the publican allowed the two boys, not yet twenty-one, to drink in the bar; a fishing trip for freshwater perch in the river; a spin up the mountain range behind town on a borrowed motorbike; kicking a football about the park with old school mates; or a quiet yarn about the days when they were kids, before a uniform changed their lives.

Clem liked the change of pace and was relieved to see that it also eased the tensions caused by Thommo's over-indulgence in grog and gambling in the army. He had gone a bit wild gambling at cards and two-up, and was always trying to keep up with the older and more experienced drinkers. But back home in the valley Thommo calmed down and once again they were two best mates, doing things together like in the days before the war. They spent time with each other's family but it was hard to relax at the farm and Clem was pleased that the Thompsons treated him like a second son.

One evening Clem had a chat with Mr Thompson as they sat in the lounge room waiting for the call to the tea table.

'Well, Clem, I suppose you must be thinking beyond the battle to come, or battles probably. It's good for morale to have some idea of what you'd like to do when you come back, duty done. Something beyond marrying Elizabeth,' he added with understanding. 'Maybe have a crack at making it in Sydney?'

Clem wasn't surprised at the reference to Elizabeth. They hadn't hidden their deepening relationship from Thommo or his parents. 'A lot of the country blokes in our unit talk about heading for the big cities when they get discharged. Having some leave in the city with money in our pockets has opened our eyes a bit,' admitted Clem.

'Elizabeth definitely wants to get out of here . . . we've sort of talked about it,' he added shyly.

Frank patted his shoulder. 'You do what you think best. Don't worry about your dad and the farm.' Frank Thompson left it at that. He'd heard enough from Thommo to appreciate how tough life was for Clem at the farm because of his father. 'For now you've got a big job ahead of you. We're very proud of you two.' He paused, and took Clem's hand. 'Keep an eye on my boy for me, Clem. I'm sure he'll be keeping an eye on you.' Then Frank turned away and changed the subject.

The Williams' family party for the young men was a big success. Emily, helped by daughters Mollie and Elizabeth, had made supper and set it out on the long kitchen table. The Gordon boys, two of them with their girlfriends, Elizabeth's friend Cynthia, Clem and Thommo and several other young couples, were all having their first sundowners of the evening in the back garden or on the back verandah.

In the kitchen Emily and Mrs Gordon fussed with last-minute food preparation and crushed up a block of ice to cool a jug of orangeade, while the men sat on the front verandah enjoying a quiet smoke over a bottle of beer. Emily didn't allow any strong liquor like whisky in the house, though an occasional glass of sherry was tolerated. She accepted the boys liked their beer and had their 'little indulgences'. Emily had taken up smoking some years before and while she limited herself she did enjoy the luxury of her Capstan 'ciggie' at morning and afternoon tea, then after dinner in the evening.

The boys all smoked. Some rolled their own as it was cheaper but Thommo now flashed around English cigarettes he'd won in a card game. Dressed in their uniforms the young soldiers looked handsome and carefree. Mollie posed them in front of the water tank and took their photo with her box brownie before the sun set.

'Mollie, take one of me and Elizabeth,' asked Clem, taking Elizabeth's hand.

'Not in front of the tank. We take all our family pictures at the front steps,' said Elizabeth.

They sat together on the brick flower box beside the steps at the front of Cricklewood. Elizabeth leaned in close to Clem's shoulder, her arm possessively through his. Clem pulled off his hat and ran his hand through his military-cut hair, smoothing the once luxuriant curls. They both smiled broadly, fresh faced, happy. There was no hint of the shadows yet to come into their lives.

After supper they all crammed into the lounge room, opened the French doors and spilled onto the front verandah for what Emily described as 'a bit of a concert, a sing song'.

Elizabeth played the piano and Emily accompanied her on the violin she'd brought from England. They all knew 'Bless 'em All', 'Kiss Me Goodnight, Sergeant Major', 'A Sleepy Lagoon', 'Red Red Robin'.

Mid evening, while music sheets were being sorted between songs, Harold called for everyone's attention, ringing a little brass bell that sat on the mantelpiece.

'Thank you for your attention, dear friends. Please forgive this little formality but I wanted to express the feelings of myself and my dear wife,' he gave a nod towards Emily who smiled and fluttered her hand. 'Feelings that are born of the circumstances reflected in the uniforms being worn here tonight,' continued Harold. 'We are very proud that our boys are marching for a just cause.' There was a burst of applause. Looking at the enthusiastic and eager faces of the young men, Harold tried to smother images of dead comrades and brave soldiers lying in the muddy horror of Flanders. He raised his glass. 'Would you join me in a toast. To Empire, freedom, democracy and, above all, to victory.'

There was a roar of approval and a great chorus shouting 'To victory!' When everyone had drunk, Emily took her place at the keyboard and in seconds 'Rule Britannia' was being sung loudly and passionately. Harold then went around and shook the hand of each of the boys and wished them a safe return.

He had a special word with Thommo, who declared he'd 'make a bloody good fist of it'.

'Listen to your officers and save your money, young man. When you get back you could have a tidy packet to get you started in a home or a little business,' advised Harold.

'She'll be right, Mr Williams. And I'll keep a lookout for Clem,' he added, wondering if Harold knew about Elizabeth and Clem's future plans.

'You rely on your mates in war, that's for sure,' said Harold, thinking of his old friend Scooter. 'Don't underestimate the enemy – and there are plenty of them. At least you're better armed and equipped than we were, I reckon.'

Later, Mrs Gordon, Emily and a reluctant Mollie washed up. Mollie went to bed, exhausted by the long day, to read another chapter of *Anne's House of Dreams*. The Gordons and their girls, along with other couples, drifted off, and Cynthia was escorted home by Thommo. Finally there was just Clem and Elizabeth sitting beside each other on the back steps.

Emily popped out to say goodnight. 'Don't you two sit up too long. You have to work in the morning, Elizabeth, and Clem, I'm sure you'll have milking in the morning.'

'Hopefully for the last time, Mrs W,' he said, then shut up as Elizabeth dug him in the ribs.

'Well, goodnight, dears.' Emily went to her bedroom

357

where Harold was already fast asleep. She was pleased they'd given the boys a good party, one they'd no doubt remember in the dark days that were inevitably ahead. Emily remembered the shocking scenes in the First World War when the troops wounded in France came to London in their tens of thousands, including her own brother. She had already signed up with the Red Cross and hoped Elizabeth would do her bit as well. They had to support all the home-town boys.

Clem held Elizabeth in his arms and kissed her, then whispered, 'This is too cramped. Let's get on the couch.' He led her to the old couch that doubled as a spare bed in the sleep-out section of the verandah screened by lattice and a well-worn and faded canvas blind.

'Going to miss me?' he asked pulling her down to his side.

'Maybe.'

'You're a tease, Lizzie Williams.'

'Don't call me that. I've told you so many times, Clem,' she said crossly.

'Sorry. Keep your hair on.' He silenced her with another kiss, his hands roaming over her body, sliding under her skirt.

Elizabeth stopped his hand with hers.

'Aw, c'mon, darlin'. I'm going off to war, for gosh sake!'

'You don't know that for sure, do you?'

'Yeah, we got word we'll be going abroad. Could be the Middle East.'

Elizabeth didn't answer but slowly lifted her hand and pulled his body to her.

Clem counted it as his first sexual experience. It had been exciting and he felt satisfied and relaxed. Then came the worry.

'You're not sorry?'

It was Elizabeth's first time but the practical girl was now fussing about her underwear and pulling the blanket off to soak in the laundry tub. 'I'll tell Mum beer got spilled. Clem, you'd better go. Dad sometimes gets up at night.'

'Throwing me out, eh?' He yawned and pulled on his pants.

They hugged goodbye at the front gate.

'Don't you tell Thommo what we did,' she admonished.

'No. Course not.' It suddenly hit him. 'Hey, um, you won't get pregnant or anything . . .?'

'Hope not,' said Elizabeth cheerfully.

But afterwards, as she lay in bed, she realised how little she knew about these things. There was no way she could ask her mother about such matters. Especially now as it would raise immediate suspicion. She'd talk to Cynthia, she had friends in Sydney who were more experienced and knowledgeable. Elizabeth then cast the pregnancy concern to one side and relived the highlights of the evening. She'd enjoyed holding centre stage briefly as she played the piano, the envious glances from the other girls when Clem was so openly demonstrative towards her, and finally their love-making. It had been a bit fumbled and awkward trying to be quiet. She began to think of more romantic and exotic scenarios of how it would be next time. What she'd wear, how'd she look and behave. Scenes from films of Rita Hayworth and Joan Crawford came to mind. One day, she and Clem would have a life together as man and wife in their own home, in the city. How exciting it would be.

A train rumbled. The bridge creaked. A night bird called. Oh yes, after the war she would leave the country behind . . . with Clem.

*

Isabella, 1854

Isabella had been living in the cottage at Birimbal some distance from the burnt remains of her mansion while she waited for her home at the river to be completed. She decided to call her new home Riverview as she loved the peaceful vista of the river. She stayed at Birimbal till the last crop of lucerne had been harvested and stored in the remaining barn. There was still some stock on the property including five hundred head of cattle, half of which she had instructed an agency in Sydney to sell. She had been juggling finances with the two properties so had taken a loan from the firm, putting up her cattle as security. Her loan would be paid off from the sale of the cattle.

Most days her company was limited to a stockman and two female native servants, so on hearing approaching horses Isabella went outside to see who her visitors were. Three men dismounted, one she recognised as a gentleman she'd met briefly when he stopped by for a courtesy call a month before. He seemed to be the leader of the three.

'Good morning, gentlemen.' She recognised the man in charge.

'Good morning again, Miss Kelly. I am Charles Skerrett. You graciously extended hospitality to me some time back.' Although humbly dressed his manner and speech impressed Isabella. He seemed a man who'd been well educated.

'Well, Mr Skerrett, cool water is the least one can offer a thirsty traveller. What brings you this way?'

'May I introduce my companions, Mr Millar and Mr Anderson.' They raised their hats as Skerrett continued, 'They are accompanying me on business. As you may recall, I have been a magistrate in Melbourne for several years but I moved to Port Macquarie where I have cattle and horses.'

Isabella thought quickly. If Skerrett had a proven record as a magistrate perhaps he could act as one in the valley and solve her contentious dealings with local magistrates.

Charles Skerrett continued, 'I am looking for a property further north. I've heard you are leaving here and so I wish to enquire about a lease.'

'I am not selling Birimbal, but I could consider a lease. You have family, Mr Skerrett?'

'Indeed, ma'am. Eight girls and one son.' He gave a disarming smile. 'I am travelling through to Sydney to collect power-of-attorney from the firm of Brierly, Dean and Co. and to collect an inheritance of one thousand five hundred pounds that has come my way.'

'My cottage is small, though I believe the bails close by could be converted to sleeping quarters. They are clean and dry.' Isabella suddenly thought having Skerrett in residence would not only provide some income but would be a deterrent to anyone with malicious intent. She still firmly believed her grand home had been deliberately set on fire. 'Do come inside where we can discuss matters in more comfort,' said Isabella.

Over tea Skerrett and Isabella came to an agreement. He would lease Birimbal for ten pounds a year.

'And your cattle, Miss Kelly? I am interested in purchasing some.'

'Well, the cattle I have for sale are listed with an agent in Sydney. If you are in Sydney and wish to contact him, I will give you the name and address.'

Several weeks later Skerrett reappeared and told Isabella he had bought all her cattle from her agent in Sydney.

Isabella was shocked. 'But I only authorised the agent to sell half of the stock on this property. I planned to take the other two hundred and fifty to Riverview.'

'They fetched a very good price.'

'There must be some misunderstanding. Can I see the documentation, Mr Skerrett?'

'I do not have it as it is in my goods coming from Sydney. However, you can expect a letter from the agent very soon. I can assure you he sold me the entire herd.'

Isabella rose and paced the room to calm the anger Skerrett's announcement stirred in her. Perhaps she had not been clear enough in her instructions to the Sydney agent and cursed herself for not making a copy of the selling instructions.

'I understand that you must be concerned at this turn of events, Miss Kelly, but I have gone into a complex financial arrangement in Sydney to pay for this herd. I cannot go back on the sale. So until we have the papers concerning the sale, can we draw up an agreement to allow me to muster the cattle.'

Although she was not happy about the arrangement, Isabella believed her cattle were now Skerrett's and he could sell, slaughter or breed with them as he wished. She hastily wrote out two copies of a mustering agreement which they both signed and countersigned.

Skerrett and his family arrived the day before Isabella left for Riverview. She was surprised at the bedraggled appearance of Mrs Skerrett and the thin and ragged children. Their belongings appeared to be mostly bedding pulled behind in a dray.

'Have you not brought supplies with you, Mr Skerrett?' asked Isabella.

'The wagon with food and grain supplies was destroyed when it went over a flooded causeway. Those two fellows you met with me were quite careless. I dismissed both of them after the loss. So I would be grateful if we can impose on your store until I can replenish our needs.'

Isabella gave them flour, sugar, wheat and some grain seed. She felt sorry for the group of thin girls huddled around their mother who had a baby in one arm and held the hand of a toddler.

'I have left some horses here until my man Florian comes from the river to fetch them and other remaining necessities. You can take the milk from the cows,' offered Isabella.

'You are a kind lady. Many thanks, Miss Kelly.' He doffed his hat in a courtly gesture and Isabella wondered how it had happened that such an educated gentleman appeared to be in such strained domestic circumstances. His wife appeared to be totally unsuited to be the partner of a gentleman and magistrate. Skerrett continued, 'I am unable to muster the cattle as planned, so I suggest we tear up the agreement.' He produced a paper and tore it into pieces, throwing them into the kitchen fire.

Isabella retrieved her copy of the contract from her writing box and tore it up as well. 'I hope fortune smiles on you,' she said as she took her leave.

When she left Birimbal for the river she met her neighbour Mr Andrews on the road.

'Ah, Miss Kelly, I've been meaning to call by and enquire about buying a fat bullock from you.'

'I'm sorry, Mr Andrews, I've sold all my cattle to my tenant, Mr Skerrett.'

At Riverview Isabella applied herself to the many tasks of upgrading the property. It was some time before she became concerned at not hearing from the agent in Sydney about the sale of her cattle to Skerrett, so she sent a letter.

The agent's reply shocked her.

Miss Kelly,
We regret to inform you we have had no dealings with a Mr Charles Skerrett, or that any sale of your cattle has taken place. Certainly no monies have been received. Would you please instruct us in how you wish

to proceed in the matter of selling the 250 head of your herd as requested.

Isabella confided in Florian. 'I fear there is some misunderstanding, at least I hope that's all it is. I must go to Sydney.'

The meeting with her agent was no more illuminating. He advised her to put an advertisement in the local paper cautioning anyone not to buy cattle or horses with the Kelly brand on them. Isabella returned to Birimbal to confront Charles Skerrett. There she found only Mrs Skerrett and the children. Isabella demanded to know what had happened.

The woman dabbed at her eyes and whined as several children hovered around her skirt. 'We are in great difficulty. We have little food and my husband ordered a beast to be killed for us to eat. I don't know about any cattle. He's gone to see the neighbour Mr Turner.'

Isabella looked at the cringing woman, the dirty and untidy room, the snivelling children. 'Tell your husband he will face greater difficulties for what he has done,' she snapped as she turned on her heel.

Isabella took a fresh horse from the few that remained on Birimbal and rode around the hill to the property belonging to Luke Turner. She found Turner's stockman at the slaughter yards and he told her that the farmer was away. Isabella spotted several hides hanging on the rails and saw they each had her brand on them.

'Cut out those brands and give them to me,' she demanded.

The stockman didn't argue. He knew Isabella Kelly was not a woman to contradict or ignore. The boss could sort it out. He was relieved when Isabella rode off with the pieces of hide hanging from her saddle.

Back at Riverview she told Florian she was charging Skerrett with cattle stealing.

Florian looked at the hides and nodded. 'He seems to be very sure about where he stands in this matter to sell some of the stock,' he said in some puzzlement.

'Or plain treacherous, Florian. And he appeared to be a gentleman. I am not going to the local magistrate, I shall go to Dungog Police.'

'Miss, please do not travel alone. Take my son Kelly with you. The lad is bright and can help you.'

They rode out, Isabella side-saddle on her black horse and Kelly on a chestnut mare with a white blaze on her forehead. He rode easily, having been on a horse most of his ten years. He was shy but excited at this adventure.

A short distance from Dungog township they came upon Luke Turner who was returning to his property. Isabella hailed him, noting that the horse he rode looked like one of hers. He was clearly embarrassed at meeting her.

'I wish to enquire why you purchased my cattle from Skerrett. Surely you recognised my brand?' she said.

Turner looked uncomfortable. 'I enquired and Mr Skerrett said he'd bought them from you and needed to make a sale. He showed me the paper you had signed, so I went ahead and took six beasts.'

'Paper? What paper? I signed no paper. Those animals belonged to me and I am on my way to have him arrested.'

Turner looked shocked. 'Oh, don't do that, Miss Kelly. It will cause trouble. I am not sure what the paper said . . .' he looked uncomfortable. 'I have never learned to read or sign my name properly. I believed him. Surely he would not sell cattle to me knowing they belonged to you.'

Isabella stared him down. While Turner was quite possibly a fool and had made a mistake there was something about his manner that disturbed her. She glanced at Kelly who had dismounted and was studying Turner's horse. 'What is it, boy?'

'This is your horse. I know it. I rode him.'

Turner flicked his whip towards the boy. 'What rubbish this native boy talks. Get away from my horse.' Turner lifted the whip in a threatening gesture.

'That will do, I demand you dismount, Mr Turner, and let me look at the brand on that horse.' The saddle blanket and saddlebags behind covered a fair portion of the horse's rump.

'I will do no such thing. The horse is mine.' And with a flourish, he kicked the horse into a canter and rode away without looking back.

'I fear Charles Skerrett has taken great liberties. I should never have let him and his miserable family onto my property,' said Isabella. But the thought that Skerrett was showing a document purported to be signed by her caused her deep misgivings. She was also disturbed that a man of breeding, as Skerrett seemed to be, could be so blatantly dishonest. One part of her still wanted to believe there had been a misunderstanding that would be cleared up. But there was no dismissing the fact he had taken and sold her cattle.

The police conducted a lengthy enquiry and Charles Skerrett was arrested. The case finally came before the Central Criminal Court in Darlinghurst, Sydney, early the following year.

Charles Skerrett looked calm, almost cocky, and stated his defence in a straightforward manner and on a simple premise – he owned the cattle. Miss Kelly had sold them to him so he could do with them as he wished. He flourished a bill of sale, a receipt and an agreement to muster the cattle.

Too late Isabella realised that Skerrett had torn up some other paper and not the mustering contract. She hadn't read them, and now realised that what he had destroyed in the fire was an irrelevant letter. So now Skerrett could produce an authentic document allowing him to round up all the cattle on Birimbal and sell them. Isabella sat still and straight stifling her rage and shock at the other forged documents he produced.

Her near neighbour, Mr Andrews, gave evidence that he had asked to buy a fat bullock. Miss Kelly told him she had none to sell as Skerrett had already bought the cattle. However, when Andrews was shown the bill of sale he did not think it was Isabella's signature as he knew her handwriting well. However, he thought the signature on the mustering agreement was genuine.

When Turner took the stand he was nervous and could not satisfactorily explain how he paid for the cattle or was in possession of the horse with Isabella's brand on it. When pressed he said that Skerrett had shown him a bill of sale so he purchased the horse and cattle. However, when asked to read to the court the bill of sale, Turner admitted he could neither read nor write.

It didn't take long for the jury to convict Skerrett of cattle theft and he was sentenced to ten years' labour on the roads.

The trial had taken a toll on Isabella. She learned that Skerrett had been transported for theft and forgery and her anguish that he had duped her grew. She returned to Riverview in ill health. She was cared for by Hettie who gave her teas brewed from bush leaves Noona brought her, and soon Isabella recovered. She was disappointed that her judgment of men had failed. The yardstick by which she gauged others, and they her, had been shaken. She vowed to be even more alert to the devious ploys of people wishing to take advantage of her.

In this new colony the old values did not apply. Rascals pretended to be gentlemen and no one was the wiser. A man could hide his past and create a new life. She compared Florian and Skerrett, two convicted felons. One had been rashly and unfairly sentenced but had come through to begin a new and honest life, hard as it may be. The other preferred to live by deceit, his wits and his charm. Isabella vowed she would never be taken advantage of again.

She found solace in the new orchid conservatory she'd had built. There was a thick stand of rainforest along the river where she found a variety of interesting plants for potting. It provided a little relief from the demanding work required to build up Riverview. She had had a big financial setback but hoped to recover from the costs involved in prosecuting Skerrett. Even though she felt vindicated she was deeply disturbed that a man could so easily forge documents to cheat her.

Isabella had sadly come to the conclusion that men were not as her guardian William Crowder had led her to expect. That a man of education, social standing, manners and apparent wealth was a man to be trusted and respected. It now seemed to Isabella that, with few exceptions, in the wild colonial world even gentlemen were bastards.

13

Dani

DANI FELT THAT SHE was painting herself into the picture. That she was melting into the oil paint as she worked. It was a large canvas of the deep part of the valley at Kelly's Crossing – shadowy trees with leaves limply hanging in the heat of noon, slashes of sunlight on the slow-moving stream, no movement or sound from birds or animals. The still, hot scene radiated from the canvas in the slick of oily colours.

Dani felt the sting of perspiration on her body and moved her brush into the cooler green-greys of under-growth further up the creek and touched up the water of refreshing rock pools. She imagined she heard the snap of a twig, the rustle of a bird seeking shade. How wonderful it would be to slip out of her clothes and lie in the shallows and shady pools.

'Dani?'

She jumped, leaping back a step as if discovered naked in the water.

'Hey, sorry, Dani. Didn't you hear me drive up?' Barney poked his head through the studio door. 'Helen's picked you some vegies.' He stared at Dani smudged with paint, beads of perspiration shining above her lip. 'You look a bit hot and bothered. Am I disturbing you?'

'I felt I was right in the middle of this scene . . .' Dani couldn't describe the sensation adequately. The unfinished canvas drew her in, she was there, in every sense. But it wasn't the present moment. She was in Isabella's time. She felt the pangs Isabella must have felt at the deceit of Charles Skerrett, and the love she must have had for the valley and her home in Birimbal in the high country and Riverview on the river.

'It's okay, Barney.' Dani put down her brush, severing her connection with the past and the sensations evoked by the fresh paint strokes of feeling part of the painting.

Barney came and stood beside her, contemplating the picture. After a moment's silence he said softly, 'It's like a doorway. You go right in there.' He paused for another deep look at the work, then asked, 'Who're the people?'

Dani peered into the shadowy reaches of the trees. 'I haven't painted any people.'

'They're there though. I can see 'em.'

Dani shivered. 'Must be spirits you can see, Barney.'

'Yeah, it happens a lot. I see things, y'know?'

'What sort of things?' asked Dani, studying the wiry man in his uniform of khaki shorts and shirt.

'Dunno. Sometimes it's a fleeting figure, a face. Or I'm somewhere and I know people are there with me, even if I can't see them. Or, I might be walking somewhere I haven't been before and I'll know exactly what I'm going to see when I get around the corner. And bingo, there it is. Sometimes when I go fishing, I know exactly where the fish will be. It's like a voice in my head.' He gave a grin. 'Funny, eh?'

'You're very intuitive, Barney,' said Dani with a smile and nod of understanding.

Barney accepted the comment as if he'd been told that before. 'I'll put the vegies in the kitchen. Now, the other thing is, I wanted to ask you if Tim can come camping with me and Toby tomorrow night. Just us boys.'

'I'm sure he'd love it, where are you going to camp?' Dani thought there must be a few good spots on the ninety acres of Chesterfield.

'We're going down the river to one of the little islands. There's one that's got a bit of a gravel beach where we can pull the boat in. Helen's grandfather used to graze cattle there in the old days. The other islands are too thick with mangroves and rubbishy growth to get through,' said Barney.

'How'd they get the cattle across the river to the island?' asked Dani. It seemed an odd place to graze cattle.

'On the punt, or swim them if it was calm. There were a few farms on the islands that grew food for the markets in Hungerford and Riverwood in the old days. One island still has a decent farmhouse on it.'

'And what's on this island where you're going with the boys?'

'Nothing anymore. There's a sheltered possie where we can pitch the tent. It's only small, maybe four acres. Real good fishing off one end of the island, you can cast into a deep channel. We'll light a bonfire, tell stories, you know, boys' stuff.'

'It sounds great, Barney. Tim doesn't get to do that sort of thing very often.' Dani was grateful her son could share a grandfather.

'Rightio then. Drop him over with his sleeping bag and

fishing gear. I've got everything we need.' He turned and took another look at the painting. 'That's real good, Dani. You've certainly got the feel of the place.'

'Even if it feels a little creepy?' she asked.

'There's history, good and bad, in every bit of the landscape, long before we came here. Take those people who think they're buying a house in that new community Jason is building. They're only breathing new life into old land, they should appreciate what they're part of. It's good he's trying not to disturb some parts too much,' said Barney.

'Perhaps that's what I hope people will understand when they see these paintings. They're part of something that goes way, way back,' said Dani thoughtfully. Barney had clarified for her what she was instinctively painting.

Barney nodded. 'Like waaay back. Dreamtime territory.'

'I wonder if the pioneers had any idea,' mused Dani.

'Doubt it, the way they whaled into clearing the land and pushing the Aborigines around. S'pose there wasn't anyone to tell them what was what. If anyone learned to speak a native dialect they didn't comprehend what they were being told, most likely.'

'From what Max has told me, Aboriginal culture and beliefs are very complex,' said Dani. 'I don't know much about it.'

'Sad thing is, same thing applies to a lot of modern Aboriginal people. Well, I'd better be going. See you tomorrow.'

'Okay, Barney, and I'm looking forward to cooking those nice fresh vegies. Ta.'

'No chemicals or sprays either. Just my chilli and garlic bug spray. See ya.' He waved.

Dani gazed at her painting, then decided to take a break and go for a walk. She'd been meaning to get into a routine of a brisk walk before breakfast each morning but even though she got up early with good intentions, she'd make a cup of tea and wander to her studio and look at yesterday's work, tidy her paints and brushes, and before she knew it an hour or more had passed and she was ravenous. She always had a hearty breakfast and if Tim was with her they'd be into the day's plans, all thoughts of a walk forgotten. So now she put on her walking shoes, whistled Jolly and headed down towards the creek.

It was mid morning, comfortably warm and clear, and Dani took a deep breath, inhaling the smell of the lemon-scented gums. Seeing Juniper and Bomber across the creek, she called them to come and get the carrots she'd promised Tim she'd give them each day. The horses ignored her so she crossed the creek on the stepping stones Tim and Toby had dragged into place a few weeks earlier.

Despite the lure of the carrots the two horses were wary and by the time they decided to take the snack, she was halfway up the long, partly cleared slope.

This was Kerry's land and, as she'd never explored this side of the creek or visited her neighbour, Dani decided to press on in the hope of running into the rather reclusive woman.

It was pretty country with several fenced paddocks with stands of trees as windbreaks and shade but, apart from the two horses, no sign of livestock or cropping. The whole area seemed empty, no, lost. So different from the scene she was painting.

Jolly raced ahead, her nose to the ground following the zigzag route of a rabbit. Then she stopped by a dense thicket of trees, lifting her head and listening.

'What is it, Jolly? Are we near Kerry's place?' Dani walked through the trees, glancing back to note the way she'd come as there was no path or track to follow. Juniper and Bomber must have their own route to wherever they went to shelter. Or perhaps they were left in the open all the time. Again Dani thought it unwise for Tim to consider riding these big unworked horses.

She came out of the trees on top of a small rise and, looking down, saw Kerry's cottage nestled in the cleft of the knoll and behind it, a steeper hill ringed with large formal, mostly introduced, trees. These must have been planted many years ago – large pines and fully established beech and elm trees that looked like a fortress ringing the top of the hill.

The cottage was a classic picture of Australiana with a bullnose roof over the front verandah, lots of lattice and a pretty garden shaded by a large magnolia tree. Some way behind the house and up the slope was a lazily turning windmill pumping water into a pipe that led to a tank. There was a fenced side yard with a shed and she could see chickens pecking around the clothesline.

As she walked towards the cottage Jolly raced ahead and Dani expected a dog to come and greet them or Kerry to emerge. She called out. 'Anyone home? Kerry? You there? Hello?'

There was no answer. Dani paused at the front of the house, the door was open and she could see down the hall-way to the open back door and a small deck. From this closer range she realised how old the cottage was, judging by the style of weatherboards used for walls, the sagging front verandah and the odd windows. She reckoned it could be at least eighty years old. But with no answer except a possessive and alarmed squawk from a large white hen, Dani and Jolly continued their walk. Having come this far she decided to go to the top of the hill to the stand of big trees and see what the view was like. It might be a good vista to paint.

It was a surprisingly long climb, the cottage shrank to doll's house proportions, and soon she was lost in the grove of magnificent trees. A dry-stone wall wound to the top of the hill and Dani was reminded of lush English countryside, as the recent rain had turned the ground cover a fresh green. There was an old-fashioned wooden gate that swung open easily enough so they went on, following a faint path through the grass.

Dani was so interested in the fruit trees, flowering shrubs, old garden beds and overgrown hedges that the sight of the house caught her completely by surprise. She had come from behind so she was confronted with stables, servants' quarters, a wash house and a cookhouse that appeared to have been converted into a storeroom reached by a covered walkway. To one side was a large private courtyard surrounded by a walled garden smothered in climbing roses. Further from the house in a largely overgrown remnant of garden was an ornate wooden summerhouse in desperate need of repair.

Dani walked along a meandering path to a formal circular driveway and stood gazing in absolute wonder at the magnificent old homestead that stood before her. It was double-storeyed and made of bricks that had mellowed with age. The upstairs windows had large shutters under the deep eaves of a slate roof with elaborate chimneys. The downstairs front portico was flanked by a wide, stone-flagged colonnade shaded by sandstone columns where a prolific wisteria vine climbed. Double French doors opened onto this frontage from which short courtyard wings curved around to either side. There was a large fountain in the centre of the driveway with huge angophora trees on both sides. The lawns and rose beds must have been magnificent once and the view over the valley to the mountains and shimmering river was unobstructed. It was all quite breathtaking.

The house must have been built in the late 1800s, surmised Dani, but it was sadly neglected. Peeling paint, broken trim and architraves, dirty windows, untended gardens. Nonetheless it didn't appear abandoned. Some efforts had been made here and there – some pruned cuttings, leaves and twigs raked into a pile. The flagged front verandah looked like it had been swept, the fountain was clean but dry.

Dani went to the front door and rapped the iron knocker then turned to appreciate the view framed by the colonnade and wisteria vine. What a place to sit and meditate on the scene. Several unravelling wicker chairs and an old wooden deckchair were positioned between the stone columns. Dani shaded her eyes and peered through a set of French doors where the curtains were pulled back. It looked like a lounge or drawing room, bulky shadows suggested furniture covered by sheets.

She walked slowly around the side of the house and discovered a swimming pool, a more recent addition, maybe in the 1950s.

Jolly stopped and gave a low growl, looking towards the house. At the back entrance a large door stood ajar. Curiosity was gnawing at Dani and she was keen to see inside, but she had an overwhelming feeling that she was trespassing. She knew she should call out in case anyone was around, but she couldn't shake the feeling she would not be welcome.

She stepped into the vestibule and went down the wide central hallway, Jolly padding behind her. There was a familiar smell and then a rattle and a clatter from a room towards the front. Dani turned towards the noise, pushing open a heavy, carved cedar door.

And gasped in astonishment.

It was the dining room – completely furnished down to a rose crystal epergne on the centre of the table, silver dishes and a tea service set along the ornate rosewood credenza. What was more surprising was the sight of Kerry, wearing a large apron smock, busily polishing the table.

Kerry caught her breath and stared at Dani in the doorway.

'Furniture oil. That's what I could smell. A lovely smell,' said Dani, struggling to sound friendly and defuse the obvious tension her arrival had created.

'You shouldn't be here,' said Kerry shortly. Her hair was tied back with a scarf, she looked flushed and harried.

'I'm sorry. I started walking, there wasn't anyone home at your cottage . . . I assumed it was your place . . . and I saw the trees on top of the hill.'

Kerry straightened up. 'They're supposed to screen the house. Not invite people to come exploring.'

Dani immediately apologised and tried to sound neighbourly as she reintroduced herself and Jolly. 'I'm Tim's mum, from over the creek. I didn't even know this was here. Whose house is it? Is this where you live?' she asked, quite confused. The grand house appeared to be intact, with all its original furnishings down to bric-a-brac.

'No. It's not my place. I just look after it. I live in the old manager's cottage in exchange for keeping this place in order.'

'Well, you're doing a lovely job,' said Dani. 'It's extraordinary. Whose place is it? Could I look around?'

Kerry gathered up her duster and bottle of polish. 'Don't mention this to anyone. I'm not to let visitors inside. Not that many people remember this place anymore. Not since the old man died and the rest of the family moved out.' She gave a flick of the duster and headed through an archway into a small sitting room.

'I won't say a word,' Dani promised. She glanced around the sitting room filled with Victorian memorabilia and spied the library with floor-to-ceiling bookcases. It was amazing everything was still intact. She wondered if Barry and Maree from Isadora's knew of this place. They'd go crazy over everything in here. 'Does anyone come and stay? What will happen to this place? Be a magnificent B&B, wouldn't it,' she said lightly.

Kerry looked at Dani as if wondering whether to tell her something, then turned away. 'It will never go out of the family. Passed down from father to son. It'll just fall down eventually, I suppose.'

'What about the National Trust, surely this is heritage listed?' exclaimed Dani.

'No way. The old man wouldn't hear of it. Anyway, I think it should stay just as it is. Excuse me, I have a lot to do.'

'I hope I haven't got you into any trouble, Kerry, I'll keep this to myself. But as I'm here, I just thought . . . it's not often you get a chance to see how the other half lived, all that time ago,' said Dani softly.

'Turn right when you get to the upstairs landing,' said Kerry shortly. 'You're an artist, you'll probably enjoy the gallery. Take the dog with you, no problem.'

Dani began to explore the house, entranced by the spacious rooms, the relics of generations of a family's existence, the extraordinary views from every window. The landing ran into a modest gallery, a mezzanine floor suspended above the lobby. It featured a few interesting portraits, some works of local scenery and prize livestock as well as a few competent works of bucolic English countryside. Dani wandered up and down imagining how her Isabella pictures would fit in. This house was probably built after Isabella's time, but how many other historic relics were scattered about the valley, she wondered. She loved the master bedroom though she thought she'd update the old-fashioned bathroom and turn one of the four bedrooms into a study.

As she went back downstairs it occurred to Dani that, although it was fully furnished, there was nothing personal in the house. No photographs, no personal little things, just the formal portraits. Obviously no one had lived here for a long time, so it was odd Kerry was kept on as housekeeper. She was a strange woman. There was something about the way she'd been so feverishly rubbing and polishing the table. She obviously loved the place.

They parted on pleasant terms after Dani enthused about the contents, the art, and the single-handed effort being made by Kerry to maintain order and cleanliness in the huge home.

'Do drop over to The Vale sometime for a cup of tea,' offered Dani and Kerry smiled and nodded as she worked but made no commitment.

Walking home across the creek Dani glanced over her shoulder at the ring of trees on the far hill hiding the strange and beautiful old house. She thought about how homes had developed in the area from the first settlers in a one-room sapling-frame hut covered in strips of bark with leather hinges on the door and a slab of bark as a window shutter. Then would come the mud-brick chimney, extra rooms or a larger, separate dwelling made from felled timber with a tin roof or wooden shingles. Pioneer housing was simple and organic, a style dictated by abundant bush and limited cash until the wealthier and more successful landholders built mini-mansions, many in the style of what they knew back in the old country. And now Jason was evolving housing that was reverting to how it had been in the beginning – modern but modest, harmoniously existing within the landscape. She had more of a sense of what Jason was trying to do and decided Isabella would probably approve.

*

Cedartown, 1942

Harold was sitting in the lounge room reading the newspaper with the latest war news when he heard the brass knocker fall against the front door. He opened the door to find Clem standing there in uniform. He gave Harold a bit of a smile and whipped off his slouch hat.

'Morning, Mr Williams.'

'Clem, lad! How wonderful to see you. Elizabeth said you were hoping to get leave. Come in, come in.'

He ushered Clem into the lounge room where Clem sat on the edge of the lounge suite, holding his hat between his knees. 'Sorry I couldn't give any notice, they move us around pretty quickly and we're never sure where we'll be next week.'

'I understand how it is, of course.' Harold looked at the man he'd known since he was a youngster now back from action with the 9th Division in the Middle East. Harold saw the strain in Clem's once bright and mischievous eyes, the tightness around his mouth, the tautness in his body. The boy had been blooded, seen how war could be. 'I'll get Elizabeth for you.' Harold paused. 'How long have you got?'

'A week, maybe a bit more. We're waiting for the rest of the 13th to remobilise then we're being sent to New Guinea, we hear on the grapevine.'

'Those wretched Japs are storming down from Singapore. After Pearl Harbor they think they can walk into Darwin. Or come through the Sydney Heads.'

'Not if we can help it, sir.'

'Good lad, that's the spirit.' Harold disappeared down the hallway calling for his elder daughter.

'She's down in the fowl yard getting me some eggs,' said Emily who was busy kneading dough to bake bread. 'Was that the door?'

'It's Clem. Back on leave, wants to see Elizabeth.'

'Oh my goodness,' exclaimed Emily, immediately wiping her hands on her apron. 'Elizabeth will be furious, she's got her old clothes on. Trousers, no less. Keep Clem chatting while she tidies herself up. Where's Mollie?'

'Don't fuss, Mum. I don't think Clem is going to care what she's wearing.'

Clem appeared in the kitchen doorway. 'Hello, Mrs Williams. Did I hear you say Elizabeth is down the back?' Emily nodded and Clem grinned. 'I'll just pop down there and give her a big surprise.' Clem shot through the kitchen door and down the back steps before Emily could say anything. He wanted to see Elizabeth alone, hold her and kiss her.

Elizabeth was on her hands and knees in the chook yard, reaching under the laying boxes where there were several eggs in the cool dirt.

'You damn girls, why'd you lay under here when you've got nice straw boxes.'

'Just to annoy you probably.' Clem gave her bottom a cheerful pat.

'Clem! You wretch! Oh my! Why didn't you tell me!' Elizabeth scrambled to her feet, dusting off her shirt and cotton trousers.

Clem grabbed her and held her tightly burying his face in her hair, which was partly covered with a bandana. 'Ah Jeez, Elizabeth. I've missed you. Real bad.' He kissed her and would have been content just to stand there, holding her in his arms, tasting her lips, smelling the pine-freshness of her hair.

Elizabeth wiggled from his embrace. 'Goodness, Clem. I wish I'd known you were coming today. Just look at me. How long are you home for?'

'You look good to me. Dunno about the time. Not long.'

'So . . . how was it? Terrible?' When Clem didn't answer immediately she continued, 'Dad told me not to ask. But I was so worried. And Thommo? He back too?'

'Yep. So what do you want to do? Are the Gordon boys home?'

'Not that I've heard. Say, there's a dance tomorrow night. Or what about the pictures? Mr Thompson has got a John Wayne showing.'

'I was hoping we could just kind of be, you know, quiet like. Just the two of us,' said Clem holding her hand as they walked back to the house.

'Oh. I s'pose so.' Elizabeth was hoping she could show off her soldier, home from the front.

She won the day and the town closed its collective eyes to the carousing, singing, drinking and partying of the group of local boys on a brief reprieve before 'going north'. There was talk of jungle training and going to the islands to stop the Jap invasion.

'Where're you going for tropical training?' Cynthia asked Thommo. 'Maybe me and Elizabeth could get the train to Brisbane and see you up there!'

'Fat chance,' laughed Thommo. 'You two girls got to keep working, keep the home fires burning. Anyway, some blokes didn't get any leave at all. Straight off the ship from the Middle East and on the ship to New Guinea and Borneo.'

'So you'd better make the most of this leave then,' said Elizabeth.

'I thought we were,' said Clem. 'But I gotta spend some time at home. Dad's fuming over practically everything connected to the farm and Mum is looking very down in the mouth.'

'That farm, I thought when you joined up you'd never have to work on it again,' said Elizabeth in an exasperated voice.

'They are my family.'

'Hang about you two,' soothed Thommo. 'What say we go for a walk down to the river.'

'I'd better be getting home, I promised I'd be there for tea tonight,' said Cynthia.

'Me too,' said Elizabeth, even though she'd hoped to spend the evening with Clem.

'I was going to meet a couple of pals, want to come along?' Thommo asked Clem.

'Nah, I'll head out to the farm. I'd better get Keith's truck back.' He grinned at Elizabeth. 'See ya tomorrow then. Just you and me, eh?'

'After work. Hooroo then.' She took Cynthia's hand and the girls walked off.

'So whaddya want to do then? You don't really want to go home, do ya?' Thommo stuck his hands deep in his trousers pockets as they sauntered back down the street from the Australia Hotel.

'Maybe I should. I feel sorry for Mum. I haven't spent much time with her this leave,' said Clem. 'And your folks would probably like to see more of you.' Clem thought about the Thompsons' packages. While his mother had written simple, heartfelt letters about life on the farm and sent the socks she knitted, Thommo's parents had sent parcels with raisins, biscuits, cigarettes and his favourite lollies, which he'd shared with Clem.

'All right. Maybe the Gordons will lob in and we can muck around with them. See ya.'

The following day when Elizabeth skipped out of the All-farms Stock and Station Agency, she found Clem standing outside, dressed in his civvies, twisting his hat in his hands, looking solemn. 'Why didn't you come inside and say hello to Donald? Whatever is the matter with you?' she asked, linking her arm through his and giving him a quick peck on the cheek.

'There's been news, bad news from Syria . . .' he began.

Elizabeth stopped, her hand flying to her mouth. 'Has someone we know been killed?'

'Yeah.' He swallowed and took a deep breath.

'Clem! Who, for goodness sake?'

'Andy. Andy Gordon. Your mum and dad are pretty upset. They're with Mr and Mrs Gordon right now.'

Elizabeth stood still in shock. 'But he was coming home, like you, on leave . . . They were so looking forward to it.' Tears began to roll down her face. The three Gordon boys had always been the boys next door since she could remember.

Awkwardly Clem took her in his arms, feeling incapable of comforting her.

Elizabeth suddenly drew back and looked at him. 'What if something happens to you?'

'Nah, nothing's going to happen to me. Never fear. Come on, let's go down the road and I'll get you a shandy.'

'No, I hate sitting in that ladies' lounge. I want to be with you.' She clutched his arm as they walked down Isabella Street. Shops were closing and as they passed the jewellery store, Elizabeth stopped. 'Let's get married, Clem. I don't want you to go away and leave things so . . . up in the air.' She peered at the display of rings.

'What do you mean, up in the air?' said Clem. 'We're engaged, sort of, you said.' He was slightly taken aback at this turn of events.

'I don't want to wait. I want us to get married. Please, Clem, it means a lot to me.'

'There's no time! I leave in three days.'

'We can do it. Just a simple thing. And later, when it's over and you're back we'll have a proper wedding.'

Elizabeth's eyes were shining and she looked so pretty, Clem's heart lurched.

'What will our parents say? We have to get paper-work . . . I dunno.' Clem shook his head.

'I'll look after everything like that, Clem,' said Elizabeth, suddenly businesslike. 'You just get the ring. We'll go to the registry office in Hungerford. You ring up and book us in. Wear your uniform and have Thommo for your best man of course.'

In the few minutes they'd walked together since breaking the news, Clem felt his life revving into high gear. Elizabeth chattered on, her tears over Andy gone. Where was he going to get a ring for her, pondered Clem. He had some money saved but he'd promised it to his mother so she had a little nest egg of her own that his father didn't know about. What about Thommo? He had a ring he'd won in a poker game in Syria. Maybe he'd loan it to Clem. Or give it to him. Thommo owed Clem a few quid borrowed for card games.

'Let's ask your parents first. I'll have to speak to your dad.'

'It's my mother who'll dig her heels in,' said Elizabeth calmly. 'Dad'll talk her round, you'll see.'

Clem couldn't begin to think what his parents would say. He'd never told them how serious he and Elizabeth were. He shuddered. 'Elizabeth, are you sure you want to do this? I mean, it's a big step. What difference is it going to make to us? We love each other no matter what.'

'Clem Richards, you stop this. How do you think I'll feel if you get killed?' demanded Elizabeth. 'At least if I'm your wife I'm left with something.' Her voice choked up and she was close to tears again. A woman walking past glanced at them.

'All right, settle down. Let me think about this. You're

right, I should look after you. You'll get my allotment. We can save up, maybe get a house . . .'

'Don't forget I'm saving money from my job. We just need enough to get us to Sydney, start a new life. Oh Clem, it's the only way we're going to get out of here. You're already gone, I'm still stuck here.' Elizabeth was rigid with impatience. 'I wish I could join up.'

'Your mum said you were working with the Red Cross, and maybe joining the VAD,' said Clem but stopped as Elizabeth dismissively waved a hand.

'Heavens, Clem, rolling bandages, learning first aid and wrapping parcels to be sent to the troops. That's not getting me out of here.'

'You have a good job, you save your money, yeah, that's the best thing to do,' said Clem. He couldn't see Elizabeth in the forces, working like the nurses he'd seen. There was a gentleness, a calmness about them, a sense of humour that he couldn't see Elizabeth producing when the heat was on, all hell breaking loose, wounded everywhere. She was so emotional. So driven.

Elizabeth interrupted his thoughts. 'Then that's settled. Come on, let's break the news.'

As they walked towards Cricklewood Clem felt his life spinning out of control.

Clem waited till after the dishes had been done and Keith was reading the newspaper while his father took his nightly turn around the yard with his final cigarette of the day, 'Just checkin' on things.'

Nola folded a blanket on top of the kitchen table, spread a sheet over it and pulled the basket of damped-down clothes to hand.

'Mum, I got some news.'

'What's that, Clem, love?' She wrapped a flannel

around the handle of the flat iron, lifted it from the top of the wood-burning range and spat on her finger, testing the hotness of the bottom of the iron.

'Here, sit down, stop fussing with the ironing.'

She realised this was important so she put the iron back on the stove and drew up a chair at the kitchen table. 'Is something the matter?' she asked, seeing Clem's serious face.

'Nope. But, well, me and Elizabeth Williams, we're real close, good mates for a long time. And . . . Well, it's got a bit more serious . . . and with me going away and . . . we're getting married,' he finished in a rush.

'Married! Oh, Clem, love, that's a big step.' She fiddled with the tablecloth brushing away imaginary crumbs. 'She's not, you know, in the family way?'

'Cripes, no! It's because, what with Andy dying, she wants us to feel, well, married.'

'What's her family say?'

'She's telling them tonight. So what do you think? She's a real nice girl, Mum.'

'I know that, dear. A good family.' And that's half the trouble, she thought. 'I'm sure Mrs Williams has big plans for those two girls of hers.'

'We have big plans too, Mum,' said Clem with some passion. 'We're going to move to Sydney, I can get work as a mechanic. Mr Thompson said he'd help me get a job.'

'Did he now? You have been making plans,' said Nola dryly. 'I just want you to be happy, pet. But your father –'

'What about me?' Walter appeared in the kitchen and sat by the stove to take off his boots. Phyllis trailed in behind him.

'Young Clem here wants to get married. He and Elizabeth Williams want to tie the knot before he ships out. Lot of young people are, love.'

'Ooh, can I be a bridesmaid?' squealed Phyllis. Her parents ignored her.

'I don't want no shotgun weddings in this family,' snapped Walter Richards.

'It's not like that at all. She wants to be married, God forbid anything should happen to him . . .'

'So she can get his pay allotment I suppose. She's too good for the likes of him. She'll never live here with us.'

'We don't want to live here, Dad. We want to try our luck in Sydney.'

Walter stood up. 'Well, seems you've made your bed, you lie in it. Don't you come whining back here when it all goes bust. Kev and Keith and me will manage. And don't you expect any of this place to be left to you neither.' He stomped out of the kitchen.

'So where's the wedding going to be?' asked wide-eyed Phyllis.

Nola didn't answer as she tried to stifle the anger she felt at her husband's outburst.

'I simply will not hear of it, Elizabeth. And you can do much, much better than Clem Richards.' Emily's mouth snapped into a tight line.

'He's a bit of a rough diamond, but he's a good lad,' said Harold. 'He'll look after Elizabeth.'

'I can look after myself, Dad. I've got a good job, I've passed my book-keeping test. And Clem is going to get a job in Sydney with a big engineering company when the war is over.'

'Well, why not wait till he comes back when peace is declared and do things properly? Nicely,' added Emily, who was a stickler for doing things in the correct manner.

'Where's the ring?' asked Mollie and retreated at the glare from Elizabeth.

'Mum's right. Why, not wait, have a slap-up wedding with all the trimmings when life gets back to normal?' Harold gave her a pleading look.

'And what if he doesn't come back? No one will ever know what we meant to each other,' exclaimed Elizabeth.

'Well, if he doesn't come back, there's nothing you can do about it. Life goes on.' Emily rose and picked up her cup of cold tea. 'I have a headache. Mollie, get me a powder. There'll be no more discussion about this, young lady.'

The three of them sat in silence at the kitchen table staring at the bright oil cloth with the doily in the centre where the sauce bottles stood in crochet holders beside the sugar bowl and milk jug topped with the beaded covers that Emily had made. Elizabeth put her face in her hands and started to cry.

'There, there, love. It's not the end of the world . . .' began Harold, but his daughter wasn't listening.

She lifted her stricken face. 'Dad, please, can't you talk to her? You got engaged in the war and I bet you would've got married had you the chance . . . like we have.'

'I don't know about that, but I know how you feel. You want something to hold on to, to remember . . . if the worst happened . . .' his voice trailed off as he remembered the longing he'd felt for Emily while he was away fighting. He knew she'd wait for him, still be there if he was crippled or blinded.

'It's just a piece of paper, Dad. I'm not leaving home, nothing will change. But I'll have the ring, his name. Please, Dad, it means so much to me.'

'Yeah, c'mon, Dad, talk Mum round. Or else Elizabeth will rush off and elope or do something stupid,' said Mollie.

'If your heart is set on it I'll see what I can do.' He gave her a hug and a gentle kiss on the forehead. 'Chin up, lass.'

Elizabeth never asked what her father said to her mother but some time later he emerged from their bedroom, put his head in the lounge room where Elizabeth was playing a gentle tune on the piano, gave her a small wave and a thumbs up, then quietly went out the front door for a walk. Elizabeth sighed and began a fresh tune on the piano. She didn't miss a note of 'The Last Rose of Summer', her mother's favourite.

The wedding was simple and low key although Emily had persuaded Elizabeth to be married in the small Anglican church in Cedartown. Elizabeth wore her smart navy suit with a shallow saucer hat perched to one side with a wisp of veil that drew attention to her eyes. Pinned to her lapel was a double rose corsage with maidenhair fern. Foamy lace edging from her blouse showed at her décolletage and wrists. She carried a bouquet of small pink rosebuds and Emily and Harold also wore a rosebud on their lapels. In a symbolic touch Harold had added the small gold horseshoe that had been his welcome home gift from the community after the Great War. He never wore his service medals and Emily wondered if he still had them. Mollie stood beside her older sister feeling very special in her spotted voile dress, holding a posy of roses.

Walter had borrowed Keith's suit and Nola wore her Sunday dress with uncomfortable best shoes, gloves and a straw hat decorated with a silk flower. Thommo and Clem looked dashing in their uniforms. During the service the immediate family – Mollie, Phyllis, Keith, Kevin, home on leave, with both sets of parents – sat in the first pew of the church.

Other guests included Thommo's parents, Frank and Vera; Cynthia; Donald and Mr and Mrs George Forde from Elizabeth's office. A few curious neighbours who lived next to the church and went to every wedding made up the group.

Afterwards Emily, helped by Mollie, had arranged a light supper in the hall next to the church. Harold had been given a hand of pork which was baked and sliced cold, along with a good salad and boiled potatoes. Harold had also made one of his specials, a triple-decker sponge cake thick with cream and sliced strawberries. They toasted the happy couple in beer and homemade lemonade though Thommo slipped Clem a small bottle of whisky 'For a snort to keep your strength up, seeing it's your wedding night.' They exchanged mischievous grins.

Thommo had also generously given Clem the little diamond ring he'd won. 'Keep it, mate. Jeez, you can't take it off her finger once it's on!'

Emily gave Elizabeth a brooch that had belonged to her mother. 'Your grandmother gave it to me when I sailed to Australia. Don't lose it, darling, it's a little link with our past, and the past is important, it really is in the long haul.'

Elizabeth didn't really like the ornate marcasite figure of a bird and didn't want responsibility for a family heirloom. 'It's lovely, Mum, but I'll worry about it all the time. I'll wear it as something borrowed, and give it back to you.'

It was an evening service to suit the minister who had a heavy schedule around the district giving support to families who had lost sons at war, or were coping with wounded lads. And there were more weddings than usual as couples tied the knot before the young men left for war zones, just like Elizabeth and Clem.

Clem and Elizabeth left the church hall arm in arm under a shower of confetti to drive the short distance to the large Commercial Hotel in Hungerford where Thommo had booked the best room for them. It was a classic country hotel of large proportions, iron lace around the upper balcony, a sweeping staircase of dark wood flanked by brass urns planted with ferns. Along the hallway that smelled of beeswax were pictures of Scottish castles, the Lakes District, and the King and Queen.

Their room had a large brass bed, heavy velvet drapes at the window and a washstand with a china jug and bowl. Elizabeth was impressed. Apart from the boarding house at the beach where they holidayed each year and the occasional night when she'd been allowed to stay with her best friend from school, Ruby, who lived out on a farm, she hadn't ever stayed anywhere outside Cricklewood.

After the rush and frantic arrangements of the wedding, now finding themselves husband and wife, alone in a strange room together, they felt uneasy and busied themselves putting clothes away, brushing confetti from their hair. When Clem came back from the bathroom and toilet down the end of the hall wearing a dressing gown to find Elizabeth standing in her petticoat, they both looked embarrassed and apologised, before Clem started grinning.

'Oh, sorry, ma'am, I was looking for Mrs Richards.'

Elizabeth threw her rolled-up nylons – also procured by Thommo – at him. 'Never heard of her. Oh, wait a minute.' She looked at her diamond ring and the plain gold band on her finger. 'Oh, yes, I'd forgotten. Must be me!'

Laughing, Clem lunged at her, pushing her onto the bed. 'Get this stuff off. Let's see what married life is like.'

In the dining room the next morning they ordered a big breakfast of fruit juice, fresh fruit slices, and bacon and eggs. Elizabeth couldn't help displaying her left hand on the white linen tablecloth but as the waitress took their order she showed no sign of seeing the rings, or having heard the inevitable kitchen chat about the newlyweds. She didn't react when Clem said with some emphasis, 'My wife will have tomatoes with her bacon and eggs, thank you.' The waitress simply licked the stub of pencil again and made a note.

For Elizabeth it didn't matter because Clem took her hand and gave it a loving squeeze after he stroked her ring finger.

The waitress was taking away the plates when Thommo arrived with Cynthia and strode across the dining room.

'Hi ho, newlyweds. Congrats on making it safely through the challenges of the night.' Cynthia gave him a hard dig in the ribs with her elbow. 'Rightio, let's get a move on, a lot to do before you two have to be torn apart.'

The reality of the day hit Elizabeth. Her new husband and Thommo were catching the midday mail train from Cedartown to return to camp up north.

There was quite a crowd on the platform seeing off the dozen or more local boys of the 9th Division. Harold was there in his railway uniform feeling more comfortable than in his suit at the wedding. He came over and shook hands with Thommo and Clem, and smiled at Elizabeth who was clinging to Clem's arm.

'Chin up, lass, they'll be back before you know it,' he said softly.

'Atherton, then the jungle, and victory,' said Clem with bravado, hoping it would cheer up Elizabeth. 'But who knows, we might get another leave before being shipped out.'

'Good idea to get you acclimatised to the humidity,' commented Harold.

'Where's Mum?' asked Elizabeth.

'Over there on the verandah. Didn't want to get upset, or see you upset,' said Harold. 'Excuse me while I sort out some luggage.' He went to the luggage trolley loaded with kitbags, boxes and suitcases.

Elizabeth glanced across the road junction to Cricklewood and saw Emily standing on the front veran- dah. 'Doesn't seem right after getting married to have to go back home. Sleep in a room with my little sister,' she sighed.

'Was good, last night, eh?' said Clem putting his arm around her. 'I'll remember every minute of it while I'm away.'

'Me too. Oh, do be careful. Well, as much as you can, I s'pose.' She turned and buried her face in his chest, feeling the rough prickle of his uniform.

Clem didn't speak, but held her, at the same time watching the public display of affection and emotion from all the other families. Thommo cracked jokes and did the rounds saying cheerio to everyone while Frank and Vera watched their son, always the joker, with tight, sad smiles.

Clem pulled his box camera from the small haversack slung on his shoulder. 'Stand over there by the Cedartown sign.' He snapped the picture of Elizabeth leaning against the wooden platform sign, a wisp of hair blowing round her face as she gave a wistful smile. He took a few pictures of families embracing their boys and, spotting an aged border collie sitting close to a kitbag, he took a picture of the dog guarding his master's belongings.

The puffing and whistle shriek of the approaching steam train silenced the chatter on the platform. Backpacks, kit bags and suitcases were thrown inside, there was a rush of last goodbyes, kisses and hugs and a dash for seats where windows were flung open and arms and heads crammed out for one last touch of loved ones.

Elizabeth held Clem's hand as he pushed his head and shoulders out the window to kiss her once more. Thommo hung from the doorway for a final kiss and hug for his parents. Then too swiftly there was the hissing of steam, the blast from the horn, the station master calling 'All aaaaa-board', a final slam of doors and the imperceptible inching forward of the train pulling away from the platform.

Shouts and cries, 'Good luck', 'Give the Nips curry,

lads' and 'God bless', rang out as handkerchiefs dabbed at eyes and tears ran unchecked down men's faces as they watched their sons proudly waving, covering the emotion they felt at what could be the last time they'd see their family, or this place.

Elizabeth tried to hold on to Clem and, as the train picked up speed and Thommo's head poked out beside Clem's, she started to run to prolong the contact between them for as long as possible, until Clem's fingertips were wrenched from hers and she stumbled to a stop as the crowded carriages whizzed by.

As the train curved down the track, soldiers still waving and calling from windows, she felt the comforting touch of her father's hand on her shoulder. 'He'll be all right, love. Clem and Thommo, they'll make it back home, don't you worry.'

Harold hoped his words rang true. And if the two childhood mates made it through, survived war and returned home, he prayed they would be unscathed, and carry no wounds to their bodies, hearts or minds. He knew, he'd been there and would never forget.

Clem had never imagined so much rain could fall so heavily for so long. It came down in a constant curtain the men couldn't see through for more than a few yards. The grey-green jungle world around them was blurred, all they could hear was drumming rain sluicing through the bamboo and heavy tropical trees, drenching the ground that was already running and slushy, unable to absorb another drop. The men had been so wet for so long they'd given up trying to remain dry. Now it was a matter of dealing with bugs, leeches, itches, the stings from swarms of mosquitoes, and aching bodies exhausted from creeping and climbing through treacherous trails or unmarked terrain.

The occasional crash through the wet trees of an animal or bird stretched nerves. And in the brief moments when the rain unexpectedly and suddenly ceased, the silence was scary. Then there was the drip of sodden leaves, the rivulets of cascading water and the imagined sounds of snakes slithering.

They knew the Japanese were dug in near here, an enclave from which they moved silently and swiftly, ambushing and targeting the Australians from well-hidden positions in trees, in hides on the rise of a ridge, or at the edge of a scarcely defined track. The Japanese moved lightly and silently.

Thommo summed it up. 'The little bastards seem to treat this bloody jungle like home. Stuff 'em. We've had them falling arse over head backwards for months now, why don't they just give up and go back to climbing Mount Fuji.'

Clem would never feel at home here in New Guinea. Thommo, a few feet away, adapted to and accepted whatever conditions he was in. His inevitably cheerful, 'Gotta make the best of it eh, cobber?' sometimes irritated the tired men around him. Only Clem could tell when Thommo was dispirited or worried, for then the jokes would come thick and fast and he'd chatter until someone would snap at him to 'Bloody shut up'. He knew to shut up when action was likely, when they were playing a deadly cat and mouse game with a ruthless enemy.

As they waited for the signal to move forward Clem wondered just how much longer they'd be wallowing in mud. Their campaign on the north coast of New Guinea near Lae was going well, despite the determined defence of the captured port by the Japanese. Clem and his mates knew the Japanese were in big trouble fighting on two fronts, the coastal enclave and high up in the mountains splitting the great tropical island. On the Kokoda Track the Jap drive towards Port Moresby had been checked and the exhausted remnants of the force were falling back towards Lae. Yeah, Clem told himself with some satisfaction, we've got the little slant-eyed bastards on the run. He looked around for Thommo and gave him a thumbs up signal. He and Thommo had worked out a series of small conversational signs at these times of silent lull and one would mime to the other a gesture that recalled fishing down at the river, the time they jumped the train down to the beach, the Empire Night fireworks when Clem had first kissed Elizabeth. It helped pass the time, which to the men seemed to run backwards, especially the sleepless hours awaiting dawn and a possible attack.

The latest downpour eased, mist curled wraith-like through the tangle of vines, the weird shapes of thorny trees and the matted green thicket where giant spiderwebs hung. The patrol leader gave the signal to move out. The Bren gun, oiled and wrapped in a groundsheet, was lifted, the point scout given whispered instructions and, with his Owen gun at the ready, moved ahead.

Thommo exchanged a look with Clem: Better him than me, it said, first man around a bend or through the thicket of bamboo is going to cop it. All remained silent though every man was alert. The dozen men crept forward, crouching and pushing through the jungle that constantly clawed at exposed skin, entangling clothes and equipment.

In the twilight gloom where only a feeble ray of sunlight penetrated, they approached an exposed rise and the patrol leader signalled them to fan out.

They were almost back in the cover of the jungle canopy when a machine gun opened fire on them and men instinctively flung themselves to the ground, rolling into the cover of the trees and undergrowth.

They retaliated and Clem heard a grunt, a shout, and a crash of scrub behind him. Glancing round he saw at once that Thommo had been hit. The firing continued in bursts before an Australian grenade found its mark, knocking out the enemy machine gun, and the men scrambled forward. Each man was on his own, every man for himself, seeking an enemy in a tree or behind a clump of bamboo before he picked you off.

As suddenly as it began, the clash was over. The surviving enemy disappeared, the Australians consolidated as support came forward.

Clem, however, slipped back. He moved carefully, fearful that a sniper may have stayed behind and would get him as he headed back to where he last saw Thommo. Hearing a low groan, he cautiously inched down into the gully at the side of the track where Thommo had rolled. Spotting his mate, Clem ran in zigzags to a cover of low jungle growth where Thommo lay.

He'd copped a bullet in the shoulder close to his neck, there was a lot of blood and a heavy graze to the side of his head. Clem lifted Thommo's head, his eyes opened and he gasped, trying to speak. Clem put a water bottle to his mate's lips and, as Thommo swallowed, put a finger to his lips to shush him.

But Thommo, eyes wide with fear, dragged at Clem's arm, pulling his face close to his, to hoarsely whisper in his ear. 'Don't leave me here, mate. Shoot me. I don't want them to get me.'

It was the greatest unspoken fear among the men, being captured. The rumours of what the Japs did if they found an Australian, dead or alive, haunted every man. They took no prisoners here and the Australians had heard of horrible rituals inflicted by the enemy on dead soldiers.

'We promised we'd look after each other, cobber. I'll get you out,' whispered Clem, though he wondered how. It all looked impossible, and time was running out. Another attack was certain and what passed as a front line was forever fluid. It suddenly could be behind you.

He tied up Thommo's shoulder with a sleeve torn from his shirt, sat him up, leaned him against a tree and waited. The spasmodic firing had stopped and he wondered how far ahead the main section of the patrol had gone and in what direction. Where was the medico or the fuzzy wuzzy angels when you needed them, he thought grimly. One look at Thommo, who was watching with desperate eyes, convinced Clem he couldn't leave him here.

'Righto, matey. Seems quiet. You game to chance it? Don't reckon they'll be coming back looking for us.' They both wondered about other small Jap patrols but didn't say anything.

'Bloody hell, I'm not hanging round here. Let's go.' Thommo struggled to get to his feet.

'Easy does it.' Clem slipped an arm around him but as Thommo took the weight on his feet a leg buckled.

'Flaming hell.' He gazed down at his leg. 'Get me boot off, something's wrong with me foot.'

Clem pulled off Thommo's sodden boot to find it full of blood. Pulling up a trouser leg he found a bullet wound that had shattered the shin bone. 'Crikey, another hole. You collecting lead for souvenirs or something? Hang about.' Trying to sound chirpy Clem stuffed his handkerchief into the wound, tying it with another strip of shirt.

'I can hop a bit.' Thommo leaned on Clem who shouldered both their small battle rucksacks, each slinging a rifle across his back.

'Wait, you need a stick.' He took his bayonet and cut a length of stout bamboo. 'Hook your leg around that, let it take the weight.'

'It makes me look like a bloody cripple,' muttered Thommo, but he found the pole gave him extra support and they were able to slowly scramble along until they reached a slope that fell away sharply.

'On my back, hang on round my neck. Piggy back,' instructed Clem.

Thommo was too weak to argue. Clem laboriously pulled them both to where they'd been when the Japanese had struck. At least Clem had a route to follow for a while at least, but the going was slow. They edged downhill to a rushing stream.

'Gotta stop, mate. Rest up, let's wash that leg.'

Thommo sprawled on the ground. 'Leave it. Might bleed more. If I got any blood left.' He put his head on his arm and closed his eyes.

Clem filled his helmet with the clear water and poured it over his head. It felt good. They were in a gully and he had no idea where to go from here. Although the sun was high, it was shady by the stream where tall trees thrust through the rainforest towards light. The trapped air was fetid, steamy. He was about to wade across the stream for a recce when he saw, through a gap in the trees on the other side, up on the edge of the ravine, some figures moving through the jungle. They made no noise but there was no mistaking they were Nips. Clem hit the ground and lay by the stream hoping Thommo remained quiet.

The Japanese disappeared and Clem realised he'd have to strike out on the side opposite the Japanese patrol and hope for the best. But Thommo had curled on his side and was rambling incoherently about taking a little kip.

Clem shook him and hauled him to his feet enough to take his weight and drag him forward. 'Keep moving, Thommo, you can't sleep here. C'mon, matey.'

They made slow progress and Clem was tiring. Thommo seemed barely conscious though he kept shoving his good foot forward, limping badly on the other. The wound on his shoulder was bleeding again. Clem lost track of time or distance. He knew he couldn't continue too much further and had no idea where he was going, conscious only of steadily staggering downhill, away from the jungle in which they had been fighting. He began praying.

He knew he wasn't as alert or paying attention to his surroundings as he should be, not that he could reach his rifle quickly, hampered as he was by Thommo. Then to his astonishment they burst out of the jungle on to a track, admittedly not much more than a blur of crushed undergrowth, but slashed branches beside it clearly indicated a native trail.

'Prayer answered, Thommo,' he whispered.

His mate just groaned and slumped to the ground.

Clem sat beside him and drank from his water bottle. What now? And as if in answer to the unspoken question, he heard voices, a sing-song language, and through the bushes he could see some natives coming along the track. 'Angels,' said Clem almost in disbelief. The struggle was over.

Six natives took the two men to their village only a short distance further along the track, carrying Thommo and the two packs. News of their arrival was spread by one of the men who ran ahead, and the whole village turned out to chant a welcome to the two soldiers. In pidgin English their chief indicated that an army medical unit had just set up camp in a whitefella plantation nearby.

Two days later Thommo awoke in a rough bed, merely a canvas stretcher mounted on some empty ammunition boxes. As he slowly opened his eyes and figured out it was a mosquito net that gave a misty look to the world around him, he saw Clem dozing in a camp chair beside the bed. He then noticed that his wounds were neatly dressed, leg in splints, and that there was little pain. Anaesthetic or something like that, he figured.

'Hey Clem,' he called, and when his mate stirred added, 'Pub's open. I've ordered you a schooner.'

Clem got under the net and took Thommo's hand. 'Bewdy fella, well done. Good to have you back with the living. Been touch and go, I can tell you.'

'Sorry if I still sound a little confused,' confessed Thommo, 'but I'm having trouble getting the world in focus. What's been happening. Where are we?'

'Still on the plantation in the field hospital. But now that you're getting with it, that schooner may be closer than you think. While you've been sleeping word has come through that some of our mob have won a leave break back home. So I reckon we might just get home together. That'll be worth a beer.'

'Or two,' added Thommo with a big grin. 'Thanks for saving me. You're a hero and deserve a medal.'

'Come off it. You'd have done the same for me. We're mates, not heroes.'

'Okay, buddy,' chirped Thommo in a comic American accent but Clem had suddenly gone serious, his face creased with lines of agony. 'What's up?' asked Thommo.

Clem stood and stretched, took some deep breaths and sat down again. 'Wish to hell I knew. The doc reckons I'm suffering from malaria. Been feeling a bit funny while I was waiting for you to come around. But bugger that, let's celebrate. I'll see if I can rustle up a mug of tea.' He winked at Thommo and strode out of the tent, not wanting Thommo to see how he felt. The fever was coming back, and sweat was streaming from his body that ached like every joint had been hit with a sledge hammer. He hoped to hell leave came through quickly for both of them.

14

Dani

DANI GAZED AT THE length of sand. Turquoise waves followed each other in lazy undulating rolls, foaming onto the near-deserted beach. A few early risers were on their surfboards or walking their dogs towards the point. Wrapped in a towelling bathrobe, sipping her first morning cup of tea, she began to think about her plans for the day. Dinner and a sexy night with Roddy had been very pleasant, but already her mind was beginning to turn to her own life.

'Pretty special view, huh?' Roddy, in a matching robe, sat on a deck chair beside her holding his coffee and his mobile phone.

'It is. I feel like I'm on holiday.' Dani didn't add that the block of swish apartments where Roddy was renting the penthouse seemed like a resort even down to the matching robes. She actually missed her morning view of the valley and the river with mist rising over the hills and dew shining on the grass. 'So what are your plans for the day?'

'Waiting to hear back from NZ about Russell's latest draft of the script. He's put in a lot more locations. Could alter the budget breakdown.'

'Outside the valley? Like where? Sydney?'

'No, up north. Isabella's arrival in Australia. She's shipwrecked and is saved by natives, rescued by a wealthy sea captain –'

'Roddy! It's the Isabella Kelly story, not Eliza Fraser!' Dani wanted to laugh but it was too ludicrous. 'She came out here by choice with money and valuable possessions.'

'So where'd she get it? She was an Irish orphan,' he retorted.

'Who was adopted by a wealthy guardian in London. It's true, no one knows where her money came from, Garth assumes William Crowder gave her an inheritance when she left England.'

'Well, if the investors like Russell's idea, let them put in their money and we'll change the script back later,' he said easily. 'And it's attracting interest from Hollywood names. Couple of agents for American actresses have been in touch.'

'Ones who can do an English accent, I assume,' said Dani.

Roddy missed her facetious tone. 'We've set a shooting schedule so we could pin the locals down and then block out the time. Food people, accommodation, transport guys. Going to bring a lot of business to town. Not to mention the flow on after the film comes out.'

Dani didn't probe further. Roddy always had an upbeat answer or skimmed over questions about nitty-gritty details. 'So what will you be doing when filming starts?'

'I'll be on the road. Stitching up sales hopefully.'

'Before people see the finished film?' asked Dani.

'Well, when we have a rough cut. I want to strike when the iron is hot and get on to the next project.'

'Oh, another film? So you're staying in the movie business? Have you got any ideas?' Dani's instinct was that Roddy flitted from one thing to another.

'Could have. I'm putting out feelers now I've got this one up and running. Might dabble in something else. This development thing is interesting.'

Dani put her cup down with a thud. 'You mean what Jason is doing?'

'Nah, that's too finicky, too hung up on eco stuff. But this tree change, sea change thing is big. I hadn't realised it till I came here and saw the drift from the city turning into a bit of a flood.'

'And it's not such a backwater either,' said Dani defensively, surprising herself. 'What do you have in mind?'

'Round here there are a few spots I've checked out on the way down to Sydney. On the coast. You could clear big areas of patchy scrubland behind the dunes and whack up holiday homes or retirement properties. Nothing too expensive, no fancy architecture. Then they'll need shopping centres, amenities. I can see a lot of money to be made.'

'Once you get the land,' said Dani tightly. 'It's mostly state owned that hasn't been released, isn't it?'

'Ah, there are ways around that. Money speaks. And I know the voices.' He stretched. 'So what're your plans?'

Dani stood up, tightening the belt on her robe. 'If you mean today, I'm meeting Mum and Tim with friends as it's the first day of the Cedartown Show. If you mean the future, as in past next week, I'm unsure except I don't want to see this little valley or the countryside and coast around here exploited. I'm thinking I could live here. Settle for a bit.'

Words were coming out of her mouth that Dani hadn't

thought about before. Roddy had struck a painful nerve, just as Jason had when she first heard about his Birimbal project. But after listening to Jason, she could see that Birimbal was going in a direction that could be the way of the future, while Roddy was talking eighties and nineties quick-buck development. Her mother's memories, and the knowledge she had roots here, as Max had brought home to her as well, had made Dani protective of the valley. Selfishly so perhaps, but she'd hate to see Roddy and his 'investors' rip into the valley and the coast just to make money with no benefit to the people or the place.

Roddy was staring at her, recognising the tension in her body language that signalled he'd upset her. 'I don't like the word settle. And if you think I'm going to exploit this place, look around, there's a queue forming.' He smiled, trying to soften his words. 'Look to the future, think of what's best for the people living here, the opportunities for their kids.' When Dani didn't look convinced he added, 'Once the movie is out you won't be able to stop it. Get real, Dani, get on the bandwagon or be left behind.'

She sighed, letting go of the anger she was feeling.

'We really are coming from different places, aren't we?' She studied the good-looking, happy-go-lucky entrepreneur beside her. 'We really don't know each other very well at all, do we?'

'Hey, does it matter? We're here for a good time, not a long time. You enjoyed last night. You made it clear you didn't want any kind of commitment, just a bit of fun. And I certainly don't want to be tied down.' He almost shuddered.

'Nor do I, Roddy. And we have had fun but there's got to be more to a relationship,' began Dani but Roddy held up his coffee mug, shielding his face.

'Ah, c'mon, Dani, don't start on that song and dance. I know every word. Listen let's put the cards on the table.

I'm not interested in a meaningful, full-on partnership. I like my freedom. I thought what we had going was perfect. When I'm here we have fun, no strings attached. You're interested in the movie I'm doing –'

'I told you about Isabella if you recall.'

'Yeah, but who's taken it to the next level? You and Jason don't own Isabella. Seems to me since you got here you've got too involved with this little community and your family stuff. Maybe if we were in Sydney it'd be different. We both have lots of other things going on there, friends, deals, happenings, you know.'

'Yep, I do know,' said Dani, thinking back to her life in Sydney.

She knew the world he described. Launches, events with the smart youthful set being photographed for the social papers and magazines. Where men like Jason – genuinely wealthy – and men like Roddy – wannabe entrepreneurs who talk the talk and look good – mingled with pretty girls shipped in for decoration. Some, like Ginny, were real models, most described themselves as models. The way Dani saw it men like Jason and Roddy only ever met those sorts of women. Dani felt she was quite different – independent, divorced with a child, and a definite ambition. And she no longer cared about the latest fashions, accessories, or going to the hip new places to be seen.

Dani gave Roddy a frank look. 'And you know what, Roddy? I don't care about that kind of lifestyle anymore.'

'You've been in the bush too long, Dani. Seems you and I are moving in different directions, babe.' He paused as they stared at each other, reading more than they wished in the other's eyes. Roddy was first to drop his gaze. 'I'd better get dressed.'

'Right. I'll grab some breakfast down the road,' said Dani, knowing there was never food in Roddy's apartment.

After she'd dressed she found Roddy on his mobile phone so she leaned over and gave him a peck on the cheek as he talked.

'Hang on, George, one tick. See ya, Dani, sorry, this is LA. I'll be in touch.'

'Sure, Roddy, don't let me interrupt. See you. And thanks for dinner.'

He gave a smile, a wave and resumed talking to LA and didn't watch as Dani quietly left the apartment, knowing she wouldn't return.

Each time Dani passed the Cedartown showground she admired the heavy old log fence and row of rusting corrugated-iron horse stalls under the shade of the big gum trees, thinking it would make a nice painting even though it always looked rather forlorn and unused. But today it was thronged with people, animals and vehicles.

'My God, look at the crowd. Horse floats and caravans from Queensland and Victoria, people have come from everywhere,' exclaimed Dani. 'This show must be a popular event.'

'Lots of them have tents and campervans, they must be staying here with their animals, I guess,' said Lara. 'Just look at the people. I hope Tim doesn't get nervous.'

'I can't believe he's going in a competition,' said Dani. 'I hope he doesn't get upset if he doesn't win anything.'

'We had a talk. Seems Mardi his instructor has covered that. Competing is the way to improve your riding skills,' said Lara. 'They went off together early this morning for a run through.'

'Never thought I'd see the day,' said Dani. 'This is more nerve-racking than soccer.'

Lara stopped the car in the roped-off parking area, where a man in a white coat with a badge on his hat directed them with a big smile. 'Main entrance to your right, ladies, enjoy the show.'

'Heavens, where to start?' said Lara.

'The livestock pavilions . . . and down there the agriculture section . . . Let's look at the animals before we find Tim,' said Dani.

They passed a children's farmyard with big fluffy rabbits, baby lambs, fat pink spotless piglets and baby ducks all being cuddled and petted by children under the watchful eyes of two attendants. Next door was a pen of prize goats, their silky coats brushed and shining.

'I've always wanted a goat. Maybe I could get some at The Vale,' said Dani. 'Keep the grass down.'

'They eat the flowers and vegies too. And they're very smart. Too much trouble, I think,' said Lara. 'Jolly would go bananas.'

'I'll keep getting the goat's cheese from that little cheese factory in town then,' laughed Dani.

They wandered through the breezy open-sided sheds where the prize cows were being groomed, their huge udders near bursting. Several youngsters were leading their calves or sheep from beribboned stalls and massive docile bulls stood stoically as though they'd been here, done that a dozen times before.

'There's a boy from Tim's class with that little heifer. I hope Tim doesn't decide he wants one,' said Dani.

'I lay odds he'll want some sort of animal before the day is over,' said Lara.

As they wandered around, they smiled and nodded at people they recognised from shops, the bank, the post office, and the library, all transformed in smart country outfits either as a competitor, entrant with a prize animal, or working in some capacity. Others wore dustcoats and large badges and passes on a ribbon round their neck signifying they were judges or officials.

'Morning, ladies. Come to cheer on the lad?' Henry Catchpole approached dressed in moleskin pants, a checked shirt, woollen tie and tweed jacket. He swept off his Akubra hat. 'Glad you came along, this show is a great tradition. Goes back to the early days of the valley.'

'It's amazing. We might not have come if Tim wasn't in the gymkhana,' said Lara.

'What should we see? Are you doing anything official?' asked Dani.

'See everything. This is on for the whole weekend. Rodeo Saturday night is not to be missed. I'm judging a few cattle entries and doing an auction. I wouldn't miss it. First came to the show with my prize black Australorp when I was eight. Have a look at the poultry, you'll be surprised.'

'Is Patricia here?' asked Lara.

'She is. Presenting a prize and yakking to people, keeping the mayor in line. The usual. We're set up under that big tree over there, there's a few chairs and refreshments on the go. Pop over any time.'

'Thanks, Henry.' And as they moved away, Dani said, 'It's like a small version of the Royal Easter Show, polo match, country fair, and farmers' market all in one.'

'But a lot more friendly and a lot more fun, I think,' said Lara.

'There's the riding arena, let's find Tim. He came here right after breakfast.' Dani looked at the horses and riders dressed immaculately in their riding jackets and hats, polished boots, regulation tie shirts and jodhpurs. 'Look at those girls, they look about four!'

They watched the little girls on their ponies step through their paces and edged around the back of the ring to find Tim brushing Blackie, his pony.

'Hey Mum! Ma! What do you think? Doesn't he look good?' He smoothed the pony's plaited mane.

'You look pretty good yourself,' said Dani, giving him a hug.

'Did Mardi help you get ready?' asked Lara, pleased to see him so nattily and neatly dressed.

'It's how you have to dress or you lose points,' said Tim. 'I'm not going on for a bit, but you're going to watch, right?'

'You bet, and good luck, darling, just do your best.'

'It's my first time,' he mumbled.

'And it won't be your last. You'll love it, sweetie,' said Lara. 'Do you want to look around with us, Tim, before you go in the ring? There's so much to see.'

'Sure. I have ages yet.'

They went into the long shadowy poultry pavilion with rows and rows of clean small boxes where preened and cleaned fowls of all description strutted and posed for the parade of judges.

'They seem to take it very seriously,' whispered Lara, watching the judges confer, make notes, and lift out the prize specimens to give them a swift and thorough examination.

'I've never seen hens like them,' said Dani, peering to read a sign beneath a puffed ball of white feathers. ' "White Pekin Pullet". And this rare breed: "Silver Campine". That looks like a rubber chook, it's got no feathers!'

'Can I stroke it?' Tim asked a judge holding a black and white strong-legged bird with feathers round its feet and beautiful barred silver markings on its wings. 'Wow, are they are hard to look after?'

'They need a bit of attention, depends if you're going to show them or not. You go and talk to old Mr Perkins down there in the red tie. He knows everything there is to know about breeding show birds.'

'Can I, Mum?'

'What, breed chooks? You talk to Mr Perkins first

411

though. I think you have enough on your plate, Tim,' answered Dani as Lara grinned at her. 'Let's go next door to the agriculture pavilion.'

As Tim shot off Lara shook her head. 'You know who'll be looking after those show chooks, don't you?'

Dani laughed. 'I don't think so. I'm happy with the couple scratching around in the backyard giving us eggs for breakfast. Thankfully we haven't had a visit from a fox yet.'

In the long airy agriculture pavilion they found rows of laden trestle tables and displays of flowers, pickles, jams, vegetables, handiwork and elaborately decorated cakes.

'My God, look at this stuff. Is it real?' exclaimed Lara. 'Those pumpkins are as big as an armchair,' she said. 'Sit on one and I'll take a photo.'

'Let me take one of the two of you,' said Patricia Catchpole, looking very official in a flowered suit, with a large badge on her lapel. 'Have you seen the preserves? They're works of art.'

'They certainly are,' said Dani, who'd noticed the rows of big glass jars filled with carefully and artistically arranged chillies and fruit and pickled vegetables. 'Can you buy any of this produce? I love the roses and orchids.'

They were walking along the rows admiring the crochet work, embroidery, macramé, and painted ceramics when Tim found them.

'Hi, Mrs Catchpole. Can we buy one of those cakes?'

'Some people won't part with their entries but when everyone is packing up at the end of the show you might pick up a bargain, Tim,' said Patricia. 'I'm looking forward to seeing you in the ring. All your pals are here to cheer you on.'

'Where? Who's here?' asked Tim.

'Max and Sarah and their kids, and all the group from Chesterfield. The kids are on the merry-go-round. I tell you, that thing has come out every year since before Henry was a youngster. And that's going back.'

'I'll just go and see them,' said Tim.

'Don't get messed up,' called Dani.

'So is this a fundraiser for the community? There are a lot of out-of-towners,' commented Lara.

'The committee choose a charity every year or so. This year it's to benefit the Cedartown Hospital. They want a cardiac treatment room, save patients being rushed over to Hungerford. Now, I have a few duties to perform. Come and have a drink with us at lunchtime. Under the cedar tree.'

They bought mugs of tea and a butterfly cake filled with fresh cream and wandered over to greet Helen and Barney, and Max and Sarah who were watching all the kids spinning around on the old steam-driven merry-go-round that was a centrepiece at fairs and shows.

'That music brings back memories. I only went on it once that I remember,' sighed Lara. 'Poppy told me how it had been rescued and restored. I just love that rinky-dink organ music.'

'Isn't this divine!' George and Claude joined them.

'This is fun, I've never seen such food,' said Claude.

'These country women know a thing or two about presentation.'

As the merry-go-round came to a halt, George grinned at Tim. 'Come on, Tim, hop on one of the ponies, you're dressed for it!'

'You know you're dying to have a go,' laughed Claude to George.

Tim hesitated, but seeing Toby, Len and Tabatha were all on it, he ran to grab a colourful horse with flowing silver mane and a carved gold-painted pole. Dani took a photo.

'Want to join me in the flying swan?' Jason was walking towards them.

Lara took the camera from Dani. 'Oh, do get on it. It's nearly full, I'll go next turn.'

Dani began to protest but somehow Jason propelled her towards the double seat on the back of a swan with outstretched wings.

'It's a Cedartown tradition,' he said. 'My favourite was always the Indian elephant, but George has got that one.'

The attendant blew a whistle and the organ wound up and began playing as the beautiful creatures suspended around its mirrored, kaleidoscopic centre began to rise and fall.

'So you have memories of growing up here too?' said Dani. 'I thought you were a city kid.'

'We used to come back sometimes when I was very young, even though we lived in Sydney and I went to school there. I must have been your Tim's age when I last did this.'

Dani glanced back at Tim, her city kid, dressed in his riding habit, face flushed with laughter with his friends as they whipped on their painted charges. Would he remember this and return with his children? Would he consider Cedartown part of his heritage, the place his roots sprang from?

The music was loud, drowning chitchat, and Dani closed her eyes as the merry-go-round spun and the swan dipped and gently dived. The laughter and squeals around her seemed to come from a long way away. She imagined her mother as a little girl riding this merry-go-round. Had her father come to the show too? Dani understood better now her mother's urge to find out more of her family story. What had happened to her father's side? She was becoming aware of her mother's upbringing and how her grandparents' lives continued to influence them. And above all the strength of connection to this valley where they had all lived.

Dani opened her eyes to find Tim tugging at her sleeve. 'Do you feel sick, Mum?'

'Ah, no, I must have been dreaming. That was fun, wasn't it?' She stood up, her legs feeling a bit shaky. Jason was chatting to George and Claude.

'I have to go over to the stalls to go in the parade. You coming, Mum?'

'You bet.'

They all trailed behind Tim as he raced to the stalls and they made their way to the show ring.

'Ooh, look, there's Carter,' said Lara. 'What's he doing?'

'He's got an information booth about the National Parks and Wildlife stuff,' said Barney. 'He's got birds and snakes and plants and spiders to show people. He's such a good entertainer, spins a great yarn.'

'I'll just go and say hello, tell him we'll stop by after Tim's event,' said Lara.

Dani and Helen exchanged a grin as Carter spotted Lara and gave a wave over the heads of the crowd around his booth.

Perched along the wooden benches on the grassy knoll Dani watched Tim's group line up waiting for the judge to call the first one out. Tim sat straight, if stiffly, in the saddle, one of three boys among six girls.

'I'm so nervous for him,' whispered Dani.

'There's Mardi, his instructor,' said Lara. 'She seems very good. Just think he'd never been on a horse till a few months ago.'

'And there's Kerry. What's she doing there?' wondered Dani, as she spotted the slight figure and wild curls of her neighbour.

'She's very into the horse scene. Used to be a show jumper herself before her accident,' said Helen.

'Oh, don't mention the word,' said Lara. 'Look, there's the first round.'

They watched each competitor bow to the judge, then go through the set course, from walking to sitting trot to rising trot at the designated spot, completing the circles and diagonals they'd memorised and practised. The judges marked each competitor on how well they handled their horse, how comfortable they were and how well they held their riding position in the saddle, and how the horse responded to their commands.

Tim's round went well, though he lost a few points for beginning his rising trot a little too late and allowing his horse to drift slightly from the arena track. But he earned a round of applause and when he slid from the horse at the gate, Dani was surprised to see Jason there to take the reins and slap him on the back. Mardi joined them and spoke to Tim, smiled and patted his shoulder.

'He seems to have done quite well,' said Lara.

'Let's go and tell him he was terrific.' Dani raced around the show ring to hug Tim.

'You were fantastic, Tim! I'm so proud of you. Were you nervous?'

'Not much once I started. You have to concentrate,' he said.

'I can see that. Was Mardi pleased?'

'She said I did okay.' He took off his riding hat.

'You did better than well considering how little time you've been riding,' said Jason.

'So can I go out riding with you now?' asked Tim.

'If your mum agrees. And we'll take Mardi with us too, how about that?' Jason shot Dani a questioning look.

'It depends, where you go and what horses. We'll see,' said Dani.

'Aw, Mum, it'll be fine . . .'

'You'll soon be good enough to get on Bomber. Good lad.'

Dani turned to see Kerry.

Jason gave a slight nod and turned on his heel. 'Catch you all later.'

'Hello, Kerry,' said Dani. 'I thought he did very well. But then you'd know more than me. But really I don't think he's ready for a big horse like Bomber.'

'Figure of speech. Jason'll fix him up with a suitable pony,' said Kerry. 'That's one of his that Tim rode today.'

'Jason said we can go riding now. Can he bring some horses to The Vale?' asked Tim excitedly.

'He doesn't ride there,' said Kerry. 'Plenty of other places. Round Dingo Creek. Down by the river there's a nice track. Good one, Tim. See you.'

She turned and left them and Dani thought again what an odd woman she was. She suddenly thought of the big old house and made a note to ask Helen or Henry about it. They watched the prize giving and Tim receive a white ribbon rosette. Dani took a picture of him nearly bursting with pride, draping the ribbon round the pony's neck.

'Wait till Dad sees this,' he said. 'I got to go, Mum. Catch you later.'

'We'll be around or under the big cedar tree with the Catchpoles,' said Dani.

Almost everyone had brought a picnic basket and in between watching, participating in or judging events; rides; games and competitions, they settled in groups and wandered between them visiting, gossiping, sharing news and friendship.

Tim had changed into shorts and the boys were taking turns trying to stay on the mechanical bull. Tabatha had entered one of Chesterfield's Angora goats in the show, hoping for a prize.

Lara settled into one of Henry's fold-up chairs in the shade as Patricia passed around a plate of cheese, olives and biscuits. Helen and Barney sat on a rug on the grass.

While Tabatha and Toby were busy, their parents, Angela and Tony, were off looking at a display of farm machinery. Dani relaxed between Max and Sarah, thinking how content she felt here.

Patricia sat down and glanced at her watch. 'I have to go and hand out prizes in the floral display in a little while. So, Dani, you excited about the Isabella movie? Roddy's been quite a find, eh?'

'I hope so,' she answered uncomfortably. 'Seems like townspeople are expecting big things.'

'The tourist attraction of the movie set of Isabella's house with sulky rides and so on could bring in people. Once they're here and discover there's a lot more to see they'll stay. That means they spend money on food, accommodation, souvenirs, seeing the sights,' said Patricia.

'That's still a long way off,' said Dani.

'And what about you and Roddy?' asked Helen with a smile.

'Like you said, Helen, I'm just using him for sex!' They all laughed, and Dani added quickly, 'It's nothing serious, I'm still looking for Mr Right.'

'You girls are too picky,' said Helen. 'Young women today want to run everything themselves and be in charge, or else opt out and turn into femo-crats. Botox, the gym, get someone in to care for the kids and a rich husband who's bored out of his skull.'

'Now they're fighting words,' said Patricia.

'I wish,' laughed Sarah.

'You're generalising. Don't tell me feminism has delivered, because ambitious women still get demonised,' said Dani. 'And I think it's true, men marry down, women try to marry up. At least there's not the social stigma about marrying younger men that there used to be. It's just hard to meet people, let alone find a match.'

'I'm so glad I'm past that,' sighed Patricia. 'I'd hate to

be in my twenties or thirties today. Go on the Net, Dani. Everyone does.'

'What a load of codswallop you women talk,' interjected Henry, reaching for a refill of tea from the Thermos. 'Walk around here, there are a pile of healthy single farmers come to town for the show. Used to be the rodeo and the Saturday night show ball was where you'd find the love of your life. No trouble.'

The women laughed and Max and Dani began discussing his exhibition he was readying for the New York agent, now Greta had told him.

'I have to lock up the studio and keep the key,' said Sarah. 'To stop him creeping back in at night and redoing a painting, or starting over. As soon as one is finished I whip it over to Greta to store.'

Dani laughed, but she understood Max's feelings of insecurity. 'No matter how good you become, or how famous, or collectable – whatever you want to call it – seems to me each painting is like starting from square one again.'

As everyone chatted, Henry turned to Lara. 'Been meaning to tell you. Had a woman contact me at the museum the other day. Said she'd heard about you and that her elderly mother could help you with your family search. I've got her details at the museum. Pop by next week.'

Lara was surprised at the casualness of his remark but decided not to get too excited by it. Once again the spectre of the mysterious letters came back to rattle her. She was about to quietly mention it to Henry when Dani came between them, handing around biscuits.

Max and Sarah rose to go and check on the children, and Helen and Barney went off to see a few more exhibits with an offer to join their mob where Angela and Tony had set up their picnic.

'Now there's something you don't see very often,' commented Henry.

'What's that?' asked Dani.

'Jason and Kerry being sociable.' He nodded in the direction of where Jason was standing talking to Kerry who was about to get into her truck.

'Why not? Don't they have horses in common?' asked Dani.

'They've a lot more in common than that,' commented Patricia.

'Some of us can relate to sibling rivalry,' grinned Henry. 'Patricia has a very difficult sister. Jason and Kerry have never had much in common. Big falling out when their father died and left everything to Jason.'

Dani sat down. 'They're brother and sister? I had no idea.'

'It's common knowledge. Jason moved away when he was very young and didn't come back till he got involved with the Birimbal project. His great-grandfather was a lawyer and his grandfather too. His father, also a legal man, moved to Sydney and became a judge. Jason's mother was a Sydney society matron, so he cut his ties with Cedartown pretty early. When their father died the family estate here went, as it always has, to the oldest son. Girls did not inherit as they weren't considered capable of managing money. Their husbands did that, hence the idea was to marry up, as you were discussing earlier.'

'So Jason hardly lived here but what happened to Kerry?' Dani was shocked she knew none of this. But then she and Jason were more professional associates, why would he talk about his family?

'She was into horses and on the show-jumping circuit. Got married, her husband was killed and later she had a bad accident so she came back home. Except she had no home. So Jason lets her live on the family estate,' explained Henry. 'There's more to it, but you'd have to talk to Kerry and Jason to get the story.'

'It feels like prying,' said Dani. 'Nothing's ever been hinted at, and if they don't get on, I don't feel I should ask.'

'Quite right too,' said Patricia, standing up and smoothing her skirt. 'There's enough speculation and gossip in this town. Always has been. Right, I'm off to do what I have to do.'

The group broke up with plans to join Tony and Angela and Helen and Barney who had Eskies full of cold beer and chicken in the back of their four-wheel drive. To make a day of it, Lara invited everyone back to Cricklewood for an impromptu supper.

Tim and Dani stayed the night at Cricklewood and after everyone had left and they'd cleaned up and Tim had gone to bed with his prize ribbon hanging on the bedpost, Dani and Lara sat in the crisp night air on the front verandah.

'That was a surprise about Jason and Kerry,' said Lara.

'Mmm. I've found Kerry to be a bit . . . stand-offish. Maybe it's shyness. Maybe she's bitter.'

'Who wouldn't be? It's how it was in the country, the property always divided up among the boys,' said Lara.

'There's this amazing old house filled with antiques on the property, it must be Jason's family home. But it's like a mausoleum and Kerry lives in a farm cottage. Weird,' said Dani. 'There must have been some falling out.'

'Sounds cosier than a big place full of stuff to look after,' said Lara. 'That must be where the things in your cottage came from.'

Dani was thoughtful, remembering Kerry slaving away cleaning the big house. Why didn't Jason get a cleaner rather than let his sister do it?

Lara changed the subject. 'Speaking of weird. I've been getting these letters, Dani. Well, a couple dropped in the mailbox here, by hand.'

'What sort of letters?' Dani was unsettled by the strain in her mother's voice.

In reply Lara handed Dani the letters, which she read swiftly in the light coming from the lounge room.

'Mum, who would send these? Whoever it is sounds unhinged, and who'd know about what you're doing? Did you go to the police?' said Dani.

'No, I let it go, it's some kind of a prank maybe. There was that article about us in the local paper . . .'

'Mum, these are threatening.' Dani felt unnerved and glanced out into the dark street.

'What puzzles me is the idea there's some secret, something bad I shouldn't know.'

'Like what? Is there something you're not telling me?' asked Dani.

'No, of course not, it's something I don't know and whatever it is someone doesn't want me to find out.'

'About your father? His family? That's the only gap in your family history, isn't it?' Dani had become so swept up in reading about Isabella's history and life that she hadn't thought too much about her mother's search. She now had the feeling, following her thoughts on the merry-go-round, that there was some convergence. That past histories – linked to her family, the present, the future and the valley – were somehow merging.

'Mum, did I hear Henry say he had some contact? Someone who knew your family? You'd better look them up.'

'I will. I just hope whoever it is has all their marbles and I'm not going to have to sit with some oldie in a home who can't remember their own name.' Lara got up. 'It's been a big day, I'm going to bed. You should too. Don't you have some work to do tomorrow?'

'Yeah. I'm seeing Jason and going with Max to the gallery to help him select which paintings to show the agent.'

'Honey, maybe you should show the agent some of your work too,' suggested Lara.

'No way, Mum. I'm nowhere near Max's league, and it's his connection. When I feel I'm ready Greta will set me up I'm sure.'

Dani had her own creative insecurities and wasn't ready to put herself out there for public comment. She was still trying to find her own style and the best technique to express it. For the moment she was absorbed by Isabella, her life and country, which was giving her a focus and also providing something of a crutch. She just hoped her work would be what Jason and his backers wanted. At the thought of investors she thought of Roddy and his mysterious film financier and hoped he'd come up with the full budget for the film. Dani wanted the film to be made, not so much for Roddy's sake but for all the people in the community who were supporting it.

Dani shut the front door and wondered if the strange letter writer was out there, watching. You're not going to spook us. There are too many strong family vibes around this house protecting us, she decided.

Lara

It was the usual chaotic jolly atmosphere in the back room of the historical society. Lara greeted Garth and nodded at the others whose names she couldn't recall. Henry emerged from the front display area and produced a scrap of paper.

'There you go. She says her mother knew your family.'

Lara glanced at the name. 'I'll give her a call. Hope her mother is still alert, she must be getting on.'

'Only one way to find out. I'm off to the Cedartown RSL for lunch. You joined yet? Best and cheapest food in town,' said Henry.

Lara did some shopping at the local organic fruit and veg shop, popped into the cheese factory deli to stock up and made a note the next time she was in Hungerford to go to Rudi's smallgoods for some of his tasty German bratwurst sausages and his smoked and pickled meats. She hadn't entertained or had people drop in to visit so regularly in a long time. She'd got out of the habit in Sydney. She had dinner parties when she was married and after that she met friends in cafes or restaurants. Preparing food for guests had become a chore. Here she was enjoying discovering all the local delicacies and, most of all, the company of friends she'd made in the valley.

Back at Cricklewood she poured herself a glass of iced rainwater from the tank, sat at the telephone desk in the hallway and dialled the number Henry had given her.

The woman who answered, Barbara Ellmore, sounded very pleasant and said her mother had read the article in the local paper and knew who she was.

'So your mother is pretty active?' asked Lara.

'Oh, she's amazing, fit as a flea, I have trouble keeping up with her. She'd go to the club every day if I had the time. She plays cards three nights a week.'

'How wonderful. How old is she?'

'She's seventy-nine, still drives, has a bad back and arthritis, so she moved out of her big house and has a nice unit on the outskirts of Riverwood. She lives alone, cooks, tidies her unit, potters in the garden. We insisted she get someone in to do the heavy cleaning. Would you like to meet her?'

'Indeed I would. Perhaps I should chat to her on the phone first,' said Lara.

'Fine. If you can catch her at home,' added Barbara.

Lara wrote down the phone number and directions before realising, 'Silly, I haven't even asked her name.'

'It's Phyllis Lane. She was Phyllis Richards. She's a really decent old stick. And I'm not just saying that 'cause she's my mother. Everyone loves her. From the few things she said, I'm pretty sure she'll be able to help you. She wants to talk to you, wouldn't tell me anything.'

'What sort of things?' asked Lara cautiously.

'Look, it's not my place to say. At first she said she didn't think you should be raking over the past, it's all dead and gone. But I figured anyone who moved up here to research their family history needs to know anything Mum remembers that could help.'

'Thank you,' said Lara.

'That generation, they're very proper, conscious of not stepping out of line, breaking confidences, that sort of thing,' said Barbara cheerfully. 'You have to admire that.'

'Indeed. Well, I'll give Mrs Lane a call.'

'Call her Aunty Phyllis, everyone does.'

Lara hung up the phone, quite rattled at so easily finding a member of the Richards family. What relation were these people to her father Clem Richards? She hadn't wanted to ask someone like Barbara who probably didn't know, sounded busy, and seemed not that interested anyway. All Lara knew about her father was the name on her birth certificate. She hoped this 'Aunty Phyllis' would be honest and give her unbiased information.

But there must be some reason her own mother had refused to talk about him. Elizabeth said she'd told Lara about him when she was little. Lara protested that she was so young she had no recall of the conversation, but that the subject was closed as far as Elizabeth was concerned.

Her stepfather – whom she believed to be her father until she saw her birth certificate for the first time – was a loving, gentle man whom she adored. Lara had never wondered about her biological father until she was pregnant with Dani. By then she was living abroad and the subject of her real father had become such a taboo subject Lara let it drop. Now there were many unanswered questions.

How she wished she'd probed her grandfather more deeply when she'd come to visit him with baby Dani after her grandmother Emily had died. Lara knew her grandparents tended to put a positive, light-hearted coating on unpleasantness. Vague references from her grandmother about not raking up the past, or certain things being best forgotten, had slipped under Lara's childhood radar at the time. She knew there had been a falling out between her mother and her grandmother, but neither of them were easy personalities. With the instinctive wisdom of a child, Lara found it safest never to repeat anything either said or did to the other.

It took two days to reach Phyllis by phone. Lara caught her one evening and found her to be chirpy, bright and chatty.

'It's taken you a while to come back and visit, what took you so long?' asked Phyllis.

'I've visited a few times. And I used to come on holidays,' said Lara feeling chastised. 'But you're right, I have left it a long time. Maybe too long. You don't think about the past when you're busy getting on with the present.'

'You were little when you left here, weren't you? I only remember you as a baby.'

'You knew me, saw me then?' exclaimed Lara.

'I was young, not interested in babies at that stage,' chuckled Phyllis. 'My dear old mum was more interested in you, not that your grandmother allowed that.'

Lara was feeling overwhelmed, the past had caught up with her in a rush. 'So what relation are you to my father, Clem Richards?'

'Little sister.' Phyllis sighed. 'He was my favourite brother. If we could turn back the clock, eh?'

'What was he like? What happened between him and my mother, she refused to talk about him.'

Phyllis paused. 'Dear, I don't think it's my place to tell you things your mother never told you.'

Lara wanted to shake the phone. 'Come on, it couldn't be that bad, could it? A lot of water under the bridge. My mother isn't here, how am I going to find out anything? It's not just for me, my daughter wants to know her history too,' said Lara in exasperation.

'I don't know a lot, and I'm not going to repeat gossip unless I know it to be true. I was young, more interested in my own life. There was a lot of pain, the war changed families . . .' she broke off.

Lara tried another tack. 'What about my grandparents, Emily and Harold Williams, did you know them?'

'First time I met them properly was at the wedding. I so wanted to be a bridesmaid in a long dress with flowers in my hair. But it was wartime, it was an evening wedding as I recall. I remember having a dance with Clem, he always made a fuss of me. 'Cause I was the only girl and the youngest in our family.'

'What was the wedding like? What do you remember?' Lara was thirsty for any details.

'It was small, simple. I remember there were a few friends but the two families kept very separate. Your grandmother didn't approve. She kept her nose in the air. Not that it bothered me.'

'And after that?'

Phyllis sighed. 'It's a bit late, I haven't had my tea. I think it's best we have a chat another time. Face to face?'

'I'd like that. Can I come and see you? I'd really appreciate it. Do you have any photos?' asked Lara suddenly.

'Well, now. I suppose I have kept some. I had a big

clean out when I moved here. Gave a lot of stuff to Barbara and her daughter.'

'Is tomorrow too soon?'

Phyllis chuckled. 'Steady on. I have to do a bit of digging in boxes and I have a card tournament, and a few things on. What about morning tea on Friday?'

Four days away. Lara sighed, she had little choice and she didn't want to frighten her off. 'Whatever suits you. I'll come to you. Barbara gave me the address. Can I take you out somewhere?'

'No, let's stay here. Easier with pictures and things.'

'Of course. Thank you so much, Phyllis . . . Can I call you that?'

'Everyone calls me Aunty Phyllis, dear. Of course in your case I really am your aunty. Be real nice to catch up with you, Lara. Bye.'

Lara sat still, holding the phone, staring at the black and white tiles of the hallway floor. It hadn't registered with her till that moment that the woman she'd been chatting with, a complete stranger, was family. Her father's sister. Her aunt.

Lara poured herself a drink and sat in the lounge room, the TV flickering with the sound off, unheeded. Photographs and cuttings were still piled on the coffee table. Idly she began to flick through them deciding which ones she'd take to show Phyllis in the hope she could identify them. There were lots of pictures of soldiers in uniform. Some obviously taken at Cricklewood, on the front verandah, on the front lawn beside Emily's roses, and some more casual ones of the boys with Elizabeth and another girl cuddling on the back steps.

Then a photo caught her eye and she lifted it from the pile and studied it, looking at the boyish happy face, with his arm around a beaming Elizabeth in a very forties frock with padded shoulders, round-toed high heels, her hair rolled around her face in a stylish copy of Joan Crawford or Loretta Young or whatever movie star was the current favourite.

Then Lara shivered and turned slowly to glance over her shoulder into the shadowy corners of the room. Could this be the man she'd glimpsed as a ghostly figure standing in this room the first night she stayed here? He looked familiar.

Lara threw the photo down on the pile and rushed from the lounge room, shutting the double glass doors and retreating to the kitchen. She went to bed early with her book, the phone and a glass of hot milk. She slept. A determined sleep. Eyes squeezed shut, pillow clutched close. She barely moved during a dreamless passing of the hours. But in the morning a sixth sense, a feeling of dread sent her to the letterbox.

As she suspected, and feared, another letter waited.

Do not believe the lies and fabrications of those with fading memories. No one knows the truth. It is too late to repair the damage and fix the pain. Go away before you and yours are punished too.

In the bright light of morning, the letter seemed less intimidating than it would have at night time, but it was nonetheless threatening. Lara decided to put it to one side and try to ignore it. She didn't want to worry Dani. But it was a creepy feeling, like someone had intruded into her home. She knew she was watching faces in the street, wondering if anyone was following her.

So Lara was pleased when she saw Barney pull up at the front gate and unload some wire and tools. Then he carried a plate covered in a tea cloth into the kitchen.

'Hi, Lara. Fresh scones Helen's just made. I thought I'd repair that fence you wanted done.'

'Great, thanks, Barney. I don't want Jolly getting out through that hole. I'll put the kettle on. We'll have it outside, I'm doing a bit of sorting.' Lara waved at the coffee table in the lounge room, littered with letters and photographs. To one side there was a fraying bird's nest.

'Blue wren. What's this for?' asked Barney.

'I'm finding bits and pieces for Dani's new art project. She wants to do something different when she's finished the Isabella paintings. She's still struggling to find her niche.'

'Can we contribute to her collection?'

'She's happy to accept any acquisitions. What did you have in mind?' said Lara.

'Oh, some blue feathers, a couple of feathers from a bowerbird. An old Aboriginal stone-cutting tool and a couple of shells that have been sharpened.' He paused. 'I was going to give them to Max, but I've decided to keep them.'

'Where did you find them?'

'At Chesterfield.'

'I bet Dani would love to borrow the old implements and use them on a plate image and run it off,' said Lara. 'Then return them to you.' Barney was fidgety and she felt he was leading up to something. 'What say we have that cuppa?'

He settled himself at the old cane table and chairs on the front verandah as Lara put down the tray with the tea things. 'Y'know how I went down to Sydney couple of weeks back because my great-aunty died?' he began.

'Yes. Sorry to hear that. How did it go?'

'Blew me away, actually. You're not the only one with family gaps . . . secrets.' He reached for a scone.

'Why? What did you find out?'

'Jeez, Lara, I hardly know where to begin. My mother has always been tight-lipped about the family. Told me my paternal grandmother – Dad's mother – died when I was a kid. Never knew much about Dad's side. He died quite a few years back. Well, now it turns out my grandmother lived till she was in her eighties.'

'My God, where was she?'

Barney's scone sat untouched. 'She was sent to Callan Park mental institution in Sydney. She died a few years back. In a mental home out in Orange.'

'Why did they keep it a secret? I mean, she must have been ill . . .'

'Lara, she wasn't mad, she had depression. But she was Aboriginal. Mixed blood. They framed her, locked her up, to keep her ancestry secret.'

Lara stared at the olive-skinned, wiry man with the warm black eyes. 'Really? And you had no idea?'

'Not really. Helen's not surprised.' He turned and showed his thin legs sticking out from his shorts and ending in his work boots. 'Says I have skinny Aboriginal legs,' he smiled. Then looked thoughtful. 'Looking back now I kinda wondered about things. When I was in a country town out west, a few blackfellas gave me a "Hi, bro" in the street. Lots of other weird stuff. And, you know, my father, he was olive-skinned, Spanish blood I was told. But he'd never sit in the sun, always under a tree, or he wore long-sleeved shirts and a hat.' Barney began to spread jam on his scone.

'Well, that's a bit of a surprise. What're you going to do about it?'

'First I got mad, not knowing about my granny. I could have gone and seen her. That made me sad. How did she feel being in there? I don't think there was anything wrong with her. I wish my father was alive so I could ask him questions, Mum's ashamed and that's why they kept it quiet all these years. Poor old Dad, lost all contact with his people, I guess.'

431

'Do you know where he came from?' asked Lara quietly, she could see Barney was deeply hurt.

'Yeah. Out west, I've already made contact with them and I'm planning a visit. They sent pictures and stuff. I can see family resemblances all over the place. They're planning a big reunion.'

'What do Angela and the family think?' Lara was thinking of Barney's striking dark-eyed daughter.

'Thrilled to bits. Think it's great. Toby wants to know what tribe he comes from.'

Barney bit into his scone and Lara slowly sipped her tea. Barney had been hit with quite a bombshell, but at least he was finding family and filling in the jigsaw of his life. 'So is that the reason you want to hang onto the Aboriginal artifacts?' she finally said.

'I had a long talk to Max, we're wondering whether his people and my people ever connected. I think my mob were originally desert people while he comes from this area. But he's glad Chesterfield is in a brother's hands.'

'Your place was his traditional land?'

'Apparently. We thought we'd have a little ceremony of some kind. Just small, just family. That includes you and Dani of course,' said Barney.

'Thank you. Do you feel any different, Barn . . . knowing all this?' asked Lara, trying to sift through her own feelings.

He broke into a wide smile. 'You bet. While it's hurtful at how they hid so much, I feel settled inside now. I'm hearing family stories, there's a whole pile of rellies who want to know and accept me. That's a good feeling.'

'So is this public knowledge?' Lara wondered what she might eventually find out about her father, and if she'd share it.

'Not taking out a newspaper ad, but I'm not hiding it either. Been too much of that,' said Barney. 'It'll just come out naturally I s'pose. Though Toby and Tab want to tell everyone at school. They think it's cool.'

'Thanks for telling me.'

'I just thought you'd appreciate what it means to me. Finding out stuff, finding family. I hope you do too, Lara.'

'Yes, me too. I just know there's someone out there who knows something.' She stifled the impulse to mention the letter.

Barney was already on his feet. 'How about I tackle that fence.'

15

Riverview, 1852

Isabella

THEY RODE IN A leisurely style, young Kelly in front on the colt Isabella had given him. Florian rode beside Isabella, and Noona with her baby daughter propped in front of her followed. Florian and Isabella were discussing her plans to rebuild at Birimbal once they had evicted Mrs Skerrett and her children.

'I've given her fair warning and been lenient in letting her stay past the lease while her husband is in gaol. But she must realise she cannot stay on indefinitely, especially when she hasn't paid rent,' said Isabella.

Florian nodded, though he had reservations. 'Charles Skerrett has many friends, even though he's locked away. I think there could be repercussions when he hears his wife has been evicted.'

'The law is on my side,' said Isabella firmly. Then

she started to discuss plans for rebuilding her mansion. 'The first matter to take in hand is the main house, I still believe an inn providing quality accommodation is sorely needed on this route to and from Port Macquarie. Mark my words, Florian, one day this part of the country will be in great demand.'

'I hope the workers know what they're doing, Miss Kelly. You know I'm really not much more than a bush carpenter.'

'I've employed a man who is an excellent cabinetmaker and wood turner, he'll see to the details and instruct the labourers. I'll rely on you to manage the cattle and the staff when I'm not there.'

Isabella was enjoying living at Riverview, the house on the river. She was close to a pocket of rainforest where she'd found many more interesting plants for her collection. The view across the river gave her a great sense of serenity. It was a very different feeling from being on her hill where the bush was constantly creeping forward, swarming over the fences, making her feel an interloper trying to impose her will on the wilderness. At the river with its wide sweep of water, broad alluvial flats, flooded or not, she always felt she had a means of escape, that she wasn't surrounded. Not that she felt threatened and she loved the solitude of the mountain, but the river was a different world again and she sometimes sat and contemplated the bird life, fish leaping and the many moods of the stretch of water. She could see it would not be long before coastal ships would be sailing regularly up this river with supplies and passengers from Sydney and other ports along the coast.

Already there were men logging the hills of its rich timber, dragging logs by bullock teams to the river, then floating them downstream to basic bush mills to be used for building. There was a demand in the city for quality wood for furniture and Isabella intended to use local red cedar and white beech in her new home.

Florian interrupted her thoughts. 'And Noona and the children, Miss Kelly?' It still worried Florian, and indeed Isabella, that his Aboriginal wife and their half-caste children presented a potential problem in the eyes of white society and the law.

'Keep to your own affairs, Florian,' she said shortly. 'And your own dwelling. Be discreet when there are others around.'

Florian understood. They'd established a custom at Riverview where Florian was occasionally invited to join Isabella for an evening meal at the dining table because Isabella wanted to discuss business matters or enjoy the company of the younger man who had been schooled in manners and conversation. At these times Noona and the children stayed in their simple quarters. So when a passing visitor, coming to the house one evening, had been invited to share the meal, as was the bush custom of hospitality, he had carried the gossip to the next town of Miss Kelly entertaining the handsome young ex convict at her table.

Isabella had also taken it upon herself to call for Florian's son Kelly and had begun to school him in reading and writing as well as the basic niceties of table manners and courtesy.

Noona understood more English than she spoke and continued to speak to her son and baby daughter in her own language. She was a diligent worker when shown what to do in the laundry, house and garden, but preferred her own ways, unlike the other native girl who'd been trained by a missionary and worked in the kitchen. There was a strong cultural barrier between her and Noona.

Noona explained to Florian she would die if she lost her links with her traditions and he did not argue when she occasionally flung aside the clothes provided by Isabella and went walkabout, Kelly at her side, the baby slung in a woven string pouch in reach of her naked breasts. Kelly understood that it was important to know the bush and the spirit of the land and knowledge of country that came from his mother. With equal firmness his father encouraged him to learn well what Miss Kelly taught him.

Kelly, who had ridden ahead as they were now on Birimbal land, had disappeared from sight but he suddenly reappeared at a gallop. He pulled up beside Isabella and his parents.

'There are two men at the crossing,' he said breathlessly.

'Why do you look so concerned, lad?'

'It's the bad man,' he gasped. 'Mr Skerrett.' Kelly had been in the background often enough to hear about the trouble between Skerrett and Isabella.

'Impossible. He's in gaol.' Isabella spurred her horse forward nonetheless. On reaching the crossing she couldn't see anyone, but there was a saddled horse drinking a little further downstream.

Then two men stepped from the scrub and stood in the middle of the track on the opposite side of the creek. One was Skerrett, hands on his hips, a cocky grin on his face. Isabella didn't recognise the other surly-faced man with a thick moustache.

Isabella challenged them at once. 'What are you doing here, Skerrett? I'll report you to the authorities.' Isabella glanced over her shoulder as Florian and Kelly rode into view.

Skerrett gave a harsh laugh. 'Then do so, Isabella Kelly. I'm a free man. My wife petitioned to have me pardoned. It seems I have good friends in positions to help me.'

Isabella felt a ball of anger in the pit of her stomach. She had heard stories of Skerrett's wife Maria, travelling around the countryside protesting her husband's innocence to anyone who would listen. She'd visited him at Cockatoo

Island Prison and there had been rumours of Mrs Skerrett orchestrating a campaign to get her husband released. She was known to have visited Magistrate Henry Flett – no friend to Isabella – several times. Isabella had given little credence to the talk though it had given her cause to pause before asking Mrs Skerrett and the nine children to leave her Birimbal property. But she had not expected this. That Skerrett's barely-educated wife had got him pardoned.

'Then I expect to find my home vacated immediately and you and your brood gone from my property. Rent and repairs are owing to me,' snapped Isabella.

'You owe me, not the other way around,' said Skerrett brusquely. 'I'm going to collect what is my due.' Here he gave the scowling man beside him a broad smile. 'And I intend that Mr Parsons here assist me and be my witness: I am claiming what is mine.'

'And what might that be? I owe you nothing. I demand you leave my property.' Isabella moved her horse to the edge of the creek.

Skerrett's companion spoke for the first time, sounding rough and hostile. 'I seen the paper. He wants his cattle and horses you tricked him out of. We're goin' to take 'em. It'll do you harm to try and stop us.'

Isabella was outraged that Skerrett would attempt to steal the stock she'd left at Birimbal. 'You have no right, no authority and no piece of paper. You'll be back in gaol before you know it,' shouted Isabella.

'Take care, Miss Kelly,' warned Florian behind her. 'He has a pistol.'

'And so have I. Out of my way, you've caused me enough trouble, Skerrett, leave my land immediately. You're tres- passing.' She kicked her horse forward and charged across the creek at the two men, taking them by surprise. In his haste to get out of the way of the large black horse, Sker- rett tripped and fell, rolling to one side to avoid her horse's hooves. But Parsons leapt to the side and managed to fire a shot after Isabella as she thundered up the slope where she reined in the horse and turned and shouted to Florian, 'Ride to Mr Andrews' property, tell him these men have threatened and attacked me.' And she raced away.

Florian turned his horse as Noona and Kelly came into view and called to his son, 'Follow Miss Kelly, go to Birimbal. I'm going to Mr Andrews' place. Cut downstream.'

Seeing the two men fetch their horses, Kelly pushed his strong young colt into the stream and splashed away a few yards before riding back onto the bank. He was swiftly lost between the trees.

Florian shouted at Noona in her language to take the child and hide from the men. He'd send Kelly to fetch her. That these white men were bad men. He saw her clutch the baby protectively in its sling and turn her horse away. He assumed the two men would go after Isabella. Mrs Skerrett and the children must still be at Birimbal. Skerrett was cunning, and Parsons looked to be an unsavoury character – clearly they'd hatched some plan to claim Miss Kelly's cattle. Florian knew Isabella to be honest in her dealings, but he thought the men of the region, especially those like Flett and other magistrates, treated her most unfairly. In any dispute the men were always believed over Isabella.

'Damn bitch of a woman,' snarled Skerrett. 'Always making trouble.'

'I should ha' pegged her one, or shot her damn horse from under her. Teach her a lesson,' whined Parsons. 'Who're them people she's with? Servants?'

'A convict and his gin. He works for the Kelly woman.'

'That's agin' the law, ain't it?' Parsons' interest was piqued. 'What say you and me do the law a favour and see that bit o' black rubbish is sent back to the bush where she belongs.'

439

Skerrett was now mounted. He pulled a hip flask from a coat pocket and took a swig. 'Kelly's breaking the law allowing her people to mix with the blacks.' Skerrett had heard the gossip about Florian and his native woman, that they had children and Isabella afforded them shelter. Now it occurred to him that the cold-hearted Isabella Kelly might have a soft spot for the mixed-race family. He turned and grinned at Parsons. 'What say you and me do a little hunting?'

'Whooa, you an' me goin' to catch us a wild one, eh?' Parsons brandished his pistol and kicked his horse across the creek.

Skerrett rode noisily along the track in the direction Noona had taken while Parsons, from behind scanned the bush then decided to take an alternative route and plunged into the undergrowth.

Noona had dismounted and hearing the thrashing of the following horses had crawled into a thicket, cradling her baby. She'd circled back and waded upstream after sending her horse in the other direction.

Parsons wished he had his dogs with him, the thrill of the chase was not the same without them. His horse picked its way through the overgrown scrub as he slashed at the bushes with his whip, cursing under his breath. Skerrett followed the track, his thoughts still on Isabella, so he didn't notice the crouching figure of Noona, her hand over her infant's mouth, smothering its whimpers.

Her abandoned horse had instinctively turned towards the creek, and Skerrett, hearing the hooves splashing across the creek, quickly turned and raced towards it. Seeing the horse without its rider, he swore under his breath, hesitated and decided to leave Parsons to hunt down the native woman. He continued across the creek and headed for Birimbal to have a showdown with Isabella. In his pocket he carried the document giving him permission to muster and sell the cattle on Isabella's land. The document that Isabella believed had been destroyed in the fire months before.

Parsons soon realised that Noona had sent her horse in the opposite direction to which she'd fled. It had now become an obsession with him to find the black woman. He had a deep hatred of blacks. He had once slept with a gin he coveted and been attacked by men of her tribe. In the skirmish his best mate had been speared. Parsons swore that at every opportunity he too would 'pay back' the blacks.

'I can smell you, bitch,' he shouted in anger, and urged his horse forward, smashing through the bush. His fury became a slow burn that consumed him, pushing aside Skerrett and his plan to grab Kelly's cattle. He decided to be cunning and reined in his horse and sat still, listening to every small sound around him. He felt that every nerve in his body was on alert, seeking to sense the slightest signal that might indicate where the woman and child were hiding.

'C'mon, bitch,' he hissed.

Noona knew there was a horse and rider close by as she lay rigid with fear, her child clutched close and kept quiet by sucking at a nipple. She hoped the white man would give up looking for her, or that Kelly or Florian might return and scare him off.

But Parsons was not giving up. He dismounted and, leading his horse, began to search methodically. While no black tracker, he'd observed how the natives read the land and he began to see the crushed grasses and broken twigs where the woman had fled from the creek. He remounted and pushed his horse into the water, walking close to the bank.

He quickly spotted where she'd left the stream and plunged into the bush. Noona could hear him coming in her direction. There was only one thing in her mind now, the safety of her daughter. Like a female kangaroo in times of danger, Noona abandoned her baby, tucking her under a low thick shrub. She then took off swiftly through the scrub. She was fleet-footed and forced her way into the thickest part of the bush, hoping the white man would give up as it was too dense for a horse to get through.

But Parsons had a fire in his belly, a raging desire to destroy the woman in a deranged attempt to settle the ghosts and nightmares that had haunted him for so long. If he could kill her perhaps it would end the torment he suffered in the dark hours. The torment of having lost a mate in a dirty struggle with black scum.

He knew he was closing in on her, he could hear her frantic crashing in the undergrowth. Then it stopped as she paused, gauging where he was. He waited. He was coolly patient now and drew his pistol from its holster, patting his hip, feeling the sheath of the long knife he carried.

Noona suddenly realised she was in trouble. The way ahead was blocked with a great pile of boulders, then a sheer cliff. Perhaps if she could scramble upwards there might be a slit of a cave she could roll into.

Parsons also saw the cliff and grinned in delight, knowing his quarry was cornered. Then he glimpsed her trying to scramble up the rocks. 'Like a bloody monkey,' he scowled. 'Gotcha now.' He moved faster and as soon as he was in range he cocked the pistol, took aim and fired.

The lithe figure jerked, twisted, lost her grip and seemed to float in slow motion backwards to land out of sight with a soft thud.

Not in a hurry anymore, Parsons returned the gun to its holster and drew out the knife, slashing his way to the rock face.

Was she dead? Or playing possum? Parsons didn't care, for the sight of the crumpled near-naked woman aroused in him a fury that sent blood rushing to his head so that he was seeing everything through a red scrim. He kicked her onto her back and paused for a moment as the dark pained eyes bored into him with a look that sent his mind into a turmoil.

The lethal knife had a life of its own as it slashed at her throat and the more the deep red blood stained her skin and splashed him, the more the knife sliced at her breasts, her belly, between her legs and finally back to her neck until he straightened with Noona's head hanging from one hand, the bloodied knife in the other, its work done.

Parsons fell to his knees, panting, totally drained. He stayed there until flies, drawn by the sticky congealing blood, began to swarm around him. He lifted the knife and slowly wiped it clean with his kerchief. Then he slipped the knife into its sheath. He got to his feet and, looking at the woman's body, scowled at the dead, blank face, then turned back towards the creek crossing.

When he reached the bank where his horse still waited, he fell into the water, soaking his clothes, washing away the stains of his deed. He felt cleansed now. But there was more to be done.

For several hours he searched the bush until he heard the baby crying.

He killed the baby girl swiftly. As he wiped the blade clean he felt good. He had got rid of her and saved men from the pain she'd bring as a woman.

Satisfied, he rode the track to Birimbal, his mind at peace for the first time in many a month.

Isabella and Skerrett met angrily at the homestead. They argued, then Isabella broke away, strode to the house and stormed inside. She was stunned at the filth and disorder. Mrs Skerrett and her tribe of children had gone and there appeared to be no one at the property. Skerrett had no doubt seen to that before accosting her

443

on the track. Her cattle and six good horses were in the yard ready to be taken away by Skerrett. Florian was standing guard, watching Skerrett who was waiting for his partner to arrive. It was a stand-off, both ignoring each other.

Isabella wondered what Skerrett's offsider was up to. And where was Noona? She hoped Kelly would arrive back with Mr Andrews before nightfall. Florian wanted to look for Noona and the baby but Isabella needed him with her. She assured him they would be safe in their own environment, and fussed around in the kitchen to make a billy of tea.

Some time later Florian came to the door. 'Mr Andrews and Kelly are here,' he announced with relief.

Isabella went outside and greeted her neighbour warmly. Florian sent Kelly to the back of the house and ordered him to keep out of sight.

'Thank you for coming, Mr Andrews,' said Isabella, not disguising her relief at seeing him.

'That's all right, Miss Kelly. The lad had some wild story that didn't make much sense to me. So, what seems to be the trouble?'

He glanced around looking faintly annoyed as all seemed peaceful.

'Mr Skerrett and his friend bailed us up on the road at the crossing, harassed my party and fired a pistol to stop me returning to my property,' said Isabella.

Andrews swung off his horse and glanced over at the yards where Skerrett was leaning against the railing. 'Matters seem to be in hand now. What was the altercation over? I was led to believe from the half-caste child that you were in danger, Miss Kelly.'

'It appeared so at the time. He has a companion who hasn't arrived here.' She didn't want to mention Noona though she assumed the neighbours knew of Florian's family. 'I'm afraid he might have returned to my river property.'

'I'd heard Mr Skerrett was discharged from gaol and his family are moving on, is there some issue?' Andrews didn't repeat that he'd been told that since Skerrett had been pardoned people were inferring that it must be Isabella who was guilty.

'He claims to have the right to take my cattle and horses with him,' said Isabella. 'I never agreed to such a plan. I left these animals here as breeding stock while I sold the rest.'

'Miss Kelly, I have no wish to enter into any disagreement between you and Mr Skerrett. I was merely concerned for your welfare.'

'Thank you, Mr Andrews. I felt threatened and frightened for my life. Could you please come inside?'

Andrews hesitated, glancing over to Skerrett who looked quite cocky. But he did not want to be called to court yet again on one of Isabella Kelly's disputes. 'Thank you, but I will speak to Mr Skerrett and be on my way before dark.'

Just then Parsons cantered up the path towards the house and, seeing Skerrett, turned to the yards and dismounted.

Andrews led his horse to the yards and greeted Skerrett, nodding at Parsons who was unfamiliar to him.

'I was sent for by Miss Kelly. She says she was threatened, you fired at her?'

'Miss Kelly is a proven liar, Mr Andrews. I've come to collect these animals she agreed I could muster and sell when I leased this property.' He produced the agreement.

Andrews studied the paper and handed it back to Skerrett. 'It seems to be in order.'

'That woman is crazy. Now my associate has arrived we're taking these animals,' said Skerrett. 'And no one can stop us.'

Andrews shrugged. 'It is no business of mine.' But he knew if called upon he'd have to vouch that Skerrett appeared to have authorisation from Kelly, whether she'd changed her mind since or not. 'I will be returning to my home. Good day, gentlemen.'

Parsons merely gave a smirk as they watched Andrews walk away. Skerrett began to lower the yard rails. 'We'll push out of here and make camp and settle the beasts. What took you so long?'

Parsons merely shrugged. 'Cunning little bitch ran off.'

Skerrett was more concerned with getting the cattle and horses on the road. 'I'll take the lead, you bring up the rear.'

Isabella came out of the house and shouted, 'I forbid you to take those animals. It's theft.'

Florian ran around to the front and said to Isabella, 'Leave them go, Miss Kelly, they will make trouble. Mr Skerrett seemed to convince Mr Andrews he has a right to them.'

'He tricked me, Florian. And I fear it will not go my way in a court,' said Isabella sounding defeated and tired.

'Then leave it be, miss. I'm going to look for Noona and the child. Kelly will stay here. Or do you want him to follow Skerrett, see where he camps?'

'Find Noona and the baby. Tell Kelly to stay with me. I will deal with Skerrett another day.' Isabella turned and went inside.

Florian did not return until sunrise. Kelly heard his horse and ran to meet him. He stopped when he saw his father riding along alone, his head bowed as if a great weight had settled on his shoulders. Florian appeared not to see him and went to his quarters and fell onto his bed.

Kelly crept to the door and, hearing the great wrenching sobs that seemed to howl from the bottom of his father's boots, he knew something terrible had happened. He turned and ran to where they had first confronted the two white men. He reached the crossing as the sun fell on his shoulders. All was still and quiet. But Kelly knew, knew in his bones, his mother and sister had died here.

Later Isabella found the young boy curled on the bank by the creek. She shook him and Kelly opened his eyes and stared at her. Isabella shuddered. They were no longer the eyes of an innocent boy. They were the anguished, empty eyes of a boy-man who had seen visions and been given knowledge too terrible for anyone to bear.

She lifted Kelly and sat him on the saddle in front of her and they turned their backs on the crossing and the terrible events of the previous day. One day, swore Isabella to herself, justice will prevail.

Dani

The Hungerford Regional Art Gallery was closed to the public when Dani and Max pulled his paintings out of the storage area and began to hang them under Greta's supervision.

'That blue night scene, put it in the centre, pride of place,' said Greta.

Their footsteps echoed in the old house that had been renovated to provide spacious display areas with high ceilings, skylights and extra light fittings. With the pictures given plenty of white space, distance to enable viewers to see them in full perspective with the correct lighting and nothing else competing for attention, they seemed to come to life and breathe.

'Max, aren't you proud? Look at your work. It's stunning,' said Dani in awe. She stood back trying to take in the work that had such depth. 'The more you look at it the more things you see. Each is an unfolding story, you keep going back to see what's evolved, what comes to mind, every time you look at them,' said Dani.

'They're a feast, you have to absorb them one at a time,' agreed Greta. 'They're unique, unlike anything I've seen before. And there's no way of knowing whether a white, black or pink artist did them. You've created your own genre, Max,' she said lightly.

'Yes. Stories beneath the paint. It's going to be hard to part with them,' said Max softly.

'No, it won't be hard. Not when you've got a cheque in your hand, Maxwell,' said Greta briskly. 'Ken Minton will be here tomorrow morning ten sharp.'

'And then what happens?' asked Dani.

'He's on his way north, Cairns, I think. If he likes any he'll buy them. If he really likes them he might buy the whole collection, commission more, fly Max to New York for the opening. Who knows?' said Greta.

'Max, what are you going to say to this dealer, agent guy?' asked Dani, wondering how she'd present herself, what she would say to a dealer to get them interested in her work.

'Oh, I won't be here,' said Max shaking his head. 'No way. Let the work speak for itself. Greta can do all the talking.'

They left the art gallery as Greta began to catalogue and photograph Max's paintings.

'Do you feel like you're losing kids?' asked Dani. She'd noticed how Max glanced around at each picture before they left.

He gave a sheepish grin. 'Yeah, a bit. There's just an awful lot of me in every one of them. Don't you find that?'

'I'm still fumbling along, I'm nowhere near your level,

but occasionally I feel, I know, when it's working. It's like someone else is holding the brush, it sort of paints itself,' said Dani. 'My strongest feeling is that I'm actually in it, at the place I'm painting. Well, with these Isabella pictures anyway.' Max gave an understanding nod as she went on, 'Barney said a strange thing. He reckoned he could see people in one picture. I'd painted a stand of big trees that created a lot of shadows, so I suppose you could imagine shadows that looked like figures.'

Max gave her a sharp look. 'Really? That's interesting. Barney doesn't know what he knows yet. He's still coming to grips with his Aboriginality.'

Dani thought that an odd remark. 'Well, he seems very intuitive in some ways and yet he's such a simple, down-to-earth bloke, isn't he?' When Max didn't answer she added, almost to herself, 'People aren't always what they appear to be.'

'What was the place you'd painted, where Barney saw the figures?' asked Max.

'Kelly's Crossing. Or should we be calling it Isabella Kelly's Crossing?' said Dani flippantly, trying to jolly Max out of his sudden serious mood.

'No, we shouldn't call it that. It's a bit confusing really. Carter is trying to get National Parks to rename it, and your developer mate Jason is well intentioned, and it's good he doesn't want Isabella to be forgotten, ignored. But there was another Kelly.'

'Really? Who?' Dani instantly thought of Roddy's film, this could add or possibly detract from his story. 'Who was that? A relative? I thought she was childless.'

'In a manner of speaking. But there was a boy, a mixed-blood born to one of her white workers and an Aboriginal woman. Isabella must have been attached to him, because he was named Kelly.'

'How do you know this?' asked Dani as they reached

449

his car. She had the feeling Max was telling her something he didn't often speak about.

'My grandmother told me. Family is very important to Aboriginal people. They keep track of relatives as best they can.'

'Was he a relative?' Dani was beginning to understand Max's deep association with this valley.

'Apparently. Kelly ended up living on a mission, and married a mixed-blood girl. Their son was my great-great-grandfather. It was a side of the family we'd lost touch with for years. Didn't really know about them until my mother found a cousin and suddenly the family got bigger than we could have imagined. We all had a big reunion a few years back.'

'Max, have you told anyone else about this?' asked Dani. 'People here, Patricia and Henry, Barney and Helen?'

'Not really. That's just part of my family story. Kelly's mother was murdered by a white man according to Grandma. Why bring up that painful stuff?' said Max, getting into the car.

Dani got in beside him. 'But, Max, it means you have a very strong family tie to Isabella! Kelly's Crossing might be named for your ancestor. Maybe Isabella left something to him in her will.'

Max started the car and gave a wry grin. 'Nah, there's no hint of that in what we've been able to uncover. From what we know of how Isabella was treated I doubt they'd let a half-caste kid gain anything, even if she didn't have children. There wasn't actually much left after Isabella died, according to Garth.'

'But even so, I think your family should be recognised as having a special tie to this place.'

'I don't need recognition, I know in my bones I belong here. And it would upset a lot of the locals. Descendants of people who did Isabella a bad turn.'

'Yeah, I see your point,' said Dani. 'I wonder if there's a family anywhere without some secret deep in their past waiting to be uncovered.'

'If you look hard enough there's sure to be secrets. So maybe it's best you don't start looking.'

'I wish my mother hadn't started on this search for a father and his family she never knew, never cared about,' said Dani. 'There's someone trying to stop her.'

'What do you mean?'

'Mysterious anonymous letters are being dropped in the mail box at Cricklewood. She just told me about them.'

'Really? That's strange. Any idea who it could be? Or why?'

'Nope. I don't think it's something awful or we would have had some kind of an inkling. She's found an old aunty on her father's side and is going to see her, maybe learn something. Seems odd there's someone who's a rellie we've never had any contact with at all,' said Dani. 'It's a pity I never knew my grandmother's sister Mollie.'

'Not in my experience,' said Max. 'Families can split up real easy, have a falling out over something and the bitterness is carried on through generations. And by then no one knows what the original dispute was all about.'

'Hopefully this aunty still has her marbles and can throw some light on the family,' said Dani. 'It doesn't make a lot of difference to me, but Mum has got a bit swept up by it all.'

'You get to a stage in your life where answers to those questions mean a lot. Generally when you're on the wrong side of fifty or you lose someone close,' said Max gently. 'When you have children you eventually want to know the links that make up the chain of people you're descended from. Who've made you the person you are.'

Dani was thoughtful. 'You might be right. I guess I'm

hoping Mum will do the hard work and give me the full story. Whatever it is.'

'You're busy getting on with your life, following this new path, exploring your abilities, and that's good, Dani,' said Max. 'And spending time with your son away from the city. He'll probably remember this time here as being special when he looks back later in life.'

'I know that. I felt a bit guilty about him spending the weeknights with my mother at Cricklewood. But they both seem to get so much out of it, now he's into soccer, messing round in boats with Toby and Barney, playing with your two, riding and hanging out at the Nostalgia Cafe.'

'They teaching him to cook or got him peeling potatoes?' asked Max.

'Bit of both, I hope,' sighed Dani. 'But for someone who thought food came out of plastic containers in a supermarket or a takeaway, he's had his eyes opened.'

They arrived at Max's house. Dani had left her car there and Tim was playing with Len and Julian.

Sarah came out of the gallery beside the house. 'So how did the paintings look, hung together?' she asked.

'Sensational,' said Dani. 'If that dealer doesn't grab the lot, he's mad.'

'I don't know about that. How about a coffee, Dani? What are the boys up to?' Max asked Sarah.

'They've been dealing with an injured bird they found. A baby galah. And Tim has been skiting to Len about his camping trip to the island, and now Len wants to go,' said Sarah.

'An island camp? Where was that, Dani?' asked Max.

'Barney took Tim and Toby for an overnight camp on an island in the river, Tim hasn't stopped talking about it. They caught a fish and a crab and cooked it for dinner over a fire, and Barney told them stories. Boys' stuff.'

Max smiled. 'Excellent. Barney, he's special all right.'

Tim dashed in to greet Dani and tell her about the bird. 'It's still little, only got a few pink and grey feathers. Can we keep it, Mum? Len says you can teach them to talk.'

'You'll have to find out how to look after it. I wouldn't want you to keep it in a cage,' said Dani.

'He'll manage it. The WIRES people will give you some tips. When it's grown it'll fly away, and maybe come back to visit,' said Max.

'Can I take him to Ma's at Cricklewood too, please, Mum? Toby and Tab have a pet wallaby, so I want to keep this one,' pleaded Tim, his eyes shining.

'If you want it, darling. But it will be your responsibility.'

Dani smiled at Max. 'Seems a low-maintenance pet, provided Jolly doesn't hassle it.'

'Keep it out of the house, bird poo stains,' advised Sarah. 'Let the bird have its freedom but keep it safe from wild birds till it can defend itself.'

'No cage though,' insisted Dani.

'He can stay in my room, I'll clean up,' said Tim fervently.

Sarah laughed as she exchanged a look with Dani, both women knowing who would be cleaning up bird droppings. 'Can't argue with that. A bird in a cage sends heaven in a rage,' Sarah said.

Tim chatted comfortingly to the bird nestled in a shoe-box as they drove back to The Vale.

'He'll be all right, won't he, Mum? What'll we call him? Maybe it's a girl? How do you tell? When will it fly? Do you think it will learn to talk? Can you paint its picture when its got all its feathers, please, Mum?'

Dani nodded, but her mind kept drifting back to Max's comments. In his low-key, gentle way he always made her think about things. About her art, about Barney, about Tim, about her mother and her search. She suddenly found herself reflecting on what had preoccupied her when she lived in Sydney. It all seemed relatively unimportant now, though at the time her job, her son, the divorce, and dealing with her ex had been big issues.

Here in the country she had found a sense of herself again, a feeling of peace, an appreciation of things beautiful and life enriching – her son and his riding, the sunrise over the hills and river, the easy warmth of new friends, the bond she shared with her mother through this place. And a sense she was getting closer to some kind of a breakthrough with Isabella.

The shadowy woman with a rich history had become part of her daily existence. Dani thought about Isabella every time she looked at the land around her, land that Isabella had owned, traversed and must have loved. The paintings she'd done of that land had taken on a life of their own and Dani wondered if any other subject she painted would come close to making her feel what she felt while doing these. Jason was pleased with them and told her the bigshot behind the corporation had liked them too. It suddenly struck Dani that when she turned over the paintings to Jason she'd be at a loss again, facing a blank canvas.

The following day Dani lightly raised this with Jason as she showed him photographs of her most recent paintings.

'You've really got into Isabella's story, haven't you? These works of Kelly's Crossing are very powerful.'

'Jason, maybe you shouldn't use those particular paintings in your brochures and presentations,' said Dani. 'There are so many other pictures. Max told me his great-great-grandfather came from round there and there's bad energy at that place.'

Jason was intrigued. 'I had no idea Max had such a strong connection here. We should tell Carter and, I agree, it's not the kind of thing that's a sales angle to push.'

'They might worry about a native title claim or something you mean?'

'No, it's just white Australians don't like to be reminded of the hurt and wrongdoing done to indigenous Australians.'

'I'd like to give one to Max if that's okay with you. Do you think it's good enough?' asked Dani shyly.

'Dani, that's a great idea! It's come from your heart and I think you saw something there without knowing it,' said Jason. 'From the commercial side we'll go with the colourful character depictions of the feisty free-spirited Isabella and the beautiful landscapes of the hills, valley and river that you've done.'

'Well, I hope they help sell the concept of Birimbal village development,' said Dani, feeling relieved.

'It's going well. We'll have to start thinking about the official launch now the landscaping is in place around the nature areas, lagoons, wetlands, parks and village streets. Most of the infrastructure is happening and the construction of the community centre is underway. We'll have the launch there. Your paintings will be hung and for sale.'

'When are the sales brochures going out and the media campaign starting?' asked Dani.

'A month or so. The international CEO is coming over to give the final nod. We'll be making a TV ad as well.' He paused. 'There are two prongs to the ad campaign, we're swimming against the flow trying to persuade people to downscale.'

'You mean smaller is desirable. Streamline, simplify our lives,' grinned Dani. 'I hadn't realised how much stuff – unnecessary stuff – I had till I moved up here.'

'That's part of the village concept, we don't need gigantic homes with media rooms and plasma TVs in every bedroom, ride-on lawnmowers and eight-thousand-dollar barbecues,' said Jason. 'Some things are best shared as a mini-community cum family, rather than isolating yourself in a house that cuts out interaction with people or your environment.'

Dani nodded in agreement. 'I've noticed the difference with Tim and me since we've been here. In Sydney he spent a lot of time in his room with his computer. We ate with the TV in the background all the time. There wasn't imaginative play, or real living. Things were so organised, not spontaneous like here.'

'No campfires, catching eels or swags on an island, eh?' smiled Jason. 'I missed my life here when I was in boarding school. I hated it.'

Dani gazed at the images of her paintings scattered across Jason's desk. 'I love the cows trudging across the paddocks, the pelicans cruising on the glassy river. They sum up the tranquillity of this valley which hasn't changed so much since Isabella's time,' she mused.

'You've done a terrific job with these paintings, Dani. Putting a name, a woman's dream and a location to the whole concept will make a big difference.'

'And don't forget the movie!'

Jason pulled a face. 'I'm not worrying about that. We'll be launched way before the movie is released. Of course, if the film is a hit, it will raise our profile but I'm not associating Birimbal with the movie. Have you told Roddy about Max's connection with Kelly's Crossing? Would be a powerful scene in the film.'

Dani shook her head. 'No. Max doesn't want to dwell on the past. It's still a sensitive issue. And I don't see much of Roddy actually.'

Jason gave her a look, but said nothing for a moment as he gathered up papers on his desk and slid a cheque across to her. 'Your final payment. So you're at a loss for ideas for your next subject?'

'Kind of. I liked painting a series of pictures that had

a sequence of events, a storyline, rather than just isolated subjects,' she said.

'Didn't you say your mother was delving into your past, your family association up here? Why not explore that?' suggested Jason. 'Kind of illustrate what she's going to write about when she's got the history sorted. You could start with your grandparents' house, their story. Take a trip to London, see where they came from. Be a visual contrast, wouldn't it?'

Dani laughed. 'I can't just dash off to London. But one day I might do that.' She stared at him, hesitating. 'Speaking of houses and family history, may I ask about your family home? I went for a walk and came across the estate. I ran into Kerry there, but she didn't gossip of course. It's an extraordinary building.'

Jason didn't look at her while there was an awkward pause and Dani wished she hadn't mentioned it. Finally he gave a small smile. 'It's a bit of a family sore. Created some friction a while back.'

'Oh, I'm sorry. You don't have to say any more.'

Jason leaned back in his chair. 'Families, we all have 'em, and they all come with some heartache or headache. My great-grandfather built the house and in his will it was left to the eldest son. It was stipulated that this should always be the case. So my grandfather left it to my father. Both were barristers – my father became a judge. We moved to Sydney when I was very young. I was supposed to study law. But I did architecture and design which interested me far more. When he died he left the house to me with a lot of stipulations and restrictions. My sister Kerry has very different views from me. I wanted to modernise the house, even turn it into a boutique hotel or health retreat. She wants it left intact, in mothballs. So I figured if she wanted to keep it like that, she could look after it.'

'What happened to her husband?' asked Dani.

'They were working in Europe in an equestrian centre in Belgium when he was killed in a car smash. And later she had a bad riding accident, so she came back and has buried herself ever since. She got upset when I moved up here, though I have no intention of living in that museum.'

Dani couldn't see Jason and especially his girlfriend Ginny feeling at home in the old house. 'Why doesn't Kerry live in the big house?' asked Dani.

'I wish she would,' said Jason. 'She's become a bit funny, insecure, keeps to herself. Says it's not right to ignore the wishes of our father and grandfather and great-grandfather.'

'It's a shame it's just sitting there . . . unappreciated,' said Dani.

As if reading her mind Jason suddenly said, 'Why don't you document it? Paint it? The house, the grounds, the gardens, the rooms . . . I mean, it's maybe not what you want to paint, but it would be an interesting exercise. Though maybe not very commercial. I guess the paintings wouldn't be of great interest to anyone else,' he added. 'I could buy some of course.'

'Leave it with me, Jason. It's an interesting idea, and I don't expect you to commission me. I'll chew it over. Well, I'd better be going.' She got up, glancing towards the room where she had her desk with the writing box on it.

'Hey, you don't have to move out, if you want to keep this as your town office, you're very welcome.'

'Well, I will for a while if you don't mind.' Dani had no reason to continue to keep her few possessions in the desk but for some reason she was reluctant to take them with her. She glanced down at the cheque Jason had given her. 'Jason, this is too much. You've overpaid me.'

He brushed it aside. 'A bit of a bonus, spend it on Tim. He tells me it's his birthday next week.'

'Yes, he's going down to Sydney to stay with his father

for the long weekend and birthday. I've no idea what to give him.'

'How about a pony? I'm happy to part with Blackie, the one he's been riding. I know he's fond of it.'

'Jason! What will we do with a pony when we move back? He'd want to keep it and that would be a hassle.'

'Oh. It hadn't registered with me that you'd be moving back to Sydney. You both seem so settled into the valley now. Well, why not buy him his own saddle? There's an old bloke in Cedartown who makes great saddles.'

Dani glanced down at the cheque. 'That's a good idea. Thank you, Jason. You've been so kind to Tim.'

'I enjoy his company. I've promised to take him out riding around the old place, and on the track along the river – with your permission of course. He's quite proficient now.'

'If you're sure the pony is steady and okay. I must say I thought Tim managed him very well at the gymkhana. Thanks, Jason. Tim will be excited. I'll let you two organise the ride.'

She drove to Cricklewood to see Lara and wait for Tim to come home from school. She found Carter and her mother sitting on the front verandah.

'Hi, darling, Carter has come to rescue Tim's galah,' said Lara.

'Hi, Dani. I contacted the local WIRES wildlife rescue service and really the bird should go to them, it's tricky feeding a fledgling as you have to crop feed it, can't just shove food in its beak,' said Carter.

'Oh no, he'll be disappointed,' said Dani. She could hear the insistent squeaks from the shoebox by Lara's feet.

'Carter brought over some porridge and a special mixture of crushed seeds to feed it. We'll let Tim have a go at it and decide what's best.'

'Fledglings are very demanding. I'm sure he'll be happy to let someone else do it,' grinned Carter. 'Also, it's against the law in New South Wales to keep a native animal.'

'Where have you been?' Lara asked Dani. 'Cup of tea?'

'Yes, please. I just got my final pay cheque from Jason. I'm looking for something new to throw myself into and Jason suggested I might like to paint his old estate – I've dubbed it Miss Haversham House.'

Carter laughed. 'It's a white elephant all right, antique dealers keep circling. Be a shame to see it broken up. Mind you, that Kerry is a fierce little guard dog.'

'What's the story?' asked Lara.

'You're wondering what you might dig up in your family history! Well, Jason's family history would be a rich dig with a few surprises, I'm sure.' Then he changed tack. 'Y'know, Dani, maybe you could paint some of the more unusual features of the valley – that incredible old house, Isabella, the wild men on the mountain – put 'em on postcards and make a buck.'

'I'm not in commercial art anymore. Excuse me, I'll get some more milk.'

'What wild men on the mountain?' asked Lara.

'Old hippies who went feral and still live in 1972, or who've gone organic with green toes and are into biodynamics, hydroponics, wind farms, quantum heating and so on,' said Carter. 'Mind you, there are some pretty smart people in Jumbai doing good things. One bloke up there was an early follower of Peter Andrews' farming techniques and he's stopped soil erosion, built up his water. Great stuff.'

Tim arrived and rushed to see the bird. Lara listened to him chatter with Carter for a while then took the tea tray inside. She found her daughter sitting on the back steps.

'Tim's home. He's getting a feeding lesson from Carter. I don't think he'll feel too bad about letting the bird be taken away.' There was no reaction from Dani, who seemed to be deep in thought. 'What's up, sweetie?'

'Ah, just wondering what to do next. Jason wanted to give Tim a horse for his birthday and I said what would we do with it in Sydney. And it came to me – I'm not ready to go back to the city. But I can't afford to stay here, and there's Tim. Jeff has been relaxed about him being up here, but for a while longer? I don't know about that.'

'Mmm. Maybe you should ask Jeff to come up here for Tim's birthday instead of Tim going down there to see him,' suggested Lara.

'Tim wants to get the train, not fly. His father has planned stuff for the birthday.'

'Maybe you should go down to Sydney with him on the train. See how you feel about the city again,' said Lara.

'I might. Well, Tim and I are going shopping. Hopefully without the bird. What are you doing?'

Lara gave her daughter a small smile. 'Going off to meet Aunty Phyllis. I'll let you know what she has to say.'

'Yeah, I'll be interested to hear what secrets she knows about the family.'

When Dani finally got home there was a message from Roddy on her phone at The Vale sounding worried and almost pleading that she call him.

'Hi, Roddy, what's up?'

'Hey, Dani. Man, have I got problems. These movie people are nutters. Russell Franks has pissed off to Europe – and taken one of the local girls with him. She's only seventeen.'

'What a dirty old man! Will he still direct the film?'

Roddy sounded despondent. 'That depends. If we have a film. There're a few money problems.'

Dani felt the sudden pang of a long-suppressed worry becoming a reality. 'How bad is it?'

'The contracts haven't been signed and the money has stalled. The guy I had lined up in New Zealand has run into tax problems, he can't access the offshore money he had allotted for the film budget. Of course the other investors have run a mile.'

'Can it be resurrected, can you find other backers?' Dani suddenly thought of all the valley people who'd put up seed funding that must have been over a hundred thousand dollars. 'What's happened to the initial money private investors put up?'

'That's gone. The launch, media junkets, Russell ran up bills everywhere. I'm out of pocket too,' he added defensively.

'I don't know what to say, Roddy. It's bad for all the local business people too. Have you talked to Patricia?'

'Not yet. I'm trying to come up with an alternative plan to put to her. I was hoping you might have some ideas. Can I come and talk to you?'

Well, at least he wasn't skipping town, thought Dani. She felt partially responsible for the movie fiasco, having introduced him to Patricia and others. 'I have no ideas right now, Roddy, I don't think I can help. How are you going to break the news? Who knows?'

'No one yet, but things will come out pretty quickly. I really thought this one was going to come off.' He sounded forlorn and bewildered.

Dani recalled his tales of bravado – dabbling in vineyards in Western Australia, a resort in Fiji, other projects he'd mentioned but she'd taken little interest in the details. Roddy was well meaning, but always looking for the quick and easy big money. She recalled Jason picking up on this and not trusting him. 'Come over tomorrow for a coffee. Frankly, I think you and Roz better nut out a media statement.'

'Roz the PR whiz kid has gone too. I'll see you round eleven. There must be some way of milking Isabella to recover a dollar or three,' said Roddy hopefully.

Isabella has been used and abused too much, thought Dani with some anger. She wanted Isabella's name to be part of something far better than the common perception that had prevailed for so long. She didn't want her to be taken for a ride by ambitious and greedy men – yet again. 'I'll see you tomorrow, Roddy, I won't mention this to anyone of course.' She hung up the phone. Poor Roddy. She dialled her mother.

'Mum, you'll never guess what's happened. I need some advice!'

16

Cedartown, 1944

IT WAS A QUIET homecoming. So different from the carousing of departure. Men, damaged in body and spirit, limped home or sat in the repatriation hospitals trying to heal. But minds were still tortured, nightmares raged, and sights and sounds of war could not be erased. When the Richards received the news that Clem was coming home on ten days' leave, even Walter managed an affectionate embrace with Nola and Keith cracked open a bottle of beer to share with his father.

'Clem will be leaving Sydney on the seventeenth, they say. I suppose he'll get the train,' said Nola reading the formal notification. 'I hope he's well enough to travel.' The news that Clem had been hospitalised for malaria had shaken Nola.

'Could do with a hand, been bloody hard work for

Keith and me,' muttered Walter. 'Kevin and Clem can pull their weight around here again once the war is done with.'

'Not before they're ready,' admonished Nola.

'I s'pose Thommo will be with him,' said Keith.

'He was wounded, maybe he's not ready to be discharged from the rehab hospital at Concord. The Thompsons are so anxious to see him. Mr Thompson hasn't been at all well, I hear,' said Nola, and Keith wondered again at his mother's talent for picking up news when she rarely left the farm and there was no telephone. But he had seen how she offered cups of tea to delivery people, the postman, the hawker who brought his little wagon filled with knick-knacks and housewares.

'I imagine Clem will want to see Elizabeth straight away,' said Nola. 'We'll just have to wait our turn.'

Walter grunted and picked up his newspaper. Keith and Nola exchanged a look. Walter still refused to mention Clem's marriage.

Elizabeth crumpled the letter in her hand and took deep breaths, clutching the kitchen chair.

Harold came into the kitchen and, seeing her eyes squeezed shut and mail scattered on the table, asked with a tremor in his voice, 'What is it love? News of Clem?' His mind was racing, Clem had been in the repatriation hospital at Concord, he was safely in Australia, what could have happened? Thommo was the one who'd been wounded. 'The boys, they're all right aren't they?'

'Clem's got leave. He's coming home.'

'Well, that's good news. Wonderful!' He smiled and gave her a loving hug. 'You two can soon start your new life together. I know it's been hard for you, pet.' He held his daughter.

Elizabeth was thinking the same thing. But she had no plans to start their married life back on the Richards' farm. Or in Cedartown. The war had rent an unpleasant interlude in her plans to move away from Cedartown. She hadn't felt especially patriotic and on the whole the war had bored her. Although now that the Americans were coming through Cedartown and staying for a week or two at a time en route north, there had been a greater demand for the company of the town's pretty girls. Their social life gained a fresh excitement because the Yanks were good fun, very polite and lavished the girls with gifts like nylons, cigarettes and chocolates. The local boys considered they were buying their women, bunging on an act with their fancy accents and exaggerated charm, and there had been a few bruising blues out the back of the pub. Young boys trailed the Americans hoping for an illegal smoke, or sweets. Boys with pretty older sisters scored handsomely if the soldier came to the family house. They were often bribed to leave the couple alone in the front room.

Emily and Mollie had got very wrapped up in the Red Cross activities. Once or twice Mollie had acted as the patient for the St John's Ambulance course, where she'd been bandaged, had her leg in splints, and suffered through numerous mock wounds. For Elizabeth the best part of her voluntary aid work had been learning how to drive a truck. The lessons were drawn out by a flirtatious sergeant in the instruction team who asked her out to a dance. Elizabeth told him she was married to a soldier fighting in New Guinea, so he suggested she bring a girlfriend and have a bit of fun to cheer herself up. Elizabeth and Cynthia went to the dance with the sergeant and his mate, then afterwards joined a large group for milkshakes and steak sandwiches at Costa's, the local Greek cafe. They had a good time, and she did feel better for the relaxed night out.

Inevitably Emily heard about the outing, and was angry because she believed Elizabeth had gone to the pictures with Cynthia, and the two had a heated argument. Harold stepped in and calmed them down but later took Elizabeth aside and suggested she remember that she was a married woman, and while many young people were going wild and being fast in these uncertain times, she did have to think about her reputation. And, of course, her mother's standing in the town, which Emily took very seriously.

Elizabeth pulled away from her father's embrace. 'Dad, can I use one of your passes to go down and meet him in Sydney? All that family of his will take him over once he gets home,' she said.

Harold knew she was right. It was a shame Elizabeth didn't get on with her new in-laws. The Richards were salt-of-the-earth people. Walter was a bit moody, a tough man, but maybe he had reasons for that. Harold recalled someone saying old man Richards had a bad time of it in the First World War which might account for his not getting on with his sons. Not being one for gossip, he hadn't enquired further. Elizabeth told him that Clem and his father were always clashing over even the most trivial detail of running the farm.

'Better ask your mother, love. The rail pass aside, it'll cost you a few quid here and there. And where are you going to stay?'

'I've saved my pay, Dad, and Clem's allotment. Cynthia says there's a nice little hotel not far from Central Railway. We need some time together, we've hardly had any married life at all.'

'I understand that, but you have the rest of your lives ahead of you now. You're one of the lucky ones,' Harold gently reminded her. Seeing her determined expression, he relented. 'All right, I'll see what I can do.'

Elizabeth gave him a quick kiss.

Elizabeth and Cynthia consulted over what clothes Elizabeth should take for her reunion with her husband. She borrowed Cynthia's short tartan swing coat with deep pockets and a velveteen collar to travel in with a natty matching maroon beret, then splurged some of her savings on silk scanties and a flower-sprigged sateen nightdress.

'Not that I expect this to stay on too long,' she giggled as she packed the nightgown.

'So are you going to look for a job, somewhere to live while you're down there?' asked Cynthia.

'I hope so. I have to get Clem adjusted to the idea of leaving Cedartown. He's gone on and on about the river and the hills and the valley in every letter,' said Elizabeth rolling her eyes.

'Well, after where they've been, even Cedartown must seem pretty good,' laughed Cynthia. 'Will you see Thommo?'

'No idea. I want Clem to myself,' said Elizabeth firmly.

'Do his parents know you're meeting him down in Sydney? They'll be expecting him back here, won't they?'

'Well, they'll have to wait,' answered Elizabeth, twirling in her gored skirt and favourite sweater.

Cynthia raised her eyebrows and shook her head. You had to admire Elizabeth. She knew what she wanted and went after it. She wished she was as forthright. Cynthia harboured a secret crush on the bank manager where she worked. He was married but nonetheless she often caught him looking at her in a rather special way, and he always stood very close to her when giving instructions or checking something. She had a sneaking feeling that if she gave him the nod, he'd conveniently forget he was married.

Harold, Mollie and Cynthia saw Elizabeth off on the 10 pm mail train to Sydney. Emily disapproved of the 'escapade' and had gone to bed with a headache. Elizabeth tried to sleep in her second-class carriage, but was too excited. She had a window seat and across from her a woman leaned against the window and slept soundly, her young daughter curled beside her with her head in her mother's lap. The compartment was dark and Elizabeth peered outside, seeing the occasional dim shadows of a sleeping township shrouded in the gloom of the enforced wartime blackout.

She was hungry and tired when she climbed stiffly from the train with her small case and walked along the bustling platform, through the ticket gate and into the great hall of Central Station. It was only seven o'clock in the morning but the hall was busy with people meeting passengers, or sending them off, and there were scores of servicemen and women in every uniform imaginable. A newspaper stand was doing a brisk trade, and so was the neighbouring kiosk selling tea, cupcakes and sandwiches. The milk bar was also doing a hectic trade, and there was a long queue outside the dining room, where substantial breakfasts were being served to those lucky enough to get a seat.

Elizabeth joined another queue outside the station entrance and eventually scored a taxi for the short run to her hotel, where she waited outside to meet Clem.

Every man in uniform in the street caused her to lean forward in excited expectation. She wasn't sure what he'd look like now . . . it had been so long, and he had been through so much.

But when he did appear, walking slowly, there was no mistaking his build, the tilt of his head, the shape of his face, even though he was very thin and his uniform hung loosely. But the forlorn, weary, burdened look on his face, the slump of his shoulders and the hesitation in his walk caused her to pause before racing forward. He turned to trudge down the street, the heavy kitbag over his shoulder, a smaller bag tucked under his arm, as though he had no direction or plan.

Elizabeth followed him. 'Hey, soldier, where're you headed?' she called in a breezy voice.

Clem turned, a vague, puzzled expression on his face as he saw Elizabeth smiling, walking towards him, arms outstretched. He dropped his kitbag and just stared at her in shock.

'Clem, oh, Clem, I had to come outside. I couldn't bear waiting to see you in the hotel. I just gambled on catching you here, and . . . oh Clem, darling, aren't you pleased? Oh, my . . .' She fell against him, pressing herself into him, lifting her face to his, waiting for a passionate kiss and embrace. But he seemed frozen, unable to move or speak.

Elizabeth kissed his startled face and pulled him close, allowing him to rest his head against her shoulder as she held him tightly.

'Is it really you?' he finally murmured. 'I've thought about this moment for . . .' He just couldn't find the welcoming, loving words he so dearly wanted to say.

'Yes, yes, it's me, you dill. Who else did you think it'd be?' she chirped.

He didn't answer. She felt his shoulders start to shake and knew at once that he was suffering a turmoil of emotion.

'Well, let's go down the road and get a cuppa. We both need it, right? Then we can go to the hotel. It's small and simple, but comfortable,' enthused Elizabeth as she struggled to boost his spirit.

'Er, yeah, a cuppa would be good.'

She took his small bag and snuggled up beside him. 'Darling, we can have a wonderful couple of days, just you and me.'

'What about my mum? She's expecting me home.'

'Oh don't you worry about that,' trilled Elizabeth. 'This is time for us. Come on, Clem, you must be so tired, let's get a tram, it's not far.'

Later she collected the key from the girl at the reception desk who gave them a big smile. 'My, you must be so happy to be together again.' She smiled at Clem who just stared blankly at her. 'Good on you, mate. You boys did a grand job.'

In their room he slumped in a chair, holding his head, running fingers through his hair. Elizabeth took no notice and briskly unpacked, then crouched before him, pulling off his boots and then his jacket.

'C'mon, Clem, have a rest, love. Then we'll go out and have a bite to eat. Celebrate a bit, eh?'

'Yes, I've got to rest. I'm absolutely buggered, and there was too much going on at the barracks.' Clem lay on the bed and closed his eyes, then opened them and gave a small smile. 'Thanks, darl.' He was still weak from the sweats and fevers of his battle with malaria. The physical and emotional struggle had drained his body of energy. Without opening his eyes he gently asked, 'What about Mum, the rest of them?'

'I've sent them a telegram. We're booked on Friday night's sleeper.'

Clem nodded in acknowledgment, then murmured, 'Gotta check on Thommo, help him get home.'

'Ssh,' said Elizabeth lying beside him in her petticoat. Thommo would have to make his own way home to his family. Clem had her now and didn't need Thommo.

They sat over a small supper in a restaurant near the hotel. Clem picked at his food as Elizabeth talked.

'Once you're out of the army we can move down here to Sydney, but I thought we could at least look around a bit while we're here. Maybe get some ideas about a job.'

'Job? What sort of job?'

'Clem you said you met that fellow Clive, the friend of Mr Thompson's. About learning to be a motor mechanic.'

'Ah, yeah. He wants someone to go in with him. Put up half the money and open a motor repair joint. I haven't got that kind of money.'

'Like, how much?'

'A few hundred quid. Might as well be a thousand,' said Clem dismissively.

'Listen, you've got your army money, and I've been saving like mad. Maybe we could borrow a bit from Mum and Dad.'

Clem shook his head. 'Not me. Let's not rush into things.'

'It wouldn't hurt to go round and see him, find out a bit more,' persisted Elizabeth.

Clem capitulated. 'Whatever you say, dear.'

That night Elizabeth lay beside her husband in her new nightdress as Clem tossed and turned, mumbling and shaking occasionally. In the morning she leaned across and held him, running her hands along his body, but he stopped her hand.

'Please love, not yet. Can't do anything, I'm still crook.'

'What do you mean? For how long? What's wrong with you?' demanded Elizabeth.

'Dunno. The doc said it's the malaria. I'll come good. Be patient, eh?' He squeezed her hand.

'Well, that was a fine waste of fancy gear,' she snapped, then felt ashamed and gave him a smile. 'We'll go down for a bit of brekkie and then take a walk. C'mon, sleepy head.' She got up and started to dress.

They wandered around the city, walking arm-in-arm through Hyde Park and along Martin Place where a street photographer took a snap of them. Elizabeth put the ticket in her handbag and picked up the photograph the following day. She was smiling broadly, looking very smart in Cynthia's tartan jacket, her pencil-line skirt and peeptoe high heels. She was holding on to Clem, leaning against him, and while he looked handsome in his uniform, he had a strained expression, his eyes wary.

They visited Clive who seemed keen on the suggestion that Clem might go into business with him and directed his comments to Elizabeth, recognising she wielded the influence.

'Your bloke's a natural with engines, I'm told,' he said warmly to her, then turned to Clem. 'Frank Thompson told me you should've been an engineer.'

Clem nodded. 'Yeah, well, that's easy to say. Getting there isn't so easy.'

'They say he can fix anything,' said Elizabeth with a note of confidence in her voice, then waved a hand around the garage and workshop in which they were standing. 'Is this all yours?'

'Dad started it up years ago and it's now regarded as an essential service, so I'm soldiering on here. Dad's got another business but still has a share in it.'

By the time they left Clive's garage, the deal was settled in Elizabeth's mind. She'd even found out the best place nearby to look for rental accommodation without having to pay exorbitant key money.

She clung to this dream for the future as the train steamed north on Friday night, putting aside the memory of Clem's fumbled and inadequate attempt to make love to her and blotting out the frightening scene when a car had backfired and Clem had dived onto the floor and curled up, trembling like a child. What had been the most upsetting was Clem's call for Thommo as he lay there. 'Thommo, Thommo, where are ya, mate? You all right?'

Her father had hinted to her that men came home from

473

war far different from when they went away. Her mother, too, had made veiled comments, not to 'expect too much for a bit. Let him settle down. I think you're making a mistake rushing down there. Let Clem adjust again.'

'He's my husband. We should be together, Mum.' Besides, she wasn't going to let Clem's family get in his ear and try to dominate his life, make him work on that miserable farm of theirs. Once Clem got his discharge she'd give notice at the stock and station agency and then it would be back to Sydney.

Rocking to the rhythm of the steel wheels rolling along the track, she savoured again the memory of the shops that even with rationing and lighting restrictions had a special appeal, the crowded trams and buses, the cosy cafes and interesting side streets, the spread of the harbour with the sun sparkling on the calm water.

The Richards clan was there to meet the train, and Elizabeth held Clem's arm in a proprietary fashion as they walked along the platform. Phyllis broke away and rushed to her brother. They were quickly surrounded and, seeing her father with the station master, Elizabeth slid away.

'So, how was the reunion? Worth the trip?' grinned Harold.

'Of course,' she answered airily. 'We made a lot of plans. He's going into partnership with a mate in a motor mechanic's place.'

Harold raised an eyebrow. 'That'll take a bit of capital, won't it?'

'We'll manage it, Dad. Right now we're going to rent a room in town at the boarding house.'

'Wouldn't it be cheaper to stay at home?'

Elizabeth smiled. 'C'mon, Dad, we're starting married life. For better or worse. He's spending a couple of days with the family while I get things set up. He's only got ten days then it's back to Sydney.'

'Where's Thommo? How's he doing?'

'No idea. It's Clem and me now.'

'Don't try to keep mates apart,' said Harold gently. Their eyes met and Elizabeth knew at once that what he was saying was important. 'They have a bond you'll never be able to share.'

Clem returned home, sitting in the back of the old farm truck with Phyllis and Keith. Elizabeth stayed at Cricklewood and planned to find a room in a boarding house in two days' time when Clem came back to town so they could be together.

Back at home, after a pot of tea and changing into his clean work clothes, Clem wandered about the farm noting a lot needed doing, but once he reached the river he sat and looked at the birds swooping, a ripple and splash from a leaping mullet. It was so peaceful, so soothing, he felt his body losing its tenseness for the first time in a long time. How often he'd thought about this during the war when home had seemed a dream.

He wished Thommo was here. They'd both talked and thought so much about the valley during the hard, dangerous days. He'd make sure they spent some time here together this leave no matter what Elizabeth wanted to do. Clem was worried about Thommo. While he was recovering from his wounds and resting, watched over by medical staff, he was fine. But there was a wild streak in Thommo, a restless, dangerous mood he got into when he drank too much.

Clem knew that Thommo could rustle up grog and find a place to gamble at the drop of a hat. He was in no hurry to return to his butcher's trade after the war, said he'd seen too much bloodshed and carving up of people. His father wasn't well so he'd probably help him out with the picture theatre for a while, then find something new.

By the time Clem moved into the boarding house in

Cedartown with Elizabeth, he was feeling better. The break at the farm had been healing, but also reminded him why he didn't want a life as a dairy farmer. He'd relieved Keith with the milking and farm jobs for a day, allowing him to have a special outing to continue his courtship of a girl across the river. Clem was bemused to learn Keith took a shortcut to see her by tying his good clothes in a water-proof bag he'd got from a store in town and swimming across the river. Then he changed and presented himself to her family at their farm. Walter had no idea his oldest son was interested in taking a wife, but Keith told Clem the girl had always lived on a dairy farm and accepted that's what her life would be.

'She'll settle in to our place without any problem,' he told Clem. 'So you and Elizabeth buzz off and go to Sydney. She'd never be happy out here.'

Elizabeth continued to work, Clem met her for lunch and walked her home at the end of the day. But once Thommo arrived back in town she didn't see Clem until tea time at the boarding house and even then she accused him of being 'Three sheets to the wind, thanks to Thommo. He's trouble and gives you silly ideas, Clem.'

'Ah, he's all right, Elizabeth. Poor bugger, his Dad mightn't see the year out the doc reckons. Let him have a fling before we go back to barracks. After what he's been through he's earned it.'

Clem and Elizabeth went to dinner at Cricklewood the night before Clem was due to return to Sydney with Thommo. It seemed strange to Elizabeth to be a guest in her family home and she didn't miss the fact her mother had laid out the good embroidered tablecloth and best china. Harold carved the roast beef – a treat from a cattle-man on the plateau. Clem was in good spirits, aided by a bottle or two of stout he'd been shouted by Thommo before heading to Cricklewood.

'Gravy, Clem?' asked Emily, passing the gravy boat. 'I expect you'll find army food hard to take after being spoiled silly being back home.'

'It's not bad grub, missus, though they do seem to have a helluva lot of spuds, particularly mashed spuds. And nothing like your sponge cake, Harold,' he added, knowing Harold had made one specially for the occasion.

'We've been lucky here in the valley with plenty of milk, butter and cream. Plus our own eggs and vegies. Those folk in the city with rations have had a tough time,' said Harold.

'And have you made any plans, Clem?' asked Emily pointedly.

Clem had been drilled by Elizabeth. 'Not yet, Mrs Williams. We're taking it day by day till we know we've fought off the Japs well and truly. Just doing my job and saving my pay.' He busied himself with his bread and butter.

'Thanks for dinner, Mum,' said Elizabeth collecting the plates.

Mollie followed her into the kitchen. 'So what are you and Clem going to do then? Are you really going to move away to Sydney?' whispered Mollie.

'I'm not telling you anything, missy. But, ooh, I do like Sydney. We went to a picture theatre that you wouldn't believe,' sighed Elizabeth. 'The State, and it really did look like a palace inside. Now here, take the cake to the table.'

Harold walked the couple to the front gate after Clem had given Emily and Mollie little goodbye pecks on the cheek.

'Not so hard to say adieu this time,' said Harold clasping his hand. 'You'll be back before you know it. Stick it out till the end, son. We've got them on the run now, I reckon.'

'The Yanks have been a mighty help,' said Clem. 'Wish we'd had them around during Kokoda and Lae.'

'Now, Clem, no more talk of those days. Come on, you've got to pack,' said Elizabeth tugging at his arm.

'Might see you at the station tomorrow, Harold. We're on the late afternoon express.'

Elizabeth linked her arm through Clem's. 'See you back at home tomorrow night, Dad.' It was annoying having to move back home but it was the only way they could save enough for Clem to buy into the motor business with Clive.

Harold watched the young couple walk across the railway bridge on their way back to the boarding house in town. During his chat with Clem over a glass of beer on the front verandah before tea there had been an oblique reference to some of the bad moments in New Guinea. Clem told Harold of rescuing Thommo but said little else. He didn't have to, Harold recognised the haunted expression in Clem's eyes and didn't have the heart to tell him the memories never really faded. That even now, on occasion, the scenes of Flanders and no-man's-land, of the men they never found in time and the eventual horrible death of his mate Scooter came back to him as painfully brilliant as the moment they happened.

He hoped things worked out for them. Emily thought Elizabeth had married beneath her, but Clem was a solid lad who'd probably be happy anywhere he could fiddle with engines and motors. And Elizabeth had enough drive and ambition for the both of them. He just hoped she didn't push Clem too hard too soon.

In the small room with dusty lace curtains and a metal bedstead that was brass beneath the black, under a worn, bilious pink chenille bedspread, Clem and Elizabeth made love as they had each imagined and dreamed it should be. But come the morning Elizabeth was brisk.

'I have to go to work, Clem. It's a big sale day, Donald and Mr Forde need me.'

'S'orright, love,' yawned Clem. 'Thommo and me will hang around together. I'll pop down and see you to say hooroo. I'm only going to Sydney.' He gave a grin. 'Reckon we said it all last night, eh?'

Elizabeth pulled his bare foot sticking out from the bedclothes. 'I reckon. Come down before you go to the train.'

It was an unusually big sale day. Cattle had come in from the west and down from the mountain and outlying districts. Prices had picked up and with good breeding stock in the yards, bidding was keen. Elizabeth kept meticulous records in her neat handwriting of prices and stowed the piles of pound notes in the cashbox beneath her desk. She'd have to balance the books at the end of the day. The farmers, cattlemen and agents were deferential, taking off their hats to pause a moment and chat with the pretty girl they all knew from her regular role on sale days.

George Forde was very pleased at the successful sales and went off with farmer friends to the hotel for a few beers. Donald was also busy at the saleyards arranging rail and truck transport as needed for cattle going some distance. Farmers took the opportunity while in town to stock up on feed, spare parts and odds and ends for their wives, so there was a lot of coming and going.

After lunch the stream of people through the office eased off and Elizabeth ate a quick sandwich at her desk. She kept her handbag and the metal cashbox under the desk next to her feet. Everything in her part of the office was neat and tidy, unlike the piles of papers, reports, receipts and notes stuck on the metal spike on George Forde's desk. Donald had his own filing system in his head. When paperwork was produced by Elizabeth, Donald always had prices correct to the penny as well as who'd ordered what.

Elizabeth glanced at her watch wondering when Clem would arrive. His train left at four pm and would arrive in

Sydney well after midnight. As she checked the time, the bell over the door rang and, although she was happy to see Clem, she could tell by his flushed face he'd been in the pub far too long.

'You look a bit under the weather,' she admonished.

Clem wrapped his arms around her. 'Aw, don't be cranky, Elizabeth. The blokes were shouting us drinks to see us off. Give us a kiss.'

She gave him a quick kiss wrinkling her nose at his beery breath. 'I hope you sleep it off on the train. Did you eat lunch?'

'Meat pie and peas. Baked this morning,' grinned Clem. 'So how's it been today?'

'Very good. A big sale day. Mr Forde is off celebrating. I suppose you saw him at the pub?'

'Nah, he musta been drinking at the top pub, we were at the middle one,' slurred Clem. 'So are you comin' down to the station to see us off?'

'Clem, dear, I can't, I have to mind the office. Could you wait here for a few minutes? I have to go out the back and change my stockings. I don't like looking like this with so many people around.' She glanced down at her laddered nylon stocking, a gift from one of the Americans. 'Be back in a tick.'

As she rinsed her hands, Elizabeth glanced at her reflection in the spotted old mirror. She'd been doing her hair a new way with a roll on either side of her face and thought it made her look quite sophisticated. She and Cynthia browsed through magazines in the paper shop until Mr Humphries signalled with an exaggerated cough that he had spotted them. He expected them to buy the *Women's Weekly*, not read it in his shop. Elizabeth didn't want to look like a country girl when she moved to Sydney to look for work, so she followed the emerging styles that stretched the constraints of wartime rationing and were illustrated in the couple of women's magazines still being produced. She snapped the suspender on her new stocking, smoothed her skirt then went back to the office and found Clem in her chair, feet up on her desk.

'Clem! Get your boots off that desk, they're dirty.'

Clem jumped to his feet. 'Come on, one more hug.' He held her tightly and gave her a long passionate kiss.

Elizabeth half-heartedly squirmed from his grip. 'Goodness, Clem, be careful of my hair, I am still at work you know. But it was nice,' she conceded with a smile.

'Yeah. Righto then. I'll go and get my bag, find Thommo and head to the station. Told him a short while ago to get ready.' He gave her bottom a cheeky slap and turned at the door. 'Don't do anything I wouldn't do,' he grinned.

'Little chance of that. You be careful. Don't get into trouble with Thommo.'

'Love ya, darl. Be good, we'll be down in Sydney running our own business before you know it.' He hooked the leather strap of his slouch hat under his chin and gave a wink. The door tinkled behind him.

Elizabeth looked up from her ledger when she heard the steam train whistle. She hoped Clem would sleep and not smoke and drink with Thommo on the long trip. She put down her pen, tightened the lid on the ink bottle and picked up the cashbox to add up the sale takings.

As she opened the lid, she knew something was wrong. It had felt light and Elizabeth sat there in frozen shock, staring at the empty cashbox. Madly she started opening drawers, ran around scattering papers as she went as if piles of pound notes would suddenly appear. But all the while she had a growing knot in her stomach at the memory of Clem sitting at her desk, looking cocky, fuelled by too many beers. She stopped as she remembered his parting words about being in Sydney and going into business before she knew it.

'Oh, Clem. How could you be so stupid!' she cried aloud to the empty office. Well, she'd just have to get it back from him. Maybe he'd wake up tomorrow and realise what a mad thing he'd done. But what was she going to say to Mr Forde? He wasn't back in the office so, still shaking, Elizabeth locked the door and hurried down the street to the station, hoping her father hadn't gone home yet.

She walked up the ramp at the end of the big wooden goods shed. She could see her father in his little office with his hat on, ready to leave. 'Dad, Dad!' she hurried through the door, tears starting to run down her face.

'What is it, pet? Did you miss saying goodbye to Clem? Don't tell me he didn't see you.'

'Oh, I saw him all right. Oh, Dad, it's so terrible . . .' She blurted out the story.

'Are you sure Clem took it? Maybe Mr Forde put it away for safekeeping.'

'No, Dad. I know it was there, I put some money in the cashbox not long before. Mr Forde never came back after lunch.'

'What happened?' asked Harold in a steady voice.

'Clem was minding the office when I went to the lavatory. I told him I had to change my nylons, so it took a few minutes. When I came out he looked kind of funny and he was a bit drunk. What am I to do?' she wailed.

'How much money was it?' asked Harold quietly.

'There must have been over five hundred pounds. Easy. It was a big sale day.'

Harold slumped in his chair and took his hat off, running fingers through his hair. 'Well, we can't do anything till tomorrow morning when we get hold of Clem.

482

Hopefully he'll have come to his senses. You'll just have to tell George Forde the truth.'

'I can't! What'll he think of me? I might lose my job,' sobbed Elizabeth.

'You didn't give him the money, dear girl. If we get it back quickly, Clem will be under a bit of a cloud but it will blow over. I'll talk to George with you first thing in the morning. No need to get anything official done and no one else need know about this.'

'Oh, do you think so, Dad?' Elizabeth dabbed at her face.

'Let's hope so. Dry your tears and let's face the music in the morning, eh. We'll have to track Clem down through his unit at Victoria Barracks.'

'Hopefully he'll send a message through to us. He has the phone number at the office,' sniffed Elizabeth.

'Let's go home. I was just about to pack it in.'

Elizabeth tucked her arm in her father's as they strolled towards Cricklewood. She felt better, her father was always so calm and strong. But it was going to be a long sleepless night.

Harold wasn't as calm as he appeared. All they could do was hope for the best. Five hundred pounds. It was more money than he could imagine having at any one time.

'What's up with Lizzie?' Mollie asked her father later that night as they did the washing up.

'She's upset Clem's going away. Just leave her be. And don't say anything to your mother,' he added.

They were eating breakfast when the front doorbell rang. Mollie ran to answer it and came back looking frightened.

'Dad, there's a policeman at the door. He wants to speak to Elizabeth. He called her Mrs Richards.'

Elizabeth was racing down the hallway as her father followed.

'Mollie, sit down and stay there,' said Emily firmly. But her hand was shaking as she reached for the teapot.

The policeman took off his hat. 'Morning, Mr Williams, sorry to be here so early . . .'

'That's all right, Tom. Please take a seat.' Harold led the way into the lounge room.

'It's about Clem, isn't it,' said Elizabeth sitting beside her father. Her mind was whirling. What had Clem and Thommo got up to with the money? She started praying the money hadn't been spent.

'It is about Clem. I'm awfully sorry, really I am.'

There was a catch in his voice that made Elizabeth stare at the old sergeant. 'Sorry? What do you mean? He's all right, isn't he? Is he in some sort of trouble?'

Harold gripped his daughter's hand as the sergeant looked at his feet. 'There's been an accident. Last night. A taxi and a truck . . .'

'Oh no! What happened? Is Clem all right?'

Miserably the man shook his head and looked at Harold.

'How bad is it?' asked Harold in an even tone.

The sergeant shook his head. 'Gone, I'm afraid. Terrible, terrible thing. I am so very sorry.'

Elizabeth looked wildly from the policeman to her father. 'Gone? What do you mean? The money is gone? You don't mean Clem . . . You don't mean . . . dead . . . it's impossible.' She jumped to her feet.

'He died at the scene, Elizabeth. He was in a taxi, a truck sideswiped it, killed Clem. The taxi driver is in a bad way, the truck driver seems all right.'

'I don't care about them. What about Clem? Where is he? He can't be dead. Dad, Dad . . .' She spun around to her father and fell into his arms, crying wildly.

Harold patted her shoulder, his heart aching for her.

How could this be? After coming back from the hell of war to be struck down in a traffic accident.

Elizabeth suddenly pulled away but hung on to her father's arm. 'Oh my God . . . the money! Dad!'

Mollie came racing down the hall and stood in the doorway her face white as she heard Elizabeth. 'Clem? He's dead?'

Elizabeth grabbed the sergeant's hand. 'Clem had money on him, a lot of it. Where is that? Did they take it off him? Where is he? I have to get there. Oh please, find out . . .'

'He's in the morgue, Harold. His personal effects will be there. I can get them to check.' The sergeant was anxious to leave. He hated this part of the job. 'I'm afraid I have to go out to break the news to the Richards family at the farm. Dreadful, dreadful business.'

The Sergeant closed the front door behind him, leaving Harold to comfort Elizabeth.

'I feel so terrible, Dad. About him taking the money, I kept on at him about buying into the business . . . and now this.' She broke down and Harold gave Emily a helpless look as she came towards her daughter.

It was a long walk to the stock and station agency. Harold took off his hat as he opened the door to be greeted by Donald.

'Hello, Harold. I had to open up this morning. Is Elizabeth sick or something?' He stopped as he saw Harold's face.

'Young Clem's been killed in Sydney. I need to speak to George.'

'Bloody hell. Course, of course. He's just in. Tell Elizabeth we're so sorry. She should take off as long as she likes. That's up to George though. My, the poor kid.'

Harold closed the door and stood before the man he'd known for years and haltingly told him of Clem's death and the missing money. George Forde slumped in his chair.

'Dear lord, what a mess. Poor Elizabeth. Are you sure they've been through his wallet and effects? I can't imagine Clem doing such a thing. He had the money on him?'

'Apparently he must have been drinking with Thommo and his mates. I don't know where Thommo was, the two of them must've been together and Clem caught a taxi to the barracks on his own.'

'I bet the money was spent,' said George. 'That's a big hole, Harold. I was counting on that. I feel damned bad about Clem – and Elizabeth – but I've got bills to pay. People to reimburse.'

'I understand that, George. Please don't get the police involved and make a scene about this. In the newspaper and so on. The disgrace of this will kill Emily, and poor Elizabeth has enough to deal with without her late husband being known as a thief.'

'That's all very well, Harold. But it must have been over five hundred quid!'

'George, add it up and let me know. Somehow we'll pay you back. Emily and I have some savings, I'll mortgage the house, whatever it takes.'

George shifted uncomfortably at the pleading note in Harold's voice. 'Well, I hope it doesn't come to that Harold. But if you can see your way clear, then there won't be any need for anyone to know about this.'

'Give me a day or so. And Elizabeth will need a bit of a break, the funeral and so on.'

George waved a hand. 'Whenever she's ready.'

Harold reached out and shook his hand. 'I appreciate this, George.'

'Yes, well, I'm sorry to put you through this, but I wouldn't stay in business if I didn't settle my accounts, meet my obligations.'

*

Clem's body came home on the train. The simple casket was unloaded well down the platform, unnoticed by the passengers. Harold and Mollie stood solemnly with Keith Richards. Emily and Elizabeth, like the rest of the Richards family, stayed at home, making plans for the funeral. Walter and Nola had swiftly relinquished control of the funeral to Elizabeth and the army. Elizabeth wanted a military funeral with a guard of honour and asked the Church of England minister to have the choir sing. Emily's friends in the Red Cross volunteered to decorate the church and organise a wake in the church hall after the service.

Cynthia took time off work to support Elizabeth and loaned her a black dress and hat.

'I don't want to wear black, it's so depressing and ugly,' she complained.

'Elizabeth! You must,' admonished Emily, looking to Cynthia for support.

'Wear a nice flower as well, that will help,' suggested Cynthia.

Emily sighed deeply, reached for a handkerchief and patted her eyes. She now knew about the theft of the money and was terrified some gossip about it would leak out. She just wanted the funeral to go smoothly and, after a modest mourning period, for Elizabeth to go back to work. She couldn't bear to think about the money still outstanding. Harold said he'd handle it.

It was a cruelly hot December day as the mourners gathered around the grave. Clem's funeral attracted a huge turnout. The Returned Soldiers' League stepped in to arrange the service and veterans had formed an honour guard outside the church. Mourners drove, crammed into cars, some in sulkies or on horses, others walked behind the hearse to the cemetery at the edge of town.

Men perspired in their jackets and hats, the women dabbed at their faces with hankies as much from heat as emotion. Cicadas in the surrounding gum trees thrummed loudly over the minister's words and Phyllis's hiccupping sobs.

Elizabeth was led forward to throw a flower and clod of rock-like earth into the grave. On cue the bugler played 'The Last Post', and after a minute of silence sounded 'Reveille'.

The Richards stood on the other side from Emily, Harold and Mollie, while Thommo, pale faced and looking ill, moved between both families, friends and neighbours, wandering in a state of utter distress.

Once or twice Thommo caught the undertone of talk that petered out as he drew near, and was conscious of certain looks and the faint ripple of whispered speculation directed at Elizabeth, her family and the Richards. He tried hard to keep a stiff upper lip as instructed but he couldn't keep from shaking. He felt sick and tears filled his eyes.

'Thommo seems so dreadfully upset,' commented Emily.

'They were brothers-in-arms. They survived hell and now he's lost his mate just when things were looking up. It's hard on him. Very hard,' said Harold.

The Richards family did not attend the wake, but returned with their own friends and distant relatives to the farm in time for the afternoon milking.

Elizabeth hadn't had any time alone with Thommo but that night, with Cynthia, the three of them sat in darkness on the front verandah of Cricklewood.

Elizabeth had told Cynthia about the loss of the money so she now asked Thommo, 'So what were you and Clem doing that last night?'

Thommo lit a smoke with a shaking hand. 'We slept on the train and when we got into Central I ran into a mate who knew of a two-up game. Normally Clem wouldn't go gambling but he insisted we go. He had money on him, and he won a bit and we went on from there.' He took a drag of his cigarette and slowly exhaled. 'We were at this private club at the back of the Cross, he came over and said he had to go, he was in strife, he'd blown the lot. I didn't know how much, I figured he'd dipped into his pay.' He stopped and looked at Elizabeth who was biting her lip.

'What's going to happen?' Cynthia asked Elizabeth softly.

'Dad's seeing Mr Forde tomorrow.' She stood up. 'I'm going to bed.'

'Take one of those pills the doctor gave you,' said Cynthia.

'No, I don't need it. I'm exhausted enough. G'night, Thommo, thanks for . . . everything.'

Thommo stood up and nodded, looking drained and tired. 'I'm taking my dad down to see a specialist in Sydney. Be in touch, eh?'

Cynthia touched Elizabeth's arm. 'See you tomorrow. Hope your mum feels better.'

Emily had collapsed after the wake and gone to bed without any dinner, making do with a headache powder, a cup of tea and a cigarette.

Thommo walked Cynthia to her house.

'I can't believe this has happened. Doesn't seem so long ago we were at the Empire Day fireworks does it? When you dared Clem and Elizabeth to go into the brush,' sighed Cynthia.

'Clem put me up to it. He was always sweet on her.'

'I hope your father will be all right, Thommo.'

'They don't hold out a lot of hope. They're selling the picture theatre. Mum plans to move down to the central coast with him. Her sister is there.'

489

'I thought the worst was over, just goes to show,' sighed Cynthia. 'Night, Thommo.' She watched him trudge away, the boy she'd grown up with, a forlorn soldier who'd lost his childhood mate and soon would lose his father. 'It's not fair,' she cried aloud and turned indoors.

Lara

There was no mistaking which unit belonged to Aunty Phyllis. Lara slowed the car and saw, across the expanse of neat lawn, a white-haired lady holding onto a walking frame by the open door. Pot plants and a chair stood on the tiny patio. The old lady waved as Lara parked the car wondering how long Aunty Phyllis had been standing there, looking out for her.

'Come in, come in. Tea's ready.' She gave Lara a warm hug.

Phyllis was short, slightly built, with neatly set curly hair, her face framed by pearl earrings. She was dressed in a pleated skirt and flowered blouse, wore stockings and sensible lace-up broad-heeled shoes. Glasses hung on a chain around her neck. Lara followed her into a pretty little sitting room with a small kitchenette and alcove with a table for two.

The sliding door into the bedroom opened and an attractive woman of about thirty came out.

'Hello, Lara, I'm Elaine, Barbara's daughter, Phyllis's granddaughter. I've made the tea for you two, and Gran made scones. I'm off to do her shopping so I'll leave you to it.' After a brief exchange of pleasantries, Elaine waved the shopping list and left.

'She's a good girl. Takes me to lunch at the club twice a week.'

'Does Elaine play cards too?' asked Lara as Phyllis settled herself at the table and pushed away the walking frame.

'No, she works as a nurse and has her own family. I taught her euchre but the young people aren't into cards like my lot. Now bring the teapot to the table.'

'You seem well set up here, Aunty Phyllis.' The tiny unit was very homey with cushions and photographs. A backdoor opened onto a small garden courtyard.

'I do for myself very well. Only need that frame when I go out really. A lady comes and does the cleaning but I cook, make my bed and tidy up. Never mind I'm slow, I'm not in a hurry to go anywhere.'

'Unless to cards, or the club, it seems. You're a hard one to catch,' smiled Lara. 'Those scones look good.'

They settled to the tea and scones making small talk, Phyllis enquiring about Lara's life, was she married, how many children and where she lived. Lara gave her a potted version, anxious to get the conversation back to her father.

Finally Phyllis pushed her cup to one side. 'Pull that box over here, I found some pictures of the family I thought you might like to see.' She put on her glasses and rifled for a moment and drew out a photo of a soldier posed in a studio. She smoothed it affectionately and handed it to Lara. 'That's my brother Clem. Your father. Oh, he was a lovely fellow.'

Lara stared at the picture, a small shiver of recognition running through her. 'Yes, yes, I've seen pictures of him. I wasn't sure who he was,' she said quietly. 'There's so much about the past that I now want to know, rather, need to know.'

Phyllis ignored the remark. 'Here's all the family at the old farm. That's me when I was ten, Kev, Clem and Keith. Mum and Dad. We don't have many pictures of Dad, he didn't like having his photo done. This is my wedding to Cyril, there's all the family – and Dad. Last picture of him.'

Lara studied the photograph of the young Phyllis in a long lace dress, the men looking uncomfortable in suits, and Phyllis's stout and cheerful looking mother, Nola. A flower girl with a grave expression stood beside Phyllis.

'So you've never left the area, Aunty Phyllis?'

'No, we didn't have the money. Cyril worked hard, we both did. Our first farm was up on the mountain, my, that was tough. I rarely came down, but we had good neighbours, we all helped each other out. From delivering babies, to bringing in a crop, sharing the good times and the bad times. That's how it was in a small, isolated community. Not like today where it's every man, woman and child for themselves. We all used to go to the old farm for the odd family gathering.'

They sifted through the photos, Phyllis giving a monologue of the names, places, events that had filled her life in the valley.

Finally Lara broke in. 'But what about my mother and Clem? What happened to them?'

Phyllis paused and lowered her glasses. 'So what's your mother told you? What do you know?'

'Very little. He's just been a name on my birth certificate. Was he a good man? Was he funny? What did he like? What happened after the war? Why did he and my mother split up? Did he remarry? Maybe I have half siblings out there,' exclaimed Lara.

'My dear girl.' Phyllis patted her hand, her eyes brimming. 'I don't know where to begin . . . what I should say . . . Like I said, I don't feel it's my place. I was young . . .'

'Please, Aunty Phyllis, you're my only chance to fill in the gaps. Is he still alive?'

Phyllis recoiled in shock. 'Goodness, no. Poor girl, you don't know much at all, do you?'

'Isn't it time the secrets came out? What could be so bad that no one will talk about things?' Lara felt close to tears, thinking, I'm a grown woman, yet I feel like a little kid that's been left out of the grown-ups' conversation.

'He died, Lara, dear. Before you were born. An accident and a few weeks later your mum found out she was pregnant with you. There was a lot of gossip of course . . .' Phyllis hesitated.

It seemed to Lara the scene before her froze as if it was a still frame of a film. He's dead was all she could think. After all this time to come so close. Lara realised that deep down she wanted him to be alive. She wanted to meet him, know him. And then there was the second blow, that he'd never known her. Even known she existed. She wanted to cry for the father she'd never had. The woman before her was talking. Lara tried to refocus.

'People talked about your mother's pregnancy of course. A small town, you know . . . And sadly, people love to believe the worst about others rather than the good.'

'It must have been dreadful for her,' managed Lara.

'It was, for all of us. I adored Clem. It was still wartime and there were lots of soldiers about and there'd been an . . . incident. Not that we were ever told directly. My parents didn't speak to your mother's side. But I got the impression your mother went a bit . . . wild. My father didn't approve of her at all. It was the grief I suppose.' Phyllis poured more tea. 'My family always blamed her for him taking the money. People, you know, talked. Whispers. Seems a lot of money went missing and Clem was blamed because Elizabeth pushed him. Wanted them to move to Sydney. Farm life wasn't for her.'

The knowledge Clem was dead had upset Lara more than she expected and she tried to concentrate on the

493

story Phyllis was letting out in staccato-brief bursts. 'What missing money, what happened?' Lara now recalled her grandfather telling her about some debt her mother had struggled to pay back.

Haltingly Phyllis told her that her father had been killed in a taxi near Central Station just after the train came in at 11.30 pm. 'We'll never know what transpired between Elizabeth and Clem that last day in the office where she worked. Our family found it difficult to believe Clem took the money. Or that he'd gamble, but we know how war changes men.' She paused and fiddled with the pictures then went on. 'My folks were always upset Clem died under a cloud, even if it wasn't supposed to be public knowledge. Your mother had to pay it back, I believe. Perhaps your grandfather helped. Your grandmother might have had airs and graces but she was an honourable woman. I remember my mother feeling a bit sorry for Elizabeth, working while she was expecting you and having to live at home. Can't have been easy for a young widow.'

What a messy tangle. God, her poor mother, it must have been dreadful. 'Did my mother Elizabeth ever visit your place?' she asked finally.

'Heavens, no. But your grandfather was a good man. When you were born he sent word to my mum. Your mother moved away with you when you were a little girl. By then Cyril was courting me and I didn't take such an interest.'

'Poor Clem. So he never even knew about me?'

Phyllis shook her head. 'No, dear. I'm sorry. I think he would have been a good dad to you.'

Tearfully Lara picked up the photograph of Clem in his uniform. 'I think he has been a good dad to me, you know that? I'd like to think he's been looking out for me. Quite late in life I've come to like the idea of a guardian angel.'

'Well, I wouldn't know about these things, dear. All

I can say is I think it's best you don't rake over painful memories. It's all in the past. What good is it going to do you now?' Phyllis said.

Lara didn't answer, she could tell she wasn't going to make Phyllis understand how desperately important it was to her. And how could she explain to this elderly woman that she'd seen the figure of a man, a soldier, in her grandmother's house one night? And that the man she'd seen was this man in the picture she now held. Clem, her father.

'I just wish I knew more about him, as a young man. Are your brothers still alive?' Lara asked hopefully.

'Sadly, no. There's just me now. I miss my Cyril, I miss all of them. I miss my son. I have a daughter Barbara, Elaine's mum, and lovely grandchildren, even two great-grandchildren. But I miss my son, he was my best friend after Cyril died. My son got cancer and died quickly.' She dabbed at her eyes. 'You never expect to bury your child. I cherish so many happy memories.'

Lara leaned forward and touched her hand. 'Aunty Phyllis, you're lucky to have those. I have no memories. No knowledge, nothing. And everywhere I turn there's a blank wall. I even have someone anonymously saying I shouldn't try to find out. Is there more I don't know? That I should, or shouldn't, know? These secrets, they're not worth keeping in the end. Do you understand what I'm saying?'

'She's right, Gran.' Elaine walked through the door carrying groceries. 'Secrets only hurt.'

There was something in Phyllis's eyes and her expression that Lara couldn't read. Finally Phyllis shrugged.

'I wish I could help. All the family are gone. Mine and yours.'

'What about other people that lived here during that time, would they know anything?' asked Lara.

Phyllis thought a moment and then her face cleared.

'There are a few, funny how people stayed here or came back to the valley. The Gordon boys who lived next door to your grandparents, one of their wives is still around. And, heavens, what about Thommo? He knew Clem best of all.'

'Who's Thommo? Where's he?'

'He was Clem's best friend. Martin Thompson. They grew up together, he was always out at our place. I never saw him again after Clem's funeral, but someone, now, who was it, told me he was back here. Living up on the mountain. If you could find him, he'd be the one to tell you all about your father.'

Lara began to shake with excitement, this was the closest she'd probably come to learning what her father was like. 'Oh, Aunty Phyllis, please try to remember who told you. How do I find him?'

'The mountain is a small community, Lara,' said Elaine. 'Just go and ask around. Take someone with you though, there are some strange people up there.'

'Are you serious?' Lara stood up. Her head was spinning. 'Aunty Phyllis, I can't thank you enough.'

'I'm happy to help, Lara. I often wondered how you'd turned out. If I remember anything else I'll call you.' They hugged and Phyllis said goodbye and excused herself to go to the bathroom. Elaine walked outside with Lara.

'Was she helpful?' asked Elaine.

'Eventually. She was a bit reluctant,' said Lara. 'Didn't feel it was her place to reveal what my mother had never told me. The more I hear the more secrets there seem to be.'

'Phyllis knows all about secrets, she should talk,' said Elaine with some bitterness.

Lara glanced at her in surprise. 'Really? She seems so warm and open. I wish I'd known her when I was growing up, she's the only link to my father.'

'My mother felt the same as you. We didn't find out for some time that Mum was born out of wedlock before Gran married Cyril. Gran has never told Mum who her father is. Mum was the flower girl at Gran and Cyril's wedding. She always felt like a second-class citizen. When Cyril and Gran had a son, Mum's half brother, he was treated like a king. Mum always felt like the maid, she said.'

Lara wasn't sure how to react to this information about Barbara. 'Must have been hard for Phyllis, her son dying before her,' she said as they reached her car.

'I guess so. My mum said the happiest day of her life was when Cyril died.'

'He wasn't a good stepfather to your mum?' Lara stared at the other woman. 'Did you know him?'

'Fortunately no. He abused Mum for years. She left home and got married at sixteen to get away from him.'

'My God. Did Phyllis know?' asked Lara.

'I doubt it. Or she refused to believe it. No wonder she lavished so much love on their son. Poor Mum.'

'Have you ever asked your grandmother about this?' asked Lara.

'Only about Mum's real father. I didn't see the point in bringing up the abuse issue. All Gran said was it happened, her family looked after them both, and then she met Cyril and married him. I got the feeling Mum was passed off by Gran's parents, Nola and Walter, as their menopausal baby who then went to live with Gran and Cyril.'

'How awful. Your poor mother. I guess she feels uncomfortable around Phyllis.'

'Oh, she doesn't blame her anymore. But one day I'm going to get the name of Mum's father out of Gran.'

'I can understand how you feel. Maybe his family doesn't know Phyllis ever had your mother.'

'That's what everyone says, Lara. It's the damn secrets they want to take to their graves. Don't you wish your mother had told you about your father, rather than you trying to piece bits and pieces together?'

Lara squeezed Elaine's hand. 'You're right. Well, I'm glad in a way that I'm not the only one with a secret past.' She tried to speak lightly but Elaine's story about Barbara had shaken her.

'My past is part of your past too, you know, even if tenuously. Good luck, Lara. Be careful if you go to the mountain.'

Lara drove back to Cricklewood in a daze. The afternoon sun turned the paintwork a blood-red hue. She sat on the sun-warmed front steps and closed her eyes. She was trying to absorb what she'd heard and seen in Phyllis's flat. Faces, blurred bush scenes, family groups and gatherings glimpsed in the photographs Phyllis had shown her reeled through her mind. But she couldn't get over the news her father had died even before she was born. Why had her mother refused to talk about him?

Somewhere in the jumble there was the true story. And hopefully there was one person out there who could flesh out the ghost that was Clem Richards. Her father might not have been physically in her life, but Lara now had a strong sense that he'd always been there in spirit. Certain qualities, talents, attitudes that were so unlike Elizabeth Lara always believed had come from her unknown father rather than her mother. Then apparently he'd been branded a thief and had shamed her family. Somehow, though, Lara stubbornly preferred to think of him as the eager-faced young soldier with the happy-go-lucky smile.

If she found him, perhaps this Thommo might disillusion her. Lara stood up. Whatever it is, I'd rather know, she decided. Like Elaine said, 'Too many secrets, too much pain.'

17

Cedartown, 1945

ELIZABETH WALKED SLOWLY HOME across the railway
bridge, her shoulders hunched, her head low. Watching her,
Harold's heart ached. What should be a joyous time in her
life – the arrival of her first child – was happening under a
cloud of despair, shame and hardship. Losing her husband,
especially after he'd acted so foolishly and cruelly, was shocking enough, but to discover she was pregnant so soon after
the funeral had been a difficult blow. Harold was glad they
hadn't known about the baby when he went in to see George
Forde again about the theft and the details of the money.

George had been as sympathetic as possible but, as he
looked sadly at his friend Harold Williams across his desk,
he could only say, 'I had to pay everyone what they were
owed, Harold. Otherwise I wouldn't stay in business.'

'I understand your position, George. We know the responsibility rests with us. Elizabeth feels responsible because she
left the room and even though it was her husband, that's no

excuse. The money's gone and we have to pay it back. I've managed to get three-quarters of the total sum for you. The bank has been helpful . . . and . . . we had some savings,' added Harold, straightening slightly. He didn't want George to think he and Emily were penniless. Though heaven knew this unforeseen event had wrecked whatever small financial security they had. He prayed no one in the family got sick.

'I appreciate you doing this, Harold.' George knew very well what a sacrifice the hard-working man with the gnarled hands wearing the unfamiliar tie and jacket was making for his daughter.

'Now, the arrangement we'd like to suggest for paying back the last two hundred pounds,' Harold almost couldn't get the amount out, it was such a large sum, 'is that Elizabeth continue to work for you if you're agreeable, but most of her wages be retained by you.'

George didn't answer immediately. Elizabeth was a good worker and he felt sorry for her but, while it was unfortunate that her husband had turned out to be such a disappointment, he needed the money. His business was sailing very close to the wind in these troubled times. Harold Williams was a man of integrity and honesty whom he respected. He held out his hand. 'Shake. And thank you, Harold. And Elizabeth. Perhaps staying here at her job will help settle some of the bad feelings.'

Harold winced. He knew there'd been gossip around the town but after Clem's death no one dared mention the subject. It pained Emily dreadfully to think their good name and reputation had been tainted. She blamed Elizabeth for rushing into an ill-advised marriage. 'The bank manager has the money draft all made out. We'll not mention this again. Good day to you, George.' Harold picked up his hat and quietly left the office.

*

And so Elizabeth went to work as she always had, living at home, the only occupant of the bedroom she'd shared with her sister. Mollie had joined the Women's Auxiliary Airforce when she turned eighteen and had recently moved to Melbourne. Elizabeth was envious of her younger sister's freedom and her escape from Cedartown. Here she was burdened with working for nothing for a long time ahead, still living under the watchful, sometimes accusing, eye of her mother. Now the shock of discovering she was pregnant was difficult to come to terms with. Fleetingly she had considered getting rid of the baby and had discussed it with Cynthia.

'It costs money, Elizabeth. And who'd do it? I wouldn't know where to start. You can't go to a doctor. They're not allowed. And those private places charge lots of money.'

'I heard about some ladies down south –' began Elizabeth.

'That's dangerous. Anyway, do you really want to get rid of Clem's baby? It's all you have of him,' said Cynthia, rather shocked at Elizabeth even contemplating the idea of an illegal abortion.

'I'm desperate, Cyn! I'm trapped here. I was thinking I'd go away and get a better job, send the money home and have some freedom. How am I going to manage with a baby?' Elizabeth began weeping.

Cynthia comforted her friend as best she could. Elizabeth had always been the prettiest and most popular girl in town. Now she was being shunned and her future looked bleak. 'Your mum and dad will help with the baby. I think your mum is rather looking forward to it. Maybe after the baby you can still move away. Maybe we could both go somewhere and find better jobs. The war must surely end soon.' It was a spontaneous thought, but Elizabeth clutched at it.

'That's a grand idea! Would you? Move to Sydney with me? There's still a big shortage of men, we'd get work.'

Cynthia patted her arm. 'Don't rush it, and don't mention it to your parents. Just work quietly, be the grieving widow, carrying a child. Clem fought in the war, he'd always been a nice boy. The war changes people. You can't help that. You know what your father says – hold your head up high.'

Elizabeth hugged her. 'I wish you were my sister, Cyn. Thanks.'

Elizabeth had visited the doctor and the local midwife, but she was quite unprepared for the birth of a baby. No one she knew was pregnant or had children and it wasn't a subject she could talk easily about with her mother. So when her waters broke after dinner one evening she knew her time had come. Unfortunately she was alone. Emily was visiting Harold's sister down south and Harold had gone to a lodge meeting.

Elizabeth waited, pacing up and down the hall at Cricklewood until the contractions intensified and she became too worried. She rushed next door to the Gordon's, hurrying along their long side verandah past the sleeping birds in an aviary, avoiding the dozens of cherished ferns and plans.

'Mrs Gordon, come quick.'

'Elizabeth, what is it dear? Oh my goodness, is it time?'

'I think so. Mum and Dad aren't home. What should I do?'

'Have you packed your bag?'

'No, I'm not due for two weeks at least. Is it going to be all right?'

'Don't worry, dear. Let's get your things together and Mr Gordon will take you to the hospital.'

'I'm sorry to be a trouble,' said Elizabeth as they returned to the house to get the items on the list the nurse had given her. 'I'm just a bit scared.'

Mrs Gordon felt sorry for Elizabeth. 'Nothing to be frightened of, love. Just a bit of pain and then it's all over. Too bad the boys aren't here. We'll have to let them know the good news soon, won't we?'

Elizabeth wished the Gordon boys were home from war, and Andy too. They were like brothers to her and right now she needed someone strong and cheerful.

Mr Gordon carried her small bag into the entrance of the little cottage hospital and patted her shoulder. 'Good luck, Elizabeth. I'll tell your dad as soon as he comes home and he'll be right over.' He and Elizabeth knew it would be unthinkable to interrupt a lodge meeting.

The hours passed in a blur for Elizabeth. She heard a woman shouting out in pain, a baby crying, and tapping footsteps down the wooden floorboards of the hallway. The cottage hospital was a rambling old home that served the few patients treated locally. Elizabeth groaned in pain, but no one was there to comfort her. The matron was brisk and the doctor businesslike. A few minutes after midnight, a tightly wrapped bundle was put in her arms.

'It's a girl, Elizabeth. Sweet little thing, isn't she? Does she look like her dad?'

Elizabeth was exhausted. She peered at the tiny face, all that could be seen of her daughter. 'I can't tell. Is my father here?'

'He is. I've told Mr Williams the happy news. You rest and you can see him in the morning.'

'Couldn't I see him now, please, matron?'

'You're not allowed to have visitors, but I suppose for

a minute.' She relented, feeling sorry for Elizabeth. Matron had a lot of time for Harold Williams.

Harold tiptoed to her bedside and took her hand. 'Well done, lass. She's a little corker. Just beautiful. Your mother is going to be thrilled. I'll send a telegram in the morning.'

'What am I going to do, Dad?' A tear slipped down Elizabeth's cheek. She felt overwhelmed by the responsibility suddenly laid on her with the arrival of this small human being.

'We'll manage, pet,' said Harold softly. He held her hand, remembering the thrill of seeing his first newborn daughter. After a minute he asked, 'What are you going to call the little possum?'

Elizabeth opened eyes and gave a small smile. 'Lara. I read it in a book.'

'Pretty. Just like both of you.' He leaned over and kissed her forehead. 'You just rest now.'

Two weeks after Elizabeth took Lara home to Cricklewood Harold laid a patch of wet cement under the tank stand and they pressed Lara's tiny foot into it. Harold carefully wrote her name and the date. He then went down to his old wooden shed in the backyard next to Emily's chicken run and carefully added Lara's name and birth date on a wooden plank below that of Clem's death date, which was marked with a small black cross. He stood back and surveyed the list of dates painted on the slab of timber. Cracks of sunlight shone between the roughly hewn wood and he hoped little Lara would bring sunshine into their lives. He and Emily doted on the baby, but Elizabeth was restless.

George Forde and Donald appreciated Elizabeth's

return to the stock and station agency because everything ran that much smoother. Even though they were kind, Elizabeth hated being there, constantly confronted by memories of the theft, and she found no comfort in Cynthia's declaration that it was silly to think everyone in town was still talking about her. So when Mollie told her about a well-paying job in Melbourne as a book-keeper Elizabeth saw her opportunity. She'd be able to send money home to repay debts, her baby would be loved and cared for by doting grandparents and, more importantly, it was a chance to have a new life.

After some discussion Elizabeth was surprised that her mother agreed to her leaving Cedartown. She would live in Melbourne in an old house shared by Mollie and another girl and her pay was enough to live on and send money home to her father to repay George Forde.

Elizabeth caught the night mail train to Sydney, changing to another in the morning for Melbourne. While she'd miss her baby daughter, she knew the child was safe in the caring hands of her grandparents. She hoped that, at last, she could start afresh.

Emily took over the care of Lara with proprietary enthusiasm. Harold took Lara for walks in his arms, talking to her about all they passed as they headed along the bush track, over the creek and around the sawmill. Harold pulled Elizabeth and Mollie's old pram out of the shed and cleaned it up and together he and Emily pushed their baby granddaughter into town once a week. Friends would look out for them to admire the little girl, as did shopkeepers and their customers.

If she noticed, Emily gave no sign, but on her weekly expedition she was observed by Nola Richards. Although even as paternal grandmother she was not invited to share the joy of Lara. As far as Emily was concerned, Clem Richards and his family did not exist. When Nola dabbed at her tears in their kitchen Walter Richards was brusque.

'They don't want to know us, love. They never did and never will. I bet if Clem were still alive we'd be jolly lucky to ever see that baby. Forget her. There'll be plenty of grandkids coming now Keith is married.'

'But she's the first,' sighed Nola. 'And I want to hold her. Just once.'

Isabella

Isabella's mouth was tightly clenched, her expression grim as she rode with speed and purpose away from Riverview to Dungog to see her solicitor. Over and over in her mind she ran the nightmarish events of the past several weeks.

That Skerrett had been pardoned by the chief justice, not just given a ticket of leave, was shocking enough, but that he had now made good his threat to see her brought before the courts for perjury was unbelievable. Sadly, as Florian and others had warned her, Skerrett was a contemptible man who would sink to the lowest deceit to get his way. Worse, he was clever, manipulative and a skilled liar: he had managed to convince the chief justice of his innocence. Isabella ignored the beauty of the countryside that normally soothed her. The words of the summons and warrant for her arrest kept coming back to haunt her.

Though dusty and weary from her journey, she went straight to her solicitor's office. 'How can this be?' demanded Isabella across his desk. 'Skerrett was found guilty and sentenced to ten years' hard labour.'

'It does seem quite irregular, I grant you, Miss Kelly. But he has convinced his friends and others with connections that he was hard done by in court. His wife has been persistent to the point of harassment in petitioning for his release.'

'How did he come to beg the ear of the chief justice, who, after all, was the trial judge who convicted him?' asked Isabella.

The solicitor shrugged. 'I believe Mrs Skerrett pursued and harangued the judge's wife. The judge met with Skerrett before court sittings on several mornings and was persuaded by his arguments to re-examine his case. Skerrett produced new written evidence to explain several points of doubt in his case, and so the judge wrote a letter asking the bench to look at Skerrett's argument. The magistrates believed his explanation and decided to release him.'

'And we know who those magistrates were,' declared Isabella bitterly.

'Therefore, it followed in the mind of the chief justice if Skerrett was innocent you must have perjured yourself to sway the jury at his trial.'

Isabella glared at the solicitor. 'Utter lies and fabrication. He has forged papers before, he'll do anything to get his way it seems.'

'Unfortunately whatever he has said swayed the chief justice and other magistrates in the district. Having said that, Miss Kelly, I'm sure you will be vindicated in the end. It is indeed unfortunate that you will have to endure the inconvenience of a court case to defend yourself.'

'And the expense. These past two years have been most difficult for me. Agents have let me down, made poor sales when my cattle and horses should have fetched far higher prices, and I have suffered theft and unjust claims against me and my property.'

The solicitor didn't answer, simply gave a little nod and stroked his chin. While Isabella Kelly drove a hard bargain and expected the highest prices for her good stock, privately he was convinced she had been the victim of some unscrupulous deal-making by other parties. She had indeed suffered losses and theft and, despite her suspicions and threats of litigation, she had no hope of pinning down the culprits.

'Skerrett has continued to make claims against my property at Birimbal, and my cattle, which are outrageous,' continued Isabella angrily. 'I believed once he was convicted the matters would be dropped. But he is still pursuing these claims – claims that are totally false. He is a convicted felon and forger, yet his word is believed over mine!'

The solicitor refrained from mentioning that there were quite a few local people who had run up against the wrath and high principles of Isabella Kelly and disliked her so, although they didn't actively support Skerrett, or were ambivalent about him, they were happy enough to see Isabella in trouble. The solicitor had no doubt that the fact she was a single woman alone and successful in a man's world counted against her too. 'All people in the district know that Skerrett has recently been found innocent of the charges for which he was sent to prison. Indeed, as you are well aware, he is pursuing a claim for compensation. Now that Skerrett has gone on the attack as a wronged man, it may be hard to prove him a liar.'

'All I can do is tell the truth,' said Isabella.

'Then let us discuss your situation and appoint barristers to represent you,' said the solicitor. 'My advice would also be to put your properties and assets into the hands of an agent as trustee so, if indeed it did come to the unlikely situation whereby you are convicted, the court cannot confiscate your possessions.'

Following on from the murder of Noona and her daughter, Florian and the boy Kelly were deeply distressed at this new calamity. Isabella told Florian to travel to Birimbal and stay there to protect the property. The young Kelly, Hettie, two stockmen and the overseer remained at Riverview.

But when Florian arrived at Birimbal he found Skerrett and another man in the stockyards with a large mob of cattle, all with the IMK brand.

'What are you doing with these cattle? They belong to Miss Kelly,' said Florian as he rode up.

Skerrett scowled at him and replied in an arrogant voice, 'They're mine, she sold them to me. This gentleman here is Mr Simmons, the agent. These cattle were never delivered and I've come to claim what's mine.' Skerrett casually rested a hand on his pistol. 'It's all before the court right now. I'm within my rights.'

Florian knew Skerrett was lying but felt he couldn't stop them. Helplessly he watched the cattle, along with twenty horses, driven from the yards. Skerrett must have sent stockmen to muster a large area of Isabella's property, for Florian recognised several good horses they hadn't been able to find when they'd mustered before moving to Riverview. The property was too big to fence and stock often wandered onto neighbouring properties. Florian was surprised by the number of cattle and horses that Miss Kelly's team hadn't found on the last muster, and it suddenly occurred to him these animals could have been deliberately taken to another property, or hidden on some remote reach of Isabella's property during their muster.

Florian sat on his horse in the shade of a tree as the cattle were taken away by the agent with Skerrett and a young stockman. Florian did not know about the legalities of what was happening, but he did know that Miss Kelly had sent him to Birimbal to protect her property, and he felt he had failed her badly.

The house was locked up and empty since Isabella had

evicted Mrs Skerrett and her children. Florian entered it with the key Isabella had given him and went to her desk as she had instructed. From a locked drawer he took out her writing box, also securely locked. Isabella had told him to bring it to her as it contained deeds, receipts and letters concerning her business transactions over many years. She might need to refer to them for her court case.

Florian checked the property before he left and all seemed to be in order. He paused to look at the peaceful surrounds but his heart ached at the memory of the murder of Noona and his baby daughter at the creek crossing. He resolved to ride the long way around Birimbal to avoid the crossing and its memories. It meant going through Birimbal's most remote paddock bordering the Allen property on the western side where cattle from both properties tended to graze. There had been some disputes over ownership of unbranded stock on occasion and Florian was sure Mr Allen was probably pleased his neighbour, the litigious and quick-tempered Isabella Kelly, had moved to Riverview.

It was the first time he had travelled past Allen's to reach the main track to the coast, as most people took the shorter route through the crossing on Birimbal. Through a stand of gum trees in the distance he glimpsed a clearing and what appeared to be yards. At first there was nothing unusual in that but then Florian wondered why Allen would have yards so close to Miss Kelly's property when his main stockyards were closer to his house and the road. Florian decided to take a closer look.

It was a basic stockyard with a bark lean-to shelter nearby. Florian, now driven by instinct and curiosity, peered into the windowless hut. There were some old saddles and tack, and a pile of stiff and smelly hides. Holding his breath he flipped the hides over and was shocked to see they carried Isabella's brand. Clearly they were from cattle that had been stolen and killed for the meat trade in coastal towns.

Florian rode on and later from Riverview he sent a note to Isabella telling her what he'd seen on her neighbour's property. It would only confirm what Isabella already suspected – that few people in the district liked her or could be trusted.

The court convened in Sydney one month later. Isabella walked from her boarding house in Hunter Street and sat stiffly in the courtroom ignoring Skerrett as arguments were put forward by her barrister. She was used to managing her life as an independent woman, but this was one of the few occasions where she felt the pain of being utterly alone.

As the days wore on it seemed to her to be a repeat of the trial where Skerrett had been convicted of cattle stealing and forgery. However, this time a new witness came forward to swear he had given Skerrett the large amount of money he was carrying, money that Isabella believed had come from the illegal sale of her cattle that he'd seized. The witness was a John Blake and he gave Skerrett a glowing character reference, saying they'd known each other in Sydney prior to Skerrett's moving north. Blake was taken at face value and not examined too thoroughly. It passed unnoticed that he was a distant relative of Skerrett. Nor was it revealed in court that Charles Blake Skerrett had arrived in the colony as a convict and had already ruined two honest businessmen. He was really a man of very dubious character.

When the judge called for the documents – the bill of sale and the mustering agreement – they could not be produced. They had been held by the court and were now lost, even though the chief justice had taken the documents

511

to examine them. The case now rested on Skerrett's argument that Isabella had perjured herself in declaring the documents not written by her. Without these documents it would be hard for her to prove her innocence.

Isabella's barristers argued her case but when she was cross-examined she was a poor witness, mixing up some dates, and her arrogance and annoyance did not help. The prosecution managed to infer she was not well liked in the district, and stressed that she had appeared before the bench on numerous occasions.

When Isabella tried to explain that she had won these cases where she had been exploited, she was cut off from answering. Great weight was given to the fact that the trial judge who had sentenced Skerrett to ten years' hard labour had, as chief justice, recommended his pardon. Combined with the positive evidence given by Blake, Skerrett's outrage at the injustice of his sentence, and the lack of the documents, the jury found Isabella Mary Kelly – *guilty of perjury against Charles Skerrett.*

The judge, surprised at the verdict, had no recourse but to pass sentence. He stared at the plump, fiftyish woman with greying hair and creased face who now rose in the dock and stood straight backed with chin held high as he announced that she must serve a sentence of twelve months in Darlinghurst Gaol and pay a fine of one hundred pounds.

Isabella sat back in her seat. What distressed her more than the shame and ignominy of the sentence was the fact Skerrett had lied, cheated, bribed a witness, totally fooled the chief justice and won his case. She treasured her reputation as an honest, upright person and now she was discredited.

The newspapers and many in the valley were critical of the sentence, claiming it was lenient. The prison governor, however, treated Isabella as a privileged prisoner.

She was allotted a cell of her own, rather than locked in with the other women prisoners who were prostitutes and thieves – there was even a murderess.

Isabella lay on the mouldy bed in her damp stone cell and briefly allowed herself to cry. She hoped her affairs were being looked after by the trustees she had appointed and she knew Florian, Kelly and Hettie would care for Riverview.

On the second day of her incarceration the prison governor sent word to Isabella that she would be allowed to walk in his personal garden each afternoon. For the next three weeks the too-brief hour in the fresh air of the small-walled garden was the only pleasant part of Isabella's day. She walked slowly, breathing deeply. Already the dank coldness of the sandstone cell was giving her chills and congestion in the lungs. Occasionally she paused, stood still and closed her eyes. She let the pale city sunlight soak into her clothes which constantly felt damp and uncomfortable. She tried to imagine she was back in her beloved valley. She saw in her mind's eye the spread of the ranges embracing the rich green valley where cleared paddocks and pioneer homes showed the progress of settlement. She imagined she was at Riverview where the lazy stretch of broad calm water slid past her front verandah. Or she was in her shade house with her collection of exotic plants.

It was hard to open her eyes to the grim reality of where she was.

But even this small respite was soon taken from her. After three weeks complaints were lodged that Isabella Kelly was being given special treatment in prison and the order was sent that she was no longer permitted to walk in the governor's garden.

Isabella drew herself up and regarded the unfortunate warder who brought her this news. 'Then I shall not leave my cell. I will not mingle with riffraff,' she informed him.

'There are persons in the valley I would not associate with so I am not about to socialise with inferior people here. And I certainly don't want anyone to visit me. I shall serve my time alone.'

The warder shrugged and stuck a notice to her cell door that read 'Solitary Confinement'.

Isabella, unlike the other prisoners, was allowed to write and receive letters and she saw an occasional newspaper. With her own money she was able to pay for washing and some small personal items. She wrote to Florian about her business affairs:

I have decided to sell Birimbal. Mr Lennon from the Trustees has authority to sell the property, the remaining cattle, four hundred horses and the thirteen hundred sheep. I will retain Riverview and the services of yourself and the present staff. I will reduce the stock until I am in a position to rebuild my assets. I am afraid this dreadful business with Skerrett has curtailed my finances. It is very disheartening that documents have gone missing from the court, indeed from the desk of the chief justice himself. My health is suffering badly, the food here is poor – meat – and not very good meat – is provided only once a week.

Florian folded her letter and sighed. He was concerned for his mistress and wished he could do more to help her.

Not long after, Florian was in Sydney on business for Isabella and heard gossip about the trial and the prejudice against her. In the public bar of a hotel he listened with interest as a man, about his own age, professed to have inside knowledge of the case because he worked as a clerk of the court.

Florian drew him to one side and probed further. The clerk introduced himself as Gordon Finch and, as the ale flowed, a strange story emerged that Florian had difficulty believing.

'What you're telling me is that someone, of some standing in the court, has held back or knows where the missing papers are that were supposedly written by Isabella Kelly?' said Florian, glad he hadn't mentioned that he had a connection with the 'notorious' woman. 'Why would they do that?'

'She has a lot of enemies and some have been swayed or persuaded, shall we say, by a certain person to 'lose' those papers.' He gave a little wink and smirked.

'They could be worth money if found,' suggested Florian.

The man downed his ale. 'Wouldn't do her any good now, she's in prison.'

'I believe I know someone who would be interested in, er, purchasing them,' said Florian.

Finch eyed him. 'Do you now? Like I said, them papers won't do no one any good. How much?' he added.

'I know a man who would pay a good price. I can deliver my side of a deal. Can you arrange to deliver the original papers, the forged ones?' said Florian, amazed at his daring in suggesting this.

'Perhaps.'

'Name a price then. And I will see you here tomorrow evening,' said Florian, wondering if this was just a wild goose chase. Where was he going to get the money? And if they were the forged documents, would they help Miss Kelly now the trial was over?

They settled on a sum of money and Florian returned to his lodging. He was trying to think where he could turn for help, as it seemed even the judicial system could not be trusted. He wondered which magistrate could have so ruined Isabella Kelly's case.

Glancing through the *Empire* newspaper the next

morning Florian read an article about the Reverend Doctor John Dunmore Lang and recalled Miss Kelly talking about him as a great friend whom she'd met on the ship on the way to Australia. Florian now knew where to go for help.

Reverend Lang welcomed Florian to his rooms and listened quietly. Florian produced letters Isabella had written to him from prison and convinced the reverend of his credentials, then told him the full story.

'Are you quite positive this clerk whom you met in a public house can acquire the disputed documents?'

'I believe so, Doctor Lang. Of course I would not part with any cash until I saw the papers. I am familiar with Miss Kelly's writing and if these are the ones Skerrett produced at his trial, and they are indeed forgeries as Miss Kelly swore, then perhaps they might be of some value?'

'You're a bright fellow. Indeed they would be. Her case was severely handicapped by the disappearance of the papers. If these are the missing documents which are the forgeries, she can petition the court for a pardon.'

Florian was elated. He hadn't considered the re-opening of her case. 'Excellent, if this man produces them, it will be worth the cost. It is beyond my humble means but I'm sure Miss Kelly will reimburse you. I was unsure of approaching the trustees of her estate as I didn't want anyone to know of my plan.'

'Very wise, it seems few can be trusted in this matter. I am happy to advance you the ten pounds,' said Reverend Lang. 'Be cautious and make sure they are the correct papers before handing across the money. I await your return this evening.' They shook hands and Florian left, feeling confident and impatient for the evening meeting.

He waited in a dark corner of the rowdy hotel and saw Gordon Finch enter. Finch didn't appear to be carrying anything. He glanced cautiously around and, seeing Florian stand up briefly, made his way to him.

'Evening, Mr Holmes,' said the clerk, with an impassive expression. 'Fancy meeting you again in this establishment.'

'I still have business in Sydney but I will be returning north in the morning,' said Florian for the benefit of anyone in earshot. They chatted about life and the weather until their drinks were brought to them, then they moved to a vacant table with two chairs.

The clerk sat with his back to the main room, reached into his coat and drew out an envelope before lifting his tankard and taking a long draught.

Florian looked around casually and took a sip of his drink before saying in a low voice, 'I must take a look at these before I give you payment.'

The clerk shrugged and watched him as Florian took out two sheets of paper: one the bill of sale, the other a mustering agreement. He knew the signatures were not those of Isabella. These must be the documents Skerrett had forged. There were many people who could attest that it was not the Kelly signature they knew – Miss Kelly's bank manager, Reverend Lang, business people who had never been called to verify the signature at Skerrett's trial. But he was not about to let Finch know that. He nodded and folded the papers and put them in the envelope.

'They appear to be the right ones. My friend will be glad to dispose of these for good,' he lied.

'There's a fire over there, toss them in,' suggested the clerk.

Florian kept his hand on the documents, saying quickly, 'My friend wishes to undertake that task himself. He will know then he got what he paid for, if you get my drift.' He then took out the envelope with the ten pounds in it and slid it across the table. Finch's hand reached out and the envelope was in his coat pocket in one swift movement.

They chatted amiably while they finished their ales and Florian rose and held out his hand. 'I bid you good evening, Mr Finch.'

Finch turned to the bar where men were crowded, voices loud with laughter and argument, and no one paid any attention to Florian disappearing into the night.

At the dining table in Reverend Lang's house, Florian and the minister pored over the forged papers, comparing the writing with their own correspondence from Isabella.

Lang straightened and held out his hand. 'Well done, lad, I will handle matters from here.'

Relieved, Florian thanked him and returned to his lodging house where he wrote Isabella a note, hoping it might bring some comfort to her, though he could not give details of what had transpired in case the note fell into the wrong hands.

Charles Skerrett had filed for compensation against unlawful imprisonment but when the Select Committee met to hear his case, Isabella's barrister dropped a small bombshell by re-introducing the missing documents. Comparisons with Isabella's handwriting showed them to be forgeries as she'd testified, proving she had not perjured herself. Furthermore, William Turner, who'd appeared at Skerrett's trial and subsequently disappeared, was found and brought back in to testify that he had been paid by Skerrett to say he'd witnessed the documents, when in fact he could neither read nor write.

It took only a short time for the judge to recommend that Isabella Kelly be pardoned and released from prison. She had served five and a half months and was in frail health. For several weeks she was too ill to be moved. Finally she left Darlinghurst Gaol to recover in the boarding house in Hunter Street before visiting Reverend Dunmore Lang.

'I thank you for your kindness, Doctor Lang, and for believing and assisting Florian Holmes,' said Isabella.

He dismissed her thanks but added, 'It concerns me that the acting chief justice has declined to pass a public opinion on whether you are guilty or innocent.'

'I fear there will be the inevitable rumours of "friends in high places", rather than a woman exonerated,' she sighed. 'You have noticed there has been no mention of my release nor of the report to the governor concerning my innocence in the *Sydney Morning Herald* or the *Empire* newspapers.'

'I hear there are those in your valley who know nothing of your illness and wonder at your absence. You should return as soon as you are strong enough, and put your affairs in order.'

'I wish I could clear my name. The attorney general remarked that my character is clean,' said Isabella bitterly.

'Then you must prove it so.'

Isabella spread her hands in a gesture of despair. 'I want the world to know of my innocence but when I asked the attorney general he merely said he would talk to my attorney.'

'And what did he say?'

'Dear Doctor Lang, I told him I had no money left to pay lawyers. I have been robbed by Charles Skerrett through legal actions and his theft of my assets and property ever since he was liberated from Cockatoo Island.'

The Reverend Dunmore Lang knew that, while not penniless, the once wealthy Isabella Kelly was struggling – financially, emotionally and now physically. She still faced enmity from her neighbours and fair-weather friends. 'If I can be of assistance . . .' he began.

Isabella rose shakily to her feet. 'You have done more

than enough, for which I thank you. Now I will retire as it will be a long journey back tomorrow.'

But her joy at being back at Riverview, overlooking the river, was soured by the shocking discovery of how the trustees had mismanaged her affairs while she was in prison and then ill. Birimbal and the stock Skerrett hadn't stolen had been sold off at ridiculously low prices. Skerrett and unfriendly neighbours had pounced on her stock with flimsy illegal petitions to her trustees. To redress these would mean more protracted court cases and she had neither the strength nor the funds. She hoped her case for compensation for wrongful imprisonment would recoup some of the losses.

Hettie, heavy now with her third child, was lethargic and missing her husband Richard who was away working in a timber cutters' camp. Florian, who still mourned Noona and their daughter, was not a natural farmer, and struggled with their crops and itinerant workers under the guidance of the overseer Isabella had employed. Young Kelly kept disappearing for hours, sometimes overnight, and Isabella was concerned he was spending time with the group of natives squatting near the creek. They came each season when the land was thriving, living well on plentiful fish and game, but the stockmen were ordered to chase the blacks away.

Kelly was now a tall lad of fifteen with his mother's fine features, a mop of thick black hair and dark olive skin. He'd inherited Florian's light-coloured eyes but was considered by the white population of the valley to be more native than white and was dismissively referred to as Miss Kelly's pet black boy. Few realised that Kelly could read and write and knew the customs and manners of the drawing and dining room. Kelly was tolerated but not welcomed by the settlers and was easily dismissed as another of Isabella Kelly's eccentricities. Isabella forbade Kelly from mixing with the natives and Florian did his best to persuade Kelly to avoid them as well. He never spoke to his son about his personal relationship with Noona but occasionally he'd mention to the boy something of her life or culture that she'd taught or shown him when they were out in the bush together.

'Times haven't changed much since your poor mother died. While you have the protection of Miss Kelly you have a good life. Perhaps in times to come you will be able to mingle freely with white people,' advised Florian.

But Kelly refused to deny his black heritage. It ran in his blood. He'd been taught some of his culture and his law by his mother and he could not ignore the instincts and knowledge that were intuitive. He longed more and more to be able to unite the two parts of his being. What he'd observed of white culture held little appeal for him. But he was not always welcome among the tribe that frequented the valley and it slowly occurred to Kelly he was going to have to choose. While he had a strong bond with his father and Riverview, and was grateful to Miss Kelly, the pull of his mother's people and their culture became more and more unsettling. Aborigines he knew who worked for white people and hung on the fringes of the settlements told him about the tribal elders. These men clung to the old ways and resented the intrusion of the whites.

'There's a lot of secret things goin' on, you got to be with the elders to learn it,' said one of the black stockmen who'd long ago lost links with his people. 'Don't see it's goin' t'do you much good.'

Kelly shrugged. 'I don't see me owning property in this valley, why should I pretend to be a white man like my father when my mother was Aboriginal?'

'If you're a true black man you own all this valley,'

growled the stockman. 'Them whites just come and took it. One day we gonna take it all back.'

Isabella, still struggling to recover from her illness and the emotional and financial burden of the recent years, was depressed by her loneliness and the injustices she had suffered. She began to consider returning to England.

Dani

Now that her Isabella paintings were finished, Dani turned increasingly to a different form of contemporary art. In the Isabella series she had tried to merge the past with the present, and she hoped the unseen just below the surface would be understood and that the paintings would not be viewed just as realist landscapes. She wanted people to see beyond the individual representations of trees, river and hills, and find an emotional connection to the scenes.

Dani had walked through Isabella's country with her eyes and heart open and it gave her much in return. The beauty, the tranquillity and the sense she was walking in Isabella's shoes were inspiring. It gave her fresh creative energy and in trying to capture the essence of the place she began collecting strips of bark, seed pods, leaves, grasses, tiny rocks, feathers, bits of lichen from rotting logs, wings from a dead dragonfly. She began making small collages of landscape constructions with her found objects, experimenting with textures, gluing them into position on prepared board with watered down PVA glue.

Dani then began arranging her objects on a thin card, gluing them in place and coating it with PVA so she had a hard, textured surface ready to paint with diluted acrylic paints and watercolours. She closed her eyes and ran her hand over the card enjoying the tactile feel of the picture. She decided she'd find a printing press somewhere – maybe they had one at the local high school or TAFE where Max taught – and run off some relief prints.

She glanced at the old clock she'd brought in to the studio and reluctantly stopped work. Roddy was due for coffee. There was obviously a lot wrong judging from the desperate tone of his voice. She'd agreed to see him because she felt sorry for him and a little responsible for the Isabella movie, which had obviously hit the wall.

She heard a car and was surprised to see Roddy get out of an old sedan and not his flash convertible. He gave her a warm hug and Dani hugged him back. Neither made an attempt to kiss the other's cheek.

'I've made coffee, thought we could sit outside and take in the view. It's such a lovely day,' said Dani picking up the tray.

'The view is pretty glum from where I sit,' sighed Roddy, following her with the coffee pot.

'Okay, lay it on the table. The movie deal,' said Dani as she began pouring the coffee.

'Stuffed. Money's not happening, the exec producer pulled the plug. Because Franks took off for Europe with a young girl, he's being chased by her parents. Everyone's walked away. I'm left up shit creek.'

'What about the investors?' asked Dani evenly.

'It was a speculative investment. You take your chances, honey bun.' He saw her expression and lifted his shoulders. 'Look, I feel bad but there's jack all I can do about it.'

'There's no way to recoup anything?'

'Nah. It happens a lot. Movies fall over at the last minute. Look at *Eucalyptus*, where everyone was there, ready to start shooting, and the plug was pulled. Sets built and all. No one involved was too happy.'

'I should have remembered that,' said Dani. 'I'm really

sorry, Roddy. But it's still a damn good idea. Couldn't you interest someone else in it?'

'Been down that route. Isabella has the kiss of death on her now. Have to wait a few years before shopping this script around again. At least I own that. Russell Franks got paid.'

'So how are you going to tell everyone?'

'Any suggestions?' he asked with a rueful grin.

'Go to Patricia, lay it all on the table. Call a public meeting and be honest.'

'God, how hard would that be?' He put his head in his hands.

'At least you'll be able to hold your head up and work in this town again.' Dani felt for him. He hadn't deliberately been devious or a con man. Roddy saw himself as an entrepreneur when half the time he was probably the one who was being conned.

'I feel I should just move on. The only way this can be salvaged is if I come up with another promotion that can bring media, tourists and money to town.'

Dani thought that unlikely. 'So if you're up-front about this, people might give you another go.' She poured more coffee. 'Patricia is your best bet to smooth things over.'

Roddy leaned back in his chair. 'Ah, I do have another idea. I reckon it could work, it'd certainly bring business to town, but I'm not sure how to capitalise on it.'

Dani saw the gleam in his eye and her heart sank. 'My God, you're indefatigable. Okay, run it past me but unless you deal with the film mess I can't see anyone putting up any money for another of your schemes.'

'Doesn't require investment, just media. And then you'll have people running here, could be a great tourism hook.'

'What's that?' Dani figured she might as well hear him out. Roddy was the kind of guy that could have projects and plans fall over left and right and then suddenly hit a winner when you least expected it.

Roddy leaned forward. 'The mysterious beast of the valley. The elusive, thought-to-be-extinct animal. A living wild cat-dog from the dinosaur era. We could offer a huge reward for the person that finds it. Be bigger than the Loch Ness Monster.'

Dani started to laugh, as Roddy, now carried away, went on, 'Just think, there could be trail rides, camping safaris through the valley, a model of the beast in the museum, souvenir merchandise of the valley beast, night hunts. Every TV crew would be out here like a shot. Think of the business for accommodation, tourist events, food, marketing spin-offs!'

'But, Roddy, there isn't any such beast!' Dani stood up and began putting the cups back on the tray.

'Yes, there is. You know you've seen it. You told me you took a photo of it that day with Max. Where's the picture?'

Dani stopped in shock, remembering the day she'd met Roddy. She'd almost forgotten she'd seen the creature again with Max. Foolishly, she'd mentioned the photograph to Roddy. 'I erased it.'

'Bloody hell. Why'd you erase it? Are you sure? Have you checked your camera?'

'There's no picture, Roddy. Forget it.'

He looked crushed – for a moment. Then his face cleared. 'Well, you could draw it! You're an artist. And Max saw the photo too! You're both credible, people will believe you!'

Before Dani could answer there was a call from the front door as Jolly began barking her hello bark. Jason came around the side of the house following Jolly.

'You home, Dani?' he called, then stopped as he saw Roddy.

'Oh, I'm sorry. Didn't mean to interrupt.' He looked embarrassed.

'You're not interrupting, would you like a coffee?' said Dani, relieved to see him. She was still in slight shock over Roddy's mad idea and worried he might try to go through with it. She'd have to alert Patricia who would no doubt also put the kybosh on it.

'I was just going,' smiled Roddy. 'I was just running a few ideas past Dani.'

'Another film?' said Jason with barely concealed facetiousness.

Roddy stood up with an easy grin. 'Well, it could be, eh, Dani? I'd better be going. Thanks for the advice, Dani.'

'Oh, don't let me get in the way,' said Jason hurriedly. 'I'm just dropping off the saddle for Tim's birthday.'

'Thanks, Jason.' She turned to Roddy. 'I'm giving Tim a saddle, Jason chose it for me. Well, Roddy, talk to Patricia.' Awkwardly Dani shot out her hand, feeling uncomfortable.

Roddy glanced at Jason and smiled as he pulled Dani to him and gave her a hug. 'You've been a rock, Dani. Give me a call if you spot another beastie, eh?' He nodded at Jason. 'Good luck with your development. Way to go, isn't it?' He grinned and sauntered away without a backward glance.

Dani watched him go with a feeling she'd never clap eyes on him again. Maybe read about him in a newspaper article.

'Beastie? You got snakes or something?' asked Jason.

Dani rubbed her head. 'Ah, it's a long story. Please stay. I'll make fresh coffee. There's something I have to do.'

Dani hurried into her bedroom, picked up her camera and scrolled through to the photograph of the strange animal she'd seen on the edge of the road and captured with her camera. The yellow eyes seemed to stare at her with a direct challenge. Firmly Dani pushed the 'Erase?' button and the image disappeared. She sighed and returned to Jason.

'What are you doing with yourself now you've finished with the Isabella series?'

'I'll show you if you like. I'm experimenting with some collagraphy. I'll explain later. Black coffee or white?'

'Strong and black, thanks. I'll get the saddle, where do you want to stash it till the big day?'

Jason roared with laughter after Dani told him about Roddy's great idea of the 'valley beast'. 'He's certainly a marketer's dream – but not for me. Thank God he didn't want to market Birimbal. The movie launch was enough.'

'I feel kind of sorry for him though,' said Dani. 'I don't believe he intended to rip people off, he really wanted the movie to work. I feel sort of responsible for all the locals who put in money and lost it on all the development hoopla.'

'Don't beat yourself up, Dani. If people invest in a speculative scheme they have to be prepared to lose as well as make money. I'm sure no one is going to blame you,' said Jason.

Dani didn't answer for a moment, thinking that was all very well for Jason, he could afford to lose a few thousand. People like Barney and Helen, and Claude and George couldn't. 'I just wish I could repay the people here in the valley somehow. They've been so wonderful to me and Mum. You too,' she added, suddenly realising how much Jason had helped her and Tim.

'People are happy to see you and your mother settling in, young Tim fitting in and blossoming. How is your mother's family history search working out?'

'She's suddenly got a lead. Someone up on the mountain, has no idea how to find him. She's going to ask around.'

'Mmm. What's his name? Maybe I can help. I suppose she's been told they're a very close-knit community up there.'

Dani laughed. 'Barney was a bit less diplomatic, said there are some old-time weirdos there. Helen says there's probably still an old hippy element, and drugs.'

'Maybe Lara should be careful about accepting cookies from strangers, even little old ladies,' suggested Jason.

Dani was thoughtful. 'There is something really odd about Mum's dig into the family past. I know this sounds crazy, but she got some hate mail, well, anonymous letters warning her off.'

'Did she go to the police? That sounds a bit heavy-handed,' said Jason seriously.

'I thought so too, but Mum brushed it off. There's nothing that sinister in our family tree, that we know of, anyway. But it's creepy that the letters are hand delivered and whoever is writing them seems to know what Mum's doing.'

'She's being stalked? Dani this could be serious. For you and Tim, too.'

'I guess so.' Dani had been so wrapped up in her own activities she hadn't pushed her mother more about the letters. 'I'll talk to her about it.'

'Maybe the writer lives in town and follows her moves, I wouldn't want to be trailed up that treacherous mountain road into hillbilly country,' said Jason. 'When is she going?'

'I have no idea.' Dani stood up and shrugged, as if shaking off the uncomfortable thoughts. 'Come into the studio and see my latest efforts. And thanks for getting the saddle for Tim. I've no idea where to hide it.'

'I could take it across to Kerry's cottage,' suggested Jason. 'Then when he goes to see Juniper and Bomber you can tell him to look in her tack shed.'

'Great idea. I'll stick a card and a ribbon on it. Too big to gift wrap.'

When Jason returned from his car with Tim's glossy new saddle, Dani asked, 'Do you mind if I ask you what's going to happen to your grandparents' home? It seems a shame if it just sits there like a museum but with no visitors.'

'It's difficult. I think I told you Kerry is fiercely against changing anything. She wasn't left any property and in the circumstances I've just let it slide.'

'Jason, surely you don't have to comply with the will,' said Dani. 'You know after Roddy talking about tourism here it occurs to me your place could attract the kind of visitors to the valley who are interested in history and so on,' said Dani.

'You mean strangers traipsing through the family pad? Kerry would hate that,' exclaimed Jason.

'If she doesn't want it turned into a boutique hotel or a B&B because she doesn't want anything changed, you could leave it as a living museum. It would be a terrific attraction. Kerry could run guided tours on weekends or whenever she wanted to. She'd be good at that,' enthused Dani.

Jason stared at her. 'Hmm. If we had the proper security. Kerry is retiring and private, but when she talks about horses or that house she's very knowledgeable. I wonder . . .' He paused, rubbing his chin. 'It might solve some family problems.'

'You could invent a ghost in the house, run pony rides for kids, have a picnic area,' Dani went on, but Jason held up his hand.

'Let's not get carried away here. Small steps. It's a good idea. Good on you, Dani.' He leaned over and kissed her cheek, then drew back in embarrassment. 'Sorry. I feel you may have taken a weight off my mind about Kerry. We've never been very close, we have such different interests. This could be the answer.'

'Go and talk to her,' said Dani gently. She hoped the idea of turning the house into a museum would go down well with Kerry. Families. They were never easy.

They stood quietly in Dani's studio, contemplating the textured interpretations of the landscape Dani had been experimenting with for printmaking.

'These are exquisite, Dani,' said Jason. 'How you've brought all the physical elements into the image. I'd love one of the prints when you do them.'

'Really?' Dani was pleased as he seemed to genuinely like her work. 'I've been researching more about collagraphy, it expanded from traditional printmaking like relief and intaglio printing. Flowered in the 1930s and during the Pop Art explosion in the 1950s and '60s. It's considered fine art,' she added.

'My grandfather had a printing press. He used to self-publish his legal hypotheses on how the country should be run,' said Jason. 'We might still have it and you're welcome to use it. It would need a bit of a scrub up.'

'That would be fantastic!' said Dani. 'Where would it be?'

'His old office in Cedartown was full of stuff, it was moved to the big house. Kerry would know, I'll ask her. There's a huge storage shed that even has my grandfather's old Daimler in it.'

Dani shook her head. 'Jason you've done more to support my art since I came here than anyone. I can't thank you enough.'

'I wish I could use my hands like a craftsperson,' he grinned. 'All my pictures are visions in my head of how I want the landscape to be and still nurture a community. I'll have to pick up a chisel or brush and give it a go.'

'If Birimbal and the linked village community concept

take off in other places you'll have created something really significant,' said Dani. She stopped, feeling a bit shy at the passion in her voice. 'Well, I'm thinking I should go to the beach next week, get some coastal flotsam to use in a series of sea and shore collagraphs.'

'Hey, can I come along? Might take a day off, haven't been over to the beach for ages. Can I drive you? I know some untouched beaches, maybe have lunch somewhere?'

'That'd be fun,' said Dani. 'Provided you don't mind me crawling among the rock pools and along the high-tide line.'

'I'll carry the collection bag,' said Jason. 'I'll call you to see when it suits you. Now I'd better go and hide this birthday gift. And have that talk with my sister.'

She watched Jason head down to the creek carrying the saddle and unconsciously touched her cheek where he'd kissed her. She couldn't help wondering if he was still seeing Ginny when she dropped back into Australia from her overseas jaunts.

18

Lara

IT WAS MID MORNING on a warm, sunny day and Lara was looking forward to the drive up the mountain range that provided such an enchanting backdrop to the valley. There was no great pressure to hurry back as Tim was going over to Toby and Tabatha's after school to watch Barney unveil some new 'toy' for his grandchildren. She glanced at her watch. She'd been told it took an hour to drive up the mountain. She'd have lunch and ask around and hopefully find Mr Martin Thompson, and have a chat and be back by the time Barney brought Tim home for dinner.

As Lara drove down the dirt back road out of town towards the mountain she passed a sign indicating the turnoff to the Cedartown cemetery. It was an old road lined with gum trees and she realised she'd never been there. Yet this was where her grandfather was buried. Her grandmother was buried in Maitland near Harold's sister whom she'd been visiting when she died. Lara was living overseas when her grandfather died a few years after Emily and she didn't go to his funeral. But she was so glad she'd taken baby Dani to visit him in his last years.

She turned the car along the dirt track and saw the cemetery neatly set out behind an old bush post-and-rail fence, sentinel gum trees standing guard. There was no one there, it was still and peaceful. A small sign by the gate gave a plan of the various sections, separated by religion, united by family plots.

Lara began to wander among the serried headstones and statues in the Anglican section out of curiosity, spotting family names that had become familiar to her, some she remembered from childhood as friends of her grandparents, some were well known in the town. She came across a very early section and became quite absorbed in details on the headstones of pioneers and early settlers where elaborate and simple words told of heartbreak – a child who died too young, a mother in childbirth, a young father fallen from a horse.

Before she knew it she was in a row of more recent times and then she passed a plain marker with just a name and date and nearly missed it. *Harold Williams 1878–1971*.

It hit her as if someone had slammed a fist into her belly. To see her Poppy's name like that. Unadorned, no loving phrases, no headstone, no story. And worse, in front of the granite marker, where perhaps there had once been grass or plants or some small trim around the plot, now there was only rubble and weeds. Faded plastic flowers from some place else had blown against it and Lara snatched them up and threw them away as the tears flooded from her eyes.

How could this be? She was hurt, sad, shamed.

'Oh, Poppy, I'm sorry. So sorry,' she wept, crouching down to pat the dusty black granite.

As she sat there she began to calm, the simplicity of the small head marker was probably what he would have wanted. Harold didn't like anyone to make a fuss. He was a quiet, dignified, unpretentious man. But he deserves better than this, thought Lara.

Then she said firmly, 'Poppy, I'll bring Dani to visit you and we'll spruce you up. I'm living in Cricklewood so I feel so close to you and Nana. I promise. I'll be back, soon.'

Lara, who had held back from grieving for loved ones throughout her life, suddenly felt a release of long pent-up pain. As though by suppressing the death of her stepfather, her grandparents, her mother, and now her biological father, she would somehow hold on to them. But in this quiet and peaceful place where mere symbols stood for people once loved, she felt the presence of those departed to some better place of belonging. And in letting go of those people she had held tightly in her heart, a new space opened up, and she saw how there could be a different sense of keeping close those she'd loved. A prism reflecting flashes of light, memories, pictures, emotions, moments, spun through her mind. These would never fade or be lost, and she felt the presence of her family, comforting and close.

She felt better. She began to think about ways to rejuvenate her grandfather's grave without ruining its simplicity. She looked around and studied other plots. She'd love to have growing plants but unless they were watered they'd never survive. Then she passed a Mr Bugg's grave. It was covered in a blanket of healthy lush groundcover of pointy grey-green leaves with small buds. Obviously a native that thrived here. Lara snapped off a small sprig. 'Sorry, Mr Bugg, just taking a little sample to see if the nursery can tell me what this is.'

Lara glanced back at her grandfather's resting place in the quiet corner. River stones scattered on the grave, and this plant as a border. Poppy would like that, she decided. But as she turned to walk back to the car, feeling at peace and making plans to visit every week, she stopped in shock. There was a headstone with an urn and a small plaque with a framed and fading photograph in the centre. Above it read, 'Rest in Peace', and below was a loving inscription –

Clem Wallace Richards
Brave soldier, beloved son and husband
1919–1944

And there was the same photograph of the shy, smiling soldier Phyllis had shown her. The same man she'd glimpsed as an apparition in the lounge room at Cricklewood the night she was going through the old photographs. Suddenly he was achingly familiar to her. Was this the reason she'd come back here? What had Dani started? All at once the threads of her life were coming together. Lara hoped in a few hours she'd have answers to fill in the remaining gaps.

The road took her by surprise. It was really bad. Twisting, steep and narrow, the rutted dirt had loose stones and she had no idea what she'd do if another vehicle came around one of the numerous hairpin bends. Going up she clung close to the rise of the forested mountain, coming down she'd be on the unprotected edge with a ravine dropping away with no end in sight. With the thick overhang of trees and tree ferns it would be a dark road by twilight. She'd better be on her way home before then. Lara was relieved there was blue sky, she didn't want to think what the road might be like in the wet. She drove slowly.

On the plateau the view was breathtaking. Rounded ridge tops and sharp peaks topped with foamy clouds rolled away in green waves to the horizon. The valley below was an unseen world, easily forgotten. But as she drove past farm gates and fences Lara had a sense of isolation, of a community hidden from sight. There didn't seem to be any village or any focal point of the area and Lara was bewildered as to how she was going to find anyone at all up here. Then she saw a quaint sign swinging on a board above a mail box. It was shaped like a violin and in elaborate gothic-style writing said 'Handmade Musical Instruments'.

She stopped the car and walked to the gate. A path led to a small white weatherboard cottage so she went and knocked at the door. She was about to turn away when the door was opened by a tall thin man in his sixties with thinning grey hair to his shoulders and a beaky nose.

'Morning, are you here for a lesson?' he asked peering through his rimless glasses.

'No. I was wanting directions actually.'

'You lost? Where're you headed?'

Lara gave a bright smile. 'Well, I assume I'm here, but I'm looking for someone, a Mr Martin Thompson . . .'

'Where's he live?'

'Er, that's the problem. I don't know . . . just up on the mountain. He's an old-timer so I thought locals might know him.'

'I'm not a local. Got to be born here to be a local. So how're you going to find this fella?'

'Is there a post office or shops or some place central where I could ask about him?' asked Lara.

'Have you tried the phone book? Come in and look him up in our local directory if you like.'

'Thank you.' She felt foolish. Why hadn't she thought

of that? She followed him into a house that had stained-glass window inserts, hanging chimes and glass mobiles, and furniture covered in books and piles of music. Photographs of earnest guitarists hunched over flamenco guitars and concert violinists and pianists lined the walls. In a room that obviously served as his working studio was a long table covered in bits of instruments, wood shavings and small tools. Instruments and their cases leaned against walls and sat in piles. A grand piano dominated the room though it too was almost buried beneath notebooks, sheet music and leatherbound books.

'My goodness. You seem to have a lot of work happening. You actually make instruments?'

'Repair, restore, as well as make new ones. Lot of musos up here.' He shuffled papers, uncovered a telephone on a side table and began searching for the phone book.

'Really? That's interesting. Is there a hall, somewhere for concerts?'

'Yeah. Kinda. More for the kids though. Not a lot to do on the mountain, but we manage to entertain ourselves.' He gave a hint of a smile as he handed her a small booklet of typed pages stapled together.

'I'll just see if he's listed.' She thumbed through the small population with local phone numbers, some with hippy-sounding names. No Thompsons were among them.

'No luck?' He picked up a piece of fine-grained wood in the shape of a guitar top.

'No. That's beautiful wood.' She watched him fit it then sand an edge.

'American beech. I use Aussie wood when I can get it. Need a friend in forestry to find downers – dead wood, stuff that's going to be bloody woodchipped unless someone like me uses it.'

'I have a friend in National Parks I can put you in touch with if you like.'

'Beaut. Write his number down. I'm Sagaro by the way.'

'Lara Langdon.' She wrote down Carter's number for him. 'There you go, Sagaro. That's an unusual name.'

He grinned. 'From my orange days when I was a Sanny-asin. Few of us up here. Maybe your friend has a Sannyasin name?'

'I doubt it. He's an old codger from Second World War days.' She paused. 'I wonder. Could I look at that direc-tory again, please?' It was such a local list of names it might be possible. She thumbed through it. 'Bingo! Here it is! Under Thommo. Nothing else. Eighteen, The Ease-ment, Falls Road. Where's that?'

'By Glenborough Falls. You seen them? Lot of water running at the moment.'

'No. I can see I'll have to spend some time up here. Is there a lot to see? It all seems so . . . tucked away,' said Lara.

Sagaro nodded his head vigorously. 'People like their privacy up here. The biodynamic farmers are fussy about a dog or anyone unknown setting foot on their land – bugs and such. And, well, you never know what people are farming, eh?' He grinned and put down the tool he was working with.

Lara suddenly realised the sweet musty smell in the air probably wasn't Indonesian cigarettes as she'd thought. 'Well, thanks very much, Sagaro. You've been very helpful.'

Following Sagaro's directions Lara drove towards the scenic waterfall. There was a slightly sinister under-tone to this place, she decided. She spotted a sign to the falls and was surprised to see a small general store. Aha. This must be the centre of the universe on the moun-tain, she thought. There was a petrol pump, a sign for the post office, a banner for a newspaper, a few tables and chairs under a bit of shade cloth, and a basket of fruit or vegetables of some kind with a sign on it 'Free'. Lara decided she'd call in for a coffee after visiting Thommo and before embarking on the drive back down the mountain.

The road turned into a carpark and small picnic area where the scenic walk began around the falls. Lara stopped the car and then saw a laneway on the opposite side of the road marked The Easement. She drove along it until she spotted a letterbox with the number 18 on it. There were no other farms or houses nearby that she could see. She got out of the car to open the gate, then closed it behind her and followed the grassy driveway. Tall trees – heavy pines, mountain ash and a rainforest variety she couldn't identify – screened the house from the road.

It was an old weatherboard home thickly shaded with a carpet of rotting leaves around the entrance. Lichen, like grey acne, pitted the trunks of the trees and even on a sunny afternoon the place looked moist and dank. A weeping kind of house. It would be hideously cold and miserable in winter, thought Lara. She parked, walked to the front door and rapped the knocker.

She could hear movement inside and was debating with herself about going to the back door but hesitated. She should have rung him. But then the door opened cautiously and a man peered out at her. Her immediate impression was of a man in pain. Deep furrows in his face, a downturned mouth, a pinched expression. Yet she could tell he'd been a good-looking man once. Flashes of the smiling youthful servicemen in her grandparents' photographs came to mind.

When he didn't speak but simply stared at her, Lara smiled at him.

'Mr Thompson?' He nodded briefly and Lara went on. 'My name is Lara Langdon, my grandparents were Harold and Emily Williams from Cedartown. I believe you knew them?'

'I might have,' he finally answered non-committally.

'I'm sorry to drop in out of the blue, but I was wondering if I could chat to you for a few minutes? I'm doing my family history and I thought you might be able to help me.'

'I doubt that. I keep to myself these days.' He hadn't opened the door and he was still regarding Lara suspiciously.

'I understand that. But you did grow up here and were known as Thommo, is that right?' persisted Lara. She knew she was right, there was a flicker in his eyes as he thought what to say, then he merely held the door open and stepped to one side.

'You'd better come in.'

Lara followed him down the hallway to the neat kitchen. It was a sparse bachelor's or widower's kitchen – the basics were laid out for one person. One mug beside a small teapot, one plate with a knife on it. The only incongruous item was a rifle leaning in one corner. For snakes, she assumed.

'Did you drive up here from Cedartown to see me then? I s'pose you'll want a cup of tea?'

'Tea would be lovely. Can I help?' Lara hoped he might be more forthcoming over a cup of tea. 'Yes, I came up here hoping to find you.' Some instinct told her to hold off mentioning her father Clem just yet.

He didn't say anything as he took another mug and a bigger teapot from a cupboard. 'Nothing much in the way of scones or cake. Digestive Oval biscuits okay?'

'Thank you.'

He kept his back to her as he turned on an old-fashioned electric jug and spooned tea from a Bushells tin tea caddy into the brown ceramic teapot. 'So who told you about me then?' he asked as he sat down at the little table.

'Phyllis Lane, who was Phyllis Richards.'

He nodded. 'Haven't seen her for many years.'

'She's very spry and active,' said Lara brightly. 'Has most of her family here.' She paused. 'Do you have any family up here?'

'All gone. I spent most of my life on the central coast. My mother moved there after the war when Dad was sick.'

'Was he in the war?' asked Lara.

'No. He was too old for the war. Had heart problems.'

'He ran the picture theatre in Cedartown, I believe,' prompted Lara.

'Yes.' As Lara waited for him to elaborate he gave her a hard stare. 'Why do you want to know all this old stuff?' It was a challenging question but Lara answered gently.

'I need to know where I come from. I have a lot of gaps in my immediate family history. It's time I knew what the real story is.'

'Real story? What do you mean?' He was defensive, almost aggressive. 'What's your mother told you?'

'My mother never told me anything, that's the problem. I just have names on a bit of paper. Photographs I can't identify.' Lara had them in her car but although this man probably knew more than he was letting on, he wasn't ready to identify the people in pictures as she'd hoped.

He stood up as the jug boiled and busied himself making the tea. He put the pot and a jug of milk on the table, added the sugar bowl and a plate with the flat oval biscuits arranged on it.

Lara went on. 'The main person I'm interested in is Clem Richards. As it turns out he was my father. And I don't know anything about him.'

'He's dead. Killed in Sydney in an accident.' His tone

was bitter and he sat and poured the milk and tea into their mugs.

'He'd just left my mother after being on leave. Must have been dreadful for her to lose her husband home from the war in some traffic accident and then find out she was pregnant with me.'

'Yeah. S'pose so.' He added sugar to his mug and stirred it, studying the swirl on the surface of the tea. His clinking spoon was the only sound in the room.

Lara took a breath. 'I understand you two were best mates. Grew up together, went through the war together. Must have been awful for you too.'

'War was awful. Changed people. I never got over it.'

'The war? Or Clem's death?' asked Lara.

He dropped the spoon on the tablecloth. 'Why'd you say that?' Again the defensive challenge. 'I didn't have anything to do with that. Why can't you just let things be?'

Lara was shocked she'd hit such a nerve so early in the conversation. Thommo's eyes were bright and fierce. A little scary. 'Because I want to know what he was like. I never knew my father! I never even knew he *was* my father!' Her vehement response startled them both.

'That's not my fault,' he snapped.

'So what's wrong with sharing some of your memories, reminiscences with me?' said Lara. 'At least tell me about my father. You were with him so much.' Lara meant the question to encompass their childhood, their war experiences, but Thommo seemed fixated on her father's accidental death.

'I wasn't there. He got a taxi back to the barracks. We'd been gambling up the Cross and he did his dough. Three am it was and a truck hit the taxi. The truck driver was going to the markets.' Thommo repeated this quickly as if it had happened yesterday.

Having just heard the story from Phyllis, Lara was puzzled at the discrepancies in their versions of what happened and she wished she'd asked Aunty Phyllis more about the 'incident' over the money. 'I've been told Clem Richards never gambled.'

'He had money. A whack of money.' Thommo rubbed his eyes.

'And where was the game? Why would he go there if he didn't gamble?' Lara wondered aloud.

Thommo didn't answer for a moment. 'The Cross,' he said.

Lara continued, 'So how come the accident happened near Central Railway Station if he was coming back from Kings Cross? Phyllis said he was heading to the barracks in Oxford Street, and was killed near Central, which isn't anywhere near the Cross.'

Thommo just shook his head.

Lara persisted, sensing he was holding something important back. 'And if he had no money on him, how was he going to pay for a taxi?'

'I could have paid for it.'

'Let me get this straight. Phyllis said the accident happened close to midnight because he got in on the eleven-thirty pm train. Yet you say it was three am. It sounds to me like he was killed just after he got off the train.'

At this, Thommo jumped up. 'You'll be sorry. You dig around you'll regret it. Maybe there *are* stories you shouldn't know. Don't start poking your nose in things dead and gone. Leave the past alone. Go back to Sydney, whatever you find out won't do you any good!'

Lara was stunned at this outburst. It came out of nowhere and seemed quite irrational. Then she went cold as she stared at this angry old man. 'It was you! You've been putting those letters in my mailbox!'

She expected a rebuttal, some bluster of denial but

instead he started to shake and turned away, his hands gripping the back of his chair.

'Why, why didn't you leave us alone?' he whispered shakily.

'I'm sorry. It's an issue for me . . . I didn't realise it would affect you so much,' began Lara.

'You don't understand, you don't know!' he said through clenched teeth.

'So why don't you tell me?' said Lara quietly.

He was still facing away from her breathing deeply, obviously thinking hard. He straightened and turned to face her, strangely calm. 'I've got letters, some pictures. They might help you. They're in my shed. Out the back.'

'That would be great. Thank you.'

'Come and I'll show you.' He opened the kitchen door and went through a small laundry and pointed to the aluminium shed. 'They're in there. In old biscuit tins on a shelf.' He shuffled along the path and held the door open.

'See the Arnott's tins. Help yourself.'

'Which one?' asked Lara looking at the four or five rusting square tins above some tools and jars of nails and screws.

'Lift down the red ones. I've got bad arthritis.'

Lara had a sudden flashback to her grandfather's old wooden shed at the bottom of the garden at Cricklewood and how he stored things in Arnott's biscuit tins with the distinctive label of a parrot on a perch with a cracker. She took down the top layer of tins to reach the ones with the red labels wondering what was in them. Perhaps letters and photos of Clem and Thommo as young men?

There was a clang and bang and the shed went dark.

'What's going on? Thommo?'

The door had banged shut and for a second she thought it was a gust of wind, but then she heard the scratching metallic noise of the bolt being slid in place.

She remembered seeing the padlock hanging off it. Then she remembered the rifle in the kitchen.

'Thommo! What're you doing?' Lara rattled the door and banged on it.

She shouted. There was no answer. She remembered the remoteness of this house. Shouting wouldn't help. The unreality of her predicament spun in her head. What did he hope to gain by this? Lara slumped to the cement floor in the dark shed where chinks of daylight seeped under the door and along the roof line where the walls were bolted to the roof. She'd left her bag with her phone inside the house. Probably wouldn't work up here anyway. Dear God, what was he thinking?

The shed smelled musty, with an odour of stale newspapers and rat droppings. She was trying to remember what she'd noticed when she walked in here. Nothing much, her eyes had been focused on the row of biscuit tins. She got up and began groping slowly and methodically along the bench, shelves and wall trying to identify implements. Maybe a heavy hammer or wrench would bust through the outside lock. As she felt her way she tried not to think about what might happen to her. Who would ever know where she was?

Tim had gone to Chesterfield with Toby and Tabatha after school. Lara would pick him up at about five pm. Toby's 'new toy', as Dani called it, had Tim very excited. Barney had bought Toby a second-hand power boat, a racy little 'flattie' fibreglass hull with a six-horsepower outboard engine. It looked to Tim like a shallow seagoing skateboard and he was very envious of it and Toby dressed in his helmet and lifejacket. Barney had painted it bright orange with big purple flames along the sides. It was christened *Chesterfield*, and smaller script was added on the inside of the hull: *Driver Toby Poole, Pit Crew Len James and Grandad, Sponsored by Long River Gallery*.

Now that Toby had turned nine Barney had been coaching Toby in boat handling, waterway rules and flag knowledge for the past year. In two weeks he'd enter his first big competition down the coast. This afternoon Tim was holding the stopwatch and timing Toby's laps along the river.

As the sun sank Tim helped Toby hose off the boat after Barney had towed it on the light trailer behind the tractor back to the shed where it was stored next to the hay bales. The family of guinea pigs raced backwards and forwards taking no notice. The wallaby, now hopping around, followed the boys.

Tabatha appeared and asked how Toby's times had been.

'Good. He's going to thrash those big boys,' said Tim.

'I hope so,' said Tabatha. 'Mum wants to know if you're staying for dinner, Tim.'

'No, my Ma is picking me up. What time is it?'

'After six o'clock,' said Tabatha. 'She's late.'

Tim went into Angela's kitchen where she was preparing dinner for the kids. Helen was sitting watching with a cup of coffee.

'Ma is late. Should I call Mum? Ma's never late.'

'Let's call your grandma's mobile first,' suggested Helen.

When there was no answer Helen said, 'Well, not to worry, we'll set a place for you.'

But Tim was suddenly anxious. 'She'd ring me if she was going to be late. Why doesn't she answer?'

'Lara was going up the mountain, wasn't she? I hope she's not driving down in the dark. What was she doing up there?' Angela exchanged a look with her mother.

'I dunno. Trying to find someone, I think.' Tim was

worried. 'Can we call my mum please? She's been out getting stuff for painting.'

Dani was instantly concerned. 'I'm out in the scrub, Helen. It'll take me forty-five minutes to get to your place. Keep Tim there if you don't mind. I'm not sure what to do.'

'There's no point in you driving up that dreadful road in the dark. We'll hear soon enough. Don't worry, love,' said Helen. But she didn't sound very convincing.

'I'm going back home. Keep me posted.'

Dani hung up and picked up the bag of items she'd collected to use in her collagraphy. As she was driving back to The Vale her mobile rang. She hoped it was Lara.

'Dani? This is Jason. I wanted to suggest a date to go to the beach –'

She cut him off. 'Jason, tell me about that mountain road again. My mother went up there and hasn't come back when she said. I'm a bit worried.'

Jason was immediately concerned. 'She's not driving down now, is she? When was she due back?'

'Nearly two hours ago. It's not like her. I hope she hasn't had an accident.'

'Have you checked with the police? Do you want me to call?'

'No. But I just feel I should drive up there, is there mobile reception? She'd call if there was some problem.'

'I'll check with the local cops. Reception is patchy, doubt you'd get it at all. Listen, if you're really worried I'll drive you. It's a bad road but I know it. Where are you?'

'I'll be home in about twenty minutes.'

'I'll meet you there, we can go in my four-wheel drive.'

She hoped by the time Jason turned up that she would have heard from her mother. But neither Helen and Barney nor Dani had any news.

'There's no reports of any accidents. She could have broken down, got sidetracked, who knows? And with no mobile reception, there's no way of letting you know,' said Jason striding into The Vale.

'But she'd know we'd worry. Surely she'd knock on someone's door and use the phone,' said Dani.

'Places are scattered, farms tucked away. What was she doing up there anyway?' asked Jason.

'She was going to try to find some old friend of her father's. I'm worried, Jason.'

'Get a torch and a jacket. I'll call Helen and tell her I'm driving you up. I've got a satellite phone, Helen can reach me on that.'

'Jason, you don't have to do this –'

'Nonsense. It's a hideous road, worse in the dark. And I don't think you should wander around alone up there.'

'Thank you,' said Dani gratefully, taking her jacket off the hook of the door.

In the beam of the headlights the road seemed to be barely the width of the car. A thick tangle of trees loomed from inkiness as they swept around each hairpin curve, the boulders at the edge of the road on one side, the ravine on the other, picked out in the roving flashes of the lights. Dani found she was periodically holding her breath and even though Jason was a confident driver she shuddered to think of her mother negotiating this road in daylight let alone darkness.

Jason was trying to take Dani's mind off her worries. 'So who was it your mum was looking for up here? Do you know where?'

'God, I didn't tune in too well. I haven't a clue about this bloke's name. Thommo something. He's an old bloke who knew Mum's real father. It hadn't registered with me she was just going to hop in the car and cruise around. I didn't think she had an address.'

'Who told her about him?'

'An old aunty she found. I have no idea where she is either. I've been so wrapped up in all the Isabella stuff, I didn't take in the details. I thought she was just pottering through the museum and so on. It wasn't until she told me about those letters that I took some notice.'

'Do you think Henry would know who this fellow was?'

'I'm sure of it. Can we ring him?' Dani reached for the sat phone.

Disappointed, she left a message on the Catchpoles' answering machine. 'They're out. God, what if she really found the letter man and he's a nutter?'

'The letters did sound a bit threatening. But wouldn't she have told you if she was going to see him?' asked Jason.

'I guess so. My mother can be rather impetuous. She probably thought she'd race up there, look around and hope to find him. The thing is, from her TV producing days, she's pretty good at walking into a story and finding what she wants.'

'Let's hope she didn't luck out this time,' said Jason grimly.

They didn't speak much, each wrapped in their private thoughts. They saw only two other vehicles, a ute and a kombi. When they reached the plateau, Jason slowed, trying to decide which direction to take.

'Where's the town? Village, whatever is up here?' asked Dani peering into the darkness.

'Not much here. There's a town further across, went to a nice lunch there once in a cafe craft shop thing. I seem to remember though . . .' He swung the car along the paved section of road where occasional mailboxes of various shapes, from utilitarian to artistic creations perched, the sole indication of habitation.

'There's bugger-all up here! No streetlights, no houses, nothing!' exclaimed Dani in exasperation. 'Where the hell would she have gone?'

'It's very pretty, stunning scenery in daylight,' said Jason.

Dani didn't answer, she was starting to become very frightened. The thought that her beautiful mother was out there somewhere, either in trouble or involved in some adventure or story, was driving her crazy with fear one moment, exasperation the next.

Jason was feeling frustrated at his helplessness, they couldn't just drive around in the dark. Then in the distance he saw lights. Red and green lights blinked outside a rundown house where figures lounged outside. Dim lights shone through the windows. The house looked to be one of the original cottages built on the mountain. He pulled over and as soon as they opened the car door the sound of amplified rock music assailed them.

'What's this, the local club?' commented Dani.

Jason approached several of the young men outside. 'Hi, guys. How's it going?'

'Okay,' said one warily.

'Sounds good in there. Is this the local music centre?' said Jason.

'Yeah. Kinda.' Two of the boys had guitars.

Jason went to the doorway. A band was playing with someone thrashing a set of drums. A sound console was rigged up and a girl was listening through headphones.

'You can record in there?' asked Jason looking at the dilapidated state of the house.

'Take a look if you like,' offered one of the boys as Dani joined them.

'This is kinda neat,' she said in his ear over the loud music.

The walls were covered with posters, music graffiti and a board with notes and flyers pinned to it. There were some broken-down tables and chairs, a sink and a rusting fridge.

'What goes on in here?' Jason asked a girl watching the band.

'Music, dance parties. Just a hang out,' she said.

'Who runs it?' asked Jason.

'Anyone can use it. It's always open.'

'Not locked up? What about the gear?' Dani thought how Tim would love to get onto the drums.

The girl shrugged. 'Nah. It's for all of us. If anything got knocked off, we'd find them. Not worth it.'

'You could do with a bit more gear, some better facilities,' said Jason.

'No money up here, mate,' said the girl. 'You lost?'

'We're actually looking for a lady who came up here today. Is there a local copper, someone who keeps an eye on things?' asked Jason thinking this place could be a popular drug outlet. He'd heard about the drug scene on the mountain.

'Nah, we have a few oldies on the committee. If you want to find someone go down to the general store.'

Jason and Dani exchanged a glance.

'Is it still open?'

'Yeah. If the door is shut go round the back, there's always someone hanging out,' advised the girl.

'Thanks. Where is it?'

She waved an arm. 'Two minutes down the road.'

They hurried to the car and drove slowly down the dark road.

'There . . . lights. Thank God. This place is like another planet,' said Dani.

'Civilisation!' said Jason.

There was an antiquated petrol pump. A large sign decorated with flowers and faded hippy artwork said

'General Store'. There were tables and chairs outside with several people sitting smoking, holding bottles of beer. They hurried inside. A few people were buying takeaway food, browsing through newspapers and standing around chatting.

'What can I do for you?' asked the man behind the counter.

Jason did the talking. 'We're looking for a lady who came up here today. She was looking for a local bloke . . .'

'Heard that before,' grinned the man.

'She seems to have been sidetracked,' said Jason carefully.

'That's not unusual.'

Jason turned to Dani. 'What's his name?'

'I don't know,' she said, suddenly close to tears. 'My mother is Lara Langdon, in her sixties, blonde, very pretty, warm kind of lady. Did she come in here asking directions or something?'

The man caught the note of desperation in Dani's voice and glanced at Jason. 'Can't say that rings a bell. We haven't had many tourists round today. Who was she looking for?'

Dani was aware people were coming and going. A man waited behind them to be served. 'I don't know his full name. He's an old local who's known as Thommo. She didn't know where he lived, she came on a whim, I think.'

'Did you say Thommo?' The man behind them spoke up and Dani turned to a tall thin man with a grey pony tail, beaky nose and granny glasses.

'Yes. Do you know him?' asked Dani eagerly.

'Can't say I do, but I had a lady drop into my place – I'm Sagaro. I repair musical instruments and she saw my sign. She was looking for the main part of town, which is here,' he gestured.

'So what did you tell her?' prodded Jason.

'I suggested she look in the phone book and she found him. He had an address on The Easement,' said Sagaro.

'Let's look in the phone book,' said Dani quickly.

'Where's this Easement?' asked Jason urgently.

'It winds around the backwaters of the big falls. Only a couple of houses are there.' Sagaro crinkled his eyes as he concentrated. 'Let me think, I'm pretty sure it was eighteen. Might be hard to find in the dark though.'

'Thank you so much.' Dani headed out the door.

Jason hung back a moment. 'What time do you close here?'

The shopkeeper lifted his shoulders. 'It's ten pm, depends how long that mob hang around.' He pointed to the drinkers under the awning outside.

'Listen, this fellow could be a bit of a nutcase. If we don't pop back by here in an hour or so, could you send out some sort of patrol?' asked Jason.

'No worries, mate.'

Sagaro watched them drive away and commented, 'How much trouble could some old codger be?'

Lara sat on the cold floor hugging her knees. She'd shouted, she'd cried. Now she felt drained and, while scared, resigned to waiting out this ordeal. There was no way anyone would know where she was. She just hoped Thommo would come to some sort of sense in the daylight. Or that someone else just might come within earshot – if she heard them or they her.

Jason drove slowly, the headlights on high beam.

'There! Look, number eighteen,' said Dani. 'Do we just drive up or what?'

Jason stopped the car at the entrance to the long tree-lined driveway. 'I don't think we should announce ourselves. You wait here and I'll take a look first.'

'No, I'm coming with you.'

'Dani, let's not both get into trouble. Stay here, lock the doors and if I'm not back in ten minutes or so, drive back to the store and tell them,' said Jason firmly. 'Where's the torch?'

'I suppose you're right. Be careful. Don't let anyone see your torchlight,' said Dani.

'I'll be okay. Don't worry, okay?' He squeezed her shoulder and got out of the car.

She watched him shine the torch along the driveway, shading its beam with his hand, then he turned it off and set off. Dani pushed down the locks on all the doors and sat there feeling tense and nervous. The tips of the pines swayed in a breeze, the moon was behind wet cotton clouds. She hoped it didn't rain. The whole place was creepy. She longed for the open expanse of The Vale with its paddocks, the winding clear stream and distant ranges. Being up in these peaks was strangely claustrophobic. As she strained to hear any sound through the tightly wound windows she thought she heard a bird or an animal call and in the background a steady low murmur which she realised must be the waterfall. She was trying to hear sounds far away: faint voices, a dog barking, a generator, a car, anything that gave some indication that people lived around here.

Her mind was focused on the middle and far distance, so when there was a bang on the window beside her, she let out a scream and jumped.

'Jason?'

The window was foggy from her breath in the car. She could just make out a figure and a face moving around the car. Dani scrambled across into the driver's seat, fumbling for the ignition key. She turned the engine on and the headlights flared to life. She was frozen in shock at what the lights illuminated – an old man stood there, pointing a rifle straight at her.

Shit! Should she drive at him, would he shoot through the windscreen before she hit him? Instead she punched her hand on the horn, a long loud blast.

He reacted so swiftly, the rifle must have been cocked ready to fire. A headlight was shot out and he was by the driver's door wrenching at the door handle.

'Get away!' screamed Dani, bashing at the face at the window. She threw the car into reverse and shot backwards, but then braked as she saw Jason in the beam of the one headlight lunge forward to grapple with the old man.

Dani leapt from the car and stumbled towards them. Jason had hold of the rifle in one hand and a firm grip on the man under the armpit. He seemed to have crumpled, the threat and fight scared out of him.

'He's insane. Did you see Mum?'

'I only reached the house when I heard you blow the horn, but her car's there,' panted Jason. He turned the man to face him. 'Where is Lara? Mrs Langdon?' he demanded.

'Elizabeth?' mumbled the man, twisting his face away. 'I'm sorry, so sorry.'

Jason glanced at Dani. 'Where's the lady who came to see you?' he asked.

'She doesn't know, nobody knows. All these years, no one knew 'bout Clem and me . . .'

'What's he mumbling about? Where is my mother?' snapped Dani. 'I'm going to look in his house.'

She grabbed the torch from Jason. 'Come on.' Dani ran ahead, the torchlight bobbing through the blackness as Jason, still holding the old man and the rifle, followed as best he could.

Reaching the house Dani saw one small light shining inside. She pushed open the front door and ran through the cottage shouting, 'Mum? Mum? Are you in here?'

All the rooms were empty. Dani began to shiver. Oh God, what had he done? Had he shot her? . . . Oh please no. Then she heard a noise, a banging, out the back.

She ran through the kitchen into the overgrown back-yard and saw the shed.

'Help . . . Who's out there?'

'Mum! It's me, Dani. It's all right. We're here.'

'Oh my God, thank God . . .' came Lara's relieved and weeping voice.

Dani couldn't open the padlock. 'Mum, hang on, we'll get this open.'

Lara was beyond wondering how Dani had found her. 'Thommo, the man, he has a gun . . .'

'I know, it's all right, Jason has it. He's got him. We'll get this open, hang on.'

Dani ran around the house, banging her shins against a ladder and shouted for Jason.

At first she couldn't hear or see anything. 'Jason? Where are you?' She started back down the driveway and then saw the torchlight, but only one figure. She stopped, ready to hide in the bushes until she saw it was Jason.

'Jason, what happened? Where is he?'

'Cunning old bastard, somehow he gave me the slip, I couldn't see him in the dark, but he can't get too far.'

'The gun, where is it?'

'I have it. Is your mum there?'

'Yes, yes, she is. She's locked in a shed. I can't get the padlock open.'

Lara stood at the back of the shed, her hands over her ears as Jason shot off the padlock and then she fell out into her daughter's arms.

Weeping, they both kissed Jason as he led them back inside, turning on lights in the kitchen.

'We'd better go and find that crazy old bugger,' said Jason.

'Jason, Mum is safe, let's just get out of here,' said Dani. 'This place gives me the creeps.'

'No. I haven't come through all this not to know what the hell is going on with him,' declared Lara. 'Where did he go?'

'There must have been a track he knew about. He just wrenched himself free, shoved me to one side and disappeared in the undergrowth,' said Jason.

'Right, let's find him,' said Lara. 'We've got the rifle, what harm can he do to us?'

Jason retraced his steps. 'I think it was around here.' He waved the flashlight.

'There, a track,' said Dani pointing to the one-person path winding through the thick scrub.

They followed it single file, no one speaking for the rushing and roar of the waterfall could now be heard clearly. The trees thinned and there was a grassy patch with several large boulders, beyond it a shining pool of water.

'Must be the headwaters where it comes down from the hill,' said Jason waving the torch back and forwards.

'Be a lovely swimming spot in summer,' commented Lara.

'Is that a path at the edge?' asked Dani. It was easier to see without the overhang of trees.

'Yes, it must go to the falls, there's a lookout somewhere, I recall,' said Jason.

'Let's not go near the edge,' said Lara. 'Heights worry me.'

Dani was more concerned that the crazed Thommo was hiding and would rush at them, pushing them into the flowing water.

They followed the path until it branched into a clearing with a picnic seat and steps leading up to an area that appeared to be a parking lot. From there steps and a paved track wound away towards the signposted lookout.

'This goes for some distance so you look across the gorge at the falls from the opposite side. I think there's a side view near here too,' said Jason in a low voice.

'You go, I'm staying here,' said Lara.

'We're not leaving you, Mum,' said Dani.

'I'll be fine. Leave the rifle with me then.' She was half joking, but Jason handed it to her. 'We won't be long. Fire it in the air if you need us.' He showed her the safety catch.

'I know how to use this,' said Lara calmly, startling Dani, who filed her question 'How come?' away for a future conversation.

Jason reached for Dani's hand and led her along the path, shining the torch behind him so that she could see and he had enough light to also see where he was stepping.

'Your mum seems to be coping well after that ordeal,' he said.

'Yeah, she's full of surprises. Thanks for helping us, Jason, I don't know what I would have done without you.'

He didn't answer but squeezed her hand. The sound of the rushing wall of water was increasing.

Lara wasn't really coping, she was feeling numb. The hours since her long drive up the mountain were blunted by the stark shock of the expression in Thommo's eyes. What was he so afraid of, so frightened of he'd been prepared to harm her. Or was he? Had he acted out of panic, or had it been premeditated? He couldn't have known she was going to come up here and find him, it had been an impulse on her part. But somehow he had known what she'd been doing, who she'd been talking to, knew enough of her activities in Cedartown to leave the notes at timely moments. It occurred to her that perhaps the old soldier was more afraid of her than she was of him.

Lara got up. The pale moon had shed the filter of clouds and gave a shimmer of light. Slowly she picked her way back to the rock-strewn water and looked upstream to the thick overhang of trees and the deeper pool, and then downstream to where ripples of shallow white water were beginning to trail on the surface. She imagined throwing a stick into the water – it would spin and swirl along until it easily slid over the glassy edge of water to dance in the white rushing curtain before splintering on the sharp rocks in the deep gorge below.

Cautiously she moved along the barely discernible track that only animals and intrepid kids had trampled. She watched where she was stepping until she paused and saw up ahead a chain with a small sign swinging from it. 'Do not proceed past this point,' she read.

It would be too easy to duck underneath and slip into the water. How many kids had dared each other to cross this line? She remembered the radio report of the young man who'd been found dead in the gorge when she'd first driven up here. Drugs, foul play, or a seemingly simple solution to overwhelming problems?

As she stood there, the rifle slung on her shoulder, she knew she wasn't alone. On the other side of the chain, under the heavy branch of a tree, stood Thommo. His back was to her and he was gazing at the ribbon of water that was swiftly spinning to the abyss and oblivion. There was something about the hunch of his shoulders, the droop of his head.

'Thommo!' she shouted. But he didn't hear her above the rushing water. Lara ducked under the chain and went towards him. She didn't want to frighten him, so she picked up a small stone and flicked it against his back.

He swung around and saw her standing there.

Lara lifted an arm and waved at him to come towards her. Although she was holding a rifle, it wasn't a threatening gesture. She called him to her again.

He lowered his gaze and simply stood there, and Lara had the impression the old man was crying. She went to him, touched his arm and gently tugged him back along the path.

He followed meekly and when they reached the picnic seat he slumped and Lara sat beside him.

'I wasn't going to hurt you,' he mumbled.

'Why'd you do that? What are you doing here?'

'Figured it'd be best to do away with m'self. Couldn't face it. After all these years.'

'Well, I'm glad you didn't. Who'd you think was going to find me?' said Lara briskly. He wasn't to know no one knew where she'd gone. Then more gently she asked, 'Why did you leave the notes? How did you know what I was doing?'

'Historical society. I usually go in there every Tuesday as a volunteer. Saw you in there, heard them talking about you. Had 'em all looking for stuff.'

'Well, they didn't find anything of much use. What's the real story, Thommo? The truth?'

He didn't answer but sat there twisting his hands.

'I need to know. It's really important to me,' said Lara.

He straightened. 'Me and Clem went through good times and bad times. We were mates. I don't know why I did it, but then it was done. In a minute I ruined all our lives. His family, your mum, her family, buggered them up. And I was too much of a coward to say.'

Lara began to realise the enormity of the weight of guilt this man had carried for years. 'What did you do, Thommo?'

'I took the money. From Elizabeth's desk. I met Clem in the office then Clem stepped out to see someone in the street, Elizabeth was in the lav. I needed the money. I gambled, I had people after me.' The words rushed out. 'I was going to square it with them, I swear I was. Then Clem got killed . . .' he winced, the pain still as fresh as the night it happened.

Lara was struggling to take this in. 'So Clem never went gambling with you that night? He never took that money? And when he died no one would ever know what you did. Even Clem.'

'I reckon he knows all right. Never forgive me for it. I get punished every day of my life.'

'You don't think if you'd told what you'd done, come clean about it after it happened, that things would have been better?' asked Lara, trying not to sound accusing.

'I was scared, love. I didn't have any money. I was in trouble. And I was sick in the head, I reckon. From the war. We was all different after that. Clem too.'

Lara drew a deep breath. 'So what did you do?'

'My father was sick and my mum moved down the coast, I went and lived near there. Haven't had much of a life. Never married, no kids . . . serves me right, I s'pose.' He lifted his chin. 'I gave the Williamses some money but. Saved up and dropped it in their letterbox years later. Harold was a good bloke. Musta been hard for them.'

Lara was silent. Her poor mother. The years she'd slaved away to repay the money that Thommo had stolen. The accusations against her husband, the struggle to raise her daughter on her own. The shame and struggle of her grandparents. She felt a flash of anger, but, looking at this pathetic man, it subsided.

'What're you gonna do?' he said. 'I couldn't live with people knowing. I had to live with meself every day. I'll go away.'

561

'I see why you never mixed with anyone from the old days. I thought it strange you didn't see Clem's sister Phyllis.'

'She was a nice little kid. All Clem's family were. Good people. Even if your mum's lot didn't think so. I guaranteed that.' His shoulders started to shake. 'Jeez, Clem, mate . . . I'm sorry . . .'

'Mum, Mum, you along there?' Dani's piercing voice echoed along the path.

'Yes. We're here,' Lara shouted back.

Jason and Dani ran towards them but slowed as they saw Lara and Thommo sitting quietly.

'You all right, Mum?' Dani dropped a protective arm around her shoulders. Jason took the rifle.

'Yes, this is Thommo. An old friend of my father's. He panicked a bit, didn't mean any harm,' said Lara.

'Didn't mean any harm!' exclaimed Dani, but stopped as Lara gave her a shut-up gesture.

'What do you want to do, Lara?' asked Jason.

'Go home,' she answered in a tired voice. 'Call Tim, they must be worried.'

Lara stood up and they prepared to walk away. Thommo didn't move.

'You can't stay here. Come back with us,' said Lara.

'Leave me be. I'll be along shortly.' He sounded calmer, if drained, after unloading the guilt of sixty-odd years.

Dani started walking quickly away. 'Tim, Barney and Helen must be frantic.'

Jason gave Lara a querying look as she stood gazing down at the old man.

Lara briefly touched his bony shoulder. 'Thank you.'

Jason followed Lara, Dani was racing ahead now she could see by the moon.

'So was this excursion worth it?' asked Jason.

'For me, or him?' Lara was still sifting through thoughts

and feelings. 'It's all a bit late, the damage has been done. I feel so badly for my mother. But it's in the past. I can't restore my father's good name. It's crippled Thommo's life. What good does it do to tell anyone? Besides, there's no one to tell.'

The hurt in her voice touched Jason. 'It sounds like you've got a lot of sorting out to do, and things to share with Dani and Tim. There are always unanswered questions. Why people did what they did. We find out stuff too late. Tim will want to know later when he's interested in family matters.'

'You're right. Maybe I should write it all down,' sighed Lara.

They reached the main track back to the house and Jason dropped his arm around her shoulders. 'Dani once mentioned you wanted to write a book. Maybe this is it.'

Lara almost smiled. 'Truth being stranger than fiction? We'll see. Oh my God, what's going on?'

In the driveway at Thommo's house there was a fire truck and a knot of people. Dani raced to them. Sagaro stepped forward.

'You said to send out the patrol if you didn't get back. Here we are. The house is empty. Did you find your mother?'

'That's her. We went to the falls,' said Dani lamely.

'So all's well?' asked Sagaro.

'Thanks, mate,' said Jason, shaking his hand. 'Bit of drama but it's all okay. I think.'

Dani raced to the car and grabbed her mobile. 'Damn, there's no reception. I'll use the phone in the house.'

'This is Lara,' said Jason.

'We've met,' grinned Sagaro. 'And just as well I remembered who you were looking for.'

'Thanks so much,' said Lara.

'Is the bar still open down at the store?' asked Jason.

'Must be, we're all here, left the joint open,' said Sagaro.

'My shout,' said Jason. 'For everyone.' He looked around at the young men leaning against a wildly painted kombi van; the storekeeper, a big bloke with a beard and tattoos astride his motorbike; and the effete-looking Sagaro.

'See you there.'

Lara's car was parked around the back of Thommo's house and so she followed Jason and Dani to the store where party lights strung in a tree had been turned on and a man was playing a guitar.

'It's a party!' laughed Jason.

'Poor Mum, she's had a big day. It's nearly one am,' said Dani.

As drinks were poured, Dani clinked glasses with Jason. 'Thanks. You were right, it's another world up here. But I don't fancy that drive down the mountain.'

'You can't do that,' said Sagaro. 'Against the law to drink and drive. We'll rustle up a couple of beds, no worries. Cheers.'

Jason and Dani smiled at each other as Sagaro pulled the cork on a bottle of red. 'They have their own laws up here,' said Jason.

Much later at Sagaro's house Lara slept in a room full of violins, a cello and a viola. Helen had asked what she had found out, but Lara had pleaded exhaustion. She fell asleep but woke at dawn. Dani and Jason had been put up at the back of the general store where the storekeeper kept a couple of spare rooms. 'People crash here a lot,' he explained.

Lara tiptoed outside, slipped behind the wheel of her car and drove slowly to Thommo's house.

All was quiet. The shed door was shut. She opened the kitchen door and stepped inside. The rifle was in its place, the tea and biscuits Thommo had made her were still on the table. A cold shiver went down her back as she walked through the little house. She'd left him feeling vulnerable and guilty. Should she have stayed with him? No, she wasn't going to be responsible for his life. Lara paused at the closed door to a bedroom. Quietly she turned the handle and looked inside.

Thommo was lying on his side on his bed, fully clothed. He'd kicked off his shoes and Lara had a sudden urge to straighten them. She stared at him wondering if he was alive or dead, too afraid to step inside. Then she saw the rhythmic lifting of his chest and an occasional wheezy breath. She closed the door and left the house.

Breakfast at the general store of hamburgers in homemade bread was a subdued affair. Several people from the night before were still there and others had turned up for an early feed to help their hangovers.

Jason and Dani followed Lara down the mountain. Halfway down, as they rounded a bend, through the trees they saw the valley and the river spread before them glistening in the sun.

'Looks like home to me,' said Jason.

'Me too,' agreed Dani. She tried to imagine herself back in the city. Like the mountain, Sydney seemed a strange planet she'd once inhabited but she couldn't see herself settling there again. Had her mother settled her family ghosts and would she now return to her pretty suburban home? Who knew. The valley had changed their lives.

19

Cedartown, 1948

THE WINTER SUN WARMED the air and glittered on the creek as Emily and Lara walked slowly towards Isabella Street. Harold watched from the railway yards, pleased to see Emily and the toddler Lara enjoying the fresh air and sunshine. What a difference the little girl made to their lives. Sweet natured, happy and curious, she was an absolute joy.

Elizabeth made the trip home to her little girl every holiday, even though the trains were uncomfortably crowded. She always found Lara warm and affectionate towards her, but when unsure of anything she ran to hide behind Emily's skirt and clutch her hand.

It was on one of these trips home that Elizabeth met up again with an acquaintance of her teenage years, Charlie. Charlie was a good-looking lad who had lived across the valley. As a youth he seemed to be rather shy, and of course he didn't ask the popular Elizabeth for a dance or an outing once she'd become known as Clem Richards' girl. She'd always known him as just one of the gang of local boys, and had sent him cheerful letters about home-town doings when he was away at the war. It was a duty of the local girls to write to several of the boys. Charlie had been a POW in Changi and had come back to Cedartown to recuperate. He'd worked in the local sawmill and driven a milk truck, but was now planning to move to Sydney to try his luck. Several of his army mates had great dreams and schemes for cashing in on the postwar building and industrial boom, and he thought he might throw his lot in with one of them. Plenty of jobs for willing workers, he told Elizabeth.

A chance meeting where he'd thanked her for her letters – though he got them all at once after he'd got home from Singapore – had led to them sharing their feelings and frustrations of those years, and some of the difficulties of postwar life. It led to a whirlwind romance and when Charlie travelled to Melbourne to see her they were convinced they had to be together, and they decided to move to Sydney.

Emily was not pleased. While she and Harold liked Charlie, considering him a solid and reliable lad, he was still unsettled and had no definite prospects. Elizabeth had to work, as she was still reimbursing her father and George Forde, but what upset Emily most was hearing that Elizabeth planned to take Lara to live with her in Sydney. Not only had Emily become devoted to her granddaughter but she did not approve of Elizabeth and Charlie gadding off to Sydney, unwed, with a young child and no firm plans.

She and Elizabeth argued time and again in the kitchen after tea, while Charlie and Harold smoked in the darkness of the front verandah. Charlie was firm about their marriage plans and long-term future.

'I want to do right by her and the little one, Harold. I want to have a good job, some money behind me, so we can build a good life in the big smoke. That's where it's all happening these days,' he said.

Harold had no doubt Elizabeth was the one pushing Charlie along, but said quietly, 'You're a good man. I know you'll do the right thing, but it's a lot to take on.'

'Lara is a good little kid. She didn't know her real father so the sooner she gets used to having me around the better, eh?'

Harold finally succeeded in persuading Emily to let Elizabeth and Lara go without too much fuss.

'They have to make their way in the world as a family at some stage. Little Lara needs to know her mother. With Charlie looking out for them, they'll be all right.'

'How's she going to work and look after her?' demanded Emily. 'And when will we see her? We'll miss her growing up.'

'I think you'll be surprised how often little Lara will be here to stay with us,' said Harold. 'Elizabeth has always been resourceful. She'll manage.'

And so she did. Lara had blurred memories of living in the middle of a big city. She remembered a fish and chip shop and a smiling lady who gave her long, hot chips in a cone of newspaper. She remembered an organised play-group with children who were very different from her country friends. They spoke to her with strange accents, and to each other in strange languages.

Lara remembered a man coming to take a photograph one day in the tiny yard behind the shop which they lived above. A blanket was hung over the back fence of the narrow rear lane as a backdrop. Wearing a good dress and a bow in her hair she posed sitting in a small cane chair. It was not a happy picture. She remembered hating having to get dressed up for the event.

When she was older her family moved to the fringe of the city, to bush and trees and a bay. Perhaps the memories of her happy years there helped her feel so at home in the valley now.

Lara

Lara watched Aunty Phyllis make her way into the large glass foyer of the fancy-looking RSL club in Hungerford. She stopped her walker every few yards to greet people, including the staff, who all had a smile and a hello for the spry, white-haired lady.

'The food is good here, but let's go into the lounge and have a drink first, shall we?' said Phyllis heading towards the airy room with a bar and a poker machine annex.

Lara smiled in agreement, rather amused and hoping that at Phyllis's age she'd be out meeting friends, playing cards, going on trips, doing all the things that kept Phyllis active, busy and alert.

Settled in a corner overlooking the extensive gardens with light ales on the table, far from the large screen television and bar, Phyllis took a sip of her drink and asked, 'So dear? What did you find out from Thommo? I haven't spoken to him for fifty years or more. Disappeared after Clem died and although I heard he'd moved back to the district, I believe he's something of a recluse. I always thought about looking him up, but never got around to it. How was he?'

Lara chose her words carefully. 'At first, he was very withdrawn. Suspicious. I suppose I caught him by surprise. And he wasn't very forthcoming. Now, I understand why. It was something of a traumatic evening to say the least! Cathartic though.'

'My goodness. What did he have to say?' Phyllis gave her a penetrating look, sensing Lara was holding something back.

Lara put down her glass and wondered where to start. Slowly at first and then with more passion, she repeated the story of the night Phyllis's brother died as Thommo had told her. She revealed nothing about her tense confrontation with the old man.

Phyllis stared at Lara, her pale blue eyes filling with tears. She reached for her handbag and began fishing for her handkerchief. 'Oh my, after all this time. Poor, poor Clem. My darling brother, I always felt in my bones he couldn't have stolen that money. He was such a decent chap. I'm so glad to know this. Shame on Thommo, shame on him.' She took off her glasses and dabbed at her eyes. 'Well, at least Clem never knew how his best friend deceived him.'

'Thommo has lived with the guilt, pain, anxiety all his life,' said Lara. 'He's punished himself every day.'

'Why didn't he say something sooner?' demanded Phyllis. 'It would have been so much easier for us all.'

'He was terrified of being found out. Not just because it was a crime, but of losing face, letting everyone down. He really can't justify his actions and it's eaten away at him so badly, I think he became a bit unhinged,' said Lara. 'Now it's out I think he's relieved. But very scared of what might happen. I don't think he could face anyone, especially you.'

'So it was just an impulsive act because he gambled and needed money so badly,' said Phyllis thoughtfully. 'Shocking to think how that one wicked incident scarred so many people's lives. Our family, your mother and grandparents, your childhood. All the people in town who liked and respected Clem felt cheated. Even Thommo's parents must have been surprised that Clem could do such a thing.' She shook her head. 'All these years and now it's too late to set the record straight for them.'

'He must think about that every day too,' said Lara, suddenly realising how far the ripples of that one act had spread to affect others.

'So how did you feel hearing the truth? After what I told you about your father dying under a cloud,' said Phyllis, discreetly blowing her nose.

'Sad, terribly sad. For my mother especially, who never knew the truth and must have always blamed herself for his death because she pushed him so much about moving to Sydney. And she obviously never asked any questions about the circumstances of his accident.' Lara sighed. 'And I feel angry. That you're the only person left who knows the truth about my father being misjudged all these years.'

Phyllis nodded and took another sip of her drink and tucked the handkerchief in a pocket of her smart red jacket. 'Well, I'll make sure the rest of the family know. But really, dear, as time has gone on, it will be lovely to set the record straight,' sighed Phyllis.

'The rest of the family? You mean your daughter? And my daughter too of course.' Lara wondered if this might be an opportunity to remind Phyllis how much knowing about one's family meant. She thought of Barbara, Phyllis's first child from the brief relationship she had before she married Cyril and which she never talked about. 'It means a lot to know one's family history. Good and bad. It's not a matter of passing judgment or criticising people for something that happened at a different time. It's just needing to know the truth.'

Lara waited for this to sink in, but Phyllis let it pass. She had no idea that Lara knew the story of her daughter and she showed no flicker or any pang of guilt or hidden knowledge but sailed on with the conversation. Wily old bird, thought Lara. But then she suddenly fully understood what Phyllis was implying.

'Not just our children. The rest of the Richards clan,' explained Phyllis. 'Kevin and Keith, sadly passed on now, but each had five children, so they're your cousins. They all have kids as well. You've got dozens of cousins and relatives scattered here and there, Lara, dear.'

'Where are they?' She'd been so focused on her father she hadn't given his family much thought. 'Do they know about me?'

Phyllis hesitated. 'To be truthful, I'm not sure. Keith and Kevin knew about Elizabeth's pregnancy. I think it hurt my mother very much that she never got to see you.'

'My grandmother, I suppose,' said Lara, thinking back to the feisty and protective Emily. Sudden flashes of her grand-mother's pursed lips and comments like, 'We don't talk about that, dear. Some things are best forgotten,' came to mind.

'I doubt the boys' children know about you. Would you like to meet them? I'm in touch with most of them. Sometimes Patrick and Kev Junior and the girls pop in to see me when they're up this way. They take me out to see Mum and Dad. They're buried together out at the coast where they retired. Old Sand cemetery,' she added in explanation as Lara looked confused.

'I hadn't really considered the possibility of finding a whole family network when I started on this journey,' said Lara. 'I need time to think about this. They might not want to know me anyway as the families didn't get on.'

'Nonsense. They don't care about the old days. You have every right to look them up. You'll like them. And they'll love you. And your daughter, I'm sure. She's got loads of second cousins too.' Phyllis patted Lara's hand. 'You talk it over with your daughter. Shall we order lunch?'

*

'It's your call, Mum,' said Dani after hearing the story from Lara. 'I'm happy to meet them but we're all busy with our own lives and maybe some lost relative turning up is only of passing interest. We probably haven't anything in common even if their kids are my age.' But seeing Lara's expression of some longing, she said more gently. 'But their parents, the children of Clem's brothers, maybe you should contact them. They might have some good stories about their Uncle Clem.'

'I'll see,' said Lara. 'We have enough going on at present. Barney wants us to go over to Chesterfield early tomorrow morning. Really early, and have breakfast, and he'll take the kids to school.'

'You mean like sunrise? What for?'

'A little ceremony with Max. Just to acknowledge what Barney's found out about his family,' said Lara.

'Maybe that's what you need to do, Mum. Have a little ceremony,' suggested Dani. She gave her mother a hug. 'Let's finish tidying up your grandfather's grave. You can tell Poppy about Clem.'

'Carter has found the most beautiful piece of wood in the forest. Like a sculpture. I'm going to ask him if he'll cement it next to Poppy's grave.' Lara got up feeling better. 'I'll see you at Chesterfield tomorrow morning.'

As Dani and a sleepy Tim drove along the dirt road from The Vale on Monday morning, a delicate mist was clinging to the damp grass of the hillsides. The creek was just a silvery band glimpsed through wraith-like trails of chiffon or tulle, thought Dani. Some paddocks smelled sweetly of ploughed earth. The first birdcalls echoed across the valley.

How comfortable she felt here. She woke each morning with images and ideas sparking in her mind and grabbed her cup of tea and hurried into the studio. How different to waking and dreading going into the office that had been her life for so long.

She was doing more things with Tim. He loved what he considered his independence, living part time in town with his grandmother, having his own circle of friends and activities. But The Vale was home. 'Home,' he told Dani, 'is where my pony is.' Even though he didn't own the pony, Jason had made him feel that Blackie belonged to him and allowed him to now keep it at The Vale.

Because of Tim's enthusiasm, his father Jeff had agreed to come and see Tim compete in his next riding event. Dani suggested Jeff stay at The Vale with Tim while she took a trip to Sydney. A hit of city life and friends wouldn't go astray. Lara wanted her to check on the state of her house and garden. And Dani still had some unanswered questions about the fate of Isabella.

Lara too was out early. She drove through the sleeping town, over the old railway bridge, towards Riverwood. In the pre-dawn morning stillness gum trees arched proudly over fences and the road, layers of bark protectively hugging their silky trunks. Such dignity, she thought, taking in the variety of tranquil green curtains. In the very early light they seemed almost delicate. Yet they weather storms, they hold tight, remaining rooted in the land that nurtures them. It seemed to Lara that if only one's life, one's family, could be assured of such belonging – open to the sky, the elements, other creatures, bending and surviving harsh conditions but always reaching upwards.

The mist had lifted from the dewy grass and the clouds had risen to the top of the ridges. Lara recalled so vividly the dripping leaves and damp air of that grey morning on the mountain. She wondered if she'd ever see Thommo again. She did not plan to go to the strange mountain village any time soon. Dani had said she might go up there with Jason as he'd given money to the locals to help improve the odd little house that was the music hang-out for the young people. It was a nice gesture though Jason claimed it was just to say thanks for helping them out on that scary night.

What good friends they had in this community, how full and happy was her life here, as was that of her daughter and grandson. Lara loved her home in Sydney but it couldn't offer what she had here. And when the Clerks came back to Cricklewood from their round-Australia trip, where would she stay?

Maybe she should look into buying a little holiday cottage here in the valley, mused Lara. Jason's villas and homes in the linked villages would do extremely well, she thought, perhaps she should buy one.

She passed a farmer driving fresh produce into town and they exchanged friendly waves. Soon she drove over the hill into Riverwood, the majestic river that wound through the valley as breathtaking as ever.

As she went down the driveway to Chesterfield, Ratso raced out to bark a welcome. Max was standing on the verandah with Len and Julian in their school uniforms. Toby and Tabatha hurried across the lawn as Lara pulled up.

'C'mon, Lara, we have to do this before the sunrise,' they called.

She followed them around to the front of the main house where Max's wife Sarah, Barney and Helen, Angela and Tony, Dani, Tim and Jolly were gathered by the old flagpole on the lawn. Barney gave her a hug as Max and his two children followed.

'Thanks for coming, Lara. This is just a little flag ceremony but I wanted you guys to be here.'

Lara looked at the folded flag ready to be raised. 'The Aboriginal flag! Barney, how lovely,' she exclaimed.

They stood in a circle and watched Max, carrying his didgeridoo, move next to Barney at the flagpole.

Max gazed across the lawn to the river, the floodplain, the paddocks and hills in the pearly light where the gold of the sun was beginning to show. In his soft and gentle voice he began: 'This land has seen my people gather here for millennia. To hunt and feast, to sing and for ceremony. It has always been a bountiful place, a beautiful place, though it has seen its share of sadness too. It is a land rich in Dreaming. Ancient spirits of the earth creator live here and we are privileged to be custodians of this heritage. The old people have gone, but for those of us who've returned it makes my heart glad to see the land being cared for and respected by Barney, and Helen.' He paused and smiled at Barney and held out his hand. 'Welcome home, brother. There are ancient memories here, hold them safe.'

Barney, tears in his eyes, gave Max a brief embrace. Turning to the flagpole Barney took the ropes in his hand and said solemnly, 'I will respect this place, this country, the people who first knew this valley. From my people, to my people.' He touched his heart and then gestured towards his grandchildren, Toby and Tabatha.

Max lowered his head to the didgeridoo. The haunting sound wailed across the valley, as beautiful as birdsong, as powerful as a waterfall, a sad call to memory, a throbbing promise to the future.

Slowly Barney raised the black, red and gold flag, as Angela proudly beat a rhythm with two clapsticks she'd brought with her. Everyone joined hands and they all had tears in their eyes. The dogs sat quietly, perhaps respecting the presence of beings and creatures they could sense and feel but could not see.

At the top of the flagpole a breeze, as if freed by the first light of dawn, blew the flag out full and strong. They all gazed up at the triumphantly waving flag as the final notes of the ancient instrument rolled over the river.

Suddenly Ratso took off after a wild rabbit and the spell was broken. Hands wiped away tears and Lara and Dani gave Barney a hug.

'Breakfast on the verandah,' announced Helen. 'Then kids to school!'

Cedartown, 1954

Emily took the strand of white carved ivory beads from the little green jar, its lid topped by the figure of a clown, which sat on her dressing table. She clasped them round her neck to dress up her simple button-through, flowered cotton dress. Despite the heat she wore nylons, a girdle and white shoes with a solid small heel and straw hat. Picking up her handbag she went out onto the back verandah.

'I'll be off then, Harold.'

'Righto, love.' He put down the spade and went to the back steps, took off his gardening hat and gave her a kiss. 'Say hello to the ladies for me.'

'I'll do that. All of them,' she chuckled.

Emily went to the front gate where Mrs Glossop from the CWA was waiting in her car. They drove out of town towards Hungerford then veered along the old road to Planters Field. The scattering of fringe dwellers' homes looked so temporary – yet it had been this way for years. The Aboriginal mission settlement, known as the blacks' camp, was considered an eyesore, largely ignored by the whites of the region. The white manager and his wife were unable to improve conditions because of the lack of funds.

Some months before at a Country Women's Association meeting in Cedartown a light-skinned Aboriginal woman from Planters Field was introduced as Margaret James. She stood up and asked the ladies if they could help her get something going for the women and kids at the settlement. She surprised the members with her request and also by the fact that she was so well spoken and, as they commented over a cup of tea afterwards, seemed to be 'just like one of us'.

'Why not bake some cakes and sell them at our fete to raise some money for your community?' was one suggestion.

Margaret James stared at the well-meaning lady. 'We have no stoves in our houses, which is why we have to cook over an open hearth fire or use a camp oven,' she explained.

'Your homes have no stoves!' The ladies were shocked. And so a small group made improving the lot of the families at Planters Field a priority. Emily was one of the first to join the little committee.

'And you know, Harold, most of their little houses are very clean and tidy,' said Emily to her husband after her first visit.

Every three weeks Emily and the other volunteers visited the community where they met with Margaret James who gathered together the other women to listen to the wisdom of the white ladies. How to clean sores, treat simple wounds, make wholesome meals, bathe babies.

Emily hoped they were making some inroads, despite the lack of facilities. Over time Margaret, with her deeply wrinkled olive skin, and Emily, still proud of her fair English complexion, became friends.

Emily told her, 'I always believed England was home. Until I took my two little girls back for a trip after coming here as a bride. Back there, I started to miss things. The birds, raucous and loud, not like the sweet trills of English birds. The bush. Our town. And I realised this was my home. So when I had a chance to do this . . . I thought I should,' she finished lamely, unable to put into words her deep and confused feelings. Emily had begun to understand more clearly just how much misery and deprivation these families faced, rejected by the whites and struggling to survive.

'Most of the old ways are gone, Mrs Williams,' sighed Margaret James. 'I worry about our kids' future. Not many opportunities for them in the white man's world.'

'What happened to your family?' asked Emily tentatively. She hadn't thought it polite to enquire about her friend's personal life.

'Before I married Russell James I was raised in a mission. I had a brother but we were sent to different schools and I've lost touch with him. He was sent out west somewhere. But I went back to the orphanage and I managed to find out where my family came from. So I came back here. My great-grandfather was a white man who took up with a black girl. She was murdered with her baby. Their boy was my grandfather. My mother died when I was quite young and one day the Protection Board officer came round and nabbed me, took me away in a truck and I never saw my family again. But now, at least, I know their story.'

'My goodness,' said Emily. 'So your family has always been in this district?'

'Yes, indeed. Their name was Holmes. Grandad was called Kelly. There's a creek named for him. But it's a bad spirit place.' Margaret turned away. 'People in this town don't know what the proper story, proper history is round here.'

It was never mentioned again, but some nights, sitting by the fire at Cricklewood, Emily and Harold occasionally discussed the great divide between the people of their town: those from the wealthier families who saw themselves as the social elite, the middle class, the poor and the occasionally glimpsed people from the blacks' camp.

'Do you ever think things will change? That people will realise we're really all God's children under the sun?' mused Emily. 'Next time little Lara comes for holidays I'm going to take her out there to meet Mrs James. She's a very interesting lady. And she knows some legends and stories from her people. I'm sure Lara would enjoy hearing them.'

'You do that, dear,' said Harold, proud of his English rose who'd bloomed and flourished so strongly in this tough Australian sun.

Lara

Late each morning Lara settled on the front verandah at Cricklewood with her pot of tea and either a book or the newspaper. More often than not she simply sat there, sipping her tea, enjoying the sun and the breeze that came from the river.

This morning, after the moving flag-raising ceremony at Chesterfield, the newspaper lay unopened as she watched the postie putt-putt her way down the road on her motor scooter. She stopped outside Cricklewood and Lara walked to the gate where they exchanged chitchat about the weather, and the fish she'd caught on the weekend. She then shuffled the letters in her hand and gave Lara three.

'One from the Clerks. WA postmark, they are getting around, aren't they,' said the postie.

'Yes, a big trip. I'll be a bit sorry when they get back here. I might have to find a place of my own to buy,' said Lara.

'I'll keep my eyes open for you then, Lara. I get to hear

what's what around here. Hooroo, see you soon.' She continued down the street as Lara returned to the verandah thinking the postie probably did know everyone's business and might well hear of a house for sale.

She tore open the Clerks' letter, posted from Broome. Kristian Clerk had written in part:

> We are still enjoying our journey, what a magnificent country this is. It would take several big trips to see it all. Which we well may do in the coming years. I hope all is well back there, Dick asks if the orange trees are bearing well. Now, we wanted you to know that there has been a change in our plans for the future. Dick's mother has died in Holland and left us her house. We are considering moving back there to live to be near family and to come out to Australia and travel perhaps each year or so. Which means we would, sadly, have to sell Cricklewood.
>
> There is no rush, but if we do, Dick thought, because of your family attachment, you might be interested or your daughter might want to buy it. Think it over and let us know. I have attached the rest of our itinerary . . .

Lara's hand started to shake as she looked around her at the old red bricks warming in the sun that her grandfather had helped put in place. Her grandparents' hands were everywhere about this house and garden. Her mother had grown up here, as had Lara. It held so many memories. The thought of having the house back in the family was wonderful.

Of course she'd buy it. She'd still like to keep her place in Sydney, it was a great investment and useful for her and Dani to have a bolthole in the city.

Lara immediately began thinking of some improvements

she'd make, without doing anything to change the façade of the house. But she could extend the back verandah and make it a huge family room. There was room in the back-yard to add a lap pool, the summers were killers in the valley. So air conditioning would be a must. Her mind whirled on, imagining her books and paintings and rugs in the old house.

Her tea was cold before she glanced at the other letters and she caught her breath recognising the handwriting on the envelope. But this time Thommo had posted the letter from the mountain.

Dear Lara, if I may call you so . . . I have no excuses only regrets for what has happened, recently and so many years ago. There is no way I can make amends to your family, but I realise how much it must mean to you to learn about your father.

Clem and me were best mates. Looking back we had a magic growing up, and I started to think of the things we did, the strife we got into, and the mischief. I've never talked about the war to anyone, ever. But Clem saved my life in New Guinea. So I thought, if you agreed and wanted to, I could perhaps meet you at the historical society some time for a cuppa and I could show you the little bits and pieces I've kept. And tell you some of the tales of two country lads who grew up in a place that I realise now was pretty special and peaceful in this rough old world. Thankfully the val-ley hasn't changed too much, good people live here and people who care about keeping it healthy and not chopping down trees willy-nilly and the like. If you don't wish to see me, I understand. But I hope you might give an old man a chance to try and make good for a mate.

Respectfully yours, Martin Thompson.

Lara wiped her eyes. 'The poor old bugger,' she said aloud.

'Who me?'

Lara jumped. Carter stood at the bottom of the steps.

'Any tea left? I'm passing through, got to go up to Jason's Birimbal estate. He wants some of the old trees identified and me to check on the boundaries. He's done a magnificent job. Thought you might like to come with me.'

Lara held out her hand and Carter stepped onto the verandah and took her hand in his. 'I'd love to. A trip into the bush is just what I need. And I have lots of news to tell you. I'll go and freshen up.'

Carter heard the tremble in her voice and squeezed her hand. 'No rush, matey. We've got all the time in the world. This is the valley, remember. It'll always be here.'

Dani

Dani followed Greta through the deserted gallery. Max's paintings, carefully hung, were even more powerful now. Each one glowed, shone with an inner light, drawing your focus and heart into each picture.

'They're extraordinary,' breathed Dani with feeling. 'They're alive.'

Greta nodded, giving a slight smile of satisfaction. 'They are indeed very special. Ken Minton thought so too. He's taking the entire collection back to New York. Max too, if he wants to work in the Big Apple for six months.'

'What an opportunity. I'm so thrilled for him.' Dani knew this humble, thoughtful man would be hailed as one of the great contemporary painters and she also knew Max would stay true to his roots wherever he worked.

How she treasured the painting he'd given her. It was her inspiration, it motivated her to strive to be true to herself, it gave her physical comfort. It was hard to explain to anyone how, late at night or very early in the morning, she would stand before the whorls of paint and feel she was being taken somewhere special. Closing her eyes she would place a fingertip at the edge of the canvas and feel a tremble, a life force, a something.

Max's work would live on long after he had returned to the Dreamtime country of his ancestors. What a gift, what a legacy. Perhaps Greta would understand how she felt, but Dani remained silent as she walked past paintings she had watched evolve, grow, into these great expressive reflections of one man's heart and soul.

Greta opened the door of her office and Dani was shocked to see her collection of Isabella paintings stashed against a wall.

'What are they doing here?' she exclaimed.

'Jason brought them over, he wanted Ken Minton to look at them,' explained Greta.

'Oh no! How embarrassing. He shouldn't have. Not in here, surrounded by Max's genius.' She was furious with Jason.

Greta sat at her overflowing desk and gestured to Dani to sit in the opposite chair. 'Dani, you came here to explore your passion, your dream, to stretch yourself. See if you are an artist. I know you're not talking commercial artist, but true-to-the-heart artist. One who paints like they breathe, who does what they do because there is simply no alternative. Jason is very devoted to you, your work. He seems to know how you feel and he felt you'd want to know how you are going on this journey you've undertaken. And that a top expert's opinion would give you some guidance,' said Greta gently.

'Oh God. What did he say?' Dani steeled herself. This

was agony. It was like someone taking her child away and putting him through some painful test. If he failed how would she comfort him? Would he go on and try again? But this was her own heart and soul. No one could help her with this challenge she'd chosen. She quickly held up her hand and said breathlessly, 'Before you say anything, no matter what he said, it won't stop me! I will not give up my art.'

Greta gave a soft smile. 'I'm pleased to hear that, Dani. Now, it's not that bad.' She glanced over at Dani's vibrant canvases depicting the country Greta knew and recognised.

'Ken is unfamiliar with the country you've painted, he knows nothing of Isabella but he recognised straight away it means a lot to you. There is a great passion and they are very evocative representations with great feeling, but not the work of a world-class artist.'

Dani let her breath escape.

'He was swift to say it is only his opinion and as we know opinions are very divided in the art world.'

'Unless you're a Max,' whispered Dani.

'Yes. Now, you could become a highly competent Sunday painter, win prizes from the Royal Art Society, and sell quite well. But he hopes you won't go down that path.'

'Oh, God, I'm not going back to graphic art, commercial design,' said Dani with some heat.

'Of course you're not. Dani, maybe you'll never achieve what you want with your art. I don't know one artist who feels they've done their best work. But it's the journey, not the destination, is it not? Now, these are another matter.' Greta lifted several of Dani's collagraphs from under papers and catalogues spread across her desk.

'Damn that Jason! He's taken them from the studio where the press is!' Dani couldn't believe the arrogance, the intrusion of that man into the most tender and tentative area of her life. 'Just because he set up the printing press in the basement of the old house and lets me print there doesn't mean he can *steal* my work!'

Greta tried not to smile at Dani's outburst. 'Ken Minton thought these were very fine efforts and encourages you to keep going. They speak volumes about not just the tangible interpretation of the landscape but your own insights and emotions in the choices you make and how you construct them. Keep experimenting and be proprietary in the execution of the prints when you have one you think works well. Keep them to signed limited editions.'

'Really?'

'Fine art is executed and expressed in many ways, not just oil paint, Dani. I thought you'd be pleased.'

'I'm just a bit in shock. I wasn't prepared for this.'

'Don't be cross with Jason,' said Greta. 'Imagine how nervous you might have been if you'd known Ken Minton was going to look at your work. And by the way, not many emerging artists have the opportunity for such appraisal.' Greta stood up. 'Jason will collect these. They're needed for the Birimbal launch. I'm looking forward to it. A lot of media coming I believe. Groundbreaking stuff. Let's hope it's the way of the future.'

Dani drove back to The Vale in a daze. Emerging artist, is that what I am? she thought. She did feel a bit like a chrysalis coming out of hibernation, but she wasn't ready to spread her crumpled wings and fly off into the sunlight just yet. Damn Jason. She had mixed feelings about his gesture. He should have asked her.

She stomped into her studio and stood, hands on hips, scanning the paraphernalia of her work. She was tempted to rush around and kick and overturn everything. But then she saw Max's beautiful painting. It held her gaze, stilling her surging emotions. 'Hold on, hold on, keep going forward, it is the journey,' it seemed to say.

Dani took a long breath and walked outside, feeling the warmth of the sun, the caress of a breeze. Down at the creek Tim was on his pony trotting and turning as Jason directed.

Without thinking, Dani rushed down the hill calling, 'Jason . . .'

He turned, smiled, gestured to Tim to keep going and walked towards her. He was stunned when Dani exploded.

'How could you! How dare you take my art, show them without my permission? Just who do you think you are!' She was even more furious when she realised she was crying.

'Dani, I did it for you, would *you* have shown your work to Minton?' countered Jason.

'I'm not ready. Not yet. It's too soon,' she shouted at him.

'You could bury yourself away here and never be ready,' said Jason firmly. 'Have faith in yourself. Now you have some direction, some sense of where you're going.'

'Nowhere famous, it seems,' she snapped. 'I could be a nice Sunday painter . . . fiddling round the edges, dabbling after work. How insulting.'

'But you're not going to do that! Get on with it, Dani, you have a talent, don't waste it,' said Jason quietly. 'You needed to hear that from someone who knows. Not me, not your mother, not even Greta. Someone who knows,' he repeated.

Dani was subdued but not convinced. 'I think you're arrogant and you took a dreadful liberty with my work. You intruded on my privacy.'

'Okay, I apologise,' he gestured with both hands upward. 'But you wouldn't have let me if I had asked. I could hear you saying you're not ready. One is never ready to be judged. How do we ever know when we have it right? We just have to get on and do it, no matter what. Do you think Birimbal would have happened if I'd waited till I thought everyone would welcome it and see what I saw and think it was terrific? I just had to go for it.' He spoke fast and with feeling. Then suddenly he reached out and pulled Dani to him and kissed her hard and passionately.

For an instant she resisted. Then she clutched him wildly, kissing him with an uncontrollable release of pent-up feelings. It felt as though a torrent of old sensations were being flushed from her body. Old pains, fears and excuses left her and as she drew back, shocked and speechless, she was aware of the creeping shoots of something new feeling their way into the emptiness.

They looked at each other in silence, their eyes saying it all.

'Mum, Mum, what's up?' Tim trotted towards them, sensing his mother was crying and being comforted by Jason. He reined the pony to a halt and stared at them utterly puzzled.

'It's all right, Tim, I was just telling your mum I think she's a brilliant artist and I love her very much.'

'Oh, is that all?' said Tim. And turned the pony away. 'Can I jump the creek now?'

Without waiting for permission he broke into a canter, headed to the narrow part of the stream, leaned close and urged Blackie to leap over the strip of bubbling water, losing his balance slightly as the pony landed and sprinted forward. Tim righted himself in the saddle and let out a whoop of delight.

Dani gave a little gasp, then a smile of relief as Tim competently swung the pony into a wide arc. She turned to Jason. 'This is all your fault, you know.'

'Probably is,' he said cheerfully. 'But hey, we're all flying now.' And as Tim pushed the pony into a gallop up the rise, Jason took Dani in his arms, gently and tenderly, and kissed her again.

Jason and Dani were having lunch at the Nostalgia Cafe, oblivious to the nudges and smiles of Claude and George who kept popping out to check on 'the lovebirds'.

'They just look so right together,' sighed Claude. 'They're so into each other, both so bright and clever.'

'They just look happy. I never liked that Ginny. Dani and Jason look comfortable together,' summed up George. 'Send them out some of that raspberry slice you made.'

Jason and Dani clinked their wine glasses, and smiled.

'So when are you going to Sydney?' Jason asked.

'Jeff arrives on Thursday to stay through the weekend for Tim's riding event. I'll stay with Mum and drive down early Friday morning.

'Would you mind if I came too? I've been putting off some business things in Sydney. I'd like to take you to a flash restaurant, maybe a show.'

'That'd be great!' said Dani promptly.

'I was thinking of seafood, down by the harbour. What else are you doing?'

'I have the last pages of Isabella's story from Garth. So sad. I want to see if I can find her grave.'

'What did happen to her?' asked Jason who was now as swept up in Isabella's story as Dani.

'She got ill in gaol. Her property was sold out from under her very cheaply. Eventually – as usual she had to fight – the court awarded her one thousand pounds compensation for wrongful imprisonment.'

'Doesn't sound like much considering her losses,' commented Jason.

'She estimated she lost a minimum of ten thousand pounds plus her health and a lot of land. When she got part payment she went back to England to seek medical help. But it didn't do much for her. She had bad asthma and had to ask John Dunmore Lang to get the rest of the settlement sent to her. She eventually came back to Sydney, still ill, and I like to think she was hoping to come back to the valley,' said Dani. 'In letters she mentions that she kept a journal which she wanted to give to Charles Dickens, have him turn it into a novel.'

Jason whistled softly in dismay. 'Wow. What a shame that's been lost. Well, at least we think you have her writing box. Maybe it has a secret drawer and you'll find it. Did she ever get back here?'

'She stayed in Sydney. There was another petition to the court years later to get her another thousand pounds, but it was roundly defeated.'

'So she lived in penury in Sydney. How sad,' said Jason. 'After all she'd achieved.'

'She was cared for by a Catholic institution and although she lived her last years in poverty there was a paid ad in the *Herald* giving details of her funeral. So she must have put money aside for her funeral at some stage.'

'We'll see what we can find out then,' said Jason.

Dani smiled inwardly at the 'we'. It now seemed the most natural thing in the world to be doing things together.

In Sydney Dani saw old friends who exclaimed how happy she looked, how she'd blossomed. And sounded a little envious as Dani described her new life of freedom and fulfilment in the valley.

'Of course, she has a rich boyfriend – that must make life easy,' commented one, unaware of the journey Dani had taken.

'I'd like to downshift, give up this materialistic rat race – if I was brave enough to do it,' sighed another.

Dani and Jason stayed at the elegant Observatory Hotel in the Rocks at his insistence and took joy in discovering each other. Their bodies, their thoughts, their tastes, their habits and humour became familiar and precious to each other. They wandered hand-in-hand around the city, sharing favourite places. He took her to meet his mother, still living in their big family home overlooking the harbour. They went to Lara's house, pleased to report back that the garden was being well looked after.

'The girl who's been renting my little place at Paddington is moving back to Melbourne. I think I'll sell it,' said Dani. 'The valley is home now.'

'I sold my apartment some time back,' confessed Jason. 'When I broke up with Ginny.'

And so there was only one task left and, on a cool, blustery day, they drove to what in Isabella's day was known as the Necropolis, now Rookwood cemetery. They had the record of Isabella's burial on 25 June 1872 and a vague location of her grave. They took a section each, wandering between the rows of graves, many well-tended, others marked by chipped concrete angels, great slabs of marble with fading inscriptions and rusting iron fences around long forgotten plots. But there was not a marker nor an indication of where Isabella Mary Kelly had finally come to rest.

Jason dropped his arm around Dani's shoulders. 'If she had no relatives, no one would have tended her grave, it might have fallen into disrepair and eventually been covered over with another grave,' he said softly.

'It's so sad. I suppose there was a priest here to conduct

the service. But I wonder if anyone came to say farewell to her,' said Dani.

'Independent to the end,' said Jason.

Dani turned away, tears in her eyes. 'Stubborn, opinionated, feisty, a fighter. How lonely she must have been. At least the valley gave her joy.'

'Yes, I'm sure it did. And it's a special place for us too, Dani.'

His arm tightened round her shoulder and he drew her to him, wrapping his arms around her as the wind soughed between the graves. Jason dropped his head to Dani's hair and murmured, 'Dani, will you marry me? Make the valley home, together?'

Dani lifted her head and gazed at him but before she could answer he kissed her. She finally drew apart and smiled up at him. 'That's a yes. Oh, yes.'

Linking arms they retraced their steps as pale sunlight shone over the ghostly surrounds.

'Jase . . .'

'Yes, sweetheart?'

'I will never let our children forget that you proposed in a cemetery.'

'I think Tim will get a bit of a laugh out of it,' replied Jason.

Their laughter warmed the cold day and the place where a lonely woman from the valley had been laid to rest but was now no longer forgotten.

The End

ALSO AVAILABLE FROM PAN MACMILLAN

Di Morrissey
Monsoon

Sandy Donaldson has been working in Vietnam for a volunteer
organisation, HOPE, for four years. Reluctant to return to
Australia when her contract is up, she invites her oldest friend
Anna to come and explore the popular tourist destination of
beautiful Vietnam.

Both have unexplored links to this country, but swept up in
their own relationships and ambitions, they are reluctant to
pursue them. A chance meeting with an Australian journalist
will encourage the girls to reconnect with their past.

Monsoon is a journey into the hearts and memories of those
caught in a certain time, in a particular place.

'An intoxicating blend of drama and mystery set in steamy
South-East Asia.'
AUSTRALIAN WOMEN'S WEEKLY

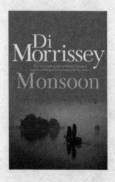

Di Morrissey
The Valley

The Valley is nestled between rugged peaks, divided by a
magnificent river. Within its peaceful green contours are held
the secrets of generations of tribes, families and loners who
have come under its spell.

But some secrets are never shared, never told.

Until one woman returns and begins asking questions . . . and
discovers the story of a forgotten valley pioneer whose life
becomes entwined with hers. But in looking into her own
family's history she uncovers more than she ever expected –
and what her mother hoped would always remain a secret . . .

'*The Valley* is a long, juicy page-turner, a generational saga
that flows resistlessly.'
THE AGE

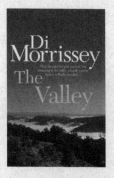

Di Morrissey
The Reef

On a small coral cay on the Great Barrier Reef two communities come together in an uneasy alliance: a tourist resort and a scientific research station.

At first glance, the island is a sexy resort, a naturalist's dream, a diver's delight. But the island holds secrets and dangers as Jennifer Towse soon discovers.

When world-famous Isobel Belitas arrives, Jennifer learns to see the world – above and below the sea – very differently. Isobel also teaches her to come to terms with her obsessive mother, as well as her disintegrating marriage. But no one, not even investigative journalist Tony Adams, could have prepared Jennifer for the stunning revelations of what is really happening on this island paradise . . .

'A story of high drama, passion and adventure within an intimate island community.'
AUSTRALIAN WOMEN'S WEEKLY

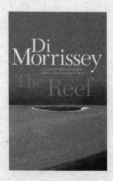

Di Morrissey
Barra Creek

In the wild Gulf country of northwestern Queensland, there's a
cattle station – Barra Creek – on a tributary of the crocodile-
infested Norman River.

It's 1963 and Sally Mitchell, the well-bred daughter of a
wealthy New Zealand sheep farmer, is on her way to England
with her friend Pru. When the young women stop over in
Sydney their plans go awry. Sally impulsively takes a job as a
governess at Barra Creek, and when the mail plane that flew
her there takes off she finds herself left in a different world.

Here Sally's life changes forever. The challenges of coping with
her three young charges, wild stockmen, the heat and the Wet,
brumby musters and cattle rushes all pale beside a great
passion, a great loss and a gruesome death.

'Beneath the surface of the fast-moving plot . . . is an intriguing
study of the human heart and all its intricacies.'
AUSTRALIAN WOMEN'S WEEKLY

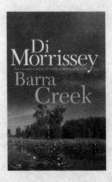